What People Are Saying
About this Book

"Who would've thought I'd learn so much about humanity through a sweet little prairie fiction book? Fantastic first novel, Corinne. I can't wait to read what happens next to these colourful characters that have crept under my skin."
Steve Erwin, best-selling co-author of *Left to Tell: Discovering God Amidst the Rwandan Holocaust* (#1 Amazon, #4 *New York Times*)

"We return to tales of arrival for good reason: reading about these risk-takers, making this country their own, is always moving. Corinne Jeffery is a very fine storyteller."
Todd Babiak, *Edmonton Journal* columnist, screenwriter, and award-winning, best-selling author of *The Garneau Block* and *Toby: A Man*

"I was quickly engrossed by the lives of the pure and not-so-pure Werner family members. They face one unpredictable drama after another as they grapple with natural hardships and human folly. A really special book."
Sharrie Williams, author, *The Maybelline Story—and the Spirited Family Dynasty Behind It*

"I can readily see this on screen!"
Leon Logothetis, reality TV show producer and author, *Amazing Adventures of a Nobody*

"Arriving is like a raw and racy *Little House on the Prairie* that throws the reader right back in time. Can't wait to read the sequel!"
Marla Martenson, author, *Diary of a Beverly Hills Matchmaker*

"An impressive debut by an author of Canadian historical fiction."
Christine Ducommun, author, *Living with Multiple Personalities: The Christine Ducommun Story* (a 2012 TV movie)

"This book has intriguing and piquant characters that will remain in my memory for years to come."
Ronald Russell, award-winning journalist and author of *Don Carina* (in screenplay production)

"Everything that happens in today's, fast-paced world occurs in Corinne Jeffery's delightful debut about German Lutheran homesteaders arriving in Saskatchewan at the turn of the twentieth century. But few of the antics are ever discussed, as those sneaky pioneers maintain their proclivity for silence and secrets. I loved my front-row seat!"
Aura Imbarus, author of the Pulitzer Prize entry, *Out of the Transylvania Night*

"Engrossing! A fun read from start to finish."
Jane Congdon, author, *It Started with Dracula: The Count, My Mother, and Me*

"I love to see other Canadian authors shine, and shine she does! Simply a wonderful book."
Charmaine Hammond, author, *On Toby's Terms*

"Corinne has done a wonderful job of researching and developing this story, which introduces us to the complexities of family relationships and offers insights into their cultural communities. The challenges of pioneer life and times in eastern Saskatchewan in the early 1900s are well captured. An enjoyable read, written from the heart!"
Dr. Peggy Quinney, PhD, University of Alberta; former dean and colleague of Corinne's at Grant MacEwan College

Arriving

1909–1919

Arriving: 1909–1919

Book one of the *Understanding Ursula* trilogy

by Corinne Jeffery

Published 2011. Reprinted 2012. Printed and bound in Canada by Friesens.

Book and cover designed by Teresa Wang.

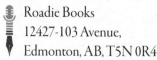 Roadie Books
12427-103 Avenue,
Edmonton, AB, T5N 0R4

Jeffery, Corinne.

Arriving: 1909–1919: a novel by Corinne Jeffery

ISBN 978-0-9869435-2-2

Dedication

To my children, Ruben and Sara,
my grandson, Aidan J., and his mommy, Heather.

And to Jack, my husband.

In memory of my grandparents,
Rudolph and Mary Gares,
for their life-long gifts of love and inspiration.

Acknowledgements

Whenever I embark upon the adventure of reading a new novel, I always begin with the acknowledgements; it gives me a sense of who has made the book a reality. It has been my aspiration to write since I was a child, and without the help of many, my dream could never have come to fruition.

Firstly, I want to thank my publisher, Faith Farthing of Roadie Books, who believed in my trilogy from the beginning. Her creativity, persistence, encouragement, and thorough eye made *Arriving: 1909–1919* so much stronger, despite my protestations against many of her recommendations. Thank you also, Faith, for introducing me to the talented Teresa Wang, who created this magical book cover and layout that, for me, immediately captured the spirit of the times.

I would like to thank my loyal friend Donna Hastings for her commitment to reading and providing invaluable suggestions and insights for the book, particularly in relation to Saskatchewan. And thank you for your role in naming the series, along with the other members of our foursome, Raylene Manolesue and Beverly Sochatsky.

When I started writing my novels, I realized I had neither the patience nor the time to read what I had written; my colleagues, Bette Hogg, Bev Verger, and Jo Whitford, pored over the pages enthusiastically. I am eternally grateful for all of the supportive words you offered throughout. I would also like to express my sincere gratitude to Donna Berg, Alexis Leclair, and my sister, Erna Lowe, for diligently reading the original manuscript.

Lastly, but most importantly, I offer special thanks to my family: Jack for his patience in waiting to read the trilogy, Ruben for his perspicacity, Sara for her unfailing belief in me, and Aidan for this: "Whenever I go into Chapters, I will look for a book with 'Corinne Jeffery' on it. I guess that's what you want to be when you grow up, right Grans?!"

Prologue
1988

The old farmhouse was standing still. It had been thirty-seven years since its cracked and paint-chipped walls had heard the voices of children. It had embodied the hopes, dreams, and realities of their life in the small farming community in Saskatchewan. It had never considered abandonment as its future.

August, the youngest son of Gustav and Amelia's youngest son, worked the farm, which was rich and fertile. But he was neither. August was the only descendant who inherited his grandfather Gustav Warner's love for the land, and his desire was for a simplistic life of raising a family on the homestead, instead of driving to and from the city every day like he and his father always did as farmers. Because he struggled with reading, writing, and arithmetic, everyone thought he was slow; his classmates always laughed at him. Many of August's teachers tried to persuade his parents to send him away to a special school. His parents resisted and encouraged him to work at his own pace. But not even his parents understood that August never enjoyed living in Melville, where he still dwelt in their basement, and that he was not interested in the fast-paced life of the city, surrounded by people. He was born into the wrong century; he envied his grandparents.

August loved the feel of earth running through his fingers. When fallowing his land, he often stopped the tractor, climbed down, and picked up handfuls of the rich, black soil. He was so similar to Gustav; he had to preserve his grandfather's legacy. His three older brothers neither cared about farming nor the inevitable fact that a stranger would buy the land their grandparents spent a lifetime acquiring. At least Hans Gerhart, his powerful neighbour, would not succeed in buying the Warner farm, which enclosed the best land in the southeast of Saskatchewan.

If only life had not changed so much, if only his father had arranged a marriage for him, as was the custom in his grandfather's time, then August would have sons and daughters to teach the joys of working with the earth. His wife would teach them to read and write at home and protect them from the lure of city life. But deep down he felt that this was not to be.

When he was honest with himself, August knew that as an old man he would be just like Hans Gerhart—alone on his vast tracts of land with no one to inherit the fruits of his labours, nobody to anticipate the thrill of turning over the soil in the spring or walk through the glowing wheat fields as they ripened in the autumn.

Perhaps he really was becoming morose, as his father repeatedly claimed. But then his spirits lightened as he remembered the invitation to the very first Warner/Werner family reunion during the last weekend of July in Neudorf. He was excited about meeting relatives he had not known existed, and just maybe he would be introduced to some healthy, young German woman—even a cousin, thrice removed, as long as she shared his interests, since he was so awkward about meeting the fair sex. If not, August knew he could always count upon his favourite Aunt Ursula to pay attention to him, and then he would not feel so different from his city-loving older brothers.

August wondered who had organized this reunion and why it was planned for July 1988. It made much more sense to him to wait until 1992 to celebrate the 100th anniversary of the Warner/Werner family's arrival in Canada. But he decided not to let these thoughts ruin his anticipation.

Arriving
1909–1919

~ 1 ~

It was impossible to sleep. Today was the most important day of his young life. Gustav still could not believe he would become a landowner the day after he turned eighteen years old. He looked at his brother Rolf and wondered how he could sleep so soundly. Then he remembered that Rolf was twenty-one, and because of the federal government's original age requirement, he had waited an additional three years to make this trip to Regina; perhaps for Rolf, landowning was not as exciting or inspiring a proposition.

Soon it would be dawn. Gustav quietly got out of bed, dressed in his work clothes, and went outside to wait for the first rays of light. He wanted to be at the station early for the train trip to the city.

Gustav thanked God for his good fortune; it was as though he was meant to become a farmer. Two events had happened this year, both of which made it so much easier for him to get started on his ambition to become one of the most successful homesteaders in the townships. He could not believe his luck when he read the article in *The Leader* in March that said the Dominion Lands Act had been amended so an eighteen-year-old single male, rather than a twenty-one-year-old, was eligible for a free quarter-section homestead grant.

The next exciting announcement was that on July 1—that very day—the Grand Trunk Pacific Railway was officially opening the branch line from Regina to Melville. When the passenger train stopped in Duff on its return to Regina, he and Rolf would be two of the first passengers to ride to the capital city from the adjoining English Methodist township.

A pink and pale-blue sunrise appeared in the east, gradually lighting the immense Saskatchewan sky. Gustav heard the jingle of Betsy's bell, and he headed across the pasture towards the slough. The three cows were eating the green grass around the water, and as he herded them towards the small barn, they continued to chew their cud. He knew it was early to milk them, but he wanted to get the barn chores out of the way so he would have time to get himself washed and dressed in his Sunday clothes.

The air was already warm; it would be another scorching prairie day. Gustav did not want to rush, and he knew it often took Rolf a long time to get moving in the morning. He could not understand how two brothers could be so different. Rolf did not seem excited at all about their trip to the Regina Lands Office to obtain his homestead grant; maybe he could only think about his wedding in September to Katie Ulmer, the minister from Lemberg's only daughter.

Gustav finished the milking, released the cows back into the pasture, and carried the pails of fresh milk to the little milk house. He stored the milk in the heavy earthen crocks to cool; his mother would find it later in the morning and would skim the cream from the top. Gustav loved the taste of the rich, yellow butter that his mother churned from the cream, especially on her freshly baked bread. These thoughts made him realize he was becoming hungry, and he hurriedly went to the well to get some water to heat for his morning wash and shave. Gustav was testing out the little tin stove he had installed in one corner of the barn; he was practising for when he and Rolf would be living on their own adjacent homesteads.

It was Gustav who had earned the money to buy some of the basic supplies such as the small stove, tin plates, and utensils that they would need as soon as they staked their claim. He had cut out the article in *The Leader* that listed some of the essential equipment recommended for successful homesteading. His father had teased him about his approach to farming, but Gustav was a planner. Since he already owned Wolfgang, his wonderfully strong quarter horse, for transportation, he knew that the next most important item was a plow.

At least for the first year, Gustav and Rolf would share their father's team of oxen and his sturdy metal plow, which he had purchased when he arrived from Russia seventeen years ago. But as soon as he could earn the money, Gustav would purchase one of the new and supposedly superior steel plows made by John Deere. Gustav had already purchased a disker to cultivate the freshly turned sod, an adze, and a strong sharp spade to dig the well. He had bought a crosscut saw for felling trees and an axe for splitting wood so he could one day build the three-storey house that he planned for his family.

His father had promised him and Rolf that they could use the round, white tent in which the family lived during the first autumn they arrived in Canada. His uncle had some stout logging chains, which they could use to drag logs out of the bush and pull them out of the mud if they got stuck. Somewhat to Gustav's surprise, Rolf seemed content to let him make all of these arrangements and to plan their future farms.

It had been up to Gustav to research where they would find prime prairie land, and he revelled in his early-morning rides through the townships that the federal government set aside for the German Lutherans from Russia. He vividly remembered that dewy morning in May when he found the stake, one that the surveyors planted in the middle of every one-mile-square section.

He led Wolfgang because he was uncertain what he was looking for; when he came across it, he was surprised it was only an inch-square, foot-long piece of dark-coloured iron. As he knelt down to examine it carefully, he saw the figures written on its side—numbers he immediately committed to memory. When he arrived back home, he wrote them down on paper to be accurate when he went to claim his land, but Gustav knew he would never forget these vital numbers for as long as he lived.

The southwest corner of section 23, township 21, and range 8, west of the 2nd meridian, sloped gently towards a slough, and Gustav decided he would farm this quarter of land. A grove of willows surrounded the small body of water, which pooled in the gully running from the northwest corner of the section. Since Rolf expressed so little interest in where he farmed, Gustav made the decision alone, determining that it made good sense for them to claim this half-section of land with its rich, black soil.

Finally, the day when they could officially stake their claims with the Dominion Lands Office in Regina arrived. Gustav finished his wash and went to the tent, which they decided to try out before living on the homestead site, to check if Rolf was awake. As he lifted its flap, he called out, "Hey, Rolf, it's time to get up. We don't want to be late for the train, and since I've milked the cows, I think it is only fair that you feed and hitch Wolfgang to the wagon."

Rolf mumbled from inside the tent, "What time is it? I didn't even hear the rooster crow. Knowing you, you have probably been up since before the sun. Did you at least leave me any water so I can shave?"

"Yes, of course. I'm going to the house. Mama will have prepared a big breakfast, and you better hurry before I eat it all."

There was great excitement when Gustav opened the door of the four-room stone house his father had so proudly finished building the first summer they lived in Canada. His two younger sisters, Hanna and Katherina, were both talking at once. "What will it be like riding on the train?" "Can I go with you and Rolf?" "Papa said we can come to the station if we promise not to fall off the back of the buggy."

Gustav laughed. As he tousled Katherina's hair, he said good morning to his parents.

He went to the stove where his mother was frying bacon and eggs. "Mama, that smells so good. I didn't sleep much last night, and I'm starving."

"Oh, Gustav, my youngest son, you have been hungry since the day you were born. But it doesn't seem to matter how much I feed you; nothing sticks to your ribs."

At that moment, Rolf came into the house. "Well, sleepyhead, we have been waiting for you so we can start breakfast," said his father. "Your mother must think that you will not see food for days; not only has she prepared a feast this morning, but she has also packed enough bread and cheese to feed everyone on the train."

The Werner family sat down at the table, and as they had done since they arrived in this country with plentiful gifts, Christian, the head of the house, said grace, thanking God for His bounty and their good fortune. He looked at Elisabetha, his wife of thirty-five years, and silently thanked his Maker for this spirited woman who had followed him first from Austria to Russia, and then to Canada.

Gustav saw the glance that passed between his parents and marvelled at the unspoken love they still shared for each other. Neither of them was demonstrative, nor did they openly express their feelings; but all of their children knew they had endured incredible hardships to give them a better life. Rolf ate hurriedly so he would have a head start, since he needed to harness Wolfgang to the buggy. His sisters' thrill about going to Duff to see the train was infectious, and with his mother's hearty breakfast, he was feeling much more energetic and impatient to be on the way. He thought it a little sad that Mama could not also see them off, but since Papa had replaced the old, green, covered wagon with the smaller, lightweight carriage, there was no room for her.

Gustav's horse, Wolfgang, was frisky this morning, and as the carriage rolled along the open countryside, the breeze was cool and refreshing. They would travel the six miles between the Werner farm and Duff in approximately one hour and still have ample time to board the train. Christian and his two young daughters would be tired of riding in the buggy by the time they returned home.

Coming down the small hill overlooking the village of Duff, they could see the big, black train, seemingly impatient, at the little station. Smoke was coming from the engine's stack, cinders were flying, and it was roaring like a caged animal wanting to be on its way. As soon as Christian called "whoa" to the horse, they jumped off the buggy; now enthusiastic about riding the train, Rolf raced Gustav in to buy their tickets.

Peter Johnson, the postmaster and now the new ticket agent, saw the young men and said, "Take your time; the train is not scheduled to leave for a half an hour." However, Gustav was as anxious to start his journey as the train appeared to be, and after paying Mr. Johnson he said goodbye to his father and sisters and immediately climbed aboard the passenger car. He wanted to sit by an open window and watch the prairie go flying by as he experienced the inaugural ride.

With a loud toot of its whistle, the engine finally started to move and quickly picked up momentum as it pulled away from the station. Rolf and Gustav waved and called out the window, "Bye! We will tell you all about it when we get home tomorrow."

"Just think, Rolf: we are making history as two of the first passengers riding on this train."

"Oh, Gustav, you always try to make such a big deal out of everything. People have been riding trains for years. Now, as exciting as it was to be the first to board the train, I want to finish the sleep that you interrupted so early this morning."

As usual, Gustav had the last word. "People have not been riding on this train. I worked on this branch line, and I know this is the first time a train has run from Melville to Regina."

Rolf slouched down in his seat, closed his eyes, and tried to go back to sleep. Instead he found himself thinking about his younger brother. Gustav seemed so different from the rest of the family; he was always full of energy and optimistic about everything, especially about becoming a homesteader. Could he not understand that being a farmer meant long, hard days filled with demanding chores, and sometimes at the end of it, there would not be enough food to adequately feed a family?

2

Even as a child, Gustav Werner knew precisely what he would do with his life. He was serious, determined, and disciplined as he planned for his future. His mother often expressed to other family members, "Of all my children, Gustav is the one who was born responsible. And yet he is also the one with boundless energy and zest for living; he seems to love everything about the life of a pioneer in this vast, untamed country."

As soon as Gustav was old enough to run after his father and older brothers, he could not wait to get his clothes and shoes on and get outside. Most of the time he was more of a nuisance because he was too small to be of much help. He was delighted with the joys of nature and would run in circles trying to catch the birds and the orange-and-black monarch butterflies. When it was time to go in for a meal, Gustav would not enter the house until he had picked a bouquet, usually of bright yellow dandelions, for his mother.

By the time Gustav was ready to start German school, which Mrs. Tressel conducted in her home three mornings a week, it was apparent he had equal enthusiasm for learning. He quickly grasped the rudiments of reading and writing and was as interested in learning about the Lutheran faith as he was in reading the German books she had brought from Austria.

Soon Gustav was reading his parents' Bible and any other books that they had managed to bring with them when they fled from Russia. However, there were chores on the farm for even a six-year-old boy, particularly in the spring and fall, when he was expected to herd the cows and pick the smaller rocks from the recently cleared land. As much as

Gustav enjoyed being outdoors and feeling important by being able to help his father and older brothers, he now resented that he had to miss many of the morning classes.

Nonetheless, by the age of ten Gustav had read all of the appropriate books in Mrs. Tressel's limited library, and he progressed through the Old Testament and started the New Testament. He was even more skilled with arithmetic, surprising her with his ability to add and subtract in his head more quickly than the other boys and girls could using paper and pencil. Mrs. Tressel became concerned that soon she would not be able to provide Gustav with enough challenges in her home-schooling.

However, before Mrs. Tressel had to deal with this eventuality, an English gentleman, Mr. Buckler, who had been hired in 1901 by the federal government to complete a census of Neudorf, came to the Werners' farm. Upon arriving at the village, he was advised to find someone who could speak and write both English and German to act as his interpreter, since most of the homesteaders only understood the latter.

Gustav could not believe his eyes when he saw his fifteen-year-old cousin, Julia Mohr, step down from the buggy, assisted by a man wearing a brown suit. He ran up to her and said, "What are you doing riding in that stranger's wagon?"

"Hello, Gustav. This is Mr. Buckler, who has been hired by the government to count all of the people in our township, and I am his assistant," she said.

As they started to walk to the house, Gustav was so intrigued that he ran behind Julia, asking, "How did you become his assistant? Do you get paid to talk to people you have known all your life? Can I get a job like yours?"

His father opened the door to welcome them, and when they had entered he turned to Gustav. "Hurry along, son; you have all your chores to do, and the chickens are hungry."

Turning away from the house, Gustav kicked at a pebble as he crossed the yard to the henhouse. Why did Papa have to send him away when he wanted to find out what was going on? Now he would have to wait until after church on Sunday to talk to Julia and get the answers to his questions. On the other hand, Julia did seem to be acting very grown-up and much too busy to bother with her younger cousin.

By the time Mr. Buckler and Julia came out of the house, Gustav was helping Johann, his favourite older brother, to sharpen the plow before beginning the spring plowing. It was not easy having three older brothers who seemed so much stronger and smarter than he was, but Johann was always ready to teach him how to do things without teasing or making him feel small and useless.

"Did you see Julia with that government man?" asked Gustav as he held the plowshare firmly so Johann could sharpen the blade. "I was carrying the milk to the shed when they drove into the yard. How do you think she got the job as his assistant?"

"You know that Julia has been going to the Methodist school in Duff, and she probably was hired because she can understand and speak English," replied Johann.

Gustav was quiet for a long time before he asked his brother, "Do you think Papa would let me go to that school?"

"No, Gustav, I know Papa will not send you to any school to learn to read and write English; he was annoyed with Aunt Margareta when she arranged for Julia to attend the Duff school. He thinks it is important for us to be able to read enough German to understand the Bible because he believes that every good German just needs to love God and to own his land. He has four sons, and even with Friedrich staying on this quarter to help Mama and him, by the time the rest of us are old enough to prove our homesteads, the Werner family will own an entire section of land. So in this country, there is no reason why we cannot all be successful as farmers."

"Don't you realize I actually want to be a farmer?" protested Gustav.

"Well, little brother, I don't understand you; but it's a lucky thing that's what you want because you don't have much of a choice."

The best part of Sunday was going to the Mohrs' house for dinner after church. Aunt Margareta was a great cook, and she usually served a variety of delicious foods without limiting the amount the hungry Werner boys could eat. Of course, Margareta had to cook for only four people on a daily basis—unlike Elisabetha Werner, who had to spend a good portion of each day trying to feed the nine hungry members of her family. It was out of compassion for her sister-in-law that Margareta planned the Sunday dinners when her older brother Christian insisted that everyone must attend the weekly church service.

Margareta Mohr was the kind of person people loved to talk about, and if the people in the village and community had only expressed to her what they said behind her back, she would have answered them truthfully. She was outspoken and fearless, saying what she meant to children, women, and even men. She was no doubt eccentric in some ways: she had been seen boxing naughty children's ears when she considered them to be disrespectful to one of their elders, and some even claimed to have seen her smoking her husband's pipe.

What surprised the townspeople the most was that her husband, Phillip, did not seem to mind her behaviour and was actually very supportive of his wife. It would be a very long time before Phillip Mohr would forget how his wife's careful planning before they had fled Russia had enabled them to smuggle their precious, hard-earned savings from the country. After safely arriving in Canada, there was enough money left to start the first general store in Neudorf, and each year their business grew.

Whatever rumour was making the rounds, no one would deny that Margareta was kind and fair. When one of her neighbours needed a helping hand or basic supplies from the store when cash was short, she would discreetly ask them if they would prefer to pay the bill after the harvest. Margareta treated everyone—man, woman, and child—the same; she did not play favourites.

Her sense of fair play was creating a dilemma for Margareta. She was so pleased with Julia's progress at the school in Duff, and she knew her nephew Gustav would learn the English language just as quickly. Margareta also realized there was no way Christian Werner would ever allow any of his children to attend the Methodist school. The one person to whom she carefully chose what she expressed was Christian, and the only time she was subtle was when she was planning how to get what she wanted from him. What Margareta really wanted was for Gustav to be included in Julia's tutoring sessions when she was teaching her parents and brother how to read, write, and speak English. Her last conversation with her friend Mary Tressel only confirmed that Gustav was the Werner boy who could most readily grasp the language of his new country. If his teacher was recommending Gustav to be singled out for additional learning, how could Margareta's sense of justice still be intact if she did not help him?

Since Aunt Margareta did not subscribe to the notion that children should be seen and not heard, as soon as Uncle Phillip finished grace Gustav started asking Julia the questions he had stored in his head since Monday morning. "How did you get the job to help count the people in Neudorf? How much do you get paid? Can I get a job too?"

"Son, one question at a time, and let Julia have something to eat before you bombard her with your inquisitiveness," chided his father. Friedrich shot Gustav an irksome glance, annoyed with his father's good humour when it came to Gustav.

"Oh, it's OK, Uncle Christian. I know how curious Gustav is and that he has been waiting for some answers," replied Julia. "Apparently Mr. Buckler stopped in Duff and asked if any students in the school could speak both English and German. When my teacher told him that I understood both languages, he came here that evening and offered me the job. I get paid for every hour I work, but I think I will keep the amount private," said Julia.

While this conversation was occurring, Margareta's plan began to take shape. With Julia away in school all day in the fall and her brother Peter too small to help in the store, she would need someone to assist her with stocking the shelves and keeping the floor clean. Instead of Phillip driving the buggy to take Julia in the mornings and pick her up from Duff in the afternoons, Gustav could drive their gentle horse, Wolfgang. In the winter, Gustav could be taught how to handle the cutter safely, and Margareta would arrange for him to stay in town with them during the week.

That evening as they prepared for bed, Margareta said to her husband, "Phillip, I need your help with a proposal I have for Gustav."

"My dear, you are always planning something for some unsuspecting person; what do you have in mind for our nephew?"

"We have often marvelled about how bright Gustav is, and the other day when I was talking to Mary, she said she has taught him as much as she can with the books that she has available. I think Gustav is capable of learning English and many of the subjects that Julia is studying at the school in Duff."

Phillip started to laugh. "Margareta, you know as well as I do that Christian is determined to keep all of the old customs and certainly his own language. He would never allow Gustav to attend an English school, even if the Lutherans ran it."

"And that is precisely why I have developed my plan, which will kill many birds with one stone. When we hire and board Gustav, Julia can tutor him in the evenings, just as she has this past year with you and me. You heard how excited Gustav was about having a job, and as he gets older, it will be very helpful for him to know English." Margareta summarized her scheme for her husband.

"Well, it seems to me that, once again, you have worked out all of the details. I'm not sure where I fit into the picture. If you want my approval, I think that it is a very sound idea. I have a strong hunch that Gustav has ambitions to be successful, and he will need to be educated in the English language."

"Ah, my dear Phillip, you have the hardest job of all. I want you to talk to Christian and convince him that we really need Gustav's help."

As he reached for his wife, Phillip teased her about always giving him the toughest tasks; then he became serious and said, "Margareta, if I am to make the arrangements with Christian, you must be patient and let me talk to him when I think it is a good time."

Phillip Mohr was as capable as his wife of being subtle when striving to reach a personal objective. He always enjoyed his curious, energetic nephew, who seemed to have more spunk than his three older brothers, and he too was eager to give him some of the advantages that he intended to provide his own children. Phillip recognized it was only a matter of time before the railway came to central Saskatchewan and that workers would be needed for its construction. One of his brother-in-law's biggest hardships was not having money to buy the equipment he needed to farm, and Phillip was determined to see that Gustav had a better start.

It took considerable time and most of a bottle of his good whiskey before Phillip finally convinced Christian that both families would benefit by having Gustav spend the winter with his uncle and aunt. He did promise to drive Gustav home every Friday night; he realized Elisabetha would miss her youngest son and that he would stay at home during the busy seasons of the year.

It took much less time for Gustav to understand how privileged he was with the opportunity to spend the winter with the Mohr family. He was delighted to spend hours with his lovely cousin as she taught him how to read and write English, and they practised speaking the new language. Gustav was astute enough to appreciate the importance of speaking German at home and intuited that he should not discuss his learning activities with his father.

The full reality of his current arrangement hit home when his Uncle Phillip took him to the Union Bank on his first Friday before driving Gustav home. "Gustav, I want you to open an account with your first week's pay. Your Aunt Margareta and I have decided to give you one dollar a week for all the chores that you do, and it would please us if you saved the money for your future."

Gustav was astonished. "Uncle Phillip, I didn't expect to get paid for helping you, especially when I am living with you."

"We believe in paying anyone who works for us, but I see no reason that your papa needs to know any of this."

The next morning when Gustav was helping his mother dig up the last of the carrots and parsnips from her garden, he blurted out, "Mama, I opened an account at the bank yesterday before I came home. Auntie and Uncle Phillip are paying me a dollar a week for driving Julia to school and helping in the store, but Uncle said not to tell Papa."

Elisabetha understood that Gustav did not feel comfortable withholding information from his parents and particularly from her. She reassured him: "Gustav, I think I know why your Uncle Phillip asked you not to say anything, so let's keep this as our little secret."

Johann was pleased for his little brother, who in time was able to teach him the basics of the English language. Rolf was indifferent, as he was too wrapped up in his physical needs—particularly in getting enough food to appease his growing appetite and adequate sleep before his father woke him at the crack of dawn. On the other hand, Friedrich was resentful that once again Gustav was the favourite son and given special considerations. He did not understand why his father was so easy on his three younger siblings.

When Friedrich was Gustav's age, their father had been much sterner: adamant about blind obedience to his orders and considerably more volatile when things were not done to his rigid standards. Christian Werner still expected conformity and orderliness from his younger children, but he seemed to be more relaxed and at times actually appeared to enjoy playing with them.

In all of his years of envy, it had never once occurred to Friedrich that perhaps Papa enjoyed Gustav because he was considerably easier to get along with and less likely to resist direction from him. What Friedrich found most irritating about this brother who was thirteen years younger than him was his smugness, as though he was privy to some truths about life of which his brothers were not aware. But then Gustav was a mystery to all of his older brothers, who did not understand his enthusiasm for hard work and his belief that work was its own reward.

As much as he disliked the arrangements his parents had made with the Mohr family, Friedrich knew better than to question them and decided to hold his sharp tongue. Besides, with his wife expecting their first child, they could use the extra space in the already overcrowded house. Gustav spent the next three winters in town with his aunt and uncle, and Friedrich gave little thought to his spoiled kid brother.

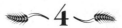

In the spring of 1905, when the Canadian Pacific Railway chose Neudorf as a divisional point to continue working west, Gustav was ready. He was fluent in English, tall for his soon-to-be fourteen years, and confident that he could work right alongside any other construction worker. However, when he went to the office to apply for a job and responded that he could speak both English and German, Gustav was hired to work with the foreman as an interpreter. With the boom of necessary construction for the rail yards, roundhouse, water tower, and station, they needed to hire as many of the local farmers as possible. These hired workers had to understand what they were being paid to do. Many men were lined up outside the office already, and Mr. Gillespie, the foreman, asked Gustav, "Young man, can you start work right away? I want to hire as many of these eager fellows as possible."

At the end of the day when he returned to the Mohrs' home, Gustav excitedly told his Aunt Margareta about his new job. "Since I am to be paid twenty dollars every week, I am going to add my wages to my account in the bank."

"Gustav, I am so pleased. Your Uncle Phillip and I always knew that learning how to speak English would be an advantage for you in the future. Speaking of your Uncle Phillip, he is waiting for you at the livery barn with some more good news."

On a day full of surprises, the best was the offer from his Uncle Phillip. "Gustav, since Julia will be going to school in Regina in the fall, I am thinking about selling Wolfgang. Now that you will be a man of means, I will give you the first choice of buying him."

"Uncle Phillip, thank you. I have dreamed of owning Wolfgang ever since I started driving Julia to Duff. When can I take him home?"

"Why don't you ride him home tonight, and we can work out the payment when you start earning money from the railway."

The first person Gustav saw when he came riding into the Werner yard was his mother, who was planting vegetables in her large garden. He jumped down from Wolfgang, and while giving her a hug, he expressed all of the exciting events of his day.

Elisabetha was fond of all of her children, having waited until she was twenty-seven before she finally conceived, but she was probably closest to Gustav. She found his enthusiasm and his sense of humour a welcome reprieve during the long, busy days of looking after her large family and helping her husband to work the land on their homestead. Elisabetha was careful not to show any favouritism—especially around Friedrich, who had always seemed to resent Gustav.

At the supper table that night, even Friedrich joined in the family's congratulations, teasing Gustav, "Well, little brother, I have always said you live under a lucky star. This time I am going to have some of it shine on me; tomorrow when you leave for work, I am coming with you, and you can get me a job on that railway too."

Christian looked at his oldest son and immediately said, "Friedrich, as you well know, I expect you to help me plow the northern end of the homestead so we can put in more wheat and oats this spring."

"Not this year, Papa. Maria and I are expecting our second child, and I need to make some money so we can finally build our own home. There is not enough room for all of us in this house, and I can make twice as much with the railway than what we earn with the grain we grow on this one quarter of land. Johann and Rolf will just have to help you with the planting."

Elisabetha quickly glanced at Christian as if to say, *Let him go. It is easier to work with his brothers, who are not moody.* Also, she would appreciate having her kitchen to herself. Over the past three years, she and Maria had worked out a tacit arrangement for meal preparation, which was necessary with so many hungry mouths to feed. But Elisabetha did not like some of the dishes Maria insisted on making, and if she expressed any opinion on the matter, Maria would simply leave and not help at all. Then she would have not only the responsibility of cooking but of all of the washing up as well.

Friedrich was certainly right about the house becoming too small. When Maria and he were having another of their frequent arguments, it was impossible to prevent Hanna and Katherina from hearing her shouting and his swearing. Elisabetha suspected that Friedrich was drinking when he went into Neudorf or to visit the neighbours on the pretext of playing cards. Each evening as he was getting ready to go out, Friedrich was as affable as he had been in his earlier years; but when he returned home late at night, the alcohol curdled his charm.

The idea that their four-room stone house with its front porch was too small was almost ridiculous to Elisabetha. She vividly remembered that first winter in this country, which was as cold as Russia, when they had arrived too late in the year to build even a log cabin; since it was far too cold to live in the tent, they had to spend their first winter in a dugout in the hillside with a sod roof. The two families had survived the bitter cold, their only heating provided by a sheet metal stove and the severe crowding of four adults with seven children. The worst of that dreaded winter had been not having a window and feeling like an animal burrowing in a hole.

She survived because Christian promised to start building a solid, warm house using the stones from their homestead land as soon as spring arrived. Fortunately, the snow melted early that year, and her husband gathered the stones and began the masonry as he promised. With the help of their large family, the neighbours, and an Indian summer, the outside of the house was completed in time for the cold weather. They worked at constructing the inside rooms during the slow winter months when farming was not possible, and they added the porch the next spring. Elisabetha insisted on a window in each of the rooms. Although they all frosted over during the winter, shafts of golden light from the sun shone through and warmed the smooth, stone floor.

The kitchen was the hub of the family's activity. Their four sons shared the largest bedroom, and Christian and she were very comfortable in the medium-sized room. At that time, they had only one daughter, and the smallest bedroom was more than adequate for Sofia. When Elisabetha delivered a second daughter three years later and they decided to give the girls their bedroom, her husband and she still had ample space in the smaller room adjacent to the kitchen.

The heavy stone walls of their home provided coolness during the intensely hot summers and protection from the strong winds and cold of the prairie winters. When it was arranged for Friedrich to marry Maria Biber, the dilemma of space for the newly wedded couple troubled Elisabetha. One night as they prepared for bed, she asked Christian, "Where will Friedrich and his new bride sleep? They clearly cannot share the boys' bedroom."

"It looks like we will have to give them this bedroom. I will sleep with the boys and you can move in with the girls until the young couple builds their own house," replied Christian.

"If we do that, where will you and I get together?" teased Elisabetha.

As Christian embraced his wife, he said, "We will have to take long walks to our grassy knoll in that grove of poplars where you love listening to the wind rustling through the leaves."

The miles of unsettled terrain passing by lulled Gustav into a trance until the train slowed for its approach into Balcarres. As he sat mesmerized, the long, green prairie grasses magically transformed to golden, flowing wheat fields on his many acres of land. Gustav was full of confidence and anticipation; he was strong, healthy, and determined to be successful. He knew that with the money he had saved in the bank, he would be able to buy better farm equipment than his father struggled with and increase the productivity of his quarter-section.

For all his optimism, something was nagging Gustav, and it took him a long time to finally put his finger on it. He was worried about his mother, who did not seem to have her usual energy and robust health. She never complained, although it had to be trying with Maria and their two children still living at home and Friedrich away working on the railroad so much. But it was something more than these daily irritations, which she had capably handled in the past. When Gustav helped her in her huge vegetable garden, he asked her how she was feeling, but she always said she was fine and to stop his fussing.

More passengers started to board the car, and a young woman with three small children claimed the seat behind Gustav. The baby she was holding was crying at the top of its lungs, and the other two children were tugging at her dress. All of them were thin, and although their clothes were clean, they looked well worn. Gustav felt sorry for this woman, who looked only a few years older than him and seemed to be overwhelmed with her responsibilities.

At that moment, Gustav shuddered with an eerie sensation of familiarity, although he was certain he had never seen her before. He looked intently at the woman and shook his head, thinking that he must still be in his trance. Startled by the young man's steady gaze, she said, "Hello, I'm Sandra McGregor. Have we been introduced?"

"I'm sorry for staring, and no, we have not met. I'm Gustav Werner. Do you need some help with your children?"

"Why, thank you. If you could seat my girls, Mary and Nancy, I would be able to feed my son and spare all of us his loud crying."

Gustav said hello to the little girls as he lifted each of them onto the train seat opposite their mother. He could not believe how light they were, and he had a sudden inspiration. "Are you hungry, Mary and Nancy? I have some fresh bread and cheese that my mother sent with me."

The girls shyly looked at him with eager eyes, but neither said anything. Gustav reached across Rolf, who still seemed to be dozing, and took the bag of food.

Rolf, instantly awake, hissed, "What are you doing? This may be the only food we have for the rest of the day. Reverend Biber said that his sister in Regina could put us up for the night if we slept on the floor, but there was no mention of a meal."

"I think we will get something to eat, but they can have my share if you are not willing to give these hungry-looking children some food."

Both girls ravenously ate a slice of bread and cheese, and when Gustav offered some to their mother after the baby was sleeping, she was equally grateful. As Sandra enjoyed the delicious food, she snatched glances at this kind young man with the handsome features.

He was tall and slender, but muscular and strong. When he spoke, he had an accent that Sandra suspected was German, since he had blond hair and blue eyes. His eyes were soft and gentle with a teasing twinkle, and she was not surprised that he soon won the confidence of her daughters.

The train ride to Regina passed comfortably for Sandra. She dozed while Gustav regaled Mary and Nancy with stories about his niece and nephew who lived in the stone house with all the other members of the Werner family. He told them about his brother Rolf in the next seat, who was usually more interested in sleeping and eating than in anything else. Rolf peered over and waved his hand at the little girls, wishing he could talk to people as easily as Gustav could.

When the conductor announced that the train was pulling into Regina, Gustav told the McGregor family that this was his destination. "This is where Rolf and I get off the train. Are you stopping here or continuing onwards?"

Sandra sat up and expressed her gratitude, "Thank you for your kindness, Mr. Werner. You have made this portion of our journey very pleasant. We have a long trip yet, as we are travelling to Winnipeg to live with my parents. Goodbye, and our best wishes to you and your family."

As the brothers got off the train, Sandra could see the resemblance between the two young men, although Rolf was considerably huskier than Gustav. Just before he went down the steps, Gustav turned and gave a final wave, still puzzled by his unusual feeling of knowing Sandra McGregor and her young family. Many years later, at one of the saddest times in his life, Gustav would remember this train ride and change his mind about his course of action.

6

Rolf and Gustav hurried to the Dominion Lands Office as soon as they left the train, and although they expected a little wait, they were in no way prepared for the huge line they saw when they arrived on Victoria Avenue. The lines of men and a few women were five people deep and extended down the entire block and around the corner to the end of the adjacent street. Rolf looked at his watch and said to Gustav, "What is going on? It is only ten o'clock in the morning and already there are more people here than in the whole town of Neudorf!"

Gustav, with his usual manner for obtaining information, simply introduced himself to the man standing immediately in front of him. "Hello, my name is Gustav Werner. My brother Rolf and I have just arrived and can't believe all these people. Do you know what is happening?"

"I'm Robert Hanson, and there is a rush for the last available land in the West. The Dominion Government has announced that the homestead grants will be stopped as soon as all of the surveyed sections have been filed at the lands offices. Good land has been scarce for the past two or three years, and there have been several claim jumps because many people have not filed on their land even though they have been living on it."

Rolf was able to understand enough English to grasp that there was a land rush, and he thought about how fortunate they were that their homesteads were within the two townships that had been set aside for the German Lutherans. In 1892 when he had arrived, Christian Werner was guaranteed quarter-sections of land adjacent to his homestead for each of his three sons living with him. Regardless of how long they had to wait to reach the lands office, Rolf and Gustav were assured of their claims.

The long day wore on, and as they slowly inched along in the line, Rolf teased Gustav about giving away his lunch. When he started to eat the remaining bread and cheese, he offered some to his brother, saying, "Those little girls looked like they hadn't eaten much in days."

By late afternoon, they had finally reached the wicket, where an officious yet tired government worker assisted them to complete and notarize the necessary documents. As the seal was placed on the form, Gustav could not prevent a smile from spreading across his face. He slapped Rolf on the back and exclaimed, "It's official: we are going to be Canadian landowners!"

On the train ride home the next morning, the brothers were quite companionable. Reverend Biber's sister fed them a hearty supper of chicken dumpling soup, fresh bread, and pickled pork hocks. After saskatoon-berry perogies and cream for dessert, even Rolf had to admit to being unable to consume any more.

The minute their heads touched the flat pillows on the floor of their host's kitchen, both young men fell sound asleep. Waiting in line for the entire day had been more tiring than working on the land, and they were relieved that they succeeded in filing their homestead claims.

Rolf was uncharacteristically talkative, and it occurred to Gustav that his older brother was shy in the presence of strangers, especially people who spoke English. Once again, he realized that his aunt and uncle had given him an incredible advantage with their commitment to his schooling. And they had been right about needing to learn the language of their new country.

"I have to admit that I was not as excited as you about filing my claim, but at least now I have the land to start building my house so it is ready when Katie and I get married. I don't want to live at home with Mama and Papa, and they have to further divide the bedrooms so everyone has a suitable place to sleep. I think Mama would have liked to keep their own room instead of sharing with the girls, separated by that thin wall from Friedrich and Maria. It doesn't look like Friedrich will ever move his family from Papa's house," said Rolf.

"One reason I got him the job with the railway was so he could earn the money to buy lumber, but he seems to spend it all on himself," sighed Gustav.

~ 7 ~

Elisabetha finished folding the last of the freshly dried laundry and began distributing it by placing each family member's clothing on his or her bed. When she came to Friedrich and Maria's bedroom, she decided that she had better knock, even though she had seen Maria walking outside with the children. She no sooner put their clean laundry on the bed and was turning to leave when she heard Maria's sharp voice snap, "What are you doing in our room?"

"I was leaving your clean clothes and linen," said Elisabetha before quickly walking away. She vowed to hold her tongue, although it was becoming harder. Her relationship with her daughter-in-law had been steadily deteriorating over the past few years. She could understand Maria's frustration with Friedrich's drinking and absences from home, but she had less and less energy to deal with either one of them.

She wanted to prepare a nice supper for Rolf and Gustav when they returned tonight from Regina, and it already seemed that so much of her day was spent working with food. In the beginning, Maria had helped her in the kitchen and the garden, but since Friedrich started working for the railway, she only infrequently contributed to the myriad tasks in this busy household.

It was as though Maria felt she did not have to work on the farm now that Friedrich rarely helped his father and brothers with the chores. Or perhaps because he was making money, she thought she should not be required to pull her weight—not that Maria ever saw much of his earnings. If it had not been for Christian's generosity, Maria and her children would have had no place to live or food to eat. Elisabetha chided herself: although she always determined to not waste her energy on trying to understand Maria, her thoughts frequently returned to that very subject.

As much as Elisabetha would have enjoyed the peacefulness of her garden, she sent Hanna and Katherina to pick the fresh green leaf lettuce for the salad with cream and vinegar. The girls were squeamish about catching a chicken, especially the task of chopping off the head so it could be plucked and gutted for frying that night. However, her two younger daughters were very helpful and actually seemed to become more solicitous as Maria became less considerate of the other family members.

The day was passing quickly, and it would soon be time for Christian to drive to Duff to pick up the boys at the railway station. Much to her delight, the girls and their father had conspired so Elisabetha would accompany Christian on this trip. Hanna and Katherina were confident they could handle making the hot potato salad and fry the chicken once it was ready for cooking.

"Get your hat, Elisabetha, and let's go for a drive on our way to Duff," said Christian.

They started off in the direction of the hamlet, but Christian pulled on the left rein to guide Wolfgang towards the secluded knoll in the poplar grove. "Christian, where are you going at this time of the day?" inquired Elisabetha. "The boys will be waiting for us at the station."

"They are old enough to make the choice to wait or to start walking towards home," replied Christian. "We never seem to have any time for each other, and I am worried about you. Things are not well between you and Maria, and you are not your spirited self."

The shade of the poplar trees and a pleasant breeze from the west created a welcome retreat from the heat of the summer afternoon and the busyness of the day. They nestled together on the soft prairie grass and enjoyed the quietness of their favourite spot on the entire quarter-section of land. "Oh, Christian, this was a good idea. I have been feeling tired this last while. This is such a beautiful, tranquil piece of God's earth. When I die, I want you to promise me that you will bury me here."

Christian shuddered with a sudden, cold fear as he studied the woman he had loved for thirty-five years. In his eyes, she was still as beautiful as that first time he had seen her in the village of Brundorf in Galicia, where her mother had hired him to assist with the chores around the manse. He was not sure what he had expected, but it had never occurred to him that his betrothed would be this tall, slender woman with the light, auburn hair and piercing blue eyes.

Over the years and with seven pregnancies, she had filled out, but she still moved with the same vigour and grace. That is, up until a few weeks ago. He caressed her now-greying but still baby-soft hair. "Elisa, don't talk like that. I need you to help me settle this wild country with its extreme weather and huge distances. We have many years ahead of us yet."

"It is too nice a day to worry about dying," Elisabetha said as she kissed Christian. "Let's go get our sons."

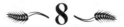

Hanna and Katherina had supper ready when the family returned from Duff. During the meal, Rolf and Gustav talked about their experiences in Regina, and as was his custom,

Gustav teased his mother about how slowly she ate. Katherina joined in and said, "I think you are becoming even slower, Mama."

The truth was that Elisabetha did not feel like eating at all, yet she did not want to upset her daughters, who had worked hard to prepare a delicious supper. She could not understand it herself. Elisabetha normally had as hearty an appetite as the rest of her family. The work on the farm was physically demanding, and the evening meal was large and nourishing to replenish energy for the next day.

Whether Elisabetha ate or not and regardless of how well she slept, she just could not seem to regain her usual level of vigorous energy and well-being. Of course this concerned her, but since she had no pain or discomfort, it was difficult to determine what was wrong. Perhaps she should listen to her own advice, which she was always giving to Gustav, and stop fussing about her health. What a good thing she had Rolf and Katie's wedding to organize; she would certainly not have time to dwell on herself.

After supper, Christian whispered to Elisabetha, "Let's go for a stroll and finish what we started this afternoon."

Once they arrived at their grassy knoll, Christian drew Elisabetha to him. She welcomed his kisses, and soon he was caressing her body and gently stroking her breasts. After so many years of physical intimacy, they both were spontaneous with each other's body. In the midst of their sexual advances, Christian stopped and asked, "Elisa, what is this lump on your right breast? I don't remember feeling it before."

"Just a minute; let me feel it. I have never noticed it before either. I don't usually go around caressing my breasts!" Elisabetha said, trying to lighten the moment.

"Maybe you could ask Margareta on Sunday. She may have some advice for you."

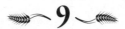

The next morning as soon as Friedrich went to the barn to get his horse ready for the ride into town, his father approached him. "Son, I need to talk to you about the house-raising bee that we are having for Rolf on Saturday. Your mama and I expect Maria and you to work alongside the rest of the family so we can build the house before Rolf and Katie get married next month. It is pretty obvious that there is no more room in our home."

Christian stopped himself from going on about the fact that Friedrich still had not built his own house because he knew how stubborn his oldest son could become when he thought someone was telling him what to do. He did decide to mention to Friedrich that his mother was not feeling herself and that it would be appreciated if Maria would help more around the house. Fortunately, Friedrich had been more intent on winning at cards the previous evening than on drinking and for once was in a reasonable mood. He too had noticed that Mama was not her usual robust self and agreed to be available on Saturday and to speak to his wife.

<p style="text-align:center">~~~~ **10** ~~~</p>

Gustav had spent every day since he had claimed his land plowing the tough, unturned prairie sod with his father's team of oxen and the heavy metal plow. It was backbreaking work because the sod was matted with the roots of grass, dandelions, weeds, and wildflowers. By the end of the day, he was so tired that if Rolf had not made supper from the food their mother sent with them for their first week of living in the tent, he probably would not have eaten.

Working for more than three years with the railway, Gustav had forgotten how physically demanding farming was, and he began to understand why Rolf always seemed to be hungry and tired. He also started to realize that if Rolf and Johann, before he had married and moved to his own homestead, had not helped Papa, neither Friedrich nor he would have been able to work away from the farm. When Gustav had offered to break Rolf's first fifteen acres so his brother could go to town with Wolfgang and the wagon to haul the lumber to build his house, he had not known just how indebted he was to Rolf.

Lying under the stars at night, it occurred to Gustav that while working for the railway he had taken a lot for granted: the stillness of the prairie, the darkness of the night when there was no moon, the silence of working alone, the sense of belonging to something far greater than him. For all of his life, Gustav would rejoice in the beauty of nature, rail at its destructive forces, and heal in its embraces. He would never lose his wonder and awe of God's world.

Each morning after a deep, replenishing sleep, Gustav was again ready to tackle the job of plowing, encouraged by the rich, black soil turned over in furrows by the plowshare. He could already imagine the flowing, silken heads of the golden wheat they would harvest next autumn on their adjoining homesteads. Sometimes it was only this mental picture of their ripening grain fields that kept him going. He made slow progress; how he wished he owned a lighter John Deere steel plow. The many hours behind the oxen handling his father's cumbersome metal plow strengthened his resolve to earn the money this winter to purchase one.

But every day when he returned to the arduous work, Gustav felt exhilarated that soon he would finish Rolf's fifteen acres and could start breaking his own land. He now understood his father's advice to concentrate on getting as many acres ready for planting in the spring as he could, rather than trying to grow a crop this year. The growing season was well under way, and between the two of them, they would not have enough cleared land to make it worthwhile.

He missed his early morning and evening rides on Wolfgang, and Gustav decided to stop early on Friday afternoon before going to his parents' for supper and to treat his horse to a gallop around the countryside. Man and beast were equally ready to exult in nature, to feel the wind in their faces and the sun at their backs as they raced across the mile-square sections of land. It was at times like this that Gustav felt at one with the universe and experienced the peace, harmony, and joy of being alive. He was no longer tired; he was young, healthy, and strong, and he had his entire life ahead of him. For as long as he could remember, Gustav had wanted to capture the pioneering spirit of his parents, and he was just beginning.

Gustav lost all awareness of time and distance while riding until he came to a small, winding, and fast-flowing creek hugged by a grove of tall poplar trees with their green, glossy leaves. Suddenly he saw a flash of orange at the top of the trees. "Whoa, Wolfgang. Be still."

He dismounted quietly and waited patiently until he caught a glimpse of three beautiful, elusive orioles flitting in and out of the treetops. When they were tired, they rested on the highest branches and sang their unique song. Gustav was mesmerized by the exquisiteness of the small songbirds and did not hear the footsteps of the man approaching him from behind.

"Excuse me, please. I don't want to disturb you, but I noticed you staring at the trees for a long time." Gustav jumped and turned to face a young man close to his own age.

"I'm sorry. I was watching some orioles, my favourite birds. I am afraid I have lost track of not only the time, but also the distance that I have ridden my horse."

"I am Andrew Thompson, and you have ridden to my homestead, which is about five miles southwest of Duff."

"Hello, I am Gustav Werner, and I'm sorry I have trespassed on your land."

"I'm happy you have come to visit. Why don't you bring Wolfgang up to the house, where you can meet my parents?"

"I think it is getting late, and my mama is expecting me for supper. May I come another time, possibly on Sunday after church, and meet your family?"

"Yes, that sounds like a good idea; maybe we can go riding. I have a horse called Sally."

～ 11 ～

Elisabetha had been preparing extra food all week for Rolf's house-raising bee, which would begin at sunrise on Saturday morning. She was looking forward to the day, even if it did include hard work: making large quantities of food, constantly washing dishes, and, if there was any time, helping to pound nails into her son's new house. But she enjoyed mingling with and feeding all of the relatives and friends who would come to help: Phillip Mohr, Reverend Ulmer, Peter and Anna Lutz, Fred and Katrina Hollinger, and Jakob Hatch and his brother Georg. She was especially looking forward to seeing her older children—Johann and Karolina, and Sofia and Karl—whom she did not see often enough since they had married and established their own homesteads.

Elisabetha reflected that she had a much better relationship with her daughter-in-law Karolina and son-in-law Karl than she did with Maria, with whom she interacted every day. Still, she sympathized with Maria and wished Friedrich would at least build his family their own house on the original farm site. Perhaps Elisabetha had warmer feelings towards Maria this week because she had been more helpful with the preparations for Saturday. As she thought about it, Elisabetha realized that Friedrich had also been at home more the last few days, and he said he would be available to work on Rolf's home. *I wonder how much of a hand Christian had in this,* thought Elisabetha, and she felt a surge of love for her husband.

The day was a success, with as many as twenty people helping to dig out a dirt basement and raise the three-room house. There was a marvellous spirit of co-operation as everyone did his or her part, even the older children, who had carried away the pails of dirt or fetched needed supplies for the men as they built the floor, walls, and roof. Rolf was very grateful but too reserved to express his thanks to his family and their friends. Before the hearty outdoor supper provided by his mother and sisters, he asked his father to include his thanks to God and to everyone present for what had been accomplished in one day.

~ **12** ~

During Sunday dinner, Margareta, who had not been at the bee, could not believe how tired and worn out Elisabetha looked, and it was unusual for her to have such a poor appetite. *How would she have the energy to prepare the wedding supper for Rolf and Katie in three short weeks?* With her typical quick thinking, Margareta had the answer.

"Phillip told me that I must kill some of the chickens before they eat all of the grain, and it occurred to me I could arrange to have Rolf's supper here after the church service. Elisabetha, would you allow me to cook for your son's wedding?"

Elisabetha was surprised again by the perceptiveness of her sister-in-law. "I would be honoured to allow you to prepare the supper. I seem to be having a lot of headaches, and I am always tired these days. As you know, I do not tend to complain, but there are times when I just have to sit down because of the weakness and pain in my limbs."

Elisabetha stopped short of telling Margareta about the lump in her breast, even though Christian had suggested she talk to her about it. It was such a private part of her body, and she was too modest to mention it to Margareta because she would insist on seeing it.

At that moment, Gustav asked his aunt if he could be excused from the table, explaining that he had met a young man who wanted to go riding with him. Margareta, delighted for him, said, "Of course you may be excused, Gustav. I'm sure that since you have become a landowner, you don't have much time to spend with Wolfgang."

~ 13 ~

When Gustav arrived at the grove of poplar trees, Andrew was already there with his horse, and the two young men started off following the crooked creek that flowed through the middle of the Thompson homestead. "How much of this land is yours?" asked Gustav.

"My father and I have the whole section because when he staked his original claim, he pre-empted the adjacent quarter-section," Andrew told him. "At the same time, my Uncle Joseph claimed the northwest corner as his homestead site and pre-empted the southwest to guarantee it for me when I turned eighteen. Then a few years ago, Uncle Joseph decided to become the lumber agent in Duff and sold his land to my father. Let's ride around the outskirts, and I will show you the entire section."

After riding for over an hour, Gustav reined in Wolfgang to a stop and stared off into the distance.

"What are you looking at now?" asked Andrew as he pulled Sally to a halt by his new friend.

"I like to see the line on the horizon where the land seems to meet the sky. It confirms for me the vastness of God's universe and makes me appreciate the wonder of this country," answered Gustav.

"I am beginning to think you are a bit of a romantic, Gustav Werner. You sound like Henry David Thoreau, who said that wilderness is the preservation of the world," teased Andrew.

"I definitely agree with him, but will we ever meet your parents?" asked Gustav.

"Sure. I'll race you back to the creek, and then we will go up to the house," said Andrew.

Andrew galloped ahead, and although Gustav and Wolfgang soon caught up and were neck and neck by the time they reached the creek, Sally was the winner of this race. As the young men developed their friendship, and before farmers started building fences on their land, they had many such contests, with each horse claiming nearly an equal number of successes. Soon their respective neighbours observed the races between the two men and their horses as they travelled across the countryside and came to appreciate the companionship between the young German and his friend the Englishman.

~ 14 ~

Maria was encouraged by Friedrich's behaviour over the last few days. He had worked along with his father, brothers, and uncles for the entire day when they were building Rolf's house. And he came home every day right after work and spent time in the evenings not only with the children, but also with her and his parents. As they were changing out of their Sunday clothes, she decided to bring up the subject of a house-raising bee for them. "I was surprised how quickly all of you were able to finish the house for Rolf and Katie. Could we use some of the money you are earning on the railway to buy lumber, and ask the family to build a separate home for us?"

"What is wrong with where we are living? We have our own room, and the children love all of the attention they receive from their grandparents. Besides, I have plans for the money that I work hard ten hours every day to earn."

"Is that money not to support your wife and to raise your children? I work around here all day so you have food to eat, clean clothes, and a tidy room," replied Maria.

"That's not what I have been hearing; in fact, it is quite the contrary. So I will damn well do what I want with my money, and I intend to buy a motorcar. It has already been ordered and will be arriving any day now."

"What in heaven's name do you need a car for when after more than six years of marriage, we are still living with your parents? All of your brothers and sisters left home and became independent as soon as they married. And who has been talking about me, and what are they saying?" asked Maria.

"There is no point to this argument. I have bought an automobile, and that is that! We will continue to live in this house because I don't think you even know how to cook and to look after your own children," answered Friedrich as he stormed out of the bedroom.

~ 15 ~

When Gustav came riding home from having afternoon tea with Andrew's parents and his pretty thirteen-year-old sister, Heather, he was surprised to see his mother sitting near the big rock under the shade of the caragana trees. He quickly dismounted, let Wolfgang loose into the pasture, and hurried to her.

"Mama, what are you doing? Are you all right? You don't look very happy."

"Oh, hello, Gustav. I came outside to get away from Friedrich and Maria, who are arguing again. Your papa took the children to see the new calf, and I have not mustered the energy to go back into the house to make supper. Actually, it is so peaceful sitting in the shade of these trees your father planted when we settled here."

Gustav sprawled on the short, thick prairie grass beside his mother and said, "What are they fighting about now? I don't understand why they can't build their own house!"

"As it turns out, that is exactly what this argument was about. Friedrich has used his money to buy a motorcar. But let's not talk about those two, who seem to get most of my attention. Tell me about your visit with Andrew."

"We had a very enjoyable afternoon: we rode for more than an hour, and then we had a race back to the creek, which Wolfgang lost! I have not been riding him very much, so I shall need to make sure I keep exercising him. Andrew's family seems very friendly, and we had tea and scones, which are somewhat like your soda biscuits. His sister Heather has the identical sandy red hair and green eyes as Andrew and is the same age as Katherina. I'm sure they would like each other. It is really nice to have a friend to talk to and do things with; I would like to bring him home to meet you and Papa."

"Oh, Gustav, you know how your papa is about anything to do with the English, and please don't ask me why because I don't know the reason. He is so firmly rooted in his German tradition that I don't think he will ever change or accept the ways of this country. We only left Austria for Russia because of the promise of land and political freedom, but when our menfolk were forced to serve in the Czar's army, we decided to flee to Canada. We had heard from some of the families who had escaped earlier that here we could be homesteaders and pacifists. But I would like to meet Andrew; one day, you can hitch Wolfgang to the buggy, and we will drive to my favourite grove of poplar trees. You can ask Andrew to meet us there, and I will bring tea and coffee cake."

⇛〜 16 〜⇚

The weeks preceding Rolf and Katie's wedding were busy for all the members of the Werner family. Gustav's gift to his older brother was money, which Rolf had decided to use to buy paint and wallpaper from his uncle's store. Rolf was very happy to have his own house and was intent on making it presentable for his new bride. He had known for a long time about the arrangement with the Ulmer family for him to marry Katie, who was three years older than his sister Hanna. Although he did not express his feelings even to Gustav, who was helping him every day, Rolf was anxious about starting married life with a young woman he had only been alone with once on a short walk.

Rolf was perfectly happy that his father selected a wife for him, and when the two families interacted at the Ulmers' home for supper, he thought Katie would make a good wife. At any rate, Rolf was far too shy to introduce himself to a woman and to have the courage to ask her to marry him. He knew that Gustav, who had the confidence to talk to anyone, would not have any problem starting a relationship with a woman, but he could never be so comfortable.

On the other hand, Rolf wondered what kind of husband he would be. He liked the respectful and courteous way his father treated Mama. Many times during the years Friedrich and Maria had lived in Papa's house, Rolf had vowed to himself that he would never behave towards his wife in the manner that Friedrich did with Maria. That meant he would need to learn how to converse and get to know Katie so he could be considerate of her, as Papa was with Mama. But what worried Rolf much more was the business of coupling with her.

Of course, Rolf had seen their farm animals working at procreating, but he had no idea what humans did. He could never ask Papa such a personal question. If Friedrich had ever been around and more reasonable, Rolf could have sought some advice from him. He knew this was an area in which Gustav would not be able to help him because certainly Gustav would be as much in the dark as he was. Perhaps he could go and visit Johann; he had always been an understanding brother. Yes, that was it; Rolf decided he would borrow Wolfgang one evening and ride over to visit Karolina and Johann.

Apparently, Rolf received very good counsel indeed. As an old man, he would frequently reflect on the rich, rewarding, and prolific life Katie and he had enjoyed in more than sixty years of marriage. He would invariably chuckle, remembering his timidity with the opposite sex, having to overcome his shyness from necessity after living in a home surrounded by women: Katie produced seven daughters before finally giving birth to their only son.

~ 17 ~

Every spring since claiming his homestead, as soon as the snow started to melt, Christian would be out in his fields from sunrise to sunset. After a hearty breakfast, he hitched the oxen to the plow and headed to an area of his quarter-section of land that needed to be broken. Elisabetha developed the habit of walking out at midday to bring him a jar of coffee, cheese, and thick slices of her delicious bread. They would look for a shady spot and have dinner together. After they ate, Christian took a half-hour nap while Elisabetha explored the landscape, searching for wildflowers and becoming familiar with yet another corner of their property. But the couple had broken their longstanding practice this year.

Christian knew Elisabetha's health was progressively worsening, and he did not want her to try walking to meet him.

He watched the position of the sun, careful to make sure he stopped plowing, tethered the oxen, and walked home for dinner before Elisabetha could leave the house to come and join him. Little did he know that he need not have worried about the time. With the increasing weakness and pain in her limbs, there was no way Elisabetha could walk much farther than her garden. She was also having more and more difficulty with her breathing. Of course, she had not told anyone about her symptoms because she did not want to worry her family, especially before Rolf and Katie's wedding.

But Elisabetha did not know that Christian had resolved to ride to Neudorf and arrange for the doctor to make a house call to examine her right after the wedding. It was Margareta who had helped Christian to make his decision. She had made him aware that Elisabetha had lost her appetite and was losing weight. Christian could not believe he had not seen these things for himself. He wondered how he could so love a person, live with and see her every day, and yet be so blind to what was happening to her. It was certainly not because he took her for granted; Christian knew how much he needed Elisabetha, and his greatest fear was her passing before he did. He simply could not imagine living without her by his side.

～ 18 ～

The Sunday morning of the wedding dawned with a bright blue, expansive sky, a gentle breeze, and the welcoming warmth of the sun's rays. Elisabetha had slept well, and as she awoke, she knew this would be one of her good days. Her head was clear, with no sign of the nagging, dull ache that she usually experienced, and even her limbs were free from pain. Before she got out of bed, she thanked God for blessing her with this day of health to celebrate her son's marriage to Katie. Then it occurred to Elisabetha that this might be the last time she would be alive to attend the most important days of her life—another of her children's weddings. This realization sent a chill through her body, and she had to struggle to regain the sense of well-being that she had experienced when she had awakened.

Elisabetha did not fear death; as a devout Lutheran, she believed in God and life everlasting, and she had lived her life according to His commandments. What distressed her the most was the thought of leaving her family—not being with them during the daily trials and tribulations, the celebrations and family gatherings, the joy of new life as her sons and daughters gave birth to their own children. How would they manage without her as the heart of the household? Elisabetha especially worried about Christian; they seemed to have become even closer since they had finally settled in this wonderful country.

As the lump in her breast became larger and she developed other symptoms, Elisabetha slowly came to accept that she would not regain her health; she was dying. Her acceptance increased as each day became harder and she could no longer deny to herself the seriousness of what was happening to her body. She managed to keep her fears, anger, and resentment to herself and eventually came to terms with the ultimate outcome while she was working—or lately, just sitting—in her garden.

At first, she had been furious with God for wanting to take her so soon. She had ranted and raved at the unfairness of it all. After so many years of struggle, hardship, and travel, they had at last started to establish a home, a future for themselves. They finally became landowners, with 160 acres of rich soil that had the potential to produce enough grain not only to feed their family, but also to sell for a profit. Elisabetha cursed God so much that on many Sundays she spent most of the service asking for His forgiveness.

When she realized she was wasting her limited energy and that it was becoming more difficult to allay the concerns of her family, she began to experience a feeling of resignation. Maybe she needed to stop pretending. Christian and Gustav, in particular, were becoming suspicious about what was wrong with her. That was part of the problem. Elisabetha did not know what was causing her body to betray her, so she could do nothing to stop it. Perhaps if she told her family, they might be able to help her, or at the very least, they could start making arrangements for when she could no longer manage all of her responsibilities.

Be brave! Get out of bed and make the most of this beautiful day, Elisabetha admonished herself. Christian would have been up at dawn and, by now, finishing the morning chores, and here she was feeling sorry for herself. Elisabetha had never been erratic in her life, and now it seemed she constantly vacillated between the extremes of thought, emotion, and behaviour. One minute she was blessing God and the next she was cursing Him. On her good days, she wanted to fight whatever this was and recover; on the days that she experienced excruciating pain throughout her body, she was ready to succumb to death. She was like the pendulum of the wall clock that they had managed to smuggle out with them when they had fled from Russia.

If she was dying, there were many things she still wanted to accomplish. Elisabetha remembered that Rolf was so excited that there was a photographer in Neudorf this week who could take wedding pictures, and the first thing she would do was arrange a family photo. She also resolved that tomorrow she would ask Christian to take her to their secluded knoll in the poplar grove, and she would tell him her concerns about her health and her future. Together they would decide what they could do and what they would tell the children.

~ 19 ~

Reverend Biber stood outside the small, wooden church on the main street of Neudorf to welcome the worshippers as they arrived for the service. Soon the handmade benches and chairs would be full, except for the two front rows, which were reserved for the families of the bride and groom. He was very pleased that both townships were coming to pay their respects for his niece's wedding. It had been a source of considerable contentment to him for some time that Katie, his gregarious and plump niece, was marrying one of the tall, handsome Werner boys. Initially, he had considered encouraging his brother-in-law, Erich Ulmer, the pastor in Lemberg, to talk to Christian about Gustav, who was closer in age to Katie; but over the years, he had noticed some disturbing changes in Gustav, particularly since he had started working for the railway.

As Gustav was maturing, he was gaining a reputation for getting too big for his britches and becoming driven to outdo others in the community. Reverend Biber was convinced that Margareta Mohr was responsible for putting these unhealthy ideas in his head, just as she was the one who had arranged for Gustav to learn how to read and speak English. And it certainly was not that he was spending any of his money in the village to help its economy. In fact, the rumour was that Gustav Werner was stingy with his money and did not seem to spend any of it. The only place he was ever seen to frequent was the newly established bank.

Why am I having these unchristian thoughts on the morning of my only niece's wedding, especially when I offered to conduct the service here in Neudorf so her father could enjoy the day? And about members of my own flock! Reverend Biber rebuked himself. It did, however, confirm to him that he made the right choice by suggesting that Erich offer Katie's dowry for Rolf when he was having his discussions with Christian. More and more, he was confident that Katie would make the quiet and complacent Rolf an excellent wife. Apparently, Katie had spent hours with her mother learning how to prepare all of the delicious and filling German dishes, and Reverend Biber had observed Rolf's hearty appetite at the many fowl suppers arranged at the church. If indeed the way to a man's heart was through his stomach, his niece and upcoming nephew would enjoy a loving and long marriage, hopefully with many grandchildren to compensate for Katie's parents' little success in producing offspring.

Just then, the Werner family arrived at the church, and although Reverend Biber saw Elisabetha every Sunday, he was not prepared for the haunted look in her eyes. In his many years as a clergyman, he had attended to innumerable individuals who were dying, and he was very familiar with their lingering but distant gaze, as though seeing everything for the last time—a look that spoke of the profundity of the bearer's feelings. He wondered if any of the Werner family had an awareness of just how ill their matriarch was, what was truly happening to this woman who had very smoothly run their household for years. He decided he must ride out to the Werner homestead this coming week and counsel Christian about this devastating turn of events.

"Good morning, Christian and Elisabetha. The union of our young people must be pleasing to the Maker for Him to have blessed us with this beautiful day. And with a breeze, yet, to help us to stay cool during the celebrations after the service."

Elisabetha was the first to respond, as she often did, unlike in many of the German families of the community where the man of the house was the only one who spoke in public. "The same good morning to you, Reverend Biber. God does indeed seem to be giving Katie and Rolf His benediction for their future together, and I, too, plan to enjoy the festivities."

When the church was full, Reverend Biber began the wedding ceremony by motioning for the bride to walk down the aisle. The talk of the town for the next week was how pretty Katie had looked in the white dress, which her mother had meticulously sewn for the occasion of her only child's marriage. Rolf Werner wore a dark suit, which seemed to make him look even taller than his six feet, and when he leaned over to place the ring on Katie's finger, he appeared very pleased with his new bride. In the German Lutheran tradition, the Sunday service followed the exchange of the marriage vows, and during his sermon, Reverend Biber was in fine voice, extolling the virtues of the holy state of matrimony. The ladies of the congregation had prepared a lunch of sandwiches, cakes, cookies, coffee, and tea so all of the townspeople would have an opportunity to congratulate the newly married twosome. The Ulmer, Biber, and Werner families would continue their celebrations well into the evening with a delicious supper prepared by Margareta Mohr, and as expected, Phillip supplied the men with plenty of whiskey to toast the groom.

⤞ 20 ⤝

The following morning, Elisabetha could not get out of bed, and Christian had to ask Hanna and Katherina to make breakfast and to separate the milk when he brought it to the shed. His daughters had been well instructed by their mother in the chores necessary to run a household, and since Maria so often refused to help, they were eager not to demonstrate the same inconsideration.

"Is Mama just tired from the wedding yesterday?" asked Katherina.

Christian looked at his beautiful thirteen-year-old daughter, who of his three girls most resembled Elisabetha. When he took the time to really observe her features, he would be transported back to the village in Austria where he had first been introduced to his wife, whom he now knew he was losing. When seen from her side profile, Katherina looked just like Elisabetha had in her youth. Katherina was already a few inches taller than her mother, and to many of the interested, available young men in the community, she was becoming exquisitely pleasing to the eye.

Christian did not know how to answer his daughter; he needed to consult with Elisabetha, and even in the midst of his dilemma, he could appreciate the irony. He wondered if they would have an opportunity to discuss what they would tell their children, or whether he would have to make the decision alone. Unlike many of the more traditional men from their homeland, Christian had come to rely on his wife during their thirty-five years of marriage as an equal partner in making the decisions that affected the family. To avoid causing his daughters any concern, at least for now, Christian chose to respond, "Yes, Mama overdid it yesterday and now needs a day to rest."

It was fortunate that Gustav had risen very early and had ridden Wolfgang to his own homestead. He gathered what food was available in the kitchen and would no doubt sample some of Rolf's new wife's cooking during the week. Christian suspected that of all of his seven sons and daughters, Gustav would be hit the hardest by his mother's untimely death. There had always been a stronger connection between the two of them, perhaps because of a similarity of character, which often resulted in a greater sensitivity to each other's needs.

Maybe this young doctor who had come to Neudorf could do something to help Elisabetha. In all of their years together, they had never had any need for a doctor, but now it was not a matter of recovering from some minor ailment. Christian resolved that as soon as he finished the milking, he would ride to the village and bring Dr. Spitznagel to examine Elisabetha. She would not be happy about Christian spending their hard-earned dollars for something she would consider unnecessary. He decided to wait to tell the girls why he had to go to town and not give any details of his real purpose for now.

$$\sim 21 \sim$$

When Christian brought Dr. Spitznagel into the bedroom, Elisabetha said, "Good morning, Doctor. I do not know whatever has possessed Christian to have you waste your time coming all the way out to our home. I am sure it is just a touch of the influenza and too much celebrating yesterday at our son's wedding."

"Good day, Mrs. Werner. Since I am here, I would like to examine you and make sure there is no serious problem. Perhaps, Mr. Werner, if you would prefer not to be present, one of your daughters could assist me during my examination."

Christian's response was immediate. "No, no, I will stay. The children do not know anything."

It did not take Dr. Spitznagel long to feel the lump in the underside of Elisabetha's right breast and, with concern, ask, "Mrs. Werner, when did you notice this growth in your breast?"

"I don't really remember. It was Christian who found it first." Looking at her husband, Elisabetha asked, "Do you recall when that was?"

"I think it was early in the spring, but I cannot say specifically now."

When he had finished his examination, Dr. Spitznagel encouraged Elisabetha to remain in bed and asked Christian to accompany him on a walk around the yard. By the time the two men reached the caragana trees, Dr. Spitznagel decided to break the uncomfortable silence.

"Mr. Werner, you indicated that your children are not aware of their mother's condition. What do you know?"

"What a clever way to ask me about the fears I have fretted about for some time. I don't know what my wife's problem is. I only know that in the past several months, she has gone from being a vibrant, healthy woman to someone who always seems tired, worn out, and lately, I suspect, to be having considerable pain. She, of course, never complains, and when any of us ask her how she is feeling, she minimizes it as she did with you today. But both of us know she is suffering from more than the influenza!"

"Mr. Werner, I am very sorry to have to tell you that if she has been having a lot of pain, I suspect that the growth in her breast has likely spread to other parts of her body and that there is very little I can do to arrest its progress. There is no easy way to tell you that your wife is dying."

Christian stopped walking and lowered his head into his hands. Dr. Spitznagel waited patiently until this proud, stern-looking man could compose himself. After some time, Christian looked at the young doctor, who appeared so sensitive to his need to collect his emotions, and said, "Thank you for your honesty. I think I have known for some time that my wife is becoming progressively worse, but I had hoped that something could be done. Will she suffer much?"

"The sad thing with these growths is that eventually most parts of the person's body are affected, and as the disease becomes more extensive, she will increasingly have more pain. She may become unaware of her surroundings and of her family members, which will make it very hard for all of you. I am so sorry that I cannot offer you better news."

⋙~ 22 ~⋘

During the last eight months of her life, Elisabetha Werner was able to return to her favourite spot, the secluded knoll with the grove of poplar trees, on two separate occasions.

A week after the doctor's visit, on another of her good days, Christian hitched Wolfgang to the carriage, arranged for Hanna and Katherina to pack a picnic lunch, and bundled Elisabetha in a blanket. The two of them spent a memorable day together enjoying the autumn weather. The leaves were starting to change to their orange and yellow colours, and with the sun shining brightly through the tall trees, the late afternoon was surreal in its beauty. Neither of them wanted to leave, nor did they want to discuss what to tell their children; they simply lay together on the grass and remembered the many happy times they had experienced over the years.

When they were finally ready to leave, Elisabetha turned to Christian and thanked him for the wonderful day. "Christian, I shall store an image of today in my mind to keep with me during the hard days ahead. I am not afraid of meeting my Maker, and you must help the children to understand it is God's will to determine when it is our time. I do want to remind you to bury me here in this blissfully serene place of the earth and to always keep it so. Will you please build a fence right around the trees?"

As hard as it was for Christian to talk about her dying, he did respond. "My dear wife, you shall have your promise."

The first Sunday that Elisabetha could not find the strength to go to church with her family served as the alarm to them that their mother was severely ill. Hanna and Katherina had frequently talked quietly together about what was plaguing their mother and stopped her from helping them in the house. But neither had the courage to ask their father about their mother's health, nor did he ever provide any information to them, even after the doctor's visit. Christian Werner could not come to terms himself with the fact that Elisabetha was dying, much less express anything to his children.

When Gustav learned that Mama was not going to church, he knocked on the door of the bedroom and anxiously approached her. "Mama, if you are not going to the service, neither am I. Please let me stay here with you, just to talk. Since I have moved to my own land, I do not see you very much."

"Yes, Gustav. I would like that, and I am sure your papa and Reverend Biber will understand. Besides, I wanted to arrange an afternoon when you can take me to the grove of trees to meet your friend Andrew."

"It will be much easier to plan now because this week I am going to walk to my place and bring Papa's oxen home. It is getting too late in the season to continue breaking sod. With the freezes at night, the ground is hard until early afternoon, and by then it is hardly worth taking the oxen to the field. Also, it is too cold to sleep in the tent much longer, and although Rolf and Katie have asked me to spend the winter with them in their new house, I would rather move back to the bedroom here."

"Of course you will come back home, Gustav, and then on one of my good days, we will go to the grove to meet Andrew."

"What do you mean, Mama, by 'one of your good days?'" Gustav asked anxiously.

After sitting together in silence for several minutes, Elisabetha began to realize that Christian had not talked to their children. Did she have the strength to be honest with Gustav, her favourite child, as he sat expecting her response? How and what would she tell him, especially since he was not aware of the seriousness of her condition?

"Gustav, I have growths in my body that are causing me weakness and some pain. Papa brought the doctor to see me, but there is little he can do. I know this is hard for you to hear, but I do not want to lie to you. I have always loved you, Son, and I don't want any deceit or mistrust in our relationship."

"What are you saying, Mama? What will happen with these growths?" exclaimed Gustav.

"I had hoped that Papa had talked to all of you about my future, but it seems he has not yet had a chance to tell you."

"I have hardly seen Papa this last while, and no one has told me anything," replied Gustav.

Elisabetha looked at her son, her eyes simultaneously full of love and pain. Before she could say anything, Gustav, with an overwhelming feeling of dread, blurted out, "Mama, you are dying?!" At the same time, he stood up, rushed to the side of her bed, and clasped his mother's shoulders. "Please, Mama, tell me I am wrong. You are too young to die. I want you to be here for my wedding. I want you to play with my children. You cannot leave us now."

"I will always be with you in your heart. Your memory of me will enable me to be at your wedding and to be there when you need me," Elisabetha answered softly.

"No, that is not good enough. It is not the same as having you here, as being able to talk to you, to ask your advice, or to visit you with my wife and children. I cannot accept that God is taking you now; you are only fifty-nine years old. You have survived too much to die just when things are finally getting easier for Papa and you." Gustav was almost yelling in his distress. "What kind of God would do this?"

"Please, son, calm yourself. You do not mean what you are saying. It is not for us to question God in His wisdom; we do not decide when we live or die."

"Oh, Mama, how can you lie there and ask me to be calm? How can you talk so rationally about your own death? I can't stay in this room; I have to get outside. I am going for a ride on Wolfgang to try and make sense of what you have told me. I am sorry, Mama. Please forgive me." As Gustav rushed out of her bedroom, Elisabetha sank heavily on her bed, the prison where she had spent most of her hours and days for the past weeks, and cried in anguish.

～ 23 ～

Wolfgang thundered across the thawing ground; Gustav urged him to go faster and faster. The prairie sod split as animal and man raced across its surface. Wolfgang's hooves left indentations in the ground, causing it to weep dewy tears as he pushed harder to appease his master. But it did not matter at what speed or how far they travelled; Gustav could not fill the emptiness in his soul. His mother, the person he loved most in the world, was dying.

Although Gustav wanted to ride forever, his horse was beginning to tire; without any direction, Wolfgang headed towards the Thompson homestead. Most of their rides over the past months had been to this destination. His light brown coat glistening with sweat, Wolfgang came to an abrupt stop in front of Andrew's house.

Andrew was hauling water up in a bucket from the newly dug well in the middle of the yard before leaving for church when he heard the sound of a horse approaching very fast. He was surprised to see his friend, who was always at the Lutheran church at this time on a Sunday morning. Andrew set the pail on the ground and ran to where Wolfgang was standing. His alarm increased as soon as he saw the dazed look in Gustav's eyes.

"What's wrong? Why are you here? Let me help you get down."

Gustav stared at him with unseeing eyes, and Andrew realized that he had experienced some kind of shock. He gently said, "Gustav, please come into the house for a cup of tea. Something has happened, and you need to tell me what I can do to help."

"I want you to come with me," Gustav finally managed to say, shaking his head to come out of his stupor.

"We are not going anywhere until you have told me what is troubling you," replied Andrew. "Besides, you have obviously ridden Wolfgang very hard, and he needs a rest. I will give him water and then tether him by the trees where he can graze."

～ 24 ～

On many occasions over the past several months, Maria did not go to church, sending her children with their grandparents and their father, if he was in any condition to go. However, it was quite amazing how on most Sunday mornings, Friedrich, regardless of what time he had come home in the early hours, was able to get up and be presentable for the trip to town. Maria's mother-in-law had learned long ago not to question any of her behaviour, and if there was any discussion about her not attending the weekly service, it occurred out of Maria's earshot.

This was the only time Maria was alone in the house, and although she missed the delicious Sunday dinners with the Mohrs, she enjoyed the quiet and the stillness of the

Werner home. She would walk through the house, going from room to room, imagining how she would change it if it were hers. After almost seven years of marriage, she had realized that this was the only house she would be able to call her own, and she thought she had accepted that reality. But her resentment had resurfaced when they held the house-raising bee for Rolf, which meant that her cousin Katie Ulmer could start her married life in her own home.

Maria had never understood why her own mother and her Aunt Julia both had had only one child, and she had always determined that she would have a large family. When she was young, her favourite game was playing house with her one precious doll, which her grandmother had made for her sixth birthday. She treated Annie, clad in gingham dress and boots, like her own baby and used a wooden box with a pillow for her bed. Being an only child was lonely, especially when all of the other families who lived close by seemed to be overrun with children. On the other hand, Maria was not very old before she figured out that there were advantages in not having siblings. She did not have to share, and she quickly learned that her parents were eager to please her. If she asked politely and with respect, Maria could get pretty much what she wanted.

As she got older, Maria spent hours planning her own home and imagining herself as a mother when she would be old enough to have a husband. So when she started to notice the tall, handsome Friedrich Werner in church and wondered what it would be like to be his wife, she decided to talk to her father. It did not take much convincing before he agreed to arrange for Friedrich to come to a family supper. The Werner family was known in the community as hard-working, experienced farmers who knew how to work their land to make it productive, and Konrad Biber considered the oldest son well worth his daughter's dowry.

At first, Maria was happy as she adjusted to being a wife. When they moved into his parents' home, Friedrich told her it was just for a short time, until he could earn the money to buy lumber to build their own home. She believed him and tried to become part of the Werner household. Maria helped Mama Werner with the chores as she had with her own mother and talked companionably with Friedrich's younger brothers and sisters. There was much more work with all the extra people in her new family, but Maria enjoyed the laughter and the conversations among them, as well as many of the activities that occurred on the farm. She particularly liked walking across the fields and carrying the lunch with Elisabetha to the Werner men as they worked their land.

In time, Maria even came to accept Friedrich's lovemaking, primarily because she knew their coupling was necessary for her to become pregnant. She desperately wanted a baby and was excited beyond belief when her monthly cycle stopped and her body started to feel heavy with the new life beginning within her. When Friedrich told his parents about the coming baby, the whole family began to plan for the first grandchild to be born. Maria had blossomed with the attention and affection that the Werner women, in particular, began to show towards her, and together they had knitted and crocheted all of the clothes and blankets for the new baby.

When Mathias was born, Maria was lost to the rest of the world. Her attention became riveted to this tiny, vulnerable, and totally dependent human being. She had had no idea of the magnitude of responsibility demanded by a newborn infant, and even though Mama Werner and her daughters were very helpful in his care, she was constantly plagued with worry and anxiety for him. Everyone tried to reassure her, explaining that because she had no younger brothers or sisters, she was just not familiar with the needs and, for that matter, the resilience of a baby. But Maria worried that when Mathias was asleep, there was something wrong with him, and when he was awake and crying, that *she* was doing something wrong.

The patience of all of the Werner family, including Friedrich, began to grow thin with Maria's unending fretting about her baby, and she started to withdraw from the many activities in which she had previously participated. She found it easier to spend most of her time in the bedroom with Mathias, although she was glad it was spring and that she could carry him outside for short walks or sit in the shade of the caragana trees. Fortunately, with such maternal vigilance, he quickly thrived and grew strong, and Maria did learn to relax and gradually made her way back into the circle of family life. Even then, it was not to resume her daily chores, but rather to bask in the attention that his grandparents, aunts, and uncles bestowed upon Mathias as he delighted them with his cooing and smiles.

When Maria became pregnant again within months of Mathias's arrival, she was rested and considerably more confident in her abilities to care for an infant. Following Julianna's birth, there was little question that Maria would not contribute to the running of the busy household. By tacit agreement, the Werner family allowed her to devote all of her time and energy to raising her children. And as much as she wanted her own home, Maria had the good sense to realize she would not have been able to dote on her beautiful, happy babies if she had been required to carry the many responsibilities of the average young farm wife. In the end, Maria again got pretty much what she wanted, as she turned a blind eye to her in-laws' obvious resentment.

25

This Sunday morning was unusual right from its beginning. Maria had awoken with a start from a restful and unbroken sleep when Mathias and Julianna had crawled onto the bed. They were wide awake and hungry, of course. Maria gave each of them a hug and asked them to put on their Sunday clothes and go to the kitchen where Aunt Hanna and Aunt

Katherina would be making breakfast. Maria felt drowsy and a little disoriented. Then she realized that Friedrich had not come home, even in the early morning hours, and in all of his years of drinking, this was the first time he had stayed away for the entire night. Not that she really cared. It meant that she had not been rudely awakened with his stumbling around, nor had she had to resist his drunken attempts to make love or to make sure, if he succeeded, that she pulled away before he released his seed into her. After having a child of each sex, Maria had decided that two babies would be enough for her, especially when her husband was rarely home.

It was so peaceful that she decided to doze for a while longer in her cozy bed with the feather quilt her mother had made for her wedding gift. She must have gone back to sleep because the next thing she heard was someone yelling. Maria could tell from the slant of sunlight through the small bedroom window that it was mid-morning, and for the second time this Sunday, she was surprised. She was certain that the rest of the family had gone to church, and it was not Friedrich, finally home, who was making the noise. In fact, it sounded like Gustav, and it was coming from his mother's bedroom. *This cannot be happening,* thought Maria, *Gustav raising his voice to his mother.* And then she heard the sound of the door slamming as someone went out.

For a few minutes, there was total silence, and then Maria heard the most unbelievable sound of all; she was convinced that she could hear Mama Werner crying. Not just soft sobs, but loud, anguished wails coming from Elisabetha's room. As Maria considered what to do, she realized that when she had seen her lately, her mother-in-law had looked dreadful. But since she tended to be oblivious to what was happening in this usually peaceful home, in which quarrels between Friedrich and herself were often the only disruptions to its harmony, she was dumbfounded.

Maria threw off the comfortable quilt, quickly pulled on her short-sleeved, flowered housedress, and opened her bedroom door. Yes, Mama Werner was continuing with her plaintive, high-pitched cries. *What shall I do now?* Maria asked herself. It occurred to her that she was totally unprepared for this type of situation, and she did not know how to console someone. In her relatively sheltered life, she had never had to care for anyone other than her children, and she was usually the one on the receiving end of compassion, primarily from her parents, who had some awareness of her marital difficulties.

With considerable hesitation, Maria knocked on the bedroom door and then waited. No response. She knocked again with a little more force. Still nothing was heard but the loud and inarticulate crying from within. Maria decided she had to enter and ascertain what was causing Elisabetha such distress.

She gently opened the door and asked, "Mama Werner, what is happening? Is there anything that I can do? You sound so terribly upset."

As Maria was speaking, she became aware of the stuffy and sickly smell that was present in the room. When she got closer to Elisabetha's bed, she was appalled at her mother-in-law's appearance. She had lost considerable weight, her colour was a ghastly grey, and she had dark, sunken circles under her eyes. Maria's mind was racing. *What is wrong? How long has it been since I have really looked at her? Why have I not noticed that she was so ill?*

Finally, Maria reached out, placed her hand gently on Elisabetha's shoulder, and said, "Mama Werner, please stop crying. I have never seen you so upset, and I cannot stand it any longer."

Elisabetha was so startled that someone was in her bedroom that she suddenly stopped her uncontrollable sobbing and peered up into Maria's face. She was completely at a loss for words. The two women momentarily stared at each other; neither knew what to say or do. With effort, Elisabetha collected herself and eventually said, "Maria, I thought that everyone had gone to church and the house was empty. I would not have carried on so had I known you were here."

"But what has happened to cause you to be so upset?" asked Maria.

Elisabetha looked at her and wondered how much to confide in this young woman with whom she had less and less rapport over the years. It was quite astonishing that she was even here in her bedroom inquiring about what was troubling her. She could hardly remember the last time that Maria and she had even spoken to each other, although they lived together in the same house. Then Elisabetha realized it had been some time since she had been out of her room and she felt a sudden compulsion to leave her bed and get some fresh air.

"Maria, I feel relieved since my big cry, and I would like to go to the kitchen to have some breakfast. Would you please help me to get up?"

Maria was actually quite eager to assist her mother-in-law, who had asked very little of her during the years they had shared the same roof. She helped Elisabetha out of bed by kindly lifting her under her arms and was amazed at how she could feel her bones through her skin. She was so thin that Maria was worried she would hurt her by merely holding her.

"It is OK, child; I will not break. Just help me put on my dress and walk beside me to the kitchen," said Elisabetha.

The impact of Elisabetha's soft, genial tone when she addressed Maria as "child" was remarkable. For the first time in years, Maria felt a spark of her earlier kinship with the family's matriarch. Together, the two women made their way to the kitchen, and when Maria had seated Elisabetha in the most comfortable chair by the stove, she went to the pantry to see if there were any fresh eggs from the morning gathering. While she scrambled the last four eggs and cut some of the homemade bread to toast over the stove, Elisabetha talked about how pleasant it was to be up and what a warm autumn day it would be.

"Thank you, Maria, for making my breakfast. I enjoyed it more than anything that I have eaten for a while," said Elisabetha after they had consumed the eggs and toast with fresh strawberry preserve.

"You are welcome, Mama Werner, but you are so thin that you cannot be eating much of anything," replied Maria.

Not wanting to spoil the companionable feeling between the two of them, Elisabetha had already decided to avoid any discussion about her illness. Instead, she wanted to enjoy this time with Maria, with no one else present to distract her from her long-overdue attempt at reconciliation. So rather then respond to her comment, Elisabetha said, "I would like another cup of your delicious coffee, please, Maria, and then perhaps you would be so kind as to walk outside with me."

They sat together, drinking from their large mugs. They did not talk about the cause of Elisabetha's distress, but rather about inconsequential things. They both felt that they had never communicated so well before.

With a warm sweater wrapped around her shoulders, Elisabetha leaned on Maria as they slowly walked to the little bench that Christian had made and placed at the edge of the caragana trees near the approach to her garden. Maria could not believe how little strength this previously energetic and robust woman now had. When they were seated and basking in the warmth of the sun's rays, Maria tentatively expressed, "Mama Werner, you are very ill, aren't you?"

Elisabetha looked into her daughter-in-law's piercing blue eyes and knew that if she was to retain any of the conciliatory goodwill she had gained, she must be honest. "I am not going to lie to you, Maria, although most of the other children do not know the extent of my illness. I have a growth in my breast, which Dr. Spitznagel has told Papa Werner will be the death of me."

As Maria opened her mouth to exclaim, they simultaneously jumped at the strange noise coming from the direction of the wagon trail. They actually huddled together; the sound was so unlike anything either of them had ever heard that they were concerned for their safety. And they were just a little annoyed when they saw Friedrich waving as he came around the trees riding in the most unusual contraption ever seen on the Werner farm. It had high wooden wheels like the democrat wagon that Phillip and Margareta Mohr had purchased two years ago for their country drives. But it also had small, solid rubber tires, which appeared to be connected and driven by chains.

When Friedrich reached the women, he came to a stop and vaulted out of the machine. "Well, what a delightful surprise! My two favourite ladies are waiting for me to show them my new automobile. And since you are here, you shall be the first passengers in my car."

Elisabetha looked at her son and replied, "I am not sure I want to ride in that strange thing you call a car."

"Oh, come, Mama. There is room for both of you in the back seat. Look, there are comfortable cushions, which are even covered in leather! I will help you in, and then when you are ready, I shall run to the front and turn the crank to get it started. Since there is just this dashboard in place of a windshield, I have practised how to jump in and drive once it is running."

The women had not seen Friedrich so excited and boyishly good-humoured for a long time, so the trio took their respective places and were driving around the Werner homestead when the rest of the family returned from the village. Even Gustav, who had been restored to his calm demeanour by his friend Andrew and tea with the Thompson family, could not believe his eyes when he rode into the yard. Most of all, he was happy to see his mother out of her confining bedroom and driving about in the fresh air, but in what he was not quite sure. And with Maria, of all people, sitting beside her? Gustav and the other Werners had no idea how this marvel of circumstances had come to be, but the fun and excitement was contagious and continued for the entire day, with every family member having an inaugural ride in Friedrich's new automobile.

At supper that evening, there was great discussion about the day's events, and not lost on any of them was the fact that for the first time in a very long period, Elisabetha also was seated at the large kitchen table in the heart of their home. What was so delightful for Christian, Elisabetha, and most particularly Maria and her children, was how Friedrich was aglow with the attention heaped on him. He was once again the outgoing, humorous young man who had attracted Maria's interest so many years ago.

26

The next morning, since he did not have any animals on his farm, Gustav helped his father with the chores before he bridled Wolfgang and set off for town. He went straight to his aunt and uncle's general store; first, he wanted to apologize for not coming for Sunday dinner yesterday, and second, he needed desperately to confide in his Aunt Margareta. Gustav felt a little more accepting of his mother's impending death since his talk with Andrew, but he knew no one would understand and be able to comfort him like his favourite aunt could. When he entered the store, Uncle Phillip was busy with a customer; he acknowledged Gustav with a nod of his head and indicated with his eyes that Aunt Margareta was upstairs in their living quarters. Gustav raced up the stairs two at a time; such was his pressing need to tell her of his anguish. She was in the kitchen and had just poured a cup of coffee for him, having heard his footsteps and remembering how he would bound up the stairs as a boy.

"Oh, Aunt Margareta, I am so happy you are not downstairs in the store. I really need to talk to you, and I am so sorry I missed dinner with you yesterday. But I just could not come. When Mama did not get ready to come to church, I went in to talk to her, and I found out that she is dying from her illness." The words rapidly tumbled out of Gustav's mouth as though he could change their impact by spitting them out as quickly as possible. Then, when his aunt opened her arms to embrace him, to his surprise and later, much to his embarrassment, he sobbed his heart out in her expansive hug.

Margareta Mohr would neither chastise her young nephew nor ever disclose his uncharacteristic emotional outburst to another living being, even her husband, with whom she shared most occurrences. She was firmly committed to this response because she knew full well that when Gustav eventually came to terms not only with his mother's death but also with his overwhelming despair, he would be very hard on himself.

Finally, as his crying began to abate, Margareta gently released him from her arms and said, "Gustav, I shall pour you a fresh cup of coffee, and we shall have something to eat before we go downstairs to see your Uncle Phillip."

"Thank you, Aunt Margareta. I would like that, and then I want to talk to Uncle to see if he can order me a musical device called a gramophone as soon as possible. In my distress yesterday, of course I took Wolfgang out for a ride. I guess I rode him so long and so hard that eventually we ended up in Andrew's yard, and he practically dumped me on the ground when he stopped very abruptly in front of the house. One way Andrew calmed me—and I do want to tell you that I did not cry in front of him or his family—was to ask me what Mama would really like to do before she died. After thinking for a few minutes, I told her she would probably love to go back to Austria, where she was born. It did not take us long to realize the impossibility of that. But then Andrew came up with an excellent suggestion."

Margareta set a plate of Gustav's favourite coffee cake, baked with apples and cinnamon, on the kitchen table with two cups of freshly brewed coffee. "I saved your dessert from yesterday because although I did not know what was happening, I sensed that you would come and see me today. Now please eat as you tell me what you and your friend decided."

"You are so good to me, Aunt Margareta. Thank you. I am hungry as usual. Andrew told me about an article he had read in *The Leader* about the hardware store selling a machine that plays music on metal cylinders. And they said they had recordings of many of the great classical composers from Austria, like Wolfgang Mozart, Johann Strauss, Joseph Haydn, and of course Ludwig van Beethoven, even if he was not a true Austrian. Andrew suggested that I order a gramophone and some music cylinders for Mama and listen to them with her since she has to spend so much time in her bed."

"Andrew is a bright young man! What an excellent idea. Let's go down to the store and ask your Uncle Phillip to get the order ready so you can run it over to the train station today. And you must bring your friend to have supper with us soon; we want to meet him."

27

It was a glorious autumn. When snow had fallen in mid-September, most of the farmers believed winter had made its early appearance. Much to their delight, at the beginning of October, the air warmed and the translucent rays of the late afternoon sun melted the snow. For three weeks, the countryside came back to life, bathed in the warmth of the unseasonably dry and sunny weather. In the mornings, the ground was covered with a heavy frost and the air was crisp, but by midday, it was very pleasant to be outdoors. It was far preferable to the intense, scorching heat of the prairie summer and certainly to the bitter cold of winter. Day after day of Indian summer passed tranquilly on the Werner homestead, and even Elisabetha experienced a time of calm and peace, comparatively free from pain.

Since he had moved back home for the winter months, on one of these mornings when Gustav came into his mother's bedroom to say good morning, Elisabetha said, "Son, it looks like it will be another beautiful day, and I would like you to arrange for us to go to the poplar grove and meet your friend Andrew. I had a reasonable sleep last night, and I am feeling strong enough to have a little excursion."

"Mama, I am so pleased. Although Andrew understands that Papa still doesn't know about our friendship, he has been asking to be introduced to you, and I was afraid you would not be able to make it," replied Gustav.

"But you forget, my dear boy, that I made you a promise, and I do not go back on my word. As soon as you have done the milking, why don't you ride to Andrew's and ask him to go to the grove for a light dinner? I wonder if we should ask Katherina to come with us in case I need help with anything during our visit."

"That is a smart idea. I shall talk to her and ask her to prepare some food and coffee to bring for dinner."

In preparation for the long-awaited introduction of his friend to his mother, Gustav had been teaching Andrew some rudimentary German, providing him with enough words and expressions to permit him to carry on a conversation. To her delight, when Elisabetha finally met Gustav's young and energetic English friend, he spoke to her in her own language. She had wondered how they would communicate, and had she been stronger, she would have continued to learn more English words while sitting with Gustav on the garden bench. Christian forbade any of them to speak English in the house, although the girls, particularly Katherina, were very interested in learning to speak another language.

Katherina was so excited to be invited to meet Gustav's friend that she prepared a tasty meal of smoked sausage, thick slices of fresh bread, potato salad, and beet pickles. As she and Hanna had regularly done over the past summer since their mother no longer had the energy, she carefully packed the food in one basket and the jars of hot coffee with thick, rich cream and sugar in another. At least this morning she did not have to carry her heavy load out to the fields; she could wait until Gustav returned and hitched Wolfgang to the carriage. Hanna was very curious about all of these arrangements and was a little annoyed, to say the least, that she had not been asked to go along with Mama, although today was her turn to take Papa his dinner. In truth, there were many times when Hanna was sure Mama favoured Katherina, not unlike the impression held by Friedrich that Gustav was the favourite son in their mother's eyes.

As they were approaching the small hill surrounded by the grove of poplar trees, they could see Andrew already waiting for them. "Your friend does have a fast horse," commented Elisabetha.

"Well, Wolfgang could not have won any race today. Look at how much he has to pull! I think Katherina has packed enough food to feed a threshing gang," teased Gustav.

"Mama always taught me that it is impolite to send a guest home hungry," replied Katherina.

"It surely will not happen today," said Elisabetha and Gustav at the same time.

When they stopped the carriage, Andrew came running over, calling his salutations to his friend and waiting to be introduced to the two women as he helped them down from their seats. After everyone had exchanged greetings, Gustav got the blanket and spread it on the ground, which was now covered in dried leaves. There still were green blades of grass poking through the heavy covering of brown and yellow poplar leaves. Andrew came up with the idea of placing Sally's saddle on the blanket as a support for Elisabetha to lean against while sitting on the ground.

Katherina's dinner was delicious, the company amiable, and the weather co-operative on this serene afternoon in mid-October. Gustav interpreted when someone did not understand what was being said, and the hours passed pleasantly. While Gustav and Andrew strolled beyond the trees on the other side of the hill, Elisabetha and Katherina dozed with a second blanket to cover them. Later, when the young men returned, they finished the last of the coffee and the strudel left from their meal. No one wanted to leave.

Gustav glanced frequently over to where his mother sat motionless, leaning on Andrew's saddle. Her blue-grey eyes were very bright and alive; she seemed to be watching everything.

"Mama, are you OK?" he asked hesitantly.

"I am fine, Son. Don't mind me; I am just drinking in the sights and sounds of nature: how the rays of the sun are shining through the trees, the wind rustling through their naked branches, the sparrows singing as they play hide-and-seek with one another," replied Elisabetha.

As she was talking, Gustav thought about how aware she was of her surroundings, of what was happening, and how she seemed to be filling up with what was going on around her. She was certainly not filled with food as the rest of them were; she had scarcely eaten a morsel. She was very focused, seeing and enjoying things that were so ordinary while he had not paid the slightest attention to them.

The sun was a bright orange and yellow ball of fire as it sank lower and lower on the horizon. When it slid out of sight, Elisabetha turned to look at the three young people and said, "Thank you, children, for a wonderful day. I am now ready to go home, please."

"I am so glad I met you, Mrs. Werner. I would like Katherina and you to come and have tea with my family sometime. My sister Heather is the same age as you, Katherina, and I am sure you could teach each other how to speak your own languages, just as Gustav and I have done these past months," replied Andrew.

28

When cold weather arrived during the last week of October 1909, it hit with a vengeance. On most evenings, the northern lights lit up the dark sky in all their brilliance. The glowing, majestic green, purple, yellow, and red colours rippled first across the horizon and then in spears that darted down to the earth. These lights continued their eerie dance as they stretched across the firmament, as though God was directing a ballet in the sky. Then one overcast night, the snow began to fall—great, fluffy flakes at first, which seemed to want to play as they drifted lightly down from the sky. But later they became more insistent and quickened their pace, as though being driven out of the heavens.

Once it had started, it did not seem to know how to stop, and it continued to snow for five days. When the snowfall finally ceased, the temperature plummeted and the bitter north wind began to blow. Soon the world was totally white and silent, except for the howling of the biting wind, which blew the snow in drifts as high as the windows. Only the men went outdoors during the blizzard to care for the animals and to carry wood for the hungry kitchen stove, which they took turns feeding during the day and the long winter nights so the fire did not go out. The thick stone walls of the Werner home offered more protection from the constant wind than most of the surrounding homesteads, but keeping the house warm—especially the bedrooms—was impossible. Every bed was covered with feather quilts and heavy blankets, which were piled higher as the temperature continued to drop.

The severity of Elisabetha's pain was in concert with the weather. Every bone in her body ached right down to the marrow, it seemed, and she could not stand the weight of the blankets on her limbs. Christian wanted to move a bed into the kitchen beside the stove, but Elisabetha would not hear of it. She would not give up her privacy because she did not want her grandchildren to see and hear her agony. Hanna thought of warming towels in the oven of the stove and using them to wrap her mother's arms and legs under the quilt to keep her warm and provide some relief from her constant pain. By now Christian had moved into the bedroom with Gustav, and the family were taking turns around the clock sitting with Elisabetha. Much to everyone's surprise, even Maria faithfully rotated regularly, trying to help Elisabetha find some measure of relief.

Gustav was devastated by the sudden deterioration in his mother's health. He rebuked himself for daring to think and to hope during that wonderful afternoon in the poplar grove that she was getting better. He remembered how serene she was as she observed everything with a childlike fascination. Now it was even harder to see her lying in her bed moaning in pain and biting her lips to prevent herself from screaming every time one of them turned her or his sisters helped her to use the chamber pot.

When it was Gustav's turn to be with his mother, he found himself becoming more and more frustrated that they could do so little to help her. As soon as this blizzard was over, Gustav resolved that he would hitch Wolfgang to the sleigh and go to Neudorf. The doctor must at least have medication to relieve the pain, even if he could do nothing to stop the progress of this terrible disease. He also wanted to check if Uncle Phillip had received the gramophone that he ordered from Regina. Gustav had decided to give it to his mother right away rather than to wait until Christmas. He was certain that the beautiful music of her homeland would at least provide some tranquility in her otherwise pain-filled, depressing existence, in which she was restricted to her bedroom.

It was a dreadful time for everyone in the Werner home. It would have been hard enough to have seven adults and two children confined in the house for more than a week, but to have their beloved matriarch dying during this bleak, bitter season in this isolated country was almost more than any human heart could bear. The children were cranky and bored; they did not understand what was happening, and whenever one of them asked, they were met with total silence. The women were bickering about whose turn it was to do the household chores, with each of them wanting to work in the kitchen where it was warm. The men could go outside, but the weather was so inclement that they could only withstand short periods. There was even less for them to occupy their time with when they were indoors, and soon the adults were at one another's throats as well. Each day it was becoming more apparent just how much of a stabilizing influence Elisabetha Werner was in their lives.

By the time the storm blew itself out, Maria was just about at the end of her tether. If she thought entertaining Mathias and Julianna during the day was trying, it was nothing compared to dealing with Friedrich at night. It was one thing to avoid him or to pull away when he was drunk, but now he was sober and much more ardent in his lovemaking. He would have none of letting Maria stop before he had finished satisfying his needs. As it was, she constantly worried about becoming pregnant again—not that she did not love her children, but she did not want to return to that demanding stage of infancy again.

The second night of the blizzard, Maria volunteered to sit with Elisabetha, and no one could talk her out of it. This tactic for avoiding her conjugal duties worked for the next three nights, but on the following day, when she was sleeping, she awoke to Friedrich's advances. When she became aware enough to know what was happening, she said, "For heaven's sake, Friedrich, it is the middle of the day; what do you think you are doing? What if one of the children comes into the bedroom?"

"I have asked Hanna and Katherina to absolutely not allow them to come in here. I told them I was very tired and did not want to be disturbed," replied Friedrich.

"But they will all hear us. Your papa will know what is going on, and everyone else will wonder."

"We will be quiet; so, my wife, stop trying to get out of your responsibilities."

～ 29 ～

The family members living in the Werner homestead became very insular during this initial snowstorm. They were so full of worry and dread with the realization that Elisabetha was dying that they literally forgot about how concerned the rest of the family who did not live in the farmhouse would be when they were unable to visit. They also seemed to overlook that there was safety, if not support, in numbers and what it might be like for Rolf and Katie being on their own. At least Johann and Karolina and Sofia and Karl had children to help with the never-ending chores and to provide some relief from the constant silence. Even when the wind stopped howling and the snow ceased its constant twirling, the world was grey during the day. The sun was a silvery metallic disk in the overcast horizon, which seemed to be closing in on them.

The first morning that the wind died down, Gustav hitched Wolfgang to the sleigh in preparation for the trip. Gustav wore his heavy winter coat, a woolen hat, and mitts his mother had knit for him last Christmas. He always carried an old comforter to wrap around himself if the fierce wind decided to return and blow its piercing wail. His first stop was to visit Rolf and Katie to make sure they had survived the blizzard and to encourage them to come and see Elisabetha. As difficult as it was to travel in the bitter prairie winter, Gustav knew his shy, sensitive brother would never forgive himself if he did not see his mother before she died. It occurred to Gustav that Rolf might not even know she was so critically ill, since Katie and he had not seen her much since their wedding.

Rolf answered the door on the first knock. "Hello, Gustav. Are we ever glad to see you. We were beginning to feel like we were the last living people in the world, and we have been so worried about Mama."

"I came as soon as I could risk taking Wolfgang out in this weather. I am on my way into town to see Aunt Margareta and Uncle Phillip and to find Dr. Spitznagel. Rolf, I don't know if you realize that Mama is in terrible pain, and I want to buy some medication to help her."

"I knew Papa had arranged for the doctor to go to the farm and examine Mama, but he never told me what was wrong with her. Katie and I were so busy finishing the house and getting ready for the winter that we have not seen much of the rest of you. It is funny how when you get married, it seems like you are a totally new person with a different life," replied Rolf.

"Well, Rolf, you seem to be happy with your new life. You look like you have already gained weight with Katie's wholesome cooking. I was thinking that since I have to go to Neudorf and home today, I would return tomorrow morning and bring both of you back to the homestead to spend the day with us. We could use some company, and you would have a chance to visit with Mama."

"Oh, that sounds like a wonderful idea," said Katie. "I will prepare some food to bring with us so Hanna and Katherina can enjoy the day as well, rather than having to worry about feeding all of us."

⟫⟩~ 30 ~⟨⟪

Well, now, this was interesting: Gustav Werner going into the bank when he was not working on the railway. Since he could not be putting money in, could he possibly be withdrawing some of his considerable sum to actually make a purchase? The group of seven, who were watching him through the windows of the hotel, decided it was worth waiting to find out if this stingy young man was about to part with some of his hard-earned dollars. Besides, it gave them something to talk about as they sat drinking coffee on this cold, wintry day, when Gustav was the only person out on the street. Sure enough, when he left the bank, he returned to his uncle's general store, and soon he was seen coming out of the building with Phillip Mohr, who was helping him carry a large box and another smaller package. But, too late, the inquisitive bystanders realized that their curiosity would not be satisfied since they had no possible way of finding out what caused Gustav to part with his cash.

On the other hand, when they saw him stop his horse and sleigh in front of Dr. Spitznagel's home, they knew full well he needed to seek medical advice for his mother. It was apparent to everyone in this small town and surrounding community that Elisabetha Werner must be seriously ill indeed for her to have missed the last two months of church. In fact, as they discussed it, they realized that none of them had seen her since Rolf and Katie's wedding. They decided that the next time one of them was in the Mohrs' store, it would be necessary to ask Phillip or Margareta what was ailing Elisabetha and when they could expect to see her back at the weekly Sunday services.

When Gustav returned home, his father greeted him as soon as he entered the house. Although he watched as Gustav opened the box, he was no further ahead than the townspeople in knowing what his son had purchased. "What is this thing that you raced into Neudorf to buy?" Christian asked.

"It is called a gramophone. It plays musical cylinders, and I bought several cylinders so Mama can listen to the music of her favourite Austrian composers. When I was a little boy, she often told me about hearing their beautiful music when she lived in Austria," replied Gustav excitedly.

"Between Friedrich and you bringing home these new mechanical contraptions, my farm will soon be littered with your junk! If you wanted to buy something for your mother, why did you not get her a useful present, like a little stove for her bedroom? You know she is always cold, and then her pain gets worse."

"Well, Papa, I will go back to town tomorrow and buy her a stove," Gustav answered tersely. He stopped himself from adding, *Why don't you buy it for her? In fact, why don't you work off the farm after you have done your planting in the spring and earn money like Friedrich and me? Then you would be able to buy her some comforts and even be able to pay Dr. Spitznagel to take care of her.*

Being confined to the house during the storm and constantly hearing Elisabetha moaning and sometimes even crying out in pain had stretched everyone's nerves to the breaking point, so there was no purpose in quarrelling with his father. As it was, since Christian had moved out of the bed he had shared with Elisabetha for the thirty-five years of their married life, he was becoming more and more distant and was speaking less and less to any of them.

Instead, Gustav walked towards his mother's bedroom and knocked lightly on the door, which was always kept open to allow in as much heat from the kitchen stove as possible.

"Mama, are you awake? I have been to town, and I have a surprise for you. I ordered a present for you from Regina, and it finally arrived in Uncle Phillip's store."

"Come in, my son. Your papa told me you had gone to Neudorf, and I am glad you have returned safely. I was concerned about you going off alone in this weather."

"It has stopped blowing, and it is beautiful outside, with the fluffy snow covering everything. The world seems so clean, white, and pure that I am sure winter must be God's favourite season. The snowdrifts are firm, and Wolfgang simply glided over them with the sleigh, so I had an exhilarating ride—especially after being cooped up in the house for over a week. Now while I am getting your present ready, you have to close your eyes and promise to wait until I tell you to open them."

"What an easy request," answered Elisabetha affectionately.

Gustav and Katherina carried the gramophone into the bedroom and set it on the small table that usually held the wash basin. He carefully removed one of the musical cylinders, and when it was placed correctly, he turned the handle to start the instrument.

As it happened, Elisabetha was unable to comply with Gustav's supplication. When the first strains of Johann Strauss's beautifully melodic Blue Danube Waltz filled her room, she not only opened her eyes, but she also sat straight up in bed and exclaimed, "Have I died already and gone to heaven? How is it possible for me to be hearing these wonderful sounds from my homeland?"

The entire Werner family came running into the bedroom, fascinated by the music, which seemed to float through the air as if to buoy them away to the ballrooms of Vienna. Christian stood at the entrance of the room, unable to believe what the music was doing for Elisabetha. Her face was rapturous, and her eyes were shining as though she was once again the young woman who had danced with him so many years ago on their wedding night. Mathias and Julianna were beside themselves with excitement, and when Friedrich reached for Maria and started to twirl her around the room, their children decided it looked like great fun, and they too joined in the dance.

Supper was very late that evening, as Gustav continued to delight everyone with more of Strauss's lovely music and also with the music of Mozart and Beethoven. When he needed a rest from turning the handle, Friedrich quickly came to relieve his brother, who had brought so much solace to his family with such a thoughtful gift. *Maybe there is a reason why Mama always seemed to favour Gustav*, thought Friedrich to himself. *When I purchased my automobile, I was really only thinking of myself and wanting to be one of the first people in the community to own a car.*

❦ 31 ❦

The gramophone changed everyone's life with its arrival. At first, Christian thought that hearing the music from Austria would only add to his already heavy burden of guilt. None of the Werner children understood that he could not openly speak to them because he blamed himself that their mother was dying. If only he had not insisted on dragging her halfway around the world, the doctors in Europe might have been able to treat her dreadful illness, which was robbing her of life at such an early age. However, as the days passed and Elisabetha continued to enjoy hearing the music over and over again and it seemed to ease her pain, Christian began to appreciate that it might assuage some of his guilt. He found himself being drawn back into her room, sitting on the chair adjacent to the bed, and holding her hand as they intently listened to the music of their countrymen for many serene hours each day.

The next day when Christian and Friedrich were outside doing the chores, Dr. Spitznagel pulled his horse and cutter up in front of the Werner house. Gustav, waiting, immediately welcomed him with a cup of fresh, hot coffee. "I am so happy that you could make the trip from town to check on my mother."

"Young man, I am relieved that you came to see me yesterday and apprised me of Elisabetha's condition. I must admit I have been worrying about how she has been coping with the pain, which I know can be considerable with her disease," replied the concerned doctor.

As soon as the two men entered the bedroom, Dr. Spitznagel saw the gramophone and said with delight, "I have been reading about this instrument in *The Leader*, and have considered getting my wife one for Christmas. She was a piano teacher in Vienna, and she misses listening to music very much. Would you recommend that I make the purchase?"

"Oh, yes. I surprised Mama with it last evening, and she was so excited that she broke her promise to wait until I told her to open her eyes. It was the first time in my life I can remember my mother not keeping her word! Then all of us spent the entire evening in her bedroom listening to music, and for the whole time, Mama did not cry out once in pain."

"Well, that settles it. I shall order a gramophone from your Uncle Phillip as soon as I return to town and commit him to silence so it will remain a secret for Mathilda's Christmas present." As he was saying this, Dr. Spitznagel realized he was being rude to his patient, and turning to Elisabetha, he said, "I am sorry, Mrs. Werner. Please excuse my lack of civility because of my fascination with your gramophone. How are you feeling this morning?"

"Good morning, Doctor. It is a nice surprise to see you, and I quite understand your interest in that marvellous instrument, which Gustav brought home yesterday. He said it was for me, but I think it will prove to be a gift for the whole family. Since I have had to remain in bed, last evening was the first time in many weeks that we have all been together in the same room."

Dr. Spitznagel looked at this courageous woman, who he suspected was enduring incredible pain without any medicinal relief, and wondered how she could still be so courteous.

"Mrs. Werner, I came with some medicine to ease your pain when it becomes too intense for you to bear. It is a drug called morphine, which must be given by injection. I have brought some syringes and needles, and I am going to teach Gustav and Hanna how to give you the medication when you decide that you need it. Since this is an arrangement between Gustav and me, I see no reason to trouble your husband with any of the details."

"Thank you, Dr. Spitznagel. You are very understanding. There are times when my limbs ache such with throbbing pain that I think I will not be able to bear it much longer; although I was so relaxed last night after listening to the music of some of the great Austrian composers that I slept much better than I have for many nights."

When Dr. Spitznagel left to continue with his house calls, Gustav, true to his word, hitched Wolfgang to the sleigh and went to fetch Rolf and Katie to spend the day with them. Elisabetha was very happy to see them, as it occurred to her just how isolated and depressed she had been feeling since she had been restricted to the four walls of her bedroom. Katie had thoughtfully brought cabbage rolls and perogies, so Hanna and Katherina put a ham into the oven, and dinner was soon ready. Once again, when the meal was over and the dishes washed, all of the family congregated around Elisabetha's bed to satisfy their fixation with the newly acquired musical instrument.

The gramophone had the power of drawing people to it, mesmerizing its listeners, and transporting them far away from the interior of the stone house on the snow-covered prairie in the middle of the bleak winter season. Everyone who came to hear it—and they did come, including all of the Werner children with their own families, the aunts and uncles, and the neighbours—sat in rapt attention, enthralled by the beautiful sounds that emanated from the enlarged end of the speaker horn. The children often started by dancing around the room and out into the kitchen, but when they tired, they too settled on the comforter on the floor and snuggled up to their parents, many times drifting off into a dreamy sleep.

Friedrich became devoted to operating the musical instrument, always ready to turn its handle and change its cylinders. Even so, the person most transformed by the gramophone was its original recipient. Elisabetha was once again restored to her pivotal role as the hub of the Werner family. Gustav had returned to town and had purchased a kerosene lamp as well as a small stove for her bedroom. Elisabetha was warm, she was no longer in the shadows, and when the pain overwhelmed her, either Gustav or Hanna gave her an injection of the morphine. But now, with her family and friends surrounding her and with the influence of the gramophone, Elisabetha was frequently able to transcend her physical suffering without the drug. Ironically, the one person who never heard the magical sounds of the gramophone in the Werner home was the one who had suggested its purchase in the first place: Andrew Thompson.

32

The weather was bitterly cold, interspersed with heavy snowfall, for months. And Christmas was approaching. Although Margareta Mohr prepared a roast goose with all of the trimmings and Phillip brought a bottle of whiskey to the farm, when they surprised the Werner family with the traditional meal of the season, only the children showed any Christmas spirit. All of the adults knew Elisabetha's life was nearing its end. She was becoming so thin that her bones were protruding at the surface of her skin, and Christian was afraid to touch her for fear she would break. For many hours each day, Elisabetha appeared to be semi-conscious, and they were certain all she could hear was the music; when it stopped, she would revive and ask them to play the cylinders again. She was no longer able to eat solid food and she existed on the chicken broth that Hanna and Katherina made sure they had available for her.

Still she lingered, and Christian wondered if she was unable to let go because she did not know whether they could manage without her. He wrestled with very ambivalent feelings: of course he did not want her to die, but he was becoming increasingly unable to see her in such a deathly state. Christian chopped more wood that winter than they could ever have used because he felt so guilty for wishing Elisabetha would finally pass into the next world. There was no one for him to talk to or to share any of these terrible feelings with; he simply could not have told them to any of their children. The one person with whom he had been able to express his innermost thoughts, hopes, and dreams seemed to be caught between two worlds and yet unable to be a part of either.

33

One night near the end of March, a wind blew in from the southeast, bringing with it much warmer air. The frost melted off the windows, and as soon as he got up, Mathias dressed in his outerwear and went outside with his grandfather and uncles to help with the chores. When the temperature had dropped below the freezing point, Maria had not allowed her children to go outdoors, and Mathias, in particular, was starting to feel like a caged animal. He did not accomplish much in the way of helping the men; after he had carried a small load of wood into the kitchen, he went back out and ran around in the snow. Then he came rushing in the house and said to his mother and sister, "Hurry and come see the trees. They are dressed in down, just like the ducks when Grandma plucks them after she has killed them!"

Maria chuckled and said, "Oh, you silly boy. It is called hoarfrost."

"Yes, I know; Uncle Gustav told me. And once the sun comes up, it will not stay long. The sun is already coming up, and it looks like a big ball of fire. It is making the sky orange and red and yellow!"

Maria got caught up in her son's excitement and quickly got Julianna's coat, hat, and boots so she could go outside. Once Julianna was dressed and ushered out the door, Maria grabbed her own winter apparel and joined her children in time to capture the beauty of the morning. The sky was an exquisite array of changing colours, the air felt lighter with the warming temperature, and the trees were beautiful, covered with their snowy vapour. Watching the scenic sunrise as her children walked on top of the hardened snowdrifts, Maria found herself taking several deep breaths of the fresh, crisp air as though she had been suffocating inside the house. She had not been outside for far too long, and the stagnant air inside was heavy with the smell of death.

It was not a false start. The temperature remained warm, and spring arrived early that year. The snow was melting, the birds were returning to fill the air with their songs, and the crocuses would soon be in bloom. Each day, the sunrise and sunset were spectacular, filling the sky with wonderful colours. The world of nature was awakening, and the season of rebirth was returning to the silent, frozen prairie.

Late that afternoon, Beethoven's inspirational Ninth Symphony ended just as the last ray of the setting sun poured through the window of Elisabetha's bedroom. It was like a beacon, and Elisabetha suddenly aroused from her semi-conscious state with a compulsion to get out of her bed, where she had lain for longer then she knew. Maria was seated on the chair beside her bed and almost jumped off it when Elisabetha spoke.

"Hello, Maria. I wonder if you would ask Christian and Gustav to come here and to hurry, please. I want to be carried to my window to see the sunset."

It took Maria some time to recover from the surprise of hearing Elisabetha speak, and with such awareness of who was with her and of the time of day. When she collected herself, she ran to the kitchen, calling for all of the family to come; Elisabetha was awake and wanting to get up. They rushed into the room. When the men carried her to the window, the sky was glorious with an incredible display of colour: pinky-rose, blue, and silver-grey with reddish and purple tinges. As she observed the spectrum of colours, the last bright light of the sun suddenly broke through. It was as though God had parted the sky with eternal light in preparation for Elisabetha, if she was judged worthy to ascend into heaven. Then the pastel hues converged into a fiery red at the horizon and the sun sank out of sight.

That evening, the gramophone was silent. After supper, the family assembled around her bedside. Elisabetha was propped up with pillows to support her. She spoke clearly and with determination.

"Over the many weeks that I have listened to the great music composed by our countrymen, I have come to accept that I am much more than this body of mine, which is steadily failing me. Now I know my spirit will live on forever when I return to our Father's house, where He has prepared rooms for all of us. So I do not want you to grieve for me. I am going home to the Lord, and every time one of you thinks of me, I shall be with you in your heart and memory. I believe this from the very depths of my soul."

Later in the evening, Elisabetha went to sleep without needing morphine for pain. During the night, she peacefully passed from this world, exactly two months before her sixtieth birthday.

In the early hours of the morning, Christian awoke from his slumber on the chair beside her bed and knew she was gone. He was glad he was with her, and as he sat in silence, he wondered what life would be like without her. How strange that Elisabetha had rallied last evening to tell them not to grieve for her. Of course, as she had throughout her life, she was trying to help her family to cope with her death and to go ahead with the business of living. Christian had always thought he would go first, and therefore he had never considered how he would manage to carry on without his strong, loving spouse, who had supported him in his lifelong quest for his own land. Now he had his land, but no one to share it with.

Christian decided to wait until daylight, and then he would call his family together to tell them their mother had died during the night. For the first time in more than a week, the sun did not shine, and it seemed to take so long for the gloomy, overcast light to come through the windowpanes. He slowly rose to his feet, feeling numb and disoriented like a ship lost at sea. His one clear purpose was to go to their secluded knoll in the poplar grove and to dig her grave as he had promised. He must go alone because he absolutely needed solitary time to work out his grief in the only way that he knew. Christian would dig through what snow remained, through the frozen ground, and dig and dig until he had a hole that was deep enough to start to bury his sorrow along with his beloved wife.

➤ 34 ≺

They had expected it, dreaded it, and if it had been their way to openly express their feelings, they might have honestly said it was a blessing. In their hearts, each knew that she had lingered between life and death not for her sake but for theirs. They knew that Elisabetha, with her strong faith, was ready to meet her Maker. The women no doubt cried quietly to themselves as they stoically went about preparing the food for the funeral and attending to the other necessary details. The men got outdoors as soon as possible and worked out their grief in whatever hard labour they decided, rightly or wrongly, needed to be done. And the children were told to not ask questions and to go play quietly so they would not be heard.

When Christian made the anticipated announcement to his family, Gustav was the first to speak. "What now, Papa? What do we do now?"

Christian stood looking vaguely at his children and grandchildren and wondered why they thought he had the answers. He had to get to the poplar grove, but he did not know what each of them should do. Their mother had been the organizer of the family, the one who took responsibility to make the arrangements and to get things done.

Fortunately, Hanna, who shared many of her mother's capabilities, stepped to the forefront and answered Gustav's question. "I think that first, you should ride Wolfgang to Rolf and Katie's house to tell them Mama has died. Then, while Rolf goes to get Johann and Karolina, you go to town and ask Aunt Margareta and Uncle Phillip to come to the farm. We shall need Auntie to show us what we must do to prepare Mama's body for burial. Also, Gustav, please talk to Reverend Biber about having the funeral tomorrow, and tell Dr. Spitznagel—I am sure he will want to come before the service. Friedrich, do you think you can get your car started so you can go and pick up Sofia and Karl and their children? Maria and Katherina can help me start getting the house and the food ready so people can come here after the interment. So now, let's have a quick breakfast and get the chores done before you head off in opposite directions to gather the rest of the family."

They all looked at her, surprised as much by her clear articulation as by the flawless logic of her arrangements. Hanna was usually the quiet and diligent daughter and sister who went about completing the multiple tasks that needed to be done to keep the household running smoothly, especially since Mama had taken ill. But she did not spend time talking, and certainly not directing any of the others in what they should do to help. They wondered if she would tell their father what he needed to do, but when she turned to him, she stopped short and waited.

Christian finally responded, "I am going to dig the grave, and I must do it alone. Friedrich, on your way to get Sofia, can you drive me to your mother's favourite spot on our farm?"

On his way back from Neudorf, Gustav still had one destination, which his sister would not have considered as part of her planning. Instead of returning home, he continued on to Andrew's homestead to tell his friend that his mother had died and to invite him to the funeral. After he had met Elisabetha, Andrew had always asked about her and, Gustav suspected, wondered why he was never invited to the Werner home. Try as hard as he could, Gustav could not think about how to tell Andrew that his father still did not know about their friendship. So he chose to say nothing and to hope he would not ask. But now Gustav could not be silent about her death; he knew that if the situation were reversed and if his friend were to withhold such vital information from him, he would never be able to trust him again.

~~➤~ **35** ~↞~~

On a cloudy and cheerless morning at the beginning of April 1910, Elisabetha Werner was laid to rest on a small hillside where the grass was starting to turn green and the surrounding poplar trees were opening their waxy, tremulous leaves. The church was overflowing with family, friends, and neighbours who had respected her for her kindness and willingness to help them. Reverend Biber was solicitous in his sermon and in his selection of hymns, choosing those that Elisabetha had particularly liked to sing. As the congregation sang "Rock of Ages," he observed the seven Werner offspring, some already with spouses and children, standing beside Christian, and wondered how one woman could birth such sturdy, healthy progeny and then not live long enough to know her grandchildren, many of whom were not yet born. Without questioning His plan, somehow it just did not seem fair.

After the interment, everyone, including Andrew Thompson, returned to the Werner home to pay his or her respects to the family. Gustav introduced his friend to his father, but Christian seemed more interested in having a drink of whiskey than in trying to understand who this young man was or why he was in his house. Christian had never felt comfortable in a large group of people, and now to be surrounded by them on the day he had buried his wife was more than he could handle. He just wanted to be left alone as he reflected sadly about how lonely and lost he was already without his anchor, his Elisabetha. Since her death, Christian scarcely said a word to anyone—not that his children had ever been particularly communicative with him.

Hanna wondered who had started this conspiracy of silence. For days after Elisabetha's funeral, the only sound of human voices was the whispering of the children. Mathias and Julianna sensed that since the house had become so quiet, they must only speak very softly to each other as they played indoors. It was not until they went outside that they recovered their vocal strength and ran around the yard yelling at each other as if to prove they had not lost their voices. It seemed like all of the adults in the house had forgotten how to talk, or if they did speak, they were being very secretive and waited until the children were asleep. Even the gramophone became taciturn, as though Elisabetha had taken its magical power with her, just as she had appropriated the heart and soul and voice of the Werner family.

Then they started to disperse. Friedrich was the first to go, returning to his job with the railway within days of his mother's death. He was especially anxious to leave because

Maria was sure she was pregnant again, and she blamed him for their frequent dalliances during the long, cold winter nights and often, at his insistence, during the day.

Gustav could hardly wait to gather his equipment and supplies, including his tent, which he promptly hauled to his own homestead. Leaving Wolfgang tethered in Rolf and Katie's yard, he walked back to his father's farm and drove the oxen across country to his land, which he would begin plowing the next day. Even though it was early in the season, he did not intend to return to his father's house. On the nights that the temperature dipped below freezing and it was too cold to stay in the tent, Gustav took his blanket and pillow and slept on Rolf and Katie's kitchen floor.

It was not long before Gustav was eating all of his meals with them, thanks to Katie's persistence; she was delighted to feed another man with a hearty appetite who appreciated her cooking. Aside from mourning her mother-in-law, Katie was in her element. With her mother's guidance, she had just determined that she was pregnant, and unlike Maria, she was ecstatic about having a baby. When Rolf and Katie had needed to rely so heavily on each other to survive the overwhelming isolation and loneliness of the long, prairie winter, they had discovered they were well-suited. Before spring arrived, they learned to love each other, and now they were rejoicing in their impending parenthood.

～ 36 ～

Gustav started breaking sod at sunrise and was soon working twelve hours a day. By trial and practice, he determined that the oxen could walk a mile an hour, and so by the end of the day, he could break one and a half acres. He maintained this pace six days a week, and by the end of that summer, he plowed 110 of his 160 acres of land. Tilling furrow after furrow through the matted grassland from dawn until dusk, he burrowed deeper and deeper within himself to bury his sorrow. With his mother's death, Gustav lost much more than a loving parent; he lost part of his soul. Still, when he trudged along behind the plow for hours on end, there was an element of peace in the repetitive motion of following the slow-moving animals and of harmony in watching the prairie sod consistently curl off the mouldboard into rich, black soil. Many days Gustav would fall into a trance, and the only feeling he experienced was a serene connection with the earth. He was frequently so detached from his surroundings that he was unaware of the time of day or where he was in the seemingly endless course of prairie grasses.

Late on one of those tranquil afternoons, he realized that a bird was dragging its body along the sod as though it had a broken wing. It had attracted his attention enough to bring him out of his daze, and he started to watch for it each time he criss-crossed that same region of the prairie. Sure enough, there it was, and as he got closer, he could see it was a killdeer. But its behaviour was very strange. It was almost as if the bird was pretending to have a broken wing because after Gustav had plowed past an area of the sod, it would right itself and walk around as though there was nothing wrong with it. When this unusual pattern was repeated three times, Gustav decided to give the oxen a rest and to investigate the cause of the bird's actions.

He approached the killdeer slowly as he walked carefully through the grass. What a good thing he had not rushed, because he saw four speckled eggs nestled in the prairie sod. Small wonder the bird reacted so strangely as he and the oxen with the plow came closer and closer to the nest, which seemed to blend into the landscape. Gustav retreated with deliberate steps because he did not want to frighten the bird. The tiny eggs in the nest caused him to reflect on the meaning of the life cycle. *All that lives must eventually die and return to the earth.* His mother had been like the killdeer; she had given him life, protected him, nurtured him, and encouraged him so he could make his own way in the world. And when her time came, she too had to die and leave this physical existence; but as she said on the evening of her death, her spirit would always be in his heart.

Katie was in the yard feeding the chickens when Gustav returned with the oxen. "Why hello, Gustav; you are stopping early today," his sister-in-law greeted him.

"Oh, Katie, I realized this afternoon that I have behaved as though I had been buried with Mama. I have done nothing but plow in my fields. I have hardly spoken even to Rolf and you, yet you have taken such good care of me. If you had not made my meals, I don't think I would have eaten much of anything. I have neglected Papa, my brothers and sisters, my friend Andrew, and even Wolfgang, who I have not ridden since the day Mama died. I feel like I have just awakened from a stupor. I am going to wash and ride home to see Papa, Hanna, Katherina, Maria, and especially her children."

"What a relief, Gustav, that you are coming out of your despair. We have all been so worried about you. Even though you have spent Sundays with us at church and dinner at Aunt Margareta and Uncle Phillip's, you have sat as silent as a stone. I don't really think that you were aware that the rest of us were with you. Auntie has been beside herself with concern that even she could not get you to talk. And Katherina has been worse off than you."

"Oh, I have been so selfish! I did not think about how the rest of the family was dealing with Mama's death. I should have known Katherina would be devastated with Mama gone and then me. She must feel terribly alone, and when you think about it, she is still so young to be without her mother. Probably Papa is not able to give her any attention; he seemed to be totally lost and unable to talk to any of us," answered Gustav.

Hanna was working in the garden when Gustav came riding Wolfgang into the yard. She put the large bowl of leafy green lettuce, the first of the season, gently down on the ground and came running to welcome her brother. She was so happy to see him that she surprised him with a hug as soon as he dismounted, which was certainly uncharacteristic behaviour for the undemonstrative Werner family. Since her mother's death, Hanna was spending many hours interacting with Maria from necessity, and was particularly aware of how affectionate she was with Mathias and Julianna. Hanna thought many times that this whole reserved family could have learned so much from Maria, who did not seem inhibited from showing her feelings. Of course, they had all heard her frequent loud arguments with her husband, but they did not seem to notice how loving she was with her children.

"Hello, Hanna. You are looking well, and I see you are taking good care of Mama's garden. She would be very happy with you," Gustav said.

"It is nice to have you come home, Gustav. I wonder if you have any idea how much we have all missed you. And you know I would never let Mama's garden become unattended, although I don't know what I shall do with all of these vegetables in the fall."

"I am sure you learned from Mama how to can, make pickles, and store the root crops, and Friedrich and I will be back home to eat your produce during the winter."

"I would be very surprised if Katherina ever moves back home," answered Hanna.

"What are you talking about? Where is Katherina, and why don't I know what is happening with her?" asked Gustav anxiously.

"Katherina has moved to Neudorf to live with Aunt Margareta and Uncle Phillip. Julia's bedroom has been empty since she was offered a teaching job in Regina, and Auntie needed someone to help her in the store. I was having a terrible time with Katherina; there were days when I could not get her out of bed, and I just did not know what to do with her. Aunt Margareta thought she could kill two birds with one stone. She would help Katherina get over her loneliness and grief since Mama's death and get some help by teaching her how to work in the store. Rolf's Katie told me that she did tell you all about it, but she said you were like a sleepwalker going through each day. We both had a laugh when I told her that you did walk in your sleep when you were a boy."

"Oh, yes, now I remember. I can understand how upset Katherina would be, and since she is only thirteen, of course she still needs a mother's love and attention," responded Gustav.

What about me? Hanna wanted to say. *I am just two years older, and I miss Mama every bit as much as anyone else does. But for some reason, you all think I will keep busy managing this house and garden and make sure all of the chores are done.* Even while resenting these thoughts, Hanna knew her family expected her to carry these responsibilities and keep things running smoothly as she had since Mama had become ill. Not for the first time, she regretted that she was so like her mother in characteristics, while Katherina's similarities were in appearance. *How did I turn out short and stout when my six brothers and sisters are tall and slender? Why am I so different?*

Hanna knew she was feeling sorry for herself. She was usually cheerful and enjoyed the satisfaction she got from working hard and accomplishing what she had set out to do. At least when Mama was alive, she expressed her appreciation for Hanna's efforts, and Hanna would then be encouraged to do even more. But now, no one even said thank you, and she felt taken for granted. Come to think of it, that was not quite true. Maria was having an awful time with morning sickness with this pregnancy and was grateful for the time that Hanna was spending with Mathias and Julianna. Both children loved her dearly and delighted in helping her feed the chickens, plant the garden, and cook the meals. Hanna knew that she was also different in temperament from her serious brothers and sisters. People often told her that she had a twinkle in her eyes, and she did like to play games and have fun.

Possibly her best attribute was her resiliency, and Hanna knew she could always find a way to get over things, even the death of her mother. When she felt really sad, she would go for lengthy walks around her father's farm, often crying buckets of bitter, resentful tears of sorrow. Eventually, though, by being out in nature, she began to heal, and her feelings of hope and optimism were restored.

Katherina, on the other hand, seemed unable to recover from upsetting events; she would not talk about Mama's death, and worse, she did not seem to want to get better. Mama used to say that Katherina was given to dark moods, just as her grandmother had been. None of the Werner children met their maternal grandmother, not because she had lived in Austria, but because she died at exactly the same age as their mother. All they knew was there was something secret about her death, which would presumably now remain a mystery that went to their mother's grave with her.

Another feature that held Hanna in good stead was her responsiveness to the situation at hand. Instead of lamenting her own need for attention, she decided to focus on Gustav and asked, "Are you feeling better now? We all realize how close you were to Mama, and it was not surprising that you were so desolate about losing her."

"I am starting to feel like I'm coming back to life. I am now aware of how wretched and alone I was feeling. The one time my friend Andrew came to see me, I could not even talk to him. It was like he was a total stranger who could not possibly understand what it was like since his own mother is still alive, so I had nothing to say to him."

"Well, at least you are talking now, and I am sure your friend will forgive you. If you are staying for supper, why don't you tether Wolfgang, then go and help Papa with the chores. He misses Mama terribly, and I am beginning to worry that he may never talk to us again. Maybe you could get him to open up by asking him something about your farm. It seems that working his land and tending to the animals are his only interests now," replied Hanna.

"I plan to stay for supper and then ride over to apologize to Andrew," said Gustav.

~ 38 ~

No wonder Hanna was often considered contented, when little events, even having her brother come home unexpectedly, gave her so much delight. While confirming that Gustav would be eating with them, her mind raced about what special food she could add to the menu. There was still some of Papa's smoked pork sausage in the smokehouse, and since it was one of Gustav's favourites, she would get a ring of it as soon as she took the lettuce into the house. It was too early in the season for the new potatoes to be ready, but a hot German salad, even with the old potatoes from the root cellar, was always very tasty with the lettuce mixed with thick cream and vinegar. Mathias and Julianna were equally excited that their uncle was visiting, and when they asked if they could help, Hanna showed them how to wash and tear the lettuce for the salad.

When Hanna looked out the kitchen window, she saw the two men coming across the yard, and although she could not determine if her father was saying much, it certainly appeared that Gustav was having an animated discussion with him. Hanna took a long, deep sigh of relief because Aunt Margareta was not the only one who thought Gustav had become as silent as a tomb. She was sure that once Gustav started to interact again, he would recover from his shock and anger caused by their mother's death, and she was looking forward to hearing conversation and laughter again in this quiet house.

The minute he walked through the door, both children came running towards Gustav. He had forgotten how much he enjoyed being with Mathias and Julianna, teasing and playing with them for hours each day during the winter months. He really had been in a stupor for weeks; how could he not have missed these two wonderful children who had lived in his house since their infancy? It was like he had completely changed and become some person he did not know, and then he realized it was not Andrew who had been the stranger when he had visited, but he himself. All he could do was hope his family and his friend would forgive him and that he could redeem himself by once again having some consideration for each of them.

Hanna lovingly prepared a delicious supper, and for the first time since Elisabetha's death, several members of the Werner family sat around the kitchen table to eat. Gustav failed to appreciate that they were all so happy he was recovering from his despair, that not one of them would have considered that he would need to be forgiven, much less worry about compensating them for his past neglect. Nonetheless, Hanna glowed with pleasure when Gustav said that her supper was the tastiest meal he had eaten in a long time. She even blushed when he started to tease her that she would make some man a fine, sturdy little wife in the near future. Mathias and Julianna took up their uncle's joshing and said that they were bored playing with each other and needed some cousins with whom they could spend time. Even Christian joined in the fun, telling his grandchildren that their uncle would get married next and provide them with new playmates. Maria then reminded them that they would soon have a new brother or sister and she would need them to help change the baby's diapers, never mind playing, since they were wise enough to take part in the grown-ups' conversation.

39

On the way to Andrew's house, Gustav rode Wolfgang at a leisurely pace. He wanted to revel in the sights and sounds of nature, since he seemed to have been oblivious to the world around him for the past months. He was amazed that he had not even noticed that it was early summer and the countryside was alive with its lush green coat of grass and the growing crops of wheat, barley, and oats. As he approached a grove of willows, the air resounded with the trill of blackbirds and the chirping of crickets, and he stopped Wolfgang so he could absorb the tunes of the prairie evening songs. Gustav's favourite trees were willows, with their long, slender, dark green leaves, partly because they were the first to leaf in the spring and the last to lose their foliage in the autumn. Mainly, though, he loved these trees that grew along the sloughs because as a boy and even as a young man, he had always watched for the return of the furry pussy willows, which he would immediately pick and present to his mother as the first wildflowers of the spring. Gustav felt a sharp pang of sorrow that this past spring he had not even noticed the catkins of the willows because there was no one to appreciate their gift.

When he arrived in the Thompsons' yard, he dismounted and tied Wolfgang to the wooden railing near the small outbuilding that served as the barn. He walked tentatively towards the house, a little concerned about how he would be received since he had not visited for so long. Gustav was met by the barking of Sparky, the family's watchdog, who was so friendly that instead of guarding them, he would have led any stranger right into the house.

"Hello, Sparky; it's me," said Gustav before stopping to pet the black and white English springer spaniel on the head.

Just then, the door opened and Mrs. Thompson expressed her delight. "Why, Gustav, how nice to see you. We have all missed you, and Andrew has been so concerned about you. Please come in and have tea with Heather and me, since we are keeping the home fires burning. Mr. Thompson is at a church meeting, and Andrew is out in the field, but he will soon be home. I think he has some news he will want to share with you."

"Hello, Mrs. Thompson. Thank you for your kind offer. I will come in to visit, but I was home for supper and my sister Hanna made such a delicious meal that I could not consume anything right now."

Of course, Mrs. Thompson paid no heed to Gustav, knowing that he, like all young men, was a bottomless pit when it came to food. Within a short time, they were seated at the round antique English oak table with expandable leaves that had made the journey from Southampton with them so many years ago. Gustav was having his second cup of tea when Andrew burst into the house. "What a welcome sight! I was beginning to wonder if you would ever return to see us," exclaimed Andrew.

"Son, is that any way to greet a guest? I sometimes worry that since you have become an adult, you have forgotten all of your manners," chided Mrs. Thompson.

"Since when is Gustav a guest? I have always considered him as one of the family," replied Andrew happily.

Turning to Gustav, Andrew said, "It is going to be a beautiful moonlit night. As soon as we have finished our tea, let's go for a race. I have missed our rides around the countryside, although we will have to be careful to not go charging through some farmer's freshly planted grain field. Soon the entire prairie will be changed forever because of the almighty plow!"

"That is a strange attitude for a farmer to have, especially since you are one of the lucky ones to own the new and superior John Deere steel plow," teased Gustav.

"You cannot possibly understand how reassuring it is to hear you banter about something again, my friend," Andrew said warmly.

The moon was full, and its luminance cast wonderful shadows over the prairie, which was still not disturbed by fences and roads. The two young men knew where there was open range still unbroken by that instrument of change, and they thrilled in renewing their favourite pastime. This time it was Wolfgang's turn to win, and when they finally came to a stop to let their horses eat some of the long, green prairie grass, Andrew justified Sally's loss. "You probably have not ridden Wolfgang for so long that he has rested and saved his energy to beat my poor horse, who has been galloping back and forth to Duff every day."

"Why have you been going to Duff so frequently?" asked Gustav.

"Did my mother not tell you?" inquired Andrew, somewhat surprised.

"Your mama did indicate that you had some news, but she said you would tell me yourself. So when are you going to share these glad tidings?"

By this time, the men were lying on the grass, gazing up at the constellations while watching for shooting stars on the warm summer evening. The vast Saskatchewan night sky accentuated the stillness and the emptiness of the prairie and the seeming insignificance of the two human beings observing its magnificence. However, Andrew felt like he had been walking on a cloud since he had first seen Sarah in church, and he was not about to feel inconsequential with the immensity of the universe.

He jokingly asked, "What makes you think my news is happy?"

"Come now, Andrew. The minute I asked why you were spending so much time travelling to Duff, your face lit up like the sun coming over the horizon at the start of the day."

"I did not realize I had become so transparent. Well, then, I better tell you about Sarah Hardy, the new banker's beautiful daughter. Her family moved to Duff in the spring, and I met her at church several weeks ago. She has eyes the colour of the sky, blond curly hair, and the prettiest little nose you have ever seen. We were introduced after the service, and when I asked her if she would like to go for a walk, she immediately agreed. I don't know if you believe in love at first sight, or perhaps, like me, you have not thought about it, but I certainly do now. I think the feeling is mutual because Sarah and I have gone walking every evening since the seeding has been finished. Her family has asked me to dinner twice, which I take as a positive sign that they approve of me. Her father is also a deacon in our church, so he attends the same meetings as my father, and by now I am sure they have talked about our relationship. I feel that Sarah is the woman that I would like to marry," expressed Andrew happily.

As his friend was speaking, Gustav listened intently, surprised that Andrew spoke about choosing whom he would marry. The possibility of making this important decision by himself and not having it made by his father was completely foreign to Gustav. Two of his older brothers and one sister had all married individuals selected years earlier by their respective parents, who had arranged the dowries to bring to the marriages. In fact, Gustav had heard his father talk about the benefits of having more sons than daughters because so far he had only been required to provide the dowry for his oldest daughter, Sofia. Although his wedding was not scheduled to occur until he was twenty-one, Gustav had already seen the young woman who was arranged to be his wife. He vaguely remembered seeing her at his mother's funeral and thinking she still looked like a child.

When Andrew saw Gustav at a loss for words, he mistakenly assumed that he was still grieving for his mother and could not share in his happiness. "Gustav, I am sorry. I have insensitively been going on about my good fortune without any regard for you still mourning your mother. Are you starting to adjust to her loss? I also wanted to ask if I could visit your mama's gravesite with you sometime. I think that with its protecting grove of poplar trees, it is one of the most scenic and peaceful locations in the district. I will never forget the wonderful afternoon we spent there last autumn."

"Of course, Andrew; I would like you to come as often as you can to visit Mama's grave. This spring, as he had promised, Papa built a fence around the trees and Hanna planted some peonies, my mother's favourite flowers. I am pleased for you, and I look forward to meeting this young woman who has so captivated your feelings."

Gustav knew Andrew had misinterpreted his lack of response, but he needed time to think about what Andrew was telling him. Was this just another one of the differences between their two families, or was it because of the diversity between their cultures, customs, and traditions? Perhaps it was both. Although Gustav was starting to feel more like his previously assured self, at this time he had the confidence neither to explore these questions with his friend nor to deal with their possible answers.

~ 40 ~

The week before Christmas, Maria gave birth to her second daughter. The Werner family was happy to rejoice in a new life rather than to remember the previous year marked by death. Christian, in particular, was very pleased when Maria expressed to the family that she had decided to call her baby girl Elisabetha. It clearly was her choice since Friedrich did not even come home for the birth of his third child. After a short visit at Thanksgiving, he had returned to Melville for the winter to work on the railway. This hamlet had grown rapidly after the last spike of the railway had been driven in 1908, and it had become the second divisional point on the Grand Trunk Pacific Railway west of Winnipeg. By 1910, Melville was a town with more than one thousand people and "many more things to do than to sit and languish on this little farm," as Friedrich loudly expressed to his wife in yet another argument, on his second day home after months of being away.

Interestingly, though, he did not suggest that his wife and family move to Melville so they could all live together. Even Christian could not understand how his oldest son could be so irresponsible about providing for his own offspring. Not to be there when one of your children was born was unforgivable, as far as Christian was concerned. Once again Hanna was the dependable and hard-working one who sat with Maria and then helped through her labour and delivery. The two women had become remarkably close over the past year, which was not surprising since they were the only females left on the farm. Hanna had accurately predicted that Katherina would not return, and Christian had been considerably relieved that Gustav had come home for the winter. He would have been even lonelier with no other male to visit with and to help with the chores.

It was a milder winter, and whether it was because their mother was no longer alive to sustain the family or because of the new babies, Johann and Karolina, Sofia and Karl, and their families made many more return trips to their papa's homestead. They often gathered Rolf, Katie, their new daughter, Sabina, who was born two weeks later than little Elisabetha; arriving with food and sometimes even whiskey for Christian, the entire family would spend the day together. If the weather turned and the company had to stay the night, there were almost enough beds and certainly plenty of comforters to sleep on the floor in the kitchen beside the warm stove. In many ways, the Werner family seemed to be unifying in the absence of their matriarch, which would have pleased Elisabetha greatly. Surprisingly, though, their socialization never again took place to the sound of music.

To be honest, Johann had an ulterior motive for his frequent visits to the farm. One day, while they were carrying wood to take into the house, Johann hesitantly asked Gustav, "Do you think I would be able to learn how to speak and read English?"

Gustav reassured his brother that he thought anyone could learn whatever he made up his mind to and then asked, "Would you like me to teach you?"

"Yes, I would really appreciate your help. Neither Karolina nor I seem interested in farming, and when we heard that Friedrich could get a job working full-time for the railway, we talked about the possibility of my doing the same. I realize that Friedrich can speak and understand English because he has worked for so long with other Canadians. I know I will also have to learn the language of this country if I am ever to be anything but a farmer."

"Sure, I would happily teach you, but I think I should come to your house. Papa does not like the fact that I learned English, and although I had my friend Andrew come to the house on the day of Mama's funeral, I have never invited him back. At first, I resented that I could not have Andrew come here, but now I think I don't ask him because I do not want to upset Papa. As it is, he is disturbed that Katherina has left the farm and is learning English while helping Aunt Margareta with the store. I sometimes think that if Uncle Phillip did not treat Papa so well, he might disown his younger sister altogether."

"I agree with you, and we were going to ask you to come to our house anyway because the whole family wants to learn from you. Eventually, we will move to Melville so Barbara and Jakob have an opportunity to go to a proper school. See how well Julia is doing! Imagine having a cousin who went to normal school and now has a teaching job in Regina. I don't like to upset Papa either, but we just cannot keep all of the old German customs and traditions in this new country."

When Johann was saying these words, Gustav suddenly remembered what Andrew had said about choosing his own wife, and then he wondered why he had put it so completely out of his mind. Perhaps the idea of having to make such important decisions on his own seemed confusing and overwhelming to him. Everything was so much clearer when Mama was alive because whenever he had serious questions, she always provided a satisfying answer. But it was different now. Gustav knew he was not the only one who hesitated to go to Papa to ask for advice. In fact, it was interesting how they had all rallied around their father to try to fill the void created by their mother's passing—all of them except his oldest and youngest offspring, who seemed to be more interested in meeting their own needs.

Even while thinking these negative thoughts, Gustav knew it was terribly unfair to include Friedrich and Katherina in the same category. Friedrich was considerably older with responsibilities, and yet he seemed to be purely selfish when it came to caring for his own family. Katherina was still a child, and although she was only two years younger than Hanna, she had an entirely different temperament. Gustav suspected that he was not the only family member who was worried by how long it was taking Katherina to bounce back, even with Aunt Margareta's love. More than a year later, Katherina still had deep periods of despair, and as was known only to Dr. Spitznagel and her aunt, she often just wanted to die.

<h2 style="text-align:center">➤~ 41 ~✦</h2>

It did not take Margareta long to see absolutely no levity in her favourite niece, Katherina, although she would not have verbalized it to anyone. She would never forget the haunted, desolate look in Katherina's eyes as her mother's body had been lowered into the grave that Christian had dug single-handedly the morning of Elisabetha's death. Margareta saw that barren and inconsolable stare before, many years earlier in Austria, just hours before the bearer, Elisabetha's mother, had chosen to take her own life. That memory had sent shivers up and down her spine, and Margareta knew she could not wait long to intercede on Katherina's behalf. But how could she ever convince her stubborn and sometimes overbearing brother to allow his youngest daughter to live in Neudorf, especially after what the Mohr family had supposedly done to Gustav?

Furthermore, Margareta knew that this time she would need to find the solution by herself rather than ask her husband to get involved in her plan. It had taken Christian considerable time to forgive Phillip for persuading him to allow Gustav to work in the store during the winter months when he was a boy. As far as Christian was concerned, it was when Gustav learned to speak, read, and write English that he started to question and want to change the German customs and traditions that had been part of the Werner family for generations. There was no doubt in Margareta's mind that her brother knew she was the impetus behind Phillip's actions and that he probably never would completely absolve her of the responsibility of putting all those newfangled ideas into Gustav's head.

As it was, Katherina's change of residence happened so subtly that it was several weeks before Christian even realized that his youngest daughter was no longer living in his home. It certainly helped Margareta's planning that he was so grief-stricken and, unbeknownst to his children at the time, so overwhelmed with guilt because of their mother's premature death that he was unable to focus on anything other than his usual chores on the farm. And Hanna was beside herself with worry about Katherina, as though she could compensate for Christian's manifest disinterest in his offspring. Then there was also the problem with Gustav, who like his father seemed to have lost the ability to speak; but at least he was moving and apparently working through his anguish by toiling for lengthy hours every day on his land.

So that Sunday at the beginning of May, when Margareta noticed Katherina falling asleep at the dinner table, she suddenly knew she had her solution. She quietly got up from the table, went to Katherina's chair, and said to her niece, "Come with me, Dear. I am going to take you to Julia's bedroom, where you can lie down and have a sleep." As she rose, like a sleepwalker, Katherina replied, "Thank you, Auntie. I have been so tired this past month, and it doesn't seem to matter how much I sleep; I am still fatigued."

They walked down the hall and up the four stairs, which took them to the cozy attic that Phillip had converted into a bedroom for Julia years ago when she needed a private place away from the hustle and bustle of the store to study her lessons. Julia had a knack for decorating and making her own space very comfortable, with a pastel floral covering for her quilt and matching curtains for the small window. As soon as she got into the room, Margareta went to the dresser and pulled out a flannelette nightgown.

"Put this on so you will be warm as you snuggle under the comforter. Julia always said she felt so secure and sheltered, even on the coldest winter nights when the wind was howling outside her window, once she was safely tucked into her little bed." Margareta walked over to the window to draw the curtains, allowing her niece some privacy as she changed from her clothes into the nightdress and then got into bed.

"Good night, my darling. Have a restful sleep, and don't worry; I shall not let anyone wake you until you are ready to get up," Margareta said lovingly as she pulled the light down quilt up to her niece's chin and kissed her on the forehead. She was certain that Katherina was sound asleep before she tiptoed out of the room, closing the door quietly behind her.

When the family was ready to leave and return home, Margareta asked Hanna to come with her and check on her sister. As she had surmised, Katherina was sleeping like a baby, and it did not take much to convince Hanna to let well enough alone. In fact, the minute Hanna saw her little sister resting so peacefully, she asked her aunt if they could bring her home another day. "I would be only too happy to keep her with me today, as long as you can talk your papa into letting her stay," answered Margareta kindly.

"Papa doesn't seem to even notice us anymore, and I am having a terrible time getting Katherina to do anything. Sometimes I can't get her out of bed all day and then she is awake most of the night, which interferes with my sleep. I am tired when I go to bed because I have to do all the chores, and Maria needs help with the children. Auntie, I just don't know what to do. I know Katherina misses Mama very much, but so do I," said Hanna, as tears started to run down her cheeks.

"Oh, you poor child, come here," Margareta responded, as she hugged her sturdy, hard-working niece. "Katherina can stay with your Uncle Phillip and me until you have had some time to look after yourself. What both of you really need is a restorative night's sleep to regain your energy and, for you, Hanna, your wonderful sense of optimism. I know you are very different from Katherina, and I think your life will always be easier because you are able to see the brighter side of things. Katherina is so like your grandmother, who always seemed to view life from a darker perspective. Nonetheless, I want you to remember that I love you too, and whenever you need someone to talk to, I am also here for you."

~ 42 ~

Even Margareta could never have predicted how long Katherina would sleep before she finally awoke from her slumber in Julia's bed. After twenty-four hours, she went to Dr. Spitznagel's office to seek his advice and was relieved when he suggested that she give her niece more time before she tried to awaken her. The doctor was a kindly man who explained that Katherina might need a prolonged sleep to allow her adolescent body and mind to recover from the dreadful shock and loss caused by her mother's death. Given what Margareta told him about her niece's behaviour in the month since Elisabetha's passing, Dr. Spitznagel encouraged her to keep the child in Neudorf, where she could provide her with much-needed motherly love. His clear recommendation was that Katherina needed an environment in which she could restore her body, reanimate her mind, and renew her spirit.

Since Christian knew and respected Dr. Spitznagel, Margareta quickly understood that she had found a powerful ally in her plans for her lovely young niece. Even as he was expressing his medical opinion, Margareta was mentally formulating her proposals for Katherina's future. First and foremost in her mind, Margareta Mohr knew that if she had anything to say or do about it, Katherina Werner would never return to the farm to lead the life of drudgery and toil that was the lot of the pioneering woman. She had too delicate a constitution to work like a slave for fourteen to sixteen hours a day milking cows, churning butter, baking bread, cooking, cleaning, and washing clothes with a scrub board after carrying and heating the water. That did not even include planting and tending to the huge garden and then canning and preserving the produce each fall to feed the seemingly endless number of children that most of these women produced.

Margareta fully intended to involve Gustav in her design, just as soon as he recovered from his own doldrums. She knew he would rebound, by virtue of his frantic plowing of his land, as though he was churning the demons from his soul into the prairie sod. Then Margareta and Phillip would teach Katherina English and, when ready, get her to work alongside Margareta in the general store so Phillip could finally open the lumberyard which he had talked about doing for years to their son Peter.

Sure, the Silent Critics would gossip that Margareta Mohr was doing it again. As she had before, she was sticking her nose into her brother's business and ruining another of his children with her meddlesome ways. At some time in their conversations, no doubt they would wonder again why Margareta seemed to have such a great love for children and yet had only produced two of her own. It did not matter to Margareta what the Silent Critics said or thought about her actions because they never expressed their questions or opinions to her face, only behind her back. Her only concern was to save her niece, to open her mind, and to revive her spirit so she could develop into a fine young woman.

～ 43 ～

Time vindicated Margareta, and with Gustav's frequent visits to Neudorf, within two years Katherina was fully fluent in English. And, in addition to being skilled at selling, she had demonstrated her aptitude for mathematics and had taken on all of the financial accounting for the store. When she had an opportunity to learn and to use her mind, Katherina blossomed like a budding rose, and now people came into the store just to chat with this charming young girl. Her family had thought that she had reached her full height when she was thirteen, but at fifteen, she was only a half a head shorter than her six-foot-tall brother Gustav. One day, it occurred to Margareta to have Katherina try on some of the new dresses that she had added to the store's inventory for the customers; within days of that idea, they all sold. Soon this experience sparked yet another idea in her fertile mind, and Margareta discussed with Phillip the possibility of opening a dress shop in Neudorf, where Katherina could encourage sales by wearing samples of the merchandise.

Even Phillip Mohr had stood and stared at his elegant young niece that day in September when she waited for Gustav to arrive and take her as his guest to Andrew and Sarah's wedding in Duff. When Andrew asked Gustav to the wedding, he asked if Gustav thought Katherina would like to accompany him. She was delighted to be included in the festivities. Margareta instantly decided the two of them must take the train to Regina to search for a new dress that would be appropriate to wear to an English wedding.

When Phillip asked, "My dear, why the sudden rush to travel all the way to the capital city?" Margareta readily responded. "I have not seen Julia for far too long, and I thought Katherina might enjoy the new experience of a ride on the train." Once again, she confirmed the one conclusion that the Silent Critics had reached years ago: that Margareta Mohr was a quick thinker.

Julia was a great help, taking them to the shops in Regina on Broad Street until all three women agreed that they found just the right dress for Katherina's first real party. Although she had been to weddings before, none had concluded with a dance, and when they returned to Neudorf, Margareta coaxed Phillip into teaching their niece some basic waltz steps so she could enjoy the evening fully.

"Aunt Margareta, I don't know how I can ever thank you for all the things you do for me," said Katherina as her aunt put her long, light auburn hair up in a French knot, held in place with Margareta's pearl-studded hairpin and a bow that matched the colour of her dress.

"Seeing the wonderful changes in you will always be more than enough thanks for both your Uncle Phillip and me," answered her aunt graciously.

"Katherina, where did you get such a dress?" asked Gustav as soon as he arrived with Wolfgang hitched to their father's lightweight carriage.

"Well, good afternoon to you too, Gustav," Katherina teased with a twinkle in her sky-blue eyes.

As they were about to leave, Margareta came running out of the house with her beige crocheted shawl. "Katherina, wrap this around your shoulders to protect your dress from the dust, and it will keep you warm when you return home much later in the evening. Both of you look so handsome and full of youthful energy. Have a delightful time at the wedding."

～～ 44 ～～

On the way to Duff, Gustav kept glancing at his youngest sister, unable to believe how beautiful she looked in the long, straight, emerald-green gown with the patterned silver design stitched around the collar and running down both sides of the dress's slender skirt. The long, puffed sleeves seemed to enhance her tall, slim body, and the silver scarf around her neck held in place with a pearl brooch further emphasized the ruffled bodice of the satiny evening gown.

"Katherina, if only Mama could see you now!" Gustav exclaimed. "I think she would wonder what had happened to her little girl, and I don't know that Papa would even recognize you. Aunt Margareta has made you into an attractive and charming young lady."

"Thank you, Gustav. You look very handsome yourself in your new suit that matches the colour of your eyes. I am so glad you didn't get another dark brown or black one. And I do think that Mama is looking down on us right now and is happy that Uncle Phillip and Aunt Margareta take such good care of us all. Do you know that when she bought my dress, she also picked out a pretty red skirt and white blouse for Hanna? Besides, the other day Auntie told me that I look more and more like Mama when she was young, so I think Papa would easily know me, even when I am very dressed up for an English wedding," laughed Katherina.

When the two strangers walked into the Methodist church in Duff, first one head then another and another turned, until every person in the building was looking at the tall, handsome, blond man and the exquisitely beautiful woman of almost his height at his side. It was a surprise when they chose to sit at the back of the church rather than joining either family in the pews at the front, which had been set aside for the relatives. Who, then, were these young people? With curiosity piqued, they had no choice but to wait until after the marriage ceremony; even then, not all of the guests would have their inquisitiveness appeased. But one English gentleman resolved, the minute they entered the church, to not wait beyond the customary time needed for a formal introduction before meeting this enchanting-looking woman.

Fortunately, David Hardy, the older brother of the bride, did not have to break social conventions to be introduced to Katherina Werner. When Andrew and Sarah were pronounced man and wife by the minister and then marched down the aisle to the front door of the church, David, the best man, quietly asked Heather, Andrew's younger sister and the maid of honour, "Do you have any idea who those people are, the ones who sat near the back of the church?"

"Oh, sure. That's Katherina Werner, my friend who is my age, and her older brother Gustav, Andrew's friend," replied Heather beguilingly. "They are German, and they live on a farm not too far from our land. Well, actually, Katherina now stays with her Aunt Margareta and Uncle Phillip in Neudorf. They have come to tea and dinner at our house many times, and even I was included when Gustav invited Andrew and Sarah to have supper at their Aunt Margareta's house in Neudorf. But I'm sure you will meet them during the wedding dinner and dance."

"Is there any chance that you could introduce me to your friend before we sit down for dinner?" asked David politely. Already he planned that by being the first man to meet her, he could reasonably lead her onto the dance floor when the music began; he did not intend to share her with any other possible suitors.

"Of course. As soon as we are outside in the churchyard and the pictures have been taken, come with me, and I shall arrange for you to meet both Katherina and Gustav. But remember that after dinner the entire bridal party starts the festivities with the first dance," answered Heather coyly.

David looked at his new sister-in-law, who had brought him sharply back to reality. Perhaps he was being too contrived in his intentions, which nonetheless he would pursue as soon as his formal obligations as best man were met.

When the delicious roast beef dinner with Yorkshire pudding and all of the trimmings had been topped off with Mrs. Hardy's trifle, which she had purportedly made with imported Bristol Cream sherry, the women cleared the dishes and the men readied the church basement for dancing. The small group of musicians began to set up and tune their violin, cello, flute, and clarinet, and within a short time began the dance by playing Mendelssohn's "Wedding March." Andrew, tall and handsome in his black tailored suit and brilliant white shirt and looking pleased with himself, led his lovely petite bride in her flowing white gown onto the dance floor. They were soon joined by the other members of the bridal party and then by the parents of the bride and groom. During the next waltz, many of the other celebrants found their partners and crowded onto the ever-decreasing space of the available dancing surface.

With the first chord of the music, Katherina closed her eyes and was transported away from this happy event, where her brother and she were being treated graciously by all of Andrew and Sarah's families and friends, back to her mother's bedroom in the stone farmhouse. What had happened to Mama's gramophone? Oh, why had they stopped playing those wonderful melodious songs when they most needed them? As Katherina sat enraptured by the music, she began to feel a hunger in her soul, a yearning to be able to transcend the human experience, to go beyond all of the limitations of her body and mind. Suddenly, she understood what her mother had been trying to convey to all of them as she had repeatedly listened, as though transfixed, to the music of her countrymen, with Papa sitting by her side. She so desperately wanted to allay their fears about her death, all the while knowing she was going to a better place, where her spirit would soar and find eternal peace forever free from the worries and hardships of this world.

Just then, Gustav tapped her on the shoulder to ask her to dance, and she almost leaped off the chair as she came back to the present.

"Do you want to dance with me? Katherina, are you all right? You had your eyes closed, and you seemed so far away," asked her brother, with concern.

"As I was waiting for you to ask me, I was remembering all the music we listened to on Mama's gramophone. Do you know that one day she told me that it was one of the best gifts she had ever received? What have you done with it?"

"Nothing. As far as I know, it is still sitting in her bedroom. I have not gone into that room since she died," answered Gustav.

"If you don't listen to the gramophone, would you mind bringing it in to Neudorf so I can again enjoy hearing all of those cylinders of music? I was no longer sad when I was thinking about Mama. In fact, I have finally understood the incredible harmony, peace, and joy that Mama experienced while she listened to the wonderful concertos and symphonies of the great composers."

"I would like you to have the gramophone, and I shall bring it to Aunt Margareta's next Sunday. But now, should we try some of those dance steps that Uncle Phillip was teaching me at the lumberyard while you were practising with Auntie at the store?"

When the Werner siblings rose from their chairs and joined the large group of dancers, David was instantly aware that Katherina was on the dance floor. He was not the only person in the room to stare at this handsome couple again as they waltzed their way around the room. There were still those who had not made their acquaintance, such as a group of young men who had been invited by the prominent Hardy family to participate in the festivities after the dinner. David was quick to manoeuvre Heather, the woman he was currently dancing with, close to the Werners so that as soon as the piece of music ended he could recommend to Gustav that they change dance partners. He suspected that Heather would be equally happy with his adroit planning, since he had noticed her observing Gustav on more than one occasion.

Whether because of the deference afforded to the town banker's son, who the following week was starting his third year of university in Saskatoon, or rather because the other eligible young men of the community were intimidated by her elegance, David was able to monopolize Katherina for the rest of the evening. Aside from allowing Andrew and Gustav an occasional waltz, David was seen constantly twirling Katherina around the small dance floor or sitting at one of the tables chatting amicably with her. By the time the evening finally ended, David had extracted a promise from Katherina to allow him to call on her when he returned to the community next spring at the completion of his university year.

~ 45 ~

Spring did not seem to want to stay in the year of 1912. At first, it had seemingly arrived early, with its warming temperature and gentle breezes dancing between the willows and enticing the soft, furry, silver catkins from their cocooning slender, graceful wands. Then, when it had everyone convinced, it receded once again to the cold, strong wind from the northwest with its blowing snow, and to a freezing winter. This seasonal teasing continued for more than two months until it seemed that nature was simply confused. On the warm spring days, the crows cawed in the poplars, where the sticky buds started to appear on the branches, the meadowlarks trilled in the greening grass, and the gophers cautiously stuck their heads out of the holes in the ground. It was a mystery where all the birds went when winter came back to stalk the prairie and reclaim the country with its lingering, bone-chilling cold and harsh, withering winds. At least the gophers could retreat underground and try again later when spring decided to prevail.

The indecision of the weather weighed heavily on Gustav because this was the year that Rolf and he could file the applications at the Dominion Lands Office in Regina to confirm the titles for their land. Both of them had exceeded the cultivation requirements stipulated by the Dominion Lands Act before the Crown would award the land patents for their homesteads. Actually, Gustav had been surprised by how marginal the specified improvements were and never would have considered only breaking the required fifteen to fifty acres of his land. In the three years since they had filed on their land, Rolf and he not only plowed most of their combined 320 acres, but by this spring they would also plant most of it in crops. It occurred to Gustav that two reasons so much of their land was broken were that Rolf had become more enthusiastic about farming since he was going to be a father, and Gustav had slaved, as though trying to break up his grief with each bite of the plowshare at the same time he severed the roots of the matted sod of the unturned prairie.

That summer, Gustav had learned some important lessons. Hard work helped him to heal and to finally come to terms with his mama's death. And by working from dawn to dusk six days a week, he broke almost a quarter-section of land during one season. Of course, he really had no other responsibilities: he did not have a wife or children who needed his time and energy, and by living in the tent, he had no housekeeping chores. As far as his few items of laundry, when Katie was washing clothes every Monday anyway, why would she not just do his at the same time? Even when Sabina was born, Katie and Rolf persisted in including Gustav in their lives, which were filled with happiness and love for their first daughter.

Gustav often marvelled at the changes in his previously quiet and diffident brother, who appeared to have come to life with his wonderfully outgoing and caring wife. Katie was exactly the kind of woman Rolf needed, capable of helping him make decisions and realizing that his easygoing nature was a strength rather than a liability. Gustav always knew that Rolf's needs to own land and to make money were not nearly as insistent as his own and that his older brother was much more easily satisfied than he would ever be. Rolf was content with his wife, his beautiful baby girl, his new house, and his quarter-section of land. He could not understand why Gustav was so ambitious and so driven to work most of the time, although Rolf certainly appreciated it when he helped him to break his land. The brothers, although very different by nature, quickly adopted the co-operative spirit of the Western pioneers and helped each other on their adjacent homesteads.

But there was another reason Gustav was so troubled by the lateness of the spring in 1912. He had yet to comply with one of the conditions that had to be met before Rolf and he could go to Regina to prove their homesteads. Since he had been so welcome in Katie and Rolf's home, and because the tent was more than adequate for him to live in during the summer months, Gustav had never built the required domicile on his land. Quite frankly, he considered it a total waste of money to build a house when he far preferred to live in the outdoors and to sleep under the stars on the warm summer nights. Besides, he needed to actually live on his land for only six months of each year, which he did, and his father appreciated him coming home for the winter months to help him with the chores.

Nonetheless, Gustav knew he had to act quickly and build some kind of a dwelling before the Dominion Lands Board dispatched the homestead inspector to confirm that the proper improvements had been undertaken. The last thing Gustav would dream of doing was to not adhere to the government regulations and to jeopardize the title deed to his land. One April morning, when the air was warmer and lighter without its icy crystals and spring was emerging as victor of the vacillating seasons, he hitched Wolfgang to the carriage and drove to Rolf's home on his way to Neudorf to discuss a proposal that he hoped would solve his problem.

Rolf was carrying a pail of milk to the house as Gustav drove Wolfgang into his yard. After the long winter and uncertain spring, Rolf was looking forward to having his brother return to his own homestead and to working together over the summer months. "Good morning, Gustav. You are just in time for breakfast, and you can be sure that Katie will have more than enough food. I hope this weather changes for the better and you will soon be back with us every day."

"Thank you, Rolf. I have already had my meal, but I will come in for coffee because I need to talk with you about putting up a building on my land," replied Gustav.

As the men approached the house, the door opened and Katie welcomed them into her kitchen, which smelled of freshly baked bread, brewing coffee, and sizzling bacon. "Gustav, it is so nice to have you back." Even as she spoke, Katie placed a third plate on the table, and Gustav knew there was no point in protesting that he had already eaten. It was a good thing he worked such long hours during the summer; otherwise, he would put on weight eating Katie's delicious meals, as Rolf had done over the past three years. He looked at his brother and realized that Rolf had become really pudgy over the winter. As Gustav observed that Rolf and Katie were starting to resemble each other, a tall and a short version, he looked closely at Katie and saw what he had not noticed before: that she was heavy with child again.

When the men were drinking their coffee, Gustav said, "Rolf, I have been thinking that we could build a shed with a small window to be my domicile, and after the inspector has seen it, you could use it for a smokehouse. Since we built your house so close to my property line, it would be near enough to carry the meat home, yet allow plenty of distance for the smoke not to bother you."

"But I thought you would buy lumber this spring to build your own house," Rolf responded with surprise.

"I am not going to build a house on my homestead. I like living in the tent during the warm weather, and over this past winter, I realized that Papa is failing and soon will not be able to manage his own farm. Now that most of our land is broken, I will have time to help him with his seeding and harvesting each year, so I will just continue to live in his house."

"You will be getting married this fall, and do you want to bring your bride to live in Papa's house? Look at what happened with Friedrich and Maria's marriage, living under the same roof as Mama and Papa and all of the rest of us. They did not have a chance to get to know each other," answered Rolf with disbelief.

"The problems in their marriage have nothing to do with where they live. Those two were ill-suited from the start, mainly I think because they are too much alike. They are both selfish and thoughtless people," replied Gustav.

"Well, I don't think you are being fair to Maria. You forget how she changed when Mama was dying and how she took her turn sitting with her day or night. And think about how loving she is with her children. The selfish one is Friedrich; I don't think he cares about anyone but himself. He never once sat up during the night with Mama!"

"I don't want to argue about Friedrich and Maria. And besides, I am not even sure I want to get married this year."

"What are you talking about, Gustav? Papa made the arrangements years ago, and you are to marry Amelia Schweitzer this autumn after the harvest. Katie and I were married early in September because there were no crops to take off, but now that we all have our own land, it was decided that we are too busy for a wedding until the fall. Where were you when we had this family discussion at Easter? Good heavens, Aunt Margareta is already planning your wedding supper!" Rolf was starting to get frustrated with his youngest brother, who questioned everything.

"I remember seeing Amelia at Mama's funeral, and she looked like a little girl. If Papa is deciding that I am to be married, I would at least like a woman who is close to my own age. But what I really want is to be able to select the person that I spend my life with, as my friend Andrew did when he married Sarah Hardy last September. They met at their church and after they had spent time together, he proposed to her. Of course, they had met each other's parents, but Andrew and Sarah made their own decision to get married. I too would like this freedom of choice instead of always having to obey Papa and having him decide what I do," Gustav replied heatedly.

"I am starting to understand why Papa didn't want you to learn English, and what does he know about your English friend? You are beginning to think just like him, and you forget that their ways are very different from ours. The Germans have arranged their children's marriages for generations and usually with very good success. Think about it: Mama and Papa, Aunt Margareta and Uncle Phillip, and all of your brothers and sisters except Friedrich and Maria are happily married. This way we can keep our own language, our religion, and our German customs, which is why Mama and Papa fled from Russia to Canada in the first place." By now Rolf was standing and yelling at Gustav, who had also jumped up from his chair.

Katie came rushing into the house from the clothesline, where she had been hanging up the freshly washed diapers. "What is the matter with you two? You have awakened Sabina with your noisy arguing. Rolf, if you are not going to get your daughter, at least go outside and do some work."

"I'm sorry, Katie. I will go and bring you Sabina from her crib," answered Rolf sheepishly.

"We were being inconsiderate, Katie—sorry. Thank you for breakfast. I am going into Neudorf to buy some lumber to build your future smokehouse. I will come back tomorrow when both of us have settled down and can behave like adults," responded Gustav.

~ **46** ~

On the way to town, Gustav thought about his argument with his brother, and once again, he recognized how similar Rolf was to their father. Neither of them wanted to accept that things would change in this new country and that they simply would not be able to continue with all of their old German traditions. Gustav could not understand why his father would want to come to Canada, this growing, progressive, and vast land where the opportunities seemed limitless, and then try to make it just like the two countries he had left behind. What was the point of dragging the family halfway around the world to stay the same? If they were still living in Russia, or Austria, where there most likely was better medical care, maybe Mama might be alive today. The instant Gustav had this thought, it occurred to him that this was exactly what had made his father feel so guilty about Mama's death and why he had not been able to talk to any of his children. Oh, poor Papa. He could not be held responsible for their mother's terrible illness.

With this insight, Gustav resolved to be more understanding of his father, and even of Rolf, who had always worked complacently alongside his father without question, contempt, or disobedience. Certainly, Friedrich had been the most difficult of all of the children and the one about whom there were now so many questions. What was he doing in Melville, how could he abandon his wife and children, and who did he expect to care for them when Papa died? But Gustav knew he would be the reason for even more distress for his father when Johann, whom he had been teaching English for the past two years, also decided to leave his farm and move to Melville to work for the railway. At least Gustav shared his father's love for owning land and planned to keep Johann's homestead in the Werner family by buying it himself. But in many ways, Rolf was the only son who aspired to be like his father by raising strong, healthy children to farm the land and to pass on the Germanic heritage for posterity.

The air was considerably warmer in the late morning, and Gustav decided it was too nice a spring day to dwell on the expectations, similarities, and differences of the Werner family. And then there was the question of him marrying the Schweitzer girl, who at the very least was two years older than when he had last seen her. Maybe she had matured and had become a lovely young woman whom he could learn to love and respect. Rolf did have a point about most of the families' arranged marriages being happy, and he certainly did not know who else he could take as his bride. But since he could not solve any of these dilemmas right away, he determined that as soon as he got to Neudorf, he would go to Aunt Margareta's store and take Katherina for a ride in the country. Gustav knew his aunt would be pleased that even as his busy seeding season was fast approaching, he was spending time with his sister, and no doubt he would be invited to stay for supper.

Gustav's relationship with his Aunt Margareta had become even stronger since his mother's death, not just because she was now the only female with whom he could share his thoughts and feelings as he had with his mother, but also owing to her insight into Katherina. Margareta Mohr may well have been the only person to realize the depth of Katherina's despair at the time of Elisabetha's demise, and Gustav now came to believe that she had probably saved his youngest sister's life. To be fair, Hanna knew there was something seriously wrong with Katherina, but aside from trying to encourage her to get out of bed and lose herself in nature and work, she could not find the answer for her sister's sense of hopelessness. Nor could Hanna totally understand how someone as beautiful, tall, and graceful as Katherina, the Werner daughter who was always the first to be noticed, could have such dark feelings in her heart.

Once again, Margareta had risked not only the prattle of the nosy group of seven of the small town, but of much more serious consequence, the possible wrath of her older brother, Christian Werner, when she decided to have Katherina live with her. As far as her busybody neighbours were concerned—who, of course, were also her customers in the general store—Margareta knew she would eventually dispel their inquisitiveness about her niece by giving them something else to talk about or by being totally mute on the subject. She had long ago suspected that her nephew Gustav and she were probably the two people most frequently gossiped about in Neudorf by those individuals she ironically came to identify as the Silent Critics, knowing full well they were anything but silent, except when they came face to face with the recipients of their rumour mongering.

To be sure, they were an eclectic collection of individuals, with a widow, a widower, a bachelor, two spinster sisters, and even a husband and wife whose children with whom they lived were happy to have their parents out of their hair for the better part of the day. These seven old people had come together, one by one or in pairs, as in the case of the sisters, who hesitantly joined the coffee clique out of a sense of loneliness and the feeling of not being needed anymore. They knew the townspeople referred to them as the Silent Critics; they even knew that Margareta Mohr had coined the name, believing that they talked about people only behind their backs and became silent in their presence. But instead of being upset about the appellation, the Silent Critics revelled in their role. At least now everyone in town noticed them, and they had a purpose. And when times were frivolous, Margareta had to acknowledge that she sometimes deliberately played along with these prying individuals and went out of her way to give them the fodder to inspire their next rumour.

⟫⟩~ 48 ~⟨⟪

By the time Gustav reached Neudorf, the fresh, sweet-smelling air of blossoming spring flowers had dispelled any residual anguish from his fight with Rolf. He bounded up the three small steps into the general store in one flying leap, nearly knocking his aunt off her feet as he threw open the door.

"Hello, Aunt Margareta. How are you this nice day? I am convinced that spring is finally going to stay," said Gustav.

"Good morning, Gustav," replied Margareta. "You certainly are in high spirits, which is so nice to see. And are you here to make a purchase or just to visit before you get wrapped up in your seeding?"

"I have come to town to buy some lumber to build a smokehouse, but before I go to Uncle Phillip's yard, I thought that since I have the carriage, I would surprise Katherina with a ride in the country. We may even be able to pick some crocuses and bring them back for you to use as a centre for the supper table," said Gustav.

"It seems you will have to stand in line if you want to take your sister out. She had a surprise visitor earlier this morning, and they have already gone for a ride."

"Who has come to take Katherina out? She doesn't know anyone other than her family."

"It seems she knows a very pleasant, polite young man called David Hardy. He said he also knew you from Andrew and Sarah's wedding last September, and he asked how you were doing," replied Margareta.

"Oh, sure, I remember David. He is Sarah's older brother and was Andrew's best man. But why has he come to see Katherina, and did he ask Papa whether he could go out with her?" inquired Gustav.

"I very much doubt that he talked to your father, since he would not know him or where he lives," answered Margareta with some surprise.

"Well, then, did you send him to talk to Uncle Phillip about taking Katherina for a ride?"

"No, Gustav, I invited him into the house for a cup of coffee and called Katherina, and he asked her if she would like to accompany him on a ride into the country. After we finished our coffee, Katherina asked me if I could spare her from the store for a few hours, and I told them to have an enjoyable time." Margareta was becoming a little frustrated with her nephew, who by this time was peering at her with an astounded look on his face.

"Aunt Margareta, are you telling me you let Katherina decide for herself to go away with David Hardy?" asked Gustav in disbelief.

"She has gone for a ride around the countryside on a beautiful spring day and not to the end of the world, Gustav. Would you listen to yourself? You are starting to sound like your father!" replied Margareta with exasperation.

"But Auntie, she cannot be seen driving around town with a strange man. Katherina is only sixteen years old!"

When she stood completely upright to her fullest height, Margareta Mohr measured, at best, five feet two inches, although most people, including the Silent Critics, would argue that she was considerably taller. On this spring morning in April 1912, she took her six-foot nephew by the arm, led him to a chair, and forcibly sat him down before responding to him.

"You are full of contradictions, my fine young nephew. You have frequently told me how frustrated you have been with your papa because he wants to keep the ways and traditions of the old country rather than to change and learn about the different customs and the language of this new country. I also remember you saying repeatedly that you want to think of yourself as a Canadian and not as a German, since you are now a landowner in Canada. I know you want the freedom to make your own choices; therefore, you have to be prepared to allow others to do the same."

"Aunt Margareta, as you very well know, I am twenty-one years of age, an adult, while Katherina is still a young girl," said Gustav with a feeling of irritation that surprised even him.

"I don't think that you have looked very closely at Katherina for some time, or you would have noticed she is becoming a young woman. And you may be interested to know that Amelia, the woman your father has arranged for you to marry in five short months, is exactly Katherina's age. Now, I grant you, Amelia Schweitzer is a very mature young woman, given that she has had to run her father's household and look after her two younger siblings since her mother's death when she was seven, but she is nonetheless sixteen years of age."

"Are you sure? Whatever is Papa thinking? He can't seriously want me to marry a sixteen-year-old; she is still a child. In fact, I just had an argument with Rolf before I left his farm because, as I told him, I am not certain that I am ready to get married at my age, never mind to someone only sixteen!"

"Well, you are having an interesting day, Gustav. I think this is the closest we have ever come to having words, and rather than continue, why don't you come in and have some dinner before you go to the lumberyard," Margareta said calmly.

Gustav began to laugh and said to his aunt, "I have had two meals already today, and it is not yet noon. I had better get back to my fields before I start gaining weight like Rolf and end up quarrelling with every member of the family!"

49

It seemed that Gustav was prophetic, at least when it came to initiating family arguments, and the worst one on that April spring day was yet to come. He had continued to talk with his aunt, although both of them had returned to their usual congenial interaction, until Phillip and Peter arrived home for dinner. And since he was still there and now could not go to the lumberyard until his uncle and cousin had eaten, Gustav joined them for their meal.

When he purchased enough lumber, four small panes of glass for a window, and a door to construct a home that was convincing enough to satisfy the homestead inspector, Gustav was ready to leave Neudorf. The truth was that he lingered in town hoping Katherina would return from her excursion with David. He was careful not to be too obvious because he did not want to upset his aunt again, but by mid-afternoon, he knew he would have to leave without seeing his sister.

Finally on his way, Gustav told himself that it was probably just as well that he missed Katherina and David because he was feeling both annoyed and worried that they had been together, unchaperoned, for such a long period of time. It was a very good thing Papa was not aware that his youngest child was driving around unattended with a man who had neither been formally introduced to him nor had sought his permission to call on his daughter. And an Englishman at that.

Instead of driving to his homestead, Gustav headed towards his father's farm and then decided to stop at the little cemetery to visit his mother's gravesite. Perhaps he could find some crocuses to put at the head of her grave, although he sensed he was rushing the return of one of the first prairie wildflowers. For as long as he could remember, Gustav had eagerly awaited the coming of spring, the season of rebirth and reawakening of the earth, with its warmth and vibrancy. When the air became alive with the sounds of the birds and the unique scents of the budding flowers, opening leaves, and sprouting spears of grass, it was like being released from a dark, freezing-cold prison. He seemed to become more alive, as though he was able to absorb the surging forces of the world around him, and the wonderful gifts of life and nature buoyed his spirit.

His mother had teased him that he had far too much energy in the spring after the long winter months, and she had always given him extra chores to keep him busy. Now as an adult, when he was honest with himself, this time of recreation sometimes made him feel as frisky as a young stallion. Had Gustav understood his own sexuality, he might have been more aware that his strong urges and those dreams from which he would awaken shamefully wet were perfectly natural for a healthy, youthful, and virile male. Of course, he knew that Papa's farm animals procreated in the early spring, and many times he watched in fascination as the hired bull coupled with their growing herd of cows. But Gustav was not only a virgin; he did not know how humans went about the business of having sexual intercourse and whether he could even do it. Part of the reason he had loitered at his Uncle Phillip's lumberyard was because he hoped to have a private talk with him, but Peter, who idolized his older cousin, was constantly underfoot.

Gustav called, "Whoa, Wolfgang," and the carriage came to a stop. He leaped down and tied the horse to a tree where a clump of fresh green grass thrust up through its dried, brown perennial roots. He searched in the areas where the ground was protected from the wind, but the prairie crocuses had yet to produce their silky purple flowers. As he opened the gate to the fence that his father built around the grove of poplar trees, he was startled to see his father lying on the ground beside Elisabetha's grave. He rushed over to him, calling, "Papa, Papa, what is wrong? Are you all right? Why are you on the ground?"

Christian sat up quickly and brushed the dirt from his overalls.

"Yes, Gustav, I am fine. I had been cleaning the leaves and mud from the spring's runoff away from your mother's headstone when I decided to have a little rest. What brings you here today? I thought you were going to start building your smokehouse."

"Oh, Rolf and I had a little dispute over breakfast, and I don't think either Katie or he would be all that happy to see me again this afternoon. So I thought I would take the carriage and the lumber back to your farm and call on Andrew and Sarah to see how they are doing."

"I cannot believe that you had another breakfast after what Hanna prepared for you before you left. And what was your quarrel about?" asked Christian.

"It was rather ridiculous, and I am not even sure how it got started other than I told Rolf that I wasn't sure I was ready to get married," replied Gustav.

"Well, of course it is time for you to have a wife; all of the Werner men are married by the age of twenty-one. And on that subject, I went to see Mr. Schweitzer this morning. He invited you and me for supper this coming Saturday so you can properly make Amelia's acquaintance and he and I can finalize the balance of her dowry. We thought that the last Sunday in September would be a good day for the wedding, as it gives all of us time to finish the threshing. This next Sunday after church, I shall talk to Reverend Biber," answered Christian with the satisfaction that accompanies careful planning.

"But Papa, this is what I quarrelled with Rolf about this morning. Then when I went to see Aunt Margareta and she told me Amelia is only sixteen years old, I was so astonished that I came close to having another argument with her. You can't possibly want me to marry a child!"

"Gustav, what are you saying? Your mother and I made the arrangement years ago with the Schweitzer family for you to wed Amelia, who, by the way, is a very sturdy, comely, and hard-working woman. She has run her father's house since her mother died, and he told me himself that she has done such a fine job that he is worried how he will manage without her. She will be a great help to Hanna and Maria, especially with the children, as she has practically raised her younger siblings. And besides, I have already accepted some of her dowry, which I needed so I could pay for your mother's casket," replied Christian. As he spoke, he continued to pull up dried grass and weeds from around Elisabetha's grave, possibly with more force than was needed.

Gustav knelt down on the opposite side, and following his father's example, he too dislodged debris from the small headstone. He heard the determination in his father's voice; although at times he appeared frail, Christian Werner could still be a formidable figure. Gustav was not necessarily opposed to marrying Amelia, and he knew that the last thing he wanted to do was to raise Papa's ire by questioning him. Nonetheless, he felt compelled to voice his concerns.

"Papa, I am not saying that I don't want to marry Amelia, but perhaps it would be better if we waited a couple of years until she is at least eighteen. Then I would feel that she was an adult who was ready to take on the responsibilities of a husband and a home."

"Son, you clearly have not been listening to me. I just told you that Amelia has been looking after her father's house and raising her younger brother and sister for the past nine years. What difference does it make that she is sixteen?" Christian answered gruffly as he stood up and glared at his son. Although he had ended with a question, he clearly considered the conversation to be over.

"It makes a great deal of difference to me. Heather, my friend Andrew's sister, is also sixteen, and it would not even occur to me that she would be old enough to get married. What's more, her father would never allow it, especially to a man who is five years older than she is! And think about it, Papa: would you consider marrying off Katherina when she turns sixteen in June?"

"I don't seem to have any say in what happens to Katherina, and I become very angry when I think about how your Aunt Margareta has taken over my parental responsibilities with my youngest child. And don't you talk to me about your English family and their strange way of doing things."

"Did it ever occur to you that maybe our ways seem odd to them? Why do you decide whom I am to marry? Last year, when Andrew got married, he was able to choose the person he will spend his life with, rather than having his father decide," replied Gustav angrily as he too rose to his full height of six feet.

Gustav had finally articulated the thoughts that had been recurring in his mind since that day when Andrew and he went riding and Andrew said he planned to ask Sarah to be his bride. But Gustav could not have chosen a worse time to question his traditional German father.

"How dare you defy me by asking those questions, and here, of all places, on this sacred spot that your mother requested as her final resting place!" Suddenly, Christian understood what had been weighing him down since Elisabetha's death. Yes, there was guilt, but he worked through those feelings, and yet there was still something he could not identify. Now his youngest son's open defiance about one of his most important responsibilities as his parent made him aware of his burden. He was losing control over his own family and, with that realization, Christian Werner unleashed the frustration, the resentment, and the anger he had bottled up for two years in a tirade directed at Gustav.

"The Werner family has arranged the marriages of their offspring for generations and with great success. Most of the couples have enjoyed happy and productive relationships, which have resulted in the continuation of our family name for over a century. Your mother and I barely knew each other before we wed, and yet we learned to love each other, raised seven strong, healthy children, and endured the hardships of immigrating to not one but two new countries. You have no idea how much we loved each other, how we could talk things through, and how lonely I am without her. When you arrived I was lying by your mother's grave because only by touching the earth can I feel connected to her. But what do you know about love and commitment when the only person you ever think about is yourself?

"You would never have considered disobeying me if your Aunt Margareta had not ruined you by taking you in and teaching you English. Then you make friends with those English people from Duff and suddenly you think you are too good for our German customs and traditions and that you will decide when and to whom you will marry! Well, I have news for you, Gustav Werner: I am still your father. You will marry Amelia Schweitzer, you will marry her in September, and you will obey me because I know you will come to love her. And when you have your own children, you will be just like me, and you will decide what they do. Understand?" Christian finally stopped shouting and took a breath.

Gustav could not believe his eyes and his ears; he stood looking at his father with shock and amazement. Christian was yelling so loud that Gustav was sure he could be heard in Rolf's yard. He scared away birds that had been singing in the trees and caused gophers to retreat hastily to their holes in the ground. As he made his long speech, which consisted of more words than Gustav had heard him express at one time since Mama's funeral, Christian seemed to grow in size and to tower over his son. Of course, Gustav knew this was not possible, yet he felt strangely small and frightened, as though he had become a child again. He had never seen his father this angry, and certainly not with him.

At the same time, Gustav was worried for his father. He was sure it was not good for him to get so excited and overwrought. He remembered when Mr. Gillespie, his supervisor at the railway, had shouted at one of the men and then dropped dead in the middle of a sentence. Dr. Spitznagel said he had had a heart seizure, and Gustav did not want the same thing to happen to his remaining parent. "I am sorry, Papa; I did not want to upset you, and I promise to mind my manners when we go to meet the Schweitzers on Saturday," replied Gustav, surprisingly meek after his father's harangue. "Let's go home, Papa. You can ride in the carriage with me, and I will stay home to help you with the chores before supper."

$$\approx\!\!\sim 50 \sim\!\!\ll$$

Christian Werner was not the kind of man to hold a grudge, and he had surprised himself with the vehemence of his reaction to his son's behaviour at the cemetery. On the ride back that day, both men were subdued, neither saying another word to each other, although they worked side by side doing the chores when they arrived home. Even during supper, if the women and children had not spoken, there would have been no conversation at all. Fortunately, Hanna and Maria were too busy attending to Mathias, Julianna, and Baby Elisabetha, who, at almost eighteen months of age, was a handful by herself, to notice the strain between the two remaining men of the household. At the same time, while Christian did not harbour ill will towards anyone, he rarely apologized for anything he said or did.

On the other hand, Gustav was not as quick to overcome his resentment that his father was still so adamant about exercising control over him as an adult, and the silence between them continued until it became an almost insurmountable barrier. Gustav would be true to his promise of being polite and mannerly when he was introduced to his future bride because he knew his mother would have played a dominant role in choosing Amelia Schweitzer to be his wife. Still, he had considerable misgivings about marrying a sixteen-year-old girl, wondering if they shared enough in common that they might eventually learn to love each other.

Come what may, Gustav vowed that he would speak openly with his family, that he would express words of encouragement and praise, and that he would allow his children to make their own choices. And yet when the time came, he followed in his father's footsteps and similarly demanded that they obey him. Long before his death, Gustav often considered that it was this retreat to silence regarding their innermost thoughts and feelings, this need to control, and this expectation of blind obedience, even in the face of what they truly believed, that resulted in the whole German race becoming a part of the atrocities committed in the name of the fatherland. Like so many of his countrymen for generations to follow, Gustav would carry the legacy of guilt and the shame, the horrible disgrace of the Nazi regime under its evil dictator, with him to his grave. Gustav's only consolation was that at least some of the people he had loved and respected the most never had to know.

~ 51 ~

Several days passed before Gustav rode Wolfgang over to his friend's house. When he arrived, Andrew and his father were busy unloading a large pile of lumber from their sturdy, green wagon that had carried them across the windy Saskatchewan prairie. As soon as he dismounted and tethered Wolfgang, Gustav returned to where the men were working and started to help. "Hello, Mr. Thompson, Andrew. What are you going to do with all this lumber?"

"Good morning, Gustav. You have a wonderful sense of timing," responded Andrew while Mr. Thompson nodded to his son's friend. "We are planning to build an extension to Father's house, adding two more bedrooms and a living room to support our growing family. We have just found out that Sarah is with child, and we will have our first baby in time for Christmas," Andrew answered excitedly.

"Congratulations, Andrew. That is great news, and I will be very happy to work on your house-raising bee today. I remember how quickly we were able to build Rolf and Katie's house when everyone pitched in to get the job done. Then if we have some time, maybe we can go for a race across the countryside. Wolfgang will get sluggish again if I don't soon take him for a long ride," said Gustav wistfully.

Now that Andrew was married, there did not seem to be much opportunity for the two men to spend time together, and Gustav missed the companionship of his only friend. And after the huge fight with his father, he had been hesitant to ride over to the Thompson farm until things had cooled down with his father.

"Well, my friend, do you have enough energy left to challenge our horses to a race?" asked Andrew as he finished the last mouthful of his mother's delicious apple pie at the end of a very busy day.

"After all that I have eaten, I don't think it would be fair to expect Wolfgang to carry me around," teased Gustav. "But I would like to go for a stroll, and then maybe when we are not so full, we could have a race."

Gustav wanted to share his news with Andrew in private rather than in front of his whole family and had waited for this opportunity to tell his friend about his wedding. As the two men walked leisurely around the Thompsons' farm, Gustav said, "You must be very pleased with how much of the extension was built today. I really like the way you constructed the add-on; with Sarah and you having the upstairs, it will seem like you have your own house."

"My father and I spent hours discussing how we could build onto the existing house to give us some privacy and still share the kitchen and the water pump. It was Father's idea to build upward and to include an extra room where Sarah could sit and rock the baby if he wakes up during the night," replied Andrew.

"What makes you think your firstborn will be a boy?" chuckled Gustav.

"Actually, I would prefer a little girl just like Sarah, but we will be happy with either as long as the baby is strong and healthy. Gustav, what about you? You are getting behind; here I am already becoming a father, and you are still a bachelor!" ribbed Andrew.

"One of the reasons I wanted us to go for a walk was to invite Sarah and you to my wedding the last Sunday in September. As much as I would like to ask you to be my best man, I shall keep peace in the family and have my brothers as my groomsmen, although I have decided to ask Johann and Rolf because we never know when Friedrich is coming home. He has not seen his family since the fall, which I think is one reason why Papa is so annoyed with his children."

"Just a minute here, Gustav. You have lost me with all of this news at once. And first things first: Congratulations! Who is the lucky woman? Aren't you the sly one! You never said a word about seeing someone," Andrew teased.

Even before he had finished speaking, Andrew knew something was wrong. Gustav had stopped walking, lowered his head, and pretended to play with Sparky, who had leaped up from his nap to run along with the men. Andrew decided to wait until Gustav responded.

After a few deep breaths, Gustav said, "Oh, we Germans have some peculiar ways that I am not sure you know about or want to hear on such a beautiful evening."

"Of course I want to know what is going on. You are my best friend and this is one of the most important times of your life," Andrew earnestly replied.

"Well, Andrew, I have not been having a courtship such as Sarah and you had before your wedding. You see, according to our custom, years ago when I was a boy, my parents arranged with the Schweitzer family that I would wed their daughter Amelia when I turned twenty-one years old. At that time, they had apparently talked about the dowry, which she would bring to the marriage. I met her for the first time last Saturday, when they had Papa and me to supper. We will not see each other again until our wedding day on that last Sunday in September," Gustav answered, keeping his gaze focused on the ground.

"I still don't understand what is upsetting you. Did you not like her?" Trying to lighten the conversation, Andrew teased, "Is she the ugly duckling of the family, or is she just bone lazy?"

Despite himself, Gustav had to laugh. "No, Amelia does not fit either one of your negative descriptions. Just as Papa had said, she is a pretty young woman, although considerably shorter than me. And if anything, she can work as hard as any man. She has been running her father's household since she was seven years old and raising her younger siblings. She made a delicious supper of stewed chicken with dumplings that even filled me up, and plum perogies, one of my favourite desserts. It was almost as if she knew which foods I like best," said Gustav, just coming to this realization as he spoke.

"Good. Now at least, my friend, you have your head out of the dirt! But I still want to know what is disturbing you when you should be excited about this wonderful time in your life."

"Sometimes I am not able to figure out my papa. We had a big fight at Mama's gravesite about my marrying Amelia. Papa was yelling so loud that I thought he would strip the bark off the poplar trees and knock the budding leaves to the ground. I guess what bothers me the most is that Amelia is only sixteen and that I had no choice about who was to be my wife, as you did," answered Gustav.

"Oh, Gustav, you didn't bring me into this argument with your father. No wonder he was so angry! I have only met him once at your mother's funeral, and I could tell he is a proud man just by the way he held himself, so upright, so stoic, even though from what you had said he was devastated about losing his wife. And then you challenged him on what he would consider one of his most important decisions as your father and perhaps one of the last resolutions he would have made with your mother."

"How can you take his side? Your parents let you make your own decisions, discuss things with you rather than telling you what to do, and even tell you that they love you. I think the first time I ever heard Papa use the word *love* was during our quarrel when he told me how much he loved Mama? It seems that the German way is to control their children, to bring them to a new country but keep them steeped in all of the conventions of the Old World. I think that one reason Papa has been so miserable is that we are all growing up and he can't tell us what to do anymore," replied Gustav heatedly.

"Gustav, please calm down. I am not taking anyone's side."

"I am sorry, Andrew. I don't know what is the matter with me lately. I seem to be such a hothead. I'm starting quarrels with everyone, including Aunt Margareta, who is wonderful with all of us. She has become like a second mother to Katherina and Hanna, and she has always been available to help me through things," said Gustav.

"What you need is to settle down with a woman who will look after you and will help you deal with those physical urges that are likely the real problem," said Andrew knowingly. "But I must say that my sister will be very disappointed."

Gustav blinked. "Of course you can invite Heather to the wedding. I would also like your parents to come and finally meet all of my family. If Papa is going to have the say of whom I am marrying, I will at least decide who I want to come to the wedding."

"Gustav, sometimes I think you spend too much time in your fields. Have you never seen how Heather looks at you, how her eyes follow your every move, and when she thinks you are not aware of her, how she gazes at you with pure love and devotion on her face? I think my little sister has been in love with you since that first day I brought you home for tea. Heather worships the ground you walk on, and now you are going to invite her to your wedding to another woman."

"Well, Andrew, I really like Heather too, but nothing could ever come of it! Papa would never allow me to marry someone other than Amelia, and especially not an English girl."

Andrew looked intently at his friend. At first he thought Gustav was being glib and insensitive about Heather's feelings, until he realized he was simply being truthful. There was no guile or arrogance on his face; although he objected, Gustav believed that he had to obey his father and spend the rest of his life with a woman he did not know, even if he did care about another. Finally, the full measure of control that Christian Werner exerted over his children dawned on Andrew.

⚡ 52 ⚡

Even the potatoes in their cool, darkened root cellar were ready for an early spring, having started to sprout their eyes, their white tentacles reaching and waiting to be quartered into pieces for seeding in the rich, black soil. Hanna gathered several of them, carefully placing them in her upturned apron, and carried them to the kitchen table, where Maria and she were getting ready to begin planting the garden for another year. In this third season of nurturing her mother's garden, Hanna assiduously followed in Elisabetha's footsteps as though still guiding her every movement. On one occasion while Maria was helping her, she asked Hanna why they had to do everything in exactly the same order each time. After

Hanna's terse response, "Because this is the way Mama wants it done," Maria knew better than to question her again when she was performing one of her many rituals.

The two women had become very close over the past two years, and Maria understood that Hanna was keeping her mother alive in her mind by running the household, planting the garden, and even helping to care for her nephew and nieces precisely as Elisabetha had done. Almost all of her actions had become like rites to honour her mother. It was Hanna's way of remembering Mama and withstanding her Aunt Margareta's influence. She would never be like Katherina, who now lived in Neudorf and seemed to be forgetting not only her dead mother but also her father, who missed his youngest daughter terribly. Oh, Hanna loved her Aunt Margareta and Uncle Phillip just as much as the rest of them and was very grateful for their many invitations to dinner and their thoughtful gifts, but she would not lose sight of her responsibilities as an obedient daughter.

Last year when Elisabetha was a baby, taking care of her consisted of placing her on a blanket on her tummy and checking on her periodically to make sure that she was still safe. This spring, however, the women decided that they would need to enlist the help of Mathias and Julianna to play with her if they were to finish planting the huge garden in a timely fashion. The problem was that both of her older children would rather follow behind Maria and drop the seeds into the carefully dug straight furrows of overturned earth. Hanna and Maria eventually determined that a suitable incentive for Mathias and Julianna would be to allow them to stay up an hour later each day that they entertained their little sister, not knowing that at least for one of those evenings, there would indeed be strong enticement.

It was nearing the end of their third long and tiring day of back-breaking toil, which involved constant standing and bending to hoe the ground, plant the seeds, and then rake the earth over them. In the protective and nourishing soil, the tiny seeds would germinate into healthy plants, producing enough vegetables to feed the family during the entire winter. Hanna thought she heard a strange yet familiar sound. She stopped working; resting her hands on her hips, she listened intently until she realized what she was hearing was the chugging noise made by that thing Friedrich called his automobile. Her first thought concerned the whereabouts of the children, especially Elisabetha, who would run right up to the contraption without any regard for her safety. Rather than take any chances, Hanna ran out of the garden, calling for Mathias and Julianna to bring the toddler to her.

But Hanna was not quick enough. As she ran to the dirt road, she saw that Mathias had outdistanced her, and trailed by his two sisters, he raced towards the noisy machine. As if by divine intervention, Elisabetha tripped on her untied shoelace and fell down. When her siblings left her behind, she decided to stay put and have a good cry. She was quite content to be picked up by her Aunt Hanna, who soothed her, saying, "There, there. I shall carry you, and we will catch those other two, who didn't even stop when their precious baby sister fell!"

By this time, Maria, who was hoeing near the end of the garden farthest from the road leading to the house, became aware of the commotion and also took a break from the demanding work. Seeing that her sister-in-law had rescued her baby from being run over by Friedrich's car, Maria was not in any hurry to welcome her absentee husband.

Friedrich had barely stopped his automobile before he jumped out and ran to meet his children. Mathias reached him first, yelling, "Papa, Papa, you have come home!" When Friedrich lifted him up to swing him around in the air, he was surprised by how his son had grown and how sturdy a lad he had become. Similarly, he marvelled at how pretty and tall Julianna was. When Hanna approached him carrying Elisabetha, he realized he would not have known his youngest child if she had not been in the arms of his sister. Julianna was hesitant to greet her father, and after a few minutes of wavering, she chose instead to retreat to her Aunt Hanna's side and take her offered hand. Elisabetha would not look at this stranger and buried her face into her aunt's shoulder.

All three children had the same amber hair, with light brown interspersed with blond tips, which would brighten with the intense sunlight of the long prairie summer. Later that evening, when Elisabetha finally warmed up to him and sat on his lap before he tucked her into bed, Friedrich noticed that her eyes were an even deeper sky-blue than her siblings'. When he looked into them, he felt a pang of guilt and remorse that he missed so much of her infancy, but then he justified himself by thinking he had been working to support his family. Why, then, were they all so aloof with him? Even Mathias, after his initial rush to welcome him, receded into the uneasy silence of the adults, which continued throughout the meal and well into the evening.

Christian barely spoke to his eldest son, which had as much to do with his regret for shouting at Gustav as it did with Friedrich's lengthy abandonment of his family. Oh, he was disgusted with the way that Friedrich treated his family, but he was starting to realize it might be wise to keep his opinions to himself. In truth, Christian kept hearing Elisabetha's repeated caution to him about letting their offspring live their own lives. By now Christian recognized that Gustav was distant with him, and he had a distinct sense that his youngest son was obeying him more out of respect for his dead mother than for him. Besides, he just did not have the energy or the will to become embroiled in another taxing and disorderly family argument, so Christian sat quietly and ate the smoked sausage and sauerkraut with potato dumplings in silence.

When Maria slowly approached Friedrich outside, she tersely said hello and then rebuked him for bringing the children silly toys when they all needed new shoes and Sunday clothes for church. Of course, Mathias and Julianna were old enough to recognize their mother's displeasure and scarcely played with the ball and the rag doll that their father so proudly gave to them. But it was the soft brown teddy bear that coaxed Elisabetha to come and sit with him, and at long last, Friedrich felt a small measure of warmth and love from the family he had deserted so many times. The real surprise was yet to come when Maria asked him to carry the sleepy baby with her new possession into the bedroom.

"Before you place Elisabetha in her crib, please change her diaper if you know how," said Maria calmly.

Friedrich looked sharply at his wife, thinking she was being sarcastic; but she was busy gathering her bedclothes from under the pillow. She continued in a quiet voice. "Mathias and Julianna can sleep in this bedroom with you, and I am moving in with Hanna during your stay."

"What do you mean? I did not drive the long distance home to have my wife sleep with my sister. What the hell are you thinking?" asked Friedrich angrily.

"I will be staying in Hanna's bedroom while you are home. I am tired of you expecting the children and me to be at your beck and call whenever you decide to grace us with your presence." Much to his astonishment, instead of shouting at him as she had in the past, Maria persisted in speaking in a low tone. Friedrich could not believe that this was the same petulant and immature woman who had always been so quick to scream at him when she was angry about his drinking and staying out late at night. She was trying a new tactic with him. Well, he would make short work of that. Placing the sleeping baby on the bed, he started to cross the room to where Maria was standing.

In an icy voice, Maria said, "You will not touch me. I will not have you come home only to plant your seed and then leave again while I cope with another pregnancy and child to raise. I don't know what you do with all of the money you supposedly earn; if it were not for the generosity of your family, the children and I would be homeless, not to mention starving to death. I am just as glad that my parents have moved to Melville, as I am too embarrassed to even tell my own mother and father how you treat us."

As she spoke, Maria moved steadily towards the door, knowing that Hanna and Christian would come to her rescue.

When Friedrich realized that she meant what she was saying, he yelled, "What a way to talk! Who do you think you are? As your husband, I will damn well do what I want with you, and if you walk out of that door, it will be a hell of a long time before I will return to this dumpy, cold stone house in the middle of nowhere."

"You are a husband and father in name only," said Maria as she confidently and proudly walked out of the bedroom without a backward glance. And for once in his life, Friedrich Werner was true to his word: he stormed out of his father's home, not to return for more than a year, and missed the wedding of his youngest brother.

~ 53 ~

The Silent Critics of Neudorf were delighted with the comings and goings at the Mohr household, and when one of them overheard Margareta in the general store referring to David Hardy as Katherina's young man, their tongues really began to wag. Little did they know that on this subject, at least, Margareta would have been more than happy if any one of them had chosen to break their code of silence in her presence. She would have been thrilled to talk with them and to extol the virtues of the bright, handsome university student with the wavy brown hair and gentle amber eyes. But the Silent Critics were not interested in the young man per se. They were much more curious about what Christian Werner, the traditional German patriarch, thought of his youngest daughter stepping out with an Englishman, and a Methodist at that.

There were those who argued that Christian could not have known what Katherina was doing because they were convinced he would never allow it. Now, had any one of them involved Margareta in this discourse, she would have been mute indeed. She knew only too well what her brother would say and do if he had the slightest awareness of the developing relationship between these two compatible and charming youths. On the other hand, every day Margareta could see how Katherina was flourishing with the increasing attention she received from David since he started calling on her. As much as she had progressed since living in Neudorf, there was no comparison to the glow in her cheeks, the shine in her eyes, and the bounce in her step of late. When Margareta saw the couple together, she knew this was their destiny.

Even Phillip was becoming concerned about the number of times he would come home for a meal and learn that Katherina had gone for a ride in the country with David. As a rule, he did not interfere with any of his wife's plans or, as he had overheard the Silent Critics say, her conniving schemes. But he too knew that when his brother-in-law discovered what was going on, he would forbid Katherina from ever seeing David again. And Phillip's biggest worry was that his beautiful niece was too fragile to cope with losing another person she cared deeply about, so he tried to convince Margareta to discourage David from coming around so much.

"My love, that was a delicious dinner, but before I go back to the lumberyard to let Peter come home to eat, I think we need to talk about this budding friendship between Katherina and David Hardy."

"Oh, yes, isn't it wonderful? Have you noticed how Katherina has come alive since she met David? I have never seen her so happy, so energetic, as though she has found the sun, which is allowing her to blossom like a rose in the spring. As we both know, Katherina is a very bright young woman who needs stimulation to keep her mind occupied rather than to dwell on the negative things in life," answered Margareta.

"My dear, I very much doubt that it is Katherina's mind that has captured David's attention. There have been many times when I have seen him just stand and stare at her beauty. You forget I was once a young man too, and I can assure you that although I had been told that you were a clever little woman, your brain was the farthest thing from my mind," said Phillip as he stood up, walked around to her chair, and kissed his wife of twenty-seven years firmly on the mouth.

"So now the truth comes out," laughed Margareta after Phillip released her. "And all the while I was convinced that you loved me for the head on my shoulders and for my abilities to plan, to organize, and to scheme!"

"So you have been eavesdropping on the Silent Critics too. But all bantering aside, what are we going to do about these two young lovebirds?" questioned Phillip.

"I am not sure we have any say in what happens with Katherina and David. As much as I would like to take credit for the relationship between them, I have had nothing to do with it. David is a persistent and decisive man who clearly knows what he wants. One night at supper, Sarah shared with me that the minute David saw Katherina at her wedding to Andrew he had eyes for no one else. What's more, he totally monopolized her and did not allow anyone other than Andrew and Gustav, the only men who would not compete, to dance with her all evening. And the fact is I am thrilled for Katherina. David is a fine gentleman who, when he has completed his studies to be a lawyer, will be able to give Katherina the kind of life she deserves."

"Well, I can see I will not get much support from you, my dearest, but I do think that at the very least we should try to make sure they are chaperoned most of the time. Since you always seem to be having someone to supper, let's try to include David and Katherina in a group with the other young people, so if Christian gets wind of what is going on, he will be less suspicious. He knows we often have Gustav's friends Andrew and Sarah to visit. If we invite David, he may just think, as I am certain the Silent Critics do, that we are trying to get on the good side of that English banker in Duff—especially now that we have been talking about opening a dress shop here in Neudorf," said Phillip pensively.

"And the Silent Critics think that I am the Mohr who is responsible for the many intriguing plots of this household," teased Margareta.

～⟫⟫～ 54 ～⟪⟪～

The morning air was warming in the brilliant sunshine as Ben, the Hardy family's chestnut-brown quarter horse, pulled the light, elegant carriage with its two occupants along the dry dirt road between the carefully measured square sections of land. The vast Saskatchewan sky was majestic from horizon to horizon in its blueness; fluffy, white cumulus clouds like gigantic pillows floated lazily in its midst. Overhead, a gaggle of geese could be heard honking as they mysteriously crossed this sphere of their domain in long wavering Vs, coming out of the south and disappearing into the north. Hawks circled nearby as they keenly searched for their prey, knowing that the young gophers would come out of their holes and the field mice would scurry around hungrily looking for their own meals.

"Oh, David, I love these early morning rides with the refreshing air blowing in my face and hair," said Katherina as she held firmly to the front railing of the carriage. "It is a wonderful way to embrace the day, but I am starting to feel very guilty about always leaving Aunt Margareta to mind the store, especially when we are so busy with the plans for my dress shop."

David looked at Katherina's perfect hair and wondered how she could feel the wind, which was unable to whiffle any of her beautiful auburn strands from its pile high on her head. He realized that every time he saw Katherina, she had her hair pulled back in one stylish fashion or another, and he longed to see how she would look if she just let it fall around her lovely face. There and then, David determined that when Katherina became his wife, he would insist that she let her long, shiny locks of hair fly in the breeze during their daily morning rides.

"When we are married, we will start every day with a ride in the country, rain or shine," teased David. "But seriously, I know your aunt needs you at work, and once again I am trying to monopolize your time; except that this morning we have an important appointment at my father's bank in Duff. I told him about you opening a dress shop in Neudorf, and of course I told him it would only be a matter of time before you would expand your business to Lemberg as well. He thinks you have an excellent idea for a commercial venture, and he is prepared to offer you financial backing to encourage you to open a shop in Duff also. In fact, he said that a pretty, young woman like you should really consider setting up a tailor shop because all the men would flock to your store just for the opportunity to gaze at you!"

"I think you are getting ahead of things on every count, David. First of all, what is this talk of marriage? And second, I will need to see if the store in Neudorf is successful before I even think about planning another. I know Uncle Phillip and Aunt Margareta are taking a risk in opening another business in Neudorf, and the Silent Critics, as they call them, are saying that the Mohr family is becoming greedy," Katherina answered. But her expression suggested she was considering that in a few years she could have several shops in different towns and that she was enjoying this forward thinking.

"I have no concern about how successful you will be. Your Aunt Margareta has told me several times that since you started working in the Mohr General Store, she has not been able to keep ladies' wear in stock because her sales have more than tripled; not to mention that during the past two years, the other two general stores in town have struggled to stay afloat, with most shoppers coming through the doors of her business. And let's face it: the Silent Critics will always find something to talk about, particularly when someone else is getting ahead and progressing with the changing times. I think Canada is going to be a great country, with flowing wheat fields, fat cattle grazing in its green pastures, and a good life for those of us willing to work hard," said David with conviction.

Katherina started to laugh and said, "You sound just like my Aunt Margareta! She believes a person can do whatever she wants to get ahead in this New World, as she calls it. And I have no doubt that you will be a very successful lawyer with your vision of the future for this land. You are right, David: we can all help to develop and make Canada a great place to live. It is a wonderful country, and I am glad to be young and alive," said Katherina with a poignancy that David could not possibly begin to understand. As she spoke, Katherina moved her left hand off the railing and placed it gently on David's right arm.

Aside from their customary handshake salutation, this was the first time Katherina had touched David, and suddenly his heart soared. He had been captivated with Katherina from the moment he had set eyes on her, and he had thought about her every day over the winter while at university. However, he had sensed a hesitation in her. While David understood that she was still only sixteen and almost five years younger than he, it did not stop him from planning their marriage as soon as Katherina turned eighteen. His timing was perfect; by then he would be finished his degree and his articles, he would be called to the bar, and they could begin their life together.

"Well, now that we have settled the fate of your businesses and of the country in our usual serious manner, we can enjoy the rest of our short journey. With the number of trips Ben makes, I think he will soon be able to travel this road blindfolded," David said happily, feeling as though he could conquer the world, as young men in love do.

~ 55 ~

Prosperity had made its appearance early in the lives of the younger Werner brothers, and its momentum continued with each deposit from Gustav's railway income. It had revealed its presence to him from the moment he had opened his bank account at the age of thirteen with his Uncle Phillip's encouragement and payment for services rendered. But it really started to demonstrate its leverage after spring breakup in 1910, when Gustav purchased his John Deere steel plow and then the McCormick reaper prior to that year's harvest. It drew Gustav into its forceful hold, caressing him with its promise and enticing him with its power. Oh, the Silent Critics were right: prosperity, with its tools of money and land, hooked its claws into Gustav Werner and would exert its controlling influence over him throughout his life, and Rolf went along for the ride.

The steel plow immediately proved its superiority, and with approximately 300 acres plowed and seeded within the three-year improving period for their homestead grant, both men had abundant grain to sell each fall. The price of wheat, in particular, was high, and because the seed for planting during this initial time span was provided by the federal government, Rolf and Gustav sold every kernel of grain that they produced. From that first time when Gustav negotiated a higher price for their produce from the grain buyer in Duff, Rolf had the good sense to recognize his younger brother's mathematical skills and his ability to talk with people. Then when Gustav introduced Rolf to the notion of opening a bank account in Neudorf for the secure storage of his money, and he learned that while it was in safekeeping it would actually increase in value because of something called interest, it was firmly settled in Rolf's mind that Gustav would handle all of the important business matters related to their farms.

On one beautiful, warm afternoon, when the two men had finally finished the spring seeding and Gustav was unhitching the oxen from the plow, he said, "Well, Rolf, now we are ready to choose a day and return to Regina to file the applications for our letters patent. Then this land will really belong to us, and the Werner family will own their first section of land in Canada."

Rolf was quick to agree but was curious. "Yes, I will talk to Katie to see when it is a good day for me to go, but what do you mean by our first section? Who do you think will be able to get another homestead?"

"Oh, I realize none of us can apply for any more land from the Crown, but as the years go by, I will buy other quarter-sections to increase the size of my farm. I fully intend to own at least a section of this rich farm land myself," answered Gustav with confidence. With Gustav's fierce determination to be the most successful farmer in the townships, his formidable strength of will, and his seemingly boundless enthusiasm for working, it would never have occurred to Rolf to doubt any of his brother's plans. To be truthful, Rolf was just as happy to let Gustav take the lead once again, as he did when he chose to claim the adjacent quarter-sections for their homesteads so he could enjoy his time with his loving wife and his steadily increasing family.

⋙⁓ 56 ⁓⋘

The Monday that Christian drove his sons to the train station in Duff for the second time dawned bright and sunny with an early morning haze, which often preceded a scorching prairie day. He glanced at his sons with pride as they climbed down from the carriage.

Both were wearing their Sunday suit of clothes, were clean-shaven, and had recent haircuts. Christian remembered the day three years ago when his daughters and he had made this journey to send Rolf and Gustav to Regina to claim their land, and he realized just how much progress his youngest sons had made in such a short time. Whenever he visited their land, he marvelled at how quickly they had turned the prairie sod into fields of grain and in the fall had harvested all of those acres of wheat with that reaper machine they had bought. Now Rolf and Gustav looked like successful men rather than the farm boys who had been so excited and, at least Rolf, a little nervous about their first ride on a train to the capital city of their new province.

This trip the young men did not carry food on in small cloth bags, and although they had arranged with Julia to get a room in the boarding house where she lived in Regina, they had enough money in their pockets to surprise their cousin by taking her out to a restaurant for a meal. As soon as they finished their business at the Dominion Lands Office, Rolf and Gustav planned to meet Julia and to spend the rest of the day with her. Gustav, in particular, looked forward to seeing Julia, who came back to Neudorf only when the children she taught were out of school on holidays; he missed her and their usual lively conversations. When she first left home to go to the city, Gustav thought she would return to the community when it was time for her to marry; but when the years went by and she stayed in Regina, he finally asked his Aunt Margareta about it, only to be puzzled by her answer.

At the time, Gustav had been too young to fully understand what his beloved aunt had meant when she said that Uncle Phillip and she did not intend to arrange marriages for Julia and Peter, but instead would let their children make their own choices. Now, as he rode on the train with nothing to do but to look out the window and reflect, Gustav recalled their discussion, wondering whether Julia would ever marry, and then remembered his argument with his father about his own impending wedding, which was rapidly approaching. Maybe one reason Gustav seldom stopped working these days was that he did not want time to think about how his life would change by autumn. He liked his independence, and there was no point in talking to Rolf about his uncertainties about married life because his older brother always reported that marriage was the best thing that ever happened to him.

As the train moved along the fleeting prairie, Gustav looked across the aisle, expecting to see Rolf fast asleep in his seat as he had been on their first journey. To his surprise, his brother was gazing out the window with a smile on his relaxed face.

"What are you thinking about with such delight?" asked Gustav.

"I was remembering what Sabina said to me this morning as I was shaving. Katie was telling her that I would be away overnight, and she came running to me with tears rolling down her healthy, fat cheeks and said, 'Papa, you will not be here to tuck me into my bed when I go to sleep.' Do you know, Gustav, that being called Papa is one of the most wonderful experiences I think you can have? There is so much joy in hearing your own child speak those first words to you and look at you as though you are the most important person in the whole world. But I'm sure you will make a good father also since you spend so much time with Mathias, Julianna, and Elisabetha. I sometimes think Friedrich must be sick in the head for the awful way he treats Maria and his children," said Rolf.

"Yes, I completely agree with you about our disgraceful oldest brother, but I have to laugh at how much you have changed in three years. It used to be as hard as pulling hen's teeth to get you to say anything or even to keep you awake, and now you are so open and expressive about what you think and feel. I guess you are right, Rolf, that being a husband and a father are the keys that have unlocked your heart."

"No, Gustav, it is not just being a husband and a father, as Friedrich has repeatedly proven. Now I know exactly how Papa felt when Mama died, and once you come to love Amelia, it will also be true for you," said Rolf with as much eloquence as Gustav had ever heard from his kind, gentle older brother, who was also, Gustav began to realize, a loyal friend.

The train started to slow down as it approached the station, and when Rolf looked out the window, he suddenly exclaimed, "Oh, what a nice surprise! Julia has come to meet us."

Gustav rose from his seat, crossed the aisle, and saw his cousin standing on the platform, looking as beautiful as ever in an emerald-green dress and a matching hat, which sat stylishly on her auburn hair. Julia, watching for them, smiled when the brothers saw her and returned her wave.

"How thoughtful of Julia to come to the station," replied Gustav. "Now we can all go to the lands office, and as soon as we have filed our applications, we can take her to dinner."

The train had barely come to a full stop when first Gustav and, right behind him, Rolf emerged from the black, snorting beast of metal, not even waiting for the small set of stairs to be lowered, but jumping down to the wooden surface of the platform. After a quick salutation since they could scarcely hear above the noise of the train, the two men followed Julia to the north side of the brick station, where a man held a skittish black horse by the reins.

"Rolf and Gustav, I would like you to meet my betrothed, Robert Cameron, who has kindly offered to drive us around the city today in his carriage. His horse Dixie is frightened of the train, so he decided to wait here for us," said Julia as she walked around to the tall man with the flaming red hair and tucked her hand into his folded left arm.

When the introductions were completed, Rolf and Gustav climbed into the back of the comfortable four-seater carriage, which even had padding covering the wooden bottoms of the seats. It was quickly evident that Robert knew their purpose in coming to the city as he headed Dixie in the direction of the Dominion Lands Office. When her cousins had asked Julia if she had plans for the day, she had said with a smile that after they finished their business, Robert and she would show Rolf and Gustav some activities of city life.

The foursome had a memorable day, which was heightened for the Werner brothers as they emerged from the Dominion Lands Office imbued with the power that accrues from owning property. Robert Cameron stood down from the carriage where Julia and he waited, and as he extended his right hand to each of the young men, he said, "Congratulations on becoming a landowner. I have tremendous respect for farmers, as you are the real pioneers who will make Canada a prosperous country."

It was Rolf who noticed Robert's carefully manicured, soft hands, and surprisingly he was not fazed by Robert's answer to his question, "What kind of work do you do?"

With some hesitation because Julia had warned him that educated people usually intimidated Rolf, Robert responded that he was a surgeon and then quickly changed the subject.

Little did he know that not much could dishearten either Werner brother, who had worked from dawn to dusk for the last three years towards this eventful day. Once they climbed back into the carriage, they were taken on a whirlwind tour of the thriving capital city of Regina, which had originated from the site of a pile of buffalo bones rather than from the typical proximity to water. Like all other towns and villages in the new province of Saskatchewan, Regina was quickly increasing in size due to the influx of people coming west daily on the railway.

Even though they ate dinner in what was rumoured to be the best restaurant in the fledgling city, attended live theatre for the first time in their lives, and slept in very comfortable beds in pleasant surroundings as Julia and Robert's guests, Rolf and Gustav boarded the train the following morning without parting with a single penny of their hard-earned cash.

~ 57 ~

The Schweitzer rooster seldom had the chance to crow and awaken the family ahead of Amelia, who was already in the henhouse gathering the chicken eggs for their breakfast. Summer and winter, she was up and working before the emergence of dawn, preparing the first meal of the day for her papa, three brothers, and little sister. Since her mother's death when she was only seven years of age, somehow or other Amelia Schweitzer had managed to take care of them all. It was much easier now that she was a woman of sixteen, but she could still remember those nights when she went to bed so tired that her head did not touch the pillow before she was asleep. With each year, as her siblings grew older and could do more, life became less trying for her, particularly since Papa had insisted that the boys also work in the garden. His rule was simple: "If you want to eat, you help to grow the food!"

The Lemberg township homesteaders quickly became aware of Amelia's prowess for running a household and had nothing but admiration for the way she helped her father to keep the family together and to raise her siblings. They were certain that when Karl Schweitzer had lost his wife, just months after his oldest daughter had married, he would have to give away at least his two youngest to a childless couple; but with fierce determination, his seven-year-old had taken on the tasks of cooking the meals, washing and mending the clothes, tending the garden, and performing the multitude of other responsibilities of a pioneer farm woman. It was just short of a miracle to see how Amelia worked; although many conjectured that the reason the child did not reach her full height was that she never had the time to grow. And the more Amelia heard their praise, the harder she laboured, until it seemed she could not sit still for a minute.

When it was learned that there was a marriage arranged between Amelia and Gustav Werner, during all of the speculation there was little doubt that these two young people, with their reputations for hard work, would become the most successful homesteaders of the two townships; but would they have time to produce any offspring? Of course, none of this concerned Amelia, as she had to prepare for her wedding in just three short months. Fortunately, her older sister Wilhelmina offered to give her the dress that their mother sewed for her wedding, and although it had to be shortened, it would require few alterations. And months earlier, Wilhelmina gave her younger sister the gift she would appreciate above all others: she declared that Amelia would not be allowed to prepare food for anyone on her wedding day and would spend the night at Wilhelmina's home so she could get ready without having to look after any other family member.

There were, nonetheless, many things still troubling Amelia as the time for her nuptials drew nearer. Who would keep the house just the way her papa always wanted it? Could her youngest sister, Katie, manage all of the cooking, cleaning, and washing by herself? Were her brothers, especially the older two, Ludwig and Heinrich, likely to heed Katie when she needed help in the garden? And how could Franz, although turning ten was still her little brother, go to sleep at night without her telling him a story and tucking him into his bed? She was doing it again; she was filling her mind with worry and concern about everyone else so she would not think about what would happen to her. Even though Wilhelmina told her many times that she must realize her life was about to change, Amelia could not seem to become aware of what she wanted or how she felt.

When she finally got a quiet moment to herself, Amelia admitted that she was a little afraid of Gustav Werner, not that he did anything to warrant fear the night his papa and he came to supper. But he was so silent, only talking when introduced and saying nothing else until it was time to leave. She learned nothing about him except that he had a good, healthy appetite and he seemed to enjoy her cooking. Gustav was polite and thanked her for the delicious meal, recognizing that although it was her papa who had invited them to supper, Amelia had done all of the work. Naturally, Amelia had heard the talk in the townships about Gustav's ambitions: how he worked so hard only to hoard his money and that he was becoming English in many of his ways. And then he was so tall and handsome, older and mature; maybe he had not spoken during the entire evening because he had little interest in her.

It was the first time in her young life that Amelia felt inadequate. She always solved any problem by working through it, but the only men in her life were her father and brothers, whose main concern was that she had the meals on the table when they came in from the fields. Now, when she was making her father's bed, she found herself looking into the hand mirror from her Mama's ornate, pink dresser set that she had brought with her from Austria, and trying to decide if she was pretty. Amelia had not had the time to learn how to do her hair in a stylish fashion like Katherina Werner, who she had seen that one time in Lemberg, nor had she the clothes to dress the way she heard that Gustav's youngest sister did even during the week. The more she thought about Katherina, the worse she felt. Although she had always wanted to be tall and slender, Amelia had come to accept that, at sixteen, she had likely stopped growing and would go through her life as short as her mother had been; she would probably become just as stout after she too started having babies.

On the other hand, she understood that if she persisted in comparing herself to Katherina, she would soon be overcome with doubt and uncertainty about marrying Gustav. And that was not going to change. She had already talked to her papa, telling him she was too young to get married. When he refuted that argument and she then said he needed her to run his household, he had adamantly said, "Amelia, consider yourself lucky to be getting a man as hard-working and determined as Gustav. I thank God every day that Christian Werner and I made the arrangement for your marriage years ago. In time, he will come to understand what a good woman you are, and he will love you."

"Oh, Papa, I want to believe you, but I don't think he even liked me. He never said a word to me all evening. I'm sure he would prefer someone as beautiful and elegant as his sister Katherina rather than a short person like me," said Amelia plaintively.

"Don't be silly, child. A man wants a strong woman who can produce his offspring so he has heirs to inherit and farm his land—especially Gustav, who will never be content with just his quarter-section from the homestead grant. Besides, what do you know about Katherina Werner? She may well be pleasing to the eye, but I have heard that she has troubles of her own, things that will never plague you. When Katherina's mother died, Margareta Mohr had to take her into town and look after her because her mind was weak and fragile, and apparently the whole Werner family feared for her safety. And she was thirteen at the time. Just remember how when your mama passed away and you were only seven years old, you rallied all of us so Katie and Franz could stay with our family. So don't liken yourself to someone you have only seen once," said Karl as he turned back to his Bible, which was tattered from being passed down through generations to the oldest Schweitzer son.

Amelia had the good sense to accept these words as praise from her usually taciturn father, but she was sorry that he returned to his reading—not that she would have had the courage to ask him what she should know about lying down with a man. So many times when she was visiting Wilhelmina, she had been on the verge of talking to her older sister about what she needed to do as a wife, but she just could not bring herself to discuss this unspoken subject. And yet Amelia wanted to be able to satisfy Gustav, not only in the kitchen but also in those matters that went on between a man and a woman in the bedroom. Deep in her soul, Amelia admitted that she was pleased to be marrying Gustav Werner, a man who was noticed and talked about in the townships because of his appearance and his success.

If anyone had ever bothered to ask, it would have come as a surprise that Amelia Schweitzer herself had aspirations—if not for herself, then certainly for her children—that might challenge those of her soon-to-be husband.

⇛ 58 ⇚

Gustav and Rolf's reminiscences about the enjoyable day changed to alarm when they saw that it was Uncle Phillip waiting for them at the station in Duff. Not wanting to hear bad news, Rolf and Gustav bided their time until the train came to a full stop and the man who had taken their tickets lowered the steps to the platform. True to form, Rolf allowed his younger brother to greet their uncle and to ascertain what brought him instead of their papa to meet them.

"Hello, Uncle Phillip. We were not expecting you to meet us."

"I knew you would think something was wrong, but I did not want to hold a sign saying everything was all right," said Phillip teasingly. "I had to come to Duff on business, so I stopped at the farm and told your papa that I would save him the trip. He was busy hauling stones from the northwest quarter, and he was quite happy for me to pick you up. Your papa seems to be getting back his good spirits, even telling me that he thought the stones on his homestead were reproducing because he was sure he had already cleared that particular field!"

"I think you're right, Uncle Phillip," replied Gustav. "I've also noticed that Papa is more like himself this spring. I'm glad, since Amelia and I are going to live in his house rather than on my homestead. That way, if I want to work in town during the winter, Amelia will have the company of Hanna, Maria, and the children. And when the weather is not too bad, I can ride Wolfgang back and forth and continue to help Papa with the chores."

"Well, as usual, Gustav, you have carefully considered your plans for the future. But have you thought about how Amelia will feel starting out married life in her father-in-law's home. Not to mention that I'm sure you would like a neighbour, wouldn't you, Rolf? Especially during our long, cold, and lonely winters."

"It would be company for Katie and me to have Gustav and Amelia living on their land, but I learned a long time ago that there isn't anything I can say or do to get my resolute brother to change his mind. So we will just be happy when they come to visit," said Rolf. "Anyway, now that we have our little girls, we always seem to have something to keep us busy, and I can hardly wait to see them."

"I will drive you home first, Rolf, because I'm sure Katie needs you to help with the chores," said Phillip. "It must be hard with the two babies for her to get much done other than what can't wait. She was probably up at the crack of dawn to do the milking while the girls were still sleeping in their cribs."

Before starting his journey, Phillip decided to wait until he had delivered Rolf home and they were on their way—not to the Werner homestead as Gustav would expect, but rather to Neudorf—so he could have a private discussion with his nephew. Although he was uncertain how to broach the subject, he agreed with his wife that it was his duty to have this talk with Gustav. On the many occasions that Margareta had rebuked him for not taking Rolf aside before his wedding three years ago, he stood firm in his belief that it would have been a waste of time. Phillip was convinced that Rolf and Katie wanted to start their family right away and, furthermore, that they were intent on having many children. Rolf's contentment with his life as a husband and father was apparent to all.

When Katie came running out of the house and asked the men to come in for coffee, Phillip said, "Thank you, Katie, but I need to get back to town."

Although Gustav offered to walk to his papa's farm, Phillip insisted. "What would your mother have thought if I expected you to tramp across the fields in your Sunday suit? Let's just be on our way."

But at the junction of the dirt road, instead of turning left towards the farm, Phillip pulled on the reins so his new black stallion, Kaiser, veered to the right and headed towards Neudorf.

Surprised, Gustav said, "Uncle Phillip, where are you going? I thought you were going to drive me home."

"Actually, Gustav, we are going for a ride so we can have some privacy. If I take you home, your papa is always around, and if we go to town, Peter never leaves your side."

There and then, Phillip decided that the best way to approach his touchy topic was to get it out in the open.

"We Germans don't talk about the more important subjects in our lives, and I must say that in our many years of married life, your Aunt Margareta has taught me the folly of our secretive ways. I am convinced that your papa will not have told you much, if anything, about the relations between a man and a woman, so I will take on this responsibility, with your aunt's repeated encouragement, I must acknowledge," Phillip said, trying to introduce some levity to the situation.

"I wondered what you had up your sleeve, Uncle. You talk about me being predictable, but you seldom do anything either without a well-thought-out plan. And you are completely right: no one in the Werner family ever discusses how we all just happen to be here on this Earth. Even Mama, when she was alive, never said anything about it, unless she spoke to the girls and expected Papa to talk to us boys about sex," said Gustav. He seemed pleased with himself that he had actually said the forbidden word out loud. "But Papa has yet to mention anything to me, unless he is waiting until my wedding day."

Phillip was relieved that Gustav could use the right word, and it occurred to him that he had not heard another member of the Werner family ever say it. But he smiled to himself as he realized just how much like his dear outspoken wife his nephew was becoming. And so, Phillip Mohr decided to plunge right into the shadowy, nebulous realm of the sexuality of the Werner male.

"Gustav, when you lie in bed with Amelia on your wedding night, you will become aroused, as no doubt you have many times before since you are a healthy, vigorous young man. Only, you will finally be able to satisfy your natural physical urges in the way that God intended man to have his needs met, by coupling with the female member of the species. You will no longer have to experience those shameful wet dreams or the guilt of those times when you had to find relief by handling your private parts."

At this point in his conversation, Phillip understood that he needed to give Gustav a chance to digest what he was saying, and thus he turned his attention to his horse. "Whoa, Kaiser. It's time to let you make a meal of some of this tasty prairie forage." He climbed down from the democrat wagon and tethered Kaiser to a willow beside a clump of long, green spear grass.

As Phillip turned to his nephew, he saw that he had already jumped down onto a patch of fescue. Phillip said, "I would not let you walk across the fields, but if you roll up your pant legs, I don't see why we can't go for a stroll through this pasture. I think your mama would approve of the advice I am about to give you."

As the two men walked alongside each other, Phillip continued. "Gustav, both your aunt and I know you are resolved to get ahead, and unlike the Silent Critics, we admire your zeal and determination. One thing we want you to realize, though, is that if you start having children right away, as all of your older siblings have, and if you don't exercise some control, you can quickly end up with many hungry mouths to feed. Then, quite naturally, you will have little money left to acquire more land or to purchase the latest farm equipment, which, as you know, has allowed you to grow your homestead so much quicker than your papa, for example.

"Now, it is no accident that your Aunt Margareta and I only have Julia and Peter. In fact, we had always planned to have just two children so we could develop our business when we came to this land of opportunity."

His uncle's candour was a little unnerving for Gustav, who did not want to retreat into that Germanic characteristic of keeping the silence, but he just did not know what to say. Fortunately, Phillip did not appear to expect any kind of response other than Gustav's rapt attention, which he certainly had as his uncle continued to make his point.

"I will not suggest that you abstain from conjugal relations with Amelia—far from it—because the truth is that if you are gentle and loving with your wife, she will enjoy it. Most women who are honest with themselves also enjoy the pleasures of sexual union. But what I want to teach you is that when you are having intercourse, just as you are reaching your orgasm and releasing your semen, you need to withdraw from inside Amelia." Phillip glanced at his nephew, whose face now clearly wore an expression of astonishment.

"Oh, Gustav, I know that this information is difficult for you to grasp right now because your only frame of reference is what you have seen with your barnyard animals. When I was planning for this conversation, I deliberately chose not to use them as an example since I don't think there is any similarity other than the physical act. When a man makes love to his wife, it is the ultimate expression of his feelings for her, a way for him to convey how much she means to him. The act of lovemaking is kind and gentle, never base or bestial; otherwise, it is just the man satisfying his physical lust, and that does make it animalistic. And the woman always knows, so remember to show love and respect for your wife's needs, and both of you can enjoy the natural relationship between a man and a woman."

Phillip knew he had said enough, and as the older man walked beside the young man, who was more like a son than a nephew, he waited for a response. Margareta would have been pleased with how sensitively he handled what he now knew was Gustav's introduction to the delicate subject of sexual intercourse. Phillip was also aware that Gustav would think about and recall his words many times as he came to his own understanding of sex and, eventually, how he would treat Amelia in their bedroom in the years to come. Most importantly, Phillip hoped that he had conveyed the normalcy and the joy of the union between a husband and his wife.

When he stopped blushing and could finally look at him, Gustav replied, "Thank you, Uncle Phillip. Already I know that I am lucky to have received your words of wisdom, and I promise you I shall remember them as Amelia and I start our life together. But there are things that are really bothering me about marrying her. She is so young, and I know hardly anything about her. When I tried to talk to Papa about waiting a couple of years, he became very upset with me, so I don't dare bring it up again. I agree with you that so many of our traditions and ways of doing things are unusual in this new country, but again, there is no discussing making any changes with Papa. In fact, I have a really strong hunch that Papa is not aware you are having this talk with me, or for that matter, whether you had this conversation with any of my brothers. I realize it was not easy for you to express your personal feelings with such honesty, but I appreciate your frankness. No one has ever spoken so openly with me before, and I think you did it out of love and respect for me. And tonight, please also thank Aunt Margareta for always being so considerate of my needs and of my future."

⟫⟫⟫～ 59 ～⟪⟪⟪

The next morning, when Gustav arrived at Rolf and Katie's door, he knocked lightly and waited until Katie came to answer it. "For goodness' sake, it's you, Gustav. Why didn't you just come in as you usually do?"

"Good morning, Katie. Now that Rolf and you have officially filed on your homestead, I thought I should start by showing proper respect to the landholders," Gustav teased his sister-in-law. She was consistently cheerful and willing to serve any visitor food and drink; however, today, before she even asked, he said, "Your coffee always smells so good, and I will come in for a cup, if I may."

As Gustav came through the porch and entered the kitchen, Rolf arrived from the girls' bedroom, carrying one of his daughters in each arm. "Well, you are bright and early and just in time to hold one of your nieces. The baby woke up as I finished dressing Sabina, so I thought I would bring them together. Gustav, why don't you take Sabina, and I can go back to the bedroom to change Barbara's diaper. Katie usually prepares breakfast while I get the children up and dressed, and then we can all sit around the table as a family."

Sabina wrapped her chubby little arms around her uncle's neck as soon as Rolf brought her near Gustav, who then carried her to a chair at the table. After he sat down, he placed her comfortably on his lap.

"Now, Katie, please do not make me any breakfast," Gustav requested. "I only want a cup of coffee while Rolf and I decide what we need to do today."

"Are you sure, Gustav? If you go to the fields, you will be hungry," said Katie as she brought steaming bowls of oatmeal porridge and set them on the table along with a glass pitcher of milk covered by a layer of rich cream.

"I don't think we have much left to do in the fields now that we have finished the seeding and the summer fallowing, so I was going to suggest to Rolf that we make the new building look lived in until the homestead inspector has seen it. After his inspection we will put boards across the rafters so in the fall you can hang the slaughtered porker and smoke your own hams, hocks, and bacon for the winter."

"That will be a real treat; but as you know, I don't speak for my husband, so you will have to wait and talk to Rolf," answered Katie.

Rolf returned to the kitchen, cooing to his younger daughter, and as he sat down at the table Katie and he engaged in the banter and warm interaction of a husband and wife as they planned the activities for the day. Gustav listened to their comfortable exchange and thought about his conversation with his Uncle Phillip the day before. Suddenly, he started to look at his brother and sister-in-law with an increased awareness of the love and respect between them. It was as if he just had his eyes opened; for the first time, he observed the ease and familiarity with which they related to each other. Previously Gustav had dismissed the depth and true meaning of their marriage, but now he realized how little he had understood about the intimacy of Rolf and Katie's relationship.

Later that evening, when he rode Wolfgang to the Thompsons' homestead and was welcomed into Andrew and Sarah's newly finished sitting area, he again noticed the warmth and companionship between this married couple. Gustav was pensive as Sarah talked excitedly about some of the names they picked out for the baby when he or she would arrive.

"You seem very quiet tonight, my dear friend. Are we boring you with all this chatter about our domestic concerns?" Andrew asked as he handed Gustav a cup of pleasant-smelling tea and a plate of cookies.

"No, not at all. I was just thinking you could have a son or daughter to bring to my wedding in September," responded Gustav.

"The doctor has told us we can expect the baby to come sometime during the last two weeks of September, so you may well have an extra guest for your big day. By the way, how are you doing with the preparations, and do you need help with anything?"

"It's good of you to ask, Andrew, but my wedding will be a much smaller event than Sarah's and yours. We will have the ceremony before the church service on that Sunday and then have a meal with family. Amelia's older sister was going to cook the dinner, but Aunt Margareta convinced Papa to arrange with the Schweitzer family to let her prepare the food in Neudorf. Since everyone has to come to town anyway, they are quite happy to stay and eat after church rather than having to drive to Wilhelmina's farm, which is actually closer to Lemberg. I know that Aunt Margareta is again looking after my interests because she knows that I want to invite your family, and she has apparently encouraged Katherina to ask David."

"David was telling me the other day that he will be back at university in Saskatoon by the end of September, but he is planning to take the train home to Duff that weekend so he can be Katherina's guest," Sarah replied as she refilled Gustav's cup with hot tea.

"That might be interesting," said Gustav, almost to himself. "I wondered if she would ask David since Papa has never met him and doesn't even know she is keeping company with him."

"Well, I am looking forward to finally introducing my family to the rest of your relatives, Gustav. Do you realize we have been friends now for over three years, my parents have never even met your father, and I only saw him the day of your mother's funeral? Leave it to your perceptive Aunt Margareta to figure out how to get us all together," responded Andrew.

On the way to his homestead, Gustav rode Wolfgang at a slow trot, enjoying the gentle breeze that blew on that warm summer evening. The cobalt-blue sky was alive with silvery white clouds dancing in its immenseness and lurking stars waiting for their turns to shine. Many times during his evening rides, Gustav felt as though he alone occupied the universe with the crickets and the coyotes that shared a secret language across the plains with one another. Now more often than not, he raced Wolfgang against the wind since Andrew so seldom could compete with him. With each passing year, he realized just how much he valued his solitude and his freedom. But everything seemed to be changing, even the openness of the prairie, which was becoming defined by the one-mile-square sections of land forcing him to ride Wolfgang along the dirt road allowance between the fields of grain.

The most important transition in his life had yet to occur. Soon he would have a wife, and he would no longer be able to come and go as he pleased. He would always have to consider her and find out what she wanted to do, this woman about whom he knew virtually nothing. More and more, Gustav wondered if Friedrich had left his family because he needed his independence, and he worried that in time he might follow in his oldest brother's footsteps. Then he thought about the two couples with whom he had spent time over the course of the day: his friend Andrew, whose marriage had come about because he had chosen Sarah as his wife, and his brother, whose partnership had been arranged by their respective parents. Yet there seemed to be little difference between the relationships. In each of the marriages, it was obvious that the individuals were happy, and because of the love between them, they had worked things out compatibly.

Perhaps he would come to love Amelia as everyone was saying he would and they too would have a good life. Gustav knew he definitely wanted his own children. Why else would he be so determined to build a legacy if he did not have sons and daughters to whom he could bequeath the considerable acres of land he intended to acquire? Then, of course, he would have the freedom and enjoyment of his solitary work outdoors on his land for most of the days of his life, and he would have many opportunities to commune with nature, revelling in its beauty and harmony. And he was still a free man, at least until the harvest, but if he did not soon begin to deal with the ubiquitous weeds in his fledgling wheat fields, he would have no grain to thresh.

⟫⟩~ **60** ~⟨⟪

The summer was hot and dry, but the moisture from the many snowfalls during the past winter and some rain throughout the month of May was enough that the fields of wheat, oats, and barley were growing tall and full. Now, if nature co-operated and did not send hail, premature frost, or heavy rains and strong winds to flatten the stalks of grain before they ripened and were safely harvested, it would be a bumper crop. Gustav prayed that there would be no setbacks this year, either from the weather or grasshoppers, which could devour an entire field of maturing grain in a matter of days. He wanted to start his life as a married man by having a prosperous year with money in the bank. If he was to have a wife, he wanted to be able to support her.

On one of the rare days when there was precipitation, Gustav decided to ride Wolfgang to his father's homestead. When he entered the stone house, everything was in an uproar. Hanna and Maria had moved practically every piece of furniture in the house into the kitchen, and even the three children were running around, involved in their flurry of activity.

"Good heavens! What is going on here? It is a good thing Mama is not alive to see what you women have done to her home," exclaimed Gustav as he removed his raincoat.

"Don't get bossy with us, Gustav Werner," Hanna answered with a brisk tone. "Since you seem to be taking little interest in getting anything ready for your new bride, we are determined that Amelia will, at the very least, have a freshly cleaned and painted bedroom when this becomes her new home. We have talked to Papa, and he is quite content to have the bedroom beside the kitchen, since it is the warmest in the winter. Mathias will move into the smallest one, and Maria and her girls will sleep in the same room with me."

"It was my idea," said Maria, quickly coming to Hanna's defence; although since Katherina had moved into Neudorf and the responsibilities of the household had fallen totally on her shoulders, Hanna had emerged as a strong woman quite capable of standing up for herself. However, she did appreciate her sister-in-law's support.

Gustav looked at the women and was about to say he was only asking and not telling them what to do, when the truth of Hanna's comments dawned on him. He had not even given a thought to how he would welcome his wife into his father's home or, for that matter, where they would sleep.

"I'm sorry, Hanna and Maria," Gustav said. "You are right. I did not think about Amelia having to leave her home and family to start a whole new life when we are married. I have just wondered what it will be like for me to be a married man, without considering that she will have to make many more changes than I will. No wonder Andrew kept asking me how I was coming with my plans! It's time I woke up and realized I have much to learn about caring for a wife and that I should be thanking both of you for making these preparations. So what can I do to help?" Gustav said sheepishly.

His forgiving sister readily accepted Gustav's apology on behalf of both women and took him into the bedroom that had initially been their parents' room and then, for the past several years, where Maria and her children had slept. "You can begin by removing the old, faded wallpaper from all of these walls, since we have bought paint from Uncle Phillip's lumberyard to give the bedroom a fresh, new look."

"Who paid for the paint, if I may ask?" Gustav inquired carefully, not wanting to again ruffle the spirit of co-operation that existed between the women and children as they beautified this room for the new family member.

"We have all contributed to the cost of the supplies to fix up your bedroom," Hanna answered. "The children have been doing extra chores and picking berries to sell at Aunt Margareta's store to buy the material for new curtains that Maria has offered to sew. Actually, we were going to surprise you as well as Amelia, but since you have now caught us in the act, you can make our work much easier by pulling all of the wallpaper off." She handed her brother a sharp knife and a bucket of hot, soapy water.

It did not take Gustav long to figure out why Hanna was so anxious to get him busy stripping the paper that had probably been on the walls since Papa had built the house. The paste had long ago adhered to the stone, and the paper now clung like a layer of skin, refusing to give way even after he gave each small section a thorough sopping with an old water-soaked cloth. He soon learned to soak, wait, and then scrape until the paper reluctantly parted from the stone walls that had held it secure for years. As Gustav worked, he developed a rhythm, becoming lost in his task. Other than helping with his mother when she was dying, he had never done any of the chores required in the house; he had thought that women's work was easier. It was a day of enlightenment; his arms and legs became tired with the constant soaking, rubbing, and bending required by his laborious and tedious job.

But he also experienced a sense of satisfaction as the strips of old, dried wallpaper pulled away, already giving the room a cleaner look and smell before the walls were washed and painted. The more Gustav worked, the more he appreciated Hanna and Maria's initiative of getting a bedroom ready for Amelia and him. What had he been thinking? Why had he decided against having a house-raising bee on his homestead, as the family had done for Johann and Rolf when they had married? Then he remembered that unsettling, recurring dream from which he would awaken shaking with apprehension. It was always the same: he rode to Papa's home and found him alone, sitting at the kitchen table with no food to eat or wood to heat the house. With each repetition, Gustav became more alarmed about what it meant. It did not make any sense, none at all.

Although Hanna would marry next autumn, Maria and her children would most certainly always live on Papa's farm, waiting for Friedrich to make his infrequent visits. His father was getting old, and Gustav worried about how much longer he would be able to manage his farm and tend to his animals. But it was not as definitive as that. It was just an eerie feeling that something unusual was going to happen. There were times when Gustav worked on his land for many long hours, and in his peace and solitude, things around him became hazy, as though he was blending with the earth. He could feel the energy of the universe, his oneness with it, and then occasionally he would experience a presentiment that enabled him to know and see well beyond the field of vision afforded to him with his eyes.

⇒~ 61 ~⇐

Katherina knew she wanted to help this thin, tall stranger the moment Wilhelmina Strauss walked into her new dress shop in Neudorf and opened the box, revealing a yellowing wedding gown. Without any introduction, she started, "I was going to shorten this dress for my sister to wear at her wedding in September, but unfortunately I have not taken proper care of it. Since you must know about dresses, perhaps you will be able to tell me what I can do to get it back to its original white colour? My mother made it for my wedding nine years ago, but she died shortly after, without teaching any of her daughters her craft of tailoring."

As Katherina lifted the dress from the box, she saw the uneven streaks of colour and felt the aging fabric, which had become stiff and parched. She knew instantly that no bride could be expected to wear this dress for her wedding. "I must advise you that even if I were able to wash and bleach this dress to white again, the material would likely disintegrate in the process."

"It may be just as well. Why should poor Amelia, who works so hard to take care of everyone, have to wear a second-hand dress on her wedding day? As it is, the only time she gets something different to wear is when I need a change and shorten one of mine," Wilhelmina said, more to herself than to the beautifully dressed young shopkeeper.

"Forgive me for being so bold, but did you say your sister's name is Amelia?"

"How silly of me. I neglected to make your acquaintance when I came into the shop. I am Wilhelmina Strauss and my sister is Amelia Schweitzer."

"As soon as you said your sister's name I wondered if she was the young woman who is to marry my brother, Gustav. I am very pleased to meet you. My name is Katherina Werner, and I am Gustav's youngest sister."

Wilhelmina was completely taken aback; before she could stop herself she blurted out, "But I was told that Gustav had a sister the same age as Amelia. You cannot possibly be only sixteen and be in charge of this store!"

"I am frequently told that I look much older in my appearance than my actual age. This is my shop, which I opened but two weeks ago with the help of my Aunt Margareta and Uncle Phillip. Now let's put your dress back into its box, and the two of us arrange to procure a new gown befitting your kind sister for her wedding day," Katherina said, a wonderful plan already forming in her mind. After all, as the Silent Critics were heard claiming, she was becoming more like her Aunt Margareta Mohr every day.

"Would you really help me to buy or make a dress for Amelia?" Wilhelmina said, unable to disguise her amazement at this confident and sophisticated woman who seemed years older in the ways of the world than Amelia, or for that matter herself. Yet she was perfectly amicable as she proposed a much more appealing option than trying to salvage her gown, which had definitely seen better days.

"If you know Amelia's measurements and would trust me to select a dress for her, I would be very happy to go to a special shop in Regina when I am in the city next week."

"Oh, but how much money would you need to buy a wedding dress in Regina?"

"Why don't you let me worry about that? Since I have not yet bought a gift for Amelia and Gustav, perhaps you would consider allowing me to buy the dress as their wedding present. Gustav is very excited about me owning my own store and when the people at church ask and learn where Amelia got her gown, it will be very good for my business. I would also like to suggest that you and I keep this little intrigue between ourselves," replied Katherina in a warm, reassuring voice.

Wilhelmina was surprised and then delighted by Katherina's eagerness to help her to get a suitable dress for Amelia; she was thrilled to be complicit with this enchanting, quick-thinking girl. Imagine Amelia wearing a wedding gown purchased in Regina. Their father had probably given no thought to what his daughter would wear, and here was a total stranger offering to not only shop but also to pay for it. To be fair, Katherina's occupation was buying dresses, whereas Papa made his livelihood farming.

"I know Amelia will be very pleased with a new dress because she is expecting to wear the same one I did. And if your brother will not be upset with your present, I am more than happy to let you make the choice. Naturally we will need Amelia to try it on before the wedding, but it will certainly be a surprise for all of the guests," Wilhelmina said with a smile. "And thank you for your kindness. My husband and I live on a farm near Lemberg, and we always go there, but it does not have a dress shop. I had heard about this one opening in Neudorf, and I am so happy that I decided to come to you. When shall I come back to pick up your purchase?"

"Thank you for entrusting me with a task I shall thoroughly enjoy. Since we still have time, please give me a couple of weeks to make sure I have it here for you."

⁓ 62 ⁓

Not wanting to antagonize her brother any more, Margareta, at Katherina's request, asked David Hardy to eat supper with them on Saturday, as she so frequently did at her own behest. She was very careful to never include him in their customary dinners on Sunday after church, agreeing with her husband that before he was accepted into the family it was David's responsibility to call on Christian Werner and ask his permission to court his daughter. But she saw no reason why her family could not enjoy the company of this engaging gentleman with the polite manners and stimulating conversations on other occasions. Since Gustav had become a homesteader, he was not able to spend nearly as much time with them, and Peter particularly missed the companionship of someone closer to his own age. David understood his loneliness, and always made sure to involve Katherina's impressionable young cousin in some of their almost-daily outings.

During the meal, Katherina told them about meeting Wilhelmina Strauss in her shop, sharing that she was pleased to make the acquaintance of one of her soon-to-be sister-in-law's family members, completely omitting, of course, any mention of their contrivance.

"She is a tall, slender woman, unlike how Gustav has described Amelia. She was very friendly and seemed just as happy to meet me," Katherina said. She turned to David, who was sitting to her right at the big round oak table, and passed him the fried chicken, which was one of his favourite meals. "I am planning to take the train to Regina on Monday morning, and I would like to ask you to accompany me, David, if your father can spare you from the bank."

"Thank you for asking me, Katherina. I would very much enjoy spending a day in the city with you. As it happens, I finished at the bank yesterday because I have to get ready to return to university, and I can purchase many of the supplies I need in Regina and have them before leaving for Saskatoon the following week." David was delighted with Katherina's invitation, recognizing that this was the first time she had ever initiated an excursion with him. Even his many meals with the Mohr family came at the request of her aunt, and David was worried that when he left for school he would be out of the running for Katherina's attention. On the one hand, he knew it was too soon to propose to her; on the other, he was concerned that when he was away, the many young men in the community who had been kept at bay by his frequent presence at Katherina's side would finally have their chance to pursue her.

On Monday morning, David was up before the sun; he washed, dressed, and ate breakfast, anticipating the moment he could hitch his father's horse to the carriage and drive to Neudorf to pick up Katherina. He had not been so excited since he was a boy, when his parents often gave him little notice about special outings to make sure they could all sleep the night before the event. When they had finally reached the decision to immigrate to Canada, it was not possible to keep the news from David, and their then-five-year-old son had nearly driven them crazy with his constant questions. From birth, David did not seem to require much sleep and frequently he would not even bother going to bed before an important examination. But not wanting his nocturnal activities to disturb his parents who were getting older, David forced himself to lie down and, in the midst of planning for his future, he fell asleep.

David simply could not exist without a plan. He was constantly setting goals and devising strategies, one of the many reasons his father had suggested that he become a lawyer. It was a good calling for him and until he met Katherina he fully intended to practise law in the city, perhaps even in eastern Canada, where he thought his skills would be better challenged and honed. But over the summer, he realized beyond a shadow of a doubt that he was in love with Katherina, and moving to Toronto was quickly losing its appeal. Last fall when they had met at his sister's wedding, David knew it was love at first sight, and he could not get Katherina Werner out of his mind when he returned to Saskatoon. Now the more time he spent with her, the more he wanted her. David was determined that no one and nothing would keep him from marrying her in two years, after he finished his last year of law and his articles and was called to the bar.

On the train at last, with Katherina to himself, David chose the seat by the window, hoping to keep her gaze focused on him rather than on the expanse of the ripening prairie, which would race them all of the way to the outskirts of the young city. He heard his mother's voice in his head, telling him to sometimes give others a chance to decide; but as he so often did, he ignored her advice. Katherina did not seem to mind where she sat as she excitedly told David the reason for their precipitate trip to Regina.

"I'm going to buy Amelia's gown for her wedding to my brother at the end of this month, and it is to be a complete surprise for her. She thinks she will be wearing the same dress her mother made for Wilhelmina when she was married nine years ago. She hasn't the slightest idea of the arrangement her sister and I have made."

"I would think not. What woman would let someone else select the dress she would wear on her wedding day, especially a total stranger?"

"At first I was surprised too that Wilhelmina would choose Amelia's gown, and then when she asked for my help, an idea came to me. And since I will never be a bride, Amelia Schweitzer will have the kind of gown that I would have worn."

"What are you talking about, Katherina? Of course you will get married, perhaps sooner than you think." David had to bite his tongue because he so impulsively wanted to take advantage of this unexpected opportunity to propose to her right there and then. The only thing stopping him was a sense of respect for her one remaining parent, whose approval he had yet to seek. Instead, he asked, "What would ever possess you to say something like that?"

"I can't explain it, and although I don't know what Papa has in mind for me, I just know I shall spend my life as a spinster and over time will probably become one of the Silent Critics of Neudorf," Katherina said with a chuckle. "But not while Aunt Margareta is still alive."

It struck him like a bolt out of the blue. *Of course, her father would have made plans for Katherina's betrothal, and he would need to ask him to pre-empt the arrangement before he could seek her hand in marriage.* Trying to digest how he could have overlooked such an important consideration, he could only respond, "I don't want to hear you talk so glibly about your future. Why would you plan for a lifetime of loneliness without a husband and family?"

"Oh, David, don't be so serious. Of course it is not my intention to be an old maid, but as we all know, the best of plans can go awry. Anyway, let's forget that I even mentioned it. I want to enjoy this exciting day in the city with you and to find a lovely wedding dress for my new sister-in-law. Are you going to buy your notebooks and supplies while I do my shopping?"

David turned to face her directly. "Not a chance. I am not going to let the most beautiful woman in the city be left unattended while I go searching for books. Just promise me, Katherina, that you will never again bring up the subject of you not being a bride."

～ 63 ～

They had nearly finished the supper dishes when they heard a team of horses pull into the yard. "I wonder who is coming to visit," Amelia said to her younger sister, Katie. "We need to get back into the garden and pick more of the beans, and I want to dig up some of the carrots to pickle."

"Haven't we done enough already? All summer long we have spent every day in that garden or here in the house canning vegetables and making jam, jellies, pickles, and anything else you can think of to keep Franz and me working constantly. At least Papa lets

Ludwig and Heinrich have some time to do what they want after working in the fields all day," complained Katie as she hung the towel on the rack beside the cupbord.

"The men are older and have their own things that they need to do, and when I am not here in the winter, you will be very happy that we grew and preserved so much food for you to eat. With the pig that Papa will soon slaughter and smoke, there will be plenty to feed the family until next spring," replied Amelia, placing her arm around her sister's shoulder. "Then I will not worry so much about how you are taking care of Papa and the boys."

"I am sorry, Amelia. I should remember that you are just trying to look after us, even when you will not be living here. I will miss you very much," said Katie, with tears in her crystal-blue eyes.

"I shall come and visit you so often that you will be tired of seeing me; now let's go and welcome our visitors in for a cup of coffee," Amelia responded.

"Oh, no! We have only finished the dishes and now we are going to start all over again."

With a laugh Amelia answered as she was walking towards the door, "Soon you will realize that's what life is like; we are always going in a circle and we will never get everything done."

She reached for the knob when Franz came rushing in and said, "Amelia, you cannot come outside. Peter and Wilhelmina sent me into the house to tell you that you are to sit down on a chair in the kitchen and to keep your eyes closed until you are told that you can open them, and not one minute before, or you will ruin the surprise. And this time Peter said you have to listen to me."

"Franz, don't be silly. This is not the time to be playing games when we have company."

Since his sister, who was more like a mother to him, would not heed him, Franz turned to Katie and said, "You take Amelia's right arm and I will take her left, and together we will get her to sit down." Of all the Schweitzer children, Katie loved a surprise the most and was instantly ready to assist their youngest brother. Once they managed to seat her on the chair Katie ran to the cupboard, took out a clean dishtowel, and tied it around Amelia's eyes so she could not peek.

There was a great deal of commotion as several people came into the kitchen. In addition to Peter's voice, Amelia was curious when she heard her father's voice telling him to "put it down here on the mat." He had told his daughters that right after supper he was riding into town because he had to attend to some business. When Heinrich called out, "Papa, watch that you don't set it down on my foot," had it not been for the cloth Katie had wrapped around her head, Amelia could not have followed Franz's directions. What was happening? Amelia was exactly the opposite of her sister, always wanting to plan and to be prepared rather than to be confounded by the unexpected.

After what seemed like a long time, particularly for Amelia, and following some insuppressible expressions of awe, a complete silence descended on the room. Finally, Wilhelmina said, in a clear voice, "Franz and Katie, you may now remove the towel so Amelia can see."

Sitting in the middle of the floor on the braided oval rug was the most beautiful handmade hope chest, its soft, freshly stained, tawny-brown wood gleaming in the rays of the evening sun, which poured through the kitchen window. Amelia's hands flew to her mouth; she was speechless. Watching her response with delight, her brother-in-law, Peter, knew he did not need to ask if she liked the gift.

He said, "Wilhelmina and I decided to give you your wedding present ahead of time because we know you have been busily crocheting doilies, pillowcases, and tablecloths in preparation for your marriage to Gustav. Now you will be able to store them until you move to the Werners' home; but you may want to open it and see what is inside."

With some hesitation, Amelia walked over to the chest and gently caressed its surface. She had never seen such pliable wood. Finding her voice, she said, "This feels as smooth as a piece of fine fabric. What kind of lumber did you use to make this lovely gift?"

"When we decided to give you a hope chest, I went to Phillip Mohr's lumberyard and he ordered this cedarwood, which is supposed to be very durable. And because of its fragrance, bugs and insects stay away from it. Come on Amelia, open it up," Peter insisted with the support of everyone in the room.

Not certain that she could handle any more surprises, Amelia slowly turned the latchkey and lifted the lid of the chest. If Ludwig had not been standing right beside her to catch it, the top of the chest would have come slamming down. The sight of what appeared to be a snowy white wedding dress was just too much for Amelia, who, to the astonishment of all of her family, burst into tears. No one could recall her crying about anything for years, and here she was sobbing on what she would later remember as one of the most wonderful evenings of her life. Understanding immediately why she was so overcome with emotion, Wilhelmina walked to her younger sister who had carried the burden of their mother's premature death, enveloped Amelia in her arms, and allowed her to cry until she got it out of her system.

~ 64 ~

The Sunday morning of her wedding dawned bright and sunny, with a lustre promising another splendid autumn day. Amelia slept soundly in the bedroom that her sister arranged for her and that, for the first time in her life, she did not have to share with her siblings. True to her word, Wilhelmina insisted that Amelia was to have the cozy guest room, which Peter built in the attic of the farmhouse. The bed was very comfortable with its soft mattress and down-filled quilt, and although Amelia thought she would be too excited to sleep, she scarcely had time to think about anything before a gentle slumber claimed her. Once, during the night, she awakened and had a start when the bright moonlight streaming through the small four-paned window fell upon her wedding gown hanging from the doorframe, looking like an apparition.

When she recovered from her fright, Amelia climbed out from under her snug comforter feeling like a butterfly emerging from its cocoon. She walked over to the door and just stopped short from burying her face in the soft, gossamer white dress. She gently touched the material to make sure it was real, and she pinched herself yet again to prove that it really did belong to her. She still did not know who was responsible for purchasing this beautiful gift; the only thing her sister would tell her was that it was a surprise. Ever since that evening when Peter and Wilhelmina had given her the cedar hope chest filled with its snowy fabric, Amelia had felt like a child basking in the glow of a mother's love. She had a radiance about her that even her usually unobservant father noticed, but rather than comment to his daughter, he kept his silence and simply attributed it to her impending marriage.

Peter and Wilhelmina's open expression of love and appreciation was new and unfamiliar to Amelia, filling her with a feeling of warmth and at the same time exciting her. She had been too young when her mother died to completely remember her love, although Wilhelmina constantly told all of them that their mama had been a kind and gentle person. Then she became so busy mothering her younger siblings and running the household that she spent no time thinking about herself. Karl Schweitzer had never been demonstrative towards any of his children, and after his wife's death he became more and more silent and morose. Even Heinrich and Ludwig turned to Amelia when they needed solace from their father's demanding expectations and frequent tongue-lashings, and the rest of the time they were too wrapped up in their own interests to consider that their little sister might require human comfort. There was no doubt that Katie and Franz loved Amelia dearly, but understandably they were equally selfish when it came to reciprocity.

Not wanting to linger away from her restful haven, Amelia returned to bed, and the next thing she heard was Wilhelmina gently calling to her that breakfast was ready. Her sister was right when she said having a room to herself would be one of her best wedding presents, but it had never occurred to Amelia that it would include having the morning meal prepared for her. For years, she had been responsible for gathering the fresh eggs from the chickens and milking the cows before feeding the family at the start of each day. And here she was, languishing under the covers while Wilhelmina obviously had awakened at the crack of dawn and bustled about getting a plethora of things done before they all left for church. Amelia could not believe she had slept while everyone else was up and doing their chores; it was incredible to her that she had not heard a sound.

Sheepishly, Amelia came down the short flight of stairs into the kitchen where Peter and his three sons were already seated at the large wooden table, waiting for her to appear.

"Well, good morning, Sleepyhead," said her brother-in-law with a childish grin on his ruggedly handsome face. "I guess we don't need to ask if you had a good repose. I never thought anyone could sleep through the uproar that occurs every morning in this household, but you have certainly proven me wrong."

"I have no idea what happened to me. I have never slept past dawn in my life, not to mention that I did not even hear your rooster crow," Amelia said with her head lowered as she sat down in a vacant chair.

"Don't pay any attention to Peter's teasing. That's exactly what I wanted you to do and now you will be well rested and relaxed on the most important day of your young life. Do you want one egg or two, Amelia, as I just have yours and mine left to fry?"

"Two, please and thank you, Wilhelmina. It has been a very long time since someone has made breakfast for me. This has been a wonderful gift; but you know, I have been worried about how I will keep my beautiful dress from getting dusty on the way to Neudorf."

"Oh, you will not be wearing your gown to town; right after we have eaten, we shall go back upstairs and wrap your dress so not one fleck of dust or dirt will land on that delicate fabric," said Wilhelmina, with a mischievous look in her clear blue eyes.

"But where am I to change my clothes and what else do I need to do to get ready? I thought that was the reason we took turns bathing last night," replied Amelia, becoming more skeptical about her sister's kind if not dubious arrangements.

"You will just need to wait patiently and trust me as the events of this day unfold. The only thing I shall tell you now is that soon you will have the opportunity to meet my charming accomplice in many of these plans," Wilhelmina said as she brought two plates with large, over-easy eggs and toast to the table and took the chair beside her sister.

~ 65 ~

Few of the townspeople or the farmers around Neudorf had ever met her, although the story of the little seven-year-old girl from Lemberg who had managed to keep her family together after her mother's untimely death had been told often. Fewer still were prepared for what they saw when Amelia Schweitzer walked down the aisle of the Lutheran church on her father's arm on that Sunday morning. Gustav Werner had been more than a little concerned when his bride's family had arrived for the service and taken their seats in the pews on the left side of the small building and she did not appear. Gustav had become quite agitated, repeatedly turning his head and anxiously watching the door of the church.

Finally Reverend Biber asked everyone to stand and motioned with a wave of his hand for Karl Schweitzer to begin the wedding procession. An audible gasp rose up to the rafters in the house of worship as, one by one, every head turned and saw the lovely, virtuous, childlike woman with her pale blue eyes focused only on the young man waiting for her at the front of the church. Unable to remain facing forward any longer, Gustav slowly inched his head around and suddenly felt himself become weak at the knees as he stared into the face of an angel. Amelia steadily returned his gaze, her eyes radiating innocent love and purity, accentuated by the immaculate whiteness of her wedding gown and the veil positioned on the top of her head, trailing down her back to the floor.

Amelia was so nervous. She had only ever been around her family and the considerably smaller congregation of the Lemberg church, and she had certainly never been the centre of attention. Now she had to walk down the aisle with everyone watching her. And what they would see was possibly even more incredible to her. After Wilhelmina had introduced her to Katherina, this future sister-in-law quickly styled her soft, short, auburn hair so it curled towards her round face, and then she produced another surprise. A long delicate veil matching her wedding gown was carefully placed on her head as Katherina completed the finishing touches of her hair and makeup. When the two women helped Amelia into her dress and then directed her to a full-length mirror, she could not believe her eyes.

What a good thing that Wilhelmina had hinted at the transition in her appearance by clasping both hands to her face in awe and then telling Amelia that any sign of tears would only undo all of Katherina's efforts. Katherina had the perspicacity to realize that she could not taint the sublime effect of this naïve young woman dressed in her wintry-white apparel by making the slightest public reference to its purchaser. She did, however, mentally congratulate herself for her selection, equally pleased as Wilhelmina was with the results. The delicate, turned-down collar that attached to the bodice of the dress with the same gossamer lace that bordered the floor-length veil made Amelia's face radiant. The satiny fabric of the flared skirt falling from its A-line waist to just below her knees and the short, puffy sleeves of satin made Amelia look doll-like.

"Oh, when I tried on my dress before, I didn't have a long mirror to see what it was really like, and now I don't think I can walk down the aisle in such a beautiful gown," Amelia said timidly.

"Of course you can, Amelia. You look wonderful and you don't have much choice because they are probably waiting for you right now. So, my dear soon-to-be sister-in-law, when we get there, I want you to keep your head high and your eyes only on your handsome groom, and do not pay attention to anyone else," answered Katherina, with a mischievous gleam in her eyes.

When the three women arrived at the church, Karl would not have recognized Amelia if her older sister had not been with her. He could not begin to imagine where she had obtained the store-bought clothes and shoes she was wearing, not that he had given a moment's consideration to what she would wear on her wedding day. Feeling a pang of guilt, he waited patiently for the minister's signal, and then proudly walked his middle daughter down the aisle, presenting her to the awestruck Gustav. During the ceremony and throughout the day, Gustav, Karl, and many other members of the congregation stopped in the middle of their conversations and gazed at Amelia with open admiration. People she did not know approached her to make her acquaintance and to offer their congratulations. Although she was totally unaccustomed to so much attention and did not want it, Amelia managed to politely thank her well-wishers, remembering Katherina's confidence in her.

Never before had two fathers been so observant of their respective daughters. Karl Schweitzer had to keep asking himself how he had failed to notice that Amelia had developed into such a mature and seemingly assured young woman. He felt honoured to be her father and experienced more than a little pride when Reverend Biber came over and complimented him for raising such a fine family. His gratification continued to grow as one by one the members of the Neudorf congregation grasped his hand in a firm handshake and told him that he had done an outstanding job keeping his family together. But by the end of the day Karl had a gnawing feeling in the pit of his stomach as he realized that all the praise being heaped on him really belonged to Amelia.

Christian Werner, on the other hand, was alarmed by what he saw. He could hardly recognize the charming, outgoing, and impeccably groomed Katherina as his daughter. His annoyance started when she did not take her seat in the pews with her family for the ceremony, and the minute Reverend Biber had blessed the newlyweds, a man had sought her out. He decided that he was in no mood to be introduced to him; but he did not have much choice in the matter, since Katherina immediately brought him over. Christian soon realized that this Englishman, with his fine clothes and polite manners, was no stranger to his sixteen-year-old daughter. Coffee and cakes were served after the exchange of vows and sermon, and if she was not attending to Amelia, Katherina was mingling with all of the congregants with that David Hardy by her side. That did it. This time Margareta had gone too far.

The day was exactly what Margareta had hoped for when she was planning Gustav and Amelia's wedding dinner. The rays of the bright sun had burned off the chill of the early morning, and it promised to be a warm Indian summer afternoon, perfect for eating and relaxing outdoors. As soon as the members of the congregation began to disperse, Phillip and Peter arranged for the men to carry the sawhorses and planks of lumber to the churchyard to be set up to hold the food. No sooner were the boards of the makeshift tables placed than the women covered them with an array of coloured cloths and began bringing out the food that each had contributed. Hams, pork hocks, smoked sausages, fried chicken, hot potato salad, dilled carrots with yellow beans, perogies, cabbage rolls, dill pickles, fresh-baked bread, cottage cheese buns, strudel, and coffee cakes; there was more food than some of the children had ever seen in their young lives.

As soon as Reverend Biber said the blessing, more than thirty adults and easily as many children stood and waited for Gustav and Amelia to lead them to the feast. With heaping plates, parents led their children to a shady spot under a tree where a blanket was placed on the prairie grass so they could begin eating. Gustav directed Amelia to the head table and chairs where his father had joined Rolf, Katie, and their girls, deciding that when they had finished eating, he would introduce her to Andrew, Sarah, Katherina, and David. He realized that Amelia could not converse with his friends, but he at least wanted them to meet her. He remembered how well Andrew and Sarah had treated both Katherina and him not so long ago at their wedding. Before this day was over, Gustav wanted his father to get to know his friends, and he was glad to see that Katherina had finally introduced David to him.

Long after the Werner and Schweitzer wedding, the people of Neudorf and Lemberg would talk not only about Amelia's unique dress, but also offer much commentary on how her cherubic appearance suited this young woman who had already made so many sacrifices in her life. They took great delight in trying to determine what she had in common with her husband's already worldly sister, whose solicitude was apparent from the start of the day. It came as no surprise that Katherina Werner had a hand in buying such an exquisite wedding ensemble, but it took the Silent Critics of Neudorf considerable time and a slip of the tongue by Margareta Mohr to accurately confirm the identity of its purchaser. To be fair, many had had their suspicions right from that very first moment when Amelia had made her demure entrance into the church.

～ 66 ～

It felt so strange to be going to the Werner home on the democrat wagon with her husband by her side. She had felt like her heart would break when Katie and Franz had both clung to her when it was time to say goodbye. Poor Franz; even when Papa had admonished him for crying like a baby, he still kept his arms tightly clasped around Amelia's neck through his flood of tears. Finally Wilhelmina coaxed him to let go by promising him that he could spend the night with his nephews. Amelia had to stop herself from asking if she could come too. During the day, Katherina's attentions had helped her to overcome her shyness and to quietly acknowledge the many strangers who spoke to her. But now it occurred to her that, with the exception of an occasional word during the delicious dinner, Gustav had scarcely spoken to her, even as they had talked to each other's families and thanked them for coming.

On what seemed like the longest ride of her life, Amelia kept telling herself that if Gustav was even half as nice as his youngest sister, she would soon come to love him. Once they reached his papa's house and had a chance to be alone, maybe both would feel more at ease with each other. Still, here they were, sitting beside one another, just the two of them, and neither seemed able to say anything. At least Amelia had some awareness of what to expect on her wedding night because of Wilhelmina's talk last night in the privacy of the guest bedroom. And she ardently wanted to believe what her sister had repeatedly told her: that Gustav would quickly come to care for her because of her excellent cooking and the tidy, orderly house she would keep for him.

The sky became overcast, with clouds clinging to the horizon. As soon as they reached the stone house, Gustav jumped down from the wagon and offered Amelia his hand to help her descend. "Hanna and Maria will be waiting to show you where you can put your things. I want to get Wolfgang in the barn before it starts to rain, and then I shall be in to change my clothes."

"I will get into my work clothes too, and come to help you milk the cows," Amelia said, eager to prove that she was prepared to immediately contribute in the Werner household.

"No, either the women or Papa will look after the chores today. You can go into the house and make yourself comfortable," Gustav replied definitively.

Just then, Mathias came running up and said, "My mother sent me to welcome you to your new home and to help you carry in your belongings."

"Thank you, Mathias. If you carry this valise, I can bring the suitcase," replied Amelia, grateful for Maria's gesture. She wondered how it had been for her when she arrived as a new bride to this same house and if she had been anywhere near as nervous as she was feeling at this moment. It was strange that her husband Friedrich had not been at his youngest brother's wedding. Instead it was Hanna, her sister-in-law, who had been at her side all day, helping her with her three children as though they were her own.

"Mama had all of us, even Uncle Gustav, clean and decorate your bedroom before you came, and she told me I could show it to you," Mathias said excitedly as he picked up the small flowered bag by its corded handle.

Mathias was tall for his seven years and eager to get to know his new Aunt Amelia. She had looked so pretty and small in her wedding dress and now that she changed her clothing for the ride to the farm, she seemed even more like someone with whom he could play his favourite game of hide-and-seek. He hoped she would like his little sisters and him because with Mama and Aunt Hanna to do the chores, she would be able to play with them just as Uncle Gustav did when he was not working at his farm.

Amelia looked at the boy with the tow-coloured hair and clear blue eyes shining with enthusiasm, and then around at the tidy yard with the bench made from rocks at the entrance to the large garden. The solid stone house looked inviting with the flicking light from a kerosene lamp shining through its patchwork apertures of glass. She returned her gaze to the expectant child who stood patiently waiting, and suddenly her anxiety was replaced by a feeling of engulfing warmth. It would be all right. She would earn her place in this new family of hers.

"Let's go and see the room that you have prepared for me," she said kindly as she gathered up her sister's old suitcase in her left hand and reached out with her right to grasp the relaxed, chubby fist of her friendly nephew.

Maria glanced out the window to see her impressionable son bringing Amelia towards the house and up its two wide and steep steps, and her heart swelled with love. Mathias was a sensitive child, always wanting to please people and be ready to help them; he was so unlike his father, who had such little sensitivity even towards his own wife and family. There were many times when she felt grateful that her husband was not at home most of the year; he would have belittled Mathias for his responsive and gentle temperament. Instead her son reminded her of her father, and she now knew that she had mistakenly chosen for appearance rather than for character and disposition when she had insisted on marrying Friedrich Werner.

Opening the sturdy door, Maria said, "Please come in, Amelia, and make yourself at home. We have the fire going, and as soon as Papa has finished the milking, we will have a light supper of chicken soup. Hanna and I thought that after Aunt Margareta's wonderful dinner, no one would want much to eat. And since Gustav is outside, I told Mathias that his sisters and he could help you settle in your bedroom."

As she stepped into the spacious kitchen, Amelia was pleasantly surprised to see a large, round table at its centre; a large kerosene lamp illuminated the blue-and-white soup bowls set around its circular edge. She felt heartened by this sign that, at least at mealtimes, there was no head of the family. In the Schweitzer home, her papa always sat at the upper end of their rectangular table; none of them had ever dared to sit in his chair, although she pretty much had her say when it came to running the household. As a child, she had heard the stories about how Elisabetha Werner had made many of the decisions in the family. But why was she thinking about her husband's mother at a time like this? Where was Gustav? If he wanted her to feel comfortable, why did he not come to the house? Could it be that he was as uncertain as she about what was to happen between them tonight?

Turning away from the black iron stove, which was situated off to the left of the table, Maria said, "Come here, Mathias. I have lit the small lamp for you to carry into your Aunt Amelia's bedroom. Give the valise to Julianna and I shall hand you the light."

"Me too, me too," cried Elisabetha scarcely before Maria finished uttering directions to her son.

"Yes, my darling. You can take one of the handles of the bag while your sister holds the other and then you will both be carrying it," Maria fondly reassured her youngest.

With Mathias in the lead, the little entourage started towards the master bedroom of the house. Feeling very important that his mother had entrusted him with the lamp, Mathias rose to the occasion and said, "All of you wait here until I have carefully placed the lamp on the bedside table. I will give you the signal to come in, when I am ready for you."

Getting into the spirit of his plan, Amelia motioned to the two little girls to wait beside her. Solemnly they came to a halt, placed the bags on the floor, and waited together in a huddle, with Julianna and Elisabetha staring up at Amelia.

After a few minutes, Mathias opened the door and said, "Aunt Amelia, please enter the room, which we have made ready for you."

Touched by the eagerness of these delightful children, Amelia crossed over the threshold into her new bedroom with her nieces firmly in tow. Before she was able to spot them, she smelled the fragrance of the late autumn sweet peas, and again she experienced that warm sensation of acceptance. As she looked around in the light cast by Mathias's lamp, she saw the comfortable double bed with its feathered quilt, the night table, a dresser, and her cedar chest, which Peter must have delivered last night. The lower part of the walls were painted a baby blue, and the upper portion featured wallpaper with a tiny floral pattern of green, pink, and blues; it still held the scent of flour.

"Thank you, children. What a beautifully decorated room, and with wallpaper yet! How did you know that I have always wanted such a pretty room?" If her new husband was not ready to welcome her, his family had certainly gone out of their way to make her feel at home.

Instead of putting away her belongings, Amelia knelt on the braided mat beside the bed and hugged all three children at once. They were still sitting on the floor when Maria and Hanna came to the door to tell them that the men had come in for supper. Disentangling herself from the arms of Julianna and Elisabetha, Amelia stood up and placed her bags on the bed. She took out her hatpin, removed her hat, and then set it on top of the dresser.

"I will unpack later. Mathias, could you please go around the bed and bring the lamp out to the kitchen for your mother?"

The evening meal was a quiet affair. Even the children were subdued after the fun and games of the day, topped off with the excitement of showing their new aunt where she would be sleeping. Aside from saying grace, Christian Werner never said a word, and Gustav only asked Amelia if the house was to her liking. Hanna and Maria talked quietly to each other about the wedding before Maria rescued Elisabetha from falling asleep in her bowl. The chicken and dumpling soup was delicious, and although Amelia did not think she would be hungry, she relished eating food for a third time in one day that she did not have to prepare. When Hanna got up and started to clear the table, Amelia rose at the same time, carrying dishes to the sunken porcelain sink where the hand pump was secured to the base of the cupboard.

"Oh, I can wash these few dishes, Amelia. Why don't you go and put your things away?"

"Thank you, Hanna." Turning to see what the men were doing, Amelia whispered to her, "Could you please point me in the direction of your outhouse?"

"Sure, I will show you where it is, but there is a chamber pot under your bed if you don't want to go outside in the dark," Hanna replied in the same muted tone of voice.

The very thought of having Gustav walk into the room when she was using this receptacle was enough to make Amelia blush and Hanna to observe the reddening in her face even in the shadowy light in this corner of the kitchen.

"Could we use the small lamp that Maria gave Mathias earlier?" Amelia continued in her low whisper.

The two women slipped quietly out the door; Hanna held the light and led Amelia on a path behind the house and through a row of caragana trees. After walking the length of a churchyard, they descended a small hill, and straight ahead looming in the darkness was the wooden building, which housed the outdoor toilet. "I will hold the lamp while you go inside but don't worry about closing the door completely. There is just you and me here," said Hanna reassuringly.

When they returned to the house, Christian was still sitting at the table now with his elbows ensconced on its surface, reading his well-worn Bible. The children had most certainly gone to bed, and Gustav was nowhere to be seen.

"Now, you take this lamp and go to your husband. Good night, Amelia," Hanna said.

As she opened the door to the bedroom, she saw Gustav's silhouette as he sat on the far side of the bed. He had changed his clothes and was already in his nightshirt. Looking for her bags, she noticed that he had moved the suitcase and valise over to a chair on the other side of the dresser.

"I put your things over there, thinking that you would prefer to unpack tomorrow morning, when you can see where to arrange your clothing in the drawers of the dresser. I hope that is all right with you. And if you give me the lamp I shall set it down on the table and you will have some light as you prepare for bed," said Gustav gently.

Once again, Amelia felt her mind going blank and her tongue becoming tied, exactly the same as it had on the ride from Neudorf to the farm; all she could manage to mumble was "Thank you."

Not wanting her husband to see her, Amelia sought the darkest corner of the bedroom and quickly took off first her dress and then her petticoat, and with equal haste pulled her nightgown over her head. She tried to remember what Wilhelmina had told her about how to treat her husband on her wedding night, but she was too frightened to recall any of her sister's advice. Finally she decided that the only thing she could do was get into bed and wait to see what happened. At least she had the side of the bed nearest to the door. The minute she had this thought, Amelia admonished herself for her silly cowardice. But as she was pulling down the quilt to get in the bed, she nearly jumped out of her skin when Gustav asked, "Is it all right if I blow out the lamp?"

"Yes, please," was her instant reply.

The room became totally dark, and even if the night had not been heavy with rain clouds, the single four-paned window would not have admitted much light. Gustav slipped under the quilt and settled his six-foot body as near as he could to the edge of the mattress. In his mind's eye, he was still seeing Amelia as she had been when she entered the church, an angelic-looking child in a milky-white dress. Gustav recalled Uncle Phillip's advice about when he was to withdraw to make certain that he did not sire children right away, which he was not about to do with this young girl; but try as hard as he could, he did not remember if Uncle Phillip had told him what to do to begin his lovemaking. But it was much later, long after he knew that Amelia was asleep, likely tired of waiting for him to reach for her, that Gustav came to realize that he had not experienced the slightest sexual arousal. And what was even worse, he felt nothing for this woman who had become his wife and now lay on the other side of his bed.

~ 67 ~

Could she have done it again? For the second consecutive morning, Amelia awoke to the sound of voices and of people bustling around, rather than to the crowing of the rooster, which always began its loud cry at the break of day. She glanced over to the other side of the bed, and seeing that it was empty, quickly rose and changed into one of the dresses she usually wore to the garden. As she was coming through the door, she heard Julianna say, "Mama, can I go and tell Auntie Amelia it is time to come for breakfast?"

"Hello, Julianna. I don't know what is the matter with me. At home I was always awake long before anyone else was up, but the last couple of days I have become such a sleepyhead!"

Maria looked knowingly at Amelia and said, "I am glad you had a restful night, and there was no reason for you to get up early. The chores have all been done and we are just sitting down to our meal. Do you like coffee to drink or would you prefer milk?"

As Amelia sat in the same chair as she had the previous evening, Gustav stopped talking with his father and said, "Good morning, Amelia. I hope that you slept well and found the bed comfortable."

"Yes, thank you, Gustav, and I hope that you did too. Maria, may I please have some coffee?" Perhaps this was a good indication. At least they were beginning to talk to each other, even if it was just about niceties.

Christian acknowledged her before he said grace. When they began eating, he turned to Gustav and said, "As soon as I have finished breakfast, I am going to hitch Wolfgang to the democrat wagon and return it to Phillip."

"Oh, Papa, I was planning to do that since I am the one who asked Uncle Phillip if I could borrow it; I want to go into town anyway."

"No, Son, I have a very important reason to go to Neudorf and it is something that I must do alone," Christian replied emphatically without looking at Gustav.

Now everyone's curiosity was piqued. But the adults, especially his own offspring, knew better than to inquire, although Gustav stopped just short of reminding his father that Wolfgang was *his* horse. And Maria's children would never have considered the possibility of questioning their grandfather about anything; they knew he was always right.

～ 68 ～

Life in the Thompson household was turned upside down with the arrival of Sarah and Andrew's petite baby girl, whom they christened Emma. She made her long-awaited appearance two weeks before Gustav's wedding, and almost immediately seemed to have confused her days and nights. Although she tried her best, Sarah was unable to keep Emma awake to feed her during the day, when she was the sleepiest baby that Grandma Thompson had ever seen. But come the night, when the rest of the family was weary and ready for their restorative sleep, Emma's slate-blue eyes were wide open. At first she seemed very hungry, but shortly after being at Sarah's breast, she would become colicky. Her loud anguished cries would persist for hours, keeping them all awake—even Andrew's father, who usually had trouble hearing. No amount of walking with her or rocking in the chair seemed to offer relief to the poor little infant.

It was fortunate that the harvest was finished and only the root vegetables needed to be dug from the garden because whenever Emma finally closed her eyes in repose, the adults took to their beds in desperation and also succumbed to the delights of sleep.

Andrew and his father took turns milking the cows and feeding the livestock each morning and night and his mother made soups and stews, which could be left simmering on the kitchen stove. One evening when he came into the house from doing the chores, Andrew found his wife sobbing as though her heart would break.

"Sarah, whatever is the matter?" She was so distressed that Andrew ran to Emma's tiny cot to check on his daughter. But no, she was lying on her side sleeping peacefully. This was cause for rejoicing, not despair.

Returning to the sitting room, Andrew perched his tall body on the arm of the sofa, placed his arm around Sarah's shoulder, and waited until she had calmed down. At long last her tears subsided, and she motioned to Andrew to sit down on the seat beside her.

"Now, my darling, are you ready to tell me what is upsetting you so much?" Andrew asked again.

"It is hard to put into words. I feel like such a failure as a mother because I can't get Emma to eat at the right time."

"Well, who said she was eating at the wrong time? Emma is much too young to know how to tell whether it is day or night, and maybe she eats when she is hungry. And when you think about it, that makes good sense, so she is really a smart little baby," said Andrew lovingly.

"But your parents and Heather must wonder when they will have a normal life again," Sarah said woefully. "Not to mention that at Gustav and Amelia's wedding yesterday, I realized that we have hardly had a chance to talk to each other since Emma's birth, and I miss the quiet evenings we used to spend together."

"I think that all first-time parents must have to make adjustments and learn how to deal with the demands of a newborn. And look on the bright side: because Emma slept most of the day, we were able to enjoy that wonderful dinner and visit with all of the guests. Now tell me, what did you think of Amelia?"

"She is a pretty little woman. She looked so young and sweet in her beautiful gown, but I felt sorry for her. In fact, all day I wondered what was wrong with Gustav. He was very different than when he has been here or when we have seen him at his Aunt Margareta's house. It was like he was far away or at least wanted to be anywhere else rather than at his own wedding," Sarah replied thoughtfully.

"You noticed that, too! In the three years that Gustav and I have been friends, I have not known him to be so quiet and distant. He didn't even seem to want to talk with us, and at one point I was beginning to think he would not bring Amelia over for introductions. Do you suppose he was nervous about becoming a married man?"

"I don't seem to remember you being very anxious about marrying me, but I was trying to think what it would have been like if you and I had only seen each other for the second time on the day of our nuptials. Gustav and Amelia would know nothing about one another, as though they were strangers meeting in the night. I just hope someone sat down with Amelia and told her what to expect when they went to bed."

"As I recall, on one of our walks, Gustav talked to me about how some of the German customs were so different. At the time I didn't really ask him what he meant; I just told him that the English had some unusual traditions also. I think I am starting to understand what he was trying to say. Oh, why didn't I listen to him? If I had only paid attention to him, I might have encouraged him to visit Amelia, at least on her father's farm, even if they were not able to go courting like we did. I feel so badly; I let my friend down. What a pair we are. Two failures together!" Andrew said despondently.

"Andrew, I think it is futile to blame yourself for not helping your friend, when all he needed to do was ask for your advice. I won't hear of you referring to yourself as a failure," said Sarah as she reached over to caress her husband's arm.

"Well, then, I will not allow you to consider yourself an unsuccessful mother. After all, you have only had two weeks to learn how to care for Emma, whereas I have been Gustav's friend for years. And now I think we should get some sleep while our precious baby daughter is snugly in her bed." Andrew took Sarah in his arms and kissed her gently on her petite, heart-shaped mouth.

⇒≫〜 69 〜≪⇐

Feeling slighted that none of them had been invited to the wedding dinner, the Silent Critics all arrived very early at the hotel the next morning. Not one of them considered it the slightest bit audacious to have expected to be included in the festivities. After all, they had been involved with Margareta Mohr for so long that they viewed themselves as members of the family.

They had scarcely sat down by the front window with their cups of coffee when one of them saw a man racing his horse down the main street of Neudorf. What was the matter with the fool? He had a heavy democrat wagon hitched to the horse, and if anyone had happened to cross the street, it would have been at their peril.

On the other hand, it might prove more interesting than sitting around and complaining about being excluded yesterday. By this time, several of them had recognized that it was Christian Werner driving at such breakneck speed on the busiest street in town, pulling the wagon in which Gustav and his bride had departed in the late afternoon of the previous day. Well, he certainly had a bee in his bonnet, but as a family man he should know better. It was dangerous to gallop through a thriving, booming town, which was flourishing with new businesses opening every week.

"My dear Phillip, you are slow to get going this morning. But since you are lingering, would you like another cup of coffee?" Margareta asked her husband as she was already pouring more coffee into his mug.

"Ah, what a good idea; why don't you sit down and join me? I sent Peter off to open the doors at the lumberyard, and I'm sure Katherina is more than capable of handling both the general store and her adjacent dress shop. Yesterday was delightful, and of course your dinner was delicious, but we were both so busy that we never had a minute to talk, and then it was too late last night."

"I shall sit awhile. I must be getting old because I am tired this morning, but I am ever so glad that we hosted the wedding dinner and that Gustav's English friends were able to come."

"I'm not so sure it was a good idea. Did you have any opportunity to observe Christian yesterday? He spent most of the day watching Katherina and David with the most menacing expression on his face. He even turned down my offer for a drink of my best whiskey, which I considered a very revealing indication of his displeasure," Phillip said pensively as he reached for another slice of Margareta's apple strudel.

As Margareta got up from her chair and walked to the cupboard to cut more strudel, she said, "Well, did Christian do or say anything to either one of them?"

"I don't think he spoke much to anyone yesterday, and he definitely did not talk to David or Katherina. But I have a strange feeling we will hear more about the relationship between Katherina and David Hardy. I think that since Elisabetha's death, Christian has become much more adamant about keeping the customs of the old country. What progress Elisabetha had made in terms of getting him to change and accept this New World was lost when she went to her grave."

"Are you worried about what Christian will do?" Margareta asked her husband as she began to realize there might have been another reason for Phillip's tardiness to leave the house this morning.

"Oh no, I think Christian is a reasonable man; besides there isn't much that he can do," replied Phillip, although he was careful not to tell his wife that she also had been the recipient of her brother's malevolent stares. But even as he spoke these words of reassurance he again experienced that feeling of apprehension with which he had awoken this morning.

Not wanting to succumb to his unease, Phillip decided to put it aside, got up from the table, and said, "Enough about Christian. I better get to work or Peter will wonder what has happened to me." He walked around to Margareta's chair, lowered his head to kiss her, and was reaching for his hat and light coat when the front door of the house was flung open.

Startled, Phillip turned to see Christian stomp into the small porch and climb the three steps into the kitchen with more speed than he thought his brother-in-law could muster.

"Where is she? I want to talk to her right now," he demanded.

"Good morning to you too, Christian. Is that any way to enter my house?" Phillip replied.

"I am not concerned with your house or any of you. All I am here to do is gather up my daughter and bring her home where she belongs," snapped Christian.

There was no way Margareta Mohr would allow her brother to talk to her loving husband with such rudeness. She stood up and tried to make light of the situation.

"What is the matter with you, Christian? Did you get out of bed on the dark side this morning? Why don't you sit down, and perhaps a cup of coffee will calm your nerves."

"I have had more than enough of your hospitality. I don't know where you get some of your ideas, sister of mine, but the last thing you are going to do is arrange for my flesh and blood to marry an Englishman. Once I have removed Katherina from this household, none of the Werner family will ever darken your doorway again. Now, where is she?"

"You make more than your share of assumptions, Christian, but you forget that you are standing in my house," Phillip said angrily. "Your sister and I will decide who comes and goes here, not you. And don't think you are the only hotheaded, stubborn German in this room. Now if you can't be civil, you can leave with as much rapidity as you burst in here." He moved closer to Christian, ready to escort him out of the house.

Before he reached him, Christian turned, jumped down the stairs, and slammed the door on his way out. Phillip walked over to Margareta, took her in his arms and said, "Are you all right?"

"Yes, I am fine, but I fear that Christian has gone to the store to get Katherina. Please go quickly to her. It has been years since I have seen Christian in such foul temper."

～ 71 ～

Although there were several customers in the store and in the dress shop for a Monday morning, sales had been slow. It was just as well, since Margareta had yet to arrive. Katherina was starting to worry about what could be keeping her aunt when her papa burst into the store. "Finally I have found you. So now you work in their store while they sit around drinking coffee. Well, I am going to put an end to all of this right now. Get your things, Katherina. You are coming home with me, and you will work with Hanna and Maria on my farm where you belong."

"What are you talking about, Papa? I am not leaving with you. I now live in Neudorf, and I own this dress shop. Aunt Margareta and I work together, and when one of us is not available, the other looks after both of the stores," Katherina told her father with pride.

"Where did you get the money to buy property? And what does a sixteen-year-old girl like you need with a store? This is Margareta's influence again, but I am going to change that once and for all. Gather up your belongings and we are going home."

"Papa, I don't think you understand what I have been saying to you. My home is here in Neudorf and I have my own business to operate. The last thing I will do is move back and waste away on your farm," Katherina said emphatically.

"What do you mean? It is good enough for your sister and for even your sister-in-laws. Who do you think you are that you can tell me, your father, what you will be doing? There is no doubt that you have become more than a little mixed up during the last two years. A father tells his daughter, not the other way around. So hurry up, before I lose my temper with you."

As father and daughter were engaging in their escalating discussion, Phillip quietly opened the door and entered the store; but when he heard how capably Katherina was handling her father, he decided to wait. Fortunately Christian's back was to him so he was not aware that Phillip had entered. Phillip realized that Christian was being considerably more controlled with Katherina than he had been earlier with either Margareta or him, but he was not convinced that it would last. Still, Katherina was holding her ground, and if Margareta had been present she would have been proud of her young protégée.

"I am not going home with you, Papa, whether or not you become angry with me. I am living my life the way I choose, regardless of how you think I should. Now, if you will please excuse me, I have customers that I must assist," Katherina said firmly. She turned to walk into the dress shop, where Mrs. Spitznagel had been trying on a blouse and skirt in the one available change room.

"How dare you turn your back on your father? If you walk away from me now, I shall no longer consider you my daughter. This is your last chance to come home with me, and if you refuse, Katherina Werner, you are dead in my mind and heart," Christian yelled at his youngest and, as he had always known, his most highly strung daughter.

Katherina stopped in her tracks, and as she hesitated, she knew her papa meant what he said—but so did she. She just could not go back to the drudgery and boredom of living on the farm where she knew that without stimulation and challenges she would return to that dark place where she thought more about dying than about living. She had to risk losing her father in order to keep the person that she was becoming; she had to be herself.

As she turned to face her father, Katherina looked him squarely in the eyes and said, "Papa, I love you very much, but I cannot go home with you. I know you don't understand, and the only thing I can tell you is that if I return to the farm, I will die."

Christian took one long last look at his beautiful child, the one who most resembled his beloved Elisabetha, before he swung around and charged out the door, nearly taking Phillip with him even though he never saw him standing at the entrance of the store.

If one of them had been close enough to see and hear the exchange between Christian and Katherina Werner, the Silent Critics would have acquired enough gossip to sustain them for a month. As it was, Mrs. Spitznagel and her two friends who were in the store might appreciate that this confrontation between a father and his defiant daughter could symbolize in many ways the clash of traditions, customs, and transitions between the Old World and the New. Furthermore, for the protection of the persons involved, Katherina prayed that their discretion could be relied upon in the days to come. Time did confirm that the only information the Silent Critics ever learned was limited to what they saw from the window of the hotel—that Christian Werner left the general store with more umbrage than they could have imagined.

～ 72 ～

Winter dragged on and on with fierce blizzards and snowfall so heavy that on many occasions Gustav had to shovel the fluffy white frozen flakes away from the windows before the family could look out and see the assailing weather. His father and he trudged through the snow, trying desperately to stomp down a narrow pathway between the house and barn. No sooner had they created an open path than the west wind would start to blow again, swirling the flakes around and about until large drifts stretched across the entire yard. Depending on its ferocity, there were many times when the banks of snow that accumulated were packed so hard that they could gently walk on the top, only to break through when they least expected it.

It was such hard slogging that Gustav tried to get his father to stay in the house. It did not take both of them to tend to their animals, but Christian was adamant about getting dressed in his outerwear every morning and night to go outdoors. Although Gustav did not think it was possible, his papa had become even more taciturn; the only time he seemed to talk was when the two men were in the barn. But after that fateful day following his wedding in September, when Christian had insisted on going to Neudorf alone, Gustav had been convinced that they would never engage in any kind of conversation again. When Christian rode Wolfgang into the yard at a frantic pace, as though man and horse were being pursued by demons, Gustav came running from the garden to find out what happened.

His father dismounted, threw the reins at Gustav, and said, "Wolfgang is your horse and you can look after him. Since I don't ever intend to go to Neudorf again, I won't be needing him."

"Papa, what is the matter? What a strange thing to say! We go to church every Sunday because Wolfgang faithfully pulls the carriage or the cutter. Without him, this family would have no means of transportation," Gustav replied in defence of Wolfgang, the animal he often considered his best friend.

"Well, that is done. You can go to church if you want, but no member of this family will ever set foot into the Mohr home again, or for that matter, talk to anyone who lives in that household," Christian told his son as he shook his fist at him.

"I think you should go in the house and get something to drink to calm yourself, Papa. You can't possibly mean what you are saying. Your own daughter lives with Aunt Margareta and Uncle Phillip, and of course we will continue going to church, and if they are willing, having Sunday dinner with them."

"Listen to me, Gustav Werner. I mean exactly what I say, and I forbid anyone of this family to even consider that there is another daughter."

As Christian yelled at him, Gustav remembered their quarrel at Mama's gravesite, and once again, he was worried about his father's state of health. However, this time he simply was not prepared to acquiesce to his unreasonable and dictatorial demand that he deny the existence of his youngest sister.

"Papa, I will not hear what you are saying; nothing in this world would compel me to ever forsake Katherina. What could she possibly have done that would have turned you so against her that you would treat her as though she was dead?" Gustav shouted at his father with equal wrath in his voice. "Aunt Margareta and Uncle Phillip have always been very good to this family, especially after Mama died. How can you turn your back on your own flesh and blood?"

By this time, the three women and three children had come running from the garden, where they had been digging out the last of the carrots, parsnips, and turnips. They stood huddled together as though to ward off an attack as they watched the men sling words at each other with unexpected rancour. Hanna had lived her whole life in the same house as these two men and she had never seen either of them so angry, both so ready to explode. Suddenly it occurred to her that they were on the verge of becoming embroiled in fisticuffs, and she knew Papa was no match for Gustav.

Quickly Hanna withdrew from their protective circle, and turning to Maria, she said, "Take your children into the house. They do not need to see these grown men behave as though they were the youngsters."

Then she looked at Amelia and motioned for her to come with her. "Please go around to Gustav's left side and grab his arm, and as I take his right, together we will swing him away from Papa. Be prepared that he will try to push you, but I know you are strong."

The women succeeded in pulling Gustav full circle so that now he was facing them.

In a very cool, calm voice, Hanna said, "Stop your arguing this minute, before one of you hurts the other. Gustav, I will not allow you to hit Papa."

As soon as she had uttered these words, Gustav came to his senses. He looked around, bewildered; he stared at his father, who stood now with his arms at his sides. Gustav realized just how close they had been to fighting each other. He gently removed the women's hands from his arms and started walking towards the barn. When Gustav reached it, he kept on walking, overcome with shame that he had been so volatile with his papa, and more than a little surprised by the courage and strength of his wife and his sister.

His father was true to his word about not returning to the Mohr household or in any way acknowledging his youngest daughter. And, to his family's disbelief, he entirely stopped attending the Sunday church service even though Reverend Biber made several trips to the farm trying to invite Christian back into the fold. None of them was ever able to learn what had transpired because naturally there was total silence on the subject. However, bit by bit his father slowly began to converse with him, due, Gustav suspected, to loneliness and isolation rather than any feeling of contrition. Neither man ever apologized or talked about what had caused them to rage against each other.

73

For days following Christian's precipitant trip to Neudorf, Katherina had been quiet to the point of withdrawing even from the conversations at mealtime. She hastily ate, replied in the tersest manner that would not preclude her customary politeness, and as soon as the dishes were done, retreated to her bedroom. There she remained until early the next morning when, as reliable as clockwork, she appeared in the kitchen, had a light breakfast, and left for work. During the day, Margareta watched her closely, concerned that her changed demeanour would affect her relationships with her customers. She was pleasantly surprised and very pleased that Katherina maintained her affable and professional bearing at all times in her dress shop, which once again confirmed for her aunt that she had the potential of being a successful business woman, even at the age of sixteen years.

One evening, when Margareta could no longer stand to see her niece consumed with guilt and shame, she went to her bedroom and tapped gently on the door. No response. Not easily deterred, Margareta knocked again, this time with more force. "Please open your door, Katherina. I must talk with you and I shall not leave if I have to pound away here all night."

Being well aware of her aunt's insistent nature, Katherina got off her bed, went to the door, and opened it. As Margareta entered the eerily lit room, which had been Julia's private domain before she had moved to Regina, she made a mental note to have Phillip provide Katherina with a larger kerosene lamp so she could at least read if she was going to spend her evening hours sequestered in this small loft with its sloping ceiling.

"Come sit on your bed with me, Katherina. I am going to divulge a family secret, which I overheard when I was a couple of years younger than you. To this day no one knows that I know." Margareta fluffed up the pillow, placed it by the headboard, heaved her short, stout body up onto the comfortable three-quarter bed, and patted a spot for Katherina to sit beside her.

Katherina readily complied, snuggling her tall, slender body alongside her beloved aunt. "Mama used to tell us stories all the time and it is one of the things I miss most since she died. But she seldom ever told us any secrets, especially the carefully concealed ones about our family members."

As Margareta hugged her niece, she realized that if she said nothing at all she would still be helping her in the best possible way. Why had she not just taken the child into her arms and held her on the day of her father's devastating edict?

With her head propped comfortably on her aunt's ample bosom, Katherina started to feel the tension being released from her muscles, like the fluffy smoke from the puffballs she used to find in the pasture as a little girl and loved to squeeze. The dark cloud that hung over her since her fight with her father began to dissipate; the weight was lifted off her shoulders and she became more relaxed than she had been for days. In her Aunt Margareta's loving arms, she again felt young and vibrant, her mind alert, alive and curious.

"I am waiting to hear your story, Auntie. Come on now, you promised," Katherina insisted.

Chuckling, Margareta said, "Well my darling, it is obvious that you are beginning to feel like your usual impatient and inquisitive self. And I don't remember making any kind of promise, but I will keep my word, on the conditions that you wait until I have finished before you ask any questions, and you stay just as you are, curled up like a child, since I do not have any grandchildren to cuddle and hold."

"I think I shall have an easier time with the latter than the former of your stipulations, but I will do my best," Katherina answered honestly.

Margareta began, "This is the story of Elfrieda Reiner, the only daughter of the minister and his wife, who lived in the little village of Weisenberg, Austria. They had a large family, with ten sons born before the tiny and frail baby girl made her appearance in the world. Apparently she came out screaming, and everyone said that if she ever grew to match the strength of her lungs, she would be stronger than any one of her husky big brothers. Naturally her parents took her to church every Sunday, and as her mother was the choral conductor, to all of the choir practices during the week. Much to the surprise of the congregation and eventually the entire village, Elfrieda started to sing before she was able to speak any words. It was not long before the petite child who had to stand on a stool in the choir loft of the small church was sharing her beautiful voice at every wedding and funeral in the community.

"Soon people came from the surrounding towns and villages to the services to hear the remarkable child sing, and her mother was beginning to formulate a plan for her youngest child to have voice lessons. Elfrieda's mother was an ambitious woman who was frustrated by the demands of her very Prussian husband; but with the support of many of the other women in the village, she was determined that her daughter would do more with her life than look after a man and conceive a houseful of children. Old Mrs. Lutz, the village doctor's mother, had recently moved from Vienna to live with her only child's family. Now, it was well known that Julianna Lutz had been an opera singer with the Vienna State Opera, and Mrs. Reiner was confident that she could find the way to entice the famed diva to pass on her artistry to a promising young protégée.

"Sure enough, it was soon learned that Mrs. Lutz had over the years acquired a taste for fine foods, and with her sweet tooth, was particularly partial to pastries, strudels, and German coffee cakes. As it happened, her daughter-in-law was far more capable as a nurse assisting her husband in his ever-increasing practice than she was with any of the culinary arts. Although the Lutz household now had two women residing within its walls, neither one could cook, much less bake, in the manner to which Julianna was accustomed. Before long, so committed were the women of this hamlet to helping one of their own to rise above the drudgery of a life dictated by a man, that they took turns preparing the evening meal for the family in exchange for singing lessons for Elfrieda Reiner.

"All went well, until one morning in the spring of the year that Elfrieda celebrated her twelfth birthday, when the minister from the town of Brundorf paid a visit to the Reverend Reiner. After a hearty meal, the two men retired to the church where the aging Reverend Wirth told his colleague his tragic tale. His wife had recently died giving birth to a baby, whom she had conceived at her change of life, and although the infant had also succumbed, he needed a strong girl to cook and clean for him and his four sons. The solution was quickly obvious to the Reverend Reiner, who had never approved of all the fuss that was being made over Elfrieda; why, it was wrong in the eyes of God for a child to call so much attention to herself. On the spot, Reverend Reiner decided to send Elfrieda to the Reverend Wirth's household that very afternoon.

"It made no difference that Elfrieda's mother sobbed, yelled, and even flung herself at her husband's feet, begging him to change his mind and keep his only daughter at home. He had determined that she was going, and he would never renege on his commitment to any man, much less to one of the cloth. Nothing could be done; Elfrieda was forced to throw her few belongings in an old valise and be pulled kicking and screaming into the carriage to go away with Reverend Wirth. Keeping in mind what the good Reverend Reiner said about his daughter always causing a commotion when she sang, Reverend

Wirth decided on his way home that his servant girl would not be allowed to sing in his church choir."

Katherina could not bear to hear what was happening to this young girl, but when she started to fidget and was on the verge of speaking, her Aunt Margareta perceptively said, "Tsk-tsk, remember my conditions or I shall not continue with the story."

As Katherina settled back to her cozy position, Margareta resumed. "Well, by the time Elfrieda was fifteen, she was with child, and although it was unknown whether the baby belonged to the Reverend Wirth or to one of his two older frisky sons, the minister who was thirty years her senior decided to take her as his second wife. Even though she was pregnant, her position in the family changed from that of the servant to the lady of the house, and Elfrieda immediately set about improving her lot in life. Her most important accomplishment was convincing her husband that his two oldest sons were ready to leave his home and have wives and families of their own. When she had initially arrived, the two younger boys so desperately missed their mother that they quickly learned to please Elfrieda in exchange for her love and affection. Now, she was confident that she could continue to persuade them to be her allies as she began to exert her influence over her elderly spouse. So it was that over the years Elfrieda seemed to have overcome her tremendous unhappiness with her fate, which in large part was because of the delight she took in her own family of two sons and two daughters.

"Once again, she became active in the church, where it was expected that the minister's wife would be responsible for the choir, and soon the number of congregants began to swell as Elfrieda resumed her role as the soloist. Reverend Wirth, unlike Elfrieda's father, welcomed the attention, which reflected on him because of his beautiful and youthful wife's prowess as a songster. Many in his flock were certain that it was the vitality and assiduity of Elfrieda Wirth that enabled their endearing Reverend to continue to preach well into his twilight years. Even more were adamant that it was because of her gentle persuasion that he had become considerably more tolerant and accepting during his advancing years.

"Almost forty years after his unfortunate visit to Weisenberg, the old man passed on, and although a new minister was sent to take over Reverend Wirth's church, Elfrieda and her two youngest children were so ensconced in the manse that he did not have the heart to ask them to leave. As it happened, the much younger Reverend Hollinger considered the singing of chorales and, on special occasions, even oratorios, essential for his ministry, since he viewed himself as being quite a capable tenor. He was jubilant when he learned that the choral conductor was known throughout the township for her lovely soprano voice, and it was not long before Elfrieda and Reverend Hollinger were singing duets at every church service. As time went on, he became more ambitious, wanting her to sing some of the wonderful arias he had heard when he was in seminary in Vienna. After years of his persistence, Elfrieda finally consented to prepare for a concert, singing arias from Schubert's German lieder repertoire and Mozart's Requiem.

"The much-awaited concert was held on a beautiful autumn Sunday afternoon, with every person from Brundorf and all the villages and hamlets within a day's journey filling every corner of the churchyard. By the time Elfrieda finished her performance, a complete hush fell over the audience until first one adult, then another and another, with children scrambling to do as their parents, rose to their feet for an extended ovation. When the applause eventually died down and Elfrieda stopped bowing, Reverend Hollinger stepped onto the small raised platform and told his congregation that they had heard as fine a soprano as if they had been sitting in the balcony seats of the Vienna State Opera. Then he made his momentous announcement, which he never would have made if he could have predicted its outcome."

Suddenly Margareta stopped talking, and sat gently caressing her niece's soft fresh scented hair. By this time Katherina was so intrigued by the story that she could not bear to wait much longer to ask questions, and she started to feel annoyed that her aunt seemed to be testing her. But this was not the case at all. Instead, Margareta was hesitating, wanting to choose her words very carefully; she was fully cognizant of the impact they could have on her sensitive niece. After what seemed to Katherina like a long time, Margareta shifted her position and began again.

"I must tell you, to be fair to Reverend Hollinger, that as a boy and youth he had lived in Salzburg before he went to Vienna to study for the ministry, and coming to Brundorf was his first foray into the parochialism of small Austrian towns and villages. Therefore, it was much to the surprise of everyone present when the kindly Reverend Hollinger in a voice full of recrimination went on to loudly declare that it was a sin, why, almost a cardinal sin, that no one had ever recognized Elfrieda Wirth's God-given gift as a singer. It was manifest that she was meant to sing, to sing for Austria and on the stage of every renowned opera house of Europe. How was it possible that her incredible talent as a soprano had been wasted, that as a child and young woman she had not been sent away to the best schools that our wonderful country with its history of musical genius had to offer?

"That evening, Elfrieda Reiner Wirth returned to the manse, and during the night she knotted the bedsheets together and hung herself, precisely two months before her sixtieth birthday. She was found the next morning by her beloved younger daughter."

A chill went through her entire body. With a shudder, Katherina abruptly moved away from her aunt's sheltering embrace and said in an agitated voice, "Auntie, can I talk now? Who was Elfrieda Reiner Wirth, and why ever did you tell me her dreadfully tragic story? Especially when you know that Mama died exactly two months before she turned sixty!"

Margareta righted herself on the cozy bed, turned to her niece, and looking directly into her teary eyes said, "My darling Katherina, Elfrieda Reiner Wirth was your grandmother, your mama's mother, and it was Elisabetha, her youngest child, who found her that terrible morning when she was only nineteen years of age.

"Most of us in Brundorf were very afraid for your mother; the shock almost killed her and it took her a long time to recover. She just could not accept that for all those years, her mother had been so unhappy that she would take her own life. Particularly since in many ways she was considered a liberated woman for her time, as she had raised her sons and daughters alike to believe that they could determine their own destinies. At the time of your mama's death, I did think it a strange coincidence that both mother and daughter left this world at the same age."

Margareta continued, "The only reason I have shared this dark family secret with you is because I cannot ever let such a fate happen to you. Katherina Werner, you are meant for so much more than being a cheerless farm wife, slaving away your life for a man and a houseful of screaming, demanding children. One reason I like David Hardy is that he knows you have a good head on your shoulders, and that you are capable of being a successful businesswoman. He encourages you to be who you are instead of giving in to what other people, especially your papa, expects. I know it is hard for you not to feel guilty, but I believe that in good time your father will come to accept that you are able to make your own decisions."

"Oh, poor Mama. It must have been terrible to find her like that, and then to have the whole town know that her only parent had killed herself!" Katherina said as she gazed off to the darkest corner of her bedroom, as though seeing what her mother had found that morning so many years ago.

"Your mother was at least spared the gossiping of the townspeople because Reverend Hollinger did not want them to know how she had died. When he was called to the manse, the young minister asked her older siblings to conceal the manner in which their mother had passed on, and he arranged a ceremonious burial service. Then, apparently because he felt so guilty about her death, he soon left Brundorf, returned to Vienna, and to the best of the townspeople's knowledge, never again ministered to any congregation."

"If the minister covered up the truth, how did you find out what really happened? Did Mama tell you how her mother died? Were the people in the community not suspicious about her sudden death?" Katherina asked, her curiosity now fully aroused. No one had ever shared any family secret with her before in her life, and even if Mama were still alive, she doubted she would have heard this story from her mother's lips.

"I was about eleven years old and I shall never forget that concert. Your grandmother sang so beautifully that I was enthralled with her. After the fowl supper in the church, I went to tell her how she had captivated me with her singing; but when I did, I saw a haunted, inconsolable look in her lovely light violet eyes. Of course, I knew nothing about her past. I only knew she was this wonderfully warm woman who had always been kind to me, and I could not understand why she seemed so distant and forlorn. Like everyone in Brundorf, I was deeply saddened to find out the next morning that she had died during the night, but it was not until six years later that I heard what really happened," Margareta said in a faraway voice.

"But, Auntie, you have not answered my questions. How did you learn the truth?" By now, Katherina was becoming more excitable because she knew her aunt had to have come by this obscure family secret surreptitiously.

"I am not proud of the way that I heard about your grandmother, and to this day, I have never told a soul—not even your Uncle Phillip. The summer that I was seventeen, I lived with your parents so I could help your mama after the birth of Friedrich. As it happened, one evening I woke up thirsty, went to the kitchen to get some water, and I heard your mama telling your father about Elfrieda's life. I knew it was wrong for me to eavesdrop outside the kitchen door that summer evening, but I was fascinated by what I was hearing. To this day, I think your papa and I, and now you, are the only family members who will ever know the truth about Elfrieda Reiner Wirth. And now it is getting late, and if I have answered all your questions, I think we both should get ready for bed," Margareta said, feeling very weary after dredging up such old traumatic memories. Even so many years later, she still felt disillusionment and pain when she realized how a daughter's extraordinary talent had been wasted and her chance for happiness ruined by her own father.

"Auntie, as you know, my questions will never all be answered, but I agree that it is time to go to sleep." As Katherina kissed her aunt on the cheek, she said, "Thank you, Aunt Margareta, for having the confidence in me to reveal my grandmother's history. Even though I never knew her, I feel privileged to at least have learned something about a woman who must have been remarkable. Now I can finally understand why Mama so adamantly encouraged each of us to be the person that God meant us to be, and why you have always had the strength to stand up to people, even Papa, who can be very overbearing at times. But why should the memory of my grandmother be relegated to the realm of a deep, dark family secret because of her death, rather than her descendants being proudly told about her talents and accomplishments during her life?"

With a chuckle, Katherina said, "Oh dear, here I go again! If I live to be a hundred I don't think I shall ever stop asking questions."

74

Although the winter of 1912 was long and bitterly cold, it seemed to pass virtually unnoticed in the Werner household. The atmosphere within the heavy stone walls of the comfortable home was warm, harmonious, and peaceful, reminiscent of when Elisabetha was alive. The children sat at the kitchen table each morning learning their lessons, capably taught by their mother, and when Amelia asked if she could be included, they were delighted. The truth was that Mathias, Julianna, and Elisabetha worshipped the ground their new auntie walked on, and when it was discovered that she had not learned how to read and write when she was a child, they quickly welcomed her to be a pupil with them. In fact, they found it quite novel and inspiring that a grown-up would sit with them to study the rudiments of the written German language.

Correspondingly, the children's consistent enthusiasm helped Amelia to acquire the ability to read and write almost as quickly as they accomplished the task. Finally, even Gustav became involved and assisted Maria in instructing basic arithmetic to the four willing students, and although he dearly would have loved to teach them English, he did not out of deference to his father.

During the afternoons, every family member quietly went about his or her delegated chores since Elisabetha still needed her daily repose. Christian and Gustav often cut and carried wood and tended to the farm animals at that time of the day when there was some warmth in the thin winter sun. When the men returned indoors, Gustav would sit in the kitchen; he frequently found himself watching his young wife. Most interesting was that Amelia had been accepted into the fold by her sister-in-laws like a member of the family who had been born and raised in the household. He was fascinated by how the three women so skillfully co-operated, as though they could read one another's mind. One would require a cooking utensil while another was already handing it to her. It dawned on Gustav that Amelia had brought the glow back into the Werner home.

The more he observed, the more Gustav came to understand how subtly Amelia had worked her way not only into the hearts of the children but also into those of the two women who previously had the full run of the household before her arrival. To begin with, Amelia was assiduous in taking on any of the chores that either Hanna or Maria asked of her. Because she could complete a task so quickly, whether making the beds or preparing breakfast, she would immediately carry on with sweeping the floors and washing the dishes. Amelia made work appear effortless, as she chatted amiably with adults and children alike, and then when everything was done, she beguiled them with the results of her labour; she somehow made it seem that she had been sitting while Hanna and Maria had slaved away, rather than the reverse. With each passing day, Gustav gained increasing respect and admiration for Amelia as she endeared herself to his family, remarkably without awareness of her charms.

In truth, Amelia was in many ways as innocent as Maria's three children, which explained their immediate affinity for their new aunt. She quite naturally accepted each individual for whom he or she was without envy, resentment, or judgment, and it was soon apparent that she had a great capacity to love others. Even his uncommunicative father, who had, if possible, become even more silent since his hasty trip to Neudorf, could not resist talking to Amelia when she sat down beside him and patiently waited for him to respond to her questions. When Christian Werner started to tell Amelia stories from the old country, Gustav and Hanna could not believe their ears; their father had never before shared much information about his past.

Nonetheless, the most unlikely friendship was the open and genuinely fond relationship between Amelia and his youngest sister, Katherina. Sure, they were the same age, but they were as different as night and day. What did the tall elegant Katherina, now the proud owner of a business, have in common with the short, unassuming farm girl? At first Gustav thought his sister was just being kind, and maybe even deliberately befriending his wife to give the Silent Critics something else to gossip about when a member of the Werner or Mohr family was not present. However, Amelia seemed to be the first one Katherina acknowledged as soon as they arrived for church each Sunday. After dinner, the two young women would wash the dishes and chat and laugh in the kitchen like schoolgirls before disappearing to Katherina's bedroom for their private discussions until it was time for Amelia to leave.

It soon became perfectly obvious to Gustav that not only Katherina but all of his family had come to cherish Amelia. Yet when Gustav retired to the privacy of their bedroom every night with his wife, he still could not consummate his marriage. It was not that Amelia put any pressure on him. She would quickly change from her day clothes into a nightdress, climb under the heavy down quilt, and lie absolutely still on her side of the bed. Gustav wondered if Amelia even knew what to expect, or perhaps she was just as happy to go to sleep at the end of her busy days. He did know that he would have to make the first advance towards her. Amelia had not asked anything of him since she had given up her home and family to become a Werner. For that matter, she had made no requests nor appeared to have any expectations of her new family members. Amelia was the one who was always unconditionally giving to them, so why was he not able to love her?

The weeks passed and finally Amelia did appeal to her new family, when she quietly expressed one evening after supper that she hoped her father and siblings could come to the Werner home for Christmas dinner. Since Christian had made it abundantly clear that he was not returning to Neudorf, either for church or for family dinners at the Mohrs', it seemed like the best answer to a potentially thorny dilemma. Papa could not be left on his own for Christmas, regardless of how stubborn the old man had become, and Aunt Margareta would most certainly understand. When the Schweitzer family arrived for Amelia's roast goose on Christmas Day, not one of the Werners was prepared for the joyous reunion between Amelia and her relatives, particularly with her youngest siblings, Katie and Franz. When it was time for them to leave, the two children, who had only known Amelia as their mother, wept tears of sorrow. Gustav finally realized just how much his wife had given up for him.

That night when they went to bed, Gustav waited until Amelia was snugly under the covers before he reached over, gently kissed her on her cheek, and said, "Thank you, Amelia, for preparing such a delicious dinner, and for bringing love back into this house. But I want to apologize for the entire Werner family. We have been so caught up in the radiance and warmth that you have given to all of us that we have completely forgotten about your family, especially poor little Katie and Franz. From today onward, that will change, and you and I will make sure we either invite your family here or we go to see them at least once every week.

As Amelia turned to her husband with gratitude, he lovingly took her into his arms, and for the first time in their married life he loved her as a man loves a woman. And he was surprised by how natural it was once he accepted his feelings.

~ 75 ~

Since the evening that Amelia left to stay with Wilhelmina before her wedding, life in the Schweitzer household had become progressively more chaotic. None of her family had really appreciated how much she did for all of them. Even Karl had not realized the extent that Heinrich, Ludwig, and he depended on Amelia, never mind his youngest children. Amelia had been so efficient in running his home that as the years passed the family had come to expect the meals to be on the table on time, the laundry washed and folded, the cleaning done, and the larder full of canned meats, vegetables, and berries. Well, the storage cupboard had been filled to the top with the fruits of Amelia's labours from the summer, but it was of little benefit if there was no one to plan and organize the meals. If Karl had expected Katie to step in and replace Amelia in handling the responsibilities of managing his home, he could not have been more wrong.

The flaw in Amelia's nine years of filling the gap left by her mother's death was that she preferred to complete the household chores by herself. When she tried to get Katie and Franz to help her, it seemed to take twice as long, so in the end she just let them play while she did the work. It did not take Katie long to figure out that if she dallied or did a sloppy job of an assigned task, Amelia would come along, tell her to leave it, and then redo the chore herself. Actually, many times Katie liked to sit and watch Amelia as she worked; so proficient was she that she made the work look easy and almost enjoyable. Katie did not grasp that hard work brings its own rewards, and when Amelia left home, she was ill-prepared and even less skilled to take care of her father's house and her family members.

Then there was the problem of Franz, who, even at the age of ten, still thought of Amelia as his mother, not as a sister like Katie. He had always been a frail, sickly child and his most frequent recourse for dealing with life's irritations was to burst into tears and sob until Amelia held and soothed him. To prepare him, Amelia told him repeatedly that she would be moving away when she married Gustav, but Franz did not really believe that she would leave them. He remembered when Gustav had come for supper that one evening being so relieved that he was a grown-up and that he lived in a house with his father and sisters; there was no need for Amelia to look after her future husband. His realization after her wedding dinner that Amelia was not coming home hit Franz like a thunderbolt, and he cried through the night and the better part of the next day.

Finally one evening in October when Karl was trying to get some food on the table and Franz was snivelling about one thing or another, Karl said, "If you don't stop that right now, I will damn well give you something to cry about and it will be a lot worse than what you're crying about now."

"Oh, Papa, how can you talk to little Franz like that, especially when he misses Amelia so much," Katie admonished him, opening a jar of pickled carrots and yellow beans.

"It's not how I talk to your brother that has caused the havoc in this house, but the way first Amelia, and now you, constantly treat him as though he was still a baby," Karl snapped, and then, as much to his surprise as Katie's, he stretched out his hand and slapped her hard across the face. Franz stopped crying instantly, while Heinrich stood silently with his mouth open. Both Ludwig and Heinrich had had their share of beatings from their father when his hot temper erupted while they worked in the fields. But Karl had never struck one of his daughters before, or even his boys when they were inside their home.

Katie was so stunned that she dropped the jar of pickles, and as she was picking up the broken glass through her tears, she felt a sharp pain as a jagged piece of glass stabbed into her left knee, nearly reaching to the bone. When she cried out, her father quickly knelt down beside her and removed the glass with one swift movement.

Feeling very ashamed, Karl helped Katie to her feet, led her over to the kitchen sink, and washed her wound, which was bleeding profusely. After the blood flowed freely, cleansing the gash, he carefully wrapped her knee with a clean cloth, securing it with several strands of Katie's crocheting thread.

Supper was a very quiet meal of bread and canned saskatoon berries, which Karl placed in front of each of his children after Heinrich had cleaned up the mess of broken glass and ruined pickles. The Schweitzer family spoke not one word that entire evening, and from that time forward, Franz completely stopped his crying, in front of his father at least. If only his father had learned his lesson as well. It seemed that after crossing that boundary, whenever Karl was angry or frustrated with any of his offspring he took it out on Katie. After each beating, he was filled with remorse and vowed not to strike her again; but time and time again, he pounded his fury out on his youngest daughter's body, making sure to avoid hitting her face and head. Heinrich and Ludwig seemed unable to do anything but stand and watch while Franz wept on the inside, careful not to let one sob escape from his pursed lips.

➤➤～ 76 ～⧫⧫

During the year of 1913, a wedding and a funeral would occur within the Mohr and Werner families respectively, and Christian would consider both equally tragic. He did not hesitate to express his views about the celebration in the Mohr household, although he would not go near the event when it happened. His absence, of course, gave rise to considerable speculation by the Silent Critics, who once again had to observe from the sidelines. But when the patriarch of the Werner family did not even attend the church service to bring closure to the misfortune that had befallen one of his progeny, the Silent Critics were beside themselves with conjecture. For weeks they talked amongst themselves until their tongues were sore from wagging. They were barely able to complete their daily chores, and yet they could not reach any reasonable conclusion.

Timing always had a profound impact on his life, and yet it rarely seemed to work in Friedrich's favour. He had been firstborn to a stern, domineering father who did not mellow until his three youngest children were born, and then he became the son who had worked on the original homestead in Canada because his aging parents needed his help to break the matted prairie sod on the family farm. Then he was forced to sit and watch all of the advantages that fell into Gustav's lap, staring from the sidelines as his youngest brother became the golden-haired son—in the stone house that Friedrich nearly broke his back to build—and then spent the winters of his youth in the comfort of the Mohr home in Neudorf. And if that was not enough, when both Werner men had been working on the railway, Friedrich slaved away building tracks while his youngest brother stood and translated orders from English bosses to German workers and then made more money than Friedrich did at the end of each day. At least now that Gustav had his own farm, he no longer had to contend with his insufferable brother telling him what to do.

It never would have occurred to Friedrich that he had spent the better part of his adult life competing with Gustav; yet it seemed that every minute he had to himself, Friedrich would mull over how privileged his little brother was in comparison. When

Friedrich did remember that he was a husband and the father of three young children, he thought about how he had been forced to marry that spoiled, selfish woman, and then he had no choice but to live in his father's house. Of course by now Gustav would have married Amelia Schweitzer, and although Friedrich felt quite vindicated for not going to the wedding, he wondered if he even had a bedroom in the home that, as far as he was concerned, he had erected. Yet from his perspective, Friedrich felt that over the years he had come to accept that life would always deal him a poor hand. But nothing could have prepared him for what he saw through his alcohol-glazed eyes on the dawn of that early spring morning when he returned unexpectedly to the Werner homestead.

When Margareta first suggested to Phillip that they install a telephone in the general store, he had resisted, telling his wife they had no need for such a gadget. One evening, as they sat at the supper table enjoying a second cup of coffee with their poppy-seed cake, he teased, "My dear wife, I suspect your real reason for wanting a telephone is to stir up the rumour mill for the Silent Critics."

"Naturally, that is part of my intent, but it is not my primary purpose," Margareta replied with a broad grin on her pleasantly plump face. Then her countenance changed and she said wistfully, "I really miss not being able to talk to Julia, and in her letter last month, she wrote about her boarding house getting a telephone. If we had one also, I would be able to call her at least once a week and then I would feel that she was still involved in our family. Julia has been away from home for so long that I sometimes forget I have a daughter, not that I don't thoroughly relish having Katherina here with us."

"Yes, I understand how you feel. I often think that maybe we made a mistake when we encouraged Julia to get her education. Neither of us fully appreciated what it would mean until she moved away to Regina. She doesn't seem as interested in coming back home to visit as she did when she first left. Well, I suppose if we had one of these new devices of communication, we could fill our orders more quickly than with the telegraph or by mail," Phillip answered pensively.

Then, realizing that Margareta had once again cleverly convinced him that they needed what she wanted, he burst out laughing and chided her. "I think that the Silent Critics are absolutely right when they whisper that you have me wrapped around your little finger."

But if Phillip was in the store when the new telephone rang, he was always the first to rush behind the counter to answer it. Furthermore, Margareta started to notice that her husband was spending much more time with her in the store than he had for months, leaving

Peter to handle the customers at the lumberyard. When she mentioned this observation to him, he readily explained that he was short of supplies for his business. So it was Phillip who received the call from Julia on a late Wednesday afternoon when she rang to ask if she could bring a guest home for her Easter school break. Her father delightedly answered in the affirmative but neglected to obtain any details; so later when Margareta wanted to confirm the identity of their guest, Phillip was unable to provide his wife with information.

On the Saturday morning that Julia was arriving on the train, Katherina offered to mind the store as well as her dress shop; she knew her aunt was looking forward to seeing Julia again and filled with curiosity about who her daughter was bringing home. In fact, every mealtime conversation since Julia's telephone request had focused on the mysterious visitor who was coming to Neudorf with her. Although Margareta must have asked Phillip a hundred times whether they were expecting a male or female caller, all the poor man could do was shake his head and say that he did not know. When he became sensitive about her persistent inquiries, she promptly reminded him that she was the one trying to get the house ready and make the appropriate sleeping arrangements.

Phillip countered by telling his wife that she worried far too much about such minor details. After all, if their guest were a man, it would be perfectly acceptable for him to room with Peter for one week; if a woman, no doubt she could share Julia's bedroom loft with her and Katherina. Indeed, Phillip conjectured that the three females would probably have a great time chatting and giggling all night long. Phillip even ventured that if she absolutely had to know, all she had to do was telephone and ask her daughter. True to her nature, however, Margareta had the last word when she insisted that it would be rude to inquire at this late date, and the person would not be an enigma if only Phillip would develop the habit of paying attention to the fine points of the art of communication. When Peter and Katherina could no longer stand their uncharacteristic bickering, they put an immediate and effective stop to it by threatening that Phillip and Margareta would be required to mind their respective shops while they went to the train station to welcome Julia and her friend.

~~ 78 ~~

Since his new automobile was so much quieter than the old rattletrap he had previously owned, Friedrich determined that he could probably drive into his father's yard without waking any of the family from their sleep. As he thought about it, he decided that once he found the bedroom in which Maria was sleeping, he would quietly slip into the bed beside her. Since he had been away for such a long time, she would surely be willing to couple with him—unlike the last time when he had come home and she had promptly moved out of his bed. And if she was not eager, this time he would damn well show her who was boss in this marriage.

When he was about to park his car, Friedrich remembered that he was still having trouble getting it started and elected to drive to the top of the little knoll on the east side of the house. He turned his pride and joy so that it faced the lazy, flowing creek at the bottom of the hill; that way, if it gave him any bother, the momentum from a push might coax the engine alive. After Friedrich turned off the motor, he opened the door, stepped out on a patch of grass that peeked through the last of the snow, and then quietly closed the door behind him. As he walked towards his father's house, the sun was peeping over the horizon, chasing night away and bringing in another day. The puddles from the melted snow had frozen over with jagged edges, and as he crunched through them he was reminded about how much he had enjoyed hearing that sound as a youth during his first spring in Canada.

Reaching the short flight of stairs into the house, Friedrich paused, looked around the tidy yard enclosed by the caragana and poplar trees, and breathed in the crisp, refreshing, Saskatchewan morning air. Vaguely he wondered what had happened to that energetic young man who had been so excited about immigrating to a new country full of promise and opportunity. Standing on the sturdy doorstep of the stone house while pondering that question, Friedrich concluded that it was the women in his life who had kept him back and prevented him from reaching the success he had envisioned for himself. If that silly Maria Biber had not insisted on marrying him and then promptly producing three hungry mouths to feed and clothe, he would not have been trapped on his father's miserable farm for all of those years. If only he had gone to Melville right away and started working on the railway, he would now have a better position so Anastasia would not always be at him about making more money, especially now that she was pregnant.

Then, just like Maria, Anastasia started telling him how he should spend his hard-earned dollars. After their fight yesterday, Friedrich drove to the hotel to have a drink to calm his shattered nerves; but when the barkeeper later said it was closing time, he was not ready to face Anastasia. It was when he had cranked his automobile by hand and finally got it started that the idea to drive to Neudorf, instead of going home, occurred to him. Let her sit by the window waiting for him and worrying about where he was; he would show Anastasia Schmidt. Friedrich drove slowly since he was the only vehicle on the road; he drank too much and was tired after working for six days before the week ended with another quarrel. At least his three children would be excited to see him when they awakened and found that their papa had come back to the farm.

～ 79 ～

The stationmaster was full of apology when he told Phillip and Margareta that the train from Regina would be at least forty-five minutes late. Since their businesses were in good hands, Phillip suggested that they go to the hotel for a cup of coffee. As they walked towards the establishment, one of the Silent Critics caught sight of them and immediately sounded the alert to the other members of the group. No sooner had the Mohrs entered the doorway than they were called over to share the table with those individuals who delighted in spreading rumours behind their backs. This was quite novel, to have the opportunity to sit down with their critics and to break through the silence. Phillip hesitated, however, because all too often he had come across them when they were not aware of his presence, and the things the Silent Critics said about his wife were less than kind.

On the other hand, Margareta seemed to have no qualms about joining them; she walked straight over to their table, pulled out a chair, and sat down. The minute they had ordered coffee, the Silent Critics changed their tactic, obviously intending to obtain as much information as possible right from the source. As Phillip sat and listened to how aptly Margareta deflected their questions and then redirected their inquiries so the Silent Critics provided all of the information, he marvelled at her skill. Time passed quickly and then Phillip said they must go; only then did one member of the group realize that they had not found out why Phillip and Margareta Mohr were out on the town so early on this sunny spring morning rather than tending to their customers.

～ 80 ～

Opening the heavy door as quietly as he could, Friedrich went into the house and again thought about how easily a total stranger could let himself into the unlocked home. Years ago, he had encouraged Papa to get a watchdog but his father had adamantly refused, saying that he would not live in the same building as an animal. Even the first year, when the family had arrived to the townships in Saskatchewan so late in the fall that they had to live in a dugout in the hillside with a sod roof, they had still erected a hasty shelter for the team of oxen. Friedrich stood for a few minutes, familiarizing himself with the positioning of the furniture in the kitchen; he was still feeling the effect of his many drinks, and who knew if those two women had moved everything around while he was away? The last thing he wanted to do was awaken everyone by crashing into a misplaced table or chair.

It occurred to Friedrich that Gustav and Amelia would have taken over the large bedroom, so it made sense that Maria and the children would be occupying the medium-sized room. In the eerie first light of dawn, Friedrich soundlessly made his way to the door;

before he opened it, he straightened his clothes and smoothed back his hair, remembering that he was looking forward to surprising his wife and to satisfying her in bed. As he gently turned the handle and slowly pushed the door wide enough so he could enter the east-facing room, a bright shaft of sunlight flowed through the window, slanting towards the head of the double bed. But wait, what was he seeing? It looked like two adult bodies were under the cozy quilt, and it appeared that one of them was awake and stroking the other person's hair and face. Surprised into immobility, Friedrich watched as the other individual stirred and then moved closer to the person who looked like Maria.

Clearly, the two individuals were totally unaware of this invasion of privacy and now Friedrich held his breath, not wanting to be found out. As he stared, he heard his wife say, "Are you awake, or do you need some gentle coaxing from me?" Then, to his amazement, his sister Hanna responded, "My dear, you know how much happier I am during the entire day when you awaken me with your tender loving."

Friedrich's mouth dropped open as he witnessed the inexplicable behaviour of his wife kissing his sister as a man would a woman. Stunned but unable to watch any longer for fear of what he might see next, Friedrich stepped back through the partially closed door and, trembling, escaped back to the kitchen and then to the outdoors.

As soon as he was outside, he took several gulps of the fresh morning air to try to clear his head. He could not believe what he had seen. Maybe his mind was muddled from the alcohol he had consumed. Had he just imagined their bizarre conduct? Then why did he feel sick to his stomach? Friedrich turned around and listened at the door, but as far as he could tell, neither his wife nor his sister knew he had been in the house, let alone in the bedroom. Should he go back into the house and confirm his observations? The very thought of even being near that bedroom caused Friedrich to bolt to the back of the outhouse, where he promptly vomited. Disgusted with what he saw, he suddenly wanted to get as far away as possible from both women, his father's house, and this damn farm, which seemed to hold nothing but bad experiences for him.

When he started to bring up bile, which bitterly symbolized how he felt about discovering his wife in bed with his sister, Friedrich forced himself to stop spewing from his empty stomach. Breathing slowly, he walked towards his automobile, aware that it was almost daylight and that Gustav would soon be getting up to herd the cows into the barn for milking. He wanted to leave before anyone saw him, as though he had never been here. Friedrich reached into his vehicle, took out the hand crank, and went to the front of the car. He inserted the handle into the shaft and began the rotating motion necessary to get the engine started. He cranked and cranked without success. Of course, even his automobile would let him down when he needed it the most. He tried again, this time with more force, as the shock of his wife's grotesque behaviour began to wear off and be replaced with increasing fury that she could prefer his sister to him. But try as hard as he could, the damn thing would not come alive, and the day was upon him.

Frustrated, Friedrich went around to the side of the car, opened the door, and, leaning in, put it into gear. He knew it was hazardous to be in front of the car because it would move as soon as the engine fired, but he figured he could jump to the side and leap into the open door as it went by him. This new automobile seemed to require some impetus to get going, and he made a mental note to have it checked out when he returned to Melville. But as he had done so many times in so many ways throughout his life, Friedrich Werner overestimated his ability to accomplish what he set out to do. Or perhaps, in this particular instance, he minimized the effects of age and alcohol upon his body, specifically on his reflexes and mobility, and miscalculated the incline of the hill.

At any rate, he returned to cranking the car and scarcely completed the second full rotation when, to his surprise, the engine roared to life. Friedrich had no chance to move aside before his newly purchased automobile, of which he was so proud, was on top of him, over him, and then dragging him down the slope of the hill. It sputtered and eventually came to a full stop just beyond the edge of the shallow creek that continued to flow at a snail's pace under the thin layer of ice from the overnight freeze.

As it happened on that beautiful spring morning in April, the Werner cows were not eating the fresh green grass that heralded the return of the season by sprouting through the last of the snow at the side of the creek. Instead, when Gustav came out of the house not thirty minutes after Friedrich's unfortunate accident, the only sound he heard was Betsy's bell on the west side of the barn at the other end of the pasture. Since the cows were so near, he was in no hurry, and he stopped to enjoy the crispness of the air and to appreciate the arrival of his favourite time of year. Gustav decided to walk through the row of caragana trees, and then, being so close to the poplars his father had planted years ago as a windbreak, he chose to continue towards the barn by strolling the extra distance along the tree line.

When he reached the poplar trees Gustav could not resist stopping and touching the tiny sticky buds that had started to form on the branches. As a boy, he had played for hours among the saplings, which seemed to grow taller so much faster than he did, until their tops were quickly beyond his reach. Each spring he had measured himself by one particular tree that was less hardy than the others, and he had talked to it every day, encouraging it to grow faster. However, as he had watched its buds enlarge until they unfurled to their waxy green leaves, he was convinced that his favourite tree had the brightest foliage of the lot. On windy days, Gustav had always run to the poplar grove where he would lie down on the thick grass and listen to the rustling of the leaves in the gentle breeze.

Sauntering along, Gustav continued with his reminiscences; he had not been to visit his mother's grave since the fall. He realized that now when he remembered his mama it was no longer painful; instead, he thought of her with fondness, recalling the happy times they had spent together. It occurred to Gustav that he was much more at peace with himself, and once again he felt in harmony with God and nature. He had regained his buoyant spirit and his youthful aspiration to be one of the most successful farmers in the townships. But perhaps more importantly, his enjoyment of the company of other people had returned, and he had the good sense to know it was in large part due to Amelia. With each passing day, Gustav realized he was coming to love his tender, caring young wife and her family, whom they had visited at least once or twice every week since Christmas.

As he herded the cows into the barn, Gustav decided that after he finished the milking he would ride Wolfgang to the cemetery to do the usual spring cleanup. Papa did not seem to have much energy these days; in fact, his bedroom door had still been closed this morning when Gustav had put on his work clothes to go outside. In many ways, it was quicker for Gustav to do the chores alone, because his father moved slowly and often stopped to talk about one thing or another. Then Gustav would feel compelled to let him finish because he had no interest in upsetting his only remaining parent. As it was, all three cows had just delivered their calves, and it seemed that the minute he sat down on the little three-legged stool their milk began to flow. Within the hour, Gustav had completed his task, untied the cows and released them back into the pasture, fed the calves, and given Wolfgang some oats before closing the barn door.

Coming out of the red barn that the entire family had painted a couple of years ago, Gustav was halfway up to the house with a pail of milk in each hand when he thought he saw something shiny near the creek. The low-lying sun was brightly reflecting off an object, but what could it be? Gently setting the overflowing pails down on the path, he walked through the long, dried grass, flattened by the winter's heavy snowfall, towards the creek. Soon he realized that a car was stuck in the slushy mud and tangled grass of the half-frozen water. It did not look like Friedrich's automobile, so whose could it be and why was it here? It was not until Gustav went to the front of the vehicle that he saw a man trapped under it.

"Oh, my God, it is Friedrich!" Gustav exclaimed. "Friedrich, can you hear me? Just say something so I know you are alive."

When he received no response from his eldest brother, Gustav knew he had to act quickly, but he could not free Friedrich on his own.

"I am going to the house to get Papa and the women to help, and we will have you out from under your car in no time," said Gustav, as much to convince himself as his unresponsive brother. Running up to the house, he burst open the door and yelled, "Papa, Hanna, Amelia! Put on your coats and boots right away and come with me. Maria, you stay in the house and keep your children here with you, including Mathias. I have found Friedrich down by the creek and I need help to carry him up the hill." Knowing that something had to be very wrong for Gustav to order them around, the three family members he had named rose from the breakfast table and did what they were told.

As soon as they arrived at the scene of the accident, Gustav positioned his father at the front of the car nearest the creek's edge and told the women to come with him so that one was on either side of Friedrich. Then he waded through the ice-cold water to the far side of the vehicle before giving them his directions. "On three, Papa and I will use the crowbar to jack up the car, and then Hanna and Amelia, you will pull Friedrich out from under it." If they were not stunned by what had happened to Friedrich, the Werner family rapidly reached that state the minute they entered the freezing water. Each dreaded learning the truth about Friedrich's condition once they rescued him from the icy brink. Perhaps it was the desperation of the situation or the synergy of the people involved because the plan worked on the initial attempt, and within minutes they were carrying the comatose Friedrich up the path to the house.

Mathias, who had been glued to the small window, could wait no longer and flew out the door before his mother could stop him. "Papa, Papa, are you all right? What has happened to you?"

Gustav was the first adult to respond.

"Mathias, go back into the house and tell your mother to get ready for us. Ask her to draw the quilts on her bed down to the bottom so we can lay your papa on it. Then go around to the other bedrooms and gather some extra blankets because we will need to pile them on top of your father. He is very cold and we must return his body temperature to normal. Go quickly now."

When they had laid him on the bed, Gustav, with his father's help, gently removed Friedrich's clothes, which were stiff with ice, just as Maria came into the room with towels she had warmed in the roaster in the oven. After wrapping Friedrich's body in the heated flannel, they quickly covered him with the piles of quilts. Gustav lowered his face to his brother's and confirmed that he was still breathing, although his breaths were shallow at best. Turning to Maria he said, "I am going to change out of these wet clothes and then ride to Neudorf to bring Dr. Spitznagel as soon as I can find him. The warmed towels are an excellent idea; while I am gone, keep changing them because they will help to restore his body heat."

Chastising himself for strolling through the trees and dallying instead of taking his usual route to the barn, Gustav knew he might have found Friedrich at least an hour earlier. His guilt almost overwhelmed him as he ran to his bedroom, threw his soggy clothes uncharacteristically onto the floor, and changed into a dry shirt and trousers. Grabbing his Sunday coat as he dashed out the door, he raced to the barn, hastily put the bridle into Wolfgang's mouth, and left before his family could say anything to him. It was not until years later that Gustav could recall his hasty trip to town. It was as if he was possessed by demons as he urged Wolfgang to go faster and faster, so that when man and beast reached Neudorf, they nearly ran into the train coming in from Regina as it pulled across the track.

Fortunately, Wolfgang was able to pull up short and veer to the side as he reared back onto his hind legs. When Phillip Mohr came running from the platform, where he could not believe what he saw, he grabbed Wolfgang's bit as soon as his front legs were back on the ground and brought him under control.

"Gustav, what are you doing? You just about ran Wolfgang and yourself into the train!"

Gustav, jolted back to his senses, blurted, "Uncle Phillip, do you know where I can find Dr. Spitznagel? Friedrich has had an accident at the farm and needs a doctor right away."

At that precise moment, Julia was descending the short flight of stairs from the train onto the wooden platform, immediately followed by her betrothed, Dr. Robert Cameron. Without waiting for an introduction to Julia's parents, the tall, handsome man with red hair and green eyes jumped down from the train and ran over to where Wolfgang stood frothing at the mouth after his hard ride. "Gustav, we met in Regina and I could not help but overhear that you need a doctor. Let me jump up behind you and I shall come with you right now." Before any member of the Mohr family could speak, Robert had climbed up onto the horse's rear. He held on to Gustav, who turned Wolfgang around in the direction of the Werner farm, and with the two men on his back, the horse galloped out of sight.

After Julia's parents had hugged and welcomed her home, Phillip turned to his wife and said, "Well, Margareta, at least we know our houseguest is a man, but clearly we will have to wait until he has attended to Friedrich before we have a chance to make his acquaintance. I wonder what our irresponsible nephew has done now!"

"Phillip, you should not talk about Friedrich like that, particularly in front of Julia." As they spoke, the whistle blew and the train slowly started to move forward, continuing on its journey to Melville. "Come, my darling, let's go to the house and prepare dinner. Perhaps by the time it is ready, your young man will have returned to town and your father can finally meet him. I do concur with your papa that it is disappointing that we must bide our time," Margareta exclaimed as she fondly took her daughter's arm and together they began the short walk home.

If Margareta Mohr experienced a sense of disgruntlement because of the delay in having her husband meet Julia's interesting gentleman friend (whom she speculated her daughter had brought home to seek her father's approval), it was nothing compared to the feelings with which the Silent Critics had to contend. Once again they obsessed over whatever had possessed Rudolf Schultz to build his hotel on the wrong side of the tracks. Why, every time the train came into town, their vantage seats at the front window did not allow them to immediately see who had come to visit because the train station sat north of the hotel.

81

Mathias reclaimed his perch on the kitchen cupboard by the window after Gustav dashed away on Wolfgang. The men had not dismounted before he was outside again, running towards them.

"Uncle Gustav, what is wrong with my papa? Nobody will tell me anything and Mama won't even let me go into her bedroom."

When Robert had started courting Julia and discovered that she was German, he had insisted that she teach him her language. Regardless, he would not have needed to understand his words to appreciate the distress of this little blond-haired boy, whose bright blue eyes would have sparkled under more favourable circumstances. Although Robert felt for the child, he refrained from making glib comments about his purpose in accompanying his uncle. Gustav had told him about finding Friedrich under his car in the creek, but had said virtually nothing about his brother's overall condition, and Robert was hesitant to make any remarks to raise the tyke's hopes.

They had no sooner entered the house than Christian was at the door questioning his son.

"Gustav, who have you brought? I thought you went to town to bring Dr. Spitznagel. This is no time to bring a stranger into our home."

"Papa, I want to introduce you to Dr. Robert Cameron. He was just getting off the train when I arrived in Neudorf, and Rolf and I met him when we went to Regina last spring. He promptly offered to come with me and I decided that in the interest of time I would not try to locate Dr. Spitznagel. Now, please let me take him to his patient."

The three women had been constantly changing the warmed flannel towels, which they wrapped around Friedrich's body, particularly around his limbs and on top of his chest. Dr. Cameron first said, "You have done an excellent job of restoring his body temperature, but I will need to remove the quilts and towels to thoroughly check the state of his injuries. At first glance, he appears to have limited external injuries, which is amazing; although he could have sustained internal damage when the car ran over him. Perhaps his wife can stay to assist me and the other two ladies can exchange the cloths when I have finished."

Just then, as everyone in the room watched, the unconscious man lying in his wife's bed let out a rush of air from deep in his lungs, and expired before the doctor could commence his medical examination. It was strangely ironic that Friedrich's last breath came in the bed where he had witnessed the scene that precipitated his death.

Moreover, there were those, especially among the Silent Critics, who, when they pieced the story together, considered it paradoxical that the only time Christian Werner acknowledged Robert Cameron was when the English doctor pronounced his oldest offspring dead. Not one person in the entire township would have believed Christian would hold true to his word to never again step foot in the Neudorf church. So it was that Julia Mohr and her young Englishman were in town to attend Friedrich Werner's funeral, while Christian stayed at home alone on the farm, verifying the accuracy of the oldest son's repeated claims that the homestead was the bane of his existence. Indeed, Friedrich, who had shared his father's dislike for the English, would have been surprised by the number of them in attendance at his burial.

82

After each time Gustav brought her to visit them on the Thompson farm, Sarah felt that Amelia was becoming a little more comfortable in their presence. She was still very shy if Andrew was in the sitting room with them, but when the men went outside to study the crops or to race their horses, Amelia visibly relaxed and tried to express herself in her broken English. Sarah was becoming very fond of her reserved young friend, who, although the same age as her husband's sister, was mature beyond her years. It was distressing for both women that they were so limited in their conversations because of their different languages, and Sarah became increasingly irritated with Gustav.

One evening, shortly after Friedrich's untimely demise, the Thompson family invited Gustav and Amelia for supper. Andrew's father was trying to cheer everyone up by regaling them with stories of his boyhood in England, and it was Sarah who noticed that Amelia kept her head lowered and did not join in the laughter.

Then it struck Sarah that Amelia could not enjoy her father-in-law's wry sense of humour and delightful way of making the most mundane events seem interesting when she could understand very little of what he was saying. On the other hand, ever since she had known Gustav, he had had an excellent command of the English language and spoke fluently on most topics.

That night as they were preparing for bed, Sarah asked Andrew, "Why doesn't Gustav teach Amelia our language so she can take part in the conversations with us? I am getting annoyed with him. He thoroughly enjoys our company, but he seems to expect his wife to sit like a bump on a log when they come to visit."

"Perhaps Amelia does not want to learn to speak English," Andrew answered lightly as he hung up his trousers.

"I don't believe that for one moment. As soon as the two of you go outdoors, Amelia asks me to teach her more words and to listen to her as she repeats to ensure that she is enunciating correctly. And I know she is embarrassed when she cannot understand what we are saying," Sarah replied.

The truth was that Andrew had often wondered the same thing, and although he had searched his mind for some plausible answer, he too was stymied by his friend's behaviour.

Walking over to the bed, he sat down and leaned his head on his wife's shoulder. "I think Gustav is full of contradictions. When we became friends years ago, he told me how he was able to learn English, and that even as a youth, he realized that for him to be successful in Canada, he would need to be able to speak, read, and write what he called 'the language of the New World.'

"However, from what I can ascertain, his papa is totally against him using it in the house; so out of respect, they only speak German. But what confuses me is how Gustav thinks that Amelia and the rest of his family, especially Maria's children, will adapt to life in this country if they don't speak English. Between you and me, Sarah, I have frequently thought that Gustav should stand up to his father and insist that the entire family learn both languages."

"That would make very good sense to me; although all too often I get the impression that Gustav does not want Amelia to participate equally when the four of us get together. Don't misunderstand me, Andrew, I really like Gustav, except for the way he seems to ignore Amelia in our company. I know she is considerably younger and more diffident than you and me, but how will she become confident with us if she is a wallflower because of her language barrier? I am not sure that Gustav expects women to be kept at home in the kitchen."

"Well, I think that may be another one of Gustav's inconsistencies," said Andrew, gently brushing a strand of soft hair back from Sarah's forehead. "I strongly suspect from how he talks that, as the man of the house, he wants to make all of the decisions. But I am almost certain that is not the kind of relationship his parents had when his mother was alive. I remember a wonderful day when Gustav arranged dinner outdoors in a beautiful spot so I could meet his mother, and although we were gathering there because she wanted to keep peace at home with Christian, Elisabetha Werner was not a meek, docile woman. In fact, she was the opposite—easily as outgoing and, I dare say, outspoken as Margareta Mohr. From what I can determine, I am sure that both of these strong women insisted on parity with their husbands and then taught their children the importance of equality—if we look at their daughters, Katherina and Julia."

With Sarah's head now nestled on his broad chest, Andrew continued: "On many occasions Gustav told me that his father does not want to give up any of the customs and ways of the old country and therefore has refused to change. I know Gustav did not like his father choosing Amelia as his bride because he told me about the huge quarrel they had when he tried to tell Christian that he did not want an arranged marriage; it was obvious to me that Gustav wanted to make his own choices about what he did and whom he married.

Then, not much later, when Katherina wanted to decide where she lived and worked, Gustav was so upset that I questioned who was the real traditionalist in the Werner family."

Snuggling into Andrew's embrace, Sarah responded, "Oh, yes, thank you for reminding me that Gustav and Amelia did not choose to become husband and wife. Perhaps we are being unfair, since we don't know what it would be like to marry before knowing anything about or having a chance to develop feelings for each other. I certainly appreciate why Gustav would want to break away from such a custom, but I can also understand that it would be hard for an older person like his father to adjust to a totally different way of living and speaking in a new country."

"I think it is more than Christian Werner wanting to cling to German traditions. I have sensed a deep-seated animosity in him towards the English. Do you recall how Christian could barely say hello when Gustav introduced him to our families at Gustav's wedding? Furthermore, I know that the reason Margareta would invite David, you, and me for supper on Saturdays was to avoid an encounter with Christian. Of course, that was in the days when he was still going into town. Wasn't it unbelievable that he did not even go to Friedrich's funeral? Then, the other day, Gustav let it slip how his father was embarrassingly rude to Dr. Cameron when he arrived at the farm to help the day Friedrich died. As I add it all together, I suspect it is much more than Mr. Werner adhering to conventions. At least on the issue of bearing ill will towards the English, we can be thankful that Gustav has not followed in his father's footsteps."

"Nonetheless, he might be well advised to treat his wife the way he says his father treated his mother," Sarah quietly responded as she turned to her husband and kissed him on the cheek. "Anyway, I think that as soon as Amelia gives Gustav a child, he will feel much more loving towards her."

"Unfortunately, Amelia may have to wait for some time before she has a baby. Just the other day, when I was teasing him about becoming a father, Gustav said that he did not intend to start a family until he was much better established and had purchased at least another quarter-section of land."

"What a shame! Amelia is wonderful with Emma. I can be walking the floor with her wailing her lungs out and the minute Amelia takes her in her arms Emma stops crying and falls asleep."

"Well, my darling, I still love you," Andrew replied as he tilted Sarah's face towards him and planted a kiss on her petite mouth.

When Sarah firmly kissed him back, Andrew whispered in her ear, "I think we have discussed enough of the Werner family's idiosyncrasies for tonight and it is time for us to focus on the Thompson proclivity for having more than one offspring."

"Oh, Andrew, whatever are you talking about now? I think that you read books every chance you get so you can deliberately confound me with new...."

Sarah could not finish her sentence with her husband smothering her mouth with his ardent kisses.

⟫~ *83* ~⟪

It was not the kind of week that she had excitedly planned when Julia invited Robert to come to Neudorf for Easter to meet her father before they announced their engagement. When Gustav and Robert rode into town doubled up on Wolfgang's back at least two hours later than expected, it was apparent when they dismounted that something was tragically wrong. Instead of coming directly to the house, the men stood engaged in conversation in the small yard, which was surrounded by a white picket fence.

"I know how badly you feel about your brother's death, and I can't seem to reassure you enough that there was nothing you could have done to save him. Friedrich likely did not die because he was submerged too long in the creek, but because of his extensive internal injuries caused when the car ran over him. Although I don't know your Uncle Phillip, I am prepared to be the one to tell the Mohr family that Friedrich is dead, if that is your preference," Robert said to the reticent Gustav, who was clearly still furious with his father since leaving the farm.

Gustav looked at the tall man in his early thirties, with his bright red hair and deep-set greenish eyes, which conveyed a sombre but kindly expression. This learned man, who was practically a stranger, had already done so much for the Werner family. In the silence that had followed his pronouncement that Friedrich was dead, all any of them could do was stand and stare at the lifeless body on the bed. Then when Christian had stormed out of the room and Mathias came running in through the open door, even his mother had not been able to stop him from repeatedly shaking his father and screaming at him to wake up. Gustav had remained immobilized, deep in his anguished memories of when his mother had died. It was Dr. Cameron who finally took the distraught eight-year-old boy by the hand, led him out of the bedroom, and patiently explained to him that his father had passed on to a better world. Realizing that his father was gone forever this time, Mathias burst into tears, and the considerate doctor held him in his strong arms and told him to cry until he felt like stopping.

Quite naturally when they saw their older brother sobbing, without knowing why, both Julianna and Elisabetha immediately followed suit. Amelia, hearing the bedlam outside of the bedroom door, left Hanna to console her shocked sister-in-law and went to comfort her nieces.

Although Maria was able to hold back her tears, she said in a monotone voice to no one in particular, "I may not have loved Friedrich these past few years, but I would never have wished him dead at thirty-seven."

Her honest utterance seemed to shake Gustav out of his trance; finding his legs, he too decided that Hanna could best deal with the visibly shaken Maria. Arriving in the kitchen and uncertain what to do next, Gustav pulled up a chair and sat at the table beside his father.

When Dr. Cameron finally calmed Mathias, his sisters ceased their crying like clockwork and Amelia went to the stove to put the kettle on to make coffee for their guest. As she started to set cups and saucers on the table, Gustav rose, walked over to the hallway where Robert was still standing, and invited him to come and take a chair. Turning to his wife before he sat down, Gustav said, "Amelia, I would like you to meet Dr. Robert Cameron." After her salutation, she instantly asked him if he would stay for dinner.

"Thank you, Amelia, for your kind offer, but after a cup of coffee I must ask Gustav to take me back to Neudorf where Miss Mohr is waiting." As he pulled out a chair, even Robert was taken aback by the rapidity with which Christian jumped up and, without a word, strode away to his bedroom.

In the ensuing silence, which was fraught with tension, Gustav had to stop himself from going after his father, taking him by the shoulder, and returning him to the kitchen to apologize for his uncharacteristically rude behaviour. *What was the man's problem?* Gustav had never seen his father treat a visitor so disagreeably. Once again, as was happening more often in the Werner household, the gentle Amelia eased the strain in the air by responding as though nothing had transpired and asking Robert if he would like to try a piece of her fresh-baked bread.

"Why, yes, I would enjoy something light to eat since we had a very early breakfast. I know Mrs. Mohr will be expecting me for dinner, but what could it hurt to have a sample of your delicious-smelling bread?"

Gustav was too upset to eat anything; but as he watched Robert eat his third slice with chokecherry jelly, he hoped Julia's friend had a hearty appetite, knowing full well the quantity of food that Aunt Margareta would have prepared in anticipation of her guest's arrival.

Things had just settled down when Christian came striding back into the kitchen and walked over to where Gustav was seated. Even though Christian had been present when Robert was speaking to Amelia, he addressed his comments to his son.

"You can give your friend this money to pay for his services to Friedrich. I do not accept charity, especially from an Englishman."

Gustav was dumbfounded, but before he could recover his voice, Robert graciously rose from his chair and said, "Thank you for your hospitality. Amelia, your bread and jelly are wonderful, and if I don't leave soon I shall not have any appetite left to do justice to Mrs. Mohr's dinner. I shall need you to return me to Neudorf, Gustav, if you are able, or at least to point me in the right direction so I can walk."

"Of course, I shall take you back on Wolfgang. We have used up way too much of your time as it is," Gustav replied.

Robert then turned abruptly, and with his long, deliberate gait quickly walked away from the table, without so much as a glance at the money. He was already in the yard before Mathias was able to catch up to him and ask, "Dr. Cameron, am I ever going to see you again?"

"Yes, son, you will see a lot of me since I shall become part of your family by this fall," Robert answered with a wink as he tousled Mathias's hair.

When they arrived in Neudorf, after having been with Mathias in his time of need and then being subjected to the uncivil Christian, Dr. Cameron was ready to take on the unpleasant task of breaking the news of Friedrich's tragic end to a man whom he had yet to meet.

"No, Robert, I cannot allow you to accept any more of my responsibilities. I shall tell my Uncle Phillip and Aunt Margareta that Friedrich is dead; but before we go into the house, I must apologize for my father's ill manners. I have never understood his dislike for your nationality, and I am ashamed of the way he treated you—especially when Julia no doubt brought you home for a happy event and not to deal with her ungrateful relatives."

Gazing intently at the earnest young man, Robert replied, "Yes, Gustav, you are quite right. Julia was so happy that I could, during a week she was not teaching, get away from my busy practice and finally come to Neudorf to make her father's acquaintance. I know your Aunt Margareta well because of the many trips she makes to Regina, but I have yet to meet Mr. Mohr. It is my intention to ask him for Julia's hand in marriage, and we will begin making our wedding plans for the fall; although now the timing may be inappropriate."

Then clasping Gustav lightly by the shoulder, he added, "I accept your apology, although you don't have to feel guilty about your father's conduct. Many of my patients in Regina are of German origin, and I have encountered similar responses from some of them. Yet others are quite delighted with me, particularly now as I am becoming more fluent in your language."

From the corner of his eye, Robert could see Julia anxiously standing by the window as he continued, "I think that it will be our generation and our children who will adapt best to this wonderful country and establish its identity. In a few years I won't be English and you German, but we will all blend together as our families become a melting pot of Canadians. Where our ancestors came from will be of little consequence. But now we should go inside and break the bad news so we can get on with Margareta's meal. Thankfully, some people of our parents' age are much more open and accepting of our ethnic differences, and if your Uncle Phillip is at all like his wife, I am looking forward to a relaxing and enjoyable week."

Feeling more comfortable after Robert's compassionate words, Gustav responded, "I know you will find Phillip Mohr to be a good man who equals my aunt in terms of receptiveness and progressive thinking. As a boy, I was fortunate to be able to live with them during the winters, and they have had a huge impact on who I am today. But I want to clarify that my mother was similar to them in her beliefs. It has only been since her death that my father has become so narrow-minded in his regard for others, and it seems that the older he gets, the more insular he becomes."

As soon as the men resumed their approach towards the house, Julia grabbed a light coat and was out the door like a flash to meet them.

"Hello, Robert and Gustav. Whatever has kept you so long? We have been worried sick about what has happened and it has not helped one bit when the two of you stand in the yard looking so ominous. The least you could do is come and tell the rest of us," Julia said indignantly.

"You are quite right, my darling—although we did need to sort out a couple of things before we came in to convey our news," Robert replied as he gently embraced Julia.

⇒∼ 84 ∼⇐

Well, now, this was worth the wait. One of the Silent Critics who happened to be in the general store when Phillip received the telephone call that day was certain she had overheard him quietly say to his wife that Julia was bringing home a guest for Easter. Yet, when the train finally departed and they could again observe all of the goings-on from their choice seats in the hotel overlooking Main Street, they saw only Julia walking home with her parents. That was most unusual, particularly because Phillip was carrying not one but two suitcases while Margareta and Julie leisurely strolled along, each holding another. What had they missed with Rudolf Schultz's poor positioning of the restaurant that they practically supported with their daily patronage?

After lengthy conjecture that started over morning coffee and resumed after dinner, the Silent Critics were about to leave the hotel when one of the less vocal men of their group noticed Gustav Werner riding into town, sharing his steed with another person. Deciding they could not leave yet, they returned to their seats and were rewarded by observing the surreptitious exchange between the two men in the Mohrs' front yard and, much more importantly, the highly irregular demonstration of affection between Julia Mohr and a man. That did it. How could they go home now, when presented with such grist for the rumour mill of Neudorf?

Given the gravity of their tidings, Gustav asked Julia to expedite the introduction between her father and Robert so he could apprise his aunt and uncle of the events of the morning. However, the moment the three young people reached the house, Phillip flung open the door, extended his right hand to his guest, and said, "Welcome to Neudorf. I am Phillip Mohr, Julia's father, and I am happy to make your acquaintance. Hello, Gustav, good to see you on a Saturday. Both of you, please come in and have some dinner; you must be starving by now. Or have you eaten already? I know Margareta will be most disappointed if you had your meal at the farm."

Robert noticed that his host's greeting was the antithesis of how he had been received at the Werner household. He warmly replied, "Hello, Mr. Mohr. I am Robert Cameron. I have looked forward to meeting you for some time now. Fortunately, I still have an appetite even after three pieces of Amelia Werner's sumptuous fresh bread with my favourite jelly. She told me where she had picked the chokecherries and promised that next fall she would take me with her to the best berry patches."

"Well, Robert, I'm glad you have a healthy appetite, as my dear wife believes that the way to a man's heart is through his stomach. She has had a feast ready in anticipation of your arrival for the past hour, so let's go into the kitchen."

Before they could proceed, Gustav had to intercede. "Uncle Phillip and Julia, I have to tell you that Friedrich has had an accident. I found him this morning partially immersed in the creek, which had frozen lightly during the night. We don't know when he came home or what he was trying to do, but it was obvious that he had been run over by his car. He died shortly after Robert and I reached the farm. Now we will never find out anything except that he had bought a new automobile, which looks very different from the previous one he owned. Oh, yes, and we also know that Papa wants it removed from his land as soon as possible, which he made abundantly clear after hearing that Friedrich was dead. The rest of us are very grateful to Dr. Cameron. In addition to confirming that Friedrich had passed away, Robert was the only one who could calm poor Mathias, who naturally was devastated by seeing his father lying dead on his mama's bed."

"What a wretched way for a little boy to see his father," Julia sighed.

"I suppose that thoughtless Friedrich had been drinking again. I'm sorry, Dr. Cameron; I don't mean to speak ill of the dead, but unfortunately Friedrich Werner had a reputation and I often wondered how alcohol and driving an automobile would mix," Phillip stated emphatically.

"There is no need for you to apologize, Mr. Mohr, and as it happens you are quite correct. The smell of alcohol was very apparent when I leaned over your nephew to check if he was still breathing. It was a tragic way for a man to die, and particularly when he had such a young family. No doubt he will be sadly missed," Robert said compassionately.

The three relatives furtively glanced at one another and tacitly decided to go into no more details about the disreputable Friedrich to a man newly introduced to Julia's family. But Gustav could not leave the subject yet.

"Uncle Phillip, we have to tell Aunt Margareta. Should we do it now or wait until after we have eaten?"

"No, Gustav, I have never been able to keep anything from your aunt; she instantly knows when something is wrong," Phillip answered. "We will go into the kitchen before she comes out and immediately give her the news, so that right after dinner I can go to the lumberyard to tell Peter, and you can accompany her to the store to let Katherina know that her eldest brother is dead. Then we must arrange to meet with Johann and Karolina and Sofia and Karl, and on your way home, I am sure you are planning to stop in to see Rolf and Katie. In fact, there will be many arrangements to make, and we will need to rely on Margareta's wonderful ability to organize the lot of us." Phillip finally led them to the kitchen, where his wife was busily making a fresh pot of coffee.

⚡ 86 ⚡

It was almost midnight before Gustav finally climbed into bed exhausted. He cautiously slid under the quilt on his side of the iron-framed double bed so he would not disturb Amelia, who was sleeping soundly. He often marvelled at how quickly his young wife could fall asleep, while lately his own mind kept him awake sometimes into the early hours of the morning. But such would not be the case tonight. The day had been so full of tragic and unexpected events that he was completely drained of energy, and he did not want to think about the fact that his oldest brother was dead. Then there was his father's unusual response to the death of his firstborn. As the sweet, compelling grip of sleep carried him away, Gustav puzzled over what was happening to Christian Werner.

True to her nature, Margareta had started to formulate the necessary arrangements for Friedrich's funeral almost as soon as her husband had apprised her of the calamity at the Werner farm. She knew immediately that her nephew would feel responsible for his negligent brother, and said, "Oh, Gustav, I am sorry to hear about Friedrich, but you must not blame yourself that you did not find him sooner."

Robert turned and looked at his future mother-in-law with admiration for her astuteness: "Thank you, Mrs. Mohr," he replied. "Regardless of what I have said, I have not been able to convince Gustav that he could not have saved Friedrich's life. Perhaps he will believe you and let go of his misguided feelings of culpability."

"I assure you, Robert, that I shall not allow my nephew, who is like my other son, to carry the burden of guilt for a man who has been irresponsible and courted disaster for most of his life. Now before we talk any more about Friedrich or make plans for his funeral, let us sit down and enjoy the meal I have prepared to welcome you into our home." Margareta linked one arm around him and the other about Julia and led them to her table, which was heavily laden with delicious-smelling food.

When everyone at the table was satiated to the point of not being able to move, Margareta was ready to deal with the essential details to properly bring closure to a deceased person's life.

"As it is not fair to expect Maria or even Hanna to handle what has to be done, I will need to prepare Friedrich's body for burial; but I know it is not a good idea for either Phillip or me to go with you to the farm. Gustav, I think the solution is for you to hitch Wolfgang and Kaiser to the democrat wagon and pick up Rolf on your way home to help you. Once the two of you have placed the body in the carriage, you can return to town, and while Phillip meets with Reverend Biber, I will perform the necessary preparations. It does mean another trip to Neudorf for you, Gustav, but it may keep peace in the family."

Once again, Gustav was astonished by his aunt's uncanny prophetic sense about what would transpire; although, as it turned out, on this occasion she was inaccurate in at least one aspect of her prediction. Instead of making two trips to town during the course of the long day, Gustav would be required to return to town for yet a third time before nightfall. All had gone according to Margareta's carefully orchestrated plan until Gustav and Rolf were about to leave the Werner farm with Friedrich's body securely positioned in the back of Phillip's wagon. The two men had just climbed up onto the wooden seat when Christian charged out of the house.

"I suppose that meddlesome sister of mine has put you up to this, and for once in her life she is right! It's a damn good thing you are taking Friedrich's dead body out of my house, but I have news for you. I not only want him off my farm today, but I also want that noisy contraption gone as well."

"Papa, that may have to wait until tomorrow. It is already getting late," Gustav replied and prepared to give the horses the command to start moving.

To both Gustav's and Rolf's surprise, their father started to yell. "I will not take no for an answer. As soon as you have delivered your dead brother to your relatives, you will come back to pull his piece of junk out of the creek and get it off my land. I do not want it scaring my cows when they go for a drink of water."

By now, Christian was ranting and raving as he had done that unforgettable day in the cemetery, and Gustav knew it would be impossible to try to reason with him.

"All right, Papa. I will bring the horses back and haul Friedrich's car away today. Now go back into the house and calm down before you drop dead from all your exertion."

As soon as they were out of Christian's earshot, Rolf turned to his younger brother and said, "What was that all about? I have never seen Papa react so violently, especially considering that one of his children has just died."

"Well, I have certainly witnessed Papa's outbursts before, but I am as dumbfounded as you by the way he is responding to Friedrich's death. He has been acting strange lately, and you should have seen how he treated Dr. Cameron this morning. I have no idea what is wrong with him. What a good thing that Phillip did not come to the farm with me. He might have taken Papa aside and told him to smarten up, and who knows what would have happened then. Aunt Margareta was definitely right about me bringing you."

Gustav hesitated for a moment and then added pensively, "More and more it seems that Amelia is the only person Papa is civil to, and occasionally his grandchildren, when he takes them for a walk to show them his land."

"So, what are you going to do? There isn't much point in me coming back with you to pull the car from the creek because I don't know how to drive it, and I need to help Katie with the girls. Now that she is close to her time, she becomes tired so quickly that I don't like to leave her alone for very long," Rolf asked earnestly.

"I don't want to keep you away from your family, so I will drop you at home on the way to Neudorf and maybe get Peter to come back to the farm with me," Gustav answered. He cracked the reins and commanded, "Giddy-up, Wolfgang and Kaiser, giddy-up."

Eventually it was Peter and Robert who climbed onto Kaiser's back to make the trip to the Werner farm before the sun set in the western horizon. Phillip had been furious when Gustav had told his aunt and uncle about his father's unreasonable demand, and tried to talk his nephew into waiting until the morning. "I have just met with Reverend Biber and he has consented to arrange for Friedrich's funeral after the church service tomorrow. We don't have room for Friedrich's body in our house any more than your father does, so we will keep his coffin at the lumber store overnight. If you take Kaiser to pull the car from the creek, how will one of us let Johann and Sofia know that their brother is dead? It would be cruel to wait until they arrive for church and then tell them they have Friedrich's burial to attend."

"Uncle Phillip, you have not seen Papa for a long time, and you don't understand that lately when he has made up his mind about something, he is as ferocious as a dog watching over his bone. If I don't do what he ordered, no one will get any sleep tonight at the farm. I realize it is complicated, but like Aunt Margareta, I want to try and keep peace in the family at this dreadful time. Perhaps you could ask Reverend Biber if you could borrow his horse. I think he would understand, and after all, as Friedrich's father-in-law, he is a relative. Besides, first thing tomorrow morning, I want to ride over to tell Andrew and Sarah because they will want to come and be with us."

"Even if I am able to get his horse, who will go back to the farm with you?" Phillip replied, beginning to relent. It was unlike Gustav to be so insistent and, as Phillip looked closer, he saw weariness in the young man's eyes. Phillip was not alone in his observations. Robert Cameron had also been watching Gustav as the men sat at the table drinking coffee. He saw the strain on Gustav's face, and thought he was trying to shoulder far too much of the responsibility for the morning's catastrophic event.

Wanting to come to his aid, Robert suggested, "Peter, what if you and I accompany Gustav to the farm? I have been learning to drive an automobile and I could steer while you and Gustav guide the horses to pull the car out of the creek and haul it to town."

In the short time he had known Julia's gentleman friend, Peter was quickly starting to like this man who treated everyone with a natural openness and respect. "Sure, I will come with you, but after what Gustav said about Uncle Christian's reaction to you, do you want to return to the Werner farm?"

For the first time that day, laughter was heard in the Mohr home when Robert wryly replied, "If I see him coming, I shall start running in the opposite direction!"

～ 87 ～

When he woke in the diffused light of dawn, Gustav saw that Amelia's side of the bed was empty. As he lay on his back for a few minutes to stretch his limbs, he was reminded of his father's words, not so long ago, about Amelia's singular capacity for work. Gustav was an early riser, but it was rare when he was out of bed before his wife—although this morning she must have awakened even earlier than usual. It was as if she knew today would be onerous, although he had not told any of them that Friedrich's funeral had been so quickly arranged.

Rising and pulling on his work clothes, Gustav went into the kitchen to find Amelia setting the table and boiling the water for porridge. The scent of the freshly brewed coffee was instantly appealing, and Gustav said, "Good morning, Amelia. Sit down and have a cup of coffee with me before everyone else comes in for breakfast. I would like to talk to you about some important matters."

With more than a little trepidation, Amelia glanced at Gustav as she reached for two mugs and did as he requested. She never sat down at the table until all of the food was ready and she had served the entire family. Fortunately, her husband came straight to the point, and as soon as she was seated, said, "Uncle Phillip has arranged for Reverend Biber to have Friedrich's funeral today right after the church service. We realize it looks like we are rushing things, but we really don't have much of a choice. Papa was so angry with me yesterday that I don't think I should be the one to tell him. When he has finished his breakfast, would you ask him to come to Neudorf for his son's burial? I have noticed that you are able to talk to him and get him to help you do things, whereas he always seems to be cross with me."

It took Amelia a few minutes to respond. She was so touched by Gustav's comments that she felt tears rush to her eyes. She had often wondered if her husband had any awareness of her contributions to his family, since he never said a word. When she was certain she was in control, Amelia answered, "Yes, when I am serving Papa his coffee at the end of his meal, I will find a way to let him know about Friedrich's funeral. But I am not sure he will listen to me either. As much as I have thought about it, I have not been able to understand why he acted so strangely yesterday when Friedrich died, and I could not get him to tell me why it was necessary for you to move his automobile off the farm right away. Now, if that is all you wanted to say, I must get back to work; if I hurry, I will still have time this morning to do some baking for the lunch, which will probably be at the Mohrs' house. Oh dear, your papa will figure that out too and then it will not matter what I say to him. As we both know, he is fiercely determined to never set foot in the Mohr household again."

Gustav looked at Amelia with surprise; he had no idea that she knew about his father's quarrel with Uncle Phillip and Aunt Margareta. As he got up from the table, he made a mental note to pay more attention to his wife whose involvement with his family members was startling, and perhaps exceeded his own. "Well, do the best you can, and thank you, Amelia. Would you also ask Hanna to do the milking? I want to ride over to the Thompsons' farm and tell Andrew and Sarah our bad news."

88

The little church in Neudorf was filled to capacity, as it was every Sunday morning. For some time now Reverend Biber and the deacons had talked about the need for a larger building, but they had yet to involve the members of the congregation in their discussion. From the moment he woke on that bright spring morning, Reverend Biber had mulled over whether to tell his flock about Friedrich Werner's funeral before or after his sermon. He still felt some resentment towards Phillip for urging him to arrange the burial so hastily, but as he was shaving he had to acknowledge that he once again had readily acquiesced to his affable friend. Konrad Biber and Phillip Mohr had known each other for their entire lives, and even as a middle-aged man, Konrad had retained his admiration and its accompanying sentiment—envy—for Phillip, who made a success of his every venture.

While Reverend Biber stood at the pulpit waiting for his congregants to file in and take their seats in the wooden pews, it occurred to him that he needed to develop a better sense of reciprocity. Since he had done a favour for Phillip, maybe he could scratch his back and get a very reasonable price, if not an actual donation, of the lumber needed to enlarge their place of worship. The thought instantly improved his state of mind, and Konrad Biber decided on the spot to shorten his usually lengthy sermon, and while he had a full house, deliver a heart-rending eulogy for his son-in-law, who had regrettably run over himself with his most prized possession. So, on that warm day in April when the radiant sun promised the end of winter, the only folks in the overflowing church not surprised by the most unlikely short Sunday morning service were the Silent Critics.

Glued to their perches at the hotel like birds patiently waiting for their quarry, they saw all of the action outside the Mohr household on the previous day. At first when Gustav returned to town with the democrat wagon pulled by the two horses, and the men filed out to help him carry a carefully wrapped body into the house, they immediately thought Christian Werner had died. The irony that he was being taken into the Mohr home was lost on none of the Silent Critics; although, as one was quick to point out, he was not exactly entering on his own two feet. Since it was now mid-afternoon, the Silent Critics decided to stay longer and have a farewell drink to a man whom they had all respected, if for no other reason than that he had adamantly stood up to Margareta Mohr.

It was not until the late afternoon, as the sun was going over the horizon and they could scarcely see through the darkening shadows, that they observed the same two horses, now pulling an automobile that was delivered to the rear of the general store. The Silent Critics clearly had to revise their initial assumption. The only option was that it must be Friedrich's body that had been carried surreptitiously into the Mohr home, since he was the only member of the Werner family to drive a car.

Hence, when Reverend Biber announced that the morning service would be shortened to allow for Friedrich Werner's funeral, the congregants began to understand the presence of the family's English friends in their church. Nonetheless, not one faithful congregation member rose to leave as their kindly minister began the obsequies for one of the younger men of their close-knit community who abruptly departed from their midst. During the lunch served at the Mohr home, it was repeated that Friedrich would have been well pleased with the numbers in attendance for his final appearance in the church that he had rarely frequented. Although many must have thought it, there was not a whisper that the only obvious person missing was the dead man's father.

89

He had never stayed out all night before. There were countless times when she had sat by the small window into the early hours of the morning, anxiously watching for him to come staggering down the street. When he was close to the building she would go down to the door, open it to let him in, and then help him climb the two flights of rickety stairs to the one-room flat above the bakery. But this morning, the sun would soon be up and she had to go into the shop and begin baking the bread and sweets for the daily sales. Anastasia rose slowly from the uncomfortable chair, rubbing the lower portion of her back, and wondered how much bigger she would get before this baby finally decided to come into the world. As she struggled into a dress that barely fit over her expanding belly, neither for the first nor the last time she admonished herself for having a child with a man who was so similar to her own father.

Shuddering, Anastasia suddenly remembered how when she was thirteen years of age, she had thrown her meagre belongings into her treasured pillowcase, lovingly embroidered for her by her mother before she died, and walked away from the Litzenberger farm seven miles north of Neudorf. It was not until her father had started to come very close to her, patting her hair or caressing her arms and upper body, that Anastasia had become alarmed.

Over the years, she had come to expect his beatings, and now was frequently able to circumvent them by jumping beyond his reach. She did not understand what her father intended to do with her, but that afternoon when he had kissed her on the mouth, she felt sick to her stomach, as much from his unnatural behaviour as from his rancid breath. She managed to pull away from his clumsy grasp and run out of the house. She kept running until she reached the ravine, her favourite place on the farm, and hid among the trees and underbrush. At first she heard him yelling at her to come back in and cook his meal; but then he must have returned indoors. Once again, only the songs of the meadowlarks and the sound of the gentle breeze whistling through the willows pierced the stillness of the prairie.

The warm autumn sun was overhead when Anastasia's hunger interrupted her hiding. She knew her father would never find her in the ravine where she came on Sunday afternoons to play in her make-believe home surrounded by the protective branches of the trees. Venturing beyond the imaginary walls of her tree house, Anastasia found a chokecherry tree still laden with berries and ate until she had appeased her appetite. Then, feeling tired, she found a thick patch of prairie grass and lay down to sleep. When Anastasia awoke from a dream in which she had run away from the farm, she rose from her resting place and knew that was exactly what she would do. She crept back to the house, quietly opened the door, and listened for any sounds of her father. Hearing a welcome silence, she sneaked into her tiny bedroom tucked behind the wall of the kitchen, quickly gathered her few possessions, and grabbing the half loaf of bread on the table as she rushed by, was back out the door and gone.

A full moon lit the boundless Saskatchewan night and with no idea of how she would make her escape, she steadily put one foot in front of the other until she reached the outskirts of town, just as a fiery red sun peeped over the horizon. Anastasia knew she had at least until mid-morning before her father would arouse from his drunken stupor, realize that he was hungry, and then wobble into the kitchen demanding his breakfast.

When Anastasia came to the railway tracks, she saw the open door of the boxcar of the stationary freight train and immediately scrambled inside, going to the farthest corner to hide in the dark. It was not long before she heard the whistle blow; then the train slowly started to move. When it picked up speed, Anastasia finally started to relax, realizing that she succeeded in her flight. She did not take the time to check the position of the engine, and therefore she neither knew nor cared in what direction she was headed. Sighing with relief, she reached inside her pillowcase, took out the bread, and tore off a piece to eat as she leaned back against the secure side of the railway car.

It seemed only minutes later that Anastasia woke with a start; a man in dark blue clothes was shaking her and saying, "Come on, Missy. This is as far as you can go; and what a lucky thing that I saw you all curled up in the corner. Soon this boxcar will be full of grain, and it would have been the end of you. Gather up your bag and take my hand so I can help you down." Shaking herself awake, Anastasia had enough sense to ask the kindly stranger, "Please, sir, can you tell me where the train has stopped?"

"This is Melville, and the train stops here to load the grain from all of the farms in the surrounding area and take it to the elevator in Regina. Why have you stowed away on this train? Have you come to town to visit a relative?" the brakeman asked, both with considerable relief that he had averted a tragedy and more than a little suspicious about the motives of the young girl travelling alone on the train.

Fortunately, years of jumping out of the way of her abusive father's fists had quickened not only Anastasia's reflexes but her mind too; from the corner of her eye she caught sight of the sign for Helmut and Anna's Bakery.

Her reply came instantly. "Yes. I have come to Melville to visit my Uncle Helmut and Aunt Anna."

"Oh, the Schmidts will be so happy to have a young relative come to stay. With no family of their own, they are always trying to entice—and with great success, I might add—the town's children into their store with their delicious sweets. Well, run along and, from now on, remember: no more stowing away in a boxcar. The next time you want to ride on the train you must buy a ticket."

The brakeman had unknowingly provided Anastasia with just the information she needed to find a place to work, and once she had proven herself, maybe even a roof over her head. Thanking the tall slender man who already saved her life at least once today, she turned away and walked into the bakery. A robust woman in her forties with bright green eyes and an expansive smile greeted her the moment she opened the door. When Anastasia returned her salutation, she felt a surge of emotion that she had never experienced before, and within the hour she had confided the squalid details of her miserable existence to the matronly woman as though they had known each other for years. By that evening, Anastasia was taken into the Schmidts' home like a long-lost daughter, and from that day forward she worked side by side with Helmut and Anna in the bakery and lived with them in their three-room flat on the second floor.

For the first week, every time the little bell above the bakery door jingled, Anastasia peered nervously at whomever had entered, afraid that it was her father coming to take her home. One day, noticing Anastasia's worried look, Anna assuaged her apprehension: "My child, you can stop fretting about that worthless excuse of a father. The only way he will ever take you away from me is over my dead body."

Anastasia looked at the woman who seemed to love her from the moment they met, and realizing that her father would never have the courage to stand up to someone so formidable, laid her fears to rest. As the years passed, everyone in the town forgot to question whence the thin child with the long, blond, wispy hair and rabbit-like movements had come. She went to church with Helmut and Anna, and visited friends and family with them until she simply became known as "the Schmidt girl."

When Anastasia became an adult, Anna asked her quiet, gentle husband to clean out the attic and to build a small flat so their adopted daughter could have a place of her own. Over the years, with Anastasia's help and her illimitable energy, the Schmidt Bakery had steadily flourished, and there now was enough money to make life more comfortable for all of them. Life was full of harmony for Anna and Helmut, who both doted on Anastasia as she grew into a beautiful and engaging young lady, and they had a difficult time containing their delight when customers commented on the relationship between the young woman and her parents. In fact, it was not until the day that Friedrich Werner walked through the front door of the bakery to buy apple strudel that there was the slightest indication of any acrimony between mother and daughter.

It was instant infatuation for Anastasia when she saw the tall, sturdy man with the deep blue eyes and ruddy complexion; at the same time, Anna took an immediate dislike to this smooth talker who was forward enough to compliment her daughter before they were even introduced. As quickly as Anna saw through Friedrich's charm, Anastasia, who had not had any other suitors, was beguiled by it, and no amount of warning from her mother could convince her that there was a lesser man within Friedrich Werner than met the eye. Soon he appeared at the bakery every day at closing time to invite Anastasia to go walking with him. Then several weeks later, on a cold rainy night when Anastasia cautiously answered the door of her flat to Friedrich's soft tapping and his story that his landlady had locked him out, she let him come in. Before the night was over, he had bedded the unsuspecting twenty-year-old.

When Anna and Helmut learned that Friedrich had moved in with their daughter, they were appalled; but regardless of their determination to have him leave their home, he returned every night and was admitted by the love-sick Anastasia, who could hardly wait for the end of the day to feel his arms around her again. Although Friedrich no longer went into the bakery, every day was filled with tension caused by the estrangement between Anastasia and her parents. Surprisingly, Helmut was more open to the unacceptable living arrangement that Anastasia had entered, trying to tell his wife that they had to allow her to lead her own life.

Anna angrily responded, "Then why does he not marry her? We don't know anything about this man!"

"And we knew even less about Anastasia," countered Helmut, "when we took her into our family seven years ago."

Finally, one morning Anastasia broke through the silence, which had existed far too long between mother and daughter; she abruptly burst into tears as they kneaded the dough to make the daily bread.

"Oh, Mama, I miss talking to you, especially now when I have so many questions to ask you. I can't stand it anymore!"

Turning to face her adoptive daughter, Anna could not stop the tears that welled up in her own eyes from flowing down her cheeks, and soon they were huddled together on the floor, both sobbing as they held each other tightly. As it happened, their reconciliation was timely; Anna soon put two and two together and determined that Anastasia was with child.

In the evenings, as Helmut and Anna sat around the kitchen table, they talked about their feelings, which vacillated between outrage and shame that their beloved daughter would have a baby out of wedlock and pure joy that they would be blessed with a grandchild. An infant had never lived under the Schmidt's roof, and the prospect was at once as daunting as it was exhilarating. At first they agreed that Helmut should try to force this man who sneaked up to their daughter's flat at night like a beast of prey to marry Anastasia, but then Anna worried that he might take both mother and child away from them. On the other hand, if she did not become Friedrich Werner's wife, what would they say to their friends and customers when Anastasia's body began to swell with her growing baby?

After much discussion they decided to say nothing at all. As soon as Anastasia started to gain weight, Helmut would keep her in the back of the bakery to work with him, and regardless of how many customers asked for her, Anna would not provide an answer but instead return to the front counter to sell to customers as she had before Anastasia had come to live with them. When her time came, they would discreetly ask Anna's sister to help with the delivery and then swear her to secrecy. As Helmut and Anna had done previously when they had taken Anastasia into their family and home, they would ignore the wagging tongues of the townspeople until they simply came to accept the infant as the

Schmidts' grandchild. The only fly in the ointment would be the baby's father, and Anna feverishly hoped and prayed that he would go away as suddenly as he had arrived.

Then one morning Anastasia told them that Friedrich had not come home the previous night. When that first day elapsed into another and another, and soon weeks began to slip by, and still there was no sign of him, Anna began to believe that her prayers had been answered.

~ 90 ~

When they were comfortably seated on the train, both Robert and Julia sat pensively gazing out the window. As the train steadily picked up speed, they watched the thawing prairie fly by and reveal its surging shoots of fresh green grass. Robert was so deep in thought that at first he did not hear Julia until she gently shook his shoulder, and then it took a minute to focus on what she was saying. He had been thinking about Mathias, who was five years younger than he had been when he lost his father, and he fervently hoped the boy would not experience the frightening nightmares that had recurred most nights until Robert was almost fifteen years old. For nearly two years he had been so fixated on death that finally his grandfather, a physician, had arranged for him to see one of his old classmates who had specialized in conditions of the mind.

None of his treatments had helped. Nothing had changed until the spring two years after his father had passed away. Robert was walking in the hills behind the family home in Sussex, when he slowly become aware of the returning signs of life all around him. He stopped and listened to the songs of the birds, heralding the reappearance of the sun's warmth after the icy grip of winter. He went up to the trees and gently touched their opening buds and watched as they unfurled their tiny, bright green leaves. A plethora of wildflowers were peeking around the slender blades of grass thrusting up from their dried-out brown roots. Everywhere the perennial essence of nature was evident, and as Robert lay down on a soft grassy knoll, where the sun had hastened the growth of what he considered God's carpet, he felt the energy and permanence of the awakening earth. Eventually, nature and time helped him to heal and it was then that Robert decided to follow in his grandfather's footsteps and become a doctor.

"Robert, are you all right? You seem so far away; I hope you are not thinking about how my relatives took over our plans this past week," Julia said with an anxious expression on her beautiful face. Robert slowly came out of his reverie and, looking into her concerned sky-blue eyes, replied, "No, my darling Julia; first of all, as a guest in your parents' home, I expected to go along with whatever was happening, and certainly no one could have foreseen your cousin's untimely demise. In fact, I am happy that I could help. Actually, I was thinking about Mathias and remembering when my own father died very suddenly, when I was thirteen. I have never told you about my difficulties at that time, but I definitely scared my mother and her family with my inability to accept that he was gone forever. I just hope and pray that Mathias can deal with the finality of death better than I did."

"You are welcome to tell me more about how you felt, but I suspect you were closer to your father than Mathias was to Friedrich. In many ways, Gustav has been like a father to those three children, since Friedrich spent so little time at home over the past few years. I think he hardly even knew Elisabetha because he left to work in Melville before her birth, and to the best of my knowledge, he only came back for brief stays at Christmas. The girls will barely miss him, and I'm sure Gustav will involve Mathias in what he is doing so he works through his grief. Gustav certainly understands the importance of coming to terms with death after what he experienced when Aunt Elisabetha died three years ago. But from what you have said, the person we need to worry about is Uncle Christian."

"Since I don't know your uncle, it is complicated for me to make a diagnosis, but I wonder if he might be showing some signs of senility. However, when he brought his money to the kitchen table and demanded that Gustav give it to me, he knew exactly what he was doing," Robert replied with a grin that made him look much more youthful. Soon after they had met, Julia saw that when Robert smiled his appearance changed from the serious demeanour of the conscientious physician to that of a boyish-looking student who had just played an outlandish prank on one of his professors.

"In all fairness, Uncle Christian was a very different person when Aunt Elisabetha was alive. I don't think he has ever really accepted that she is gone; he still misses her dreadfully. Then when he had that big fight with Katherina and stopped going to Neudorf, he seemed to shut himself off from most people. My aunt was certainly the more talkative one, but Uncle Christian did enjoy visiting my parents and his other family members. Now it seems he never leaves the farm, and almost everyone is afraid of going to see him. Gustav said there are days when the only person he talks to is Amelia."

"Well, I can't imagine anyone not getting along with Amelia. She is one of the sweetest people I have ever met—next to you, of course," Robert quickly answered with a twinkle in his soft, greenish eyes.

"You are able to recover immediately, aren't you? Although, as it happens, my dearest Robert, I entirely agree with you. Amelia looks as young as a child, and yet she seems wise beyond her years, and she brings out the best in everyone she meets. Now with three women to love Mathias, Julianna, and Elisabetha, those children will become thoroughly spoiled!" Julia said as she rested her head on Robert's shoulder.

"I wonder if you can spoil a child with love. I have never been as happy as I am now, knowing that you love me enough to become my wife and to spend the rest of your life with me. So if adults need love and affection to feel contented and whole, how can we possibly think that loving and caring for children will lead to their ruin? I think the opposite might be quite true, that the child who feels loved will mature into a well-adjusted adult and will then be concerned about other people. Indeed, I think you and I are living proof of my belief. As an only child, people were always telling my mother that she would pay for the way she indulged me, particularly after Father died. And it was very apparent to me this past week that both of your parents dearly love you and Peter. Yet neither your character nor mine seems to have been irreparably damaged or flawed because we were loved and maybe even pampered as children."

"Once again, I must agree with you," replied Julia. "I really don't see much point in having children unless you are prepared to love them, although many days I wonder about some of my students' parents. On the other hand, I hope Amelia soon becomes a mother. I could hardly watch her when she was with Maria's children; her eyes were so full of longing that it was almost painful to be near her."

The train pulled into the station, bringing their short journey to an end.

91

It would take Amelia a very long time to overcome her feelings of guilt and to forgive herself for not recognizing much sooner what was happening in the Schweitzer household. It was not because they were not visiting her father, Katie, and Franz regularly. After Christmas, Gustav was as good as his word, and nearly every Saturday, unless the weather was too inclement during the bleak mid-winter months, they had hitched Wolfgang to the light cutter and spent the day with the Schweitzer family, and sometimes the night, if a blizzard suddenly appeared and claimed the bald prairie. Once or twice as the weather warmed, and Katie wore lighter clothing in the house, Amelia noticed the black and blue marks on her arms and legs. But when she questioned her, Katie passed it off as being clumsy and having fallen down the basement stairs, and Amelia was only too eager to believe her.

In the early hours of the Friday morning of the week following Friedrich's funeral, Amelia shook herself awake from a dream about Katie. Amelia was in her father's house talking to her youngest sister as they were making pickles, but Katie would not look at her. Finally, Amelia walked in front of her and jumped back with a shriek; Katie had no face. Amelia had no idea what her nightmare meant, but she was much too restive to stay in bed; she quietly got up, pulled on her clothes over her nightdress, and went to the kitchen. She stoked the few remaining burning embers, wondering what time Gustav had arisen during the night to feed the ever-hungry, charcoal-black beast of burden. As Amelia added kindling and larger pieces of wood to encourage the dying fire back to life, she recalled her delight when she had entered the Werner home months ago and the first thing to catch her eye was the cast-iron cooking stove.

The longer she waited for Gustav to join her, the more anxious she became. Amelia hoped her husband would be the first member of the family to come out of the bedrooms so they could sit and have coffee together before everyone was up. By unspoken agreement, they had continued the practice since the morning after Friedrich's death, and bit by bit, Amelia was learning to talk to the man her father had chosen for her to marry. Until that morning almost a week ago, when Gustav had asked her to sit with him, it had not occurred to Amelia that the only time they were alone was when they were preparing for bed. Then it was far too cold in their bedroom to do anything but quickly change into their nightclothes and climb under the down quilt with its welcoming warmth. When they were lying beside each other, Amelia would remain quiet, waiting to see if Gustav would gently reach for her.

As the sky was slowly turning to light, with pastel blues and pinks streaking across the horizon, Gustav came into the kitchen.

"Good morning, Amelia. Is it just in my mind or are you getting up earlier and earlier every morning?"

"Hello, Gustav, here is your coffee. This morning I have been awake for a long time because I had a bad dream and I could not go back to sleep. Could we please go to see my family today rather than wait until tomorrow? Something is wrong at my father's house and I must go home to find out what it is," Amelia said, with more certainty than Gustav had ever heard from her.

"How can you possibly know that anything is happening with your family? You have not seen them for almost two weeks. I feel badly that we did not get to visit them last Saturday, but since they didn't know Friedrich, I didn't ride over and tell your father about the funeral on Sunday. Not that I had any time after all of my trips back and forth to Neudorf," said Gustav, as he sipped the scalding coffee.

"I have had a strange feeling ever since I awoke from my dream. It was about Katie, and I have an uneasiness that I cannot explain. I just know that things are not right." She could not bring herself to tell her husband what she had seen in her dream for fear that he would think she was being silly. Instead, Amelia sat with a faraway look in her grey-blue eyes, as though she was trying to see across the prairie into the home where she had been born and raised.

"I was planning to get the grain for seeding today, but I can go to Neudorf tomorrow. In fact, you could come with me and spend some time with Katherina in her shop. She was telling me on Sunday that she has some new dresses she thought you might like to buy. So as soon as we have eaten breakfast and have finished the chores, we will get ready to go to your father's house. I know you will want some time to prepare food to bring with us but we should be ready to leave in about two hours," Gustav replied agreeably.

Long before they could see the Schweitzer farmhouse, Gustav was inclined to think Amelia was accurate in her prediction. After having made the trip so many times during the winter, he knew at what distance he could see smoke curling up from the chimney of the three-room log house; but this morning, although the sky was perfectly clear, there was no indication of fire. Even though the weather was warming as spring reclaimed the country, he thought it unusual for his father-in-law to let the only source of heat die during the night, not to mention that they would have needed the fire to cook their breakfast. Gustav glanced sideways towards his wife and saw that she was still sitting with her eyes focused straight ahead and her lips pursed, as she had since they had left home.

The farmyard was eerily silent, with no indication of life anywhere.

"Your family must be away," said Gustav. "Perhaps they went to visit Wilhelmina and Peter after they finished the milking this morning."

No sooner had he said the words, when from the corner of his eye he caught sight of the two Schweitzer cows on the far side of the barn, their udders full, with milk leaking from the teats. Gustav had barely pulled back on the reins and commanded Wolfgang to stop before Amelia was climbing down from the carriage. "Just wait, Amelia, and I will come around to help you."

"I know they have not gone visiting. I told you that something has happened," Amelia whispered, which only accentuated the alarm in her voice.

"I don't know how you can be so sure, but you will bide your time until I have tied up Wolfgang and I can come with you into the house."

Gustav knocked as he called out his greeting, but he did not hesitate long before he opened the door. With Amelia right behind him, they entered the bone-chilling house. In the shadowy kitchen, the rays of the morning sun reflected off the tin stove, which was as lifeless as a man whose heart had stopped beating. The room was in total disarray, with chairs overturned, broken dishes on the floor, and scraps of bread strewn about, as though a gale had swept through the small house.

Taking care not to step on any fragments of porcelain, Gustav gently reached for Amelia's hand and said, "Follow in my footsteps so you don't cut yourself or trip over anything while we go to look in the bedrooms." Much later, when Amelia thought about how protective Gustav had been, she flushed with the warmth of budding love.

They went first to the larger bedroom that Karl shared with his sons. The door was ajar, and the room looked as though it had been seized by the same forceful wind, its contents scattered like the straw from the mouth of the steam thresher after the wheat had been separated from its stalks. They searched through the scattered quilts and pillows, and Gustav even looked under the beds, but no one was to be found in the disorder. They gingerly made their way to the smaller room, which Amelia had shared with Katie for years after Wilhelmina had left to marry Peter. The light wooden door was firmly closed, and when Gustav tried to open it, it would not budge. Finally, he heaved with his shoulder and the chair that had been propped up against the knob to secure it gave way.

Neither Gustav nor Amelia had said a word since they had entered the house, and it seemed they were not even breathing audibly, so afraid of what they would find. Then, through the lurking darkness in the corner of the still, dim room that had no window and where night had yet to fade into the light of day, Amelia thought she saw someone or something huddled in the centre of the mid-sized bed. Silently turning towards Gustav, she tapped him on his arm and pointed, even as he nodded to indicate he had also seen the hump under the quilt. He motioned for her to stay at the foot of the bed while he approached the side and slowly pulled back the feather tick, to reveal Katie and Franz nestled together, sound asleep. After she breathed a sigh of relief, Amelia gently shook Katie's shoulder to awaken her.

Very little in Amelia's sheltered life had prepared her for the violence of Katie's reaction; she sprang out of her fetal position like an animal frightened by a sudden sharp noise, abruptly awakening Franz. Nothing could have softened the shock of seeing Katie's face. Even in the obscure light Amelia could see that both of her eyes were black and so swollen that only slits appeared through the swelling when she opened them.

"Oh, my God, what has happened to you?" Amelia said in shock as she knelt on the bed and gathered Katie into her sturdy arms, wanting to protect her even from Gustav's sight. In the warmth of Amelia's embrace, Katie began to whimper like a small child, and then to sob as though her heart was broken.

When Gustav could no longer stand to hear Katie's convulsive weeping, he reached over the bed, took Franz by the hand, and pulling the boy towards him, lifted him onto the floor. Quietly, Gustav said, "Come with me, Franz. We will go into the kitchen and start a fire to warm the house so we can have a meal. Put your clothes on over your nightshirt so you do not become chilled, and make sure you put on your shoes." Franz looked anxiously at Katie, and relieved that Amelia was back to take care of them, willingly went along with Gustav. At ten, Franz was two years older than Mathias; but in many ways, he seemed much younger. He was a quiet, sensitive boy with a slender build, unlike his two older brothers, who had their father's robust constitution. Whenever Gustav saw him clinging to one or the other of his sisters, it crossed his mind that Franz would have trouble in his life unless he soon developed some toughness.

The first thing Gustav did was locate the kerosene lamp, which fortunately had escaped the extensive breakage of the dishes, cups, and saucers. He cringed at the thought of what Amelia and he would have found had a lit lamp been thrown into the midst of whatever debacle had befallen this household. Although the sun now shone through the window, he wanted the extra light from the lamp as the two of them began to gather the fragments of broken porcelain.

"Franz, I will pick up the larger pieces, and then I want you to get the broom and sweep the splinters into the dustpan." Soon after he started the fire and set Franz to righting the chairs, Gustav returned to the bedroom.

"Amelia, we have straightened the kitchen enough so you and Katie can bring in the food from the carriage and start making dinner. I must go to the pasture and herd those poor cows into the barn before their teats become too swollen and sore to milk."

Grabbing two tin pails as he dashed out of the house, Gustav had hardly opened the barn door before the cows were at the pasture gate; as he unlatched it, they hurried into the small lean-to, straight to their stalls. So intent was he on relieving the animals of their nourishing burden that Gustav neither saw nor heard Karl Schweitzer until he had finished the milking and was herding the cows back outside. There he was, fast asleep on a bed of straw, covered with the horse blanket; lying beside him was an empty bottle of whiskey. Immediately Gustav had the answer to the question he could not bring himself to ask Franz nor pose to Katie. Walking over towards his loudly snoring father-in-law, Gustav smelled the reek of stale alcohol.

Wanting to shake Karl awake and bash him about as he had his youngest daughter, Gustav controlled the urge, knowing he would be no better than the stupefied man, who at least could claim the despicable excuse of being consumed by drink.

He forced himself to take a pail of milk in each hand and leave the barn, and as he walked towards the house, Gustav decided to ride to the Strauss farm. He was not prepared to do anything without first talking to Wilhelmina and Peter, but he knew Katie and Franz could not stay alone with their father. Setting the milk in the kitchen, Gustav took Amelia aside and said, "I have found your father in the barn. He is passed out from drink and I just left him sleeping it off. Can you separate the milk while I go and get your sister and her husband? Together we must decide what is to be done."

Later on that day when Karl sobered up, he could not believe what he had done to Katie. Although he was very contrite and tried to tell her how sorry he was, she would not look at him. Sitting around the kitchen table, her older sisters and their husbands were adamant that Katie had to leave her father's farm. When Wilhelmina proposed that Katie come to live with Peter and her, her youngest sister wrapped her arms around her in a grateful hug and promptly went into the bedroom to pack her meagre belongings. Before Franz could protest, Gustav looked at Amelia, and knowing how much she missed the brother she had raised from infancy, suggested that Franz come to live with them. During these arrangements, as his family was being meted out like seed grain to new homesteaders, Karl Schweitzer sat in silence, with his head bowed in shame. It was not lost on him that now, ten years after his wife had died, he would lose his two youngest children, when they were finally old enough to help him.

~ 92 ~

It was impossible to know whether Margareta or her niece was more excited about Katherina's invitation. From the day David had asked her to journey with his parents to attend his graduation from law school, the Mohr household had been a beehive of activity. Whereas Katherina was filled with anticipation about travelling to Saskatoon, a city that David had often told her was much more scenic than the capital of the province, her aunt was clearly focused on the implication of Katherina's inclusion in this significant family event. Naturally, Phillip teased his wife, saying that she was letting her imagination run as wild as a grass fire across the open prairie. But Margareta was firm in her conviction that after the celebratory dinner and dance at the newly opened Flanagan Hotel where the Hardy family had booked a suite, David would most likely propose to Katherina. When Phillip countered that David had yet to seek Christian Werner's permission, Margareta quickly replied that since her brother had seemingly disowned his daughter, his consent was no longer necessary.

During the late afternoon of the day before they were to take the morning train to Saskatoon, David's father came to Neudorf to pick Katherina up to spend the night with the Hardy family in Duff to facilitate their early start. As he tethered his horses to the hitching rail outside of the Mohr home, the sun nearly blinded William Hardy as it reflected off the fender of the automobile parked in the backyard. His curiosity was piqued, but before he had even considered how he could appease it, he looked up and saw Phillip walking home from his lumberyard. "Good afternoon. You have remarkable timing, Phillip. I was just wondering if I could have a closer look at Friedrich's car, which I presume is now on your property."

"Hello, William. You are quite right. When Christian insisted that Gustav haul it off his land, Robert was the only one who had ever been behind the wheel of a car, and so he steered it while the horses pulled it into town. And now there it sits, because there is no other place to park it, and no one has made any decision about what to do with it."

"Well, I would consider purchasing it; that is, if it is for sale. Mrs. Hardy and I were just saying the other day that perhaps it is time we sell our horses and buy an automobile. With Duff growing so fast, it is becoming increasingly harder to pasture them within the town limits."

"What an excellent idea! Of course, we will need to talk with Maria because rightfully it belongs to her, but I am sure that she would appreciate the proceeds for her children and herself. I cannot imagine that she ever saw much of Friedrich's earnings when he was alive, so it would be poetic justice for her to receive the money from his car. We often thought that Friedrich paid more attention to his automobiles than he did to his family," Phillip said with a hint of sarcasm. As the men talked, they walked around to the back of the house, and William opened the half door of the Ford Model T and sat behind the wheel.

"This vehicle is certainly an improvement over the first car that Friedrich drove to Duff to exhibit for the townspeople. Hopefully, its convenience will dispel its tragic history, and I think that once I have learned how to drive, Mrs. Hardy and I would be quite comfortable riding around the countryside in style. Would you please ask Maria on Sunday if she is willing to sell it to me and at what price?" William asked as he climbed out of the seat. He began checking under the hood and looking over the tires. "I have been reading up on the Model T; Friedrich could not have owned this car for very long as it does not seem to have had much use."

"Actually, we have speculated that Friedrich had probably just bought this automobile and come back to show it off to his family. What we can't figure out is why he decided to turn around and leave the farm without talking to anyone, which makes his untimely death even more ironic and sad. And now, of course, we will never know what changed his mind on that fateful morning," Phillip answered, realizing how effortless it was to express his feelings to this man, who had so believed in his niece to arrange the bank loan for her to open her own business. "Please come into the house and have a drink with me as we try to determine what Friedrich might have paid for his automobile. I think I saw an advertisement for cars in the newspaper."

"As much as I would enjoy partaking of your hospitality, I think I must ask for a rain check until I return to finalize my purchase. The sun has nearly set and the twilight will soon turn to dusk, so I need to gather up Katherina and be on my way home. Not to mention that Martha has prepared a roast beef supper in honour of your niece's visit, and far be it from me to be late for one of my wife's delicious meals. In terms of the cost of the Model T, I shall ask David to not only search out the equitable value, but also to draw up the papers for the actual purchase on Monday morning, when he starts his articles at the law firm. It can be his first official responsibility as a practising lawyer," William Hardy replied, with more than a little fatherly pride.

93

From the moment David met them at the train station in an automobile and drove them to the hotel, the time flew by in a whirlwind of tours and activities. Walking into the hotel, with its plush red carpets, glowing chandeliers, and high ceilings, Katherina came to a full stop to allow her senses to take in the beauty and warmth of a foyer that she could not have imagined. During her many trips to Regina, she had always stayed with Julia in her boarding house, and this was the first time she had entered such an elegant building.

As the porter approached them, David turned to his parents, asked if they would accompany the gentleman to their suite, and then said to Katherina, "Would you like to walk up to the mezzanine and go out onto the balcony for a view of the city?"

Mr. and Mrs. Hardy were more than content to go ahead and start unpacking while the young people walked up the spiralling staircase with its ornamental balustrade to the balcony. When they reached the top, David opened the double-glass doors and together they stepped onto the terrace overlooking the flourishing city of Saskatoon. From the Flanagan Hotel's vantage location on the corner of Third Avenue and Twenty-first Street, David and Katherina could see the first five buildings, including the impressive power house of the University of Saskatchewan on the east side of the fast-flowing South Saskatchewan River.

"Once we have settled into our suite and had lunch, I shall take my parents and you on a walking tour of the campus," said David proudly as he pointed out the traffic bridge with the pedestrian walkway across the river. Leaning over, he planted a gentle kiss on Katherina's lovely mouth. "Thank you for coming with Mother and Father for my graduation. It is very important to me that you are here, and when I heard that you had agreed to attend, I frequently had to remind myself to study for the final examinations so my name would be called out as one of the first graduates from the university."

"I was delighted to receive your invitation. Because of Aunt Margareta's kindness, I did not need to close the dress shop. She will be busy today and on Saturday with the two stores to run, but she was almost as excited as I was that I had such a wonderful opportunity," Katherina said as she looked demurely into David's adoring eyes. This time David enveloped Katherina in his strong arms and kissed her firmly; his heart soared when she returned his ardour.

Stepping into the suite on the top floor of the hotel was as thrilling for Katherina as entering the foyer. David had ordered large bouquets of fresh-cut flowers for the sitting area and for the bedroom that his mother would share with Katherina. Mrs. Hardy chose the twin bed closest to the doorway, leaving for Katherina the one nearest the slightly open window, which admitted the warm spring breeze. The silver thread running through the deep-blue brocaded drapes matched the thick, silvery-grey carpet, making the room appear cozy and refined at the same time. The spacious room with its high-arched ceiling was aesthetically very pleasing, but what delighted Katherina most was the bathroom.

In its centre was a long white porcelain bathtub supported by four clawlike legs; hot running water flowed from the gold-plated taps by a simple turn of the hand. At the back of the room was a toilet that flushed with a handle.

After a light lunch of crepes and fruit in the dining room, the four walked down First Avenue and through the public park until they reached the bridge that would take them across the river to the university. As soon as they arrived on campus, David showed them the Foundation Stone, which had been laid by Sir Wilfred Laurier three years ago in the month of May. As their tour guide, David made sure the historical facts were at his fingertips, and he told them that Sir Wilfred had also laid the cornerstone for Saint Paul's Church, which they would attend on Sunday morning. David's father was more interested in the business details, and soon the two men walked ahead of the women, who stopped to look at the newly planted flowers and shrubs on the carefully manicured grounds.

"The architecture is beautiful, and the masonry reminds me of many of the buildings in England. But were they constructed when you started your studies?" William Hardy inquired skeptically.

"Oh, no, Father," David answered. "For the first three years we had our classes in the law office by City Hall until the academic building opened last spring for the first students to be taught at the University of Saskatchewan. The formal ceremony will be held in that building tomorrow morning, and the dinner and dance will be hosted in the ballroom at the hotel."

Turning to his father, David continued, "I am so grateful to Mother and you for encouraging and supporting me during my years of schooling. As soon as I complete my articling and am called to the bar, I plan to return to Duff to start my own practice."

Then, looking behind him and seeing that Katherina and his mother were not within earshot, David confided, "After the dinner tomorrow night I shall ask Katherina to marry me, and if all goes well there will be a family wedding next autumn, but please don't tell Mother until I have had a chance to propose."

"Your mother will be filled with joy for you, and when you are married she will immediately begin pestering the two of you for more grandchildren. I do not think she ever overcame her disappointment that she bore only two children, considering she always said she wanted a houseful," David's father said regretfully, as he recalled his wife's devastation after each of her three miscarriages. But not wanting to dwell on the past, he quickly added, "Well, well, this will indeed be a momentous year for the Hardy family: a university graduation, a wedding, and another grandchild! Perhaps you were not aware that Sarah is again with child, and on the subject of Andrew and Sarah, will you be meeting them at the train station tomorrow morning?"

"Yes, I am glad you brought up the topic, as I wanted to ask if you and Mother would walk with Katherina to the ceremony. Fortunately, I have the use of Harold's father's car for the entire weekend, and I shall have just enough time to drive to the station and arrive on campus before the graduation. And no, I did not know that Andrew and Sarah are having another baby. Isn't Emma less than a year old?" David asked.

"Emma is almost nine months old now and is crawling all over the house. She is as cute as a button, and I guess Andrew and Sarah want to try for a son. But it is interesting how distance does limit a person from knowing what is happening in your own family. For instance, when did you learn to drive an automobile?" William, with some measure of admiration, asked his son.

"Both Harold and I have been hired on at the law firm where his father is one of the partners. As soon as we received our offers, Mr. Pettigrew insisted that we learn to drive his automobile so we can quickly get around the city to visit clients. It is rather a lot of fun, and much easier than hitching up and looking after horses. Father, you should think about purchasing a car for yourself and Mother."

"How coincidental you should make that suggestion, because the first thing I would like you to do on Monday morning is to inquire of Mr. Pettigrew what he would consider a fair price for a slightly used vehicle which appears to be the same model as his. Perhaps you will have time to draw up a bill of sale, as I am planning to buy Friedrich Werner's car from his wife Maria when we return home. And maybe if we have some time on Sunday after church, you could teach me how to drive; although I can assure you that I shall never leave the car in gear when I am starting it. Rumour has it that that was the fatal mistake that cost Friedrich his life," William said to his son, as he stopped to wait for the women to catch up.

~ 94 ~

It was little wonder that her son was so captivated by this charming, young, and beautiful woman. The more time Martha Hardy spent in her company, the more she liked her, until she began to realize that Katherina's true beauty lay within her. She was consistently sweet, gentle, and thoughtful during the three days that the women lived together in the hotel bedroom. Katherina was quick to insist that Mrs. Hardy have first access to the powder room each morning, and readily acquiesced about turning off the lights when it was clear that Martha wanted to go to sleep at night. Initially, when she and her husband were planning their accommodations for David's graduation, Martha had some qualms about sharing a room with someone she only knew as her son's friend. Then she recalled the splendid story Sarah disclosed in confidence about how Katherina had secretly purchased that beautiful wedding gown for Gustav's bride-to-be, and she agreed at once.

Much to Martha's surprise, the first night they had chatted and giggled like two schoolgirls, reminding her of time spent in dormitories during her many years of boarding schools in England. Although it was late before they finally settled down and went to sleep, they were much more comfortable with each other when they awoke the next morning. Soon Martha was asking Katherina for advice on ways to alter her hairstyle and the latest tips on makeup, as it was apparent that this young businesswoman knew the current trends. On Saturday, when Katherina did her hair for the evening festivities, Martha was delighted with the results. Katherina had piled Martha's long hair into loose curls high on the top of her head, which made the five-foot-tall woman appear to increase in stature, which she very much appreciated. Naturally, Martha had expected William to notice the change in her appearance, but she was thrilled when David also complimented her on how lovely she looked as they left the suite for the ballroom for the dinner and dance.

The next morning when Martha awoke, she was surprised at the lateness of the hour. The bright sunlight was pouring through the crevice of the heavy drapes, which Katherina had asked to leave open slightly. She had explained to the older woman that she did not completely close her bedroom window, even during the coldest months, because she liked to breathe fresh air. Katherina had stopped short of disclosing to Mrs. Hardy, for fear that she would not understand, that she believed her mother's spirit was embodied in the wind—a sentiment that eventually enabled her to come to terms with Elisabetha's death. Martha glanced over towards the other bed, and seeing that Katherina was still sound asleep, she rose quietly and went into the powder room. She closed the door before she turned on the light, although it occurred to her that if she were a child, she would be tempted to flick the switch on and off, such was her delight with this novelty that instantly illuminated the room.

Thankful that the church service did not start until eleven, Martha took her time in brushing her teeth and attending to her morning toilette. As she went back into the spacious, still-shadowed bedroom, Katherina stirred, opened her eyes, and seeing Mrs. Hardy coming out of the powder room, turned over to sit up in bed. At that very moment, a ray of sunlight sparkled off Katherina's left hand, and Martha immediately wondered if the source of the iridescence was what she had anticipated for some time now.

"Oh, my dear, I am sorry to have awakened you. I did want to be quiet as I suspect it was rather late when you came in last night, although I certainly did not hear you. I was hoping to return your consideration this morning."

"No, Mrs. Hardy, I was waking up on my own," Katherina replied, almost biting her tongue, as she had been at the point of calling the older woman Mother. Unable to contain her excitement, Katherina patted a spot on the comfortable bed and said, "Come and sit so I can tell you everything about the party. You left with Mr. Hardy quite early, just as the evening was getting into full swing, and it seemed that everyone decided to join their partners on the dance floor."

Only too happy to hear what had transpired after they said good night to Andrew and Sarah and David and Katherina, Mrs. Hardy walked over and perched on the side of the bed as she chuckled, "I didn't think you would miss us if we turned in early. It was such an exhilarating day, and when you reach my age, relaxing in front of a cozy fire can be much more appealing than dancing the night away."

"We did dance until the last song was played, and then David asked if I would like to accompany him for a stroll in City Park. The night was beautiful, with a resplendent full moon, and the sky so filled with twinkling stars that it would have been a shame not to take him up on his invitation. Besides, the spring air was warm and refreshing after being indoors for most of the day and all evening. We walked and walked until I told David that my feet were becoming sore. So he led me to a park bench where we both took off our shoes and he also removed his socks. If anyone had seen us, they would have thought we were oversized children; we ran around barefoot through the dewy grass." As Katherina rhapsodized, her pretty blue eyes were as animated as a child's, and Martha stopped herself from engulfing her in a heartfelt embrace. Dreamily, Katherina continued, "Then I slipped, and as David caught me in his arms to cushion my fall, we both ended up on the grass."

Having a very good idea of what happened next, Martha waited patiently for Katherina to proceed. The young woman was clearly remembering the magic of David's kisses, and perhaps deciding how much she would disclose to her beau's mother. Finally, as though waking from a trance, Katherina resumed, "Oh, Mrs. Hardy, look at the ring that David had kept for just the right moment to give to me."

Extending her left hand with her long slender fingers so Martha could see the ring of yellow gold and its sparkling diamond solitaire, Katherina said, "David has asked me to marry him next autumn after he has been called to the bar and had a chance to open his law practice in Duff. And when I said I would be delighted to become his wife, he made sure to remind me of the time when we were on the train to Regina and I told him I had a presentiment that I would never be a bride. David does not forget anything, and he is such a tease, isn't he?"

"From the time he was a little boy, David has always enjoyed joshing, but only with the people he loves! Congratulations, my darling. I cannot think of anyone I would rather have marry David because instead of losing a son I am gaining a wonderful daughter." No longer feeling any reason for holding back, Martha Hardy reached the short distance between them and wrapped her arms around Katherina in an enormous hug.

～～～ 95 ～～

The summer of 1913 was everything that any pioneer farmer could hope, pray, or dream about after he had planted his crops. Spring arrived early, with a hoyden of a wind which seemed to announce to the bitter, withering cold northwester of winter that it had better be on its way. The crisp, refreshing breeze danced across the drifts of snow, shaking the willows and poplars until they joined in the frenzied game to seize winter by the seat of its pants and chase it from the land. Soon, the white crystals of the frozen air were replaced with a lighter, gentler atmosphere of warming sun and melting snow under a clear, bright blue sky. As winter's icy grip released its hold, the prairie reawakened and water appeared everywhere. Then, just as quickly, it soaked into the thirsty, rich black soil that basked in the radiant rays of the rising sun while retaining enough moisture under its surface to welcome the seeds of grain.

Unbelievably, Mother Nature did not send any setbacks in 1913. Day after day, the sun shone brightly, heating the earth once the seeding was completed. Then, as the fragile plants were pushing up through the ground, the rain came, falling gently at night and early morning as though coaxing each sprout to grow strong and tall in preparation for the autumn harvest. When the pioneers gathered to talk after church, they were almost afraid to comment on the ideal growing conditions, for fear that the slightest mention would jinx the perfection of the seasons. Waiting for the last shadowy green stalk of wheat to ripen to its golden yellow, they were convinced that since the grasshoppers had not appeared, then surely strong winds, hail, or frost and an accompanying early snowfall would come to flatten the grain just before the threshers could begin. But no, the weather continued to co-operate, and although it was brisk in the early mornings and late evenings, the afternoons were warm and balmy, lulling the prairie farmers into an uneasy tranquility.

It was not until the long days of threshing were over—when men, women, and children worked from dawn to dusk—and the grain was safely in the granaries that the pioneers at last breathed a collective sign of relief and finally accepted that nothing disastrous would happen this year to ruin their steady progress. Little did they know that when they were on the verge of selling their grain, the government would announce that the great wheat boom was at its end. The same statesmen who had gladly welcomed them to Canada with arms open, parceling out land and dispensing seed grain, now indicated that the homesteaders in the west had increased their production to such a level that the federal government could no longer find markets for their crops. The farmers in the German Lutheran townships of Lemberg and Neudorf were hit hard by this unexpected and, for the Werner brothers, untimely pronouncement.

This would be the year that Johann would realize his dream of selling his land and moving his family to Melville. After three long years of spending tedious hours with Gustav, Karolina and he had become reasonably articulate with the English language. Although Karl and Greta had learned to read, write, and speak English much more quickly than their parents, Johann was confident that he had grasped the rudiments of the new language. He had persevered until he reached a level of fluency that he considered adequate to gain employment at the Canadian National Railway yard. And it had been far from easy. On more than one occasion he had been ready to tell Gustav to leave them in peace, quite understanding why his father so resisted the rhetoric of their new country. Now, the three remaining Werner brothers, with a full section of cultivated land that had yielded a bumper crop, could go ahead with their carefully devised plan.

To be honest, whenever he thought about Gustav's proposal, Johann suspected that his youngest brother was again the driving force and Rolf was simply going along to appease both of them. In many ways Johann was envious of Rolf, who seemed to be so satisfied with his lot in life. He did not think that such fulfillment was possible for anyone; yet every time he saw Rolf, he was happy, glowing with pride for his increasing family and looking more and more contented. And Katie was just the same, as though their marriage was a match made in heaven. Even when Rolf had told them Katie was again with child, and Johann had surmised that he must be praying for a son, Rolf had quickly answered that his only wish was for a healthy, strong baby. Unable to believe that any man did not long for an heir, Johann cajoled his brother until Rolf ended the conversation by saying that he enjoyed being the only man in a houseful of doting women.

Johann was hitching the oxen to the plow to start his summer fallowing when Gustav came riding into the yard to discuss the government's gloomy news. It was a dark day for Johann and Karolina because they had long ago realized that their compatibility was largely rooted in their mutual dislike of farming and their desire to leave the constant hardships of the pioneering life far in the past. Each time that Friedrich had come home and filled their heads with his stories of the modern conveniences in Melville, they had talked for days about how they would enjoy living in town. In fact, Karl and Greta grew up listening to their parents discussing how much more leisurely life would be once they sold their land to Gustav and left farming behind forever. Then there was the promise that Karl and Greta had heard repeatedly—that as soon as they moved to Melville, they would go to a proper English school and have the chance of a much better life than their parents'.

Dismounting from Wolfgang, Gustav walked up to Johann and said, "Good morning. I am glad I arrived before you left for the fields. I need to talk to you right away, and I think we should go into the house because Karolina also needs to hear what I have to say."

Wary of his brother's ominous tone, Johann promptly tethered the oxen and replied, "Well, come in then, and have a cup of coffee, but you won't want to take up much of my time as I am trying to get my land ready for you to seed next spring."

As the men settled down on the wooden chairs, Karolina set three large cups filled with strong, hot coffee on the table. "Morning, Gustav. What brings you to visit so early in the day?"

Taking a sip from his cup, Gustav tried to think of the right words to help soften the blow he was about to inflict upon his unsuspecting brother and his wife, knowing too well how eager they were for him to purchase their land. Gustav had only become aware of the unusual situation last evening when he had ridden into Neudorf to make the arrangements to haul his wheat, and Uncle Phillip had given him the article in the *Lemberg Evidence*.

"I came as soon as I finished the chores because I know you always pore over the newspaper and would have read the government's announcement. I am sorry to tell you that Rolf and I will not be able to buy your homestead this autumn, even though we both realize how disappointed you will be with our decision."

"Oh, come on, Gustav. We all know that Rolf and you have more than enough money in the Union Bank to pay for our land, even if you don't sell a grain of the wheat you harvested this year. Karolina and I have made our plans to move, and as soon as I have finished the summer fallowing, I am going to take the train to Melville to look for a job at the railway yard. You can't back out on us at this late date," Johann replied, more brusquely than Gustav expected.

Becoming irritated with his brother, particularly when he thought he had broken the news as kindly as possible, Gustav answered, "Rolf and I are not changing our minds. We will have to wait until the markets improve because I am not prepared to sell my wheat when the price is at its lowest. Sure, some of the farmers are selling their grain locally for next to nothing, but I assure you it will be a cold day in hell before I become that desperate. Besides, we need the money to buy the lumber to build another granary."

"Maybe if you didn't let your wife buy a new dress practically every week, you would have all the money you need for your granary," Karolina piped up, to the surprise of both brothers.

With all three adults talking at the same time, Johann quickly ordered, "Stay out of this, Karolina. Gustav and I will settle this conversation."

Meanwhile, Gustav replied, "I don't decide how Amelia spends the money that she earns by selling eggs, butter, her baking, and the berries when they are in season, not that I can see how it is any of your affair."

For her part, Karolina was shouting, "This is also my life we are talking about and I shall have my say. Not to mention, what makes you think, Johann, that I would allow you to go off to Melville on your own and leave the children and me here on the farm. You better not think for one minute that I am going to become another railway widow like your sister-in-law Maria. When you leave this wretched land, we are all going together."

"How dare you compare me to my irresponsible, drunken brother! When have I ever left you and the children?" Johann screamed at his wife.

"Stop talking about Friedrich in such a disrespectful manner. My God, the man is barely cold in his grave," Gustav said, defending the brother he had never really understood.

The direction of the family argument changed as quickly as a squall on the open prairie during a dust storm. Husband and wife turned on Gustav, as Karolina yelled, "This is all your fault. Before you came over here this morning to renege on our deal, we were getting along just fine."

"It seems to me that both of you suffer from a very short memory. If I had not taught you how to speak and read English, neither of you would have the choice of leaving this farm," Gustav roared right back.

"Oh, yes, I wondered how long it would take before you threw that back in our faces," said Johann. He stood up and leaned across the table towards his youngest brother, waving his hands in the air.

"Mama, Papa, what is happening? Why are you fighting with Uncle Gustav?" Karl said, as he stood beside his sister at the door of the kitchen as though ensuring a safe distance from the volatile adults.

"What are you doing in the house when you should be doing your chores? Go and get about your work and leave us to our business," Karolina ordered her children.

"Hello, Karl and Greta, I am only too happy to come outdoors with you," Gustav said, as he stood up from the table and walked quickly to the door. "Thanks for the coffee. When you are ready to be more rational, maybe we will talk about when Rolf and I can buy your land."

As Gustav rode Wolfgang back to the farm, he wondered why he always seemed to be at odds with one or another of his brothers. Perhaps Rolf was content because he kept his distance and allowed his younger brother to make the important decisions. On the other hand, if he didn't proceed with his plans, Gustav knew nothing would change, and years from now he would still only be farming a half-section of land. At least Johann was as ambitious as he, and wanted to make something of his life, rather than just raise a large family on a paltry quarter-section homestead. Now, riding along the dusty road allowance on the beautiful Indian summer morning, Gustav pondered once again how the Werner brothers could be so divergent in their choices and which one would prove to be right.

Meanwhile, Johann's thoughts took him in a decidedly different direction as he watched Gustav make his hasty departure. As far as he was concerned, it was always about Gustav getting his way. Just because he had such an inane love for the land and for what he called the perfection of God's world, it did not preclude others from wanting to enjoy the benefits of man's progress. As ridiculous as it seemed, Gustav even resented having to ride his precious horse on the roads rather than across the open countryside. And why was Johann always thwarted in what he wanted to do with his life? In all of the time he had been stuck on the farm, this was the only year that he could recall no natural setback; finally when Mother Nature was on his side, his own brother was against him. More and more Johann was ready to concede that perhaps the Silent Critics were justified in their gossip about the miserliness of Gustav Werner.

96

When she had finally plucked up the courage to go see Dr. Spitznagel, she had been devastated by his diagnosis. The affable doctor tried to be as gentle as possible when he explained that her hair loss could be attributed to her change of life, and given the plethora of symptoms that women had reported to him, alopecia, as he termed it, was perhaps one of the least troublesome. If Dr. Spitznagel had only known how Margareta considered her luxurious blond tresses to be her most beauteous feature, he would not even have considered verbalizing his opinion. As she sat in the small examining room in his residence, all she could think of was the injustice of her malady, just months before her only daughter's nuptials. Already the Silent Critics had begun the rumour that the Mohr wedding would be the event of the year in Neudorf, although they acknowledged that they were unlikely to receive invitations.

Maybe if she had listened to Phillip during the many years of their marriage, her hair would not now be falling out in handfuls. He invariably teased her as she sat at her cherished dressing table each night repeatedly brushing her long hair that she would wear it out. The irony of her husband's joshing was not lost on Margareta; although even in her despair, she knew he had not literally expected that one day he would be married to a woman who was bald. Even the word brought bitter tears of resentment to her eyes as she thought about Phillip's extravagantly thick light-brown hair, and realized that contrary to many wedded pairs, in the Mohr household it was the woman rather than the man who would end up hairless. Whatever would she do? Margareta could not bear the thought that as the bride's mother, hosting Julia and Robert's wedding and dressed in her finery, she would be as baldheaded as an eagle.

So absorbed was Margareta in the image of her shiny bare head that she did not hear Dr. Spitznagel until he lightly touched her shoulder.

"Mrs. Mohr, I understand that this condition can be distressing for women, and especially for you, as you are planning your daughter's wedding. Perhaps your niece could order some wigs in her next shipment for her dress shop, or perhaps you could wear a hat. Just think: you could start a new fashion in our town of wearing chapeaux like the gentry in the old country. At the same time you would give the Silent Critics something else to talk about during their daily chinwags as they drink coffee at the hotel."

For the first time since the doctor's pronouncement, Margareta lifted her head. Looking directly at Dr. Spitznagel, she said, "My, you are observant, aren't you? I had no idea that you knew about the Silent Critics who take great delight in gossiping about my family and me."

"Not much goes on in Neudorf that I don't eventually hear about in one way or another. Although I suspect that the ignoble Silent Critics chatter about most of us in the community, they do seem to enjoy spreading rumours about you and your relatives. On many occasions, I have thought it admirable that you deliberately seem to go out of your way to give them grist for their insatiable mill. So wear the most extravagant hat you can purchase, and I promise you that I shall be the first one to compliment you on your exquisite taste within earshot of the Silent Critics. Incidentally, I am looking forward to meeting Dr. Cameron again, and Mrs. Spitznagel and I are eagerly anticipating the Neudorf wedding of the year!"

⇛~ *97* ~⇚

Initially, they had talked about having their wedding in the latter weeks of August, before Julia started teaching for the fall term of school. Fortunately, at least from her perspective, Julia overheard one of her colleagues telling the headmistress that she would marry during the summer. Julia almost choked on the coffee she was drinking when the stern and inflexible Miss Devonshire replied, "Well, so much for your teaching days. I would never consider hiring a married woman who will promptly leave me high and dry to have babies." Julia was so upset that it was several days later before she told Robert what was troubling her. He knew the first evening as they embarked on their nightly stroll that she had something on her mind; but when she denied it, he did not pry.

Finally unable to suppress her feelings any longer, Julia blurted out, "Robert, as much as I love you, I don't think I am ready to give up my teaching career to marry you."

"Just a minute, my darling. I would never expect to tell you what you could or could not do, either now or when you are my wife, and I certainly would not even consider asking you to leave your profession. I know how important teaching is to you and I want you to be able to maintain your independence," Robert answered, as he motioned Julia to a bench in the park. "Shall we sit down? You can tell me what has prompted you to think that you have to choose one or the other."

"Oh my dear, Robert, it is not you. It is Miss Devonshire, the headmistress, who will not allow me to continue teaching once we have married. I know I might be able to get a position at another school, but I have taught most of the children now for four years and I would miss them more than I can imagine. I always planned to be there until they had finished and gone on to higher schooling, and I feel like I would be abandoning them."

"Let's consider what we can do so you can secure your teaching position for next year. Perhaps we could plan our wedding later in the fall after the term has commenced, and here in this flourishing city we can live far enough away from the school to keep it our secret. In light of the fact that the wedding will take place in Neudorf, you can continue to go by your maiden name without anyone being the wiser."

"I suppose that it could work, but wouldn't that be deceitful?" Julia asked skeptically.

"Ah, in my mind, life is largely dependent on perception, my darling, and I would prefer to think of it as a creative solution," Robert answered, as he drew the love of his life into his arms and, making sure they were not being watched, kissed her lightly on the mouth.

➤➤~ 98 ~◆◆

When Robert and Julia announced that their nuptials would be arranged for the first Sunday in October, many commented on how considerate Julia remained of the farming community. By then threshing days would be done and the harvest over, and all could enjoy the festivities. To be truthful, Margareta had fully expected to be organizing a summer wedding as a welcome change, but far be it from her to question her daughter. She did, however, pray fervently for a late autumn and for one of their singularly sublime Indian summer days. If Julia and Robert's wedding was to be the happening of the year in Neudorf, Margareta wanted the church filled to capacity and people overflowing into the churchyard following the service to partake of the delectable coffee cakes. The women of the Werner family were already discussing what they would bake in preparation for the multitude of people they anticipated would be in attendance.

It was fortunate that Margareta had such a happy milestone to prepare for, as she was still dwelling on her alopecia. She had always considered herself to be a resilient individual, but her unrelenting hair loss was trying her usually buoyant demeanour. Although she stopped her nightly brushing, she continued to find clumps of hair on her pillow every morning. It was becoming increasingly more difficult to coil her hair into a bun at the back of her head in the style she had worn for as long as she could remember. Then there was the bald spot on the very top that was becoming impossible to conceal. Was she to lose every last strand of her beautiful locks of hair? Finally one morning in desperation she asked Katherina to let her into the dress shop early before her niece opened it to the townspeople, and to give her opinion as Margareta tried on some of the hats in her display.

Katherina was only too pleased to assist her aunt in the dilemma she had been aware of for some time, although Margareta had never mentioned her ailment. It was Dr. Spitznagel who had enlisted her complicity one day while he was in the dress shop on the pretext of purchasing a new scarf for his wife. After their surreptitious chat, Katherina considered how she would feel if her hair suddenly started to fall out; knowing how upset she would be, she made a special trip to Regina. Initially she looked at an assortment of wigs, but concluded that they would reveal more about her aunt's condition than they would obscure. Eventually, Katherina discreetly ordered an array of elegant hats, which she carefully hid in the storeroom. In fact, she had not the slightest intention of displaying them until her Aunt Margareta chose which ones she wished to own.

As they entered the shop, Katherina said, "Aunt Margareta, you do have remarkable timing. I have just received a shipment of hats, which are currently in fashion. I have not even had a chance to arrange them for display, so you will have the first choice on which ones you want to purchase. Come with me to the storeroom and you can try them all on to see if you like any."

"Oh, my, I never realized there could be so many lovely hats or that they could enhance one's appearance as your selection seems to do for me," Margareta said as she placed one hat after another on her head and admired her reflection in the small oval mirror hanging on the wall.

"What a clever young lady you are, my darling niece. There isn't a hat in this entire lot that does not look good on me. How can I possibly choose from among these delightful chapeaux? Perhaps I shall save myself the quandary and just buy all of them; yes, that's it, Katherina. I want you to give me the purchase cost for this entire array and you will not need to spend the time to put them on display. I shall have every hat in your collection."

"Perfect, Aunt Margareta. As you know, I have never had any affinity for arranging hat displays, and now you have saved me the trouble. Not to mention that you will be the only person in Neudorf to be wearing the most fashionable hats of the day!"

When Margareta turned her head sharply and looked at her intently, Katherina realized that she might have said too much. To quickly cover her faux pas, she said, "I must confess that I have been slightly devious with you, Aunt Margareta. There is one other hat, which I am not showing you this morning because I have selected it to match your gown for Julia's wedding, and of course you cannot see it until her special day."

"Hmm. I suspect you may have had some help in this little intrigue, but I shall never be able to prove a thing. Well, what do you think? Shall I wear this light blue one with the jaunty, turned-up rim when I open the store this morning?"

～ 99 ～

With what the Silent Critics sardonically called Margareta Mohr's unusual good fortune, the morning of Julia's wedding dawned clear and bright as the sun rose over the horizon and began to chase away the frostiness of the autumn air. By the time the congregants were filing into the church, it started to warm up, and by the completion of the service and the signing of the essential papers, the sun was almost overhead and pouring through the two small stained-glass windows. Its intense rays shone on the bride and groom as they walked down the aisle, giving them a surreal appearance, which many of the flock believed boded well for their union. Julia appeared radiantly happy in her exquisite white brocade wedding gown as she kept glancing at her husband, Dr. Robert Cameron, who looked very distinguished in his black morning suit trimmed with silk, snow-white shirt, and black tie. His formal attire was completed with a crimson red cummerbund and a black top hat, which all of the townspeople would talk about for months to come. As far as anyone could recall, there had never been such a notable gentleman to grace their church and to marry one of their own young women.

When the elegant pair reached the door of the church, they decided to form the reception line in the yard, rather than at its customary location by the front steps. With its western exposure and protection from the breeze by a grove of spruce trees along its eastern edge, the spacious area on the right side of the building was comfortably balmy. As they waited for Victoria Cameron and Phillip and Margareta Mohr to join them, Julia turned to Robert and whispered that her mother's prayers seemed to have been answered in terms of the seasonal splendour of the weather. She blushed with delight when Robert lowered his head so his lips lightly brushed her hair and quipped, "Not only Margareta's supplications will be acknowledged on our wedding day, Mrs. Cameron."

It was a resplendent afternoon, with the soft heat of the iridescent rays of the autumn sun filtering through the naked branches of the caragana trees that surrounded the north and west sides of the churchyard, dazzling the newly married Dr. and Mrs. Cameron in their contrasting wintry white and ebony raiment. Everyone wanted to wish the young people well and, of course, to be introduced to Mrs. Victoria Cameron, who had journeyed all the way from Reading, England, to attend her only progeny's wedding. To the great delight of the townsfolk, the tall, stately woman with the silvery-grey hair topped with a flamboyant hat that matched her crystal-blue eyes spoke German fluently, having begun her teaching career in languages at a girls' boarding school. Many years later, now the headmistress of an exclusive intermediate finishing college for young women, Victoria blended English and German beautifully in her decidedly British accent.

Whether it was the novelty of hearing such precise diction of their language or the animated manner in which it was delivered, Victoria Cameron quickly acquired an audience when the receiving line concluded. Initially, as the two women sat down on a bench, waiting to be served coffee and some of the delectable cakes, she told Julia how thrilled she was that her son had chosen a schoolteacher as his wife. Then Victoria started to share some of her many experiences over the years. Soon, several of the older children, hearing the bride's laughter, gathered around and asked if they could listen to the stories; they quickly joined the two adults by sitting on the dried grass beside the low bench.

One by one, the adults began to drift towards the crowd, sitting on blankets on the prairie sod, and became equally captivated by Victoria's narrative of the humorous exploits of her youthful scholars, who stealthily tried to find ways in and out of the school, smuggle food from the large kitchen, and sneak any variety of things into the premises, including an ardent young man from the school across the river. Even the Silent Critics, contrary to form, held their tongues, and were regaled by the British woman in the extravagant chapeau with a peacock feather in its brim. Only the two doctors remained aloof from the assemblage, and those who gave any thought to the nature of their discussion assumed it would be about recent medical advances.

As it happened, Dr. Spitznagel was commenting to his colleague, "It would seem that your mother has quickly intrigued the majority of the people of our community."

"Yes. Many years ago before my father died, she embarked upon a career as a writer, and after successfully publishing several short stories, was in demand to give public readings of her writing. My father was a doctor of veterinary medicine, but when I was thirteen years of age, he was tragically kicked to death by a stallion, a famous racehorse that he had been asked to treat for an undiagnosed malady. It did not take my mother long to choose the steady income and security of a teacher, rather than the risky proposition of trying to run a household and to raise a child on the proceeds of her as yet incomplete novels. I suspect it was with considerable regret that she gave up her childhood aspiration; although on many occasions I have tried to encourage her to resume her writing, she has yet to follow suit," Dr. Cameron said to the older man, who had made him feel so welcome every time he had come to Neudorf.

"In time, I certainly hope she returns to writing novels, since she clearly has a gift for storytelling. I must say I am curious that both mothers of the bride and groom share an inclination for wearing hats, not to mention the bridegroom himself!" Dr. Spitznagel said with a twinkle in his gentle hazel eyes.

Several heads turned to stare at Dr. Cameron when he burst forth with a hearty laugh. "I have never worn a top hat before in my life and I probably will not wear one again for a very long time. To the best of my memory, I cannot recall my mother ever wearing any kind of hat, not even to protect her ears when the weather was chilled. So no one was more surprised than I was when she arrived at the church dressed in such dramatic headgear. In fact, at the earliest opportunity I asked her when she had developed the custom of covering her stylish hair. Apparently when the women were dressing this morning at the Mohr home and Margareta came down the stairs wearing her elegant hat, my mother was full of envy. My mother-in-law, with her propensity for finding solutions, immediately showed my mother her rather extensive repertory of hats and allowed her to select any one of her choosing as a gift from one mother of the bridal party to the other."

On the Monday morning following the Neudorf wedding of the year, every woman who entered Katherina's Dress Shop came in expressly to purchase a hat and was disappointed to learn that none were available. As quickly as she could, Katherina placed an order from the supply books at her disposal, careful not to include any from her original selection, which entirely belonged to her aunt—except, of course, for Margareta's gift to Victoria Cameron. Regardless of how frequently Katherina brought in new shipments or how many she arranged on the shelves, by the end of the day there was never a hat to be found in Neudorf. For his part in the novel fashion that seized the women of the community, Dr. Spitznagel could take no credit; although if anyone had asked him, he would have stated that a little healthy competition goes a long way. As a matter of principle, every time he encountered Margareta, Dr. Spitznagel complimented her on her exquisite chapeau, whether or not any of the Silent Critics were within earshot.

~~~ 100 ~~~

The clouds of impending war in the old country reached across the oceans until it became the topic of conversation among the inhabitants of the New World. In many households, the men talked about taking up arms to defend their country of origin while every woman cringed in fear of the outcome. Instead of conversing about which crops to plant in the spring of 1914, whenever men gathered together in groups, even at church, they excitedly considered whether Canada would join the fight. Some stated that the minute war was officially declared, they planned to return to their homeland and join up to protect it from the invading forces. The more insightful, though, stopped and wondered about the quandary of having dual citizenship in a war against people from countries that they had been living beside and working with now for many years.

As soon as Gustav had returned from Neudorf to the Werner home with news of the continuing disputes in the Balkans and the rising tension in Europe, Christian had rallied from his seemingly disinterested state about what was happening beyond the confines of his homestead. Since he stopped going to town and his interactions were primarily limited to his family, Christian became increasingly more reticent to the point of apathy until Franz Schweitzer came to live on his farm.

Little did Amelia know what she was starting on the morning when it occurred to her that Franz could surely carry Gustav's meals out to him in the field without mishap. Asking Christian if he would mind showing Franz where Gustav was working proved to be insightful; although on the first day the women became concerned that perhaps both of them had got lost when they still had not returned in time for Franz to herd the cows from the pasture into the barn for milking.

The twilight was becoming dusk before the old man and the youth were seen talking companionably as they walked back to the farmhouse swinging the now empty pail that had contained the men's food for the day. Soon, Christian had taken the boy under his wing and spent most of the hours of each day with him, walking around his homestead, and telling him that nothing could destroy his peaceful existence on the land he had struggled to acquire his entire life.

After he gave the blessing, Christian seldom added a single word to the family conversations at mealtimes. During the evening meal, when Gustav started to relate to the women the events occurring in the countries of Europe, even the children sat up straight and listened intently to their grandfather as he adamantly told his son why he was never to talk about warfare in the Werner household.

"Hear me out, Gustav, and maybe you will understand why no man in the Werner family will ever go to war."

Gustav was, as he had been many times before, startled by the force and clarity in his father's voice, since Christian so often gave the impression that he was becoming feeble both in mind and body.

"Papa, I do not have the slightest intention of becoming involved in these hostilities, but I will be only too happy to listen to you," Gustav replied.

"Unknown to all of you except Franz, I was a peasant in my village in the Galicia territory of Austria, as was my father and his father before him. None of my ancestors were ever allowed to own property and we could never be anything but tenants; as such, we had to give most of our produce, crops, and animals to the overlord as rent for living on his land. The overlords in Austria were very wealthy and powerful, but they did not use any of the money that we earned to improve the farming methods or the lot of the hard-working vassals. Instead, the landlord who owned the large property that my family had farmed for generations sent his three sons away to England for proper schooling. Then, after they had married English women and returned to take over the ownership of the property, they demanded we pay another levy that they called taxes, when my family was already handing over most of everything that we grew and raised."

So surprised was Gustav by his father's uncharacteristic discourse that he blurted out, "Well, that would certainly explain your animosity towards the English, not to mention a few other things!"

"I have never told any of my children what I am trying to tell you, so if you want to hear what I have to say don't interrupt me again," Christian snapped, as he glared across the table at his youngest son.

"Then, if there were not enough hardships for our family, in 1848, when I was still a little boy, some country which my father had never heard of called Sardinia declared war on Austria. The sons of the overlord ordered all of their male peasants, including the boys who were older than fourteen, to join the military and to fight for their homeland. At first, Papa refused, telling the overlord that since he could not own land, he and his oldest son should not be compelled to defend it. Of course, the lord was furious and gave Papa the choice of going to war or having my mother watch as both of them were hanged as traitors. So, the next day, my father and Albert, whom I can hardly remember, were marched off to become soldiers and we never saw or heard from either of them again."

Suddenly Christian stopped talking and seemed to be very far away. No one said a word or took an audible breath. Gustav had to stop from pinching himself; he was that astounded by his father's unusual loquacity and the incredible nature of the information he was disclosing. Mathias and Julianna had a sense of the rarity of their grandfather's conversation, and even little Elisabetha seemed to know enough to stay still, while the women sat and stared in total disbelief. In fact the only person not riveted to his chair in the eerily silent kitchen was Franz, who had heard the old man's stories many times before during their daily strolls across his expansive fields. However, it would have made little difference to Christian if his entire family got up and walked away, so oblivious was he to their presence.

Memories carried Christian Werner through the heavy stone walls of the house that he had built on the land that he had homesteaded in Canada, and back to his home in Austria. He visibly shivered, remembering himself as a cold, hungry waif in shabby clothes, running around barefoot doing his chores.

"If it had not been for the Reverend Wirth's kindly wife, we would never have had clothes to wear because even though Papa and Albert went to war for the overlords, they did not excuse my mother from paying the rent and taxes. By the time we gave them their share of the produce and crops, there was scarcely enough food left to feed a family of six. To make matters worse, shortly after Papa and Albert were forced to leave, Mama gave birth to her last child, Margareta. She was as thin as a rail trying to nurse a baby and raise five children by herself.

"Our only solace was to be found in the church in Brundorf, where every Sunday after the service, the gentle-hearted Mrs. Wirth fed us a meal and gave my mother any food that her family could spare for the week. Then, much to the surprise and delight of my mother, she offered to teach Margareta and me with her two youngest children, so at least we would have the advantage of being able to read and write and to do figures. When it became known in the village that the minister's wife was schooling Margareta and me, some threatened her by saying that they would tell the landlords. Mrs. Wirth quickly silenced them by saying that the elderly reverend spoke in his sleep, revealing what his congregants had told him in confidence, and it was only because of her discretion that everybody in the township did not know their family secrets."

Christian continued in the soft faraway voice of a muse. All of his family sat fascinated by his unlikely turn as a storyteller, except for poor Elisabetha. She had fallen asleep, her head of blond curls resting on the wooden table, and for once not even Amelia jumped up to carry her into bed.

"The years passed, and after a while, Mama stopped talking about when Papa and Albert would return. I think she finally accepted that they had been killed in the war they had been forced against their will to fight, although she would never tell us that she thought they were dead. At least the overlords did not come and take my two older brothers; we lived in dread of that happening because Mama had vowed she would die before she ever allowed another member of her family to go to war. As it was, she became frailer and frailer until she seemed to give up, or maybe she just wore out. One morning, when your Aunt Margareta was about nine years old, Mama did not get out of her bed, and when the Reverend Wirth was called, he told my older brothers that she had passed away.

"One or two Sundays after we buried Mama, as we ate our meal following the service, Mrs. Wirth started to talk about how much she missed her younger daughter, whom she had sent to Lemberg, the capital of Austria, to go to a proper school. When we were getting ready to leave, the kindly woman said she would not be nearly so lonely if Margareta could stay and live with her at the manse. Well, my older brothers and sisters were only too happy to have one less mouth to feed, and they all agreed at once. Soon after, Mrs. Wirth kept finding things for me to do in the yard and around the manse, chores that she said the Reverend Wirth could no longer handle, and it wasn't very long before I was also eating most of my meals with her family.

"Then several years later, and shortly after the very elderly Reverend Wirth finally died, the most remarkable thing happened. Elfrieda Wirth took me aside one evening after supper and told me she was making the arrangements for me to marry her younger daughter. I could not believe my ears, and when I saw Elisabetha again, I could not believe my eyes! I had not seen her for a long time, and over the years, she had grown into a tall, beautiful woman and now she was to become my wife. Whenever I think about it, marrying your mother was the best thing that I ever did. We lived at the manse with her mother and would have been very happy except for the wars, which my homeland always seemed to be waging with the countries surrounding us. My older brothers and sisters had already fled with their families to Russia, where they had been promised political freedom and plots of land.

"My family kept trying to get your mother and me to join them, but we could not leave Mrs. Wirth alone in Brundorf, even though we feared every day that the overlords would come and order me to join the military. Then, one morning when I was outside doing the chores, Elisabetha found her mother dead in her bedroom. After her funeral, we sold our few belongings and left Austria to make the long journey to Russia and eventually met up with the rest of our families. It seemed as if we had barely settled and were struggling to grow enough food on the rocky, sandy soil to feed our children, when all of the men of our community were ordered to join the Czar's army. Now we would not only be sent to fight, but we would be going to war against other Austrians; so Phillip and Margareta Mohr and your mother and I decided to flee. This time, we had to steal away in the dark of night, with only the clothes on our backs and the few possessions that the men could carry, while the women looked after our children.

"After months of slow, hard travel over sea and land, near-starvation, and cold, bitter weather, we finally arrived in Neudorf, one of the townships where the Canadian government had set aside land for the German Lutherans. From that day onward, the men of our two families took an oath never to go to war, nor to take up arms against another man. And let me tell you, none of my sons will ever break that solemn family vow! So I do not want to hear another word about the constant wars and fighting in the old country. And now I am going to bed," Christian said wearily. He rose slowly from the chair, supporting himself by holding onto the table. He turned, and without a backward glance, he walked stiffly to his bedroom, went in, and shut the door.

It took the rest of his family more than a few minutes to recover from what had just happened in the kitchen of their home. Never before had Christian Werner spoken about his past, and Gustav believed that his father would not again break the silence about his life. He knew it would be his responsibility to apprise his brothers of the family oath about not going to war. Not that he thought for a second that Rolf would leave his home and family and take up arms; after all, Rolf could not step on a bug, much less harm another person. It did occur to Gustav that in the end he might have done Johann a favour by not buying his land last fall. He could not imagine that a great country like Canada would send its farmers into battle when they would be so desperately needed to grow the food to feed its army. As much as Johann longed to leave his farm, Gustav very much doubted it would be at the risk of becoming a soldier.

⟫⟫~ 101 ~⟪

The next morning as Gustav was carrying the pails of milk in the shed and then helping Amelia to pour the milk into the separator, he said, "When we have finished the chores, change your clothes and we will go and visit Andrew and Sarah."

"What a nice surprise! We have not been to see them for a while, and the baby will be getting big. But today I was to help Hanna and Maria dig up the garden and get it ready for planting," Amelia replied with an anguished look on her sweet, round face.

"Amelia, you always do more than your share of the work around here, and there is no reason why they cannot get started without you. I want to talk to Andrew, and I know how much you like seeing Sarah and the girls, so I am not leaving you at home," Gustav said. He started to turn the handle of the separator.

For some time now, he had been paying more attention to his young wife and had come to realize just how much all of his family seemed to rely on her. Sometimes Gustav wondered how they had got along without her; although at times, he suspected that Hanna and Maria were not beyond taking advantage of Amelia's giving nature. That was especially true now that Franz was living with them; Amelia seemed to think that the more her brother wandered around the fields with Christian rather than doing his share of the chores, the harder she had to work to pay for his keep.

When they pulled into the Thompsons' yard, Andrew and his father were sharpening the plow shears outside the door of the small machine shed. They immediately stopped working, and as the older man walked up to Wolfgang to grab the reins and tether him to the fence, Andrew rushed over to Amelia's side of the carriage.

"Hello, let me help you down. Sarah and I were just saying this morning that it would be nice to have a visit. Wait until you see how much little Rebecca has grown. Please come in for tea."

Soon after the guests stepped through the door into the kitchen, the women of the house were placing teacups and saucers on the table.

"Amelia and Gustav, how nice to see you again. It has been all together too long since we have had the pleasure of your company," the elder Mrs. Thompson greeted them.

Meanwhile, Sarah approached Amelia and hugged her friend. "Oh, I have been lonesome for you. These cold, bitter winters keep us apart, so I certainly hope you have planned to spend the day, as I will not let you go home before you have had a meal with us."

Over the winter in the privacy of their bedroom after Andrew had talked to him, Gustav had spent many hours helping Amelia to learn more English words, and now, as they sat around the table, she was able to understand most of the conversation. Still, she rarely spoke, particularly when the men were present, as much out of her shyness as her fear of mispronouncing a word. Then, as soon as Rebecca had awakened from her nap and Sarah brought her into the kitchen, Amelia lost interest in what was being said. When Sarah placed the infant into her arms, it was as though the rest of them ceased to exist. Amelia's eyes were as bright as the stars as she gazed lovingly at the baby staring up at her, and every member of the Thompson family recognized the yearning on Amelia's face. To his credit, Gustav slowly came to realize how much Amelia wanted to bear a child, but he considered her far too young to become a mother. Then with all the disputes in the old country, which this time could reach across the oceans to the shores of the New World, the last thing he wanted to do was father a child.

Suddenly Rebecca began to cry, and as Sarah came to take her from Amelia, she said, "I am going to nurse the baby; if you come with me into the bedroom we will not need to interrupt our visit. Oh, listen, it sounds like Emma is also awake. So now, Amelia, you won't get a minute's peace with her wanting your attention."

As Amelia rose to follow Sarah, and they disappeared up the circular stairs, Andrew glanced over to Gustav and suggested, "Since it is such a nice spring day, let's go for a walk around the farm and check if the fields are drying." Andrew was as eager as a horse chomping at the bit to talk to his friend about what was happening in Europe, but his mother had already made it abundantly clear that there would be no talk of fighting and war in her house. His father was equally reticent about discussing the information that was constantly appearing in the Duff newspaper and dominating every conversation when the men gathered in town. In truth, Andrew had been so bothered about whether Gustav would go to war that there had been many nights when he had not fallen asleep until the early hours of the morning.

The men had scarcely left the yard and were heading towards the creek when Andrew blurted out, "Will you go to war? And how will you decide whether to fight for Austria, Russia, or England? I can hardly sleep, thinking about what will happen and the possibility that you and I could end up fighting against each other. Naturally, if I go to war, I will be defending England because it is my homeland, but in a sense both Austria and Russia are your mother countries. If England declares war, Canada, as part of the Commonwealth, will immediately send its forces to fight in alliance with the British Empire."

"Just a minute, Andrew, what are you saying? Do I understand you correctly when you are telling me that, as a Canadian, you will fight on the side of the British? I think that you are losing sight of the fact that I am also a Canadian, and if I decided to go to war, of course I too would join the Allied forces," Gustav declared, with more than a hint of annoyance. Before Andrew could answer, Gustav continued, "I was only a year old when I came to this country, so what ties could I possibly have to either Austria or, for that matter, to Russia?"

Precisely as Gustav was asking his question, Andrew stopped in his tracks as though struck by a thunderbolt and stared at his friend of more than five years. No wonder he had not been able to sleep at night. If he was such a hypocrite, he did not deserve any repose. He had listened to the men as they sat around the table having coffee in the Duff hotel and in the churchyard after the services. All the while, he had been so smug, thinking how much more enlightened he was because of his lengthy friendship with Gustav. He had been in their homes, eaten their foods, attended their weddings, and even spoke and understood many words of their language. And yet Andrew had made the same distinction as every English Methodist man had: that in Duff they were Canadians, whereas the people in the next townships, separated by a road allowance, were still German Lutherans.

"Gustav, I am very sorry. Please forgive me. I don't know what I have been thinking. Of course we would both be fighting for the Canadian forces in Europe," Andrew answered, stopping short of wounding his friend's pride by mentioning his thoughtless differentiation.

Fortunately, in his haste to tell him about his father's remarkable conversation and of the Werner family vow, Gustav did not discern Andrew's hesitation. "You would not believe what happened around our kitchen table last night! For the first time I can ever recall, Papa spoke about his past, and as it turns out, my family will not go to war because of an oath that was started by my grandmother when my grandfather and uncle were both killed fighting for some overlords in Austria. In fact, that is why my family fled to Russia and then to Canada—Papa is a pacifist and is absolutely clear that none of his sons will ever fight for any country."

As Andrew listened to Gustav, he began to understand why William Thompson refused to talk about the war clouds on the horizon.

"Now that you mention it, I wonder if my father is not equally opposed to the senseless hostilities between nations. He will not allow me to even bring up the topic; but little does he know, and he won't let me tell him, that unlike many of the other young men in our community, I do not think that going to war would be an exciting adventure. Besides, I don't believe I could maim or kill another person, so I am not likely to answer the call to fight for my country."

"I think that any man who considers war to be an adventure has given little thought to the consequences—not only that he will be required to kill, but also that he will put his own life on the line. I just don't know if I am that courageous, and although I did not have a chance to tell Papa, I was more than happy to learn about the Werner family oath," Gustav said, speaking more honestly than he ever had in his life.

"Well, I really like your family oath. If you and I did go to war, even though we would be fighting on the same side, we could still be killing some of your relatives. I am sure you must have long-lost cousins and other distant connections that you may not even know about, living in Austria." As Andrew was speaking, his handsome face slowly began to transform from the unusually serious expression it had borne during their discussion. His hazel-brown eyes began to sparkle.

"An idea has just occurred to me. Could we extend the Werner vow to include me, and then you and I could make a pact right here and now that neither of us will go to war?"

"I would like that, Andrew, and if my grandmother could hear us, I suspect she would be very proud that we are honouring her oath. So now, what will we do to seal our agreement?"

"As far as I am concerned, a handshake would complete our mutual vow," Andrew answered before promptly extending his right hand to his friend. "If only nations could resolve their seemingly endless differences by talking rather than having to resort to arms, then every country would be as peaceful as Canada. My father repeatedly says that the best thing about this enormous new land is that people from countries all over the world are able to live and work together in harmony."

"My father would at least agree with yours about the peacefulness of this New World. He spends most of his days now walking around his land, enjoying the tranquility. We will consider our pact sealed for the future of our families." Gustav took Andrew's hand and shook it heartily. He jokingly continued, "I must say that I am just as glad you did not need something so dramatic as signing a contract in blood and having each of us slice up a finger or two. And now, I think we should mark this eventful day, confirming our pact and celebrating being Canadians, by taking our horses for a long-overdue run."

As the German and English friends raced across all that remained of the open plains, the dirt road sandwiched between the perfectly square fields of alternating summer fallow and stubble, they rejoiced in their Canadian identity without so much as a single thought to any possible obligation of young men to safeguard the freedom they so avidly enjoyed and took for granted, as they engaged in their innocent adventure, devoid of any destruction of man and nature.

~ 102 ~

It was one of those lazy, hazy, early summer afternoons, when weeding the garden was more about communing with the warm, comforting earth than with uprooting unwelcome vegetation. All three women had the best of intentions, and even the children were eager to help when Amelia announced as they were washing the dinner dishes that if they did not soon rescue the struggling sprouts, the family would not have much to harvest in the fall. Although Elisabetha still needed a restorative nap, her doting aunt took her in tow along with her favourite blanket, which she spread out on the thick prairie grass at the edge of the garden. Sure enough, within half an hour, the toddler was clinging to Amelia's shoulder, her right thumb firmly ensconced in her petite mouth. As Amelia carried the child back to the waiting blanket, she thought she saw something shimmering off in the distance, where the road to the farmhouse curved past the grove of encircling conifer trees.

Deciding that it was just the heat waves from the sun captured in the windbreak of surrounding trees, she resumed her place along the straight row of green beans, which seemed to pop up through the rich black soil before her very eyes. Perhaps it was twenty or thirty minutes later when Amelia stood up, rubbing her hands along her back as she stretched and then checked on her sleeping beauty. Now when she looked, the quivering image looked like two figures, one big and the other much smaller, silhouetted in the iridescent rays of the sparkling sun. Shaking her head and chiding herself for seeing things that were simply not there, Amelia returned to her stooping position to continue with a task she usually found relaxing. Today, though, Amelia was almost as inclined as her sisters-in-law to sit between the rows and chat rather than to fret about the plight of the newly germinating plants.

When a timid voice softly called out, "Is there anyone here?" Amelia almost jumped out of her skin. There would come a time when she would become quite accustomed to people seeming to appear out of nowhere at the edge of her garden asking for food or work, but today Amelia was shocked out of her reverie. Standing up and shielding her eyes from the sun, she saw a woman not much older than herself tightly holding the hand of a little boy with beautiful sky-blue eyes and long, blond hair. Not wanting to wake the still sleeping Elisabetha, Amelia quickly walked over to the spot where the stranger stood, and gently steering her away from the blanket, said, "Hello, where have you come from and how may I help you?"

"My name is Anastasia Schmidt and this is Peter. When we got off the train in Neudorf, I asked the stationmaster for directions to your farm. My son and I had no sooner started walking on the road when a kind gentleman came along in his carriage and offered us a ride. We live in Melville and I am here looking for Friedrich Werner."

Gazing intently into the stranger's eyes, Amelia was uncertain how to respond. She was on the verge of blurting out that Friedrich had been dead for over a year, but then thought better of it; it seemed apparent that the woman, whoever she was, had no knowledge of his tragic demise.

Finally, she replied, "I am Amelia Werner and if you could wait here for a few minutes, I will go and get my sisters-in-law, who are working at the other end of our garden."

As she retreated into her safe haven to find Maria and Hanna, it crossed Amelia's mind that the cherubic-looking toddler bore a striking resemblance to Friedrich, especially those lovely blue eyes. Suddenly Amelia stopped and shivered in the warm afternoon sunlight, as the reason this unknown woman had mysteriously arrived on the Werner farm became crystal clear in her mind. What a good thing she had chosen not to provide any details about her dead brother-in-law. This was definitely a matter for Maria and Maria alone. The last place Amelia wanted to be was caught in the middle between two women who had shared the same man.

Amelia walked the full length of the large garden and still saw neither hide nor hair of Maria, Hanna, Mathias, or Julianna. Finally she went to the farthest corner on the west side, where the raspberry brambles were in full bloom. Hidden from view at the edge of the garden, lying on the tall green prairie sod were the women, with the children sitting between them. At that moment, Amelia remembered what Gustav had said about her sisters-in-law taking advantage of her, and she experienced a flash of resentment. Then, thinking about how much satisfaction she always experienced when she worked hard and completed a job, her annoyance dissipated as quickly as it had come.

She tentatively called out, "Oh, here you all are. I have been looking for you. Maria, a woman has arrived from Melville with her child and is asking about Friedrich."

At the mention of Friedrich's name, Maria jumped to her feet and stared at Amelia. To be perfectly truthful, she had not given much thought to her dead husband since his body had been lowered into the ground beside his mother's grave more than a year ago.

"Who can she be and what could she possibly want from a dead man? What on earth did you tell her?" Maria asked impatiently.

"I asked her to wait while I looked for you. I never told her a thing about Friedrich since he was not my husband," Amelia replied in a tone of voice so full of pride that Maria wondered if it did not border on gloating. She turned sharply towards Amelia and was about to retort that at least her husband had been able to give her children, when she saw the innocent look on the much younger woman's face. Still, it occurred to Maria that perhaps she and Hanna had underestimated Amelia's awareness of what went on in the family, and decided they might need to be more cautious.

Maria chose to ignore the inflection in Amelia's voice and replied, "You are quite right. I am the person who must talk to this woman about Friedrich and see what it is she wants. Hanna, would you please keep Mathias and Julianna here with you?"

Walking through the garden, Maria did not hurry, as she wanted time to consider what had brought this woman to the Werner farm. She was more than a little skeptical, given that the stranger had come from Melville, where her husband had lived for the last years of his life. Approaching Anastasia, Maria did not immediately see the child, who had in the meantime wandered over to pet the children's new puppy guarding the sleeping Elisabetha on her blanket.

"Good afternoon, I am Maria Werner. Amelia came to tell me that you are looking for my husband Friedrich."

The woman, who did not appear to be much older than Amelia, turned to Maria with an astonished look on her face, and although she opened her mouth, no words came out. As the two women stood mutely staring at each other, Peter came running back to hide in his mother's skirt. Now it was Maria's turn to be shocked because in her fleeting glimpse of the little boy, she could have sworn it was Mathias; when just more than a year old, Mathias had had the same angelic face and sky-blue eyes. It was those remarkable eyes that had drawn Maria to Friedrich the first time she had seen him, and which she still believed had been his best feature. In the ensuing silence, it was as though the world had stopped, with nary a sound of the wind rustling in the leaves or the birds singing from the treetops.

It was Elisabetha, dragging her blanket and trailed by her dog Schnauzer, who brought the women back to their senses. Coming up to her mother's side she cried, "Mama, Mama, I hungry after my big sleep."

Bending down to lift up her daughter, Maria realized that perhaps Amelia was not the only member of the Werner family who was naïve. What had Maria been thinking? Where had Friedrich lived for nearly three years while he had worked in Melville? Of course he was the kind of man who needed and would find another woman to look after him. No wonder he never came home, when he had set up house with a pretty young girl who probably still doted on him and believed all of his lies.

At that instant, Maria experienced an overwhelming sense of sympathy for Anastasia; approaching her, she gently touched her on the shoulder and said, "I think you better come into the house with me. I shall give you a cup of coffee while I tell you about Friedrich Werner. This is my younger daughter, Elisabetha. What is your son called?"

Responding to the empathy in Maria's tone, the distraught Anastasia at last found her voice and replied, "His name is Peter and I am Anastasia Schmidt. My parents woke us very early this morning so we could get to the train station on time. A cup of coffee would be appreciated. Thank you for your kind offer."

She detached Peter from her leg and lifted him into her arms, and the two women walked towards the Werner farmhouse. Their only connection was a philandering man, who, if he were still alive, would never have considered that the two women in his duplicitous life would ever meet.

⋙〜 103 〜⋘

It was so annoying that they had been required to establish a rotation where at least one of them, if not two, had to arrive at precisely the moment the hotel opened its doors every morning to ensure that they got their optimal position by the big window. The Silent Critics had occupied the large round table overlooking Main Street for years now, and as far as they were concerned, the owner of the establishment should have engraved their names on it. Instead, since the entire community was anxiously waiting to hear if England would declare war on Germany and Austria, it seemed that each day more people in the coffee shop were vying for their spot so they could have their ears tuned to the hotel radio. If that was not bad enough, the men who should have been out in their fields sat at the tables with the newspaper spread all over, loudly postulating that Canada would immediately take up arms to defend its mother country.

Too often now, it was so noisy that the group of seven, who took their role as the Silent Critics of Neudorf seriously, had actually talked about forsaking their perch and finding another location to monitor the comings and goings of their town. They even toyed with the idea that together they would open their own coffee shop, which would be a standalone, rather than have the ruckus of an adjoining beer parlour. As appealing as it sounded at first to own a business, they quickly realized they would no longer be able to just sit and comment on what was happening; rather, they would be running around waiting on the very people they wanted to be observing. Besides, the point was well made that should they continue at their accustomed haunt, they were right in the heart of the activity, since anyone of any interest usually came to the town's hotel.

On the other hand, it was just that position that was beginning to erode the foundation of the masonry which heretofore had held the Silent Critics together. Over the years, the Silent Critics had tacitly agreed that they would remain aloof from the conversations they were eavesdropping on by waiting until the people expressing them had left before they began their unconstrained discussion. Therefore, it was with considerable surprise when one morning the husband of the only married couple of their group angrily asked the four farmers sitting at the table next to them how they, as Germans, had so quickly transitioned to consider England the fatherland. "You should listen to yourselves, talking in your mother tongue while you speak of fighting for the British Empire."

As the other Silent Critics frowned and hushed him, one of the farmers loudly retorted, "Mind your own business, old man. You don't know what you are talking about, so go back to your gossiping if you don't want to contend with a fight of your own making."

The angry farmer stood up and clenched his fist, but one of the other young men at their table grabbed him by the arm and led him towards the door. Soon the remaining two men also stood, but before he walked out of the room one of them turned to the Silent Critics and dismissively asked, "When will you old codgers realize that you are now living in Canada? If you are ever going to become part of this country, you have to forget about being German."

By now the other six members of the group, including his wife, glared at the troublemaker in their midst, who at least had the good sense to wait until all of the farmers had left before he began protesting.

"Do you really think I will sit here day after day and listen to all the men talking about fighting against our relatives? Why, if I were a young man, I would be on my way home to Austria to defend my homeland."

In the ensuing pandemonium, all seven Silent Critics talked at once, and in their commotion, they began to draw the attention of the other patrons in the coffee shop. To the best of everyone's knowledge, there had seldom before been any interaction between the Silent Critics and the other customers, and certainly no apparent dissension among their ranks. The bystanders could not understand the problem because of course they did not know the rule observed by the Silent Critics: to remain in the middle of the hustle and bustle of the town, but refrain from becoming directly involved. In the final analysis, the majority of six ruled, and the husband had to acquiesce to their stipulation that in the future he must hold his tongue if he wanted to seal the rift and remain a member of the

Silent Critics. The decisive utterance came from his wife, who not too kindly reminded him that the reason he had dragged her halfway around the world in the first place was because of his aversion to war.

～ 104 ～

Against all odds, Maria liked her, and more importantly, even believed her story. From the moment Anastasia had lingered diffidently at the door and would not enter the house until Amelia had come along and guided her into the kitchen, Maria knew beyond a shadow of doubt that this young woman could not have beguiled the much older and considerably more experienced Friedrich. For once, Maria directed Amelia to sit down at the table with their guests and to hold Elisabetha while Hanna and she went about preparing coffee. Maria astutely realized that Anastasia would be more comfortable in the presence of her warm, nurturing sister-in-law, who seemed able to endear herself to any stranger, than with her. Furthermore, Maria was accurate in her perception that the two women shared an alluring simplicity in addition to a similar age, and sure enough, within minutes they were chatting about the children sitting on their laps.

As the coffee brewed, Maria came to the table carrying plates heaped with bread and cheese. She set them down and said, "My youngest daughter always awakes from her nap ravenous, and then her brother and sister feel left out if I don't include them in her little repast. Julianna, would you please give our guests a plate while Mathias brings over the utensils and the chokecherry jelly. I am sure that Peter and you must be hungry after your journey, so please help yourself, Anastasia, and don't be shy. We baked bread this morning and we have a larder full of jams and canned fruit. In fact, Hanna, please get the last jar of saskatoon berries that we have been saving for special company."

"You are a very generous and hospitable woman, Maria. By the time we were on our carriage ride, we were getting hungry, even though Grandma and Grandpa Schmidt had packed us a nice lunch, hadn't they, Peter?" Anastasia responded, still directing her glance and comments towards her son rather than to his father's unusual wife, who seemed to embody the very notion of turning the other cheek.

When Elisabetha scrambled off her lap to claim her own chair in case this interloper had any designs on it, Amelia turned to Anastasia and asked, "May I please take your beautiful son while you prepare something for the two of you to eat? I love babies, and since my husband and I don't have our own yet, I long to hold other children." As she held out her arms to receive her incoming bundle, Anastasia started to say that Peter did not readily take to strangers, when he climbed down from her knees and crawled up onto Amelia's lap.

216

"Well, he has never done that before. He must sense your maternal inclination."

As the women and children went about enjoying their afternoon meal, Anastasia marvelled at how delicious Maria's basic food tasted. Whether it was the homey atmosphere or the act of feeling forgiven for her sins against this woman and her family, the fresh bread dissolved in her mouth as though she was partaking in Holy Communion. When Anastasia had decided to go looking for Friedrich, she had no idea what she would discover; but it had never crossed her naïve mind that she would meet his wife and three other children. Where was he now? Had he returned to his family and the farm and was now outdoors working in the fields? As she sat in the harmonious kitchen in the midst of these friendly women, Anastasia resolved that just as soon as she finished eating she would gather Peter in her arms and start walking back to Neudorf. As anxious as she was to ascertain what had happened to Friedrich, Anastasia no longer had the slightest intention of waiting to see him.

When Mathias and Julianna had eaten their food, they asked if they could be excused, and then Mathias said, "Mama, can we take Peter outside and show him around the yard? We will watch him with Schnauzer's help, of course."

Before Maria could respond, Elisabetha was standing up in her chair, urgently proclaiming, "I come, too."

"I think Peter and I will soon need to be on our way home, and I don't know that he would go with your children," Anastasia hesitantly replied. Once again, it seemed she had underestimated her son; she had scarcely responded when Peter climbed off Amelia's lap and reached for Mathias's outstretched hand.

"Let him go, Anastasia. Mathias and Julianna are very good about watching toddlers, and their puppy is the gentlest creature you will ever find. With the children outside, we will be able to talk, as I have some important information that I need to tell you and it is better said without too many curious little ears to overhear us. Besides, it is much too late in the day for you to be thinking about returning to town, and you are welcome to stay the night."

Anastasia simply could not believe Maria's kindness, and she experienced profound feelings of guilt and humiliation increasing with each measure of the other woman's hospitality. She had never been so ashamed in her entire life—not even when she had gone to bed with a man without the sanctity of marriage and then, several months later, given birth to his illegitimate child. All the while, she had believed that her sinful behaviour only affected Friedrich and herself and that she was harming no one. Naturally, she knew they were upset, but, if anything, Anna and Helmut Schmidt's love for her seemed to have doubled with the birth of the infant boy whom they insisted on giving their family name. Now, here was the man's wife treating her as though she was some long-lost relative who had reappeared after years of absence. Anastasia could hardly raise her head, much less say anything in response.

Maria really had not expected Anastasia to answer, and so she continued. "There is no easy way to say this, but the first thing I must tell you is that Friedrich Werner is dead. He apparently arrived home during the night in the early spring of last year, and for whatever reason instead of coming into the house, he decided to leave again. It was later determined that when he was starting his automobile, he must have left it in gear while he was cranking the engine, and the car accidentally ran over him. Even though Amelia's husband rushed to town to get the doctor, there was little he could do and Friedrich died early that morning. Of course, since we were not aware of you, there was no way to let you know what had occurred or about the day and time of his funeral."

Now Anastasia immediately lifted up her head and stared at Maria, thinking that she was being sarcastic; but there appeared to be no rancour on her gentle face. Then it slowly dawned on her that Maria had referred to Friedrich by his full name rather than with "my husband."

Unable to understand Maria's dispassionate approach to her, Anastasia finally blurted out, "I don't understand how you can learn that I have been sharing your husband yet still treat my son and me so kindly. I just can't figure you out. I am so overwhelmed with shame and guilt that I can hardly look at you, and you keep extending your goodwill towards both of us."

"Oh, Anastasia, please do not feel guilty about Friedrich. We had not been man and wife for years, and I knew from the minute you hesitated about coming into the house that you were an innocent victim of his duplicity. He could be a charming man when he wanted and was able to spin some convincing lies to serve his own purposes, so you have nothing to be ashamed of in regard to him. Over the years I have received an abundance of love from my precious children and many other people, which more than compensates for what I did not get from him. So, please let's try and be amicable since your child, Peter, is a half-brother to my son and daughters."

"I have not even told you how I happened to meet Friedrich, and the first thing I want to say, Maria, is how right you are about my being completely taken in by him. It started one morning when he came to my parents' bakery, and from then on, he came practically every evening to insist that I go out for a walk with him. Well, if I am perfectly truthful, Anna and Helmut Schmidt are not my real family. My mother died several years ago and they took me in when I ran away from my drunken father's farm." Anastasia paused and then decided that although she had no idea how she could begin to repay this family who had accepted her with such frank kindness, the very least she would do was be honest with them.

"When I finally consented to go with him, he told me that he was all alone in the world. Not only did I feel terribly sorry for him, it now seems that I foolishly believed all of his falsehoods."

As the three Werner women sat and listened, Anastasia talked as she never had before, telling them about her past, how much she missed her mother, why she left her home, and then how she found such wonderful people as Anna and Helmut Schmidt in Melville, who had taken her in as though they had been waiting for her to arrive. She no sooner made this comment than Anastasia understood why they had been so upset about her decision to search for Friedrich. Of course, they feared she would disappear as stealthily as she had come, and they would never see her and their grandson again. It was little wonder that before they had boarded the train, Helmut had shown her the papers drawn up by the town's lawyer that made Peter's and her name change legal so the Schmidt Bakery would eventually belong to her.

~ 105 ~

She knew many hands make light work. And when it was time to do the chores and make supper, Anastasia pitched in as though she had lived on the Werner farm for her entire life. The weeds survived another day, although they received more than a few desultory glances from Amelia as Anastasia and she were in the garden picking lettuce and radishes for the salad. When first Christian and Franz and later Gustav came in from the fields, Maria introduced Anastasia as her cousin from Melville who was eager to have her son Peter meet her children. She was only able to stay the night because she must return to help her parents in the operation of their busy bakery, but it was such a delight for her to breathe the fresh air of the country. Mathias and Julianna were excused from doing the dishes, which the four women dispensed with in haste, before they joined the children outdoors to take a stroll around the farm on the balmy summer evening.

The next morning Gustav hitched Wolfgang to the carriage as Amelia and he prepared to take Anastasia and Peter to Neudorf. Even the women had forgotten that the mother and child who had arrived unannounced only yesterday were not blood relatives. When Maria discreetly gave Anastasia a piece of paper with her parents' address in Melville, the younger woman exclaimed that it was but three blocks from where she lived in the loft of the bakery. Then when Maria said that her father was the reverend at St. Paul's Lutheran Church on Third Avenue, Anastasia responded that she already knew Maria's father and mother because not only was that the church the Schmidt family attended, but Maria's mother also regularly visited the bakery during the early afternoon. When they were at last comfortably on the train returning to Melville, Anastasia smiled at her good fortune.

106

Going to bed would be an exercise in futility. He knew he would not sleep, so what was the point of crawling between the fleecy white sheets? Instead, David made himself comfortable on the chair by the open window of his small flat and sat looking across the river to the hotel where Katherina would be sleeping soundly in her oversized bed. He had convinced her to stay Monday in Saskatoon while his parents returned to Duff. It was wonderful to have the three of them in attendance when he was called to the bar and then treated to a memorable evening in the hotel's dining room by his law firm. It was disappointing that Sarah and Andrew decided not to come, but he certainly understood how busy they were with Emma and Rebecca. In fact, David eagerly anticipated the day when Katherina and he would have their own children.

Now all of their plans had to be altered with the declaration of war. How could he tell her that he had enlisted? What explanation could he offer her about his profound conviction that he had to join the Allies and fight for his country, when David did not really understand it himself? All he could grasp with any semblance of reason was that from the time Britain had declared war first on Germany and then on Austria, he had known he would become one among the throngs of young men who were enlisting with every passing day. Although the federal government had not imposed conscription, it was rapidly becoming the Canadian *zeitgeist* to take up arms and defend the freedom of the British Empire. As David pondered what words he could say to soften the blow to his unsuspecting bride-to-be, his mind began to wander.

Eventually he found himself remembering when he was a boy and his mother had tried every approach in her repertory—reading, singing, and even playing the piano to try and get him to sleep. She had been so distressed by how little he actually slept that she had taken him to the doctor, convinced there had to be some physical reason for his wakefulness. David knew how worried his mother had been by his unusual behaviour, but regardless of how desperately he wanted to go to sleep, there were many nights he just lay perfectly still, hoping his mother thought he was in a deep slumber. It was Katherina, who identified the reason for his insomnia, when she said that he slept so little because of his insatiable curiosity.

Suddenly David shivered in the still, warm summer night; he had goosebumps all over his body, as though someone was walking on his grave. He hated that silly, superstitious expression almost as much as he disliked it when Katherina started talking in the fatalistic manner to which she was sometimes prone. He found it particularly annoying because she was so definitive when making those comments, as though she could foresee the future. All too frequently her predictions came true. And it had already occurred to David that regardless of how he explained his duty to fight for Canada to Katherina, she would only focus on the likelihood of him being killed in the war. Of course, the scary fact was that he could lose his life. Even as a commissioned officer, David would be in the front lines, leading his men into battle. And whether or not he survived would be up to God.

Not surprisingly given the way his mind was racing, David was still wide awake and curled up in the large cozy chair when the sun crept over the horizon, painting the morning sky with majestic strokes of pastel pinks and blues. After spending the entire night in reflection and reminiscence, David was consumed by his passion for Katherina. With his body, mind, and soul, he longed to be with her after years of waiting to make her his own. He was certain that he had contemplated all of her possible responses to his decision, and David fervently hoped she would consent to marry him before he left in two weeks to begin his military training. He was well aware that Katherina and her Aunt Margareta had already started the extensive preparations for a large family wedding in September, but he was confident that he could convince her to have a simple marriage ceremony, perhaps even this afternoon.

True to form, David had a plan. He would shave and have a long, relaxing shower, giving Katherina time to sleep in before he arrived at the hotel to whisk her away to a sumptuous breakfast in the same dining room where they had enjoyed a delectable meal on Saturday evening. Then they would go for a leisurely stroll through City Park and along the river, before the day became scorching under the blazing prairie sun. Finally they would find a park bench or a shady spot under a large elm or poplar tree and he would tell her that he had enlisted, entreating her to marry him then and there. If she agreed, they would walk to the church they attended the previous day with his parents and ask the reverend to perform the ceremony to make them husband and wife. After using the university telephone to call his parents and her Aunt Margareta at the store to tactfully announce their news, David would plead with her, if necessary, to mind the dress shop so Katherina could stay with him until he embarked upon his soldiery. Cleansing his strong, healthy body in the shower, David began thinking about the next ten days alone with Katherina in his apartment. Envisioning her in his arms as he gently loved her only increased his yearning, and as he towelled himself, he impetuously determined that now was the time to put his plan into action.

When David opened the door of the hotel and stepped into the lobby, Katherina was descending the circular mahogany staircase. He realized that she had not yet seen him and he stopped in his tracks, staring at the beautiful young woman who seemed to become more elegant with each passing year. His memory carried him back to the first time he saw her in the church at Sarah's wedding, and as had happened so many times over the past week, he was again plagued by doubt. Why would he risk everything he had planned and worked for when he was not even being forced to enlist? He was neither going to war for the excitement and adventure nor was he caught up in the *zeitgeist*, as were many of his fellow classmates. David truly believed he had a moral obligation to defend the freedom and justice of his country; it was his duty as a man. Yet he would give anything not to have to leave Katherina so soon. It occurred to David that as creatures of habit, human beings do not value the ordinariness of daily life until it threatens to cease.

"You seem very far away, my dear David. A penny for your thoughts," Katherina said as she startled David out of his trance. Indeed, he had become so engrossed in his reverie that he had not seen her approaching, although he had been looking right at her. Under any other circumstances he would have given his head a shake, but this morning he had just too many things on his mind. "Good morning, darling Katherina. I trust you slept well and are ready to enjoy our day together."

"If I didn't know better I would think you had sidestepped my query. However, I shall be more polite and answer by telling you that I slept like a contented baby full of milk," Katherina teased, as she gently slipped her hand under David's arm. When the tall, handsome couple crossed the lobby on their way into the dining room, more than a few heads turned to take notice; although it seemed neither had eyes for any other.

Their morning progressed precisely as David had planned, and he knew it was better than he could have imagined. The weather was almost temperate, aided by a cool summer breeze coming off the river, as they strolled through the park at a leisurely pace after their ample breakfast. As a rule, Katherina ate only lightly in the morning, usually having little besides a cup of coffee and a glass of juice, but when she tasted a mouthful of the fluffy scrambled eggs, delicious smoked sausages, and buttery hot scones, she was glad she had allowed David to order for both of them. By the time they were enjoying fresh wild raspberries with thick cream and aromatic coffee, she was convinced that she would not be able to move for the balance of the day. David was encouraged, to say the least, by Katherina's cheerful, buoyant demeanour, and soon found himself becoming enchanted with her playfulness.

His heart overflowing with love, David spied a shady, secluded spot near the bank of the river, under a grove of willow trees dressed in long, slender foliage that danced in the wind. With the leaves at the peak of their lushness as they darted between the sunbeams and the reflections off the river with its deep-blue hue from a distance, the morning seemed surreal. He placed his suit jacket on the soft, flattened grass, suddenly longing for a blanket and the darkness of night, so strong was his desire for her. For a moment, he wished he were not such a methodical person who had to have everything in the right order, and instead of breaking his news to Katherina he could just seize the day and enjoy his time with her. But if he did not tell her, she would return to Neudorf and they might never have a chance to become man and wife. Of all David was about to risk, he intuitively knew that if he lost Katherina nothing else would matter.

When they were settled on the makeshift covering, David took Katherina in his strong arms and asked, "Are you comfortable, my darling? I should have had the foresight to bring a blanket, but I didn't realize the weather would be so co-operative."

"Oh, yes, David. This is such a lovely place and I am glad you suggested that I stay for another day. I remember you telling me some time ago that Saskatoon was a much more beautiful city than Regina, and this morning when I looked out of my window and saw this park with all its greenery, I had to agree. As I stood there, it occurred to me that I could not recall having been this happy in my entire life."

Before Katherina could enthuse anymore, David felt compelled to speak.

"Please listen to me, Katherina. The very last thing in the world that I would ever want to do is cause you even one minute of unhappiness, but I must talk to you about our future. There is no easy way for me to say what I need to, although I have struggled and rehearsed the words as if they were lines in a play, since I have determined what I must do."

"This is so unlike you, David. I have never heard you hedge about anything before in all of the time we have known each other, so why don't you just speak your mind?" There was still a hint of jocularity in Katherina's voice, as though she was reluctant to be serious about any topic on this glorious afternoon.

Looking earnestly into her eyes, David hesitated. Katherina was so endearing when she relaxed enough to enjoy herself as she had since he greeted her at the hotel, and now he worried that he would burst her bubble. A part of him wished she had been in one of her more sombre moods when he had arrived in the morning; then at least she would not have had to experience such an antithesis of emotions. Taking a deep breath, and unconsciously drawing Katherina closer to him, David finally spoke.

"After due consideration, I have decided it is my duty as a young man to defend my country, and I must tell you that I have enlisted in the army."

The moment David uttered the words, it was as though the world stopped spinning on its axis and time froze. Nothing. Not a sound, not a movement, not even a breath. He sat with his back ramrod straight, as perfectly still as she, and waited. He dared not repeat what he had said, in case Katherina did stop breathing. The silence was deafening and yet they remained motionless, like ice crystals suspended in the frozen air of a bitterly cold winter's night. Straining his ears, David thought he heard a barely audible "No... no... no." Then he began to discern a strange sensation. Katherina was receding from his protective hold, although not a muscle in her body had moved. She was slipping away from him; she was in his arms, which he had instinctively tightened, yet she seemed to be eerily afar from him, in a place where he was unable to reach her.

What David did not know, nor could he since Katherina had never alluded to it, was that she was retreating into the deep, dark pit that she had slid into when her mother had died. She was all alone and falling farther and farther into the abyss. Terror engulfed her, and she could not see, could not think, could not feel or move, as the foreboding blackness pushed in, surrounding and then pervading her very being. As she sank once again into the depths of her despair, Katherina suddenly glimpsed a flicker of light coming from a long hallway. Focusing with all of her energy on this beacon, she was able to visualize a woman holding a small candle, and the more she looked, the more it appeared that the figure was motioning for her to draw near. Finally Katherina was able to make out the woman's face. It was Aunt Margareta coming to save her as she had so many years ago. In a flash of insight, Katherina knew she had to go home.

Gulping air as though she had been immersed in a body of water, Katherina said in a low, trembling voice, "I must go to the train station. I need to be with Aunt Margareta."

With considerable relief that Katherina was at least responding, David eased her around to face him and replied, "We have more than four hours before the train leaves for Neudorf. I was hoping we could discuss the possibility of changing some of our plans."

"Please take me to the train. I want to see Aunt Margareta," Katherina answered in a monotone voice, as though David had not spoken.

"Yes, of course I shall when the time comes; but please stay with me, Katherina, so we can talk about our future," David pleaded. He could not stand the thought of letting her go when she was so abjectly despondent. When would he see her again? How could she even think about going back to Neudorf when they had so little time left to be together?

At last, Katherina looked at David. Her eyes were wide and teary as she studied him, as if she was trying to lock a picture of his face in her memory to last her forever. With an anguished expression on her face, she cried out, "We have no future, David, because of your decision to go to war."

"I cannot let you leave now. I must help you to understand why it is my obligation to join all of the men who will be defending our country. I want to be with you more than anything in the world, but what would happen if every man chose to ignore the call to fight? Please, Katherina, stay with me in Saskatoon until I begin my training. I love you and I need you here with me."

"For how long? Two or three weeks, a month, and then I shall be alone waiting to hear what is happening to you. No, I can't live with the constant worry and dread of never seeing you again. I am going home to be with Aunt Margareta and Uncle Phillip, and if you will not take me to the station, I shall go alone."

As they sat on the bench outside the station, waiting for the late afternoon train, David and Katherina were totally silent, the war that was just beginning driving a wedge between them. They would have been more conversational if they had been strangers; at least they'd be able to make small talk about the weather or perhaps speculate about how the hostilities in Europe would affect them as Canadians. Instead, both of them sat perfectly still, eyes staring straight ahead. To his dismay, David could not convince her to even consider staying with him, and he certainly did not have the courage to reveal his intention of arranging their marriage ceremony that afternoon—not that she would have consented, so determined was she to leave him. His feelings vacillated between desolation that he would soon be alone and anger that Katherina would abandon him now. David did understand her apprehension and shock; but if only she could see beyond her fears, they could have fourteen wonderful days together to cherish and remember until he returned to her. David would not nor could he promise to come home, but he intended to do everything within his power to stay alive.

Seeing nothing as she continued to look off into the distance, Katherina was too numbed to try and talk or even to listen. How could he expect her to stay with him for fourteen days and then forsake her for a lifetime? The minute David had become serious and started his conversation in his more distant—and what she imagined as his professional—voice, she experienced a recurrence of that ominous feeling that once had seemed to permeate her soul. In the past, a heaviness would weigh down on her spirit, dragging her within the depths of her being; it would take so much energy to shake it off, until as she had felt when Mama died, she no longer wanted to live. Only her Aunt Margareta had even tried to understand her recurring episodes of doom and gloom. When she was young and still living on the farm, Hanna would become frightened and could not decide whether to stay beside her or let her languish in the bedroom.

During their courtship, as David had become aware of her dark moods and what he called her bleak premonitions, he would try to cheer her by holding her and assuring her that now and then everybody had times of melancholy. He would adamantly object when she verbalized her predictions and then try to minimize them by saying she was being pessimistic. Nonetheless, Katherina had assiduously guarded the depth to which her despair could take her, always being very careful to keep her overwhelming sensations of being swallowed by a pit of darkness to herself.

With a start, she came out of her preoccupation when she heard the conductor's voice calling, "All aboard."

They both jumped up at the same time, Katherina anxious to get on the train to be alone in her misery, and David desperate to keep her with him. He still did not believe she would go, but then all he could think of was the image that would be stored in his memory: his beloved Katherina sitting at the window looking disconsolate as the distance between them increased, although the train had yet to move. This was not part of his plan.

107

Conversations around the Werner supper table had taken on an entirely different flavour, with Christian orchestrating most of the discourse. It was as though the hours he spent during the day walking and chatting with Franz had oiled and loosened Christian's tongue in readiness for the family exchanges during the evening meal. He had started slowly at first by asking each of his family members about the happenings of their day. Initially they had all been so surprised that even Gustav had to stop and think before he could answer. Gradually, the women and children became quite accustomed to Christian's unlikely behaviour and found that as they did their daily chores they would comment to each other about different occurrences as being worthy of inclusion in the newly anticipated mealtime discussions. Sometimes Gustav would contribute and, on other occasions, he simply said he was too tired from working in the fields.

It was Amelia who seemed the most delighted with this transformation in Christian, and when it was her turn, she always spoke of things which she knew would be of particular interest to her father-in-law, whether that the baby chicks were losing their soft fluff and growing feathers or the corn had sprouted up at least another inch. When she thought about it, she realized that it warmed her heart to see Christian Werner resume his rightful place as the head of his family, instead of seeing him slouched in his chair, despondent with little or nothing to say to any of them as though he had become feeble-minded. To be truthful, Amelia never understood why his own children seemed to ignore him because from the day she had married Gustav, she had found Christian to be more than interested in what she wanted to tell him. In addition, the austere old man always took the time to listen to his grandchildren, and very often he even became involved in their games of hide-and-seek.

Of course Amelia was only too aware that Christian's changed behaviour went a long way to assuage her guilt about her siblings. She had felt dreadful about taking Katie and Franz away from their own father, even though she was convinced that it was necessary for their safety. Then when it turned out that Franz was all but useless around the farm, she worried that Gustav would soon become burdened by having an extra mouth to feed. At first, Gustav had tried to teach him how to tend to the oxen and to get the plow ready for the spring cultivation, but he soon lost his patience when Franz could not seem to get anything right. In almost two years of marriage, Amelia had come to know her husband well enough to understand that, like her, he preferred to work alone, being able to finish any job so much faster than when saddled with a helper who was not able or keen to do it in the first place. As she was so often inclined to do, Amelia blamed herself for not having expected Franz to do his share of the chores on the Schweitzer homestead; instead she had let Katie and him play while she had independently and capably handled the multitude of domestic tasks required of a pioneer woman.

At the supper table one evening, Franz excitedly told the other members of the family that Papa Christian and he had now walked every acre of the Werner farm. He was fascinated by how the land had been surveyed, with each homestead being one corner of a perfect square with an allowance for a road between each section. As Franz was talking, Gustav found himself remembering that his father had provided the same explanation when he was a boy, and it dawned on him that perhaps Franz was more alert than he had presumed. Once again, Gustav wondered if Franz missed his own father, although whenever Amelia and he went to visit Karl Schweitzer, the boy refused to go. In fact, the first time after Franz had come to live with them that Gustav had said they were going to see his father, he had run away and hid until night was approaching.

Lately, even Amelia was not eager to make their weekly trip to her former home, and quite truthfully Gustav could blame neither for wanting to stay away. As far as he could determine, some strange things were happening on the Schweitzer farm. To be sure, the land was being attended to, since Ludwig had given up his job in Melville on the railway and come back to sow and reap the crops from its rich soil, but more and more, Gustav suspected he was doing it to Karl's detriment. There was no way for Gustav to prove his conjecture, and he had certainly kept his opinion to himself, but he often wondered if Ludwig was supplying Karl with cheap whiskey just to keep his father and the man he had recently met at the beer parlour in Neudorf, Jakob Litzenberger, out of his hair. There was no one in either Lemberg or Neudorf who had ever considered that the two old men had much in common, other than the fact they both liked their liquor, and so most people were surprised to hear that Jakob was now living on the farm with Karl and Ludwig. When this fact became known, it did not take the Silent Critics long to start the rumour that Ludwig Schweitzer was buying the Litzenberger homestead one bottle of whiskey at a time, and when he was seen farming Jakob's land they were quick to say that the proof was in the pudding.

Then again, there seemed to be no limit to the amount of gossip that the Silent Critics could generate and spread about Jakob Litzenberger, until Margareta Mohr had been heard to say that he was challenging her as their preferred candidate for the rumour mill. The talk had actually started several years earlier when his daughter Anastasia, dressed in her raggedy clothing, no longer walked into Neudorf every Sunday to attend church. Well, the Silent Critics had a heyday with their speculations about what had happened to her, until the more solicitous folks in town decided that action had to be taken. Following one of his services, a group of townspeople led by Margareta approached Reverend Ulmer, who had taken over the church in Neudorf in addition to ministering to his flock in

Lemberg after Reverend Biber had moved to Melville, to ask him if he knew why Anastasia had not been seen for at least a month.

Early the next morning, the reverend knocked on Dr. Spitznagel's door to arrange for his friend to accompany him to the Schweitzer farm, where they found Karl and Jakob sleeping off their previous day's consumption of what both men considered the drink of the devil. The house was in shambles; quite possibly it smelled more like a barn than the barn itself. When they had cleared enough of the mess in the kitchen to brew some coffee and managed to get two cups of it down Jakob's throat to sober him up, they demanded to know where Anastasia was and why she had stopped coming to church.

Jakob answered in a surly voice, "I don't know where that useless girl is. Do you think I would live like this if she were around to do her chores? The last time I saw her, she was running into the ravine where she spent most of her days playing to avoid work. As far as I know, she could have been attacked and carried away by a pack of wolves because I can find neither hide nor hair of her."

The visitors were astonished by the apparent disregard that the man had for his only daughter, but they had little choice other than to return to town and explain that they were unable to determine what had happened to the girl. Although Reverend Ulmer and Dr. Spitznagel agreed that Jakob was guilty of the most despicable neglect, neither of them considered for a moment that he had physically harmed the girl. So the disappearance of Anastasia Litzenberger remained a mystery, which the Silent Critics hypothesized about at regular intervals for years to come. However, there was a day in early summer when one of the spinster sisters thought she saw a young woman who bore a striking similarity to Anastasia getting off the train with a little boy who was the spitting image of Friedrich Werner. For whatever reason she had held her tongue and did not draw the attention of the other Silent Critics to the stranger with the child, as they naturally were occupied talking about someone else.

If only the Silent Critics had not so effectively estranged themselves from most of the people in the townships, the spinster sister and Gustav Werner might well have had a mutual topic of discussion. Neither would ever know that they shared exactly the same impression about how Peter, to whom Gustav was introduced by his young mother Anastasia Schmidt, resembled his oldest brother.

He was surprised to arrive home from the fields one fine day to discover that they had guests and even more amazed to learn that the two strangers were Maria's long-lost cousins, about whom none of them had ever heard. Not for the first time, it crossed Gustav's mind that perhaps the Schweitzer household did not hold the monopoly on unusual happenings, and he had an uneasy sense that the Werner women knew more than what they were telling.

Gustav was working in his fields from dawn to dusk every day except Sunday during the spring, summer, and fall, and he realized he was becoming more and more baffled by just what took place on the Werner homestead in his absence. He had long ago decided that his young, energetic wife was doing the oxen's share of the work around the house and in the garden, and when he had talked to Amelia, his suspicions were confirmed. However, how could he refute her response that hard work was its own reward when he subscribed to the same belief? Furthermore, he managed to convince Amelia that she no longer needed to feel any guilt about Franz's contribution on the farm, since what the youth had done for Christian was far more important than any chore. In the privacy of their bedroom, Gustav, knowing that it was Amelia who would have arranged for Christian to take Franz out to the fields, thanked her for her intuitive request, which ultimately led to the healing of his father's emotional and mental wounds and restored him to his position as the head of the Werner family.

Although Gustav marvelled at what Amelia had done for the Werner family and for returning their home to the warm, harmonious place it had been when his mother was alive, he still could not believe how well the three women got along. He admitted to himself that when he brought Amelia to the farm as his bride, he was worried that his sister and sister-in-law would resent the younger woman and even make life difficult for her. Instead they had quickly accepted her, and now the three of them seemed to be the best of friends. Of course, he was happy for Amelia, and as he now knew her to be a sweet, gentle person, he was not surprised that all of his family had come to love her. The real conundrum for Gustav was how close Hanna and Maria had become over the years, until he began to question the way they treated each other; he started to think their behaviour was odd.

There had been times when Gustav returned from the fields to see the two women walking and holding hands, seemingly oblivious to everything around them. Then there was the day he had been plowing the field along the creek and decided to tether the oxen to walk the short distance home for an early dinner. He had come across Hanna and Maria lying beside each other in the tall prairie grass under the shade of the willow trees.

He blurted out, "What are you two doing?" as both sat up, straightened their hair and dresses, and responded at the same time that they were resting. Later in the evening when Gustav asked Amelia what she thought about the two women's friendship, she brusquely replied, "I think Maria is lucky to have a sister-in-law and friend like Hanna to love her and to be so caring and helpful with her children, especially since your brother Friedrich did not seem to be very interested in them even when he was alive."

It took Gustav a few days to mull over his wife's response. He could not recall Amelia ever having used a sharp tone of voice with him; if he did not know better, he would have thought that there was some sting in her words, although he readily agreed with her opinion. Gustav was not surprised that Amelia would perceive Hanna and Maria's friendship as being perfectly innocent; although, once again he was amazed by the apparent solidarity among the Werner women.

On further reflection, Gustav did not know what really bothered him about Hanna and Maria; finally one day he found the courage to ask Rolf what he thought about their closeness. As the proud father of another baby girl, Rolf was quick to respond, "Having three daughters, I live in a house surrounded by the gentler sex, and I think I have died and gone to heaven. But seriously, it is hardly surprising that Hanna and Maria have such a loving friendship since they have lived together for so many years and Hanna has helped Maria to raise her children. Mathias, Julianna, and Elisabetha are polite, well-mannered, and obedient, so in my mind, the two women are doing an excellent job in the absence of their father. I also know you have been important in their upbringing and love those three children as your own, so I don't understand what is worrying you."

"Once again, my kindly big brother, you are absolutely right. I do love Mathias, Julianna, and Elisabetha, and I have often thought they are better off not to have Friedrich around. I don't like to speak ill of the dead, and certainly not our own brother, but Friedrich always seemed to be such an unhappy man, never satisfied with his lot in life."

As Gustav spoke, the image of the little boy, Peter Schmidt, came to his mind, but he stopped short of expressing his suspicions to Rolf. As it was, lately Gustav's mind seemed to be filled with skepticism, and he questioned whether there was any purpose in involving Rolf in his uncertainties when he did not understand them himself.

⟫⟩~ 108 ~⟨⟪

As much as she loved David Hardy, had he darkened the arches of her doorway during the week following Katherina's trip to Saskatoon, Margareta might cheerily have strung him up by herself. It took her three days to even determine what was troubling her beautiful niece, who instead of excitedly anticipating her upcoming wedding, had arrived home with a dark cloud hanging over her head. True to her custom, Katherina had risen early the next morning and come to breakfast impeccably groomed and ready to manage her dress shop. However, at the end of the workday, as soon as supper was over and the dishes were washed, she retreated to her bedroom and spent the evening listening to the gramophone. It was not unusual that Katherina would take time to enjoy the cylinders of classical music that Gustav had kindly loaned to her; but, for three consecutive evenings, the only sound to be heard from her room was the plaintive weeping of the strings of Mozart's last Violin Concerto.

On Wednesday evening, unable to hold herself back any longer, Margareta climbed up the stairs to Katherina's bedroom, which she referred to as her heavenly loft since her

Uncle Phillip had constructed a window in the roof through which she could see the stars. Knocking gently, she waited patiently until she heard Katherina coming, and as soon as her niece peered through the crack of the marginally opened door, Margareta said, "My darling, if you do not let me in and tell me what transpired in Saskatoon, I shall be forced to break into your haven."

As gloomy as she had been, Katherina started to laugh at the image of her short aunt, who was becoming stouter as the years passed, taking a running leap and knocking the door from its hinges.

"Please come in, Aunt Margareta. For Uncle Phillip's sake, perhaps both of us should keep our destructive tendencies under control."

The women sat on the bed in the position that had been so comforting for Katherina during her grief-stricken days after her mother's death, and as she related David's news about joining the army, Margareta wondered if life and love would always be so hard on her favourite niece. Thinking to herself that the man needed to have his head examined, Margareta drew Katherina to her ample bosom and silently held her.

Finally she said, "Oh, darling Katherina, now I know the reason for your distress. Over the years you have been living with us, I have come to understand how your mind works, and I could tell you the very first thought that you had when David expressed his decision to you. I do not fault you for immediately contemplating that he might be killed because I would do exactly the same if Phillip were young enough to enlist. As rare as it is, I am at a loss for words since I shall not pretend to give you false reassurance and say that David will return to you. As we all know, his fate will now be in God's hands."

"I can't help thinking that if only his love for me was greater than his sense of duty, he would stay here in Canada with me," Katherina replied, struggling to stay in control. She knew if she started to cry again she would soon have spilled enough tears to overflow the creek that ran through her papa's farm. The recurring thought that haunted her was that she could not seem to retain the love of two of the most important men in her life, and many times she wondered if she was destined to always be alone and lonely.

"Katherina, you cannot continue to draw this comparison between David's love and his duty. I do not for one minute want to appear that I am taking his side for I love both of you as my own children, but I know he is a man with a profound passion for what is right and just. It was far from an accident that he became a lawyer because he has a firm commitment to uphold the laws of this new country and to ensure equality for all of its citizens. I have enjoyed many discussions with David when he waited for you to finish with your customers, and I have come to deeply respect his views. In fact, I shall never forget the time when I asked him for his thoughts about life and it then took me several days before I fully understood his answer."

"Now you have intrigued me, Auntie, since I have known for many years that your mind is as quick as a flash of lightning. So what could David have said that would take you very long to understand?" responded Katherina, sounding more like herself than she had since Saturday.

"In the end, I was so impressed by what David had said that I wrote it in my diary; but my darling niece, you are quite correct in your observation that I have been blessed with a good head on my stocky shoulders.

"I must admit that when I first met David and was getting to know him I often considered him to be a light-hearted and fun-loving young man, but I now suspect that when he is alone, the still waters run deep. He didn't score the highest mark in his class without being able to use his head for more than a hat rack, as your Uncle Phillip liked to say when he teased Peter as a boy," Margareta said, with a mischievous grin on her wholesome face.

"Yes, I could not agree with you more, and that's precisely why I think it is such a waste for him to become a soldier. All of those years of hard work and study, to throw it away to fight a war, which is hardly likely to cross the ocean and come to the shores of Canada. I have tried to understand and I know it is not fair to doubt his love for me, but in my darkest moments, all I think of is the possibility of David being killed and then wondering how I shall live my life without him."

"Even at this moment, as we sit here talking," replied Margareta, "I am convinced that David is tormented with indecision and doubt as he is savagely torn between his love and desire for you and his firm belief that he must defend his country. You see, Katherina, what I think David meant was that he knew how privileged he was to go to university and have the opportunity to study law, but he also realizes that everything comes at a cost. He understands that now he must balance his good fortune by making a sacrifice in order to seek and to achieve justice in his life. Hence, of all the young men in our community, David feels obligated to fight for the freedom of the British Empire, even though he knows he could pay the ultimate price and lose his life." Margareta began to gently brush Katherina's long, beautiful hair.

Several minutes passed before Katherina said thoughtfully, "I don't think I have been giving much consideration to David's perspective. As I recall, he did look so distressed and almost incredulous when I got on the train on Sunday, as though he never thought for a second that I would go. Oh, Aunt Margareta, what have I done? I was so absorbed in my own feelings that it never even crossed my mind that David could also be in agony."

"You were being perfectly human, since I think all of us retreat into ourselves when we are in pain, like a dog going off alone into the woods to lick his wounds. I have not had a chance to tell you what your Uncle Phillip overheard the Silent Critics talking about after church as they were having coffee at their usual table in the hotel. It seems their rumour for the day was that Peter was enlisting in the Canadian army. After Phillip told me, I was so upset and angry with Peter that I never said one word to him or even looked at him during the entire meal on Sunday evening. I could not believe our son would go to fight overseas when we had fled Russia because the Mohr family believes in pacifism just like your father. Poor Peter. I'm sure he could not understand what had possessed his usually verbose mother, and he went to bed early, no doubt feeling very dejected."

"How can you be so calm now, knowing that your only son is also going off to war? I would have thought you'd be beside yourself with despair, just as I have been for the last three days," Katherina said in amazement.

"Well, I certainly was on Sunday evening, and I too had withdrawn to the comfort of my bedroom. In fact, I had taken to my bed in my coziest nightdress and stayed there until the next morning. When I arrived to open the store, my dear friend Dr. Spitznagel was waiting for me. He is a wonderful man with such an awareness of the sensitivity of others that at times I can't believe he is not a member of the gentler sex. At any rate, he asked if he could speak to me before I let in any customers, and of course I was only too happy to oblige. Apparently, Peter had gone to him for his physical examination, which is required before he could enlist. The doctor was quick to point out that he did not want to violate his patient confidentiality, but as bad luck would have it, the widow of the Silent Critics overheard him talking to his wife about the reason for Peter's visit."

"That would explain how that information became the fodder of their incessant rumour mill," replied Katherina as she shifted her position to become more comfortable.

"Knowing that Peter would not tell his father and me about his decision to join the army unless he had been accepted, Dr. Spitznagel wanted to advise me that I need not worry. As it happens, and Dr. Spitznagel told me in the strictest confidence, Peter has a heart murmur that clearly has not bothered him up to this time in his life but will prohibit him from enlisting in military service. The considerate physician reassured me that there was nothing we could have done in terms of early detection and treatment, and he was emphatic that as Peter's parents we have no reason to feel guilty, or for that matter, anxious about his future. Between you and me, Katherina, I would far rather worry about some unusual sound in Peter's heart than constantly fret about whether or not he is still alive as he fights yet another unnecessary war in the Old World.

"Naturally, I went straight to the lumberyard to tell your Uncle Phillip, and then after we discussed Dr. Spitznagel's news, we decided to wait to see if Peter would talk to us about his decision. However, I have a strong hunch that Peter will choose to let the rumour die without making any comments about its origin," Margareta explained with a sigh as she thought to herself that it was time her son found a woman with whom to spend his life.

"I am very happy that at least Peter will be spared and you will not become old before your time because of worry and dread over what is happening to him. One of the things I have always loved about you, Aunt Margareta, is that you seem so much younger and livelier than most of the other women of your age in Neudorf, and especially the four female Silent Critics. Yet at the same time, you are so full of wisdom." Katherina hugged the older woman more tightly, knowing she would need her for the dark hours that lay ahead.

"Well, thank you, my darling. I decided long ago that I would not settle into aging like so many women do, but that I would fight tooth and nail to hold back the ravages of time. The Grim Reaper will need to struggle hard before I submit to his eternal clutches, since, as you know, I seldom go willingly anywhere that I do not choose," Margareta replied with a chuckle, making light of what she was really thinking. She had an uncanny sense that she would need to be there for her niece for many years to come.

"Oh, Auntie, I wish I had even half of your spirit and fierce determination. I seem to spend so much of my time and energy fearing the future and worrying about the past. If I could only do something to make up for the way that I treated David on Sunday, I would do it right now. As it is, I may never have an opportunity to tell him I am sorry and that I did not understand how he was feeling."

"If I know your young man, I am certain that David will find a way to see you another time before he leaves for his training. Pray that he does, Katherina, and when he comes, tell him everything that is in your heart. Always remember that we must take the bad with the good—for without sorrow, we cannot experience joy. Now it is getting late and we must get our beauty sleep," Margareta said as she shifted her position, slowly rose from the bed, and leaning over, kissed her niece on the forehead before departing from her loft.

～ 109 ～

Since the first of June, the prairie sun seemed determined to sear and bake the ground upon which it shone without reprieve from dawn to dusk. Each night it became a great red ball as it unwillingly slipped over the horizon and finally bid farewell. At daybreak it returned and relentlessly refused to allow rain clouds to form in the sky or the slightest wind to blow a welcoming breeze across the burning land. During the late afternoon, when its rays drilled down with their greatest intensity, the only movement was the heat waves rising upward from the scorched soil like apparitions, taunting anyone withering in their midst to join them in their ethereal dance until it was as though the fires of hell had come to earth as the world went to war.

The chores of farming were done either very early in the mornings or after supper, when the sun began its retreat to the faraway distance where the earth and the sky merged into one. Then the inhabitants of the prairie would surface from their resting places and resume the activities of daily living. On one particularly sweltering day as evening was approaching, Amelia was carrying two pails of milk to the shed for separating.

Franz excitedly ran up to her. "Here, let me take one of the pails. I'm sorry, Amelia, that I did not get back in time to help you with the milking, but Papa Christian and I have had a very exciting day."

"I'm happy to see you. I was beginning to worry about what happened to the two of you. Surely you were not walking around the farm during the heat of the afternoon. Even Gustav came home for dinner and has been working in his tool shed because it was too hot to be out in the fields. And right after supper, Franz, since you did not tend to the cows, you will come and help me in the garden," Amelia replied in a firm tone of voice.

"Yes, of course, but I am sure you will want to wait and listen to Papa Christian's news before we start weeding."

When Christian took his seat at the head of the table, Gustav was surprised to notice that his father's face had a healthy flush. Knowing that Christian never went walking without his trusty hat, which he had worn for as long as Gustav could remember, he wondered just where Franz and his father had spent the afternoon. Nonetheless, Gustav knew he must bide his time and wait until Christian was ready to enlighten his family, if indeed he would, about where the boy and he had been on such a stifling day. For some time now, the two of them had been venturing further and further afield, and they often returned home to tell the family about their visits with the nearby farmers. Gustav was so happy that his father had resumed calling on his neighbours and could hardly believe how much better the old man was in body and mind that he always waited patiently for him to relate the details of his daily journeys with Franz.

As soon as every member of the Werner family, including Mathias, Julianna, and even little Elisabetha, had told about their day, Christian stood up and said, "I am very happy to make an announcement, which has been a long time in coming. When Franz and I left for our walk this morning, we had not gone far when Mr. Riechmann came driving up in his carriage. He was delighted to see us because he had wanted to talk to me for some time, and so he immediately invited both Franz and me to return to his farm and spend the day with his family. As Franz has already said, he spent his time playing with their three oldest grandchildren while I sat in the kitchen with Mr. and Mrs. Riechmann talking over our plans.

"For one reason or another, their youngest son, Klaus, has never married and we determined that it would be a good match for you, Hanna, and so I am proud to tell my family that Klaus and you will wed this fall. Since your mother's death, I often felt that I was neglecting you by not arranging your marriage, and now I have done my fatherly duty by you."

It was fortunate that Christian had sat down in his chair before Hanna's response or he might well have been startled into falling because of her outburst. Initially, she was shocked into silence and disbelief, and she sat staring at Maria.

When she did recover, the young woman practically shrieked at her father, "Papa, what are you saying? You cannot possibly think I want to marry that old Klaus Riechmann! He must be at least ten years older than me; already he has lost most of his hair, not to mention that he is fat. I have never said that I wanted a husband, and certainly not one who is so long in the tooth. I am perfectly content living my life here on your farm and helping Maria raise her children."

"Don't be silly, Hanna. Every woman wants her own offspring and I have waited too long as it is to find you a suitable mate. Mr. Riechmann was so happy when I agreed you would marry Klaus that he decided on the spot that you would not need to bring a dowry. Then he offered me a drink of whiskey, which I accepted to celebrate the union of our families. Now, have you forgotten your manners? You know better than to talk back to me, and I don't want you talking about your future husband with such disrespect. Klaus is a hard-working man who will take good care of you, and you will marry him right after the harvest in September."

"I will never marry that disgusting old man, and nothing you can say or do will ever make me!" Hanna yelled as she jumped up from the table and ran outside, slamming the door behind her.

The rest of the family sat in stony silence, as surprised by Hanna's unusual behaviour as by her blatant rejection of her father's decision. Not one more word was spoken, nor was another morsel of food eaten during that memorable supper.

After several uncomfortable minutes passed, Amelia quietly got up from the table and began clearing the dishes and carrying them to the sink. To her credit, Maria exercised remarkable restraint, and instead of running after Hanna, stayed to help her sister-in-law. The very last thing she wanted to do now was raise any suspicions about the nature of her friendship with Hanna, and taking Mathias aside, she asked him to go comfort his aunt. Naturally, his sisters wanted to join him, and in the end, Maria sent all of her children outside to find Hanna. Also wanting to leave the tense kitchen, Franz rose from his chair and told his sister that he would be in the garden pulling weeds. The men stayed at the table, drinking their coffee, Christian confident in his belief that Hanna would come to her senses and eventually go along with his wishes, while Gustav sat beside his father, once again mystified by something upon which he could not quite put his finger. Nonetheless, for reasons that he could not identify, he may have been the most pleased, and if the truth were known, more than a little relieved by his father's announcement.

~ 110 ~

Two weeks had passed since Katherina's precipitous flight from Saskatoon, and without any news from her, David could not believe the depth of his dejection during his final days in the city. It was not that he did not have plenty to do, what with clearing out his small apartment, dispensing with his meagre furnishings, and being invited to a plethora of dinners by his business associates and suppers by his friends' families to say his farewells. In the midst of all this social activity, constantly surrounded by people, David never felt so alone in his life. There were moments when he told himself that he deserved to feel abandoned, and in a flash of insight, he realized that he had always been the one leaving. Perhaps he was getting a taste of his own medicine so he would have a sense of what he had done to Katherina.

Before he had reached his decision to enlist, many of his friends and even the partners in the law firm where he had articled had tried to dissuade him, not only from joining the army but also from being so hasty as to rush off and sign up before the Canadian government had identified its position on conscription. Even now, David could not explain the ineluctable pull he experienced to fighting in this war, and at any rate it was too late to change his mind. The die was cast the moment he walked into the recruiting office and signed his name on the dotted line. At night, when David was trying to sleep, he felt rather like a medieval picture he had once seen, where each of a man's limbs were tied to a team of horses pulling in opposite directions. Then he would chastise himself for being so melodramatic; but in the early hours of the morning, when David was still thrashing around in his bed, he could not help but feel that the core of his being was being ripped in half between his love for Katherina and his duty to his country.

When he finally discharged all of his responsibilities in Saskatoon, David returned home to Duff to spend his last days with his parents and to visit Sarah and Andrew and their children. The train that would take him to Manitoba where he would begin his military training as a captain in the Canadian army was scheduled to leave Duff late tomorrow afternoon. He had not heard a word from Katherina, nor had he made any attempt to telephone her at her aunt's store. To be truthful, David was not convinced that Katherina would accept the telephone call to talk to him, and he just could not bear to be the brunt of her ultimate rejection. Hence, here he was, gazing out the window from his alcove on a beautiful summer Tuesday evening when a full moon was rising in the firmament, soon after the sun had finally gone to rest, and the vastness of the Saskatchewan sky was resplendent with a multitude of stars, which only served to emphasize his insignificance in the universe. When the profundity of his despair struck him, David impulsively decided that he could wait no longer and he must make one last desperate attempt to see Katherina.

Since his parents had already retired for the night, David quietly opened his bedroom door and tiptoed down the hall in his stocking feet. He waited to put on his shoes until he had descended the stairs and reached the back door of the house. In the moonlight, which poured through the kitchen window, he found the keys to his father's car hanging on the rack by the cupboard, and he noiselessly made his escape without disturbing his mother and father. The automobile that his father had purchased from Maria Werner was parked in the shed, and David soon had it started and was on his way to Neudorf. David found his spirits lifting as he drove along the dusty road and felt the warm breeze play in his hair.

If Katherina turned out to be sound asleep, David was not quite sure how he would awaken her. He was suddenly grateful that when her Uncle Phillip had put a window in the ceiling of her loft, he had also placed a larger one on the side of the attic of the house. It occurred to him that it would be an achievable climb for him to get onto the lower portion of the projecting roof and then rap gently on the window until she heard him. Katherina had told David she always slept with her window wide open during the summer and even kept it slightly ajar during the coldest months of the winter, but he certainly did not intend to startle her by crawling through it. Perhaps the most important fact of all was that Katherina's loft was at the rear of the house and away from the other bedrooms; so if David required some time and effort to convince her to come for a ride in the country, they would not likely attract any attention.

At long last, Lady Luck sprinkled some of her fortuitous particles upon David; he had no sooner walked from the outskirts of town where he had parked the car than he looked up and saw a figure silhouetted in the upstairs window of the Mohr home. As it happened, Katherina was acutely aware that it had been fourteen days since she had left David, and fearing that she would not see him again before his departure to Manitoba, she had been unable to sleep. Looking out the window, she caught a glimpse of light shimmering at the far end of the deserted street, and she began to pray that it came from Mr. Hardy's automobile. Overcome with joy that it was indeed David, she stuck her head through the aperture and began waving to him. Then, motioning with her hand for him to give her five minutes, Katherina quickly changed from her night attire into a light summer dress and scribbled a note to Aunt Margareta that she had gone out with David. She then silently made her way out of the house.

Rushing up to David, with her long, lovely tresses caressing her shoulders, Katherina threw her arms around his neck, and to his delight whispered in his ear. "Thank you for coming. I was so afraid that I would never get another chance to tell you how much I love you and how sorry I am that I left you all alone in Saskatoon."

Wanting to bury his face and hands in her soft, flowing hair, David said, "Hush, my darling. We are together now, and that is all that matters. But let's get away from here before we awaken your family or any of the neighbours, or God forbid, one of the Silent

Critics. Why don't we drive out to our favourite knoll and enjoy this wonderful summer evening with its magnificent star-studded sky? Living in the city for far too many years, I miss the splendour of the prairie nights, and there is nothing more in the world that I would rather do than spend the next few hours with you waiting for what will be my last glorious Saskatchewan sunrise in awhile." David enveloped Katherina in his strong, protective arms.

Stopping the car, they climbed a small hill overlooking the hamlet. When they were comfortably seated upon the blanket that David had thoughtfully grabbed from his bed as he was leaving, neither of the young lovers had anything to say. Perhaps the magnitude of the moonlit night and the brilliance of the stars took their breath away as they communed with the wonders of nature. The slight cooling breeze, which played through the surrounding grove of poplar trees and rustled their waxy green leaves in a symphony of zephyr sounds, intensified the enchantment of the night.

Instead of breaking the magic of the evening, Katherina added the finishing touches when she softly said, "David, I want you to lie with me. I want you to love me as a man loves a woman."

"Oh, Katherina, I have longed to love you, and over the past few days, I have thought of little else; but my train leaves tomorrow afternoon and even if we could get Reverend Ulmer to marry us in the morning, there would be so little time. Where would we go? I don't want us to check into the Neudorf hotel and give the Silent Critics something to wag their tongues about for days and weeks after I leave you," David answered in an anguished voice.

"Not tomorrow, David, now. Here, in our favourite spot while we are encircled by the glory of God's universe. Right now in the moonlight in the time that we have left to be together," Katherina replied with assurance as she reached over and embraced David. "I made a dreadful mistake by running away from you, and you have given me the one chance I have been longing for to show you how much I love you. Please, David, I want with all my heart and soul for you to know and love me as a woman."

As he began to caress first her face and then her beautiful long neck, David was almost overwhelmed by his passion for Katherina. Kissing her gently on her mouth, he started to slide his hands along her shoulders as he carefully slipped her dress off and then progressed down to her full breasts. Wondering how something could be so soft and heavenly yet so firm and rounded, he moved his hands to ardently stroke her breasts first with his fingers. Then, lowering his head, he covered each of them in turn with his mouth and touched them with his tongue. As her nipples hardened in response, David felt as though he would explode with desire. With Katherina's hands running through his hair, he became aware of her urging him to explore her supple, virginal body. He wanted to be tender and slow to give her time to be ready to receive him, and not to climax too soon so she also could enjoy the delights of their lovemaking.

David's hands continued their search until he reached the part of Katherina's body he had imagined during years of fantasizing about this moment in time. Now he placed his fingers in her soft hair and rhythmically stroked until he found her opening. When he gently inserted his finger to prepare her for his entry, Katherina let out a gasp of pleasure, which only encouraged David to continue. She could feel his hardness pushing against her leg. The more he caressed her, the more she wanted him. Her young body yearned for him and began to arc in anticipation until he heard her say faintly, "Enter me, David, I want you so much."

"Are you ready, my darling? I will try not to hurt you." He resumed kissing her mouth, her throat, and her ears with a passion he had held in check for so long.

When they came together at last, the world could have collapsed around them and neither David nor Katherina would have known, or for that matter, cared. Afterward, lying with his head resting on her lap, David drifted off into a deep, sound sleep such as he had not enjoyed for as long as he could remember.

When the sun started to peek over the horizon, painting the sky with bright red, orange, and yellow, like a prism separating the shadowy white light from the moon into the lower colours of the spectrum, they were still in the same position. Katherina was not tired and did not want to miss one second of her time with David, even though he was sleeping. In fact, she felt more alive than she had ever felt before in her young life, as she waited for David to awaken from his slumber. Just then he stirred, and looking up into her radiant face, smiled as he rubbed the sleep from his eyes.

"Good morning, my darling. You look lovely in the waning light of our first night together. Have you slept at all, Katherina? I seem to have been resting on your lap since I closed my eyes."

"I wanted to stay awake to make sure that we saw the sunrise, since that was our reason for spending the night outdoors," Katherina answered, with a hint of amusement in her lilting voice. Then, becoming serious, she continued, "As I watched the firmament change from night to day, it occurred to me that there is no better place in this world to sanctify our union than here in the presence of God; therefore in my mind, heart, and soul, we have become one as husband and wife. And now, before the sun is fully up and flooding us with the light and heat of the day, I am going to love you again, my husband, before we return to Aunt Margareta's, where I shall prepare our wedding breakfast."

～ 111 ～

The door of Katherina's Dress Shop was not opened on that particular Wednesday morning, and it would remain closed for the entire day. As might be expected, the first to see the automobile driven by a young man delivering Katherina Werner to the Mohr home very early in the morning was one of the Silent Critics. Few if any of the townsfolk would refute the Silent Critics' oft-stated claim that a person would need to get up before dawn to pull a fast one on any of them. And they certainly were rewarded for their diligence, as the driver tried to arrive at his destination as stealthily as possible by slowly coming around to the back of the house. It was to no avail. It was exactly at the moment that the husband and wife members of the infamous group chose to leave their son's house, which, unfortunately for the lovers, was adjacent to the building that doubled as the town's general store and the Mohr residence.

Knowing they were already found out, David jumped out of the vehicle as soon as he had stopped it, and dashing around to Katherina's door, he remarked, "Thank you, my dear, for agreeing to come with me so early this morning to capture my last Saskatchewan sunrise for a while. I have heard that Manitoba is not as well known for its living skies as is our province, so I really appreciate you getting up before dawn."

Instantly understanding his subterfuge, Katherina replied, "It is just as well that you appreciate my sacrifice, since I am not an early riser; although, once I was up, it was a beautiful way to start a new day. As it is, I am sure Aunt Margareta will be amazed that I will be the first person in the kitchen and have breakfast underway. The fresh air of daybreak does pique a person's appetite, so won't you please come in and enjoy a meal with my family?"

Once Katherina and David were safely within the walls of the house, they both burst out laughing.

"Wouldn't you know it? Of all the people in the town, we would have to bump into those two nosy parkers," David chuckled when he had caught his breath.

"Do you think that we fooled them?" Katherina asked, with a note of concern in her voice.

"I'm sure it really doesn't matter. They are too old to remember what we were actually doing, and regardless, they will spend all day, if not longer, speculating over coffee with the rest of the Silent Critics about their chance encounter with Katherina Werner and her roguish Englishman," answered David facetiously, with the confidence of a man who understood the nature of small-town gossips. In his many years of courting Katherina, he had fully come to appreciate Aunt Margareta's ironical name for the particular group of individuals in Neudorf, and considered it quite appropriate that everyone in the German Lutheran townships had followed suit in their appellation. David Hardy was acutely aware that Aunt Margareta, as she had asked him to address her, was a liberated woman, and he thoroughly enjoyed her outspokenness—often teasing her that he was glad to be on her side.

As they started to walk down the hall towards the kitchen, the aromatic smell of brewed coffee and the delectable scent of fresh baking alerted Katherina and David that someone had pre-empted them in the breakfast preparations, and as they turned the corner, Phillip lifted his head from the newspaper he was reading at the table.

"Well, good morning. You two certainly must have been up at the crack of dawn, and given the glow in the sky, I am sure it was a beautiful sunrise. Do come and join me for coffee and some of your Aunt Margareta's delicious cinnamon buns. Of course, you are more than welcome to have sausage or bacon and eggs, but I am afraid you will need to cook for your young man, Katherina, as I am hurrying off to an important meeting at the lumberyard. Peter has already gone ahead to make sure the store is open and we are organized for our prospective new supplier."

"It is a very good morning, Uncle Phillip, and as it happens, I planned to prepare a full breakfast for David and myself. I will ask Aunt Margareta to join us as soon as I have it ready," replied Katherina, as she reached over and gave him a peck on the cheek.

"No, your aunt woke up early, and then when she could not go back to sleep, she stayed up and baked these buns for breakfast. She left for the store when Peter went out, so you only need to worry about yourselves," Phillip answered as he stood up and walked over to where David was standing.

"Naturally, Katherina has apprised us that you are soon going to Manitoba to begin your training with the Canadian Army. You are a brave man, David, and I want to thank you for joining all the young men who will be defending Canada, and wish you godspeed for your safe return."

"Thank you, Uncle Phillip, although I must register some surprise about your gratitude. As you are probably aware, there is a fair amount of controversy among the people in many of the towns and surrounding communities, particularly in areas like Neudorf, about which side the men from the new country should join."

"In my mind, there is nothing to debate. When I chose to come to this country, I wanted to let go of the traditions and ways of the Old World, and so I immediately deemed my family and myself to be Canadians. If I were not a pacifist, I might consider doing precisely as you are, and without telling us, Peter did try to enlist, although he was rejected for health reasons. When do you actually leave?" Phillip asked, as he reached for his hat.

"My train departs from Duff later this afternoon, and I shall travel non-stop to Winnipeg."

"In that case, would you please come to the lumberyard to say your farewell to Peter and me before you drive back to your parents' home?"

"Uncle Phillip, I plan to accompany David to Duff this afternoon, and I would like you to ask Aunt Margareta to leave the dress shop closed for the day. Please tell her we shall come and say goodbye after we have eaten breakfast, and also thank her for the cinnamon buns, which she knows are my favourite," Katherina said, as David gazed at her with a pleasantly surprised look on his handsome face. Following their debacle when she had fled from him in Saskatoon, he had been afraid to ask her to come and see him off at the Duff station, and he smiled lovingly at her.

The minute he heard the outer door close behind Phillip, David crossed over to the stove where Katherina had started to fry thick slices of bacon, took her into his arms, and gave her a long, passionate kiss. When they finally pulled apart, David said, "Thank you for returning with me to Duff. Within the last few hours you have made me the happiest man on earth, and whenever I become lonely during this dreadful war, I shall savour these exquisite memories of you, my dearest. Now, show me where to find the eggs and some vegetables and I shall make you the tastiest omelet you will ever eat."

Side by side they worked, as they each prepared the specific ingredients for their wedding breakfast. David reflected on how ravenous he was, and he wondered if Katherina was equally hungry after their strenuous night of lovemaking. Had he been alone in the kitchen, he might well have pinched himself to ensure that he was not dreaming. David had yearned to love Katherina for so many years, and was now filled with such calm satisfaction that he felt rather like the kitten that had drunk a bowl full of cream. As he glanced at Katherina, he was touched by the beatific expression on her lovely face and instantly knew she was feeling as awestruck as he was with the depth and wonder of their love.

When the last dishes and spoons had been washed, dried, and returned to their places in the cupboard, Katherina turned to David and demurely asked, "Would you like to come and see my loft?"

"I can't think of anything I would rather do, especially after our delicious breakfast. I could lie down and sleep like a baby, even though those few hours before dawn were the most tranquil repose I have had for days," David answered. They left the kitchen and started to climb the stairs to Katherina's bedroom.

"What a cozy, restful room," said David as soon as she opened the door. "Ah, how convenient that your bed is still rumpled as if waiting for us to return, and come to think of it, we do have the house to ourselves. Let's lie down together for a short time and gaze out the window in the roof, which must be a wonderful feature on a clear starlit night."

No sooner had Katherina joined David on the bed than he enveloped her in his muscular arms and began to kiss her firmly on the mouth. When she finally had a chance to speak, she said, "Oh, what a devious fellow you are. I thought we were just going to look up at the sky."

"I'm not so sure I was the one who was being oblique," he replied. "As I recall, my beloved, it was you who invited me to your boudoir, right after you served our wedding repast. Besides, it may be a very long time before I am able to love you again, my darling,

243

and it would give me so much solace in the days ahead to cherish the memory of loving you in your picturesque bedroom."

Snuggling into David's warm, taut body, Katherina answered coyly before she gave herself over to him. "I don't think it is solace you are seeking, and perhaps I also want some more memories to savour while you are gone."

As David began to arouse her, Katherina could not help but think to herself that she had never had the slightest idea that coupling between a man and a woman could be so pleasurable. Even as a novice, she enjoyed the sensation of David inside her and loving her with his passion, making her feel serenely whole, safe, and in complete harmony with the man she had cherished for years. Her only previous awareness of what happened between a man and a woman behind closed doors were from Maria and Friedrich, most often when he came home after drinking, and then the noises from their bedroom that sounded almost like physical combat. It was so unlike the overwhelming feelings of fulfillment that Katherina experienced as her entire body tingled with David's caresses until she was carried away with rapturous bliss beyond her wildest imaginings.

Much later, as David was nibbling on her ear, he said, "If I don't soon get up from your soft, comfortable bed, the Canadian Army will brand me as a deserter before I have even joined their ranks. Do you suppose I could borrow either Phillip's or Peter's razor so I can shave and try to make myself presentable before we go to see your Aunt Margareta?"

"She is your aunt, too, and somehow I have a strong hunch that if she knew what we were up to she would be very happy for us."

Gently moving away from David's embrace and rising from the bed, Katherina said, "I shall show you Peter's room and get the pitcher from his wash basin to fill with hot water for your use. I am also going to have a sponge bath and change my clothes, and then we can meet in the kitchen to begin our round of farewells."

The remaining hours left to Katherina and David flew by, with both of them furtively wishing for an eternity before they had to express their final goodbye. But, much too soon, the train was pulling into the Duff station. Katherina had held up remarkably well until they had arrived at David's home and she had seen the tear-streaked faces of Mrs. Hardy and his sister, Sarah. At first, a single teardrop trickled down each of Katherina's lovely cheeks, and then it was as though someone opened a floodgate; when reality reared its ugly head, she began to sob. Mrs. Hardy instantly took her into her welcoming arms and told her to cry until she drained the reservoir; she knew from experience that it would quickly refill. As it happened, it was sound advice, and by the time she embraced David for the last time before he irresolutely climbed aboard the waiting train, she was able to manage a sparkling smile for his send-off.

In the weeks and months to come, Katherina would always reflect with satisfaction that she had been able to cheer David on as he had falteringly took each of the three short steps into the passenger car as if he were scaling one of the Rocky Mountains that he had shown her in a picture one day when they were in the university library. She knew in her heart that in his final glance, he was locking her face in his memory like a photograph. It became her fount of happiness that she had been able to give him an enduring image that was bright and spirited, rather than one with the doom and gloom insidiously residing in her soul. Katherina intuitively understood that it had been the best day of her life, and she fervently hoped and prayed it was not also the last—and that they would have many more blissful times together.

~ 112 ~

Within a month, they were gone, as though none of them had ever been on the Werner farm. The stone house that had been bursting at its sturdy seams—and bustling, at least during the long, cold winter months with the noise and activity of five adults, one youth, and three rambunctious children—suddenly became almost empty and as silent as a tomb. If only Maria and Hanna had not kept their plans so completely secret up until three days before their departure, there might have been the possibility of adjusting to the dramatic changes which would befall them all. As it was, the only member of the Werner family whom they took into their confidence was Amelia, but not before they had extracted her promise that she would remain totally quiet about their preparations. It was Maria who finally convinced Hanna that they must at least give Amelia some notice, knowing full well that their innocent young sister-in-law would be devastated by the abrupt loss of the three children whom she loved as her own.

On the fateful evening that Christian had made his announcement, night had descended on the scorching prairie and Hanna had yet to return to the house. As the sun was setting, she had sent Mathias, Julianna, and Elisabetha back indoors, asking the boy to tell his mother to meet her at the edge of the garden under the caragana trees when she had settled her children. When Maria finally arrived, the moon was full and the stars were brilliant. Under the splendour of the glorious Saskatchewan sky, the women sat on the soft grass, enjoying the slight breeze coming out of the west. Hanna had long since finished with her tears and now was ready to talk about her future. "Maria, I must get away from the farm like Katherina did so that Papa cannot make me marry that old Klaus Riechmann. I saw how Friedrich treated you during your marriage, and I have no intention of ever letting a man take advantage of me like your husband did with you."

Maria responded, "All the time I was helping Amelia clean up the kitchen, I could not stop thinking that I have been so unfair to you. By expecting you to be with me and to help me raise my children, I just presumed it was what you wanted. I did not think about you having a husband and your own children, and I fear that I may have ruined you for loving a man. Besides, you must not judge all marriages by mine. Consider your older brothers and sisters, who all seem to be pretty happy with their mates—especially Rolf and Katie, and even Gustav and Amelia are becoming more loving as they get to know each other." Maria was as earnest as she could be, but her heart was not in her words and she deliberately avoided looking at Hanna.

"Oh, Maria, I am not afraid to say what I feel. It is you and your children whom I love and want to be with for the rest of my life," Hanna replied as she reached over and gently stroked Maria's arm.

"That's exactly what I am trying to say to you, Hanna. I know what it is like to be with a man, but since you have never had the chance, you may not know if I am the one whom you really love."

"Are you asking me to measure my love by comparing you to being with a man? I just don't believe you could think my feelings for you are so shallow that I would stop loving you once I lie with a man. Well, I am certainly not going to marry that disgusting fat farmer to prove my love for you," Hanna responded adamantly, with more than a little anger in her voice.

It was a night sent to earth for lovers, and turning towards Hanna, Maria began to softly fondle her hair as she kissed her. "I admit I was testing you, my love, because I had to be sure your heart was really mine before we plot our escape. Now, we must begin to make our plans, keeping them so quiet that even the children don't know something is happening. Of course, we will move to Melville and live with my parents, who have been asking me for years to bring their only grandchildren closer so they can get to know them before they are grown. Tomorrow, I shall write them a letter telling them we are coming and that you have inquired if you can also partake of their hospitality as you are anxious to make a life for yourself away from the farm. My mother has often said that the manse in Melville is quite large; the expectation was for the reverend and his wife to have a big family, so there will be plenty of room. Besides, after all of the years I have lived on the Werner farm, they will consider it their obligation to welcome you into their home."

"I would be prepared to earn my keep, and as you know, I am a good worker. In fact, as I was waiting for you, I thought of Anastasia and wondered if I might be able to get a job in the Schmidt Bakery. Then I would be able to pay for my room and board," Hanna replied eagerly.

"That would hardly be necessary, considering that I have lived here for over ten years and have never paid a penny to your family. Any money that you make will be yours, and for the first time in your life, you will be free to make your own decisions. Indeed, once I have the children in school, I shall also look for work and we shall both become independent women just like Katherina, never again having to rely on a man for our existence," Maria exclaimed excitedly.

"What a wonderful feeling that will be, but in the first place we need to decide how we will all get to Melville," Hanna responded, once again becoming her practical self.

"Tomorrow, I shall also talk to Amelia and ask her to arrange for Gustav to take a day off from the fields to drive into Neudorf, and while you watch the children, I will go along with them. My first stop will be the bank to withdraw the money that Mr. Hardy paid me for Friedrich's automobile, and from there, I will go to the train station to buy five one-way tickets to Melville for about three weeks from now so we have time to pack our few belongings. Then I plan to take Aunt Margareta and Katherina into strict confidence and ask them for any dress boxes and strong bags they can spare for our use. Over the next two or three Sundays we will make sure we take the ones we have filled with our winter clothes and any personal items we don't need and store them at the Mohr home until we are ready to leave," Maria said, with the assurance of a person who might have carefully planned any number of similar escapes.

"You seem to have thought of everything, and you are right about us being tight-lipped about what we are doing. Papa cannot suspect anything; if he says any more about the wedding, I will quickly agree with him, and pretend I am getting ready to move my things to the Riechmann farm. We won't be able to take any of our beds or dressers, at least not at first, when we are going into town to catch the train. I guess now we will know what it felt like for Mama and Papa when they fled Russia with just the clothes on their backs. By the way, in your letter to your mother, would you please ask her the next time she goes to the bakery to inquire if Mr. and Mrs. Schmidt need any workers?" Hanna asked. With a sigh of relief, she said, "Since we have an idea of what we are doing, I feel so much better, and it will be exciting to finally get off the farm and move into a town, especially one a lot bigger than Neudorf."

"In a way it is a good thing that your father forced our hands by arranging your marriage. As I was putting the children to bed, I realized that we should have moved to Melville right after Friedrich's death, or even before—instead of 'languishing here on this farm,' as my dear husband always used to say. Then when I started to think about what I would take with me, it dawned on me that really nothing in this house belongs to me. So, all I have to show for more than ten years of my life are my children, and of course I love them dearly, but I became quite incensed when I began to figure out just how much money Friedrich must have made all those years working on the railway. What a stingy, useless man he was; he never gave me a dollar to buy anything for myself or for his children, much less built us our own house as he had promised to do when I married him."

"Well, maybe he spent some of his money on Anastasia and helped her to buy clothing and a crib for the baby he never met," Hanna responded optimistically.

With a sardonic chuckle, Maria answered, "Knowing my late husband, he would only have parted with his hard-earned cash until he had bedded her, and after that he would have returned to his usual tight-fisted nature, spending every dollar he made on alcohol and his beloved automobiles."

Thinking about Friedrich's parsimony, Maria continued, "Already it has occurred to me what poetic justice it is that we will be able to flee from the farm he hated with the money he spent on buying a new car rather than on his wife and children. However, I suggest we go back into the house now and get some sleep, as we shall be very busy in the days to come. Remember, Hanna, we must be on our guard and carry on as though nothing is going to change because my children, particularly my son, is very sensitive to the slightest difference in our routines."

~~~~~ 113 ~~~~~

Without inspiring a single doubt from the unsuspecting members of the Werner family, Maria and Hanna successfully executed their intriguing plan of escape. There was, of course, a practical purpose for letting Amelia in on their scheme as the date for their departure approached, since they needed her to arrange for transporting all of them into Neudorf to catch the train. Maria had requested that Amelia ask Gustav to hitch Wolfgang to the large old wagon, and Hanna, having anticipated her brother's resistance to using his precious horse to pull the heavy vehicle rather than the much lighter carriage, had asked Amelia to explain that they were gathering all of the children's clothing, which they had outgrown, and delivering the bags to the church. Since the children were making the contributions to the poorer families of the congregation, all three of them wanted to be present when their donations were given to Reverend Ulmer.

The day of their exodus dawned bright and clear, and the circumstance of Maria and Hanna being the first to arise would have tipped their hand had it not been so early that even Amelia was still tucked in her bed. In actual fact, Hanna had not been able to fall asleep at all, instead spending the night thinking about the enormity of the action upon which she was embarking. It was one thing for Maria to return to her parents after years of being away from their home and at long last seek their support in raising her fatherless children. Hanna, though, was acutely aware that her uncharacteristic defiance and open rejection of her father's arrangement for her to marry Klaus Riechmann would undoubtedly end her relationship with him. Christian Werner had not spoken to his youngest daughter in years, and when Katherina had left home, she at least had not embarrassed him by breaking his commitment with a neighbour.

Then Hanna had to try to resolve her almost overwhelming sense of guilt about running out and leaving the multitude of farm chores for the heartbroken Amelia, who would not only lose the children but also the comfort of the other two Werner women. In a house surrounded by men, Hanna was convinced that Amelia would quite naturally become even quieter and, worse yet, would soon start to behave as though she was their personal servant. However, whenever Hanna was filled with doubt and started becoming anxious about her impending flight, all she needed to do to heighten her determination was to consider a lifetime of depending upon a man and having to lie in bed with Klaus Riechmann's hands all over her body. Finally, tired of pretending to be asleep, Hanna rose from the bed she would never again lie in, and without waking Maria, she quickly dressed and went outside to herd the cows into the barn for which she hoped would be her last milking.

Sometime later, when Maria stirred and rolled over to the other side of the bed, she realized that Hanna was already up and gone. Stretching out her limbs the width of the bed, Maria took a few minutes to revel in the newfound freedom that awaited her by the end of this day. Then she leaped up with a broad smile on her face, and perhaps for the first time, she went into the kitchen before Amelia and started to cut thick slices of bread for breakfast. It occurred to Maria that it would be well into the afternoon before they arrived at her parents', and even though the children would eat a hearty meal when they were awakened, she should take bread and cheese for their lunch on the train. At the same time, Maria prepared the food that her father-in-law and Franz would take with them on their daily walk around the farm. Today, it was essential that the old man and the youth be hurried on their way as expediently as possible.

The chickens were fed, the eggs gathered, the fresh warm milk separated from the cream for the morning porridge, and breakfast was ready by the time Amelia came into the kitchen. Had she not known what day it was, she would have been pleased to sit down at the table and partake of a morning meal that she had not prepared. As it was, Amelia could hardly force herself to eat. Since she was a child, she had always lost her appetite when she was distressed and today would be the worst of her young life. How could she return from town this afternoon with only Gustav on the wagon and live in the cold, empty house, bereft of the two women and the three delightful children who were its heart and soul? And yet Amelia would not give away Maria and Hanna's plan at the last minute by attracting attention to herself since her sensitive brother would surely notice that she was not eating and ask what was bothering her.

Fortune was on the side of the imminent escapees, as no sooner had Christian sat down at the table than he remarked to Franz that they must leave right after breakfast because they had a busy day ahead of them walking to the Riechmann farm to finalize the date of the wedding which would unite their two families.

Maria willed herself not to glance at Hanna, thinking they were just ahead of the old man's scheme; although, of course, he would not for one minute have viewed his actions as a plot, but rather his right as the head of the household. Eating her porridge, Maria acknowledged to herself that one characteristic about men that she had always considered most irritating was that they just assumed they would determine what women would do with their lives. Well, not this time. Long before nightfall on this eventful day, at least two women in the house would be successful in their flight for freedom.

Succeed they did. It was not until Amelia and he were driving home alone that Gustav realized what had taken place during the afternoon. He had to admit that he had found it a little surprising that after they had arrived in Neudorf and picked up several more bags, boxes of clothing, and a small wooden crate at the Mohr home, Maria had then directed him to drive to the train station rather than to the church. Still, Gustav was too busy thinking about how much lumber he would need to build another granary, and that since he had the big wagon in town, he would go see Uncle Phillip as soon as the women had emptied their wagonload. Telling Amelia that he would see her at Aunt Margareta's later, Gustav departed with scarcely a word to Maria when she thanked him for bringing the children and her into Neudorf. It was strange that only Amelia was with Aunt Margareta when he arrived with Uncle Phillip and Peter for dinner, but he concluded that Maria and Hanna, since they seemed to be inseparable, must have taken the children somewhere else to eat.

It was not until it was time to leave for the farm and Gustav asked Amelia where Maria, Hanna, and the children were, that she simply responded, "They are gone." No amount of inquiring would persuade Amelia to say any more, and finally in exasperation, Gustav said, "Well, get your hat. If you will not tell me where they are, they will have to stay there because we are going home."

Gustav could not understand what was wrong with Amelia lately. Since Maria had taken her under her wing like an old mother hen, she seemed to have changed and become almost difficult and, at times, secretive, about what was happening in the Werner home. The thought occurred that it might be better if Maria were not around to influence his young wife, when the truth suddenly struck him: all those bags of clothing, asking to be delivered to the train station, not coming to Aunt Margareta's house for dinner. They must have left on the early afternoon train for Melville, and he did not have a chance to say his farewell, even to the children. No wonder Mathias had insisted on bringing Schnauzer, his little dog, into town with them.

It was beyond his belief. Christian could not, would not, accept that Hanna fled the farm just so she would not be compelled to marry Klaus Riechmann. At the supper table that evening, neither Gustav nor Amelia said a word about the empty chairs until Franz asked if they were not going to wait for the women and children. Then try as hard as he could, Gustav was unable to find the words to convince his father that Hanna had run away with Maria. The old man kept shaking his head and muttering that he could not have lost another daughter. It was days before it finally sank in that the women and children were not returning and that the family at the Werner household was reduced to less than half its size. Gustav kept chastising himself for being so blind as to not have noticed that a contrivance was afoot; he was more than a little angry that Amelia must have assisted them instead of stopping Hanna from leaving.

The impact upon Christian was much more profound. The next day after asking Gustav to drive Franz and him to the Riechmann farm, he returned to the house, took to his bedroom, and stayed there, only coming out briefly for meals. To Franz's considerable distress, it would be weeks before Christian would join him again on their daily strolls, and even then he was reticent to the point that Franz often felt he was still alone. In the end it occurred to Christian that perhaps it was not so surprising that countries fought against each other when the head of the Werner household always seemed to be at war with one or another of his own offspring.

～114～

Silence had descended upon the house as suddenly as a dark black cloud cloaking the sun on a sultry summer day. For the first time since the memorable Sunday in September when she had married Gustav, the solidly constructed Werner home offered Amelia little warmth or comfort and, saddest of all, no anticipation of the joy of the sound of children's laughter and play. When Maria and Hanna uprooted the essence of the family and moved its life and energy to Melville, they might well have ripped her heart right out of her chest and replaced it with a large wooden block. It would have been kinder, as far as Amelia was concerned. Her only solace was her garden, where she spent long hours every day until the weeds gave up their quest for dominance over the peas, carrots, and potatoes.

Even Gustav could not stand to spend any time inside, and at first he retreated to his fields as he had when his mother had died. It was not until one morning when he suddenly felt the urge to talk with Andrew and asked Amelia to come with him that he began to understand the depth of her inconsolability. He had come upon her as she was weeding the row of beans and found it interesting that the soil where she had been was damp; he then realized it was her tears, falling like raindrops, that were providing the moisture. Choking back his own feelings, Gustav croaked, "Come on, Amelia, you have been working much too hard lately. Change your dress and hat and let's go visit Andrew and Sarah and their girls."

Springing up from her squatted position, Amelia quickly wiped her face with the back of her hands, not wanting her husband to see her tears. She was completely taken by surprise when she stepped out on the path between the rows and Gustav wrapped his arms around her in a spontaneous hug. It was the first time he had demonstrated any sign of affection for her outside the closed door of their bedroom. Amelia longed to stay enveloped in his embrace and to ask him why, after almost two years of marriage, they still did not have a child of their own, but she could not find the courage. Besides, she desperately wanted to see Sarah, Emma, and Rebecca and she thought she might irritate Gustav by broaching a subject that usually caused him to become wholly annoyed. Instead, Amelia moved out of his arms and replied, "I can be ready before you will be able to hitch Wolfgang to the carriage."

As they approached the southern boundary of the Thompsons' section of land, they encountered Mr. Thompson and Andrew seeding a row of evergreen trees where their homestead came to an end.

"Whoa, Wolfgang," Gustav called out. As he jumped down from the carriage, he said, "Good morning. I have never seen anyone plant as many trees as the two of you. Are you trying to make Saskatchewan as green as you have always described England to be and according to the books that Mrs. Thompson has shown us?"

The men simultaneously rose from their crouched position. Mr. Thompson replied, "Hello, Gustav and Amelia. You are just in time to help us with these saplings."

He continued with a chuckle, "It would take a very long time indeed to make this country as lush as my homeland. I suspect the only time it will be green is when the fields of grain have germinated through the rich black soil and are growing towards maturity for harvesting. Rather, the colour most likely to characterize this land will be the golden yellow of its ripening wheat fields, not the luxuriant verdancy of the English countryside. Nevertheless, the very best advice I can give you is to plant trees wherever you can because this country is so large and open—too open for some of the strong winds we get out of the west and north."

By this time, Amelia had climbed down from the carriage and was getting ready to plant the precious little seedlings, which were no more than two inches in height. To Gustav's astonishment, since she rarely said more than the usual salutations in the presence of the men, Amelia turned to the elder man and said, "I really like how you have caragana and poplar trees growing around your house and barn like a ring to keep you all safe and sound. I have often thought I would like to plant more trees on our farm, but I seldom see these small trees in the stores in Neudorf. You must tell me where you order them and when is the best time of year to put them in the ground."

If Mr. Thompson was surprised by Amelia's unusual talkativeness, he did not show it; without missing a beat, he answered, "You are absolutely right, Amelia. When I brought Mrs. Thompson to what she still calls 'this godforsaken land,' she insisted that the only way she would live in such a barren country was if I planted a protective circle of trees to surround her house and garden. After our first winter, she was convinced that the winds coming out of the west could pick us up and blow us all to kingdom come without anyone being the wiser, since at that time our closest neighbour was miles away. Then, in the summertime when I saw whirlwinds come down out of nowhere, pick up the precious topsoil from our fallowed fields, and carry it away, I decided that I would eventually grow trees around our entire section of land. But I most definitely do not expect you to do my planting, so get that husband of yours to drive you up to the house where our womenfolk will be delighted to see you."

When they arrived, Sarah and the girls were walking out of the garden, carrying buckets of peas to be shelled for dinner. Seeing Amelia, Emma dropped her small pail at her feet, spilling its contents all over the ground, and started to run towards the carriage as Gustav pulled on the reins to bring Wolfgang to an immediate halt.

On this occasion it was Amelia who leaped down, and quickly gathering the child into her arms, said, "Oh, Emma, you must never run up to us until Uncle Gustav has stopped the carriage. Although Wolfgang would never want to hurt you, it is hard for him to come to a full stop. You must give me your word that you will always wait by your mama's side until Wolfgang has reached the fence and we have climbed down from the carriage."

"But I wanted to see you, Auntie Amelia. You have not been here for a long time," Emma wailed.

Still holding Rebecca in her arms, Sarah came dashing up, and when she caught her breath, said, "Thank you, Amelia. Emma, we are waiting to hear you make your promise to your auntie and to me. Do you understand why it is so important for you to wait?"

As soon as the child complied with the women's request, they walked over to join Mrs. Thompson, who, seeing what had happened through the kitchen window, had gone outside to gather up the spilled peas.

"No, Mother, please leave those for Emma, since she dropped them."

By the time dinner was ready to be served, the Thompson women had learned of Maria and Hanna's abrupt departure from the Werner farm and were beginning to appreciate Amelia's uncharacteristic loquacity. Mrs. Thompson was the first to give Amelia another hug and express her support, saying, "You poor child, you must miss them terribly, and I suppose you have hardly had a chance to say a word as the only woman in a houseful of men."

Chiming in, Sarah said, "It must be dreadful for you not having the children around since you love them as though they were your own; your days will have been so lonely and quiet from morning until night. I just can't imagine going through the entire day alone without having someone with whom to speak. It is quite understandable why you need to get all of this off your chest, and, Amelia, it is lovely to hear you use so many English words. I cannot ever remember you opening up to Mother Thompson and me as you have this morning, and now we will expect you to tell us everything that is happening with you. As my mother always says, 'every cloud has a silver lining,' and as unfortunate as it may be that Maria and Hanna have left, this can be your opportunity to find your voice. I have suspected for some time that you just let Maria and Hanna do the talking and make the decisions around the house, and now you can determine how to run your own home."

As the elder Mrs. Thompson nodded her head in agreement, a thought that had crossed her mind many times over the past few years occurred to her again. She would be the first to tell anyone that her daughter-in-law shared many of her own traits and that the two women were perfectly compatible when it came to matters like running a house and even raising Emma and Rebecca. Nonetheless, she often sensed hesitancy in Sarah in her presence, which really was not a true reflection of the capable and confident younger woman. The only conclusion that Mrs. Thompson had been able to reach was that Sarah longed to be the mistress of her own household. Nor could she fault her, and at that moment, a seed was planted in her mind which, once this atrocious war was over, she resolved to bring to fruition.

It seemed to be a day for the origination of new ideas and plans, and Gustav would bring Mr. Thompson's suggestion to plant trees to its successful realization almost immediately. The two families had no sooner enjoyed the leg of lamb, roast potatoes, freshly shelled peas, and apple pie, than Andrew and Gustav excused themselves from the table and were out the door to stroll around the farm. Mr. Thompson found it interesting that they no longer raced their horses across the countryside, wondering whether it was due to the maturation of the young men or the aging of their animals. Then, too, the landscape was changing, with roads and fences marking off the fields and pastures until it seemed that the prairie had also grown up and was losing the beauty and spontaneity of its carefree, silken grasses flowing gracefully across the expansive wildness it had known in its youth.

As so often was the case, Andrew was the first to speak, giving the impression that he could hardly wait to obtain Gustav's opinion on matters he seemed to have stored up until his friend's unannounced arrival to the Thompsons' farm. More frequently than Andrew would ever admit to himself because of his increasing feelings of resentment, he reflected that he would have liked the opportunity to visit Gustav at his home when he felt the need to confer with him. During their many years of friendship, the only occasion that Andrew had been inside the Werner home was following Gustav's mother's funeral, and Christian had been too distraught to even notice him. With a sense of irony, Andrew realized that the site where he was most welcome on the Werner farm was the cemetery, which he had visited three different times. At least it was a lovely location, with its encircling grove of poplar trees.

It was equally because of his good manners and his respect for Gustav that Andrew never broached the subject of visiting him at his home. Andrew knew Amelia would have been delighted to prepare a meal for all of the Thompson family members, and that she felt sheepish about always sitting down to eat at their table. However, now—when England and Germany were at war with each other—was certainly not the time to discuss his feelings and to suggest that if not his parents, at least Sarah, the girls, and he come to call. His pressing concern was not Christian Werner's dislike or even hatred of the English, but rather how Gustav felt about their pact, when so many young men from his community were enlisting and going overseas to fight Canada's enemy. All too many times when Andrew had gone into Duff to buy supplies, he had been asked when he would do his part to defend his country.

"It seems every time I go into town lately, I hear that yet another young man has decided to join up, and in church, I seem to be one of the few men my age still around to attend the service. Have you noticed the same trend in Neudorf?"

"Actually, only three or four men from our community have signed up, which is not all that surprising since the people in our townships arrived in Canada after fleeing Austria and Russia to get away from fighting wars," Gustav answered casually, appearing to be paying more attention to the orioles flitting in the treetops between their hammock nests along the creek, where the men usually found themselves on their leisurely strolls.

"It really doesn't bother you that men will be putting their lives on the line to defend your freedom, while you stay on your farm carrying on as though the world was not at war?" Andrew inquired, with a hint of disdain in his voice.

Now heedful of his friend's comments, Gustav turned to Andrew and answered with some contempt of his own, "I don't understand why we are again talking about whether we will fight. I thought it was agreed that we would not; in fact, as I remember it, it was you who wanted to become a part of our family's pact to never take up arms against any man, so I don't know what is bothering you."

"I think I have been feeling guilty ever since we said goodbye to Sarah's brother, David, when he left almost a month ago. I have talked to my father about our agreement and he explained to me that there is a word for people who choose not to take part in wars. He said your family and you would be considered pacifists and 'conscientious objectors' because you believe that war and violence are wrong. He said that because of that, you could not be compelled to fight even if there was conscription. Furthermore, he told me that when push comes to shove, he would agree that disputes should be settled by peaceful means, and he not only accepts our pact but is happy I have decided to remain with my family on the farm."

"Well, I should think so. I can't believe you would even consider leaving Sarah and your daughters—especially now, after your news that you are expecting another baby. Although I don't have the same family responsibilities as you, I could not possibly leave Amelia alone. I have not had a chance to tell you that Maria packed up her children and moved to Melville, taking Hanna with her. If I also went away, Amelia would have to run the farm as well as the house and garden since Papa can't do much anymore, and Franz seems to live in his own world, with little understanding of the chores which must be done, never mind doing them."

"Oh, I had no idea. Amelia must miss all of them terribly, especially Elisabetha, Julianna, and Mathias..." Andrew stopped himself from adding "since she has no children of her own." He was still perplexed as to why, after almost two years of marriage, Amelia did not have a baby. It seemed that all he had to do was look at Sarah and she was again with child.

Andrew chose not to venture into what he knew would be another touchy subject. Instead, he continued, "No wonder she has been unusually talkative today. She is completely alone for long hours with no one to say a word to, and then she is outnumbered by men in the evenings."

"To make matters worse, two weeks ago when we went to visit Wilhelmina and Peter, we found out that her younger sister Katie has run off with Orville Reinhold, a man ten years older than her with a reputation for women and alcohol. Then there is her father, who is drunk whenever we go to the Schweitzer farm. Amelia feels obligated to visit the old man, although he hardly seems to know her anymore. It seems practically everyone that Amelia loves has left her, and this morning I found her crying as she was weeding the garden. So the last thing I would think of doing is to abandon her by becoming something I have never wanted to be. I am a farmer, not a soldier, and we have enough problems at home without worrying about some war between countries on the other side of the ocean." Gustav spoke with a tone which, over the years, Andrew came to know as a signal of the right time to change the topic.

"Poor Amelia. In her short life she seems to have had many crosses to bear, and yet she is always ready to give to anyone who needs a helping hand. But she must be so lonely, and come to think of it, perhaps there is something we can do for her. What if you taught Amelia how to hitch Wolfgang to the carriage, and then she would be able to drive over and visit my mother, Sarah, Heather, Emma, and Rebecca whenever she needed to talk to other women?" suggested Andrew enthusiastically.

"Good heavens, Amelia would never learn how to drive the carriage!" Gustav replied brusquely.

"How do you know unless you try? And if not, at the very least you could teach her how to ride Wolfgang, and then she could still come over by herself. Just think about it, Gustav. Amelia has been around animals all of her life, and although it is too far for her to walk, she certainly would be able to ride the relatively short distance between our two farms. Do you realize how much freedom Amelia would have if she had a means of mobility? For the first time in her life, she would be able to go wherever she wanted to, without having to depend on you or anyone else," Andrew responded equally abruptly, as he mentally congratulated himself for his brainwave and prepared to dig in his heels to find a way to assist his wife's friend. "In fact, why don't we go back to the house and start right away."

Hearing the edge once again in Andrew's voice, Gustav decided it would be better to humour him, so he turned around in the direction of the farmyard. As the men walked along in silence, Gustav considered that had Andrew indicated the slightest interest in his response, he would have truthfully expressed that it was a smart idea to teach Amelia how to ride, which could also prove useful if anything happened to his father while he was out working in the fields with the oxen. It was unlike his optimistic and cheerful friend to be curt with him, and Gustav sensed that Andrew's demeanour was about more than just his indecision regarding their pact. Was it the stifling heat of the sultry summer afternoon, or perhaps the fact that he would soon have another mouth to feed? Even as he pondered the possible reasons for Andrew's behaviour, Gustav had the uneasy feeling that the other man was skeptical of his love for Amelia and that he did not want her to become as independent as his Aunt Margareta, which, when Gustav was being honest with himself, he knew to be true.

～ 115 ～

David wrote to Mrs. Katherina Werner Hardy, as he invariably addressed her letters, two or three times each week, and the minute she received his letters, she promptly answered with her own epistles of undying love and affection. If she thought she had missed David during his years in Saskatoon, it did not compare to the longing she now experienced. Almost every night, Katherina would awaken from a deep sleep yearning for him, wanting him to be with her, lying beside her in her bed. Then when she was engulfed by blissful slumber once again, she would frequently dream of him as he embraced her passionately in his strong, loving arms. In the morning, Katherina descended the stairs from her loft with litheness in her step, a serene smile on her face, and an air of contentment bordering on smugness, as though during her repose she had been enlightened with the answers to the great mysteries of the universe.

Naturally, the Mohr family was the first to observe Katherina's transformation, although Margareta was the only member to recognize the most likely reason for the change in her niece's demeanour. As far as the men were aware, they just knew she was different in an appealing way, and even Peter started to join his parents in the parlour as they discoursed with Katherina in the evenings. The women of Neudorf returned to the dress shop day after day, hoping that some of Katherina's magical sparkle would dust down upon their shoulders, like the fluffy snowflakes that fall from the sky on a March morning as the sun shines brightly through their glistening whiteness. The Silent Critics were quick to notice what they termed the 'increased haughtiness' in an already proud and arrogant Katherina Werner. There were few, if any, people in the German Lutheran townships who would have ever questioned the young proprietor's confidence and maturity, but none could have known that now she had become a woman.

It was not long before Margareta's supposition was confirmed. The first morning that Katherina arrived at breakfast, nibbled on a slice of dry bread, and asked for a cup of weak tea was proof enough for Margareta that her hypothesis was correct. Still, she kept her conjecture to herself, knowing full well that it was only a matter of time before her uninformed niece would need to bring her into her confidence. Maintaining her silence, however, did not prevent Margareta from beginning to formulate a plan, and she knew she could completely trust the integrity of the couple with whom she would need to carry out her subterfuge. Her supportive friends, Dr. and Mrs. Spitznagel, would be only too happy to come to the Mohr home to provide for Katherina's medical attention and ultimately, when her time came, for her confinement.

With the exception of occasional nausea and slight dizziness when she arose from her bed, Katherina had never felt better in her life. Indeed, as she awoke each morning, she experienced a profound sense of peace and harmony within her being, as though she had been blessed. Stretching out her long, slender limbs under the cozy, light quilt on her comfortable three-quarter bed, Katherina luxuriated in the sensuous wonders of her young, energetic body while rejoicing in the rare tranquility of her mind and soul. Frequently, she found herself reflecting upon words that her mother had said to her many years ago and which she now understood about becoming one with another human being. Since she had been with David, Katherina felt complete, whole, and full—as if her cup runneth over.

In her rapture, Katherina did not even realize she had missed her monthly cycle, and it was well into the seventh week after David's departure that she began to notice, particularly when lying on her abdomen at night, the tenderness and swelling in both her breasts. While thinking it was strange, she certainly was not worried, since she had more vigour than she could ever recall.

Still, as Katherina liked to confide most of her thoughts and feelings to her Aunt Margareta, one evening as they were preparing supper before the men had come home, she asked, "Auntie, can I ask you a womanly question, since there are just the two of us here? We don't have much time alone anymore and I really miss our chats."

"Certainly, my child, ask whatever you want, and if I don't know the answer I shall find it somewhere," Margareta responded jestingly.

"Lately, I have been aware of some soreness in my breasts, and I wonder if you have ever experienced anything similar. It doesn't happen all of the time—usually only when I am going to sleep at night."

Instantly changing to a considerably more serious demeanour, Margareta chose her words carefully. "Katherina, I quite agree with you about longing for one of our intimate conversations, so let's plan to discuss your question after we have fed the men their meal. We could quickly wash the dishes and retire to your loft to be comfortably cozy on your bed as we spend the evening talking woman to woman. I shall even bring a pot of tea and sweets, in the event that we need some sustenance during our discourse."

When Katherina promptly responded, "Oh, yes, Auntie Margareta let's do exactly what you have suggested," the older woman breathed an inaudible sigh of relief. Margareta needed some time to assimilate the information that her niece had unwittingly provided, confirming her growing suspicions.

Later, when the two women were seated in their favourite position atop Katherina's bed, Margareta began, "Now, coming back to your question, there were only two different times when I experienced the symptom that you mentioned. On the first occasion, I had no idea what was happening to my body, but when it occurred the second time, I knew instantly that once again I was with child."

Following a lengthy pause, Katherina replied in a barely audible voice, "Aunt Margareta, are you telling me I am going to have a baby?"

"Of course, we will need to arrange for Dr. Spitznagel to come to your loft and examine you, but I have wondered for a number of weeks now if our home would not soon be blessed with the cries of a little one coming through the walls during the night," Margareta answered, as she ensconced her niece in a reassuring hug.

To her surprise, Katherina abruptly pulled away, and forcefully cried out, "Oh, what must you think of me? Have you known all this time that I had been with David as a wife is with her husband? If so, how have you been able to look at me, much less treat me as though I was still worthy of receiving your love and affection?"

With more agility than Katherina would have believed of her matronly aunt, Margareta gathered her back into her welcoming arms and said, "Stop that nonsense right this minute! I shall hear no more of it. I could not be happier for you, my darling Katherina, that not only did David and you have the opportunity to become fully reconciled, but that you will also be blessed with a child from your union."

Gently drawing away from Margareta's arms, Katherina was momentarily speechless as she gazed intently into her aunt's sky-blue eyes. When at last she found her voice, she said falteringly, "Auntie, do you really mean what you have just said?"

"Naturally I do; have you ever heard me tell a lie? Stop and think about it, my child. When have you known me to be the first one out of the house and to be at work before your Uncle Phillip leaves for the lumberyard? As it happens, I heard you leave your loft, and I watched out the window the night that David arrived and absconded with you in his father's automobile. Although I returned to my bed, when I was unable to fall back asleep I arose and decided to bake fresh cinnamon buns for your breakfast. As soon as Peter and Phillip were awake, I hurriedly bathed and dressed to go to the store before you returned. I figured that if David and you had not found a suitable place to love one another, you might bring him up here to your loft when you had the house all to yourselves."

Blushing, Katherina could not control her mirth as she replied, "Oh, Aunt Margareta, I don't think that I could ever pull the wool over your eyes! I thought that David's and my escapade was our secret, and all the while you knew everything. But I just can't believe that you would actually be happy, much less support me, for having a baby out of wedlock."

"If you expected me to judge you, young lady, then in all these years you have not learned anything about me. On the other hand, how the townspeople and, in particular, the Silent Critics would view Katherina Werner producing a child without a husband could be quite a different matter. I have no idea whatever possessed David to address all of his letters to you as Mrs. Katherina Werner Hardy, but we are going to go along with his stratagem on the pretext that you and he were married that weekend you went to Saskatoon when David was called to the bar," Margareta said with a flourish.

Beyond containing her wonderment any longer, Katherina laughingly responded, "You are just unbelievable, Aunt Margareta. In addition to knowing and understanding about David and me, it sounds like you have already worked out the details. What I find so fascinating is that David and I had rejoiced in our hearts and minds, as the sun was creeping over the horizon on that glorious morning, that we were wedded in the presence of God, with our families being represented by the trees and birds in His sublime world of nature."

"Yes, I have always believed that you and I were cut from the same cloth and share a similar romantic view of life; but fortunately, we can be practical when it is necessary. Therefore, I have talked with Dr. Spitznagel, who is waiting for my invitation to call during the evening and undertake your medical examination. Given our proximity to one of the Silent Critics, it was Dr. Spitznagel's suggestion that he come after the workday, to convey the appearance of a social visit. Now, shall we have our tea and coffee cake since it is getting late, and a young woman with child needs her beauty sleep?" Margareta prepared to heave her portly body from her niece's bed.

"Before we do, Auntie Margareta, I want to give you a proper hug to thank you, first of all, for your wonderful understanding of David's and my actions, and secondly, for having the foresight to make the essential arrangements to solve my dilemma. I think even my mother would have treated my plight very differently, and I imagine she would have been hard pressed to come up with your quick and tidy resolution." This time Katherina initiated the loving embrace between the two equally affectionate women.

~ 116 ~

Fortunately, Wolfgang was no longer the spirited animal that Gustav had purchased from his Uncle Phillip ten years ago. On the all-too-rare occasions when Gustav found the time to ride him, he could never recapture the thrill of racing his steed across the flowing grasses of the wide open countryside as if man and beast were in pursuit of the freedom enjoyed by the roving prairie winds. Now they were wholly restricted to the rutted tracks of the dirt road allowances, choked by the dust of the passing carriages and, once in a while, a sputtering vehicle seemingly intent upon destroying the silence of the land. Still, he wondered how he, like all of his neighbours, could aspire to be a successful farmer with a section or more of prime land and realistically not expect the pristine prairie to be the price of progress? Life was changing. As much as he did not want to think about it, Wolfgang was aging, and Gustav had to acknowledge that his horse could not live many more years. Deep in his heart Gustav could not imagine how lonely he would be without his faithful friend, but then he too would probably purchase an automobile.

Now that Wolfgang was docile, Gustav might well succeed in teaching Amelia how to ride him. When Andrew and he had returned to the farmyard, Mother Thompson was instantly at the door, calling them to come into the house for tea. Of course, she served scones with strawberry jam and rich, thick cream, and as Gustav was about to bite into his second delectable serving, he once again wondered how his English friends could ever get any work done during the day, given the number of times they stopped for tea. Then as he looked around, he marvelled that not one member of the entire family was stout like his Aunt Margareta whom he knew tried to avoid eating sweets except on Sundays as a treat after their dinner. It was surely a good thing that the Germans did not engage in afternoon tea, or his favourite aunt might not be able to walk around in her crowded store.

Suddenly, Gustav was annoyed with himself for thinking such unkind thoughts about a woman to whom he owed more than he could ever repay. His vexation increased when Andrew insisted they go outside and begin Amelia's riding lessons, particularly when his friend did not give him a chance to ask Amelia if she wanted to learn how to ride a horse. Consequently, and not surprisingly, Amelia became flustered and kept looking at Gustav as though he was responsible for coming up with such a strange idea. It was not until she had shyly asked if she could wait until they returned home and she changed into one of her work dresses that Andrew realized he was being exigent. Nonetheless, before they left for home Andrew took it upon himself to privately extract a promise from Gustav that he would follow through with teaching his wife, as if as soon as they were away from the Thompson homestead he would renege.

They were nearly home before Gustav simmered down enough to explain Andrew's sudden idea to Amelia and to ask what she thought about it. She immediately replied that the very notion of riding an animal had never occurred to her before. Why would she need to learn now? Especially when she had a husband to drive her to wherever she wanted to go. Even as Gustav was about to answer, the thought fleeted through his mind that if he did not convince Amelia, Andrew would blame him and persist in his erroneous belief that Gustav did not even care sufficiently for his wife to spend the time helping her to become more independent. Of course Andrew was only being relentless because he took so much pride in the fact that since he had taught Sarah how to drive their carriage, she had often expressed great delight in being able to come and go with the children as she pleased. Her parents were even more thrilled that their daughter could come to Duff to visit while her husband busily worked in the fields.

Then it occurred to Gustav that the way to persuade Amelia was to appeal to her heart and to the love he knew she had come to garner for his father. Turning to look at her, he haltingly responded, "I often worry about being away in the fields every day from dawn to dusk and wonder what you would do if something happened to Papa. He is becoming feebler, and neither Franz nor you would be able to come quickly and find me. On the other hand, if you could ride Wolfgang, you would be able to get me right away and then I could go to Neudorf to bring Dr. Spitznagel."

"I have never thought about what I would do!" Amelia exclaimed. "What a smart idea. Once I had found you, I could tether the oxen and walk back to the house while you went on to town. We should get started tomorrow as soon as we have finished the chores."

As was so characteristic of Amelia, once she made up her mind to do something she could hardly wait to begin, and as the sun was coming over the horizon the next morning she was already carrying two heavy pails of milk across the yard when Gustav looked out the kitchen window. Walking out to meet her, Gustav relieved his wife of both the laden buckets and said, "Good morning, Amelia. I didn't hear you get up, and come to think of it, the rooster has not crowed yet. Ever since I married you, that lazy bird has not needed to do his job, so maybe we should just have him for dinner one of these days. But in all fairness, you must have been awake even earlier than usual."

"I was restless, and so I got up. I think I am a little nervous about our plan for today. What if Wolfgang does not want someone else to ride him? Will he know and throw me off as soon as I get on his back?" Amelia asked warily.

"Oh, no, we will go slowly and let Wolfgang get to know you better. In fact, after breakfast, I want you to go to the garden and dig two or three good-sized carrots, which we will use to reward Wolfgang. First, I will put on his bridle and have you lead him around the yard. If he lets you, which I'm sure he will, then you can give him a carrot as a treat."

"I didn't know he liked carrots. Now I know why I am always finding the tops at the edge of the garden; all the while, I thought it was Franz pulling my carrots before they were big enough to cook. Well, it makes me feel a little better knowing that we will both have a chance to get used to each other."

Exactly as Gustav predicted, as soon as Amelia started to feed Wolfgang carrots, the animal was quite amenable to having his master hoist her upon his back and then slowly be led along towards the creek. Initially Amelia held onto his mane as though her life depended on it, but as the horse sauntered at a leisurely pace, she began to relax. It soon occurred to her that riding was easier than walking, and perhaps there was merit in being able to jump onto Wolfgang's back and go wherever she decided to go. After all, Gustav had not said that she could only ride his horse to come and get him if there was a problem with his father. As the possibilities of where she could venture began to form in her mind, Amelia became considerably more intent upon acquiring a skill that her husband had mastered years ago as a boy.

When Gustav suggested that she take Wolfgang's rein, with the instruction to tug to the right if she wanted to go in that direction and, conversely, to the left if that was the course she preferred, Amelia gingerly accepted. It was one thing to be on a horse's back with Gustav leading him along and quite another to take control of such a large animal. Fortunately, her husband continued to hold on to Wolfgang's bridle, and her first lesson of the day was soon concluded when Gustav guided horse and rider back to the barn.

"That's enough for now," Gustav said as he helped Amelia down to the ground. "Give Wolfgang another carrot and stroke his neck as you talk softly to him. It won't be long before you will be his friend, and after supper tonight we will have you walk him around the yard."

Within a few days, Amelia was comfortably riding Wolfgang alone with Gustav watching from the sidelines. She steadily progressed from a saunter about the farmyard to a slow trot along the creek until finally Gustav felt confident that he could teach her how to canter in the open pasture. Over the years, he had seen Wolfgang's pace and stamina decrease, and he knew his horse could no longer endure dashing any great distance for any length of time. So even when they were out of his sight, Gustav was not concerned that Wolfgang would leap over the fence and run away with Amelia. Truthfully, Gustav was very pleased with how quickly his wife took to riding and how she was becoming increasingly assured about going off alone until she had ridden Wolfgang the full length of the pasture.

There was a singular problem, however, which he had overlooked, and he was uncertain if Amelia was even aware of it. Every time that she was preparing to ride Wolfgang, Gustav had been present to lift her up onto the horse's back. He wondered if she might need some kind of mounting block. He had not expressed his concern because he did not want to discourage her as she became more and more excited about being able to control the animal and to go where she wanted to go. But what was the point if she would not be able to get up on Wolfgang by herself? Finally after several days, Gustav told Amelia that she had one last lesson and then she would have his blessing to ride Wolfgang over to the Thompsons' homestead.

Taken aback by the gravity of Gustav's expression, Amelia was quick to reply, "I think I am perfectly able to go off on my own right now. What else do I need to learn?"

"I want to see you get up onto Wolfgang's back, something that I neglected to teach you when we were starting, without me giving you a boost," Gustav answered as he tied his horse to the gate of the pasture.

What took place over the next half hour could have had an element of humour for a bystander, at least in the beginning; but, had Gustav dared to ask Amelia, she would promptly have shared her frustration. Try as hard as she could, she was quite simply built too close to the ground to be able to hoist herself up. Perhaps if she had a saddle, Amelia could hook her foot into the stirrup, grab the horn, pull herself off the ground, and swing her leg over until she was safely seated on the animal's broad back. As it happened, Gustav only used a blanket to cover Wolfgang when riding, so there was nothing Amelia could use to climb onto the horse, which seemed to get taller with each fruitless attempt.

At last, accepting that her legs were just too short, Amelia turned to Gustav, and with total exasperation said, "Well, what was the purpose of you teaching me to ride your horse if I need you to be here to get me on his back? I thought I would have some freedom to determine where I went without always having to rely on you!"

Trying very hard not to laugh, Gustav replied, "We need to go to Neudorf and ask Aunt Margareta to order you a saddle, and Katherina to find some riding skirts; otherwise it has been a waste of time and energy for both of us. The only one to have benefited is Wolfgang, who has enjoyed more carrots than ever before in his life!"

Shooting a quick glance at her husband, Amelia was sure that she caught him grinning, and she suddenly started to chuckle. "I suppose I must have looked pretty funny as I tried to lift my short body up onto this four-legged giant. I thought he must be at least ten feet high as I struggled, only to keep sliding back down to the ground umpteen dozen times."

"Wait. I just remembered the stool that Mathias used to stand on as he watched out the kitchen window for Friedrich to come home. I think I put it in the back of the milk house, so I will run and get it while you give Wolfgang his treat," Gustav said before sprinting towards the shed.

With Wolfgang munching contentedly on yet another carrot and Amelia thinking that at this rate she would not have any of her favourite vegetable to put in the root cellar for winter, Gustav returned, carrying the stool in one hand and a jar of cold water from their deep well in the other. "I thought you might like a drink of water since you have been working so hard. Let's have a little break, and then you can try again by standing on the stool."

After several practice endeavours, Amelia became proficient at positioning Wolfgang by the fence, then bringing the stool in beside him, taking the reins, and climbing up onto his back. Gustav wanted her to run through the procedure until it became automatic for her, and finally he gave her his stamp of approval.

"Amelia, I think you've got it! I now feel it is safe for you to go off gallivanting all over the countryside while I am slaving away in the fields so we will not starve during our long winters."

Releasing Wolfgang back into the pasture, Gustav picked up the stool and placed it inside the barn door, where it would be out of the way of the cows when they were brought in for milking.

Walking towards the house, Gustav spontaneously embraced Amelia, placing his arm around her waist and kissing her lightly. He realized that during this past week they had become closer as they worked together to achieve a common goal. Initially, he had considered that he would show Andrew a thing or two about his love for Amelia, but he soon came to understand that what had developed between them went much deeper than anything to do with his friend. Spending time alone with Amelia without the usual interruptions from his father or Franz, Gustav increasingly appreciated her as an individual, becoming more aware of her sense of humour. Until now, most of the time they spent alone was late in the evenings in their bedroom, as they were getting ready to retire after a busy day. At any rate, Amelia had certainly proven that she was a good sport as well as a fast learner.

⟫⟫⟩ 117 ⟨⟪⟪

Characteristically when she was distressed, Margareta would bake even more of her delectable sweets: cinnamon buns, coffee cakes, and strudels. Of course, if her favourite treats were readily available, she was sorely tempted to partake of ever so small a serving, just to verify that they were acceptable for the consumption of her family and any guests who might arrive. Margareta knew her friend Dr. Spitznagel would have preferred that she did not prepare and eat so many rich, delicious German desserts, which, once ingested, tended to gravitate straight to her expanding middle. He was much too kind and far too discreet of a man to tell her outright, but lately he had checked her heart each time he came to the house to examine Katherina.

Still, whenever Margareta experienced deep ominous feelings, she was inclined to appease her anxiety by devouring her desserts. Now, with the war raging, and according to what Katherina had shared from her last letter, the news that David Hardy was being sent to the front, there was plenty of inauspicious events about which to worry. Nonetheless, when the omen became reality, Margareta was taken completely unawares by its source.

The morning following their tête-à-tête, the two women immediately activated Margareta's plan, and by nightfall, Dr. and Mrs. Spitznagel had been to the Mohr home to confirm that Katherina was indeed bearing a child, whose arrival they could anticipate during the bleak mid-winter. The gentle doctor began their visit by expressing his congratulations to Katherina on her marriage to a fine, brave man whom he had always enjoyed conversing with whenever he had the good fortune to encounter him. Soon after their salutations to the Mohr men, they discreetly disappeared from the parlour on the heels of the women as they quietly treaded their way to Katherina's loft. It had been Margareta's intention to announce to Phillip and Peter during dinner that Katherina had secretly wed David Hardy, but then she decided it would be wise to wait until she began to show she was with child before apprising the other members of the family.

By now Katherina was more than willing to follow along with any of her aunt's careful contrivances. Katherina tried to remember how Maria had changed before giving birth to her three babies, but she had been too young to really notice. At that time Maria had spent so much time in her bedroom that when she did come to the kitchen, she mainly sat at the table for meals and barely acknowledged her. To be truthful, Katherina did not know what all would happen to her body, but her excitement about having her own baby far outweighed any concerns. After all, Mama had birthed seven robust children starting at an age much older than she was, and Katherina was certainly convinced that she was as healthy, if not more so, than her mother.

Then, too, Katherina was blessed with the love and support of Aunt Margareta, who she knew would be with her every step of the way. What her father would think of his youngest daughter becoming a mother when there had been no apparent wedding, and worse yet no visible husband on the scene, was beyond Katherina's imagination. In any case, she had not seen or spoken to him since their argument in her dress shop years ago. She could, however, envision his response when he found out that his grandchild had an English father, and Katherina was just as happy that she would not likely be present at the time of the announcement. When she wanted to amuse herself, Katherina even considered what the Silent Critics would say about her during their endless gossiping over coffee when she began to manifest the visible signs that she was with child—naturally she would never let any of them know of her supposed secret marriage.

The one response Katherina worried about was Amelia's. As did every member of the Werner family and most of their friends, she knew how desperately her kind, loving sister-in-law longed for a baby. The two women had become as close as sisters since Gustav had been lucky enough to marry her, and Katherina could appreciate how Amelia would feel cheated that after two years as a wife, she still had no offspring; whereas here she was carrying a child, presumably without even having had a wedding. During Dr. Spitznagel's initial examination, if his wife and her Aunt Margareta had not been in the room, Katherina might have been tempted to ask the doctor why he thought Amelia could not conceive. On the other hand, when it became apparent what Dr. Spitznagel needed to do with the private parts of her body to ascertain that she was with child, Katherina was more than relieved her aunt was present. Furthermore, she decided then and there that even when Mrs. Spitznagel, his nurse, accompanied her husband to examine her, she still wanted Aunt Margareta to be with her and reassuringly hold her hand.

In her subsequent letter to David, Katherina included a copy of the carefully prepared marriage certificate, which Aunt Margareta had requested from Reverend Ulmer, along with his subtle explanation that it could not be recorded in the church documents until David returned and he had actually conducted the ceremony. She fully understood the reverend's approach, not wanting for a minute to taint his integrity or his upstanding reputation in the townships. As it happened, Katherina was only placating her aunt since Margareta was the one concerned with having proof that her niece was married to David Hardy. Katherina did not need a piece of paper to testify that they were man and wife; nor, she suspected, would David. In her mind and soul, and especially with the new life growing within her body, Katherina profoundly believed that God had been their witness, their union sanctified in His glorious world of nature.

It did give her immeasurable delight to ecstatically write in the same letter that they had achieved the ultimate act of creation during their lovemaking and that by winter they would be blessed with a child. Katherina was already thinking of names for the baby and asked David if he would respond with his list of possible choices for either a boy or a girl. Not once did it cross Katherina's mind that she should feel the slightest semblance of shame or guilt about being with child. Each night as she said her prayers, she thanked God for His most precious gift. In fact, it seemed that as soon as Dr. Spitznagel had completed his examination and confirmed her delicate condition, Katherina no longer experienced the nausea and dizziness that had sporadically troubled her. It was as if knowing what was happening suddenly gave Katherina permission to be happier, healthier, and more rapturous with joy and wonder than she could have ever imagined.

There was nothing to prepare her for that dreadful night weeks later when she awoke with cramps in her abdomen, beyond any pain that Katherina would have in a hundred years thought possible. When the paroxysm gradually eased, she slowly arose from her bed and began to gingerly make her way out of her loft and down the hallway to her Aunt Margareta's bedroom. She just reached the door when she found herself again in the throes of another contraction, so intense that it brought her to her knees. Barely able to breathe, Katherina waited in her crouched position, moaning in agony until it finally started to abate. In the meantime, her Uncle Phillip must have been awakened by her scuffling noises outside their door because he appeared just as she was straightening herself up and gasping for air.

"Whatever is the matter, Katherina? Wake up, Margareta, and come quickly."

With a burst of speed which belied her size, Margareta was out of her bed and at her niece's side at the same time that she was giving her husband directions.

"Phillip, throw on some clothes and run down to the store to telephone Dr. Spitznagel; ask him to come immediately."

"What is happening to her? She was on the floor when I found her," Phillip said as he turned to go back inside the bedroom.

"I shall explain later. Right now, you must get Dr. Spitznagel here as soon as possible while I help Katherina return to her bed. She needs to lie down and rest quietly so that..."

Margareta stopped in mid-sentence, not wanting to blurt out the truth to her unsuspecting husband. For the first time in their soon-to-be thirty years of marriage, she had withheld information from Phillip for reasons that she had not been able to identify, and she was certainly not going to apprise him of Katherina's condition in this stressful circumstance.

It was only fifteen minutes before Dr. Spitznagel arrived, but if he had been present at the inception of Katherina's contractions, he still would not have been able to circumvent the forces which culminated in her losing her child. Much later, he was able to advise Margareta that the fetus had a very rare defect which would have prohibited the boy from living more than a few hours after childbirth, and perhaps it was kinder for her niece to experience the misfortune early in her pregnancy rather than going full term to give birth to a doomed baby. Nonetheless, Dr. Spitznagel was circumspect even with Margareta, and he spared her complete details of the flaw of the ill-fated fetus, choosing instead to take the knowledge many years later to his grave, never disclosing to anyone that Katherina Werner Hardy's child would have been born with only a remnant of a brain.

After Katherina's miscarriage, Margareta's portent of impending calamity for her niece became stronger rather than lessening, and she baked and ate even more hearty German desserts. It occurred to Margareta that if this terrible war did not soon end so David could safely return in one piece to his beloved Katherina, she would eventually not be able to move her short, squat ever-expanding body around her home and store. As it happened, regardless of how many sweets Margareta consumed during the day, there were still far too many nights when she lay wide awake in her bed, wondering if her cherished niece would only know a life of heartache and loss.

If only she had known how quickly and how much she would come to enjoy the ways of living in a town, Hanna would have left her father's homestead years ago, as her younger sister Katherina had. Even though it had soon been established that Hanna would be expected to arrive in the very early hours of the morning at the Schmidt Bakery to start the fire in the ovens and to begin kneading the dough for the daily bread, she still found the work far more preferable than the endless chores required on the farm. The very thought that she would never have to milk another cow, clean out the barn, or slop the pigs was enough to cause her to leap out of bed with more energy than she'd felt before.

But nothing could have delighted Hanna more than the toilet. At the time of the building of the manse, the sewage for the town of Melville was being developed and a toilet that flushed had been installed in the bathroom. To never have to empty another chamber pot was pure heaven as far as Hanna Werner was concerned.

As Maria had predicted, her parents had been overwhelmingly happy when, thanks to the kind stationmaster, she had been able to telephone them from the railway station to tell them that the children and she had arrived in Melville. After a short wait, Reverend Biber arrived to pick them up, proudly driving an automobile just like the one Maria had sold to Mr. Hardy following Friedrich's death. With some skepticism about riding in the same kind of vehicle that had led to her husband's demise, Maria loaded her children in the back seat with Hanna before hesitantly taking the seat in the front with her father. Once the little entourage had arrived at the manse and her parents understood that they had come to stay, with a minimum of fuss and bother, their living arrangements were capably worked out to everyone's satisfaction. Mathias and Hanna were each given a small bedroom of their own while Maria was to share the largest guest room with Julianna and Elisabetha.

Before the day was over, Hanna had her first paying job, although the full impact of having her own money would not hit her until the end of the month when she received her remuneration. As it was, Maria's mother could hardly wait until they washed the dinner dishes to walk over to the bakery and show off her three beautiful grandchildren to Helmut and Anna Schmidt. Later, the children were allowed to go up to the rooms on the third level of the store where Anastasia and Peter lived. Mathias was placed in charge of the children's activities, and the women sat at the small table in the corner, enjoying a sample of the proprietor's fare. When Helmut emerged from the rear of the bakery, he stood for a moment observing his beloved wife and daughter entertain the reverend's family. It seemed that ever since Anastasia had stepped foot across the threshold of the Schmidt Bakery, life had become better and better for Anna and him.

Now, looking at the five women chatting excitedly in their establishment, it dawned on Helmut that if he were able to employ at least one more, perhaps even both, of the young ladies to help with the expanding business, life would be near perfect. As the reputation for the delectable delights to be found in the bakery had steadily grown and the town now flourished with the completion of the railyard, they were all working longer and longer hours just to meet the daily demand, despite Anastasia's help. In addition, while he would never have expressed his feelings to either of the women in his life, Helmut was finding it increasingly difficult to get out of bed every morning at the crack of dawn. On closer perusal, he decided that he particularly liked the look of the short woman whom he had been introduced to as Hanna, with her ready smile and the mischievous twinkle in her eyes. Given her sturdy frame and lively appearance, Helmut suspected that she was no stranger to hard work.

When a customer came into the bakery and Anastasia immediately rose from her chair to attend to her, Helmut came around the counter to claim her seat. He had been standing all morning, and it was a welcome relief to take a load off his swollen feet. Automatically glancing down, Helmut could see that once again his flesh was so puffy it was practically overflowing his shoes, and he made a mental note to remind himself to ask the doctor the next time he saw him what could cause such swelling in his lower extremities.

Since he found himself sitting beside Hanna, Helmut did not waste any time before he said, "Anastasia told us about your letter saying you were coming to live in Melville and that you were wondering if there was any chance of a job here in the bakery. What do you think, Anna, about hiring Hanna to come in at daybreak to begin the morning preparations?"

For some time now, Anna had been noticing that her husband did not have his usual energy and that he was slower about getting up six days of the week to make sure the ovens were ready for her to start baking the bread, cinnamon buns, strudels, and her extensive variety of coffee cakes. Therefore, she needed no prompting to respond, "I agree with you entirely, my dear Helmut, and if you are willing, Hanna, perhaps you could begin as soon as tomorrow morning. For the first week or until you feel that you are comfortable with what we expect of you, my good husband will work right along with you, explaining and showing you everything that must be done."

By the third morning, Hanna was on her own in the Schmidt Bakery before the light of dawn made its appearance on the horizon. It was so peaceful, since the rest of the town was still in deep slumber, and she found the short walk from the manse invigorating; she became fully awake by the time she needed to set about her business. If the truth were known, the only difference in what she was required to do was in relation to the size of the ovens. From the time that Elisabetha had become ill and before Gustav had married Amelia, it was Hanna who had been the first to arise each morning and start the fire in the new stove that Gustav had purchased to heat the stone house when their mother was dying. However, as soon as Amelia entered the Werner home and saw the black iron range shining in all its glory adjacent to the far wall of the kitchen, she was so impressed that, by the next morning, she completely took over the task, with Hanna's heartfelt gratitude.

Within the month, it was clear that Hanna would be an asset to the operation of the bakery, and in the mornings Helmut confidently remained in bed for much-needed rest while Anna joined their new young employee to help her knead the dough and begin the daily baking. Soon the older woman was teaching Hanna how to make light, flaky strudels and moist coffee cakes so that before long Anna could also take it easier and sit on the nearby chair as she instructed her eager protégée. As capable as Anastasia was of taking the customers' orders and working with the cash register, she had never become very proficient or comfortable with creating the actual products to be sold. It had caused Helmut and Anna untold distress, since they worried how their adoptive daughter could keep the bakery running when they were no longer able to do the baking. Worse still, the recipes for Anna's wonderful desserts would be lost forever.

It was just as well that Hanna had readily endeared herself to the Schmidt family, as she seemed to have totally lost her popularity with Maria and her children. Hanna could easily understand how Mathias, Julianna, and little Elisabetha would be enthralled by the love and attention from their doting grandparents whom they were finally getting to know, but Maria was entirely a different matter. Night after night, Hanna would lie in her bed waiting for Maria, only to awaken the next morning with the realization and bitter disappointment that she had not come to her. Certainly they had to be much more discreet than they had been in the Werner home, especially under the watchful eye of Maria's mother who seemed to be everywhere and to know everything that took place in her house. After all, Hanna was certain the reason Maria had insisted that she occupy the small bedroom at the far end of the hallway under the alcove was so they would be unobtrusive during their lovemaking.

From the time that Maria settled with her daughters in the large guest room adjacent to her parents' bedroom, Hanna knew she could never risk going to her. However, when more than a month had passed and Maria had yet to come to visit, Hanna started to accept that their liaison must be over. Initially she could not understand what had happened; she vacillated between feeling hurt and dejected, then angry and resentful that Maria was presumably finished with her at the drop of a hat. Certainly they did not have nearly as much time together as they did on the farm, with Hanna rising very early and leaving the house long before the rest of the inhabitants were even awake. Often she worked late at the bakery, helping Anna with the end-of-day cleaning while Anastasia looked after Peter and prepared supper, which most nights included Hanna. Still, once the children were in bed and since Hanna always retired almost as soon as the house was quiet, what had prevented Maria from coming to her then?

As Hanna began to distance herself emotionally, she paid more attention to how Maria was behaving now that she had returned to live with her parents. Finally, she realized that Maria seemed to be becoming more and more like a child with her parents' continual pampering. Her mother was only too happy to take over the raising of her grandchildren, and before long most of Maria's other maternal responsibilities such as the washing and ironing, cooking all the meals, and even cleaning the children's and her bedroom. It was as though Mrs. Biber was trying to make up for the time lost when she had not been present to help her daughter during the early days and months of her trying marriage and then during her child-bearing years. As much as Hanna could understand that both the Reverend and Mrs. Biber would be eager to indulge their only offspring after her lengthy absence, she was stymied that Maria would allow them to treat her in such an infantile manner. It now seemed that Maria no longer could choose to do anything without her mother at her side.

Whatever the reason, Hanna would never have accepted anyone making her decisions or being so dependent on another person as Maria did—especially not now, when Hanna was actually earning money for the work that she did. It would be a very long time indeed before she forgot the thrill she had experienced when Helmut counted out the dollars in her hand at the end of her first month of employment. Then, remembering how Gustav always put his money in the bank in Neudorf, Hanna promptly opened her own account in the bank around the corner. The more she saved, the more she liked it, until she soon felt as though she was a person of means. As Hanna steadily began to enjoy her newfound freedom and independence, she began to question why any woman would marry and then be subjugated to the whims of a man.

Gradually Hanna came to understand why Katherina had never returned to their father's home, choosing instead to open a business so she could not only work for herself but also have her own money at her disposal. Never again would she be under Papa's thumb or, for that matter, any other man's, nor did she need to pay for her purchases with eggs, butter, or some other farm produce.

On a warm Sunday afternoon following a picnic dinner in the railway park centred in the heart of the thriving town, Helmut spontaneously offered to teach Hanna how to drive his vehicle. She knew instantly what she would do with the hard-earned dollars that she had saved. Regardless of whether Maria still loved her or not, Hanna resolved to stay in Melville and work at the Schmidt Bakery because she would never be short of money again. Unlike Katherina, though, she would return to the farm for a visit with Gustav and Amelia. However, Friedrich would not be the only Werner to own an automobile and to drive into the yard as if the road to prosperity was only to be found away from the farm.

⋙ 119 ⋘

Perhaps if she had not been so intent upon riding Wolfgang to and from the Thompsons' homestead every three or four days, and if Karl Schweitzer had not always been drinking with his new friend every time she arrived, Amelia might have made more frequent visits to see her father. From the first day when she had timorously mounted Wolfgang by standing on the stool and then practically walked him the entire distance before she had the courage to bring the animal to a slow trot, Amelia knew why it was so important to Gustav that she arrive alone to visit her friends. Of course, the Thompson family was delighted when she appeared just in time for afternoon tea, and all of them, including Andrew, joined in the laughter when she explained that she needed a footstool in order to climb on Wolfgang's back for her trip home. Soon Amelia could hardly get through her chores fast enough in the mornings so she could go visiting; she could never have anticipated the joy she would feel by being able to determine her own destination and even the time of day when she could leave the farm.

Within a short time, she was venturing further and further afield—riding to the Schweitzer farm and then one beautiful day as far as the Strauss homestead. Once Wilhelmina and Peter recovered from their shock, they asked her into the house for coffee. And then after Amelia had spent time with her nephews, the children were hurriedly ushered outside so the adults could talk.

"How fortunate that you have come, Amelia. Peter and I were at the point of driving over to see Gustav and you about what is going on at Papa's farm. Since you are now able to ride, have you seen Papa lately?" asked Wilhelmina with a great deal of concern in her voice.

"I have ridden Wolfgang home to the farm two or three times lately; but whenever I went into the house and called his name, Papa did not answer, so I rode out to the fields until I found Ludwig. I always expected Papa to be with him, but all Ludwig would say was that he was not feeling well and was resting in his bedroom. Then he would tell me that Papa had been awake most of the night coughing and that he preferred me to let him sleep. Since Ludwig has never been one to spend much time talking, I left for home. To be honest, I never checked because I didn't want to run into Papa's new friend," Amelia said tentatively.

"If you ask me, that situation has been strange since Ludwig came back to take over the farming. For a man who was not interested in the land, he certainly has come to own more than his share, as far as I am concerned. Do you know that Ludwig now has the deed to Jakob Litzenberger's farm as well as your father's land?" Peter asked as he reached for another piece of his wife's delicious cake.

"I have never paid much attention to who owns the deeds for land," Amelia replied. "Gustav handles all of the business in his family, and we don't talk about Papa's farm. I was just so happy that Ludwig came home to look after it—although I hated the mess in the house, especially after Mr. Litzenberger came to live with them. It is probably just as well that Franz has not returned to see Papa since he came to live with us; he would be very upset by the condition of his first home." She glanced back and forth from Wilhelmina and Peter, wondering what they thought was taking place at the Schweitzer homestead.

"Well, I don't blame Franz one bit, but the most bizarre occurrence of all may be what has happened to Jakob Litzenberger. You need not have worried about meeting him because for over a month now the old man has not been around when we dropped in to visit. One day when we were out in the yard, I finally asked Ludwig where he was, but all your brother would tell me was that he had left. The only place he could have gone was back to his shack that he called a home, but when we checked it had clearly been vacant for some time," Peter said. "I think Gustav and I need to go together to see Ludwig to try to determine what is going on there before something serious happens to your father. He looked dreadful the last time we did visit him. I'll be perfectly honest, Amelia. As much as I don't want to hurt your feelings, I need to tell you that I have never quite trusted Ludwig. He has always struck me as a man who will let nothing get in the way of what he wants, but even I was surprised by his devious method of buying Jakob's land."

Before Amelia left for home, she promised to bring Gustav to the Schweitzer farm the next day, so the four could determine the status of Karl's situation. When she spoke to her husband after supper about the plan, Gustav replied, "Yes, I will be happy to come with you. I have not seen your father for sometime now, and I always enjoy visiting with Peter and Wilhelmina, so we can go right after breakfast. Come to think about it, Wolfgang might balk at being hitched to the carriage since he has once again become accustomed to being ridden around the countryside."

"I thought the reason that you taught me to ride your horse was so I could go visit my friends and family," Amelia responded defensively. It occurred to her that Gustav would likely say something about her frequent absences from the farm, even though she always made sure she was home on time to milk the cows and make supper. Still, she did feel guilty that she was not working while Gustav was out in the fields most hours of the day.

"I do expect you to be able to come and go whenever you want. I was just making a joke about Wolfgang, and actually I noticed last week that he seems to be more energetic since you have been riding him. It is much better for him to do some work rather than spend the entire day roaming the pasture looking for more grass to eat. You can't imagine how pleased I am, Amelia, that you have some independence, and I was going to suggest that soon you might feel comfortable enough to ride Wolfgang to Neudorf. I'm sure that the first time you arrive at the store by yourself, Aunt Margareta will not be able to believe her eyes—not to mention you will be the one about whom the Silent Critics gossip for the next week."

By the time Gustav and Amelia drove into the Schweitzer farmyard the next morning, the Strauss boys were already playing in the grove of poplar trees that served as the windbreak for the small log house. When they came running to say hello to their aunt and uncle, Peter opened the door and quickly walked over to the fence where Gustav was tying Wolfgang to a post.

"Thank God you have come. I think we have arrived in the nick of time. Wilhelmina is in the house with her father, who does not even recognize her. He is far too ill to leave his bed, and from the smell in his room, he has been there for a long time. I was about to leave and find Ludwig because something has to be done immediately, but since you are here, one of us should go right now to Neudorf to fetch Dr. Spitznagel. Let's hope he is at home, because I am afraid the old man is dying. So, Gustav, instead of tethering Wolfgang, I think you should unhitch the carriage and ride into town."

"I can't simply leave without telling Amelia where I am going or preparing her for what she will find when she goes into the house. I don't think she has any idea her father's condition is nearly as grave as you say," Gustav hissed under his breath.

"Well, then give the reins to me because we don't have time to bicker about which of us will get the doctor," Peter replied as he tore the leather strap out of Gustav's hands and mounted Wolfgang.

No amount of haste on the early autumn day would have saved Karl Schweitzer. As soon as Dr. Spitznagel entered the room and heard the shallow, raspy respirations coming from the far corner, he knew the old man was scarcely clinging to life. He approached the bed, which still reeked of whiskey and bodily wastes; although Amelia and Wilhelmina had spent the hour bathing their father and changing the sheets and bedcovers, they had been unable to do anything about the foul-smelling mattress.

When Dr. Spitznagel gently removed the blanket and observed the skeletal body and bloated abdomen hidden by the downy quilt, he knew instantly that the liquor Karl had consumed in huge quantities over the past years had taken its toll. Looking closer and seeing the heavily jaundiced skin of the comatose man in the shadowy light cast by the kerosene lamp, his suspicions were confirmed.

Knowing he had been called far too late to do anything for Karl, Dr. Spitznagel turned to Wilhelmina and Amelia and said, "You have done your best to make your father comfortable. Now gather all the adults together as I need to talk to you."

When the Schweitzer family, including Ludwig, was seated around the table in the kitchen, which was remarkably clean considering the total disarray in their father's bedroom, Dr. Spitznagel wasted little time in apprising them that Karl was beyond any medical treatment.

"Your father is in his final stage of life; he has a few hours at best before he succumbs to a disease of his liver. I must say that I don't understand, Ludwig, why you waited so long before I was called in, or from what I can surmise, why you persisted in supplying Karl with alcohol when you could clearly see that he was sick?"

Looking at the doctor with disdain, Ludwig exclaimed, "If it were up to me, you would not have been brought all the way out here from Neudorf. I knew it was just a waste of your time and mine when I need to be out in the fields, not to mention the fact that I'm sure you must have other patients who could actually benefit from your help. As far as his drinking, I am not my father's keeper, and when he kept demanding liquor it was easier for me to give it to him than refuse him."

With rising irritation in his voice, Dr. Spitznagel answered, "As a matter of interest, I do think that you carry some responsibility for your father since you are living in and obviously cleaning part of his house as well as working his land. However, I did not come here to quibble with you. But now that I am on the premises I want to examine Jakob Litzenberger before I leave."

"For your information, Dr. Spitznagel, this is my land and you happen to be sitting in my house. If you want to see the title deed, I can quickly get it for you," Ludwig replied, with a tone of irascibility matching the doctor's own.

Then, as he stood up and walked over to the door, preparing to leave, Ludwig continued, "Jakob Litzenberger left my farm some time ago, and I have no idea where he is, nor do I care." Grabbing his hat from the hook by the porch, he strode out of the kitchen, slamming the porch door. He was gone before the astonished doctor could ask him any more questions.

The ensuing silence was as heavy as the rusted old democrat wagon still visible through the two-paned window of the kitchen. When Dr. Spitznagel looked back towards the table, all he could see was the top of four bowed heads. He knew it was shame, not guilt, that assailed the other four adults remaining in the still room—abject embarrassment that one in their midst could be so disrespectful to the man called to assist a dying parent. The sensitive doctor surmised that they were as much in the dark as he was about the possible whereabouts of their father's friend. To his inquiring mind, it did seem an unlikely coincidence that first the young daughter and now the father of the same family could just vanish as though neither had ever lived in the township. However, as far as Dr. Spitznagel was aware, there were no other relatives of the Litzenberger family. For once he was at a complete loss as to what action, if any, to take.

In the days and weeks to come following Karl Schweitzer's burial, many people, not the least of whom was Peter Strauss, were highly suspicious of the rather abrupt and mysterious disappearance of Jakob Litzenberger. In the privacy of his spacious parlour, having invited Reverend Ulmer to share a social drink with him, Dr. Spitznagel queried his friend about whether they should perhaps journey to the Schweitzer homestead and formally question Ludwig since over the years their respective occupations had come to confer a measure of authority in the community, given the absence of any law enforcement. The good minister was only too quick to point out that from what he could remember of Ludwig, he would presume that his most obvious response would be negative. As the men sat down in front of the lifeless fireplace, Dr. Spitznagel affirmed that he had already been the recipient of the farmer's denial, never mind his blatant rudeness.

In the end Dr. Spitznagel and Reverend Ulmer resolved that little would be accomplished by trying to sit down with Ludwig Schweitzer. As they travelled throughout the townships tending to those in need, they would both keep their eyes and ears open for any news regarding Mr. Litzenberger. Neither of them was prepared to give any credence to the vicious rumour that the Silent Critics had rapidly started to circulate: that Ludwig had found a way to get rid of the old man once he managed to get the deed to his land. As time passed, the gossip escalated until eventually the Silent Critics could be heard in the hotel coffee shop talking about the murder and mayhem that had no doubt occurred on the Schweitzer farm. Whereas Dr. Spitznagel could never come to believe that Ludwig would have deliberately set about to kill either his father or Jakob, he did accept that he had certainly gone out of his way to pickle the old gentlemen with a steady supply of liquor.

≫∼ 120 ∼≪

As much as she would have loved to hear the pitter-patter of tiny feet running about her home, there were many days when Margareta secretly considered that perhaps it was a blessing in disguise that Katherina had lost the baby. Of course the aging woman had longed to be a grandmother for many years now, and her own daughter seemed to be taking her time about producing an offspring. But she would never have breathed a word of her traitorous thoughts to her niece. Even as she consoled a grief-stricken Katherina and tried to encourage her to gradually resume her interest in anything other than the daily routines of her dress shop, Margareta was once again concerned about the young woman's deep episodes of unrelenting melancholy. Long after what her friend Dr. Spitznagel had advised Margareta was a normal period of mourning for her miscarried child, Katherina remained totally bereft. It took a great deal of Margareta's energy to finally convince her niece that she must tell David in her next letter that she lost the baby; Katherina persisted for some time that she did not want to upset him while he was on the battlefront.

Weeks fled by, and Katherina clung to her pattern of retreating to her loft as soon as the supper dishes were done. Even music no longer seemed to appeal to her, and the treasured gramophone sat hushed and neglected in the far corner of her bedroom. Beside herself with worry, Margareta became a slave to her stove the minute she left the general store, spending her evening hours baking and cooking more food than the family could possibly consume. As much as Phillip and Peter enjoyed her culinary delights, they were unable to keep pace; they received precious little help from Katherina, who ate like a bird. Therefore, it became Margareta's responsibility to ensure that nothing went to waste. In desperation, Phillip sat down with his wife one evening and took the stance of being concerned about her being on her feet day and night rather than make any reference to her expanding waistline, but it was of little avail. When help finally came, it arose from the most unlikely source.

During a rare visit to the hotel, Margareta was stopped in her tracks when she entered the coffee shop and heard the mention of her name. Standing in the short hallway so she was obscured from sight, she waited and listened to what the Silent Critics were about to say. Had she any forewarning of their subject of the moment, Margareta might well have chosen a more direct approach.

As it happened, the Silent Critics were making light of Margareta's short, squat body. One of the group was ready to wager that it was soon likely that Margareta would become as broad as she was tall. Now, on most topics of conversation Margareta had long ago learned to let words roll off her back like water off a duck, but there was one exception. Every member of her immediate and even her extended family knew better than to make the slightest reference to how much weight she was carrying on her thickset frame.

Quietly withdrawing through the hallway and down the stairs, Margareta turned to the back of the hotel once she had reached the outdoors. Walking blindly, salty tears brimming over her lower eyelids and streaking down her round, rosy cheeks, she hurried along the road behind the row of storefronts on the main street. She continued on until she came to the edge of town, and finding a shady spot in the tall, browning prairie grass, Margareta sat down and permitted herself the full release of a wailing woman, such as she had not engaged in for many years. Not heeding the time of day or the fact that the customers in the dress shop and store could be keeping Katherina dashing back and forth, she remained there for the balance of the afternoon, wallowing in the abject self-pity that she had always found so contemptible in others. Of course, had she not known there was a great deal of truth in what the Silent Critics were saying, Margareta would simply have ignored their wagging tongues.

When the well of her sobs had run dry, the sun had already begun its descent on the horizon, and although Phillip and Peter would still be at the lumberyard, Katherina would soon arrive home to help get supper started. If Margareta hurried, she could reach the back door of the house, slip in, and wash her puffy face and eyes before her niece could bear witness to what had kept her aunt away most of the afternoon when she had just gone to the hotel to check on Mr. Schultz's order. As luck would have it since there had not been a customer for the past hour, Katherina had closed early and was already in the kitchen when Margareta opened the door.

"Oh, there you are. I wondered how you knew so few patrons would call that you needn't return to the store." Then Katherina took a much closer look at the older woman, and with noticeable alarm in her voice she asked, "Whatever is the matter, Auntie Margareta? Have you been crying?"

Now, feeling rather foolish for the way she had spent the last couple of hours of such a glorious autumn day, Margareta was uncertain of what to say to her niece. As she struggled to think of a suitable response, Katherina was suddenly flooded with a surge of compassion for her beloved aunt and continued, "No, Auntie, don't give me your answer now. Why don't you go to your bedroom; while you are resting I shall open a jar of canned chicken for Uncle Phillip's and Peter's supper. I'm sure I can find enough food in the larder to round out their meal, and I know for a fact there are plenty of sweets for dessert. While they are eating, I shall prepare a light supper to bring up to you and then when we are comfortably seated on your bed, you can tell me what has upset you so much. It is about time that I return the favour for you, since you have consoled me many times in the privacy of my loft. Naturally, I shall explain to your concerned husband and son that you are a little under the weather and that I shall tend to you. Off you go, and please relax until I can make it to your room, Auntie Margareta."

Pleasantly surprised and pleased with Katherina's suggestion, Margareta decided to do exactly as she was told, only stopping long enough to go to the wash basin and to pump cold water on a facecloth to take with her. Once she was in the familiar surroundings of her peaceful bedroom, Margareta began to feel more and more like herself, rather than the obese person who had been maligned by the iniquitous Silent Critics. By the time her niece came to her, she had recovered her characteristic cheerful disposition and it was only with Katherina's persistence that she decided to disclose the reason for her distress.

"As I was entering the hotel, I heard my name, so I decided to hold back and hear what gossip they were spreading for the day. I had no sooner stopped when one of them placed a bet that I would soon be as wide as I am high."

Before Margareta could continue, to her utter astonishment Katherina burst out laughing, a sound absent from her lips since she had lost her baby.

Although Margareta was delighted to hear that her grieving niece had not forgotten how to laugh, she certainly did not understand what had prompted her mirth. Taking one look at Margareta's face, Katherina quickly realized that she must explain herself before she offended her aunt.

"Oh, Auntie, I'm sorry. I do not want to appear to be agreeing with the Silent Critics, but just as you made your comment, I had an image of a person looking like a round ball rolling down the street. Of course, not for one second did I envision that it was you, and I assure you that I most definitely understand how upsetting their nasty remarks would be to you. Over the past years, you have become like a mother to me, and you must know I would never make fun of you. In fact, had I been the one to overhear them making their malicious wager, I would have marched into the coffee shop and given them a piece of my mind, right then and there."

"I am feeling rather silly now that I took their idle chatter to heart. It is just that Dr. Spitznagel, in the kindest possible way, has been trying for months to get me to watch what I am eating. I know that as a dear friend his advice springs from his genuine concern for my well-being, but I can't seem to help myself. Whenever I become worried, I have the greatest compulsion to bake, and then not wanting to see anything go to waste, I quickly swallow it, barely thinking about what I am doing," Margareta said with some reluctance as she searched her niece's beautiful face. She was loath to display any of the self-pity that had consumed her mind and soul during the afternoon, nor did she want to allude to the reason for her anxiety.

Seated across from each other on the cozy bed, Margareta and her cherished niece were suddenly and uncharacteristically at a loss for words. They sat as if mesmerized, studying one another, both hesitant about what to say. Deep in their hearts, perhaps they realized that for the first time in their loving relationship they were verging on a reversal of roles and neither wanted to give voice to anything that could not be retracted. Then, almost as if her gradually illuminating thoughts were being reflected off her beloved aunt's endearing face, Katherina spoke quietly and insightfully.

"Auntie Margareta, when I hide in my loft, overcome with misery, you go to the kitchen to find your solace. Oh, how could I have been so selfish? I have been behaving like a spoiled brat! I have always expected you to be here for me, to care for me and to love me, while I have not expressed a single minute of concern about you. If it is not one thing it is another that seems to be occurring in my life, and I have just taken it for granted for years now that you will hold my hand and help me find my way."

"Come now, my darling girl. You were a child when you came to live with your Uncle Phillip and me. We would hardly have expected you to take care of us. Besides, I have never considered you to be self-indulgent or insensitive to my needs. As it is, you have matured into a remarkable young adult, running your own very successful business and being well thought of by your customers and the people of our townships," Margareta replied, with the hint of a smile forming on her heart-shaped lips. "Can I be perfectly candid with you?"

"I would be surprised and annoyed if you were anything but that when we are having one of our chats," Katherina teased, as she moved closer to her aunt.

"Please don't be upset with me, Katherina, but one thing concerning me a great deal lately was the rapidity with which the Silent Critics' tongues would wag when you became heavy with child. Of course, your condition did not bother me, but you don't know how people can talk when a baby is born out of wedlock. You know I would dearly have loved to welcome an infant into our home, but there have been moments since you lost your baby when I have honestly thought that for your sake and for the future of your dress shop, maybe there was a silver lining in your misfortune. Now, as we were talking, it just occurred to me how ironic it is that the size of the person's body in the Mohr family about whom the Silent Critics have been gossiping is mine, rather than yours.

"Perhaps it is God's way of punishing me for worrying about the idle babble of people who have nothing better to do," Margareta added reflectively.

Then, seeing the furrow of Katherina's brow, Margareta realized that now she must respond quickly and clarify her meaning to circumvent affronting her niece. She continued, "I know I was only trying to overcome my disappointment. I am just expressing my sour grapes, as your Uncle Phillip likes to say, when I allow my mind to think such thoughts."

To her relief, Katherina once again started to laugh, this time with a deep chortle that seemed to come from her core. It was such an infectious sound that soon Margareta joined her, and in a matter of minutes, the two women were collapsed together on the bed, overwhelmed with giddiness.

Later as they sat eating the cold chicken, pickled carrots with beans, and bread slices which Katherina had prepared for their supper, they revelled in the serenity of their changing relationship. Now it felt as though their bond of love had become stronger and deeper, with Katherina reaching another level of maturity and emerging as an equal to the older woman.

"Aunt Margareta, finally it is my turn to help you. As soon as we have finished our meal, we will go for a stroll, and every evening after we have finished the dishes, you and I will go walking. It will stop me from moping about in my loft and keep you out of your kitchen, so it will be much healthier for both of us," Katherina said with a flourish, signalling the budding parity of their new level of friendship.

～ 121 ～

Will it ever change? Gustav wondered as he prepared to return to the haying. If there was not one crisis, there was another; if not with this one, then with another member of the Schweitzer family, so that Amelia always seemed to either be worrying or feeling guilty about what she did or did not do. Franz had refused to go to his father's funeral, so Amelia allowed him to remain on the farm with Christian. Then less than a month later, Franz started to feel badly that he not only had not gone to pay his final respects but he also had not visited his father when he was still alive. Amelia fretted that she had made the wrong decision. As far as Gustav was concerned, there was definitely something unusual about the boy, over and above his inability to remember to do his chores or to learn how to help run the farm. Still, Franz was really Christian's only companion now that his father was no longer mobile enough to walk the considerable distance to the neighbouring farms.

Of course, Christian did not even have the heart to visit any of the other farmers in the township after the debacle of Hanna's refusal to marry Klaus Riechmann. From the day Gustav had dropped Franz and him off at the Riechmann farm to explain that since Hanna had left his home and thus ceased to be his daughter, he could not therefore compel her to marry Klaus, the old man had never ventured beyond his own land again. Probably his ears were still ringing from the loud altercation that had ensued when Old Man Riechmann, who appeared to have been consuming liquor since early that morning, heard the news. With his prominent jowls shaking like a turkey wattle, he had stood up at his table and roared at Christian that it was time he took control of his wayward daughters and put them in their place. As Franz relayed it later, Christian did not take the tongue-lashing lying down, and readily engaged in the shouting match by claiming that at least his offspring were not fat and lazy.

Nevertheless, Christian Werner knew that there was more than a vestige of truth in what Hans Riechmann had said. As Franz and he hurried home in a strained silence, he vividly recalled his acrimonious argument with Katherina not so many years ago in Neudorf. He had been far too embarrassed to speak another word to anyone for the rest of the day and had gone straight to his bedroom where he remained, even forgoing his supper. By Sunday of the same week, when Phillip Mohr had apprised his nephew of the Silent Critics' current chatter, Gustav had been assiduous about keeping the slightest hint of their gossip-mongering from his father, although he found it quite amazing how the nefarious group gleaned every minute figment of rumour in the entire township without ever leaving their roost in the hotel coffee shop. However, for all that anyone could say about both of Gustav's younger sisters having exerted their independence by leaving the Werner farm, they at least lay in the beds they had made without causing the rest of the family any undue hardship or worry.

The same was not likely to ever be said of Franz. There were more than a few occasions when Gustav would wonder how his brother-in-law would be able to stand on his own two feet since he could not remember to milk the cows without Amelia having to remind him regularly. At twelve, Franz was less responsible and in many ways not nearly as capable as Mathias had been about helping with the chores before he had unceremoniously been whisked off to Melville. Perhaps Gustav was being unfair to the youth when he recalled that when he was two years older than Franz, he had already been hired by the railway and was doing the work of a man, day in and day out for months at a time. Now that Christian ventured out for walks around his land less and less, there were altogether too many days when both the old man and the young boy would spend the long hours from morning to night sequestered in their respective bedrooms.

Then, what was happening with Amelia's younger sister, Katie? Even Wilhelmina and Peter were dumbfounded when she had arrived for Karl's funeral since no one in the family had seen or heard from her for almost a year. Other than a hasty letter to her oldest sister shortly after she had run away with Orville Reinhold to reassure Wilhelmina that her suitor had married her and thus they were not living in sin, they must have left the townships. Where they were living or how they were earning their daily bread remained a mystery during their brief visit, although there was very little question about the nature of some of their difficulties. To Gustav's wrath and Amelia's and no doubt Wilhelmina's horror, Katie was more battered and bruised than when her father had beaten her, with both her eyes blackened so she was hardly able to see her family when finally she was in their presence. Then when Peter asked Orville for an explanation, he had grabbed Katie by the arm and they had abruptly walked off in the direction whence they came.

At the time, no one thought to follow them, and soon they disappeared from sight. Later, Gustav admonished himself for not determining where Katie was living. Then he would have been able to pay her abusive husband a visit and set him straight about his treatment of his young wife. Gustav had no stomach for any kind of physical force applied to human or beast, and Orville Reinhold, a man nearly old enough to be Katie's father, should know better. On the way home, without Amelia saying a word about it, Gustav understood how upset she was by Katie's appearance and obvious situation. She seemed reassured when he vowed that as soon as the harvest was over, he would search for Katie's domicile, but he knew she would spend the time worrying about her younger sister. To be on the safe side, Gustav extracted Amelia's promise that as she rode Wolfgang about the countryside, she would not try to find Katie by herself.

Amelia was becoming increasingly adventurous about the distance she would travel now that she was very confident about riding Wolfgang. Gustav was pleased with his wife one beautiful autumn morning when she asked him if he thought she could go as far as Neudorf. Amelia told him she had run out of jars as she was pickling the abundant crop of cucumbers, carrots, and beans, and needed to buy more from the general store. He assured her that since she was capable of handling Wolfgang on the windswept prairie, she would manage fine in town, keeping his delight to himself and chuckling later when alone about her justification for the journey. Gustav was well aware that his mother had saved ample crocks and sealers to preserve enough produce from the garden to feed a family of seven. In addition, she could easily have asked Aunt Margareta to sell them to her on Sunday after dinner when they had taken the carriage to Neudorf.

There were times when the thought flashed through Gustav's mind that he should thank his friend for pressuring him to teach Amelia how to ride, and if Andrew had not been quite so heavy-handed in his approach, he would cheerfully have expressed his gratitude. During supper, when Amelia described how excited Aunt Margareta and Katherina had been to see her come riding into town, Gustav did not suppress his satisfaction with his wife's latest endeavour. Instead he congratulated her for her successful journey, even surprising Amelia with his open accolades, especially with Franz and his father still at the table. But, of course, she was totally unaware that her husband was continuing to harbour a grudge against their English friend. Even more importantly, it would never have occurred to Amelia that Gustav persisted in his misconception of Andrew thinking he did not love his wife because they had yet to produce a child.

Perhaps Andrew envied the relative freedom that Gustav and Amelia had enjoyed over the past two years, particularly since Sarah, like Rolf's Katie, always seemed to be with child or nursing a baby. In fact, during their last visit as they walked in the ripening wheat field to check out the possible yield, while he was commenting to Gustav about soon having another addition to their family, Andrew had sounded a little chagrined.

Gustav did consider sharing the excellent advice that Uncle Phillip had provided prior to his nuptials, but then he had been overcome with reserve. He recalled how embarrassed he had been at the time of his uncle's suggestion and he could not bring himself to discuss such a personal topic, even with his closest friend and confidant. Little did he know that not only would he have helped Andrew to experience increased intimacy, lessening the probable consequences, but it also would have gone a long way to alter his belief about Gustav's feelings for Amelia.

For his part, whenever he thought about their marriage, Gustav realized how important Amelia was becoming to him. In the early evenings as he was walking the oxen home, he would eagerly look forward to seeing her and hearing about how she had occupied her day. Surprisingly, instead of feeling resentment about Amelia's frequent ventures off the farm, he experienced vicarious pleasure in her undertakings. In Gustav's mind, unlike both of his younger sisters, his wife had been able to temper her quest for independence with discipline and responsibility. Never once had she neglected her chores or not served a meal on time. She quite simply had proven that she did not have to run away from her home in order to mature into a confident, autonomous woman and in the meantime still care for her family. Indeed, if Gustav were pressed, he would have been quick to admit that now he could not imagine his life without his sweet and dependable Amelia.

≈≈≈ 122 ≈≈≈

The war raged on. The harvest was over and the seasons had changed; the landscape progressed from green to yellow and then brown before the prairie was covered in white.

Few of the young men from the German Lutheran townships had signed up to fight in the Old World from which their fathers had onerously struggled to emigrate. It was more than the quandary of which country they would defend; the mere thought of the long, crowded, and arduous sea voyage across the tempestuous North Atlantic, which some of them could still remember, was enough to send their stomachs reeling and repel any adventurous notion of crossing the ocean to fight in a war of minimal importance to them. After all, the majority of their parents had been peasants in Germany and Austria, and life had never been so good as it was now. This autumn the landowners sold not only the wheat they had stored from the previous harvest when the government had announced the boom was over, but also every kernel of grain gleaned by the threshers. Perhaps for the first time many of them knew what it was like to have money in their pockets and they were more than a little resistant about giving up what they had taken years to earn.

The proprietors in Neudorf and Lemberg were similarly hesitant to leave when the time was right to bring in new merchandise to entice the willing men and women to relinquish their newly acquired dollars. After the farmers had paid off the bills that they owed to many of the merchants, they were happy to treat their wife to a new dress and their children to sticks of candy—most of them, that is, with the possible exception of Gustav and Rolf Werner, as the Silent Critics were quick to notice. As soon as they had delivered their sacks of grain to the elevator in the large democrat wagon that Phillip and Peter Mohr used to transport lumber to their patrons, the brothers could be seen entering the bank. Actually, it would be unfair to suggest that Rolf's daughters did not enjoy the treats purchased in the general store or that his wife Katie was not often observed in a new dress, albeit usually a large, floral frock to cover a body heavy with child.

Then there was Amelia Werner, whose raiment seemed to change with every passing week, and yet her husband was always going into and coming out of the bank. The only conclusion that the Silent Critics could reach was that because of her friendship with her sister-in-law, she was being supplied with her new attire at minimal or, better yet, no cost. Given his years of parsimony, it was past their belief that Gustav could be separated from his cold, hard cash to purchase something so frivolous as a new dress for his wife for practically every Sunday church service. Then again, perhaps he was trying to compensate for the fact that for some inexplicable reason after more than two years of marriage, there was still no sign of a pending arrival of a little one to grace the Werner homestead. On the rare occasion when they reached a dearth for their rumour mill, the Silent Critics speculated that perchance Gustav's stinginess extended beyond his billfold and into the bedroom.

It was at this juncture that the two spinster sisters simultaneously objected about the inordinate amount of discussion concerning only one or two families in the township. They were quickly hushed, however, by the other Silent Critics' opposing view that if the Mohr and Werner families had not provided so much fodder, they would not always be in the limelight. Indeed, it was almost impossible to stay abreast of the unusual comings and goings within these two households. If it was not one of the Werner daughters running away from the ancestral home, it was another. As much as they had faulted Margareta Mohr for her interference with Katherina's abandonment of her father's house, the Silent Critics reasonably had to deduce that she was innocent of any direct involvement with the abrupt departure of not only Hanna but also Maria and her three children from Christian Werner's farm. Other than the rumblings from Klaus Riechmann which they had analyzed in detail, they did not believe they had enough to determine what had occurred to precipitate the strange exodus.

Since it was not possible for them to objectively observe the day-to-day happenings at the Werner homestead, they could, at best, try to glean their information from those who did live in town. And just what were Margareta and Katherina up to now as they were seen strolling through the streets of Neudorf evening after evening? What could they be looking for along the same route every day after supper? Each time they could be observed, they were ambling farther and farther until they had surpassed the outskirts of the village. There was no way to describe it but bizarre. Since the scorching summer days had slipped into autumn with its cooling winds, the two women started off on their promenade without fail every evening. Soon, not only the Silent Critics were beginning to wonder what they were doing; other people were heard to comment that it was possible to set a clock by the proprietors of the Mohr General Store and Katherina's Dress Shop walking around town.

The only individual able to decipher the purpose of Margareta and Katherina's behaviour was Dr. Spitznagel, and he was delighted. In fact, one evening he asked his wife to fetch her hat and a light shawl, and when the two women were scheduled to embark upon their constitutional, the astute doctor and Mrs. Spitznagel joined them on the street and asked to accompany them. It was not long before Katherina and Mrs. Spitznagel had forged on ahead, and holding back to stay abreast of Margareta, Dr. Spitznagel said, "My dear friend, I cannot express how pleased I am that your niece and you have initiated such a healthy ritual. I must admit that I have been very concerned about Katherina's mental state since she lost the baby, particularly when at practically the same time David was sent to the front. I think that fresh air and daily exercise are exactly what the doctor should have ordered."

Turning to face her walking companion, Margareta replied with a mischievous tone in her voice: "I very much doubt you believe that the only person to benefit from our perambulation is my niece. And, my kind friend, of course you are absolutely right. Since Katherina and I started walking several weeks ago now and, incidentally, it was entirely her idea, I feel better than I have for years. I should come to your office to be weighed because I am sure I have lost a few pounds. Lately I have noticed my dresses are not nearly so snug, and I am convinced that I have mobilized muscles I did not know I possessed. Another remarkable change I have become aware of is that I am not nearly as hungry, and because I am not always in the kitchen preparing and tasting my delectable coffee cakes, I hardly think about them anymore."

With a chuckle, she continued, "Of course, I have had more than my quota of complaints from Phillip and Peter about the downturn in their daily fare."

"Well, when you have reached your limit with your husband's and son's supposed grievances, send them to me and I shall sort them out, although I suspect they are as thrilled as I am for both Katherina and you. And by the way, the two of you have now attracted the attention of more than just the Silent Critics. I hear people all over town talking about whether you are mapping off the boundaries of Neudorf for some specific reason, and if so what could it possibly be?"

"All I can say is that I hope Mrs. Spitznagel and you are able to join us regularly so we will once again draw you into the ever-churning rumour mill. Now that I think about it, since our complicity in regard to my wearing hats, you have been sadly neglected by our gossip-mongering Silent Critics!" laughed Margareta as she quickened her pace until she and Dr. Spitznagel caught up with the other two members of their party.

～ 123 ～

To kill a fellow human being. To have the blood of another man on his hands, his head, and his soul. It was not until he was well into his military training and was learning how to fire his rifle that the realization of his potential actions began to seize David. When he had made his decision to enlist, he considered it only from a profound belief in the right of justice and freedom for all mankind. When he had returned all of his overdue law books to the library, he had walked outside, took a moment to gaze at the beautiful stone masonry of the newly constructed academic building of the University of Saskatoon, and gone straight to the recruiting office. He had been advised by the recruiting officer in Saskatoon that, given his professional training, he would most likely receive a commission conferring the rank of captain in the Canadian Army, and he was given the date to report to headquarters in Winnipeg.

Even during the train ride to Manitoba, David was still lost in the ivory tower of his legal mind, thinking about each side having fair representation and time to present the facts before ultimately a judge and or a jury passed the verdict. For seven years, he had been so completely immersed in his studies to become a lawyer that some would argue he had a distorted grasp of reality. To be truthful, David often preferred to exist within the confines of his mind, where he was able to order his life with much more precision than he was sometimes able to manage in practice. As a boy, he had frequently frustrated his father who would lament that it was not possible for a pragmatic banker to produce such an abstruse son. David smiled, remembering his parent's visible relief when he had expressed that rather than follow in his father's footsteps he would like to become an attorney at law.

It was not until David had glimpsed Katherina Werner at his sister's wedding that he had come down to earth and placed his feet firmly on the ground, not that they had stayed on its surface for very long. He had never given any thought to the notion of love at first sight, and yet he was smitten just as surely as if Cupid had shot an arrow right through his heart. Soon, the mere thought of Katherina sent him soaring high into the heavens like a dove in search of its lifelong mate. Perhaps his mother had been right when she had repeatedly told him that if he would sleep like a normal person he would not be likely to get so caught up in his flights of imagination. As distressed as both of his parents had been when he asked them to come sit down with him in the parlour and then proceeded to tell them he had joined the army, he sensed his mother was secretly relieved that at least he had not chosen the air force with aspirations of becoming a pilot.

Of course as sons are wont to do with their mothers, David had delighted in his frequent exaggerations to tease her. He could be very practical when he wanted to be, and once he set his mind to accomplish any particular task, he simply focused until he succeeded. He subsequently approached his training to become a soldier with the utmost concentration and the definitive objective of surviving the war. After all, according to the reports over the wireless in the officers' quarters, the fighting would be over by Christmas and he might not be sent overseas. He could be back in Neudorf and properly marry his darling Katherina before their baby arrived. David had certainly understood why Aunt Margareta had involved Reverend Ulmer in the subterfuge of the secret marriage between Katherina and him, and he was grateful that an announcement would be made before she became heavy with child. Still, David desperately wanted to be honourable, not only in the eyes of God, as Katherina had convinced him, but in front of witnesses in the church, where he would marry her and legitimatize his son and heir.

Chiding himself for presuming that Katherina was carrying a boy, David knew in his heart he would love and adore a little baby girl just as much. He envisioned his daughter as the image of her beautiful mother, and he ached to hold both of them in his arms. Since his arrival, David had appreciated the long days of hard physical training to the point of exhaustion; when he finally dropped into his cot, he fell asleep instantly. It was when he awoke in the very early hours of the pre-dawn that he was almost beside himself with desire for Katherina. He could feel her lovely supple body as if she was with him on the narrow bed, and he longed to take her within his passionate embrace. He had to arise and walk around the barracks, so ardent was his need for her. Returning to sleep was out of the question, and as soon as the sun crept over the horizon David slipped quietly out the door and sat on the step to write his daily letter to Katherina.

It had been more than a week now since David had received one of Katherina's long, loving letters, and he was beginning to wonder if his mail was getting lost in the post. The flow of their correspondence had been so steady that he was certain there was a problem with the delivery. It definitely was not because Katherina was losing interest in writing to him; there were days when he had the unexpected pleasure of receiving two letters at once. Quite frankly, it never occurred to David that there could be any difficulty with Katherina, since in his mind she was perfect in every way. With the passing of each day since their separation, she had become more precious to him, and during his rare moments of insight, he had to caution himself to remember not to place her on a pedestal. He was sure that once they started their married life, they would experience their share of quarrels and arguments as had his own parents, and he already eagerly anticipated making up.

When he did receive the news, he was stunned. What could have happened? Katherina had always been the picture of health and vitality. How could she have lost the baby in less than three months of its conception? The morning the missive arrived, David had been the first in the line for mail call, and as he was accustomed to doing, he walked over to sit down under the large crimson-red maple tree, where it was relatively private, to enjoy his awaited letter. However, when he started to read the short note, he soon found to his dismay that it was little more than a factual statement informing him she was remiss for not writing sooner to tell him that a week ago she had a miscarriage. Dr. Spitznagel did not provide her with any sound reason for the unfortunate event, and she would write more when she was feeling better. Unable to believe that this cold, distant communication comprised his letter, David turned it over and then looked in the envelope searching for more pages, without success.

He was heartbroken. If he could have, he would have taken the next train to Neudorf, rushed up the steps of the Mohr residence, and embraced Katherina in his strong, loving arms to alleviate her anguish. David soon understood the tone of her letter, and even months later when he was sent to the front, he did not feel as far away from her as he did at that moment of grasping the reality of her agonizing revelation. The only way he could finally achieve peace of mind was to view the tragic turn of events as a portent that if he was to become engaged in active warfare in Europe he would at least survive to return home to his wife. At the risk of clutching at straws, or worse yet of bargaining with a higher power, David fervently reasoned that surely a benevolent God would not require his darling Katherina to deal with both the loss of her husband and the death of her child.

124

Christmas of 1914 was approaching, but the war continued on, and reports that travelled across the Atlantic suggested that it was escalating. It seemed so remote to everyone in Neudorf, except for Katherina who had just received word that David's infantry corps had been ordered to the front. He explained that he had tried to get leave to come back to see her before his departure, but the Allied forces had only barely prevented the Germans from breaking through to the Channel ports at a town called Ypres in Belgium—near the border with France—in November, and they urgently needed reinforcements. Katherina's despair was profound, and it was fortunate that the winter was unseasonably mild so Aunt Margareta and she could still maintain their daily strolls, although now they frequently took turns walking before the early nightfall while the other minded the shops.

It was early December when Margareta answered the persistent telephone in the store in the midst of serving several customers. There were times when she found its loud ringing jarring on her nerves, especially when she was as busy as she had been this autumn trying to keep her shelves stocked for the influx of patrons. She was ever so glad that she had started her walking routine with Katherina and had not only lost some of the excess weight she had been carrying but was also considerably quicker on her feet. Margareta knew she could well afford to lose many more pounds and the likelihood she would ever be slim was remote, but she was thoroughly enjoying her recent nimbleness. Now she could literally fly around the crowded aisles of the general store, much to the wonder of the prospective purchasers seeking specific items. Even the Silent Critics had been heard admitting that Margareta Mohr was becoming spry in her step.

Politely excusing herself, Margareta answered the intrusive black oblong box with more brusqueness in her voice than she realized, until her daughter said, "Hello, Mama. Is something wrong or is it not a good time to call?"

"Oh, my dear Julia, I'm sorry. I was in the middle of helping Mrs. Spitznagel find some fabric for her Christmas sewing, and I guess I sounded more abrupt than I intended. Of course it's lovely to hear your voice, particularly since we have not seen you since Thanksgiving. I do hope you are calling to tell me Robert and you can come home for the Christmas season," Margareta replied as she motioned to her friend that she would only be a few moments.

"Since you are busy, perhaps it would be better if you called me back later; but please do not worry. We plan to be home for the school vacation, but there are new developments that I need to talk to Papa and you about before we board the train. I am at home for the evening and Robert will soon be in for supper, so why don't you ring when Papa and you can both talk on the telephone. And remember, there is no reason for you to be anxious, Mama. I shall wait to hear from you." Julia said farewell and ended the conversation.

When Katherina returned from her walk, Margareta finalized Mrs. Spitznagel's order and resisted the temptation to pass on her constitutional; she quickly asked her niece to take charge before she embarked on her stroll. Although Julia had expressly asked her not to worry, her daughter's edict was rather like asking the sun not to shine on a stifling summer day. All of her family teased her about her propensity for fretting, and they were often wont to add that she would even worry because she did not have something about which to worry. Margareta knew that her husband and children considered her penchant for anxiety as a failing, but she preferred to think of it as a way of preparing herself for what might lie ahead. It was not because she was a negative person, but rather that she needed to analyze the possible options so she could better deal with what was required of her when the time came. Since her approach had stood her in good stead throughout most of her life, Margareta was hardly likely to change now as she was aging.

When supper was over, she asked Peter to help Katherina with the dishes, and then before Phillip could become comfortable in his easy chair in the parlour, Margareta explained that Julia and Robert were waiting for a telephone call. Walking together down the stairs as they returned to the general store, her husband did inquire if there was anything that he needed to know before they rang their daughter.

"If there is, I am as much in the dark as you are, my dear Phillip. Now that I think about it, Julia never really said anything when she called other then asking me to not worry," Margareta replied pensively.

Before the end of the first ring, Robert answered the telephone. "Good evening, this is the Cameron residence."

"Hello, Robert, you must have been waiting right by the telephone. How are you? It has been far too long since I have heard my favourite son-in-law's voice."

"Ah, Margareta, I so often wonder how your partiality would be affected if you had many more daughters to bring home their young men," Robert responded teasingly in his warm, deep masculine voice.

"I assure you that even if I had a dozen son-in-laws, hands down you would still be the best of the lot. Now, tell me you are coming home for Christmas and I shall start preparing all of your tasty requests. Indeed I think you might be pleasantly surprised to learn that since your last visit I have lost seven pounds, but what it means is that the larder is bare, especially of all of my delectable coffee cakes."

"I am very pleased for you, Margareta, although I do hope the rest of us will not be required to suffer because of your restraint, or perhaps I should be talking to Phillip to determine the extent of the deprivation in the Mohr household," chuckled Robert. "One minute and Julia will be here to speak with you."

Although they must have spoken in turns to their daughter for more than twenty minutes, as they returned up the stairs to their home, it simultaneously occurred to both Margareta and Phillip that Julia had been rather circumspect during the conversation; they were not much further ahead than when they had initiated the call. They understood that their only daughter had asked to bring some of her personal possessions home on the train and that she wanted them to meet her at the station with the wagon. But aside from this somewhat unusual request, neither Margareta nor Phillip could piece together the real reason for Julia's apparent and rather sudden change of domicile. It certainly did not seem to stem from any acrimony between Robert and Julia because when Margareta had frankly asked if they were having marital problems, they were both quick to respond that they could not be happier with each other. Instead of being pressed by her ever-persistent mother, Julia had firmly expressed that they did not want to break the bank with a telephone call when they would share all of their news once they arrived in Neudorf.

125

The morning of Robert and Julia's homecoming dawned clear and cold. Margareta had busied herself in the interim, baking coffee cakes and strudels to place in the small outside pantry that Phillip had built for her years ago. She was so proud that she had not been tempted to sample any of her fresh baking, choosing instead to freeze it as soon as it was cool enough to wrap in cheesecloth. It seemed that each time she visited Dr. Spitznagel's office, her resolve was strengthened by every pound of weight she lost. The truth was that she was feeling better than she had for a long time and now she was committed to becoming healthier. There were plenty of days in the frigid climate of her adoptive country when she would rather have stayed indoors in front of the cozy fire in her parlour; but with a fortitude she did not realize she possessed, she had pushed herself out of the door and forced one foot in front of the other until she had completed her daily walk.

Even Margareta was starting to see the favourable changes in her bodily shape, and she could hardly wait until Julia, and especially her physician son-in-law, observed her svelte figure. Laughing to herself, Margareta thought, "Oh, my, whom am I fooling?" Slender and graceful were adjectives that would never be applied to her short, squat German body. But she could dream, and she was certain that Robert would be as pleased with her as was Dr. Spitznagel, not to mention just how delighted Julia would be that her mother was finally taking better care of herself. Margareta had always been grateful that perhaps by the grace of God her daughter had taken after her father's side of the family. To be sure, Julia did not have the height and elegance of her cousin Katherina; but at least should she ever be blessed with children, she was tall enough to not become too rotund as she neared her term.

When the train finally chugged into the station, Phillip and Margareta were waiting to welcome their young people home. Although they brought the wagon as Julia had requested, neither were prepared for the amount of baggage that was placed on the snowy platform. It was clearly more than the large trunk that Julia had filled with her clothing and personal possessions when she had originally left for Regina. There were enough boxes and bags to suggest that their daughter and son-in-law had packed up their household in its entirety. Although she was almost dying from curiosity, Margareta knew it was hardly the time or place on this cold, wintry morning to ask either Julia or Robert what was happening. Furthermore, she realized she must wait patiently until they were ready to elucidate their family about what precipitated their current actions. As outspoken and opinionated as she could be, even Margareta Mohr knew when to hold her tongue.

Finally, when dinner was over, the dishes were washed, dried, and returned to their respective places, and the entire family was gathered in the parlour, Robert solicitously asked if he could have everyone's attention—as if he needed to since they had all been sitting on pins and needles wondering when one of the visitors would enlighten them about their unusual disembarkation at the Neudorf train station.

"We have two important announcements to make: one of them being very good news while the other could be said to represent tidings of a more negative nature. During the train ride, we agreed that Julia would begin, so now I shall be quiet and let her speak." Robert looked lovingly at his wife.

"Thank you, my dear. Mama and Papa, we are very happy to tell you that soon you will be grandparents, with your first grandchild expected by the end of June. Robert and I have known for two months, but we decided to wait and give you our wonderful news when we came home for Christmas."

Glancing ever so briefly at Katherina, Margareta quickly rose from her chair and rushed over to her daughter, embracing her in an enormous hug. "Congratulations, my darlings. I was beginning to think I would never know the pleasure of holding a little one in my arms again." Even in her excitement Margareta had chosen her words carefully, wanting to be sensitive to her niece, whom she appreciated was still grieving for her lost child. During their many shared confidences in the privacy of their daily strolls, the two women had agreed that since the baby's tragic demise had happened before Katherina revealed the slightest visible indication of being with child, it would remain their secret forever. Of course, they trusted implicitly in Dr. Spitznagel and David's discretion, knowing that neither man would ever breathe a word to another human being.

Following an exciting round of felicitations from everyone in the parlour, including Katherina who was genuinely happy for her cousin, Robert, who had remained standing, once again requested the opportunity to speak.

"First of all, I want to thank you for your forbearance, when we arrived with essentially all of our earthly possessions and then expected you to carry the entire lot into your home without so much as one word of explanation. Now I shall identify the other circumstance, which will have far-reaching consequences for the Mohr family, for perhaps an extended period of time. Contrary to what the news reporters were predicting—that the war would be over by Christmas—the fighting has intensified. Immediately after the festive season, I shall be shipped overseas to join the medical corps, which has a serious shortage of surgeons. With the number of critical wounds being inflicted upon our troops, every relatively young physician is expected to answer the call for the Allies."

Sitting back down in his chair, Robert continued: "I recognize that Julia and I may have been presumptuous, but we could not imagine that you would want your only daughter to live alone in the city when she was carrying her first child. Since Julia never did advise her school that she was a married woman as she could not have remained on the teaching staff, now, for obvious reasons, she submitted her resignation for the completion of this term. I have advised all of my patients that I shall not return to my practice until the end of this dreadful war, which seems to be escalating with each passing month. Therefore, for the time being we have absolutely no ties in Regina, and Julia has repeatedly assured me that since I must leave her, she wants to return to your home. We do suspect that it might become quite crowded, particularly when the baby arrives, and we are prepared to help defray the costs of building an extra room or two, perhaps at the rear of the house, for additional accommodation."

Phillip was quick to respond. "Well, Peter and I have just been talking about that very idea; although, when we were considering it, our plan was to build a more private living space for him. Ah, son, it sounds as if you may need to stay in your present bedroom, at least until your brother-in-law returns from the war.

"On the other hand, I suppose we could offer to buy some of the adjoining property from the spinster sisters and construct an addition large enough for both of you. I'm sure the sisters would appreciate their increased proximity to the Mohr home to gather more grist for the Silent Critics' rumour mill. Indeed, they will surely become the envy of the other members of Neudorf's most infamous group.

"It's settled, then. We shall begin in earnest to develop a blueprint to extend our living quarters after breakfast tomorrow morning so we can get started as soon as the ground thaws."

126

If there was any consolation for Anna, it was that at least her precious husband of forty years had died quietly in his bed and not over the intense heat of his baking oven. She cringed at the mere thought of what would have happened to him if he had experienced his heart attack while leaning over the fiery hot, black cast-iron stove. It seemed Helmut Schmidt had spent the better part of his life in front of cookstoves baking bread and his wife's delicious German desserts for most of the people in Melville. To be sure, he was always one to sample and enjoy his wares, claiming that he could hardly expect his customers to purchase what he would not consume himself. Over the past several years, Anna and the doctor had cautioned Helmut about the impact of her rich pastries on his continually expanding waistline; but, from his boyhood, he had been known for having a sweet tooth. Since his father and his grandfather before him had been bakers in Austria, it could be argued that Helmut had come by his penchant for heavy, delicious desserts quite naturally.

When she woke early in the morning, Anna had initially thought that Helmut was still asleep, and wanting him to have some much-needed rest, she had dressed quietly in their bedroom, darkened by the thick curtains, before joining Hanna in the kitchen. By the time Anastasia had opened the doors of the bakery, most of the daily product was either baked or ready to be placed in the large oven, which worked incessantly. Finally taking a break from kneading dough and making her famous cinnamon buns, Anna realized with a start that Helmut had yet to come down the short flight of stairs to have his breakfast. It was entirely uncharacteristic for her husband to sleep through a meal, and for the first time, Anna experienced a jolt of fear. Then suddenly remembering that Helmut had said he was not feeling well when they were getting ready for bed, Anna threw her apron on the table and bolted upstairs. Perhaps she should not have passed off his complaints so lightly by chiding him that it was because of the large number of perogies and bratwurst sausages he had eaten for supper.

Entering the bedroom and seeing Helmut in exactly the same position as when she had left him, Anna's heart suddenly leaped up into her throat. She was immobilized with apprehension, and it took her several minutes before she could find the courage to go over to her husband. As soon as she was close enough to observe the grayish tinge to his skin and the pallor of his usually ruby-complexioned face, Anna knew he was gone. She did not need to check if he was still breathing, but rather felt at the depth of her being that her soulmate had passed into the next world. Although Anna firmly believed they would meet again in the place where God kept a room for each of His children, she was not ready to say farewell to the man whom she had expected to have by her side when she was an old woman. She sat down on the edge of the bed beside Helmut and stared out into space, wondering what to do next.

When Anastasia arrived to determine what was keeping her dearly beloved adoptive parents, she was unable to ascertain which one was the most motionless. They both appeared to be in such a quiescent state that for a moment she feared she was once again on her own in the world. Then looking more closely, she noticed the reassuring rise and fall of Anna's chest and was comforted that at least her mother was alive. It did not take long for Anastasia to deduce the reason for Anna's immobility, and rushing over to the bed, she threw herself down to hold her father as she wept openly. Her tears acted as the catalyst to spur Anna into action, as though there now was a purpose upon which she could focus her usual energy.

"My darling, he has gone peacefully in his sleep, without pain or the distress of realizing the end was near. We must all die as part of the cycle of life, and you, with our precious grandson, brought more joy to my dear Helmut these past years than he could ever have imagined. Now we shall go downstairs to tell Hanna and then the three of us will prepare your father for his final resting place."

During the ensuing week, Hanna was a godsend. She practically ran the Schmidt Bakery single-handedly; she cooked, she cleaned, she baked, and then when she had scoured the entire kitchen and most of the rooms in the house, she took it upon herself to make the necessary funeral arrangements with Reverend Biber. She was everywhere and did everything, except for anything related to Helmut and the bedroom in which he had died. When Anna gave Hanna the news of her husband's passing and then requested her assistance in cleansing and preparing his body for burial, she bolted like a racehorse out of the starting gate. The young woman provided no explanation for her aversion to even viewing Helmut when he was resting peacefully in his large wooden coffin after Anastasia helped her mother with the provisions for his final journey.

As would be expected, Hanna did attend the church service to send Helmut Schmidt to his eternal rest; but rather than sit at the front of the new building with his few remaining family and friends, she sat alone in the last pew. Fortunately, the church was overflowing with the many patrons who had frequented the bakery for years, now wanting to pay their closing respect to a man who had sweetened their lives with his delicious desserts. Anna was very pleased that Maria and her three children sat beside her mother with Anastasia, Peter, and herself as her show of support for the family members. She did think it a little strange that during the service and the subsequent lunch, Maria essentially avoided her friend; albeit Hanna had once again resumed her role of ensuring everyone was taken care of and had plenty to eat and drink. Although it would be years before Anna came to understand Hanna's response in the face of death, it was during the hours of Helmut's funeral that she began to suspect all was not well between her hard-working employee and the reverend's daughter.

As Anna thought back to the young women's arrival in Melville almost two years ago, she recalled considering it unusual at the time that Hanna had left her own family to be with Maria and her three children. Still, Hanna was clearly so involved with Mathias, Julianna, and Elisabetha that, initially, Anna could hardly determine which was the children's mother and which was their aunt. Furthermore, it was odd that a young woman of marriageable age was allowed to travel to the city with her friend instead of being at home with a husband of her father's choosing and raising her own offspring. But then when Anna put it into the context of her adoptive daughter, she knew she would not have allowed her dear Helmut, may he rest in peace, to have arranged for her to marry a man whom she quite possibly had never met. After all, Anna had fled to Canada so she could marry the man of her choice rather than to wed the old man her father had arranged for her, primarily to gain access to his large landholdings.

The more she tried to analyze the nature of the friendship between Hanna and Maria, the more convinced she became that something was amiss. When Helmut was alive, Hanna spent longer and longer periods of time with the Schmidt family until she was with them at the bakery for practically all of her waking hours. Now that he was gone, it seemed she only went home to sleep, leaving when the moon and stars had come out to lighten the darkening sky. Invariably, Hanna would return in the quiet of the very early morning, so early that Anna started to become concerned for her safety, out alone on the streets of the ever-growing city, bustling with all of the young men arriving from the country to go to the recruitment office. Then, on closer observation, Anna began to realize that much of the love and attention that Hanna had previously directed towards Maria's three children was now being focused on Peter.

There was no doubt that the boy doted on his Aunt Hanna, and certainly Anastasia was equally delighted with the presence of another young woman on the premises with whom she could converse and share her confidences. Late one evening, Anna was once again stalling about lying down to sleep in the double bed that seemed so empty without her dearly beloved husband. Even though she had purchased a new mattress after Helmut's demise in their marital bed, frequently Anna could not bring herself to climb between the sheets until she was near the point of exhaustion. What if she proposed to Anastasia that Hanna come to live with them? There was more than enough room for three women and a small child in the living area adjoined to the bakery. Why not suggest that she move into the smaller room in the loft, and then Hanna could share this bedroom, which was now far too large for her, with Anastasia and Peter. As it was, the kitchen and parlour were already used by all of them together as a family.

Once she had reached her resolution, Anna fell asleep instantly and had her best night since losing Helmut. The next morning, before Anastasia could open the doors of the bakery, Anna took her aside and excitedly told her what she had determined last evening. "Oh, Mother, I have been thinking along the same lines and wondering how I could bring it up to you without hurting your feelings; although it did not occur to me that you would live upstairs while we would take over your space. Are you sure you want to climb the stairs every day when Hanna and I are so much younger than you?"

"Good heavens, Anastasia, the last time I counted there were all of five steps to reach your bedroom. I may be older than the two of you, but I am not so decrepit that I cannot walk up and down a short flight of stairs. In fact, it may be good for my heart so I do not suffer the same fate as your father. Lord knows, I did try to get Helmut to watch his weight, but never was a man more delighted with eating than was my dear husband. Now all we need to do is convince Hanna that she is welcome to live in our home because I sometimes suspect she has qualms about residing under the roof of people other than her own family."

"Interestingly, I too have often thought she is not all that happy at the Biber household. Mama, if you allow me to ask Hanna first, I know precisely what to say to her to persuade her to leave her present domicile and to come live with us. Of course, she will seek your approval even though I shall assure her it was your idea, and then you can confirm how much we love her and want her to be a member of the Schmidt family."

⤜ 127 ⤛

It was auspicious that he had not been able to sleep and had decided to return to his office to write up some of his patients' files. It was even more fortuitous that he had heard the rapping at the window. It had taken a long time to register as he busily made notes on the many patients he had seen during the day. At first he dismissed the noise as the fierce wind rattling the shutters that Peter Mohr had attached to the outside of the window in a vain attempt to keep out the cold. When the sound continued and seemed to become more insistent, Dr. Spitznagel finally put down the Waterman fountain pen, his prized gift from his wife this past Christmas. Paying much closer attention, he listened to the repeated knocking, which had a rhythm of urgency. Was someone out there, and who could possibly be outdoors on such a miserable night in the bleak Canadian mid-winter?

Knowing the minute that he opened the door, the bitterly harsh wind would rush into the already frigidly cold porch, Dr. Spitznagel hesitated and instead tried to look out the frosted four-paned window. But he could not see anything, and reluctantly he pushed the heavy wooden door ajar as he called out, "Hello, is anybody there? Please come into the house quickly before you freeze to death."

If a fellow human being was tarrying in such inclement weather, it could only be an emergency, and he was not surprised to hear a timorous voice respond, "Bless you for letting us into your home."

Then Dr. Spitznagel sprang into action, widening the door and reaching out to help the person up the steps, in the meantime trying to decipher the individual's reference to there being more than one of them. Once the bulky figure was inside, he quickly went back to the door and looked into the icy, crystalline darkness until he heard a soft, low voice say, "We are both here, thank you. You can now close the door, Dr. Spitznagel."

"Come into the parlour and I shall stoke up the fire so you can warm yourself." Seeing that his late-night visitor was starting to remove her shabby coat, he continued, "Perhaps you should leave your outerwear on until I have built up the fire."

"I must check to see if my baby is all right," replied the person whom Dr. Spitznagel was by now convinced had to be a woman. As she opened her coat, she revealed the reason for her cumbersome appearance. Nestled to her abdomen and cradled in a small hammocklike sling made of a tattered blanket was an infant of perhaps three or four months of age.

Approaching the woman, he asked, "May I help you remove your baby from its carrying pouch? That, by the way, was an innovative way to transport a child on a night like this."

As Dr. Spitznagel untied the blanket from around the woman, he quickly observed that the baby was cyanotic. Not knowing whether the infant was blue with the cold or was suffocating from being embedded within its protective haven under his or her mother's garments, he pulled back all clothing from the baby's face. He immediately began his examination by checking for the carotid pulse and then determining if the child was breathing. After breathing his own huge sigh of relief, he turned to the woman and said, "Your baby is alive. His respirations are shallow and rapid but his pulse is strong; once we have warmed him up, I'm sure he will be fine."

Looking more closely at the woman who had taken off her scarf and hat, Dr. Spitznagel exclaimed, "Why, is it you, Katie Reinhold? Where have you come from and what in heaven's name are you doing walking about town on a night when every living creature is taking refuge in a warm place?"

Quickly assessing that he could not provide the emergency care that both the mother and child would need without the assistance of his wife, also his nurse, Dr. Spitznagel directed Katie to the large chair in front of the fire and asked her to hold her baby while he went to awaken Mathilda. As he hastened up the stairs, he again wondered where Katie could have come from, and then he shuddered when he thought about what would have happened to mother and child had the kerosene lamp not shone like a beacon through his office window. Searching his memory, Dr. Spitznagel realized that he had not seen Katie since her father's funeral in early summer, and although he was well aware that her face had been black and blue from a beating, beyond a doubt from the brutal man whom she had introduced as her husband, he did not recall her being with child. He certainly had not been present at her confinement, so who had helped this young woman bring her baby into the world?

During one of their evening strolls, Margareta had disclosed that even though Gustav had been true to his word and had scoured the countryside with Amelia looking for her younger sister, they had found neither hide nor hair of her. With winter fast approaching, they had searched every day as soon as the morning chores were over, either doubling up on Wolfgang's back or hitching him to the carriage. Gustav even went to the extreme of taking the train to Melville and spending an entire day knocking on the doors of the men and women he knew had left the townships and moved to the larger municipality. Aside from encountering Maria at her parents' home and then having a joyous reunion with her children—especially Mathias, who was delighted to see his uncle—he had not gleaned one scrap of information about Katie and Orville Reinhold.

➵ 128 ⤸

It came as a total surprise to Gustav during his search that his sister Hanna was no longer residing with Reverend Biber at the manse after having run away surreptitiously from her family; presumably she could neither live without Maria and her three children nor with her prospective husband. When he had recovered enough to ask Maria what had happened, she had casually replied that Hanna had moved in with the Schmidt family to help them operate the bakery after Helmut had died. Her perfunctory response irritated Gustav, and as he walked down the street fuming, he could not decide which of the women vexed him more, his sister or his sister-in-law. The only consolation for his father when Hanna had left abruptly without so much as a word or hint of farewell was that she was residing with a respectable family. Now Gustav would have to advise him that she had suddenly taken up living with Anastasia, whom he did not believe for one minute was Maria's long-lost cousin.

When he opened the door of the Schmidt Bakery, Hanna was carrying a tray of sweet buns from the rear of the building to place in the front display counter. Seeing her brother, she nearly dropped the baking which she had spent the last hour preparing.

"Hello, Gustav! You startled me! You are the last person I would ever have expected to walk through the door of the bakery. When did you come to the city and what brings you all the way to Melville?"

"Well, it seems that it is a day for surprises, Hanna. I have just come from Reverend Biber's home, and Maria has informed me that you no longer stay with her and the children. I actually came to Melville to try and find Katie, Amelia's younger sister; but when I left home this morning, I did not have the slightest idea that I would also need to locate you," Gustav replied with an uncharacteristic inflection of sarcasm in his tone.

Although Hanna could not recall her brother addressing her so caustically before, she did not hesitate with her response. "As it happens, I was not lost, so it didn't take long to find me; but I have a strong feeling that it will take a great deal more time and energy to determine the whereabouts of Katie Reinhold, if indeed she is married. I have heard rumours that Orville is often seen in Melville, and in the presence of a woman who is certainly not little Katie Schweitzer from the farm."

Astonished by the terseness of Hanna's comments, Gustav realized that he had little to gain by antagonizing his sister further, and he decided to change his tack. As he looked more closely at her appearance, it occurred to him that he had never seen Hanna looking so happy and, more importantly, so confident; it brought their younger and successful sister, Katherina, to his mind. She changed her hair, seemed to be much slimmer, and was dressed in bright-coloured clothing, which she had never worn when she lived in their father's house. Perhaps coming to Melville was a good move for her; although it would be many more years before Gustav came to understand that it was neither his place to tell his sister what to do nor where she was to reside. Little did he know that regardless of what he might have said to Hanna Werner during his short visit to the Schmidt Bakery, it would have had no impact on her.

When he finally returned home after checking where Hanna had heard that Orville had been seen, without success, Gustav convinced Amelia that they had done all they could to find Katie and they must now wait until she came to see them, since at least she knew where they were. Then, several weeks later when Dr. Spitznagel approached him after the church service and whispered that he must follow him home, it was with more than a little trepidation that Gustav steered Amelia towards the genial doctor's house. Along the way, Dr. Spitznagel informed them that aside from their Aunt Margareta he had been able to keep his patients' presence in his small infirmary a secret from the Silent Critics, and thus from the entire town. Now, because he wanted to continue to maintain her confidentiality, he would wait until they were safely within the confines of his home before he disclosed the identity of the persons he needed them to see.

Sensing that Gustav and Amelia were very anxious about his unusual request, the minute they were in the cozy, warm kitchen and had removed their outerwear, Dr. Spitznagel revealed that Katie Reinhold had appeared out of nowhere this past Wednesday evening while he was working late in his office. However, before they could visit with her, he needed to prepare them that she was suffering from severe frostbite of all four of her extremities and was now heavily bandaged. Furthermore, it was far too early in her stage of healing for him to determine whether he would need to amputate her hands and feet. As much of a shock as all of this information had to be for both of them, he encouraged them to be as positive as possible for Katie's sake. Indeed, at this time his young patient was totally unaware of the gravity of her current situation.

"We will wait a few moments while you adjust to what I have just said to you, but I am pleased to share the good news that her infant son is doing very well. I must be frank with you that when I last saw Katie at your father's funeral, Amelia, I did not realize she was with child. I have made excuses to myself that I was much too appalled by her obvious beatings to have noticed; but the truth is that if I had been more observant of her condition, I would have followed her to determine where Orville Reinhold was taking her. I know that the two of you have searched far and wide since harvest to try to find her, and I honestly do not understand what about the human condition prevents us from looking in the most obvious places and sometimes right under one's nose. As it happens, for several months now Katie has been living in the shack on Jakob Litzenberger's land. What I deem as far more upsetting is the fact that for many months your brother Ludwig was aware of her whereabouts. In fact, once he accepted that they were squatters on his land, he allowed Katie to take some vegetables and to pick the berries from your father's garden."

⫸⟋ 129 ⟍⫷

Once they had adjusted again to sharing a bedroom, Katherina and Julia were like two young schoolgirls. Although Peter had offered to let his sister continue to occupy his room following Robert's departure for England, until they could build the addition at the rear of the general store in the spring, both women had been adamant that they could live together quite amicably. Julia immediately expressed her delight with the changes her father had made to Katherina's loft—specifically the ceiling window—even though it was presently covered with snow. Their one and only dilemma was that Julia wanted to be on the outer edge of the bed because she frequently needed to use the chamber pot during the night, and Katherina had a strong aversion to sleeping up against the wall. As they struggled to reach an agreement, Katherina finally admitted that her antipathy was really her fear of enclosed spaces; she stopped short of disclosing to her cousin the nature of the morbid pit into which she had always sunk during the low points in her life.

Eventually, Katherina and Julia achieved an effective resolution in a typically female fashion. They would simply rearrange all of the furniture in the room so the three-quarter bed could be in the middle, and subsequently each of them would have her own side to crawl in and out as she pleased. No sooner had they commenced implementation of their plan than there was a knock at the door. Since Julia was closest, she went to open it, and her mother rushed in exclaiming, "Good heavens, have the two of you come to blows already? What is all the noise about, when my dear poor husband is trying to get a sound sleep before he catches the early train to Regina in the morning?"

"Oh, Mother, we are so sorry. We did not realize that Papa had gone to bed already or we would have waited until the morning to move the furniture around to suit our needs. Well, Katherina, I shall sleep on the inside of the bed tonight, but I do not want to hear one word from you should I be required to use the receptacle under the bed and need to crawl over you."

Julia went to give her mother a peck on the cheek. "If we have awakened Papa, both of us will be happy to apologize in the morning."

"Your father will have his breakfast and be gone before either one of you comes down the stairs; but if he is awake when I return to our bedroom, I shall extend your most sincere regrets. Now please go to bed, and I shall help you rearrange furniture when we have time tomorrow."

Although Julia and Katherina followed the older woman's advice to the letter and climbed into bed as soon as she left, they certainly did not go to sleep. One would be on the verge of slumber when the other would start talking about some remembrance or another, and vice versa, until they both burst out laughing. Then simultaneously realizing that they were being much too noisy and were again risking Margareta's ire, they muffled their sounds by covering their heads with the downy quilt. Later when they needed to come out for air, the young women would begin in soft whispers; but as they progressed into their conversation, their voices invariably became louder. Soon the pattern was being repeated, interspersed with their giggling, until neither was in the slightest way ready to fall asleep. Finally they managed to share what had been happening in each other's life in murmurs that could not possibly be heard beyond the walls of their bedroom.

The next morning when Margareta had to climb the stairs to awaken them for breakfast, neither was quite so full of energy. Julia said that since there really was no particular reason for her to arise at such an early hour and that given her delicate condition additional rest was recommended, she would come down later. As she turned over to face the wall, Katherina insisted that it simply was not to be allowed.

"If you are going to keep me awake half the night talking about your life and telling me all about the children you taught in Regina, you will get up at the same time as I must and make yourself useful in the dress shop or the store."

Stopping on her way out the door, Margareta had qualms that Katherina's expectation would initiate the first quarrel between the two women, since she was well aware that Julia preferred to sleep in awhile on the mornings she was not required to be at work. She was pleasantly surprised when her daughter started to chuckle and said, "You have made your point, my dear cousin. We shall go through thick and thin together as we wait for our precious men to return from this terrible war. I shall arise and join you for breakfast before the three working women in the Mohr household open their thriving businesses to their patrons. Then tonight, when both of us are exhausted, we shall go to sleep straight away."

Wanting to hug her daughter for her insight, Margareta walked over to the bed and followed through on her thought, and since Katherina was sitting beside her, she embraced her niece as well.

"It will be wonderful for Katherina and me to have you helping us in the stores, Julia—at least until you become heavy with your child. In many ways, it will be a tremendous relief since we are both so busy now. Furthermore, I think you two young ladies will be able to support each other immensely over the next while until Robert and David come home."

As was so often the case, Margareta Mohr was prophetic. In the weeks and months to follow, Katherina Werner and Julia Cameron would become as inseparable as two peas in a pod. Long after they had stopped sharing a bedroom and all of the furniture in the loft had been returned to its original position, since like the vast majority of people Katherina was a creature of habit, they continued to talk endlessly about every notable and lesser occurrence in their respective lives. Julia thoroughly enjoyed reestablishing her friendship with her cousin; but it was Katherina who most deeply realized how much she had missed the camaraderie of someone closer to her own age and interests. However, not for one moment did she discount the delicate relationship she shared with her sister-in-law, Amelia. And since Amelia had started to ride Wolfgang into Neudorf during the summer, it had only been strengthened by the amount of time they were able to spend together.

Nonetheless, Amelia continued to look up to Katherina almost with a reverence that the latter neither expected nor wanted, as she did not feel she belonged on a pedestal. Katherina knew only too well that she would eventually fall off, and indeed if Amelia had had the slightest awareness of her intimate behaviour with David Hardy not long ago on a grassy knoll on the outskirts of Neudorf and its resultant consequence, her sister-in-law would have been so shocked that she might not have been able to look at her, much less talk to her, again.

Consequently, most of the time Katherina was very careful about what she expressed to Amelia. It was never to the point of being insincere or dishonest, but she was always sensitive to her childlike innocence. Conversely, she felt that she could share her hopes and dreams with Julia, and as they became closer and closer, to even progress towards revealing some of her darker secrets.

To be fair, perhaps the bond between Katherina and Julia was so quickly renewed by their common fear of the possible fate of the men they both held so dear to their hearts. Each week they waited anxiously for the mail to be delivered, and it was never a question of which one would go to the post office. At least half an hour before the anticipated time for the train to arrive at the Neudorf station, Margareta knew she had better be prepared to wait upon any customer who walked through the door, since her young ones would be making a break for the postal service. Their happiest moments were when each received a letter; but on the occasions when, for whatever reason, only one had mail, the lucky one would cheer the other bereft of her missive from the loving man in her life. They would share all of the news that was not of a very intimate nature. During the rare but bleak weeks when neither had a letter, they would console each other with the optimistic assurance that both David and Robert were simply too busy to write.

As Julia began to undergo the physical manifestations of her impending motherhood, she involved Katherina as much as she could in order to include her in what she earnestly expressed as the ultimate creative experience for a woman. Thus, on the initial occasion when the baby started to move within its protective haven and then to kick as though protesting being confined to such a small space, her cousin was the first to feel the ineluctable evidence of awakening life. The pull of her maternal instinct was so strong that Katherina could not stop herself from disclosing the happenstance of her intimate encounter with David during the last hours before he departed for his military training. When her confidante listened without making judgment, Katherina revealed her secret. By the time she told Julia about losing her baby, Katherina was speaking in such anguished sobs that comprehension was nearly impossible. Nonetheless, Julia understood perfectly and simply took Katherina into her arms and allowed her to weep.

From that moment on, once Julia had confirmed that her cousin did not find it upsetting, she shared every detail of her pregnancy until Katherina began to anticipate the birth of this infant as much as if it were her own. Every evening, the three women in the Mohr home sat cozily in front of the fire, knitting, sewing, and quilting in preparation for the baby's layette, and talking about the choice of names until Phillip and Peter had to find another place to read or listen to the news of the war on the radio. Of course, their excitement permeated the conversations during Sunday dinner, until on one such occasion Katherina happened to notice the grief-stricken look in Amelia's eyes. Her sorrow was so poignant that as soon as Gustav and Amelia had left for home Katherina requested they make a pact limiting their discussion about the baby in front of her sister-in-law unless she specifically brought up the topic.

Later in the evening as she was preparing for bed, Julia reflected on Katherina's sensitivity to Amelia's feelings. To be truthful, she had been so wrapped up in her exhilaration about her baby and all of the accompanying preparations that week after week she had missed observing how withdrawn Amelia was becoming whenever they enthused about the upcoming event. When Julia had first returned to live with her parents, Amelia had been as chatty as the other young women; but then with the news of Julia's pregnancy combined with her younger sister Katie's reappearance with her own baby, Amelia had become unusually silent during most conversations around the dinner table. In fact, it was probably fair to identify that she had reverted to being characteristically subdued again. Although recently Julia had been in her presence every Sunday, she quite honestly still knew very little about Amelia. It would seem that everyone, and perhaps Katherina most of all, seriously underestimated the quiet strength and profound depth of Gustav's innocent- and fragile-looking wife in her hour of greatest need.

~~~ 130 ~~~

As a rule, Gustav was a reasonable man, and as his loyal friend Andrew had repeatedly noted, he had become calmer after his marriage to Amelia. Whether or not he was emulating his Uncle Phillip, he abhorred violence, preferring to try and work matters out with discussion. However, if Gustav had come within a mile of Orville Reinhold, he would have run him down and beat him black and blue with his bare hands. The bruises that had discoloured Katie's face and arms at her father's funeral would be nothing compared to what her husband's body would look like when Gustav was finished with him. Every time he recalled how Orville had deserted his young wife and infant son in late fall before one of Canada's harshest winters, the knot in his stomach tightened, his fists clenched, and his jaw hurt from grinding his teeth.

At least twice every week, Gustav hitched Wolfgang to the cutter, and dressed in their hats and heavy winter coats with a feather quilt wrapped around their knees, Amelia and he paid a visit to Dr. Spitznagel's infirmary. Each time, Amelia prepared soups, cabbage rolls, and perogies, and Gustav put two rings of his smoked pork sausages and a ham into the large basket to take along to the doctor's home. Still, he felt, and he knew Amelia shared the thought, that they would never be able to repay Dr. Spitznagel and his wife for the care and attention they were administering to Katie and her son. As far as Gustav and Amelia could tell, either the doctor or Mrs. Spitznagel was changing the bandages and cleansing Katie's hands and feet every four hours, night and day. In addition, one of them would attend to the crying baby and then latch the infant onto Katie's breast to nurse whenever the young Orville needed to be fed. It was beyond anyone's understanding why Katie had chosen to name the baby after his useless father.

Not once as he was leaving did Gustav fail to offer Dr. Spitznagel cash for the extensive services the good-hearted man and his devoted wife were providing; but invariably the good doctor would shake his head and wave the money away, asking Gustav to wait.

Finally, in exasperation, Gustav blurted out, "Dr. Spitznagel, why will you not accept payment for all of the help that you are giving Katie and her child? What are you waiting for, since Katie has already been here for weeks?"

"My dear friend, your generosity belies my imagination. Never before have we eaten so heartily,—well, perhaps with the exception of when we are fortunate enough to be invited to your Aunt Margareta's table. I shall speak to you in the strictest confidence when I say I have often thought it may be a blessing in disguise that God did not grace my wife and me with children because they might well have starved to death. Please do not misunderstand me, Gustav. I love Mathilda more than I can ever express, and in addition to being a most considerate wife, she is a wonderful nurse; but she is dreadful in the kitchen. I have little knowledge myself about cooking, but it amazes me how she can ruin perfectly good food, especially given how delicious the same meal tastes when prepared by Amelia. Have you never wondered why Mathilda and I, even before we started walking regularly with your aunt and Katherina, are the skinniest people in the townships? I can assure you it is not because as doctor and nurse of the community we are trying to be an example of good health!" Dr. Spitznagel chuckled as he shook Gustav's hand. "Believe me: your gifts of food every week more than suffice as payment."

As the men stood at the door waiting for Amelia to say her farewells to Mrs. Spitznagel and her sister, and knowing how she lingered over the baby, the doctor continued: "I want to tell you again confidentially that although Katie is making steady progress, she is not out of the woods yet. I still cannot be sure that we will be able to save her extremities, or whether I may need to amputate some of her fingers and toes. So, on a serious note, I will not take any money until I have treated my patient to the best of my ability and I know she is on the road to recovery. Another concern both Mathilda and I share is about what will happen to Katie and her child once she has healed."

Then as a smile lightened his creased face, Dr. Spitznagel joked, "Unless, of course we keep them here, and Amelia and you agree to feed us for the rest of our days."

There were many reasons why Gustav admired the amiable doctor, not the least of which was his sense of humour. He frequently marvelled how in the face of life and death situations day after day, the man could always find an amusing perspective to help ease his patients' and their families' fears and tension—even the dourest members of the two German townships. Laughing in response to Dr. Spitznagel's suggestion, Gustav replied, "I don't think you would have much trouble convincing Amelia to prepare your meals, since cooking is one of her greatest enjoyments; but we have been talking to Wilhelmina and Peter about Katie. As soon as she is well enough, Amelia and I will bring her home with us until spring comes, and then we will take her back to her home on her father's farm to live with Ludwig."

"Have you involved Ludwig in your discussions? Somehow, I cannot imagine him being very happy about having his younger sister and her baby occupy the house in which he is living, particularly when the infant howls during the night. From what I know of Ludwig Schweitzer, I would be very hesitant to comment favourably on his patience. Rather, I suspect that he would send Katie and Orville back to the hovel on the Litzenberger farm where she had been residing the entire time you searched the countryside trying to find her. I just can't believe he never told anyone in the family about Katie's whereabouts; in my mind, it is criminal that he left her in that broken-down shack during part of the winter. Presumably Ludwig didn't even bother to check on her since she had to walk into town when her food and wood ran out so they would not freeze to death." Dr. Spitznagel spoke fervently and a scowl spread across his handsome face, replacing his jocularity of only a few moments ago.

"Since you have been taking care of Katie, I have had many thoughts about what I would do to Orville Reinhold if he crossed my path, and I must say that I have been tempted to ply Ludwig with some of the same treatment. So I really don't care what he thinks about our plan. In fact, I can't understand why the rest of the family has just allowed him to take over their father's farm in the first place.

"Ludwig may have extracted the title deed to Jakob Litzenberger's land, if all of the rumours are true; but he has no more rights to the Schweitzer farm than the rest of his brothers and sisters. Fortunately, Peter agrees with me entirely, and come spring, the two of us will set the matter straight," Gustav replied in a tone of voice that matched the doctor's vehemence.

In the evening as they were preparing for bed, Rolf Spitznagel turned to his wife of nearly twenty years, and reiterated parts of his private conversation with Gustav.

"I don't think I have ever seen him so worked up in my life. I could all but see his fists closing in anticipation of pummelling the two men who have so seriously maltreated Katie—starting with Orville Reinhold, and then since he was in the mood, carrying on with Ludwig Schweitzer. Not that I could fault him; indeed if I was present, I would heartily join him, particularly should I need to amputate any of the poor girl's limbs."

"Come to bed, my dear husband. You must be very distraught, since I can't recall you ever speaking of taking such action. In all of these years, I have never had an inkling of you having a mean bone in your body, and as upset as we both are about Katie and her baby, violence would accomplish nothing. Nor can I imagine Gustav being involved in fisticuffs, regardless of how angry he is, to solve the situation. Today when I inquired, Amelia told me that they will take Katie and Orville home to the Werner farm when she has recovered, so at least we need not worry about what will become of them. In fact, it has been on the tip of my tongue many times to suggest to Katie that she entrust little Orville to Amelia and

Gustav. Katie is so young, and I have a strong feeling that if her abusive husband arrives back in the townships, she will readily pack up the child and follow him."

"Have we always been of the same mind," asked Rolf, "or has it come about with living and working together all of these years? I have considered that exact thought over and over, since it is so painfully obvious that Amelia longs for a baby, and yet after more than two years of marriage, there is not the slightest indication of her being with child. Truthfully, it has occurred to me that she may have a problem conceiving; but even during our many visits lately, Gustav has never brought up the topic with me. Naturally, I wouldn't expect Amelia to talk to me about such a sensitive subject. Has she ever said anything to you while the two of you have been attending to Katie and Orville?"

Mathilda thought for a moment. "It is remarkable how Amelia is often as silent as a stone in the presence of adults, and yet you should hear her when she thinks she is alone with Orville. She talks and sings to him as though at any moment she expects the infant to respond to her. Then, when I come into the bedroom, she all but loses her voice, and other than politely answering my questions, we scarcely exchange a word. Quite frankly, I don't think that Amelia Werner confides in anyone, including her husband. I suspect she has spent her entire short life looking after other people and spared little regard for her own needs and feelings. Although Gustav treats her very well, I sometimes wonder if there is any truth to that appalling rumour started by the Silent Critics about his parsimony in the bedroom," she said.

"We must be very tired, since we are both expressing ourselves uncharacteristically. I never thought I would ever hear you give credence to one word that any member of that nefarious group spoke.

"Oh, dear, look at the hour. We must get to sleep, because it won't be long before one of us must change Katie's dressings, not to mention Orville's diaper." Rolf leaned over to kiss his wife good night.

～ 131 ～

When Julia received the letter, she felt a tremendous sense of relief. And regardless of what anyone would say to her for the duration of the war, in her mind she was convinced that Robert was much safer now that he had been transferred to London. From the time he had written about embarking for Europe, setting foot on the continent, and immediately being dispatched across the English Channel to a battlefield hospital in the north of Belgium, she was certain she would never see him again. Her father's daily commentary, gleaned from the radio in the hotel where he was spending more time than he ever had before, could not alter her perception that in the city Robert had to be much better protected by being surrounded by a multitude of other people. Even when early in the year the German blockade of England began and they heard the news of the first zeppelin attack on London, Julia continued to believe that her cherished husband could come to no harm within the heavy stone walls of the old hospital in the heart of the city overlooking the Thames River.

On the other hand, Julia worried constantly about David, as Katherina shared the news that his corps was the first Canadian division to be sent into battle at Ypres. Julia could not understand how her cousin was able to read his letters aloud to the rest of them in almost a lighthearted manner, until she began to realize that it was the vein in which they had been written. David was clearly sparing Katherina the reality of the fighting in the trenches; whereas Robert was not averse to describing the truth since they had always been candid in their discussions.

Soon, however, Julia found herself being very cautious about what information she chose to share with Katherina, shielding her from the fact that poison gas had been used for the first time in the inconclusive conflict in which David had initially risked his life. Similarly, when Robert had disclosed that there were tetanus epidemics in the trenches, Julia decided to keep her own counsel rather than being frank even with her other family members.

When Katherina began to lament that Robert must write very personal letters since Julia would share so little with any of them, her cousin readily agreed, attributing it to the fact that as a married couple of several years, they had many private matters to discuss. Since she definitely preferred to avoid any reference to her intimacy with David, particularly in front of her father and brother, Katherina would grudgingly acquiesce to Julia, at least until they were in the privacy of one or the other's bedroom. Still, rather than read directly from his letters, Julia would express in a confidential tone that Robert wanted to know all about the physical changes that were happening to her body and the complete details of her appearance as she became heavier with their child. Fortunately, Katherina willingly believed that Julia would be hesitant to discuss her bodily condition around the dinner table, and did not press for any additional information.

It was not long before Julia realized that the only way Katherina could deal with David being in the midst of bloody combat in a war was by thinking about him as if he were still away at the university. It certainly explained his letters, in which David only confined his writing to the interactions with his fellow soldiers or to commentary about the beauty of the countryside. From Robert's letters before he had been sent to London, Julia was well aware that the landscape was being destroyed with the same relentless disregard as was human life. As the weeks and months passed, Julia began to appreciate just how fragile her young cousin was, particularly following a lengthy period during which she did not receive any communication from David. Other than when she was with customers in her dress shop, Katherina underwent an episode during which she barely spoke to any of her family, and even her appearance reflected the darkness of her mood.

One evening in desperation, Julia asked her mother if they could have their tea in the privacy of her parents' bedroom. Since Katherina had all but locked Julia out of the loft, listening repeatedly to the pathos of the violin strings of a lugubrious Brahms concerto, she would hardly care, if she was even aware, that Julia was having a heart-to-heart discussion with her mother.

Carrying the silver tray to the small round table positioned between two comfortable sitting chairs, Julia exclaimed, "Mama, it has been too long since we have had a tête-à-tête in your cozy bedroom. I especially like how Papa added the window to the wall at the time he was fixing Katherina's loft. I would be tempted to mark papers at this table if I were still teaching or perhaps to spend the evening engrossed in Tolstoy's *Anna Karenina*. I know I would have a hard time blowing out the lamp and going to bed."

"I have done precisely that on more occasions than I can recall, much to the frustration of your dear father, who has threatened to completely board up my sitting area. He claims that he is unable to sleep unless the room is totally dark; although he has a nap practically every evening after supper in the parlour, not only with the lamp burning brightly but also with the clatter we make doing the dishes. So, my darling, what has prompted you to seek my counsel? Are you becoming concerned about your delivery even though Dr. and Mrs. Spitznagel have been preparing you for what to expect during your monthly examinations? Incidentally, how are you feeling? We get so busy during the day and I often don't get a chance to ask you."

"I am starting to feel as big as a house, and I wonder if I may not soon burst as my stomach continues to grow bigger. Then I think about all of the weight I have gained and fear I shall not be able to lose it once the baby arrives. But in response to your question, other than my silly anxieties about the size of my body, I feel fine except for becoming tired by the end of the day," Julia replied with a smile on her comely face.

"Once spring comes, and certainly after the baby is born, you can put him or her in the perambulator and join our walking group. In no time, you will be back to your tall, slender figure since, fortunately, you take after your papa in that department. I assure you, Julia, that if I can lose weight by taking a daily walk, you will have no trouble at all," said Margareta confidently.

"I shall certainly participate in such a healthy activity, and actually had I not become so ponderous, I would have accompanied Katherina or you during the winter months. I have been remiss in not saying before how pleased I am, Mama, that you are taking much better care of yourself. I know I have complimented you on losing weight; but I want to confirm that I admire your discipline and perseverance, even when the weather has been so inclement. I must admit I am curious: whatever got you started taking a daily constitutional in the first place?" Julia poured each of them a second cup of tea from the heavy pot before she replaced the muticoloured, crocheted tea cozy.

"Amazingly, it was Katherina, the very individual whom you want to talk about in our private conversation! She introduced the idea months ago, and we made a solemn pact that rain or shine, sleet, or snow, we would get outside every single day and walk for a minimum of twenty minutes. Before long, Dr. and Mrs. Spitznagel inquired if they could come along, and soon we were strolling, at least in the summer and autumn when the weather was fine, for an hour or more. It is no doubt much harder to be motivated when it is so bitterly cold and the strong prairie winds nearly blow you away; but I have consistently honoured our agreement, as has Katherina. I suspect that on more than a few of our fierce winter days, both of us have been tempted to renege on our deal, but we have continued to force ourselves out the door for the required time."

Moving towards the edge of her chair, as if to hurry her mother so she would finish with her comments, Julia blurted out, "However do you know that I need to discuss Katherina with you?"

"Since your papa and I have become familiar with Katherina's tendency to withdraw into her loft and immerse herself in music whenever she is upset, I did not think anything about this particular occurrence until I noticed how intensely you were trying to reach her. Then, knowing how difficult it is to break through the walls she erects around herself, I knew it was only a matter of time before you would seek my guidance."

"It seems more like a fortress in which she takes refuge, and she slams the heavily guarded door so tightly shut that a battalion could not gain entrance. I had no idea about this other facet of Katherina. It is almost like the rhyme that 'when she is good, she is very very good, and when she is bad, she is horrid!' I must tell you, Mama, that I have always had a great deal of regard for my younger cousin; but her current behaviour is lowering my respect for her."

"Please, my darling Julia, do not judge Katherina. Her conduct has nothing to do with being good or bad. She is not able to help how she responds to many of the circumstances in her life. I feel certain that she is very similar to Elfrieda Reiner Wirth, her maternal grandmother, and suffers from a disorder that Dr. Spitznagel spoke about when I finally sought his advice without Katherina's awareness. He told me he had read a paper published by an Austrian neurologist by the name of Dr. Sigmund Freud, in which he identified a type of illness he called 'melancholia.' Dr. Spitznagel has assured me that he is trying to get more information—specifically to ascertain what treatments are recommended for his patients whom he believes suffer from the disease."

"Since I know very little about Katherina's grandmother, I don't understand what you mean, Mama," Julia replied inquiringly.

"I was only a young girl when I knew Mrs. Wirth. All of our families still lived in the countryside surrounding a small hamlet in Austria, and she was the very old minister's wife. For years, I could never understand why such a lovely woman would marry a man so much older than herself. She had the most beautiful singing voice that I have ever heard, and I shall always consider her one of the kindest people I have had the good fortune to meet. Mrs. Wirth often sang in the choir, but I do remember that there were times after the service when she quickly left the church by the back door rather than standing with the reverend to shake our hands as we were leaving. Then after those occasions she would not sing again for weeks, nor would I see her in the manse or have my lessons. Finally, one day because I missed her, I asked the cook if something was wrong with Mrs. Wirth, but all she would tell me was that she had bouts that caused her to be too sad to sing."

As Margareta sat in reflection, Julia thought that her mother was reminiscing; whereas she was actually trying to decide how candid to be with her daughter. There were many times since she had disclosed Elfrieda's secret to Katherina that she regretted her frankness with her niece, fearing that she might have put the notion of suicide in her head. Sometimes when Katherina retreated to the innermost recesses of her mind, the look in her eyes frightened Margareta. As she moved deeper and deeper into her darkness, her beautiful eyes lost their lustre, until she appeared to be peering at the world through dull and dirty lenses. If that was not scary enough, there were moments when Katherina would stop dead in her tracks and focus her glance upward, as though she was being drawn to some distant light, while a blissfully happy smile spread across her face. It was then that Margareta would shudder with fear, always remembering the conversation upon which she had eavesdropped on Elisabetha and Christian Werner. She could never forget how she had trembled when Elisabetha described the horrific look on her mother's face as the young reverend lowered her to the floor from the bedsheets that had served as the hangman's noose.

Shivering as though still crouched behind the closed door where she had listened so many years ago to the secret narrative of Elfrieda's tragic demise, Margareta decided then and there to spare her daughter the ghastly details. Suddenly it occurred to her that unlike the previous episodes, this time she had not approached Katherina and tried to bring her niece out of her doldrums. Justifying her behaviour with the assertion that now her energy was being focused more on her daughter and the imminent birth of her grandchild, Margareta nonetheless felt a cold knot of apprehension in the pit of her stomach as she stood up from her chair. "We must give Katherina our love and encouragement whenever her spirits are low, remembering always that her feelings of melancholy and desolation are beyond her control. We must be very careful never to even imply she needs to pull herself together because Dr. Spitznagel advised me that it could make her worse and push her deeper into her despair."

"Oh, Mama, I am so glad you discussed this with me; lately I have been on the verge several times of taking her by her shoulders and shaking her while telling her to grow up!

Now I shall try to be more patient and understanding of her." Julia felt a sudden surge of love for her cousin, who already had experienced her share of losses.

"Thank you, Julia. I knew I could count on you, but I have been remiss in not trying to help Katherina through this bout. Therefore, I want you to go to the kitchen and make a fresh pot of tea while I go to the loft to coax Katherina to join us. Naturally it will take a fair quota of convincing; however I am feeling confident that by the time you return, I shall have Katherina in tow—even if I need to exercise my motherly authority to entice her to our cozy nest for women only. Well, at least until your father decides that he wants to go to bed and presses for our prompt exit," said Margareta as she walked towards the door.

～ 132 ～

As far as Amelia was concerned, Katie had been truly blessed. It was a benevolent God who had guided her through the blinding snowstorm to the door of two of the kindest, not to mention most schooled, people in the entire German Lutheran townships. After all, who else would have taken mother and child into their home and also have the knowledge of what to do to save her limbs, and with such total discretion? For when the final bandages were removed from all of Katie's extremities, Dr. and Mrs. Spitznagel looked on proudly at their accomplishments. Not only had her hands and feet completely healed, but they were also fully intact—all ten fingers and toes. In addition, while Katie had been recovering, her baby had thrived, gaining weight and smiling at everyone who came within his field of vision. Not even the Silent Critics were aware that the doctor and his wife had graciously opened their home for the past two months to Katie and Baby Orville.

On the fine spring morning in mid-April when Gustav and Amelia drew the wagon up in front of the Spitznagel home, the only widower of the group was the first to notice the unusual comings and goings. If they did not know better, they would think it looked like someone was moving out, but they would have been aware of any patient having been admitted to the infirmary. Since the constant level of activity in and out of the doctor's office and domicile afforded the Silent Critics a considerable ken of the relative ills of their neighbours, they had very early on positioned their table to give their inquisitive eyes full measure of the entrance. Was it possible that someone had gained access through the back door? The spinster sisters quickly refuted that theory, since they would have observed the proposed entry from their vantage point right behind the Spitznagel house. It was a mystery because the more they watched, the more convinced they were that Amelia and Gustav were preparing to depart with the young woman, and ...wait! Was she carrying a baby? They must be slipping if the doctor and his wife succeeded in pulling the wool over their eyes.

Long after the large democrat wagon had pulled away, the Silent Critics sat drinking coffee and pondering just what had transpired. It was frustrating that now they would have to keep their ears to the ground and rely on the rumours spread by other people in the town, who were not even members of their group. It had to be the height of insult to be dependent on gleaning their information from other sources. The days passed, then a week, and still they had not heard the slightest mention of the patients seen coming out of Dr. Spitznagel's infirmary. Deciding that they needed to keep their noses closer to the grindstone, the Silent Critics actually left their locale in the coffee shop of the hotel and mingled with the townsfolk on Main Street and in the shops. Yet they could not sniff out even a whiff of knowledge, and there was surprisingly very little popular interest in the mysterious woman and infant. In despair, the Silent Critics returned to their customary perch with the dubious consolation that if no one else knew the patients' identity, then they at least had not fallen down on their job.

ᨾ᨟ 133 ᨟ᨾ

With the strict instructions given at least three times by both Dr. and Mrs. Spitznagel, Amelia knew exactly how to care for Katie's hands and feet, which although healed were, without diligent attention, still vulnerable to injury. They had advised her that for some time her sister would only be able to look after her own needs and those of her son. As far as helping with any of the many chores on the farm and even around the house, Katie would be restricted to a minimum level of activity. Little did the very civilized doctor and his wife know that it had been superfluous to give Amelia directions about minding her newly discharged patients. She had been longing to bring them home so she could quite literally wait on Katie and her son hand and foot. Finally Amelia could start to assuage her ceaseless feelings of guilt, which began when she left her father's farm to marry Gustav and continued to escalate to an almost unbearable peak when her abandoned sister ran away with the disreputable Orville Reinhold.

In a matter of days, Gustav recognized the flaw in Amelia attending to Katie's every whim; but if he tried to talk to his wife, she simply quoted the doctor's orders as though every word that the man had spoken was the gospel truth. Perhaps for the first time in their married life, with tacit support from Dr. Spitznagel Amelia gained the confidence to openly question her husband rather than to acquiesce, as had been her standard practice. Torn between what he considered best for Katie and pleased that Amelia was acquiring the courage to take a stand, Gustav continued to raise his concerns periodically. With the consistency of the force of gravity, Amelia staunchly held her ground and firmly refused to deviate from her expected role as Mrs. Spitznagel's replacement. Gustav knew Amelia's show of strength was an indication of her respect for the doctor and nurse, a regard which bordered on reverence. But on the other hand, he could quickly see how Katie was enjoying her dearly beloved older sister's doting and was reverting back to the dependent behaviour of a child.

If Amelia were emerging as the winner in her contest of wills with Gustav, Katie would rapidly become the loser in terms of her independence and even her mobility. She sat in the comfortable chair which Amelia had asked Gustav to move from their bedroom into the kitchen, leaving it only when it was time to go to bed. But then why wouldn't she take advantage of the situation if her devoted sister was clearly so happy to cater to her every indulgence and also to the needs of her son? Hence, as soon as Amelia had finished her chores, she rushed back to her stove, cooking and baking all of Katie's favourite meals. It was as though with each morsel of food Amelia prepared for Katie's consumption, she was appeasing her culpability for deserting her. Regardless of how misguided her feelings of guilt were, and Gustav was not averse to telling her every chance he could, Amelia repeatedly turned a deaf ear.

In the years since Amelia had left the Schweitzer farm, Katie had forgotten just how delicious her soups, chicken and dumplings, perogies, and cabbage rolls with sour leaves tasted, never mind Gustav's smoked sausages, hams, and pork hocks. Then there were the delectable coffee cakes, cinnamon buns, and strudels to be enjoyed at the end of the meal with a strong cup of coffee and thick cream. Katie had been aware that her sister and brother-in-law never arrived at the doctor's home without a generous supply of food; but since her hands had been heavily bandaged, Mrs. Spitznagel had portioned the amount that she was fed. Now that her hands were free, Katie quite simply could not seem to reach satiation. Perhaps she was remembering how she had come close to starving while she nearly froze to death in the desolate shack on Jakob Litzenberger's land, where her husband had left her after the birth of their son.

Within a week, and most certainly by two, the effects of Katie's unlimited eating were apparent. Whether no one in the Werner household noticed, or perhaps more likely chose not to comment, matters came to a head around the Mohr dinner table one Sunday after the church service.

Perceptively, it was Margareta who recognized instantly that Katie's consumption was out of control, and when she asked for a third helping of baked ham and scalloped potatoes, Margareta, in her typically outspoken manner, said, "No, Phillip, don't pass any more food to Katie. Young lady, in my opinion you have already eaten enough to feed a man stooking sheaves in readiness for the threshers, and dessert is yet to come. Please understand that I am not being stingy; rather, I know from experience how hard it is to get around and do things when you are carrying too many pounds. Then when you try to take them off, it is harder than pulling hen's teeth."

Although Margareta's directions were well intentioned, it was clearly not the vein in which Katie chose to receive them. Since she had been taken in and diligently cared for by Dr. and Mrs. Spitznagel, Katie had quickly begun to appreciate the merits of being pampered. She had been quite used to her sister looking after her when she was a child; but as Katie was recovering from her frozen extremities, first Mrs. Spitznagel and now Amelia had unknowingly revealed to her the power that she could wield from the dependent position of a bed or an armchair. Thus, because she knew better than to talk back to her elders, when the apple coffee cake was passed to her, Katie immediately helped herself to three good-sized pieces to circumvent a similar response from Gustav's aunt. Then, as if to emphasize her point, Katie sat staring at Margareta as she petulantly stuffed every single bite into her mouth, barely stopping short of licking her plate.

But all unawares, Katie had made her first mistake. She may have thought that she had won the scrimmage with Margareta Mohr; but at the same time, she had committed a tactical error against her dedicated sister. Amelia had the utmost respect for every member of the Mohr family, dating back to their first meeting when they had so heartily welcomed her into their midst. Now for her younger sister to openly defy the lady of the house when she had been invited to sit around their ever-expanding dinner table was unthinkable. Amelia was so embarrassed that she was ready to crawl under its wooden boards and stay there until it was time to leave for home. Sitting beside her, Gustav could feel her shame, and to Amelia's surprise, he reached over and gently touched her arm under the concealment of the snow-white tablecloth. Her insistence about washing all of the dishes and making sure the kitchen was spotless before departing was a crystal-clear indication of just how mortified she was by Katie's ungrateful behaviour.

Then later when they stopped at the doctor's office on their way back to the farm, Katie was well on her way to losing the undeclared battle when she dared to question Dr. Spitznagel. On the previous Sunday when he had examined Katie, he was aware that she seemed to be putting on weight; but there was no mistaking the obvious increase in her bodily size only two weeks after he had discharged her into Amelia's capable hands.

Not having any trouble understanding how eating Amelia's excellent cooking on a daily basis could add pounds all too quickly to the waistline, and being a genial man he sensitively said, "I have good news, Katie. I think your hands and feet are now healed enough for you to start working with Amelia in the kitchen. I see no reason why you cannot help her to prepare the meals and dry the dishes. I don't recommend that you put your hands in hot water to do the washing or the laundry, but you will easily be able to manage hanging the clothes on the line to dry and bringing them in to be folded."

"Oh, no, Dr. Spitznagel. I am not nearly ready to do such heavy work. I have pains in my hands and feet almost all day, and I am too tired to do Amelia's chores. Anyway, she doesn't need my help because she has always looked after the house from the time I was a little girl," Katie replied, instantly astonishing even herself with her blunt answer.

To his surprise, Dr. Spitznagel found himself bristling in response to Katie's rebuttal. He had to stop and think about his reply for a moment because he wanted to express his disapproval of her taking advantage of Amelia's giving nature. He had no doubt that both his wife and he had played a role in determining Katie's expectations to be coddled; but knowing her sister, the doctor was only too aware that Amelia would have taken their instructions to an extreme. From the short time that they had been in the Spitznagel home this afternoon, it was apparent Amelia was also tending to most of Orville's needs. It was more than likely that the only care that Katie provided for her son was to nurse him when he was hungry after Amelia had bathed and changed him. Once again, it occurred to Rolf Spitznagel that it was amazing how quickly a human being could change from an independent, striving individual struggling for survival against all odds into a dependent clinging vine that seems unable to lift a finger to help herself.

As it happened, from the moment that Katie had refuted him, the doctor need not have worried about whether she would get out of her comfortable chair and start earning her keep in the Werner household. For the second time that day, Amelia was ashamed of her sister; but on this occasion, her response was very different from wanting to crawl under the table. Rather than lower her head, Amelia momentarily glared at Katie before she graciously thanked the Spitznagels with a basket of food for the coming week. She was suddenly anxious to change Orville and get ready to leave for home. In fact, Amelia could hardly wait until she had Katie alone in the house to put her in her place. She did not have the slightest intention of embarrassing the adults in the room any more than they already had been by Katie's rude and thankless behaviour. Furthermore, Amelia did not want Gustav to realize how right he had been about Katie all along; as hard as it was, she exercised considerable control over her increasing anger.

Of course, as soon as they arrived home, Katie laboriously climbed down from the wagon and slowly walked towards the house, leaving Amelia to carry Orville and the belongings which invariably accompany a baby in transit. When Gustav offered to assist his wife, Amelia assured him that she could manage while he fed and watered Wolfgang before releasing him into the pasture. To ensure that she had adequate time to deal with Katie prior to Gustav coming inside, she asked him to stop at the henhouse and check for eggs. Turning back to look at her more than a little strangely, Gustav wondered what was about to happen, since it was unheard of for Amelia to make such a request before he had changed out of his Sunday suit. Nonetheless, he accepted that she had something up her sleeve in relation to Katie, and as much as he would have liked to be a fly on the wall, he decided to give her the time she needed before entering the house.

Sure enough, by the time Amelia had the baby settled in his crib and returned to the kitchen, Katie was seated back in her usual spot, eating a large slice of bread slathered with thick butter and jam. The mere fact that she could be filling her face again after the sumptuous meal they had just consumed at the Mohr home was the final straw. Marching over to where Katie sat contentedly, oblivious as was her wont to the needs of anyone else, Amelia snatched the food from her sister's hand, threw it onto the plate, and sent it flying onto the table.

"That's it! I am fed up with you, Katie Schweitzer, or whatever your name is now. Get up from that chair; the minute Gustav comes in the house, it will be moved back into our bedroom, where you will never use it again. Then go to your room and change your clothes because from this second onward, you are going to be your baby's mother. As well as looking after him, you will do everything that Dr. Spitznagel said you could, and much more."

Never having seen her sister speak or act in such a manner, Katie was too dumbfounded to move, which only antagonized Amelia more. Glaring, Amelia strode over to the corner of the kitchen that housed the broom and grabbed it, but then suddenly stopped when she saw the stunned look on her sister's face.

Staring with her mouth wide open, it suddenly sank in that Amelia meant business. Katie leaped off of her customary perch and rushed into the bedroom with more speed than either of them thought possible.

"And you better be back here within five minutes ready to get to work," Amelia yelled after her.

Watching Katie retreat, Amelia slowly realized she was still holding the broom; she returned it to its place and then sat down in the chair that Katie had just vacated. To her surprise, she was shaking from head to toe, and as her anger started to subside, she wondered whence her fury had come. For heaven's sake, what was the matter with her? In her entire life, she could not recall ever having responded to anyone as she had her ailing sister, and what she found even more troubling was that she had no idea she was capable of flying into such a rage. It was as though she had taken leave of her senses. Or was she just sick and tired of Katie behaving like a spoiled brat? If so, talk about the pot calling the kettle black. Amelia was tremendously relieved that she had the foresight to ask Gustav to do the extra chores. Her embarrassment with Katie earlier in the day was nothing compared to how she now viewed her own eruption of feelings; her only consolation was that her husband had not been present to witness her unleashed temper.

True to her word, when Gustav came into the house carrying a handful of fresh eggs, Amelia immediately took them to place in the basket and then asked him to help her carry the easy chair back to their bedroom. Again, Gustav gave her an inquisitive look, but without making any comment, he set his suit jacket on the back of a kitchen chair and did as she requested. As far as Katie knew, there was no discussion of what had transpired between Amelia and her, and she was definitely too afraid to make any reference to the unprecedented outburst. If Amelia experienced any remorse, she kept it to herself, while she soon started to give Katie very clear directions of what she would be expected to do from dawn to dusk. It seemed to Katie that with the approach of spring, there was more to accomplish as each day passed until she was sure she would drop from exhaustion. Then to make matters worse, she soon realized that other than milking the cows, it looked like Franz did nothing more throughout the day than entertain the old Christian Werner.

~ 134 ~

When the snow began to melt, the water to run, and the season to change, time started to pass quickly, with all of the requirements of land and toil. After spending the long, frozen winter months in near hibernation, it was a joy to awaken to the crisp, buoyant atmosphere illuminated by the warming sun and to hear the crackle of thin ice underfoot with the heightened bounce of every step. It felt invigorating to be alive, to have blood flowing through arteries and veins all but dormant from inactivity, to revive the languished human spirit, to palpate the pulse of the earth's rejuvenation. Even hard work and drudgery, with the accompanying sore muscles and aching back, were welcomed as proof of the vitality of life and its perennial renewal.

It was not long before Katie began to wonder if Gustav and Amelia were running a race to determine which one could be first out of bed to start each day. Of course once they were up and noisily preparing to embark upon the never-ending chores, they expected her to be in the kitchen and helping with breakfast, even if Orville was still asleep. Certainly, the transformed Amelia would not have tolerated Katie lying about while she hurriedly went outside to gather the eggs and feed the chickens. At least, Katie did not want to test her by staying in bed when Amelia knocked on her door and told her it was time to get up. She was not completely over her astonishment that Amelia had seized the broom as if she might use it on her, and although Katie already had more than her share of beatings in her young life, she would have been devastated if her cherished older sister confirmed her father and husband's claim that she deserved them.

~ 135 ~

In May as they were sowing the huge garden, Katie thought her back would break from squatting over row upon row of freshly tilled earth and methodically placing the seed plants exactly one half-inch apart, as per Amelia's meticulous instructions. Since Katie was only too aware that she was coming behind her with the hoe to cover the seeds with the rich black soil, she knew she must do the job right or possibly be subjected to yet another of her sister's harangues. Surprisingly, her hands and feet caused her no discomfort at all; although by the end of the day, the muscles in her arms and legs felt like someone had set them on fire.

Katie soon found herself longing for Orville to awaken from his nap on the blanket in the shade of the caragana trees so she could finally stop and sit down to nurse him. However, her respite was short-lived; for as soon as he was satiated and changed, Amelia would press her back to her mind-numbing task. It was as though her sister had become a tyrant, and as close as she could figure, it was because she had dared just once to defy Gustav's precious Aunt Margareta.

Then slowly but surely, a strange thing began to happen. When Gustav and Amelia spoke of the progress of the spring seeding around the supper table, Katie started to contribute to the discussion. Since she worked alongside her sister all day, she thought it only fair that she add her two cents' worth rather than just sit and gorge herself with the food, which now she had also helped to prepare. When the members of the Werner family listened to her comments about the large eyes on the seed potatoes or the long bean shoots, she felt—quite possibly for the first time in her life—like an adult. Certainly Katie had rarely experienced the feeling of being considered important enough to say what was on her mind, much less to be heard when she finally gathered the courage to speak up. For most of her life, she had been in the presence of adults and told that children were to be seen and not heard. Then when her father had started to beat her after Amelia left the farm, Katie had quickly learned to keep her mouth shut in an attempt to avoid or to lessen his seemingly unprovoked attacks.

As she inevitably recovered from the aches and pains of her protesting muscles, Katie gradually began to feel stronger and more energetic. She climbed into bed early in the evenings, falling asleep as soon as her head hit the pillow, and even though she was still awakened during the night to nurse her baby, she arose in the mornings feeling refreshed rather than sluggish, as she had previously experienced. To her own amazement, she often got up before Amelia even knocked on her door, and occasionally Katie was the first person in the kitchen to attend to the dying fire. If either Amelia or Gustav was surprised by the apparent changes in Katie's behaviour, they held their silence, and perhaps waited with bated breath to see whether her willingness to do her share would last. As far as Amelia was concerned, she was relieved that Katie had acquiesced to following her directions because she was no longer sure she had the interest or desire to enforce them.

Remarkably, after years of sitting and watching Amelia make the completion of arduous tasks appear easy, what Katie was discovering for the first time in her life was how gratifying it felt to do her honest best. She began to experience the satisfaction of setting a specific goal for herself to achieve, even if it was to finish seeding five of the long rows before she had to stop to attend to Orville. When she succeeded, she found that she wanted to keep on going. Soon she was striving to accomplish more, and with each step of progress she made, the more she came to understand that she could be as hard-working as Amelia. Imperceptibly, Katie started to understand that Amelia's strength came from knowing she could do whatever she set her mind to, if she worked hard and long enough. Now as Katie considered why her older sister was so sure of herself, she came to realize that it was because she persisted like a dog with a bone until she was able to overcome whatever obstacles were in her way. If Amelia could have such enduring confidence in herself, then it finally occurred to Katie that there was no reason why she could not emulate her beloved sister.

One fine morning around the breakfast table, as if to indicate her acceptance and approval of her younger sister's coming of age, Amelia asked, "Would you be able to look after things today, Katie, while Gustav and I go to visit Sarah and Andrew, our friends who live near Duff? They have a new baby boy and we still have not had a chance to see them since he was born. You would need to make dinner for Christian and Franz, and maybe even supper, depending on what time we come home."

Scarcely able to believe her ears, it took Katie a few moments to answer, "I'm sure I will be able to find enough food in the pantry to keep us going. Also, I think I will do the washing this morning, since we finished planting the garden yesterday and Orville will soon be without clean diapers. If you want to stay later at your friends, Franz and I can milk the cows and look after the chickens."

As a hush fell over the room, it was clear that Katie was not the only one having difficulty trusting what was being said. Gustav glanced covertly at Amelia, wondering if he had been too tired to remember their plans today; perhaps he had not heard her when she had asked about visiting their friends.

Christian looked at Katie with skepticism because ever since his son had brought her to live in the Werner home, he had become more and more convinced that she could not hold a candle to Amelia when it came to cooking or, for that matter, to working.

"Now, just a minute here. I expect to have a decent meal in the middle of the day, and not something Katie is going to throw on the table. Why can't you get it ready before you leave like you always have done before, Amelia?"

"With Katie able to cook as well as I do, there isn't any reason to hold Gustav and me up from getting on our way. We want to spend the day with our friends, since we have not been to see them this spring," Amelia replied as she gave her father-in-law a reassuring smile.

It was not until they were in the carriage that Gustav had the nerve to inquire about the morning's seemingly unexpected decision to go to the Thompson farm. He certainly did not mind having a day of rest, particularly since he was finished with the spring seeding; but he just could not recall that Amelia had talked to him about it last evening. Once again,

Gustav realized he really did not understand half of what transpired between the women of the Werner household while he was out in the fields. As he was recovering from his shock of Hanna's abrupt departure with Maria and her children, he had reached the conclusion that Amelia had known all along and had chosen not to breathe a word to him.

Now he knew that somehow Amelia had managed to get Katie out of the easy chair and working as though she was determined to surpass her older sister in the realm of honest toil. However, it was equally apparent to Gustav that Amelia was also changing, and as near as he could figure, over the last several weeks she seemed to have become more talkative and sure of herself. He had started to notice her really coming out of her shell with Dr. and Mrs. Spitznagel every time they enthusiastically thanked her for the delicious food she prepared for them. Then as far as he could determine, she must have reached a turning point the day that Katie had been rude to the two people who had not only saved her limbs but also most likely her life and that of her baby. It was becoming increasingly obvious to Gustav that if he were ever to know what was taking place in his home, he would need to pay more attention to his young wife and ask her about her thoughts and plans. Quite possibly, she had decided on the spur this morning to visit their friends; but it was abundantly clear to Gustav that since he had not uttered a sigh of protest, Amelia was in charge of the happenings within the Werner household.

Instead of causing Gustav any annoyance, this sudden realization filled him with a deep sense of satisfaction. Suddenly he spied the last of the white fluffy catkins on the willow trees by the creek, and being only too aware that he had not picked them since his mother had died, he called for Wolfgang to come to a halt. While he went to gather a bundle of pussy willows and then handed them to his wife, it fully dawned on Gustav that he had been fortunate when Amelia Schweitzer had become his mate.

～ 136 ～

Finally, a letter arrived. David's wound was serious enough for him to be transported to the hospital in London for surgery, but not sufficiently severe for the army to ship him back home for the duration of the war. The opening line of the long-awaited correspondence was an abject apology for his delay in communicating with his darling Katherina. Then David excitedly went on to express how surprised he was when he saw that Dr. Robert Cameron was the surgeon who would remove the shrapnel from his shoulder and chest before setting his broken right arm.

He joked that he had always known it would be useful to be left-handed; but he also realized that he could not claim an inability to write as the justifiable excuse for his dalliance. Once again, because David was so averse to making the slightest reference to the horrors of fighting in the trenches, or of the appalling injuries inflicted on an infantryman, he simply chose not to provide a reason for his wounds, hoping Katherina was unable to read between the lines.

If he had been able to reveal his true feelings to Katherina, or to any other human being, David Hardy would have said that as he was recovering in the overcrowded hospital ward he often wished his entire right arm had been pulled out of its socket. Then surely the army would have sent him home rather than advise him that he soon would be fit enough to return to the front, to go back to leading his men into the face of the enemy fire so they could be slaughtered like cattle being butchered for food.

If he had had even the slightest idea that becoming a rifleman would be the equivalent of volunteering to be cannon fodder for the German army, he would never have joined the infantry corps. At the very least, he would have signed up with the air force and learned to fly so that he would not have to witness daily the lot of the most vulnerable of all fighting regiments, the foot soldier. Were he to tell the truth deep in his heart and soul, David knew he was completely overwhelmed with the reality of war. And had he known then what he had come to understand now, rather than enlist he would have run in the opposite direction and, if necessary, become a farmhand to avoid going overseas.

Even so, what David dreaded most about being sent back to the battlefield was that once again he would spend most of his time in the rat-infested trenches. Somehow or another, he had managed to escape the tetanus epidemics that were running rampant in the long narrow ditches that, ironically, they had dug for their shelter. Two to three hundred men huddled together in the mud that they called their home, seeking protection from the constant barrage of shells bursting all around them. When they tried to leave the trenches to attack, they would be met with a great, green cloud coming towards them, and even worse as far as he was concerned, the smell of the rotting bodies from the carnage. David did not know what he considered more horrifying, watching his men suffering from the intense vomiting caused by exposure to the deadly poison gas, or not being able to do anything as so many of them tortuously succumbed to the incessant convulsive spasms of lockjaw. Then those who managed to escape both the poison gas inhalation and the terrifying tetanus had to continue to live day and night with the ever-present vermin. How could a man survive and remain sane? When David finally fell asleep from exhaustion, he would dream of huge rats eating his ears, his nose, and other parts of his face.

No man in his right mind could write of such inhuman circumstances to his naive wife, and certainly never to his mother. The more David saw of the brutality and atrocities of war, the more he was able to understand the despair of every woman who had ever birthed a son. Perhaps it was better that Katherina had lost their son before he was born. At least she would never know the heartache of him following some idealistic notion and going to war to fight for his country, and all because of mankind's propensity for aggression and conflict. Whenever he felt strong enough, David would leave the ward of groaning, moaning men smelling of various stages of injury, illness, or death. He would invariably make his way to the small open courtyard located between the wings of the large hospital where he could see a patch of blue sky, the bursting blades of green grass, and if he were very fortunate, hear the chirping of an occasional songbird.

It was being in touch with nature where he could finally feel some semblance of normality and put his pen to paper to write to Katherina and his parents. David found that if he could limit his mind to the confines of this tiny piece of the world, he could still believe in the sanity and goodness of humanity. He could then focus on expressing his enjoyment of being able to converse with Robert Cameron who, when he had a few moments to talk, would tell David about his delight that Julia was continuing to feel well and how much he was eagerly awaiting the birth of their firstborn. Neither man could make any reference to his particular situation and talked only about their loved ones at home, firm in the belief that at least they were being spared the madness unfolding all around them. If only it had been allowed, David would have moved his small cot under the shade of the lonely beech tree, remaining there until he had recovered adequately to return to the ravage and waste of humankind on the battleground.

❧ 137 ❧

With diligent contrivance, mother and daughter had succeeded. They acknowledged to each other, but never to Katherina, that the changing seasons from winter, with its sombre grey skies and short dull days, to the promise of spring, with crocuses peeking out through the melting snow, aided greatly in the implementation of their plan. They had decided that the best way to save Katherina from her all-too-frequent episodes of wallowing in abject despondency was to prevent her from spending time alone.

When she would choose to listen to the livelier cylinders of music that had filled her mother with such sweet serenity before her death, the Mohr family enjoyed the strains of Johann Strauss's Tales From the Vienna Woods wafting down the staircase. But when Katherina was in one of her moods, she would invariably and repeatedly play a plaintive violin concerto, which would have brought tears to the most impassive eye. It was little wonder then that she would sit in her room crying as though her heart was breaking.

It therefore seemed very practical that every evening after the dishes were done, they would intercept her climbing the stairs up to her loft. The minute the kitchen was tidied, Margareta and Julia would appear, one on either side of Katherina, much like guards escorting a prisoner into the courthouse, and directed her to the front hallway. After they had donned hats, coats, and rubber footwear, they all but pushed her out the door until she appeared ready to continue along the way by her own volition. By the time the trio reached the gate opening into the Spitznagel home and inquired if the doctor and his wife planned to join them, Katherina seemed to come out of her reticence. With a sudden spurt of energy, she would soon outpace all of them with the exception of Dr. Spitznagel, and before long the other women could only hear snatches of their animated discussion from the distance. At the completion of their walk, if Mathilda and Rolf Spitznagel did not invite them in, the three women would return home to have a warming cup of tea in the cozy confines of Margareta's bedroom.

On one such evening when Julia was lagging behind even Margareta and Mathilda, she glanced over to the other side of Main Street and thought she saw several figures silhouetted in the fading light of the setting sun. Suddenly feeling fearful, she quickened her step to come abreast of her mother, who quickly slowed down as she said, "I'm sorry, Julia. I was not being very considerate of you, knowing full well how awkward it is to walk when you are heavy with child. It is a beautiful evening and I got so caught up with what Mathilda was saying that I nearly forgot about you, my darling daughter. We shall stop running as if we thought we could overtake those two racehorses ahead of us and walk at a more leisurely pace."

"Oh, thank you, Mama. Lately I feel like such a goose as I waddle along, and I just could not seem to catch up with Mathilda and you. Then I noticed that there appeared to be quite a number of people following on the other side of the street. What seems so strange is that whenever I would stop, so would they; otherwise I would have paid little attention to them. Have either of you been aware of their presence, or am I overreacting in my more vulnerable state?"

As she slowed down to hear Margareta and Julia, Mathilda turned her head, and in her peripheral vision she could see the shadows of a number of people who stopped in their tracks as soon as they observed her facing their direction. "It's odd that you should say that, Julia, because I see them too, and I must agree with you that it seems most irregular. To be honest with you, it is starting to concern me as well, and since I am not about to deliver a baby, if bad came to worse possibly I would be able to outrun them. I can certainly appreciate your disquietude. Take a quick look, Margareta, and tell me: do you recognize anybody?"

"Since they seem to be so interested in us, I shall do more than cast a furtive glance at them. In fact, I intend to stand here and stare the entire bunch down," Margareta replied as she turned completely around so she was squared up to face the interlopers.

In spite of herself, Julia burst out laughing. "I should have known that all I needed to do was to call forth my dauntless mother for protection. Let me see; how many of them are there? I count seven, but such a small number would hardly deter Margareta Mohr!"

"Seven, is it? Your eyes are definitely better than mine in this waning light. How very interesting. Shall we speculate about what group of people in Neudorf travel together like a pack of wolves, ever on the lookout for unsuspecting prey—especially when they think there may be grist for their endless rumour mill?" As she was speaking these words, to the surprise of her daughter and friend, Margareta started to walk quickly towards their supposed trackers.

In the dim illumination from the now rising moon, it took the Silent Critics more than a few moments to realize what was happening, or perhaps they could not believe their eyes as the hunted had reversed roles to become the hunter. At any rate, once they fully accepted that Margareta was striding directly towards them, in unison they turned and bolted as fast as their collective legs could carry them, back in the direction of the hotel, with the sound of Margareta's laughter ringing in their ears.

By this time, Dr. Spitznagel and Katherina had become aware that their slower walking companions had fallen well behind them, and they turned around just as Margareta had begun her pursuit. Hearing her distinct chortle piercing the stillness of the evening, they hurried back as the Silent Critics had initiated their retreat.

"What's causing such mirth, Mathilda?" Dr. Spitznagel inquired as his wife joined in Margareta's laughter.

"Well, it would seem that we are not the only people out on the street tonight, and when Margareta decided to approach the other group, they swiftly returned to their customary perch," Mathilda replied, knowing that her husband would not need her to spell out to whom she was referring.

Still, for the balance of their stroll, Dr. Spitznagel and Katherina chose to walk alongside the other members of their families. To be truthful, once everyone had enjoyed the merriment, they began wondering about the real purpose of the Silent Critics' apparent decision to pursue them, particularly when the next evening they were visible again, maintaining approximately the same distance between the two groups. Night after night, as the original five walkers embarked upon their daily constitutional, they soon became aware that the Silent Critics had joined their entourage, albeit at the seemingly prescribed twenty paces to the rear. It was strange indeed, although Dr. Spitznagel could be heard more than once expressing his delight that the Silent Critics, who for wont of another doctor in the townships, were all his patients, were all engaging in exercise, and would all benefit from a daily walk.

Then one evening after an especially vigorous walk—spurred, no doubt by the rejuvenating sensation of the brisk spring air—they were seated in the picturesque parlour of the cozy Spitznagel home when the affable doctor exclaimed, "Well, it certainly is clear that the Silent Critics' pattern is set, and for whatever reason, they are going to continue along behind us, regardless of how far or fast we walk. I thought for sure that we would lose them tonight since we all stepped up our pace—even you, Julia, perhaps intending to hasten your confinement. So once again, Margareta, as you unintentionally did with the wearing of hats, you have started another new custom for several of the people in Neudorf."

Raising his bone-china teacup, he continued, "Let's have a toast for the person in our midst who has enough influence in our town to sway a good many of its inhabitants to change their behaviours in order to be just like her."

During her many years of friendship with Dr. Spitznagel, Margareta had come to realize that he was sincere even in jest, and as she readily held her own cup up to clink his, she warmly replied, "Rolf, you are too kind, since as I vividly recall, it was your suggestion that I start wearing chapeaux rather than worry about my vanishing hair. How quickly one does become accustomed to doing certain things; now I would feel undressed if I did not have a hat covering my head."

As Margareta saw her niece laughingly joining in her tribute, she turned to her daughter and silently toasted her, knowing she would understand that their plan to bring Katherina out of her doldrums and keep her from sinking into the dark recesses of her mind had worked famously. That was far more important than the mere fact that anyone might want to emulate an aging, about-to-be grandmother.

⟫⟫⟩ 138 ⟨⟪⟪

Ever since overhearing Andrew's strange inquiry months ago now, Amelia could not help but think that Gustav was wielding some control. She had considered Andrew's query over and over, and although she was unable to make the slightest sense of what he had meant, the words had been indelibly etched in her memory. After all, surely Gustav could see how desperately Amelia longed for a child of her own instead of always caring for another woman's baby.

There had been many times when Amelia wondered if Andrew and Gustav had had words about the fact that they had yet to produce an offspring. It seemed that whenever her husband wanted to depart the Thompson homestead quickly, the only explanation had to be that the two friends had quarrelled. Yet they were so compatible that it was difficult to understand what they could possibly fight about.

One day, when Amelia was emptying the wash basin behind the house, she came within hearing range of the men. Then she heard Andrew say, "Don't you think it is about time for you to do it the right way, so Amelia could finally have her own baby?" She stood frozen with the basin clutched in her hands, not wanting to make a sound for fear her presence would be detected. Later, Amelia told herself that she had not wanted to interrupt her husband and his friend; but all the while, she knew deep down in her heart that she selfishly needed to listen to Gustav's response.

Gustav's reaction had stunned Amelia and made her wary about ever asking what Andrew had intended, even if she had been able to do so without giving away that she had been secretly listening to their conversation. Her husband had instantly clenched his fists, and as she stood gasping, she was certain that he would strike Andrew. Fortunately, Gustav came to his senses in time and stormed away while yelling at his friend to mind his own business.

As soon as he was out of sight, Amelia quietly turned and hurried back to the kitchen, just as Gustav appeared at the front door and motioned for her to get her hat and coat. Since they had scarcely finished eating their meal, Amelia considered that to leave so abruptly would be rude to Mr. and Mrs. Thompson, who always so generously shared their hospitality. Besides, she had hardly spent any time with Sarah and the children and was not near ready to go home. However, Gustav had given her another fierce look and so Amelia had thanked their friends as graciously as she could and followed her husband to the waiting carriage.

Not one word was spoken on the ride back to the Werner homestead. As soon as Gustav changed his clothes, he went out to the fields where he remained until after dark. For the next several days he was more laconic than Amelia had ever seen him, and she found herself giving him a wide berth until he worked through whatever it was that had upset him so strongly. However, before long the incident began to gnaw at Amelia like a dog with a sore paw. What could Andrew possibly have meant? Was Gustav doing something to stop her from becoming with child? Could she pluck up her courage and ask Sarah? But then, what if her friend did not know? Months had passed since she overheard Andrew's unusual question, and although Amelia's mind was tormented by indecision and doubt regardless of how much she thought about it, there did not appear to be any way to obtain an answer. Still, she was desperate enough that she knew she must unravel the mystery of what Andrew was talking about, just as capably as if it was one of her tangled balls of yarn that she used for crocheting. As it was, Amelia would become so pensive for long periods that finally Katie made the observation that whatever the problem was between Gustav and her sister, it must surely be a humdinger.

≈~ 139 ~≈

At long last, Amelia's resolve was strengthened. Lately, the more she thought about it, the more she realized that everywhere she went, she was surrounded by babies. Spending all day with Sarah and lovingly attending to her beautiful newborn son had been the last straw. The two women had enjoyed their usual companionship, and Amelia had even laughed when Sarah humourously told her about the dilemma Andrew and she had faced when it came time to name their baby. Sarah had wanted to call him after her husband, but he was adamant that it would be much too confusing as the boy grew older. Then when she respectfully suggested that they give him the same Christian name as both of his grandfathers, Andrew had openly moaned about their apparent lack of originality. Out of the blue Sarah had remembered Henry, a cousin in England with whom she had spent hours playing as a little girl, and when she proposed it as their son's first name, Andrew agreed immediately. However, Sarah was not one to be easily deterred, and eventually they had reached a compromise. Subsequently when the Methodist minister in Duff had called forth Sarah and Andrew for the baptismal service of their son, he was formally introduced to the congregants as Henry William Andrew Thompson.

Even as she chuckled at Sarah's story, all Amelia could think about was that if she was ever blessed with a baby, she would not care about the child's name. Then when they returned home in the evening and were greeted by Katie holding the wailing Orville, Amelia took him into her comforting arms and soon rocked him to sleep. As she tenderly laid him in his crib, she wondered if Gustav had doubts about her being able to look after a baby. Surely he could see how capable she was since during the first few weeks that Katie had lived with them, she had practically done everything for Orville short of nursing him. And every Sunday during family dinner at Aunt Margareta's and Uncle Phillip's home, it was Amelia who rushed to pick up Rolf and Katie's newborn daughter and soothingly walked with her until her mother was ready to feed her. And now as everyone was eagerly awaiting Julia's confinement, once again Amelia would have to take her turn in line, this time behind Aunt Margareta, to help with yet another baby in the family that did not belong to her.

Try as hard as she could, Amelia simply could not understand why after more than two years of marriage she was still not with child. Although it was a subject she could never have broached with anyone in a hundred years, even with her own sister as they worked every day side by side in the garden, she was quite certain that Gustav and she coupled as much as any other young wedded husband and wife. Yet they had no results, whereas their families and friends seemed to add new offspring to their fold every one or two years. Amelia realized that her awareness of child-bearing was limited to what she had seen of their farm animals every spring. So whenever Gustav reached out for her at bedtime, she always remained as still and as patient as the cows did while the bull went about his business. She had quickly come to learn that Gustav did not like to speak during their union; although he was often more talkative during the evenings when he seemed to want their silent coupling. On one of those evenings as they were preparing for bed, Amelia would ask Gustav why she was not yet with child rather than wait until they were lying down and he had turned to her.

To build up her courage, Amelia had carefully thought about some words she could use, and then whenever she was alone, she repeatedly practised saying them out loud until she gained a measure of comfort with them. She realized that regardless of how many times she said them to herself, she would still be so embarrassed about speaking in such a frank manner to her husband; but she just had to know. Perhaps Gustav did not understand it either and would only become cross with her for asking him such a strange question, as if he could possibly know the answer.

Finally it came to her. Amelia would do what she had done throughout her entire life. She would take the responsibility for her not being with child upon herself. Now all she had to do was wait until one evening when Gustav gave her his familiar sign of his bedtime intentions. Lately, though, he had been having spells of sullenness; he was so distant that Amelia was beginning to worry that her husband was losing interest in her. Then one particularly warm spring evening after supper, Gustav asked Amelia to come for a walk with him. Leaving the dishes for Katie and Franz, she quickly gathered her shawl and hat as she followed him out of the house. They walked along in silence until they came to the willows along the creek. By now, the fluffy catkins were becoming long, slender, and shiny green leaves.

Just then, Amelia remembered Gustav's spontaneous gift on their last visit to the Thompson farm, which gave her the courage to blurt out, "Do you think there is something wrong with me because I can't seem to become with child?"

Stopping in his tracks, Gustav turned and stared at his wife. How could she manage to always see herself as the one to blame? Was it years of doing everything for Katie and Franz that had made her think she was responsible for things that did or did not happen?

To give himself time to think about his response, he slowly started to walk again. He simply would not have Amelia think that she was at fault for not conceiving a baby when the decision had been entirely his. There were times when he still felt annoyed by Andrew's outspoken question; but after weeks of wrestling with his conscience, he was still convinced that this was not the right time to have a baby. Gustav was not insensitive to Amelia's longing for a child. Good heavens, he was not blind as his friend and even some of his family seemed to think.

The world was at war, and there was increasing commentary on the radio broadcasts that the government might have to impose conscription to swell the ranks of men needed to fight for the Commonwealth. What if he were forced to join up and go overseas like David Hardy and Robert Cameron? Worse yet, what if he was killed or maimed? No doubt with her capacity for hard work, Amelia would do her best to keep the farm going, but she already had enough on her plate. His father was getting older and more decrepit with each passing year and could not really help much in the fields or even with the farm animals. Then, if anything happened to Christian, it would most certainly be Amelia who would need to take care of him. Right now, Katie seemed intent on doing her share of the chores as well as looking after Orville; but who knew how long it would last? As far as

Gustav was concerned, she could relapse to her previous indolent behaviour at the drop of a hat.

Then there was Franz. Gustav had long since given up trying to understand him or get him to pull his weight, and what was even more frustrating was that he could put away enough food to feed two people. When he had first come to live with them, Franz was just a boy and Gustav had been certain that he could teach him how to help him run the farm. But instead of learning and improving, lately Franz had become worse, and now he could spend days moping around the house and the yard, all the while not getting one scrap of work done. If Gustav said anything to Amelia, it only led to a quarrel, so what was the point? For some time now, Gustav had reconciled himself to the fact that his wife would always coddle her youngest brother to his detriment, even after her experience with Katie. How, then, could Amelia possibly take care of all of her responsibilities if she also had a dependent infant? Knowing her only too well, Gustav perfectly understood that Amelia would work herself ragged until she dropped from exhaustion, and he could never allow that to happen to his wife.

Although he had gone over all of these reasons in his mind a multitude of times, how could he possibly express them to Amelia without upsetting her? The truth was that Gustav did not mind having Katie and her baby as well as Franz living with them since it had helped to fill the void left by the abrupt departure of Hanna, Maria, and the children.

Of course, it was unthinkable that he would try and explain what he did during their coupling to reduce the odds of Amelia being with child. He vividly remembered Rolf's outburst one day when, by trying to help his older brother avoid having a baby every year, Gustav had told him about Uncle Phillip's advice. Rolf had been furious that Gustav would take any action to prevent Amelia from having a child, and if he were not so shy, he would have made good on his threat to take his sister-in-law aside and tell her that her husband was responsible for her not conceiving.

Then without understanding that his brother actually wanted to keep on adding children to his family every year, Gustav had made the same mistake again and brought Andrew into his confidence. Although Andrew had not said much at the time, Gustav still could not believe that his only friend had thrown it back in his face, as if he had any say as to when Amelia would have a baby.

Coming out of his reverie, Gustav realized that Amelia was still waiting for his response. He turned, and tucking his hand through her right arm, replied, "There is not a single thing wrong with you, Amelia. You are a good wife. In fact, you seldom do anything that causes me any distress. I am certain that all in good time when we are ready to begin a family, you will become the mother of strong, healthy babies, and I know that you will work just as hard to raise our children properly as you do with everything else." Never having heard such high praise from her husband, Amelia lowered her head in humility and knew that she would have to let it go.

⇒〜 140 〜⇐

On the morning when Katie came back from the henhouse carrying only half a dozen eggs, Amelia was surprised; but when it happened again the next day, she knew something was amiss. When questioned, Katie indignantly answered that she was quite capable of gathering eggs but she could hardly be expected to lay them in order to make sure there were enough for breakfast.

As soon as she was out of bed the following morning, Amelia went straight to the chicken coop; but when she returned with a similar count, Katie was smugly waiting at the kitchen door.

"Well, my dear sister, it seems you can do no better than I when bringing in the eggs. Clearly many of the chickens have decided to stop laying; but at least now you will have to agree that I am not at fault."

"Oh, it is not the chickens! Something or someone must be getting at the eggs before we go to gather them, and tonight I will keep watch to catch the culprit. In all of my years, I have never had any of my chickens not lay eggs; so I will not blame them," Amelia answered with the conviction of a farmwoman who knew her poultry.

As it unfolded, Amelia did not need to wait much beyond the end of the afternoon to uncover the guilty party who was casting a dark shadow upon her trusty hens. She had an uneasy feeling throughout most of the morning while Katie and she were working in the garden; she became convinced that a pair of eyes was watching them. She stopped, rose from her stooped position, and looked around so many times that Katie started to tease her about becoming a nervous old woman. Not wanting to alarm her sister, Amelia decided to ignore her but made sure to check that Orville was still sound asleep in the old wooden baby carriage that the women had found in a shed. Even though she scanned the yard several times and on each occasion had not seen any sign of life—not even a tree stirring in the breeze—Amelia's apprehension increased until she finally told Katie to leave everything on the ground and to fetch Orville.

Just then, Amelia thought she saw a silhouette slip behind the barn. Rather than wait for her sister, she lifted the infant from his resting place as she quickly motioned Katie to follow her to the safety of the house. Once inside, she propped a chair in front of the door and made sure the broom was within her reach. Never having seen her sister so nervous, Katie began to fret that there had to be a sound reason for her unusual actions.

"Amelia, whatever is the matter? In all the years we have lived together, I cannot remember you barricading a door, and you are making me terribly skittish. It's like you are afraid that someone is after us!"

"Yes, I am worried, Katie. If there is an intruder, the blocked door will slow him down and give me time to hit him with the broom. I want you to take Orville into your bedroom and put him in his crib." Amelia grabbed the broom and held it in her left hand as she began to start making dinner. With furrowed brow, Katie hastened to the bedroom with her son in her arms, the sudden sensation of fear chilling her to the bone.

Keeping a watchful eye on the yard through the kitchen window, Amelia brought the leftover roast pork from the pantry and began slicing it to add to the potatoes and onions she was frying in the large skillet. She was glad that Gustav had mentioned earlier that he was working in the south quarter; since he was so close, he would tether the oxen and walk home at dinnertime. Franz and Christian had taken slices of bread and cheese with them in case they ended up far afield on such a beautiful spring day, but Amelia always prepared enough to feed them in the event that they arrived home. When Katie returned to the kitchen, she immediately glanced towards the door, and seeing the chair still braced against the knob, her apprehension began to subside. The delectable smell of frying onions wafted through the house, and soon Gustav would appear for his meal.

Spying Gustav strolling in the distance, Amelia quickly walked to the fortifying chair and returned it to its place at the table. No sooner had he come through the door than it was opened again to admit the wandering youth and his aging companion. All through the meal, Katie expected that Amelia would offer an explanation for her strange behaviour, but now her sister acted as though the women had had their usual domestic morning.

After his twenty-minute nap, Gustav was preparing to return to the field when Amelia followed him outside. "Before you leave, Gustav, I wonder if you would do me a favour?" Without waiting for his response, she continued, "Please check around the barn and see if you can find any sign that someone might be sleeping in one of the empty stalls."

"What are you fretting about now, Amelia?"

"Oh, never mind then. Go back to your fields. I will do it myself," Amelia said tersely, as she started to march across the yard. By now Gustav knew that when Amelia was short with him, it often meant she was worried. Rushing up beside her, he said, "Go back into the house, and I shall do as you ask right away."

Entering the barn, Gustav gave each stall a cursory glance, fully expecting to find nothing out of the ordinary; he was quite surprised when he arrived at the open space at the far end of the long, low building. Not only could he see the flattened imprint that had to have been made by a body lying on the straw, but there were burlap sacks tucked in the corner that looked as though they had served as a pillow and blanket. It seemed that Amelia was justified in her concern, and as his eyes became accustomed to the dim lighting, Gustav thoroughly searched every square inch of the barn. There was no sign of life, and given the size of the impression on the straw, the man who had likely taken respite amongst the animals was presumably long gone.

Or was he? Gustav thought to himself as he walked back to the poplar trees where he had tethered the oxen. What manner of man would skulk around the barn rather than make his presence known to the occupants of the house? How long had he been on the homestead and what did he want? No wonder Amelia was worried. Suddenly remembering the shortage of eggs for breakfast the last two mornings, Gustav knew their unannounced visitor was likely the culprit. It would be easy enough to sneak into the henhouse before they were awake, steal eggs, and eat them raw, especially when there was precious little else to be consumed.

Perhaps he had also found his way into the smokehouse and had partaken of the hams, and if particularly hungry, the sausage to complete his stolen meals. Finally, it occurred to Gustav that he must return to the house instead of plowing the field and try to ascertain who was lurking around his farm.

Deciding that he also could be stealthy, Gustav walked towards the creek and started following the willows back to the gully that was off to the right and down from the farmyard. Once he was opposite the house, he could weave his way up without being seen by running and hiding behind the shed and the smokehouse until he reached the barn. Then he would slip into a darkened corner and wait for their transient caller to appear, hopefully in need of an afternoon nap. As it happened, his surreptitiousness was unnecessary. As soon as Gustav got to the door he could hear snoring, and with three long strides, he covered the length of the barn to find Katie's husband, Orville Reinhold, curled up on the straw.

Leaning over him, he gave the slumbering man a hearty shake as he said, "Just what are you doing hanging about in my barn?"

Jumping up with a start, Orville had his fists clenched ready to protect himself until he understood what his brother-in-law was asking. Then he gruffly responded, "I didn't think I would be welcome in your home, and since I needed a place to sleep, I bedded down with your animals."

"And when you needed food to eat, you helped yourself to eggs from my henhouse and possibly meat from the smokehouse. Just when were you going to let your wife know that you were back in the townships?" Gustav demanded as he motioned to Orville to follow him.

As the men were walking to the house, Gustav had to honestly admit to himself that he had more than a few misgivings about this rough-looking man, who from all accounts had abandoned his wife and child to the brutality of a Canadian winter. Still, when Katie married him, he became part of the family; were Gustav to leave him in the barn like a common thief, he would not be much better than Orville.

Unbelievably, Katie was practically beside herself with excitement when she looked out the window and saw her husband. Quickly handing the baby to Amelia, she went flying out the door to welcome him with open arms. If she remembered her frozen extremities and her plight of just a few months ago, there was no evidence of it in her greeting, and quite possibly Orville would never be apprised of how close he came to losing both of them. Gustav had to bite his tongue, reminding himself that at the moment he was trying very hard not to clobber the other man.

It took all of two days for Gustav's sense of foreboding to be justified. He had always suspected that Katie's slothful behaviour remained close to the surface, and given the slightest excuse, would return with a vengeance. Leaving Amelia holding the hungry baby, she led Orville into the kitchen, and soon had bread and cheese cut and placed on the table, along with a bowl of canned saskatoon berries. Amelia had to bring Orville over to Katie, who had promptly sat down on a chair beside her husband, and remind her that she had been about to nurse him. While Katie was feeding the baby, Amelia put water on the stove to boil, and when her brother-in-law had finished eating everything in front of him, she motioned him to the wash basin and handed him a clean towel. As soon as the baby seemed to have his fill, Katie returned him to Amelia, obviously expecting her to burp, change, and put him down for his nap. In the blink of an eye, both Katie and Orville disappeared into her bedroom, where they remained for the balance of the afternoon.

As for Orville, it was remarkable how little time he needed to go from languishing in the barn with the farm animals to thinking he was the head of the household. It did not help that all Katie would do was wait on him hand and foot, hardly even attending to her baby and then only to nurse him. The next day, Orville and Katie spent most of their time together again in the bedroom, displaying an uncanny sense of timing by arriving in the kitchen just as Amelia was beginning to prepare another meal. Then rather than helping her sister, Katie sat down beside Orville, also waiting to be served. However, when it came time to eat, the two of them put Franz to shame with the amount they consumed. By the morning of the third day, Gustav had seen enough. It was one thing to look after a woman and her child, but quite another to support a man who would spend the day lying around the house. Finally, Gustav was ready to take action on an injustice that had troubled him now for months. Telling Amelia to get her hat and coat, they left the house to go and see Peter and Wilhelmina because it was time to put his plan to the test.

⤳ 141 ⤳

This time they would not be left out in the cold, and the Silent Critics could thank the younger spinster sister for her weak bladder. It was just as she was climbing back into her bed that she saw the glow of a light, and when she went to the window, she caught a glimpse of Mrs. and Dr. Spitznagel, who was carrying his little black bag while being admitted into the Mohr home by Margareta. Surely they were there for Julia's confinement, and all she would need to do was sit and watch for them to leave, for confirmation of the baby's arrival. If all went well, she would be able to pass on the news by the time the Silent Critics gathered for their early morning coffee. Of course, she would have no way of determining the gender of the baby unless she could glean some snippets of conversation as the doctor and his nurse were departing. Therefore, in anticipation, she opened the window wide and then gathered her eiderdown to wrap around her bony shoulders as she took up her post on the wobbly wooden chair. Had it not been so hard and Julia's intermittent screams so piercing, she would have nodded off several times; but after sitting for hours, her patience was finally rewarded.

As dawn was breaking, dressing the prairie sky in pastel blues, pinks, and the glow of the rising sun, the door opened, revealing Dr. and Mrs. Spitznagel and Margareta still deep in discussion. Pressing her ear to the windowsill, the spinster considered how fortunate it was that the Mohr family chose to use the side door as the entrance to their home rather than the front entry. "Well, Julia was never one to waste any time once she made up her mind," Margareta said as the doctor and his wife stepped out on the landing.

"I think five and a half hours for the labour and delivery of a first baby must be our best record," Dr. Spitznagel answered proudly. "Once again, congratulations, Margareta. I know you will thoroughly enjoy your beautiful grandson, and sooner than you can think you will have him in the store with you, teaching him about running the business. Seriously, though, I think mother and babe will do very well, especially after he finishes feeding and they both have a chance to get some sleep."

Hearing all she needed, the spinster swung into action. Tossing the quilt on the bed, she rushed to her sister's bedroom, telling her to get up so together they could go to the hotel with the breaking news. If they hurried, they could be the first to spread the information about the birth of Margareta Mohr's grandson around Neudorf before the new grandmother could open the doors of the general store. She was almost giddy from lack of sleep, or was it because for once the Silent Critics would get the best of their most ingenious nemesis? This improbable victory would be the direct result of her perseverance.

"There is little time to wash your face, and forget about cooking the oatmeal. The hotel is already open and I want us to be the first customers in the coffee shop so we can tell everyone as they come in that Margareta is a grandmother. Then they will go into the store and congratulate her before she even has the opportunity to announce her glad tidings. It is so exciting to finally be able to steal Margareta's thunder that this morning we will splurge by eating breakfast with our friends."

When Margareta had awakened to the sound of Julia's anguished cries and leaped out of bed, Phillip was right behind her. Responding to her directions, he had run downstairs into the store to telephone Dr. and Mrs. Spitznagel to inform them that Julia's time had come. As he came back into their bedroom, Margareta suddenly remembered how her husband had fretted and paced during the delivery of their two children, and she suggested that he might want to go to the lumberyard or take a midnight walk rather than wait around in the house. It was inevitable that Peter should also soon be awakened from his slumber, and Margareta asked Phillip to take their son along with him. Feeling like a coward, he readily agreed that childbirth was clearly within a woman's realm and retreated down the stairs.

Stepping out the front door of the general store, Phillip was reminded after all of these years why he had only fathered two children. Aside from his fear of losing Margareta in the throes of labour, which in itself was overwhelming, he could not stand to see her in pain and to hear his darling wife's ear-splitting cries as she birthed their first child. He never could fathom how a woman, after having one baby, would ever want to have another, and it was only after Margareta had begged him for years following Julia's arrival that he finally gave himself fully to her again. Then when Peter was born, Phillip thanked God for his blessings of not only giving him a son, but more importantly for sparing his wife. With a son and a daughter, Margareta seemed to be satisfied and had silently accepted Phillip's premature withdrawal during their subsequent coupling. Since her change of life, they had often jested in the privacy of their bedroom that losing her hair was a small price to pay for their much more enjoyable activities between the bed sheets.

As he strode along on the beautiful moonlit night, Phillip prayed that Julia would come through her confinement without any complications. As much as he had longed to have a grandchild, he could never deal with life without Julia. It was trying enough to constantly worry about the fate of his son-in-law existing within the very heart of the German blockade of England. Looking up at the clear sky, alive with its plethora of glimmering constellations and twinkling stars, he found it near impossible to believe that in another part of the world London was being attacked by zeppelins. What would it be like to cast your glance upward, and instead of seeing a firmament vibrant with the serene beauty of the night, to observe large dirigible airships dropping bombs upon the peaceful streets? Quite probably for the thousandth time in the past year, Phillip thanked God that his family and he had fled the continent to live in what he considered the most concordant country on earth.

Then, as he lowered his gaze, Phillip was sure he caught sight of a furtive movement in the upstairs window of the spinster sisters' house. He calmly walked over until he was adjacent to the store to ensure that he was out of sight and then waited. Sure enough, after several minutes had passed, he saw another slight motion, as though someone had leaned forward onto the windowsill to check out the comings and goings of the side door of the Mohr home. Phillip had arrived outside in time to see Dr. and Mrs. Spitznagel hurrying from their residence to be immediately admitted by Margareta, so what was there still to watch? Wondering why anyone would sit and observe a darkened street, he suddenly realized that one of the sisters might be prepared to maintain her vigil until the doctor could be seen leaving the Mohr's house. Then, no doubt she fervently hoped to eavesdrop on their parting conversation as Margareta bade her farewell to Dr. and Mrs. Spitznagel and perhaps learn what had taken place during the wee hours of the morning.

That was it precisely. The old snoop was going to spy on his family yet again so she could prattle to the rest of the Silent Critics about his first grandchild. No wonder they always knew what was happening in Neudorf, if they took turns night and day prying on the hapless inhabitants of the town. Well, not this time, if he had anything to do with it. As he slowly inched his way along the exterior of the building, Phillip developed a plan to foil the spinster sister.

Returning to the front door, he let himself in. He saw that Peter had not yet come to keep him company, and then he understood why. It was quiet upstairs, and quite possibly his son had rolled over and gone back to sleep. Either Julia had delivered the baby already or Dr. Spitznagel had given her some medication to ease the pain which, as Phillip thought about it, was the more likely option. Now, he had to implement his scheme without lighting the kerosene lamp because he did not want to alert his peeping Tom neighbour to the fact that he was in the general store.

Fortunately, Margareta believed that "everything had a place and everything in its place," and Phillip remembered exactly where he could find at least one of the items he wanted. Aided by the light of the full moon shining in through the storefront window, he quickly gathered his supplies. It was obvious what he would give to the men as they filed into the hotel for their morning coffee, but it was more difficult to determine what he could appropriately present to the women. Then he recalled his wife having enthused about the many different flavours of rock candy with their corresponding plethora of colours that she had recently added to the inventory of the store. Now where would she have placed such an attractive display of sweets? Of course, Margareta would have positioned the large jar of candy right beside the cash register, where every child who entered the store could see it and then hope to convince a parent to purchase a stick for the ride home.

He carried the glass container to the windowsill, where even in the shadowy illumination cast by the resplendent Saskatchewan night sky, Phillip could discern the variety of colours that had so enamoured Margareta. There were green-, red-, orange-, blue-, yellow-, and pink-striped sticks of the rock candy, and at once Phillip began to search for as many of the pink and blue as he could find. Then, as soon as he learned the gender of his grandchild, he could select the correct colour to give out at the hotel. Hastily rooting out the hard candy, he nearly dropped the jar when a series of tortured screams emanated once more from Julia's living quarters, and he quickened his quest. The time had come for him to again seek the silence of the night, where he so often felt the presence of his Maker, and to pray for the safekeeping of his daughter. Phillip placed his bounty on the floor beside the stairs, closed the door firmly behind him, and began walking briskly across the solitary Main Street towards the outskirts of town.

Within a few minutes, he was being hailed by Peter, who came running up behind him and said, "Good heavens, Papa, what are they doing to Julia? I have never heard such shrieks of agony before in my life."

"Her baby is about to arrive into this world, and what you were hearing is the severe pain of childbirth. I am outside walking, or you may say running away because like you I cannot stand to hear a woman suffer through such misery. Since the beginning of time, it has been ever thus; women have writhed in the throes of labour to bring new life into the universe while we men wait and pace, hoping and praying that mother and child will both survive. It can go on for hours and hours, and I personally do not believe that it gets any easier, regardless of how many offspring a woman births. Between you and me, my son, I think the Good Lord knew what He was doing when women were given the task of making sure humankind continued; I cannot imagine any man enduring such pain once, much less subjecting himself to it a second time." The two men increased the pace of their strides as if trying to get as far away from the Mohr home as possible.

"I had no idea that having a baby could be so painful. Is it dangerous? Is Julia going to be all right?" Peter asked with a tremble in his voice and an anxious look on his face, as though he had just comprehended that his sister's life could be in peril.

"That's why we walk and pray, asking our Father in Heaven not to call Julia home yet. Fortunately your mother had the foresight to tell me before I left that she would signal me by lighting a lamp in our bedroom window the moment the baby has come. In the meantime, we will circle the street until we see that beacon of light coming from the upstairs of the house. Perhaps we can begin our supplication by repeating the Lord's Prayer together."

Phillip was prepared to trudge throughout the night and all of the following day, if necessary, until he received the news of Julia's confinement. The lumberyard and the store would remain closed for the duration since he would not be able to concentrate on his customers' requirements. He could hardly be expected to invest any of his time and energy into the family businesses when his only daughter could be lying on her deathbed. After all, how many young women succumbed every year while giving birth? The truth was that as Julia had become heavier and heavier with child, Phillip was terrified for his tall, willowy

However, once he had established this point, Gustav knew he would quickly complicate matters because then he intended to suggest that Amelia's, and hopefully Wilhelmina's, allotment could be shared amongst their younger siblings. Thus, according to his plan, the Schweitzer homestead of 160 acres would be subdivided. Of course, Gustav expected that Ludwig would hardly want to waste his time farming such a small portion, but he did own the Litzenberger homestead. In addition, it was very likely that Heinrich would be only too happy to sell Ludwig his share of the land since he had not once returned to the farm after leaving to work with the railway in Saskatoon. But the real dilemma was in relation to the domicile; even if the house on the Schweitzer homestead was not much to write home about—a fact that Ludwig's wife had immediately learned and responded to by promptly returning to Saskatoon—it was still where Ludwig hung his hat.

On the other hand, there would be very little to gain by obtaining land for them if Katie and Orville had no home in which to live. Gustav could not imagine Ludwig living in the shack on the Litzenberger farm; nor did he think for a minute that they should allow his sister and her family to occupy it again since it was even more uninhabitable now. With total certainty, Gustav knew Ludwig would not permit Katie to return to their father's house with a man whom he considered useless and an infant who would undoubtedly disturb his sleep at night.

Try as he might, Gustav had not been able to find the solution as to where Katie's family would reside if he turned them out of the Werner home. Aside from the fact Amelia would be very angry should he make such a drastic decision, he could not in good conscience ask them to leave when it was clear they had no place to go. Perhaps together with Wilhelmina and Peter, they would be able to find a plausible answer—yet another reason to hope they were both available and could be counted on to uphold Gustav's proposition because, one way or another, he absolutely had to get Orville Reinhold off his farm.

Regardless of how carefully Gustav had thought it through and then discussed it with Peter, Wilhelmina, and Amelia, who were in complete agreement with him, none of them were prepared for Ludwig's response. As it happened, the four of them had spent the better part of the morning talking over Gustav's proposed arrangement, finally coming to the conclusion that, if necessary, they would organize a house-raising bee for Katie. Of course, they fully expected the Werner and Strauss families to foot the cost of the materials, but they surmised that Uncle Phillip would sell them the lumber at a reasonable price. At last, when they deemed they had worked out every contingency and Wilhelmina had prepared a meal to take with them on the premise that Ludwig might be more amenable once fed, they gathered the children and followed along in the Strauss carriage as Gustav untethered Wolfgang to lead the way.

With impeccable timing, the small entourage pulled into the Schweitzer yard just as Ludwig was coming in from the fields, no doubt to have his dinner. Although the other four adults hoped to use the element of surprise to their advantage, Ludwig gave no indication that their unlikely visit made the slightest difference to him. Nor did he bother to invite them into the house, and since it never occurred to Wilhelmina that she did not have the right to enter the family home, she walked in behind Ludwig while Peter and Gustav attended to the horses. The minute her three sons, Rolf, Georg, and Hanz, had helped their mother carry the baskets of food and place them on the kitchen table, they made a hasty retreat out the door. The boys really did not understand what was going on, but sensed it might be safer to play outdoors, waiting until they were called to come in and eat. On the rare occasions they had been around Uncle Ludwig, none had felt comfortable in his presence.

"What is this? Do you think I can't make my own meals? If that were the case, I would have wasted away by now, since none of you ever come to visit," Ludwig snapped as he waved his arms in the direction of the table laden with what he assumed was food.

"Well, if this is how you treat visitors, it's small wonder that no one wants to come near you," Wilhelmina retorted without missing a beat. For the first time since their arrival, a look of surprise appeared on Ludwig's weatherbeaten face. Up until the time he had met his outspoken wife, he had been a man who considered that a woman's place was in the kitchen, preferably barefoot and with child. What was happening with the women these days? Now his previously shy sister was talking back to him. What Ludwig could not possibly know was that after years of living with a man who loved her and respected her opinions, and given all of her responsibilities as a farm wife, Wilhelmina had come into her own. Then with three sons to raise, she was determined that her boys would grow up to be like their father and treat women with proper regard.

"By the time you have finished washing up, I shall have set the table and laid out dinner. Then when you have called the men and boys to come inside, we will sit down around the table and eat a family meal," Wilhelmina replied in a kinder tone of voice, thinking it might help their negotiations.

Instead of bristling at being told what to do by a woman, and his sister at that, Ludwig unexpectedly felt a surge of tenderness that someone cared enough about him to give him a directive. Walking over to the wash basin, Ludwig realized he often did not even bother to clean up, much less sit down at the table to have something to eat. Since he only kept one cow to milk on the farm and he certainly did not have the time to cultivate a garden other than barter wood for produce with neighbours and supplies at the Mohrs' general store, there seldom was much food in the house he could consume. Then by the time he got around to eating, he usually wolfed it down standing by the kitchen cupboard, looking out the window and wondering what the hell he was doing on this dismal farm.

When they were all seated around the old wooden table, Ludwig could scarcely believe his eyes when he saw the amount of delicious-looking food that Wilhelmina had unpacked from all of the baskets. There was cold roasted chicken, pickled pork hocks, hot potato salad, two loaves of fresh baked bread, pickled carrots and beans, and a coffee cake—more volume and variety than Ludwig had seen since he had returned to farm his father's land. Then when Peter bowed his head and asked his oldest son Rolf to ask the blessing, Ludwig realized he had even stopped saying grace before eating.

But it was not until the four adults and the boys began to chit-chat with familial ease that, to his astonishment, he felt tears spring to his eyes, and it occurred to him how he had been longing to hear the sound of human voices. Soon it seemed that everyone was talking at once; along with the clatter of utensils making contact with plates, the Schweitzer kitchen was filled with the noise of people gathered together in companionship.

It had been years since the chipped wooden walls had resounded with children's laughter; when he thought about it, mealtimes had always been hushed, strained occurrences—especially after his mother's death. Ludwig sat and listened, marvelling at how his older sister involved her sons in the conversation, even giving them a chance to have their say while Peter and Gustav good-naturedly teased them. As Ludwig absorbed it all, like a pupa drawing nourishment from within its homey cocoon in preparation for bursting forth as a butterfly in the spring, he ate and ate and ate. Wilhelmina kept passing him the platters of food, while at the same time she served dessert to the boys, who were clearly anxious to return to their play outside. When he finally reached the point where he could not consume one more mouthful, Ludwig leaned back in his chair and thanked his sister for supplying enough food to last him for the week.

Grasping the opportunity of Ludwig's unexpected expression of gratitude towards his sister, Peter decided to strike while the iron was hot.

"Well, it's easy to see you enjoyed Wilhelmina's cooking, and while we have coffee, we will get down to the business of our visit. Gustav and Amelia came to talk to us early this morning about what the family is prepared to do to help Katie, since she now has a child and a husband who seemingly has few prospects. Over the past months, while Katie and her baby have been living with them, Gustav has had considerable time to think about the possible choices and has come up with a plan which we agree can work." Peter paused, fully expecting that given his past behaviour, Ludwig would automatically protest any proposal that he had not personally put forward, and waited for his brother-in-law's barrage. When he was met with a subdued silence, Peter quickly glanced at Ludwig to make sure that the other man had not fallen asleep after eating enough to be bursting at the seams.

Seeing that Ludwig was wide awake and still listening, Peter continued until he had outlined the entire plan for dividing up the Schweitzer farm, and there was not a single interruption. By the time he had finished speaking, the three others could not believe their ears, and were looking at Ludwig with amazement. Suddenly, the old house was so quiet that it would have been possible to hear a pin drop. Almost afraid to breathe, the four proponents of the deal, which they had anticipated would infuriate their churlish relative, waited in silence, furtively glancing back and forth at one another. No doubt a similar thought had crossed everyone's mind: since they had assumed they knew how Ludwig would respond, they had never even considered his acquiescence, if indeed that was what he was doing.

When Ludwig finally did speak, Wilhelmina, Amelia, Peter, and Gustav were simultaneously startled. "Although I like your proposal, I have an even better idea. On the condition that either one or both of your families agree to buy Jakob Litzenberger's land, I shall more than willingly give my portion of Papa's farm to Katie and Franz. Then if Heinrich does not want to donate his allotment to his youngest siblings, I will dig into my pocket and pay the asking price for his twenty-seven acres of land. Furthermore, when we finalize these arrangements, I want to stipulate that we only put Katie and Franz's names on the new title deed. There is no way on God's green earth I will ever give one square foot of land to that lazy, good-for-nothing drunk, Orville Reinhold. Besides, I have never had any use for a man who beats up his woman, and I am not going to start now."

With dismay, Ludwig noticed the look of consternation on the faces of his sisters and brothers-in-law. "I don't understand why you are all staring at me like I was some kind of an ogre. The only reason I came back to farm Papa's land was because I had no faith in Orville, and little more in Katie. Perhaps now that they have a child they will both be more responsible, and Franz is certainly old enough to help with the running of the farm. I just finished the seeding when you arrived, and Gustav and Peter, if you take turns checking to see that they are doing the summer fallowing, and of course, help with the harvest, they will survive, at least this year. I suppose none of you know how much I dislike farming and I hate having to live alone for six months of the year. Yet I don't blame my wife one bit for not wanting to sit here all summer without any of the modern conveniences that we have in the city. So as far as I am concerned, we can go to town tomorrow and put our plan into action."

Deciding that a celebration was in order, and that they would all enjoy more coffee with another piece of cake, Wilhelmina rose from the table to make a fresh pot, just as her boys hesitantly opened the front door. They were uncertain about what to expect when they peered around the small porch into the kitchen, and were pleasantly surprised to hear their mother's voice inviting them back to the table for more dessert. After the rare treat of a second piece of their mother's delicious cake, eaten in the presence of the adults who seemed to be quite happy—even Uncle Ludwig—they slipped back outdoors to the freedom of their play. It was not until the Strauss family was driving home that Peter turned to his wife and said, "My dear Wilhelmina, it would appear that your idea of taking a complete dinner with us was very clever. I never suspected for a moment Ludwig could be so amiable, and I think you have just proven that the way to a man's heart is through his stomach!"

～ 144 ～

Since Katie and Orville were returning to the Schweitzer homestead with their infant who was just starting to crawl, Amelia insisted at the very least that the dilapidated house be scrubbed from top to bottom. She would really have preferred to varnish the smoke-stained walls, but she realized that any money she earned from the sale of eggs and butter could be better used to buy baby chicks and feed so Katie would be able to raise her own hens. Amelia had managed to convince Gustav to give her sister a piglet as soon as one had been weaned from its mother, and then talked Wilhelmina and Peter into making a similar offer. She knew she had to draw the line when it came to giving Katie a calf because of its expense, telling her sister instead she would help supply her with milk and cream if she did not get enough from Ludwig's only cow. Since there was still time to plant a garden, Amelia provided Katie with seeds and encouraged her to get Franz and Orville to help, since Ludwig had finished putting the crop in long before he happily left for Saskatoon. As it happened, even Gustav assisted with clearing out the overgrown weeds in preparation for sowing the garden. He was so relieved that Amelia had come to accept that Katie, Orville, Baby Orville, and Franz needed to move back to their father's farm.

～ 145 ～

The darkness of destruction and death in Europe rarely reached across the Atlantic Ocean, at least not to the German Lutheran townships in east central Saskatchewan. Had it not been for the two young cousins constantly fearing for the safety of their respective loved ones and the ever-constant wait for the mail to arrive, very few of the farmers around Neudorf and Lemberg spent their waking hours worrying about the war. In truth, everyone in the farming community as well as the inhabitants of the towns benefited from the demands of escalating conflict across the waters. Every kernel of grain that could be produced was soon on its way to market and ultimately shipped over to Britain for the war effort. Once again, as at the turn of the twentieth century, prairie farmers were encouraged by the federal government to markedly increase their agricultural production. Another great wheat boom promised to build the road to prosperity.

The townsfolk listened to the news of the fierce fighting in the old country on the radio, which constantly blared in the hotels in Neudorf and Lemberg. The highlight of the talk amongst the men was always the war, but as soon as they left the coffee shop or beer parlour, they soon forgot about the devastation in Europe. Looking across the expanse of far-reaching prairie with its changing beauty, colours, and scents of each unique season, it was near impossible to imagine a countryside destroyed by trench warfare and artillery shells that incessantly pounded the landscape. The abounding chores and labours of spring, summer, and autumn left little time or energy to think about what was happening beyond the boundary of the family farm.

As far as the young people born in Canada who subsequently became of age and proved their own homestead were concerned, they could not begin to understand the insatiable quest for land domination across the ocean. After all, it was not uncommon for families in the townships with three or four sons to eventually acquire a section or more of land through the Dominion land grants. Being eligible to receive 160 acres from the federal government to embark upon what a young man considered he was born to do was like being the recipient of an unanticipated gift. Indeed there were many, like Gustav Werner, who by dint of living on and farming their parents' homestead ultimately obtained the title deed to the original quarter-section of land. The irony was that even though Gustav had been so certain about the justice of dividing the Schweitzer farm fairly amongst the six siblings, it never seemed to occur to him that the same equity should be true for Christian Werner's homestead. Nor, interestingly, was it ever questioned by any of his brothers or sisters; although in time it would lead to serious contention between Gustav and his favourite nephew, Mathias.

⇜ 146 ⇝

What a difference a year could make. If anyone had told Hanna that she would return to the Werner homestead driving an automobile, she would have thought they had taken leave of their senses. From the moment Anna mentioned that she was thinking of selling Helmut's prized Model T, which sat forlornly in the shed at the rear of the Schmidt Bakery since his death, Hanna was determined to master the skill of driving.

As soon as spring arrived and the streets started to dry, she took several lessons from Reverend Biber and began driving around Melville. The more she embarked upon her new endeavour, the more she came to love being able to get from one place to another with unparalleled ease and, best of all, whenever she chose. Now, motoring along the packed dirt road towards Neudorf, if she had not been concentrating with all of her might, firmly holding the steering wheel with both hands, and her eyes focused straight ahead, she would have pinched herself.

Sitting in the seat beside her, Mathias seemed to be equally intent upon staring out the slanted half-window, as though willing his aunt to stay in the ruts and avoid veering into the ditch. Since they left the outskirts of town he had begun to lose his resolve to visit the farm, especially when they bounced and rattled along as Aunt Hanna started going faster. It was too late to change his mind, particularly after bothering his mother for most of the winter about missing his grandfather, Uncle Gustav, and Aunt Amelia.

It was not that Mathias did not enjoy living in town and being able to go to school, where he had quickly proven himself to be an apt student. Nor was it the absence of the company of an adult male; Grandpa Biber was so delighted with his grandson that he spent every available hour with him, even taking the boy when he made visits to his infirmed and aging congregants. Certainly he was lonely for his Uncle Gustav, whom he had always loved as much as if not more than his own father, and he often longed to be enveloped in one of Aunt Amelia's loving hugs.

The ten-year-old boy could not understand why sometimes he became so agitated that he had trouble sleeping at nights. He was popular with his schoolmates and was allowed considerable freedom to play with his friends when classes were done for the day. He did not even have any daily chores that he was responsible for, thanks to all of the modern conveniences that came with living in Melville. There was no water or wood to fetch and no animals, other than Schnauzer, that needed attending to morning and night.

Yet something was missing in Mathias's life, but he lacked the maturity to realize that the restlessness in his soul was because he had lost his connection with the land. It would be many more years before he would appreciate that, like his Uncle Gustav, he could only find peace when communing with nature. Now all he knew was that he often felt irritated with his mother, who seemed to be more interested in getting her hair done than listening to him.

As the open prairie sped by, Mathias began to relax and to breathe more deeply than he had for months. Glancing over at Aunt Hanna, he noticed that she had a smile on her face, which surprised him because when his mother had first asked her if she would consider driving Mathias back to her brother's home, she had flat-out refused. Since he had been eavesdropping at the time, Mathias decided that he might as well continue to listen to Aunt Hanna's reasons, and then he found himself agreeing with her. She had quickly pointed out that as a businesswoman, she did not have nearly the amount of available time as Maria did, and since Mathias was her son, she could take him back to the farm on the train. When his mother had promptly retorted that she would never again set foot on that godforsaken land, Mathias had to restrain himself from rushing into the kitchen and telling his mother she was starting to sound just like Papa used to on his infrequent visits.

It had taken Mathias the longest of Maria's children to adjust to their abrupt uprooting. When it had finally dawned on him that they were going to live in Melville, Mathias had angrily asked his mother why they had to leave the farm, only to be met with the silence that she always reverted to when she did not want to answer him. Julianna and

Elisabetha did not seem to care, perhaps because they were younger and had never had the freedom to roam around and explore the outdoors as he had. Julianna was much more enthralled about being given Hanna's bedroom just for herself, going out for afternoon tea with her grandmother and, most of all, having a flush toilet. When Aunt Hanna moved out of the manse to live at the bakery, Mathias felt that ever since his father died, he was losing the people he loved, one by one.

If it had not been for school and having an untold number of books to read, which opened a whole new world for him, Mathias was convinced that he would have suffocated in town with its houses built side by side and people around all the time. There was no place where he could go and just lie down on the spacious prairie to look up at the sky. There were no gophers to chase or butterflies to catch and hardly any birds to awaken him in the mornings with the sound of cheerful chirping. Whenever he would try to tell his mother how much he missed all of his childhood joys, she would brush him aside, exclaiming that he was a dreamer and had just forgotten all of the hardships of living on a farm in the middle of nowhere.

Mathias did not understand how his mother could harbour such negative feelings about the Werner homestead, and when she started to complain about Uncle Gustav and Aunt Amelia, he had to stop himself from talking back to her. He might be a young boy, but over the last few years, Mathias had gained enough sense to realize that had it not been for the generosity of his uncle and grandfather, they would not have had a roof over their heads or food to eat.

Much to his chagrin, he must have fallen asleep—something he would never have thought of doing during the daytime in town—because when Mathias stretched and looked around, he realized that they were pulling into the farmyard. He had no idea what time of day it was, although the rumblings in his stomach were a good indication that he had missed a meal. Then when he remembered Aunt Amelia's flavourful dinners, he became even more anxious to get out of the moving vehicle.

All was silent in the yard, not a soul anywhere; although at that precise moment Amelia was rising from her roost amongst the radishes and lettuce where she was picking the weeds that threatened to snuff out the fledgling plants. She heard the noise of the approaching automobile, but she thought she must have been daydreaming. She stood up just as the engine stopped and caught sight of Mathias opening the door. She started to run towards him, and when he got close, she knelt down on the ground waiting for him. The minute he reached her, she wrapped her arms around him. He was laughing and crying at the same time, and Amelia's tears of joy at seeing Mathias mingled with his tears of excitement to be returning to the farm.

Christian's happiness as he hugged Mathias eclipsed his anger towards Hanna, and then scarcely recognizing the attractive confident woman as his daughter, on the spur of the moment he decided it might be wise to bury the hatchet and reconcile with at least one of his wayward offspring. "So, you decided to come home. At least you have more courage than your sister, and Gustav did tell us after he saw you in Melville that you are much happier living away from the farm. I don't understand it, but I am beginning to realize that my children are going to make their own way. Since you are here, let's go into the house for a meal."

～ 147 ～

When the time came, Mathias simply could not bring himself to return to Melville with Aunt Hanna as she prepared to leave on the following Sunday afternoon. In the week that he had been back on the farm with Uncle Gustav and Aunt Amelia, he realized how calm he had become when he was once again surrounded by the boundless spaces of the serene prairie with its undulating landscape and beckoning horizon. Running free in the outdoors, chasing the wily gophers, and trying to catch butterflies fluttering in the soft breeze made him feel like a mustang breaking out of the paddock. Everyone had been so happy to see him—especially Aunt Amelia and his grandfather, who seemed to have perked up since once again he had a young walking companion after Gustav had sent Franz back to the Schweitzer farm with Katie and Orville.

However, when the usually obedient and quiet Mathias blurted out, "Aunt Hanna, please tell Mama that I shall not be home until after summer just before school is ready to start, and ask her to send me some of my clothes on the train," he surprised them all, including himself, as everyone then chimed in with their approval.

Driving back alone to Melville, Hanna wondered what her relationship with Maria had really been all about because lately she was aware of her inclination towards some of the young men in church. Was she feeling confused about her sexuality? Returning to the farmhouse had reminded Hanna of their intimate behaviour within the confines of the bedroom they had shared for more than a year, and she remembered how at first she had been overwhelmed with shame. It would have been easy to place the blame on Maria, who obviously was experienced in sexual matters; as Hanna recalled, it was her sister-in-law who had initiated their nighttime activities.

However, during several long walks around her father's farm, Hanna had to truthfully acknowledge to herself that she had never resisted or made any attempt to escape Maria's advances. It was strange, though, how suddenly Maria had been finished with her—almost as if with her parents' love, she no longer needed her naïve sister-in-law. Nonetheless, as she motored along the dusty road, Hanna reflected upon how thoroughly she enjoyed the freedom and independence of her life now, and she was quite confident that she was not ready to give it all up just to be with either a woman or a man.

⟫⟫~ 148 ~⟪⟪

It had never occurred to her how delightful she would feel to become a grandmother. Margareta had loved her two babies from the moment each of them had been placed into her open arms, but Julia's baby filled her with wondrous love. Perhaps it was because the Mohr family had gone much too long without an infant to thrill them with the hopes and joys of childhood, or then again it may have been Matthew's contentment. Even as his mother made her preparations to nurse him, he could be pacified in the arms of another, and it was seldom that he exercised his lungs with robust cries. During the night, either Julia must have attended to him immediately or he patiently waited in his cradle, since every morning around the breakfast table, comments were invariably made about the fact that their sleep had gone undisturbed. Very quickly, it seemed almost every conversation in the Mohr household centred on their new addition, until one evening, as they were getting ready for bed, Margareta exclaimed to her husband, "I don't know how you ever managed to convince me that our family was complete with only two babies. How I wish I had insisted on having at least five or six!"

⟫⟫~ 149 ~⟪⟪

Would the seventh chair remain empty with the passing of the widower? On the Monday morning that he had failed to arrive at the hotel, the other six Silent Critics had gone en masse to his small house at the north end of Main Street. When they received no answer to their insistent knocking, the other two men of their group were prevailed upon to enter first and determine the reason for the widower's lack of response. Finding him lying on the floor in the kitchen, the bachelor ran back to the women and urged one of them to run as fast as she could to bring Dr. Spitznagel. The younger spinster sister, being the fleetest of foot, turned immediately in the direction of the doctor's home, and was gone before he finished making his request, while the other women pushed past him into the house.

The widow was the first to ascertain that the poor man was still alive, and gently lifting his head into her ample lap, she soothed him with the reassuring news that the doctor was on his way. As chance would have it, Dr. and Mrs. Spitznagel had been called out in the early hours to assist with the arrival of Katie Werner's third daughter, and by the time they returned there was little they could do. Before the widower closed his eyes for the last time, he managed in a tremulous whisper to thank them for coming, saying it was so much more comforting to die surrounded by his friends than all alone. Indeed, when word of his demise spread throughout the community, the townsfolk of Neudorf had to agree that for once, the Silent Critics might well have served a meritorious purpose.

~ 150 ~

Had William Hardy not been so busy in the bank in addition to trying to help the recruiting officer to convince more young men to leave their farms and go to war, he would have driven to Neudorf much sooner and with considerably more anticipation to convey his son's request to Katherina. It was difficult getting the English Methodists of Duff and the surrounding area to enlist in the armed forces, particularly as the fighting in Europe continued to drag on, rather than being over before Christmas as had been audaciously predicted. To make matters worse from the perspective of recruitment, the early incentive of a regular paycheque was becoming less and less important, since the farmers' pockets were steadily being lined with the rapid sale of their grain. Why leave home and family to risk life and limb to go to battle for the old country with its depressed economy and little regard for the working man? After years of hardship in Canada, the beleaguered colonists were finally making progress and earning money, which the women would be only too happy to spend in the dress shop that David encouraged Katherina to open in Duff with the funds he had sent to his father's bank.

~ 151 ~

As Gustav would firmly believe throughout his life, the truth of the proverbial "God works in mysterious ways" was verified for him by what Mathias had been able to accomplish with Christian Werner. From the first afternoon that Mathias had accompanied Amelia and Gustav to visit with Sarah and Andrew Thompson, he seemed to be enthralled with his aunt and uncle's friends. It was not long before both of them began to tease him that he was smitten with the Thompson's older daughter Emma; but rather than acknowledge their jesting, he was soon asking Aunt Amelia when they could call on the English family again.

On the days she indicated that they might take Wolfgang for a ride in the countryside, and possibly stop in to check on how Baby Henry was doing, Mathias would be even more co-operative than usual, helping her with any task she could ask of him. As quickly as they could finish all of their morning chores and he had kindly requested leave-taking from his grandfather for their daily stroll, first Amelia and then Mathias would mount Wolfgang's back and be seen galloping out of the Werner yard. It was a sight that occurred frequently during the summer months, with the young woman and boy travelling back and forth from home to either the Thompson or the Reinhold farms, and even on many occasions, as far as Neudorf.

Of course Uncle Gustav often came along and then Wolfgang would be hitched up to the carriage so all three of them would be able to go visiting. It was on the way home from a third delicious supper with the Thompson family that Mathias was suddenly bursting with questions.

"Why does Grandpa never come with us when we go to see our family and friends? Is he too old to ride in the carriage? And how come we do not invite your nice English neighbours to our farm to eat a meal with us? Aunt Amelia, wouldn't you like to make dinner for Mr. and Mrs. Thompson and show them that you are the best German cook in both townships?"

When Mathias eventually came to understand that it was Christian who would not allow an Englishman to set foot on his land, he tentatively asked his aunt and uncle if it would be all right for him to talk to his grandfather about inviting the Thompson family. Never for one moment did Gustav expect that Mathias could make any headway with his recalcitrant father; therefore, he was completely awestruck by his determined nephew when in just two short weeks Andrew and Sarah Thompson, their three children, and Andrew's parents were welcomed into the Werner home and were seated around the table, enjoying the first of many of Amelia's savoury suppers.

⇝ 152 ⬿

Days became weeks, weeks turned into months, and all too quickly months added up to another year with life continuing in its cyclic patterns dictated by Canada's pronounced seasons. Amidst the hustle and bustle and the sheer excitement of opening a new dress shop, Katherina was able to go for hours without worrying about David and whether he would return to her. Fortunately Matthew was such a complacent baby—who once nursed and changed either cooed to his many admirers or slept in his cradle—that when Katherina approached Julia about managing the shop in Neudorf, she readily answered in the affirmative. From the beginning Katherina's venture seemed fated to succeed. As soon as she arrived at the bank in Duff, William Hardy explained to her that not three months ago, he had arranged to purchase the storefront property vacated by the confectionery, which had moved to the far end of Main Street to be closer to the hotel on the supposition that the patrons would appease their children with candy while the women sat in the coffee shop and the men in the beer parlour.

At the time, the assiduous banker had no idea what he would do with the small one-storey building adjacent to the bank, but now it was obvious it would be the perfect location for his future daughter-in-law's aspiring business. David sent all of his captain's salary to begin stocking the dress shop, and William was seriously considering making an outright gift of the real estate to Katherina. Now seated in his large comfortable office chair across the Mahoney desk from the engaging young woman, it occurred to him that the property could qualify as a pre-wedding present. He had been delighted with his only son's news that he had proposed to Katherina and they were to be married as soon as he returned from the war. William realized it was appropriate for him to welcome Katherina into the fold, since Martha already treated her as her daughter-in-law.

Later, over a roast beef dinner complete with all of the fixings, Martha offered to help in any way she could to get the shop ready, and once the business was open she would be only too willing to hold the fort when Katherina was busy in Neudorf. To be truthful, Martha could hardly wait to get out of the house, and she soon felt more productive than she had been since her children had grown up and left home. In short order, the two industrious women, with more advice than actual assistance from William, totally redecorated the premises.

To be fair, William did his share by bringing over some of the inventory from Neudorf in his automobile, and Katherina's Dress Shop in Duff was soon operational, much to the delight of the female townsfolk. Within a week, however, it became apparent that she might have hit a snag when the women in the English community did not seem pleased with the merchandise she had on display. After two weeks, when not one dress had sold, it was painfully obvious to Katherina that she had a serious problem.

Knowing she had to act quickly, she arranged to have a tea party at her future mother-in-law's home, and she invited every woman in the English township. As Katherina poured tea for several hours, she chatted amicably, asking her potential customers what she needed to do to entice them to buy a new dress. Almost without exception, each woman expressed that she preferred very different choices than what Katherina was selling in her shop. In fact, they all wanted light, colourful dresses with floral patterns rather than the tailored, sombre styles in her current array.

Finally, Katherina realized, she might have customers who would be pleased when she brought in the new fashions that she had been admiring for a long time now in the clothing catalogues. Previously when she brightened up her Neudorf stock, only she, her Aunt Margareta, Amelia, and more recently, Julia, had shown interest; none of her other customers had wanted to try dresses that suggested they were going anywhere other than to a funeral.

Enthused by the prospect of ordering ladies' apparel that was in vogue, she became caught up in studying the current catalogues and discussing the prospective inventory for the store with Martha, talking well into the evenings until it was too late to return to Neudorf. Naturally then, Katherina would stay the night, and during her first weeks in

Duff, Martha and William convinced her that she should have her own bedroom in the all-too-empty Hardy home. Before long she became very comfortable, and for reasons that Katherina was never able to understand fully, more assured in the presence of her future in-laws. It was as though her proximity to his parents lessened her fears and worries for David, and during the day she was so busy that she rarely thought of him. At night, lying in his bed in the bedroom he had occupied since he had arrived in Duff as a young boy, Katherina felt a nearness with David. For the first time since he had been shipped overseas, she slept more soundly than she could remember, often dreaming of being held in his strong arms and feeling his warm caresses, as though they were intimate once again.

Before she knew it, another week would come to an end, and on Saturday evening after she had closed the shop, Mr. Hardy would drive her home to Neudorf. On one such occasion, as twilight was claiming the horizon, Aunt Margareta, who was sitting on the rickety bench outside the general store waiting to welcome her niece home, jestingly inquired, "My dear Katherina, is this new business of yours always going to keep you in Duff for the entire week? It seems you only spend Sundays with us and then early Monday morning, either Phillip or Peter is called upon to take you away again. I wonder if you have any idea how much we all miss you."

Standing up and embracing Katherina in one of her enormous hugs, her aunt continued in her usual outspoken manner, "We actually took a family vote this week, and if it means we will continue to see so little of you, we unanimously hope the shop in Duff is not successful!"

Instantly overcome with guilt, Katherina answered, "Oh, Aunt Margareta, you can't possibly mean you want me to fail when it has always been David's and my dream to own another dress shop. In fact, we have planned to eventually start one in Lemberg as well, and surely once I have the business in Duff running smoothly, Mrs. Hardy will capably manage it."

Thinking quickly on her feet, Katherina carried on. "One of my real concerns, however, is my transport back and forth between Neudorf and Duff. I feel it is an imposition to expect Mr. Hardy to drive me home in the evenings, and similarly for Uncle Phillip or Peter to deliver me in the mornings. I just don't think it is reasonable to come home every day, even though I miss all of you, too. I especially get lonely for Baby Matthew."

It would never have occurred to Katherina to hurt her beloved Aunt Margareta's feelings by telling her she was more tranquil at the Hardys' home, particularly after residing with her for all these years. On the other hand, now that she had been able to identify the valid problem of travelling between the two towns, Katherina made a mental note to talk to Mr. Hardy the following week and try to reach some resolution. If she owned a horse, or better yet, an automobile, then she could come and go by her own volition, like Hanna who had surprised Gustav and Amelia when she came driving into the yard from Melville with Mathias in tow. Intriguingly, it did not occur to Katherina until much later to consult with her Uncle Phillip, as she naturally would have only a few short weeks ago.

As it turned out, William Hardy had also realized that Katherina needed her own method of transportation between Neudorf and Duff if she was to keep her finger on the pulse of her enterprises, and he had already contemplated the solution by the time she spoke to him over dinner on Monday. At first he was hesitant, selfishly preferring to have her stay with Martha and him as she had been doing; but at the back of his mind, William realized that Phillip and Margareta Mohr could be none too happy with the existing arrangement. It was perfectly clear that all he had to do was teach Katherina how to drive his vehicle, which essentially sat in the shed at the back of the house most of the time. Then at the beginning and end of the workday, she could travel back and forth independently rather than having to rely upon a male relative to convey her. Since Sunday was really the only day that William used his automobile to bring Sarah, Andrew, and their family into Duff for the church service and family dinner, he would simply drive Katherina home on Saturday evenings and pick her up again on Monday mornings if Phillip preferred.

Just as William expected, Katherina was a quick study and mastered the new skill of driving after only a few lessons and the absolute promise that she would always ask one of the men to start the engine for her; they both remembered Friedrich's demise. Soon she was motoring around the countryside, delighted with yet another skill she had never thought she'd acquire. In fact, one fine day she almost drove to the Werner homestead as Hanna had done, but then fearing her father's reaction, she thought better of it and went to visit Rolf and Katie's new daughter instead. At regular intervals, she did experience some qualms about driving Mr. Hardy's automobile for the pleasure of it, but he assured her that just as long as she was prepared to purchase her own gasoline, he was quite happy that the car was finally getting some use. In addition, the irony that Friedrich Werner's prize possession was now in Katherina's hands and that she was much more of a success than he had ever been was not lost on her prospective father-in-law, and certainly not on Margareta and Phillip Mohr.

Of course, the six remaining Silent Critics had a heyday watching Katherina leaving town each morning and returning at different hours in the evenings during the spring, summer, and autumn of 1916. Where could she be going every single day, and how could she be so inconsiderate, continually relegating the responsibilities of running her business to her aunt, or to her cousin who was certainly busy enough looking after her infant son? Nonetheless, when any one of them tried to elicit information from either mother or daughter, regardless of how surreptitiously, they simply got no satisfaction. The Silent Critics finally had to resort to sending the last two men in their group to the lumberyard when only Peter was present, since Phillip was as close-lipped as the Mohr women. It would take them weeks to determine that Katherina had actually started a dress shop in Duff, and months to speculate what Christian Werner's reaction would be if he ever learned from Martha or Sarah Thompson, who remarkably had become regular visitors to his home, that his youngest daughter was doing business in the English township.

➤～ 153 ～◄

Once the Canadian winter, with its fierce, blustery winds, bitter cold, and blowing snow again imposed its grip upon the still lonely prairie, travelling between the two towns every day became foolhardy. On days when the snowstorms subsided, Uncle Phillip would hitch Kaiser to the sleigh and drive Katherina to Duff. Wrapped in heavy quilts and wearing thick coats, hats, and scarves, which muffled any attempt at conversation, they travelled through the frozen landscape, the intense silence only interrupted by the runners gliding across the hard-packed snow. After stopping for a hearty breakfast and steaming hot cups of tea with William and Martha, Phillip would return to Neudorf, telling his niece that he would come to fetch her when the weather again had some clemency.

Katherina would remain in Duff for weeks at a time; during the long wintry hours, Martha Hardy and she became very intent upon ensuring the success of their new endeavour, scouring the catalogues for the most saleable merchandise and thinking up ways of promoting the dress trade. Always at the mercy of the weather, there could be a month or longer when Katherina would then be at home in Neudorf. She loved her loft, which had become like a sanctuary since it was where David and she had expressed their intimate farewell, and yet it was in this bedroom that Katherina repeatedly experienced the frightening dreams. She would be relaxed when she climbed under her cozy quilt, and there were times when she could almost feel David lying beside her. But just as she would be losing herself to the mystery of repose, she would stiffen with dread. Then after hours of tossing and turning she would finally fall into a fitful sleep, only to be awakened by ever-worsening nightmares and screams that Margareta always heard. Margareta began to consider it divine intervention that her niece's time was being equally divided between the two families. By openly sharing her belief, Margareta did much to alleviate Katherina's sense of guilt about abruptly leaving David when he told her about enlisting, but she could never help her overcome her fears for David's survival that seemed to overwhelm her in her aunt's home.

For all of her apprehension, every three or four weeks Katherina would receive a letter from David, assuring her that even though she might have terrifying dreams about his demise, he was still very much alive. Whenever Uncle Phillip was ready once again to brave the elements of the bleak Canadian winter and return her to Duff, she regained her inexplicable belief that David would continue to be safe and sound as long as she envisioned holding him close to her heart while lying in his bed. Hence, every night when she eagerly went to her repose in Duff, she enjoyed the sleep of the just until she began to feel that she was taking the easy way out. For years to come, Katherina would wonder if her nightmares had been a form of penance, and if only she had continued to reside with her devoted Aunt Margareta and Uncle Phillip in Neudorf, working and praying fervently as she had for the past three years, the outcome might have been different.

⚘ 154 ⚘

It would take Katie a lifetime to realize that Orville would not change, but not nearly as long to wish that wherever he went when he regularly left his home and family, he would just stay there. They had barely settled into the old Schweitzer farmhouse with its freshly scrubbed walls when one morning Katie awakened to discover that Orville was nowhere to be found. After the quarrel and subsequent beating she had endured the previous night, she was initially relieved he was gone, as was Franz. By the next day, as both brother and sister viewed the yard bathed in summer sunshine through blackened eyes, they began to relax, confident that Orville had left for parts unknown. Katie never knew where Orville obtained the money to buy the whiskey that turned him into a madman, striking each of them if they crossed his path—not that he was a saint when he was sober. At least as long as Katie did not ask him to help with any of the farm chores, or to look after the baby instead of lying around all day, he did not much trouble himself with any of them.

Although Katie came to accept that Orville no longer loved her because she had become stout from child-bearing, she simply could not understand his complete indifference to their beautiful son. As it happened, it did not take Katie long to learn that her husband could care less about his namesake. She was subjected to a terrible beating when she had dared to ask Orville for money to buy the baby some new clothes and a pair of shoes. Cringing in terror in the corner of the bedroom, Katie had been transported back to the whippings that her father had repeatedly dished out to her, and she instantly believed she deserved her punishment. Then when she had to resort to dressing Orville in hand-me-downs from Rolf and Katie's baby daughters, since Wilhelmina's boys were far too old for her to still have any of their infant clothing, suddenly Orville noticed his son and thrashed her again. To make matters worse, Franz always tried to intervene, only to become another recipient of Orville's fury.

Therefore, it was little wonder Katie and Franz were serenely happy that Orville had disappeared, and with constant help from Amelia, Gustav, Wilhelmina, and Peter they were able to run the farm. Although Franz was older than his cousins, Rolf, Georg, and Hans, they took him under their wing and eventually taught him how to cut and stack the wood they would need in order to survive the winter. Gustav and Peter took turns driving over their team of oxen to do the summer fallowing, while Wilhelmina and Amelia made sure there was plenty of food in the house. Everyone worked in the garden and picked berries for canning, because Katie's older siblings were in total agreement that after they had been given the original Schweitzer homestead, Katie and Franz were fully expected to make a go of it. Gustav had already made it abundantly clear to Amelia that he would not welcome Katie or even Franz back to the Werner farm, since in the back of his mind he knew Orville Reinhold would keep turning up like a bad penny.

When Katie began to swell noticeably around her middle, the rest of the family knew there would soon be another mouth to feed, realizing that Orville must have stopped beating his wife long enough to once again plant his seed.

➤➤➤ 155 ➤➤➤

Then there were five. On one bitterly cold night during the middle of February, it was the older spinster sister's need to use the chamber pot under her bed that could have saved her life, if only she had taken her own advice. Shuddering with the cold, she had quickly climbed back into her bed when she thought she could smell smoke, and then remembering the furious argument with her sister before they had retired about banking too much wood in the stove, she rose again and started down the stairs. She was halfway down when, by the faint light from the full moon pouring through the hall window, she could see smoke billowing from the kitchen. Immediately realizing their house must be on fire, she turned around on the creaky staircase and scampered back up to awaken her sister. Grabbing the quilt from her bed to cover them, she practically had to drag her foolish younger sister out of the bedroom, while insisting there was no time for her to gather up her prized possessions. As soon as both spinsters were safely outside, the elder sister gave the blanket to the younger and dispatched her to alert Phillip Mohr and their surrounding neighbours.

Doing precisely as she was told, without stopping to ask what her respected older sister was planning to do, she proved to be a capable messenger, readily warning the families adjacent to their home of the danger and briefly speculating with them how to prevent the fire from spreading. As the neighbours began to assemble outside the spinsters' home, they wondered if the fire had died out since there were no flames flickering through the walls or roof, although there was a suffocating amount of smoke pouring out through the open front door.

Unfortunately, it was not until the younger spinster returned and frantically asked about her elder sister that suspicions grew that she might have gone back into the house. By dawn, the majority of the town's menfolk were outside the spinsters' house, and as the smoke began to subside, they were convinced that the source of the problem was underdried wood in an over-banked stove. What they would not know until later was that the older spinster sister had apparently decided to retrieve the priceless portrait of her parents that hung from the wall at the top of the staircase. When they found her with it clutched in her lifeless arms, they concluded that she had obviously been overcome and then had succumbed to the smoke from the smouldering fire.

The four other Silent Critics were quick to arrive and to offer their heartfelt condolences to the younger spinster sister, although they would never be able to convince her that she was not responsible for the death of her beloved elder sister. Until the day she died, she would firmly believe she should have stayed with her instead of worrying about the very people who mercilessly taunted the Silent Critics. In fact, she was so devastated that she could not force herself to set foot into her home again. The widow saved the day by inviting her to reside in her house across the street, which had always felt so lonely and empty since her husband had died. To their credit, the townsfolk sympathetically helped the other Silent Critics to restore and move her possessions and to eventually clean up the house until there was no vestige of the damage caused by the smoke.

The people of Neudorf soon realized how fortunate they had been that the spinsters' home did not go up in flames, and at a hastily called meeting the three town councillors were requested to seek additional volunteers for their fire brigade. With their close proximity, Phillip and Margareta Mohr were particularly grateful. And it was clear that Margareta could still find her peculiar brand of humour amidst the misfortune, when in the privacy of their bedroom she remarked, "My dear Phillip, if my espoused critics continue to die off at this rate, they will soon be truly silent!"

⟩⟩⟩⟩⟩~ 156 ~⟨⟨⟨

Spring of 1917 arrived when March went out like a lamb and then remained resplendent with a plethora of crocuses, bluebells, honeysuckle, and sweet-smelling clover to speckle the greening landscape. The aspen, poplar, and willow trees, which had looked so scruffy and bare in their winter nakedness, were suddenly vibrantly and elegantly dressed in their verdant finery for spring's revival. The refreshing air was filled with the lively chirp-chirp of the robins, the warbling of the meadowlarks, the trilling of the red-winged blackbirds, and cry of the predatory hawks soaring and shrieking overhead on still-wide wings. The soft, pastel-coloured skies of the early dawn heralded warm sun-drenched days with floating clouds of butterflies fluttering lazily in the light breeze before the brilliant sunsets disappeared over the horizon. Newcomers to the prairie were convinced that they had arrived in paradise, while the old-timers rejoiced in their returning energy, feeling caressed by the vitality of the awakening earth; they could hardly wait to be renewed by nature once more while tilling their fields.

As soon as the road allowance had dried enough to be passable, Katherina politely asked her future father-in-law for the use of his automobile and resumed her travelling back and forth between Neudorf and Duff during the week. In the mornings, she revelled in her freedom, as the fresh, stimulating air cleared the cobwebs from her mind, particularly after another fitful sleep in her loft. Then on those evenings when she stayed for an early supper with Mr. and Mrs. Hardy, she invariably found herself returning home by way of the knoll overlooking Neudorf where David and she had consummated their union in the presence of God and nature. As she stood on the grassy hilltop, watching the sun sink over the rim of the prairie, always aware that she had to leave before the twilight turned to dusk, she was serenely confident that David would return to her. After all, it had now been three forlorn years since he had left. Given his steady stream of letters, it seemed he was meant to survive the atrocious battles of the prolonged war in Europe.

It was strange, however, that she only experienced her times of doubt and frightening dreams when she was back in Aunt Margareta's home. In fact, it was becoming readily apparent that Katherina was interrupting the sleep of the Mohr family much more frequently than Baby Matthew ever had since his arrival. Finally, Katherina's almost nightly disturbances culminated in a blood-curdling scream that sent Margareta upright in her bed as straight as an arrow.

As she bolted out of the door and up the short flight of stairs to the loft, she exclaimed, "Dear God, what can be happening now? Phillip, you wait here. I shall call you if I need your help to calm the poor child."

Leaping out of bed and grabbing his housecoat, Phillip responded, "I'll light the lamp and come with you, since there is not much chance I can go back to sleep with this kind of uproar."

If she would have needed to, Margareta could have made her way to Katherina's room blindfolded, so many times had she scurried up the stairs in the pitch black of night. As it was, when she opened the door, she appreciated the shadowy light of the moon streaming through the skylight that Phillip had painstakingly installed in the roof of the loft. At first, she was frozen in place because she could not believe what she saw. Katherina was violently thrashing around on her bed with her eyes closed and her arms waving as she yelled, "David, where have you gone? Come back to me. You must not leave me like this because I cannot live without you!"

"Wake up, Katherina. You are having another nightmare," Margareta said as soothingly as she could in her fright, fearing that if she startled her niece she might fall off the bed. It was actually quite astonishing that she had not already, given the pace with which she was moving to and fro on her three-quarter bed. Margareta might as well have been talking to the wall, for the impact she had on Katherina's state. For the umpteenth time, Margareta thanked God she had chosen to lose weight, as she hoisted herself up on the cushiony surface of the high mattress beside Katherina. Gently touching and stroking her arm, she managed to stop Katherina from her constant motion and then to awaken her by softly calling her name.

But the minute she awoke from her dream, and clinging to her aunt, Katherina burst into tears. As she sobbed as though she would flood all of the sloughs and creeks between Neudorf and Lemberg, Margareta quietly motioned for Phillip to go to the kitchen and bring back a pot of tea, knowing full well that none of them would go back to sleep.

It was little wonder that Katherina had been so transfixed in her nightmare, for when she finally composed herself enough to convey its contents to her Aunt Margareta and Uncle Phillip, she said, "I had driven to David's and my favourite place, a peaceful grassy knoll overlooking town, and was delighted to see him coming towards me with his arms wide open ready for my embrace. Then when he was as close to me as my bedroom door, I could see that his entire body was covered with holes the size of my thumb, and all of a sudden blood began gushing through them. I rushed to him, trying to shield his wounds with my own body, but I was unable to stop the bleeding, until eventually he disintegrated on the ground into a bright red pool of blood before my eyes."

Gathering Katherina to her bosom, Margareta gently rocked her and said soothingly, "Hush, hush, my darling. I had no idea your nightmares were so horrifying. As hard as it is, you must try to put such ghastly pictures out of your mind and remember David as he was before he left." Looking over Katherina's head, her eyes locked with Phillip's and she immediately knew her husband was probably thinking it was not so implausible that an infantryman could be torn to ribbons by enemy gunfire as he advanced on the front lines of the battleground. Silently praying that her beloved niece was not having another of her frequent premonitions, Margareta continued, "Since your Uncle Phillip has kindly made tea, let's have a cup now, and perhaps in the morning we can drop around to see Dr. Spitznagel. I'm sure he must have some medication to help you to sleep more soundly and free your mind."

"Thank you, Aunt Margareta and Uncle Phillip, for always being so understanding—especially when you lose so much sleep over me. I must be honest with you: although I cannot give you any reasonable explanation why it is so, I never have these nightmares when I stay with Mr. and Mrs. Hardy. I don't want to appear ungrateful, but after breakfast I shall pack some of my belongings and stay in Duff for a while, until I feel calmer about what is happening to David."

Time maintained its inevitable march, and still Katherina did not return to Neudorf. It was not from lack of trying, as on at least three separate occasions, Phillip and Margareta journeyed to Duff by horse and buggy to coax her to come back home. Each time they were warmly received by Martha and William Hardy, invited to partake of a meal with them, and enthusiastically welcomed by their niece. Nevertheless, the minute the subject of Katherina's homecoming was mentioned, her demeanour took an about-turn and she became withdrawn and sullen.

Her prospective in-laws were truthfully quite surprised, and perhaps even a little worried, by this side of her nature, having never witnessed any hint of it before in all their years of knowing her. Appreciating that Margareta and Phillip would want their niece home, not only for her companionship but also to assist with her flourishing dress shop in Neudorf, they gently joined in the Mohrs' increasingly insistent persuasion. Regardless of the frequency or extent of the cajoling by any and at times all of her family members, Katherina repeatedly dug in her heels and refused to listen to their entreaties, until Martha began to wonder if her impending daughter-in-law was not being just a bit petulant.

⟫⟩~ 157 ~⟨⟪

Since David had returned to the front line in the west of Belgium, he periodically corresponded with Dr. Robert Cameron in London, relieved that he finally had someone to whom he could confide his candid reflections regarding trench warfare. It was from their son-in-law's letters to Julia that Phillip and Margareta could glean any inkling of the truth about what David was experiencing, since he continued to only present a rose-coloured perspective of his circumstances and even of his whereabouts in his letters to Katherina.

It was therefore from information that Robert had written to Julia in July of 1917 that led Phillip to believe, and become immeasurably distressed, that David was most likely advancing with his corps of infantry towards a village called Passchendaele in the third battle of Ypres. At first he kept his apprehension strictly to himself. Phillip became glued to the radio broadcasts in the hotel, listening to the news of the combat; but as it raged on and on, he could no longer stand to hear every day about the appallingly heavy loss of troops as they fought their way through a sea of mud.

When the letters for Katherina stopped coming to Neudorf, all Phillip could do was pray that his niece had directed David to mail them to Duff. One evening, as they were preparing for bed, Phillip realized that unless he took Margareta into his confidence, he would spend yet another night wrestling with the covers worrying about David.

"Now it seems I am the one who keeps disturbing your beauty sleep, my dear Margareta, with my tossing and turning. And when I do get to sleep in the wee hours of the dawn, I have nightmares which I am beginning to think are comparable to Katherina's. I know you will not be able to alleviate my fears, but if I at least tell you what is upsetting me, it might appease my mind enough so I can fall asleep a little sooner."

"Well, I wondered when you were going to let me know what has been troubling you," Margareta replied. She was going to tease her husband about the possibility of another woman being in the picture since he had always told her everything, until she saw the anguish in his light-blue eyes. "What is it, Phillip? What's wrong?"

Before he answered, Phillip thought carefully about what he would relay to his wife, but then he decided that honesty, as always, would be the best policy.

"According to Robert's correspondence to Julia, David returned to Belgium last month, where the Canadian army is engaged in a fierce battle to advance the Allied forces into the heart of that small country, and eventually drive the German troops back into their homeland. Although the British broadcasts constantly draw attention to the major strategic gains of taking the village of Passchendaele, an incredible number of our soldiers are being killed and wounded. I strongly suspect that David is right in the midst of the fighting, and I'm sure you are also aware that there have been no letters for Katherina for some time now."

"Oh, Phillip, I just assumed she would have written to David and told him she was staying with his parents. Of course, I did not know about this battle, and so now I shall be thrashing around at night right along with you."

"I'm sorry, my dearest. That is precisely the reason I didn't tell you before, but it has been on my conscience and I can no longer justify you not being privy to what I am hearing on the radio news. At least now we can both hope and pray that David is still alive and will survive this godforsaken war."

～ 158 ～

The scorching heat of the prairie summer had given way to nippy, refreshing mornings, cooler days, light evening breezes, and a countryside adorned with the brilliant colours of autumn when the telegram came addressed to Mrs. Katherina Werner Hardy. Certainly the postmaster knew that Katherina was living with the Mohr family, although he had never understood the unfailing reference to the name Hardy. Since it was Phillip who always stopped at the post office on his way home from the lumberyard, he had to sign for and receive the dreaded missive. Without so much as glancing at the text, the sinking feeling in the pit of his stomach told Phillip that the contents were precisely what he had feared for weeks.

He stood rooted to the spot, oblivious of Adolph Kuss's constant chatter and questions about why an official message from the government of the country would address his niece by an English family name.

"Phillip, you have been standing there like a mute for ten minutes. Are you all right? You don't seem to have heard a word I have said, and you have the most ghastly look on your face!"

It might well have been Adolph's third or fourth query before Phillip finally came out of his reverie. Looking at the postmaster as though he was a total stranger, and realizing that if he were to speak his voice would convey his anguish, Phillip abruptly turned and walked out of the post office without saying a word. Moving briskly, he went past all the businesses on Main Street, including the general store. Soon he was on the outskirts of town and striding faster with each step until he was running, as though he could lose himself in the tall prairie grass blowing in the gentle wind.

When Phillip could no longer catch his breath, he sank down in the meadow and did something he had not done since he was a small boy. Crying for the terrible loss of a fine young man, and for what he considered such a futile cause, Phillip let his tears flow until the well that had not been used for more than fifty years ran dry. Then, when his vision had cleared, he looked at the telegram and confirmed what his gut had been voicing all along.

Margareta had seen Phillip go rushing past the store, and asking Julia to close up for the evening, she followed her husband, albeit at her own pace. When she was close enough to hear, although she could hardly believe her ears, she stopped in her tracks and waited. As it dawned on her that there could only be a singular reason for her husband's uncharacteristic behaviour since he had loved the young man like a son, Margareta dropped to her knees, exclaiming, "Oh, dear God, no!"

She was still kneeling in the fescue of the unclaimed prairie that bordered the town when Phillip came alongside her with the telegram clenched in his fist. Slipping down to the ground and taking Margareta into his arms, no words were necessary between the long married couple as he allowed her to sob. As she had done throughout her life, Margareta wailed away her grief until her suffering had eased enough for her to spring into action.

"Phillip, we must return home before Peter and Julia come looking for us. They will surely be worried, and although it will be hard to tell them this terrible news, the difficulty pales beside how we will break it to Katherina and his parents. I always considered that David had registered Katherina as his wife, and that would explain why the telegram came to her."

With their bedroom lamp burning the midnight kerosene, Margareta and Phillip finally decided that, if it could be done at all, the best time to impart the catastrophic information to Katherina was immediately after she had eaten her dinner. Since breakfast other than coffee was a rarity for her, and waiting until after the close of business and the consumption of supper meant a calamitous evening with little time for them to try and soothe her during what would be the most heart-rending night of her young life, the news had to be communicated during the light of day. Furthermore, they decided Margareta would stop in to see Dr. Spitznagel first thing in the morning and ask for a sedative which they could take with them to Duff.

Nevertheless, for all of Margareta and Phillip's compassionate deliberation and planning, when they arrived just as William and Katherina had finished their dessert and were about to leave to reopen their respective places of industry, they were still largely unprepared for her response.

The minute Martha welcomed her aunt and uncle into the kitchen, Katherina seemed to know their visit was not yet another attempt to have her return to Neudorf. Sliding sideways to the edge of her chair, she pre-empted any opportunity to break the news gently by demanding, "What has happened? I can tell by the look on both of your faces that you have come with information about David."

Then, before either Margareta or Phillip could express a single word, Katherina shrieked, "He's dead! You are here to give me the dreadful news that David has been killed in the war, aren't you?"

How could they not have considered that their countenance would reveal their purpose, particularly with their overly perceptive niece? But what could they have done to disguise their visage until they could prepare Katherina? Since neither of them had a wink of sleep during the protracted night, while still trying to deal with their own grief, of course they both looked pale and drawn.

With Katherina screaming and William and Martha looking stricken as they beseeched Phillip and Margareta to explain the reason for their impromptu visit, Phillip felt compelled to place the telegram on the table. It was as though the proverbial cat had got both of their visitors' tongues, and they stood silently watching as William grabbed the piece of paper. Soon Martha's weeping was added to Katherina's screeches, and a fleeting thought crossed Margareta's mind that it was fortunate she had done her wailing last evening. Phillip walked over to William and took both his hands into his, since he did not really know how to comfort his English friend, while Margareta stood rooted to the spot, unable to determine whether she should hug Martha or her distraught niece. Time must have passed, just as surely as the inhabitants of the town must have wondered what had happened to their conscientious banker and the two enterprising women who operated the dress shop. However, by the end of the business day when neither establishment had reopened its doors, all the townsfolk of Duff feared the worst for the courageous David Hardy.

The sedative prescribed by Dr. Spitznagel had about the same effect as giving Katherina sugar-coated candy, and her hysteria continued to heighten, until finally, in despair, Martha dispatched William to fetch Dr. Muir. With Margareta's condolences, the older woman had eventually been able to collect herself enough to recognize the depth of her daughter-in-law's sorrow. When Dr. Muir arrived and was apprised of the amount of medication that Katherina had already been given, he readily agreed with his colleague's directive not to exceed the recommended dosage. How, then, were they to calm the distraught young woman?

The only recourse any of them could suggest, given the difficulty of trying to think with her incessant and uncontrolled wailing, was to heat water for a soothing bath until sufficient time had lapsed for Dr. Muir to determine the full effects of the medication. However, by the time Martha and Margareta had managed to draw the bath, Katherina must have worn herself out; the minute she stepped into the oval tin tub, she became as limp as a rag doll.

Struggling to keep her from sliding under the water, Margareta finally had to appeal to Phillip to help them carry Katherina to her bed. It was indeed fortunate that Dr. Muir had upheld Dr. Spitznagel's instructions, for Katherina seemed to slip into an almost comatose state for several days. Although she would open her eyes when spoken to, and did take small sips of water and occasional bites of food, she did not communicate with anyone, other than frequently crying out in anguish.

In the ensuing weeks, she refused to leave her bed, lying with the quilt pulled up over her head from morning to night, and she became very perturbed when anyone entered her room. Phillip and Margareta came to Duff as often as they could to provide some measure of relief for Martha and William, who were doing the best they could given that they too were grieving, not to mention trying to keep two businesses operational. Soon fatigue began to take its toll, and Martha, in particular, found herself becoming increasingly irritated by what she deemed to be Katherina's selfish and inconsiderate behaviour.

Finally one morning when she could hardly muster the energy to get up from her own bed, Martha went into Katherina's bedroom. Pulling the covers back to the younger woman's shoulders, she exclaimed, "Katherina, you have lain around long enough. You are going to get up this minute, and get on with the business of living. William and Sarah and I have been equally devastated by David's death, but we have to get on with our lives. Besides, the last thing David would ever want you to do is to give up and lie in bed as though you were the one who had lost your life. I know he always expected so much more of you."

Walking down the corridor and overhearing Martha's reproach, it occurred to William to question the depth of Katherina's severe and prolonged despair. Was it a product of the thoughts upon which she chose to dwell or was something physically awry? In the end, though, he decided that no positive purpose would be served by pressing the issue.

159

Seasons came and went, and yet time stood still for Katherina. The morning of Martha's chastisement, she did get up out of her burrow where she had been hiding against hope that she would succumb, rather than just feeling like she had been buried alive. Life was meaningless without David. Where was he? What had happened to him? "We regret to inform you that Captain David Lyon Hardy was killed in the line of duty fighting for his country."

How could she believe he was dead and how would she bury him when there was no body? Katherina was numb with grief, and what was the point of going on into a bleak future, when she knew at the bottom of her heart she would never love another man or bear children. However, Mrs. Hardy had touched a nerve with her rebuke that David would be bitterly disappointed in his prospective wife if she simply chose to quit, particularly when he had sent her the money to start the dress shop in Duff.

Gradually, as the months passed and a new year made its appearance, Katherina reverted to her earlier pattern of behaviour: focusing energy on her business and going through the motions of living with as much efficiency, and about as much sensitivity, as Mr. Hardy's automobile, which she no longer had the slightest interest in driving.

When Martha realized she could not break down the impenetrable walls that her son's betrothed had so carefully built up around herself, she stopped going to the dress shop. At first she had been fascinated by Katherina's ability to politely communicate with her customers and then transform the moment she entered the Hardy home, becoming as silent as the tomb within which she seemed to have encased her very being. It was as though Katherina had become a petulant child, holding William and Martha responsible for David's death, and the older woman's only consolation was that Katherina alternated between being equally taciturn and explosive with the members of her own family, who initially arrived to try and take her back home to Neudorf.

Eventually Phillip and Margareta Mohr stopped coming to Duff, and finally Martha decided that in the interests of her own health and peace of mind, she must devote her time and energy to Sarah and her three grandchildren. Thus it came to pass that the two women were to coexist in the same house for more than a year, scarcely exchanging a civil word with each other.

160

At long last, Germany and Austria agreed to retreat to their own territory, and when the Armistice was signed between the Allies and Germany on November 11, 1918, the news was jubilantly received by the inhabitants in the adjacent English Methodist and German Lutheran townships. Although relatively few men from either community signed up to fight in the war when the federal government instituted conscription in 1917, even the farmers were worried that they would soon be called upon to do their duty. Now they could rejoice that peace had finally returned to the Old World and they could continue to live their busy but tranquil lives in Canada. Quite possibly, one of the only individuals indifferent to news of the end of what would later become known as the Great War was Katherina Werner Hardy. Then in late November, when Dr. Robert Cameron came home to his wife and son, her apathy turned to bitterness and resentment.

It was small consolation that Robert's chances of survival were considerably better as a surgeon in a large London hospital than David's had been as the captain of an infantry corps engaged in a two-week assault which eventually resulted in Canadian losses of more than 15,000 dead and wounded. All Katherina acknowledged was that once again her cousin Julia, who always seemed to live life as though she had been born under a lucky star, was blessed not only with a healthy child, but now also with the return of her husband. When she began to seriously erode the support of her last remaining sympathizer in the Hardy home by repeatedly remonstrating the injustice to William, Katherina felt herself sinking deeper into the black pit of her youth. By December of 1918, when entire townships were seized by the Spanish flu epidemic, which had a propensity for taking the younger members of the community, Katherina fervently prayed that she would become one of its many victims.

⇒~ 161 ~⇐

Over the years, Gustav might have become accustomed to the bitter March storms of the Canadian prairie, but there had been very little during their married life to prepare him for Amelia's tempest in the spring of 1919. Perhaps it was because of the inertia of the long, severe winter, although in retrospect he realized Amelia might well have been the only person who still cared about what happened to Katherina. Since his younger sister had completely alienated herself from her own family, and apparently had worn Mr. and Mrs. Hardy's nerves to the breaking point with her doldrums and outbursts regarding the inequities of her life, everyone had simply left her alone.

It was near the end of the month, when the sun and warming winds had turned the snow into water that filled every slough and ditch to the brim, that Amelia announced that right after breakfast she was going to ride Wolfgang to Duff.

"If Mathias could get your father to welcome our English friends into this house, I shall find the way to make him open the door and his heart to Katherina." Before Gustav could protest that Amelia had never ridden anywhere near Duff, she was gone.

As Amelia already knew, it was her anger with Katherina that gave her the courage to ride Wolfgang on the muddy road allowance to the English town. Arriving on Main Street, without any sort of plan or even knowing where she was going, she continued to proceed at a trot until she caught sight of the sign for Katherina's Dress Shop.

"Whoa, Wolfgang. There isn't any grass for you to eat, but I will give you a good feed of oats when we get home." Dismounting and tethering the horse to the hitching rail, Amelia rushed through the door, not wanting to lose her nerve before she gave her sister-in-law a piece of her mind.

As chance would have it, a customer was making a purchase and Katherina had her head lowered as she focused on the cash register. When she looked up and saw Amelia, she was quite astonished, but her amazement was about to increase dramatically. The moment Mrs. Pitcher went out the door, Amelia shut it firmly behind her and turned the sign to indicate that the store was closed.

≫~ 162 ~≪

As Amelia arrived in front of the dress shop, Mr. Hardy happened to glance out the large window of his office overlooking Main Street. It took him every minute that Amelia was tethering the horse to identify who she was, and then he could not believe his eyes. William had been introduced to Amelia Werner and had subsequently seen her at the Mohr home one Sunday afternoon and, as he recalled, on two or three occasions at the Thompson homestead. Yet other than exchanging salutations, he had never heard her utter another word. He could even remember a conversation with Martha during which they concluded that she was either an extremely reserved young woman or she had little grasp of the English language. At any rate, she was such a dear friend of their daughter, and it was obvious that she loved their grandchildren as though they were her own, that it was of little consequence whether she contributed anything to the mealtime discussions.

Now here she was in Duff, without her husband who was fluent in English and seemed much more comfortable around other people, and about to go into Katherina's Dress Shop. Good heavens, what could have driven this reticent individual to take such a bold step, since clearly if she wanted a new dress, she would have gone to Neudorf?

For the second time within one morning, no one was more astounded by her behaviour than Amelia herself. Without saying hello to Katherina or allowing her any expression of greeting, Amelia began her tirade.

"We are all very sorry you have lost David, and maybe none of us is able to understand what it must feel like for you. But what you don't seem to realize is how fortunate you are in so many other ways. I don't think there is a pioneer woman on this vast prairie who would not envy your freedom and independence, which you just take for granted. Katherina, you have been living with Aunt Margareta and Uncle Phillip for far too long, and you have forgotten that you make your own choices and decide what you do with your life. Do you have any idea how many of us would like to be able to earn money, never mind own not one but two stores? When I want to buy something, either I have to ask Gustav for money or I have to save enough from selling my eggs, butter, and maybe in a good summer, from picking berries."

The more she talked, the angrier Amelia became, until Katherina realized that her usually gentle sister-in-law was now a force with which to be reckoned and that perhaps she could benefit by listening to her.

"When I decided to come to Duff this morning, I was able to ride Wolfgang; I am one of the lucky ones whose husband has always encouraged me to do things on my own. Most women have to wait for their husbands to take them where they want to go, and all too often they sit at home alone with a houseful of children like my sister Katie. Furthermore, I don't have the nerve to learn how to drive an automobile, and here you have Mr. Hardy's vehicle, which you don't even bother to use anymore. So, as far as I am concerned, Katherina Werner, it is high time you realized that life is a gift from God, and it's a sin for me to let you squander the present by dwelling on the past instead of looking ahead to your future. Now, get your hat and coat, because the first thing we are going to do is settle the ridiculous quarrel between you and your father."

~ 164 ~

Having entered through the back door of the dress shop in time to hear Amelia's last remarks, and able to understand sufficient German to interpret her meaning, it was all William could do to restrain himself from cheering. Still waters must indeed run very deep because it never would have crossed William's mind to consider that the retiring Amelia would be capable of such a profound blend of insight and ire.

However, since he was a firm believer in striking while the iron was hot, after a brief salutation, William immediately told Katherina that he would start his automobile and she could drive both women back to the Werner homestead. Asking Katherina to assure Amelia that he would tend to Gustav's horse the moment they were on their way, he disappeared in the direction whence he had come. For her part, Amelia took her sister-in-law by the arm and led her out the door, even though she did not know the location of the Hardy home. In a rare moment of acquiescence, Katherina decided to do precisely what she was told. As they motored along the road, Amelia contentedly realized she would be home in time to get dinner on the table for Christian and Gustav.

~ 165 ~

Knowing that when they arrived home it would be up to her to break the ice between Christian and his estranged youngest daughter, Amelia suddenly lapsed into the quiet state that so often characterized her. Throughout her life, she would become totally silent whenever she needed to collect her thoughts and find the solution to a dilemma. She knew that frequently when people were speaking English, they believed she did not understand what they were saying.

Although Amelia would never become fluent in her second language, after almost seven years of marriage to Gustav, she was quite adept at figuring out the gist of most English conversations, simply choosing to allow them to think otherwise when it served her purpose. Regardless of how quickly she may have wanted to leave Duff and return safe and sound to her home, she would not have left her husband's horse unless Mr. Hardy indicated that he would stable him. Even at the peak of her wrath, Amelia would never lose sight of her responsibilities.

When they drove into the Werner yard, there was no one to welcome them; Gustav was likely walking around the edge of the fields determining when he could start working them and Christian was too hard of hearing to detect the sound of the automobile. Once again taking Katherina by the arm, although more forcibly this time, Amelia marched her into the house before either one could lose their resolve.

Christian was sitting at the kitchen table. Upon seeing the two women, he rose from his chair and slowly walked towards them. Standing in front of Katherina, he gently touched her face with both of his weather-worn hands, and after several moments of gazing into her eyes, he kissed her first on one cheek and then on the other. Katherina, overwhelmed by this loving gesture, threw her arms around him and started to weep. Amelia quietly turned towards the stove to begin making dinner, leaving a father and his daughter to renew the bond that had been broken for far too long.

166

Dinner lasted until well into the afternoon with Gustav joining in the reminiscing, which continued for the balance of the memorable day. When Amelia stood up to start the supper preparations and Gustav excused himself to do the evening chores, Katherina and Christian stayed in their positions at the kitchen table. As time passed, Christian began to regale them with experiences Elisabetha and he had shared in the old country, and in those short hours, he quite possibly spoke more than he had within the past year. As she listened, Amelia decided to make a special supper of Gustav's smoked pork sausages, hot potato salad, and sauerkraut with bacon—Christian's favourite meal.

When the unforgettable evening was drawing to a close and they were getting ready for bed, Gustav remarked, "Papa had more sparkle and life in his watery blue eyes today than I have seen since Mama died. Thank you, my dearest Amelia, for bringing Katherina home."

167

Later that night, once they were between the fleecy sheets and under the downy quilt, Gustav turned to Amelia and finally gave himself totally to his loyal wife. There was no holding back, no hasty premature withdrawal. As he experienced complete release, Gustav became one with the woman who had shared his bed for more than six years. He had no idea that it would be so much better to release when inside her, and as though to make up for all the years he had wasted, he felt himself swelling again.

If Amelia was aware of the difference in the way he was loving her, in her customary fashion she kept it to herself. When they were first married, it was Amelia's ability to keep her own counsel and to accept her responsibilities without complaining that endeared her to him. Over the years, she had earned first his respect and then his admiration with her capacity for hard work and her patience and gentleness, but now he knew he loved Amelia with all of his heart and soul for who she was, as an equal God-fearing human being. Waking in the middle of the night and wondering if he was becoming insatiable as he reached for his wife for the third time, Gustav silently made a vow. Since Amelia was so desperate to have a baby, he would do his utmost to give her one.

168

The next day, when William Hardy came riding Wolfgang into the yard, Katherina and her father were strolling around the garden. After introducing the two men, she turned to her father and asked, "Papa, would it be possible for me to visit with you on the farm for a few days before I go back to town? I have not been myself lately and I think it would be restful to stay with you and walk about the homestead." Then, looking directly into Mr. Hardy's eyes, she continued, "Thank you for returning Wolfgang. Please come in for a cup of coffee before you drive your automobile home, and I wonder when you have arrived in Duff, if you would please ask Mrs. Hardy to open the dress shop during my absence?"

As it happened, the two men who only just met could not have agreed more, albeit for completely different reasons, that it was certainly best for Katherina to spend time with her family.

≈∼ 169 ∼≈

Within the week, the Werner family reconciliation broadened to include Margareta and Phillip Mohr. At Amelia's request, Gustav had ridden into Neudorf to invite his aunt and uncle to supper. Once they recovered from their astonishment, they cautiously agreed. Amelia was delighted that after years of sitting down to Margareta's table, she could finally return the favour.

Before they left, after an evening reminiscent of the times when Elisabetha had been alive, Amelia made them promise to return the next week with Robert, Julia, and Matthew in tow. And before long, the Werner homestead would become a beehive of social activity. If not her family—Peter, Wilhelmina, Katie, Franz, and Baby Orville—it was Rolf and Katie with their three daughters or Sarah and Andrew Thompson and their three children enjoying Amelia's delicious meals, until Gustav began to worry that she was doing far too much.

Throughout the hustle and bustle, it was difficult to determine whether Christian or Katherina was most enjoying conversing with family members. It was a spring full of surprises, and none more so than on the last Sunday in April when Christian Werner walked through the doors of the Lutheran church in Neudorf. All of the townsfolk stood and stared, but perhaps the most amazed were the five remaining Silent Critics. They always arrived early and sat in the very last pew to watch members of their community file into the building or fail to appear for the weekly service. On that day when Christian Werner again darkened the church door, they at first did not believe what they were seeing. Then three of the Silent Critics turned to the two weaker-hearted of the group, fearing that they'd succumb to their shock.

≈∼ 170 ∼≈

Long before her monthly cycle had stopped, Amelia knew she was with child. Her entire body felt different, her breasts were tender and swollen, and for the first time in her life she could not keep food down in the mornings. But the real transformation went far beyond these physical changes. Suddenly she felt complete, like a woman knowing she would at last fulfil the purpose for which she had been placed on this Earth. Amelia Werner would soon become a mother and join her mother, her grandmother, and all the women who had preceded her in creating new life. She longed for a baby girl, even though she knew Gustav would want a son to carry on his name. During her reflections, it occurred to her that she should stop in and visit Dr. Spitznagel to confirm her suspicions before making any announcement to her husband.

A week later following Dr. Spitznagel's examination, they were seated in his comfortable office, where the kindly doctor verified that she indeed was with child and could expect to be holding her baby in her loving arms near the end of the year. Since the death of her mother at only seven years of age, Amelia had spent her lifetime caring for those she loved. But now the possibility of having her own infant overwhelmed her with feelings of both joy and apprehension. Ever since her wedding night, she had longed to become a mother, and now she sat immobilized with wonder. *Could this really be happening to me? What will it feel like to finally nurse my baby at my breast? Will Gustav be happy about having a family? What if something goes wrong?* Smiling fondly at his young patient as she sat quietly, Dr. Spitznagel gently spoke. "Congratulations Amelia. You are almost three months along, and everything is fine. I know you have been around babies since you were a child, but if you have any questions, please come and talk to me."

Collecting her thoughts, Amelia gratefully thanked Dr. Spitznagel and headed across the street to the dress shop. Upon seeing Katherina, she started releasing tears of joy, although it would take several moments to convince her sister-in-law that she was happy because she was finally with child. Genuinely delighted for Amelia, Katherina led her back to the door, placed the closed sign in the window, and, treating her as though she was fragile bone china, guided her into the general store. Before long, Amelia rested on the sofa with her feet up on a footstool in Aunt Margareta's parlour and enjoyed tea and cake as both women gave the mother-to-be their full attention.

The news that Amelia Werner was having a baby spread faster than a grass fire on the windswept Saskatchewan prairie on a scorching day in August, and if Gustav had worried about his wife hosting a steady stream of visitors before, now he was amazed with the number of family and friends coming to share in their glad tidings. As their guests arrived, they invariably brought baskets overflowing with fresh vegetables, smoked hams, eggs, loaves of bread, cakes, and colourful bouquets of summer wildflowers. Gustav hadn't known that for years both their families and friends had hoped and prayed for the arrival of their first child. Watching them interact with Amelia now, he wondered if he had taken his wife for granted for far too long.

If Gustav voiced his thoughts to their loved ones now, he would have received an earful, and his severest reprimand might have come from his brother-in-law Peter Strauss.

Peter had always respected Amelia, primarily because as a young child she had kept the Schweitzer family together by her sheer capacity for hard work. He would also never forget her profound joy when he had given her the cedar chest as a wedding present, and then a carved cradle mounted on rockers, and finally a rocking chair for her new role as mother. His last two pieces of intricate carpentry, which would have delighted her long ago, had sat in his attic gathering dust for years.

Or Katherina might have soundly reproached her brother for his insensitivity to Amelia's longing for a child. Now, at long last, Katherina could rejoice with Amelia, and soon the women, chatting and laughing like two excited schoolgirls, were busy knitting and crocheting sweaters, booties, blankets, shawls, and dresses since both were convinced that Amelia would have a girl. Spending hour after hour in each other's company strengthened the bond between the sisters-in-law and best friends, and then Amelia asked Katherina to be her child's godmother. After exchanging every possibility, they agreed that Ursula would be the perfect name for her daughter.

~ 171 ~

Amelia's days had never passed so quickly. During the nine months of her pregnancy, Amelia blossomed, craved pickled herring smothered in onions, and was full of contradictions. She could hardly wait for her baby's arrival, but then she had so much to do to prepare for her infant's birth. Her excitement was contagious, and as her belly began to swell and she grew heavier with child, Gustav became caught up in becoming a father. He assured Amelia that he did not mind whether they had a son or a daughter as long as the baby was healthy and strong, and she could choose the Christian name of the child since he was providing the family name. As her time drew nearer, more and more she realized that although she had plenty of experience looking after children, she did not know what to expect about bringing a baby into the world. And all anyone could tell her was that as soon as a new mother held her infant, she usually forgot the torture of labour.

When Amelia felt the first contraction one late afternoon and then the increasing intensity with each successive one, she tried to focus all her thoughts on precious Ursula rather than on being doubled over in mind-numbing pain.

~ 172 ~

As Amelia contentedly progressed through the months of her pregnancy, Gustav was surprised by how excited he was becoming about being a father. Often when working around his farm, he would come to with a jolt as he realized he had been daydreaming about walking through his fields holding his son's hand, showing him how to check the pasture fence or teaching him how to milk a cow. During these moments, he wondered why he had waited so long before starting his family, one on which he could ultimately bequeath the legacy of his land. As summer passed into autumn and the harvest was completed, Gustav could hardly wait for his firstborn son to make his appearance.

Gustav gave precious little thought to what Amelia might endure when she was bringing their child into this world. He and Christian had helped their farm animals birth their young every spring without ever seeing a difficult delivery; however, the moment he saw the raw fear in Amelia's eyes when she righted herself from a contraction, it dawned on Gustav that she might be in trouble. When she urged him to go into town to bring Aunt Margareta, he raced back to the barn and soon was spurring Wolfgang on, riding like the wind, and fervently praying that Dr. and Mrs. Spitznagel were available and could accompany his aunt back to the farm.

Amelia's tortured screams reached him long before Gustav had opened the door into the house upon his return from Neudorf. Fortunately, the doctor and his wife had not been out on calls, and they had hastened to the general store to gather Margareta and drive her back with them in their automobile. Gustav was heartened to observe that the three had already arrived. But his relief was short-lived when an uncharacteristically stern Dr. Spitznagel ordered Gustav to immediately leave his own home, to go as far away as possible, and to return only when beckoned. Gustav followed the order and appealed to his Maker as he had never done before.

Not since his mother's death had Gustav experienced such helplessness. He walked and walked on that frigid winter night until he was nearly frozen, and still he could not shake the feeling that he was at the edge of a cliff and about to fall over the precipice. He bargained with God for hours, promising to hand over anything he could think of, to allow his sweet, gentle Amelia to live. Still, her screams of agony pierced the still night air at regular intervals as though she was being ripped apart in his dead mother's bed.

At that moment, Gustav Werner came to realize that Amelia was his life, that she made him complete, and that he was certain now to lose her. And it was entirely his fault. How could he have given in now when everything in him had resisted giving her a child for so long? And how tragically ironic and sad, that by finally loving his Amelia so completely, he may have sealed her fate.

About the Author

Corinne Jeffery was born in Saskatchewan in 1945 and raised in Manitoba from the age of five. A graduate of the Brandon General Hospital School of Nursing with a Bachelor of Nursing from the University of Manitoba, she is a former educator with Grant MacEwan College in Edmonton. After many years in Winnipeg, she moved to St. Albert, Alberta, where she has been a longtime resident with her husband and family. *Arriving: 1909–1919* is her first novel.

Read an excerpt from book two of the
Understanding Ursula trilogy

Thriving: 1920–1939
by Corinne Jeffery

If the cycle of life parallels the distinct seasons of the Canadian prairie, Lydia reflected, they must surely be approaching the winter of their years. Not that William Thompson would ever admit it. As soon as the snow began to melt, her aging husband would perk up as though the reawakening of the earth imparted its energy to him.

The spring of 1920 was no exception. For a while he did have more buoyancy in his step and sparkle in his eyes; sometimes he would even reach for her as they settled into bed at night. Lydia knew William loved toiling in his fields and working alongside his faithful Percheron mares. She could well imagine the serenity of striding along in the crisp air under the clear sky while looking to the horizon, which went on and on into perpetuity. But she was becoming increasingly worried by how fatigued he was some evenings. In the depths of her heart, Lydia Thompson understood that the man to whom she had been married for thirty-eight years wistfully wanted to carry on, fearing his eventual uselessness, old age, and death.

Perhaps William and Lydia could have lived out their natural lives on the homestead had Andrew not been farming the land with his father. As a boy, Andrew had been convinced that his father knew everything. During his youth Andrew had tried so hard to learn all his father could teach him about seeding, haying, harvesting, and summer fallowing, until by the time he turned eighteen and was eligible to homestead the adjacent half-section of land, he was a proficient farmer. Working together, the two men broke and planted the vast majority of their 640 acres until each autumn their increased production of wheat attested to the thriving partnership.

But when had the rot set in? Lydia always marvelled at how Andrew had aspired to be just like William; but now that he was a man, he could hardly wait to take over the reins. Suddenly it seemed as though he thought his father should be put out to pasture along with his precious horses. No doubt Andrew still enjoyed riding around the countryside, and he would hardly question the necessity of hitching Sally to the carriage when he wanted to take his family to Duff or to go visiting in the township. But, as far as he was concerned, it was high time for them to invest in a tractor, which he expected would quickly replace horses as the source of power for all agriculture in the Canadian West. They had enough grain to sell to cover the cost of the purchase, but William was always adamant about waiting for the best market price for their wheat, so they often ended up building more and more granaries. If only his father would give him complete control of the farming, in short order Andrew would make it a much more profitable operation.